Elizabeth Warne was born in Bristol and has since moved north via Oxford and Salford to Scotland. She now lives with her husband in a Regency gatehouse situated in the beautiful wooded valley of the Water of Girvan in south-west Scotland. She sold her first short story at the age of nine and has since written a number of historical novels under pseudonyms, as well as *Ragtime Girl* – a novel praised by *Books Magazine* as deserving 'top marks for a talented portrayal of the Depression years and the wonderful range of low and high brow characters', and by the *Bristol Evening Post* as a 'red-blooded rag-trade romance' – and *Wild Silk* – praised in *Prima* for its strong characterisation, 'Ms Warne has conjured up a vivid creature in Adela, and her riches to rags to riches story is enhanced by her gritty realism'.

An Impossible Dream

Elizabeth Warne

KNIGHT

First published in 1992
by HEADLINE BOOK PUBLISHING PLC

First published in paperback in 1992
by HEADLINE BOOK PUBLISHING PLC

This edition published 1997 by
Knight an imprint of Brockhampton Press

10 9 8 7 6 5 4 3 2 1

ISBN 1 86019 639X

Typeset in 10/11½pt Plantin by
Falcon Typographic Art Ltd, Fife, Scotland

Printed and bound in Great Britain by
Mackays of Chatham PLC, Chatham, Kent

Brockhampton Press
20 Bloomsbury Street
London
WC1B 3QA

My thanks to Debby,
who reads, digests and criticises.

Chapter One

In all her fourteen years Willow never before remembered seeing her mother cry. She stared at her, feeling helpless in the face of such unrestrained grief. She was tired after her long day in the factory where she worked as a run-about, carrying bundles of corsets from one floor to another; two dozen pairs if they were heavy, five dozen if light and the foreman's idea of what was heavy or light never coincided with Willow's. By the time she finished work she ached with weariness.

As she watched her mother's thin, bent figure, her twisted features, she couldn't think what to do. 'Mum,' she murmured, putting out her hand to touch her mother's shoulder, then withdrawing it as Clara jerked away. Mum wasn't one for touching, or showing her feelings, though Willow felt secure in her affection.

She was the eldest child in the family and had watched her mother's struggles over the years. Mum hadn't broken down during the long months of too many pregnancies, of the pain of bringing children into the world, of the agony of miscarrying, of bearing dead infants. Even a month ago when her favourite child, the youngest of the family, three-year-old Clover, had died and been laid to rest in the local churchyard Mum had remained dry-eyed in public. Later that night Willow had heard her anguished muffled sobs, but the following day Clara Riches had presented her usual tough, enduring face to the world.

Lack of money, hunger, cold, Dad's failing health – even when it had led to his losing his job – had simply buttressed Clara's attempts to keep her family fed, and respectable in

1

the eyes of their neighbours. But today she wept for Dad. It was as if he had died, thought Willow. It would be much worse if he had died, wouldn't it? Surely Mum must be glad that he was still alive and would return to them?

'The disgrace,' sobbed Clara. 'Nothin' like this has ever happened in my family, nor in his. The neighbours will say they're sorry, but they'll all whisper behind their hands. Damn them!' Willow jumped. Mum really didn't like swearing. 'Damn the filthy pigs that don't know a good man when they see one!'

The doctor had recently allowed Dad to get up after his latest and worst lung infection, but he would never again be able to go back to his job with a coal-merchant. Coal dust had increased the weakness of his lungs and his breathing was now so bad that even walking meant he had to stop and rest, gasping and panting for air. Dad had begged for a job doing something lighter but his boss had pointed out that labouring was the only work Arthur had ever been able to do. Neither he nor Mum could read or write easily. Dad had missed most of his schooling through illness and Mum couldn't seem to grasp the principle. But they'd been anxious to ensure that all the children learned to read as soon as they could hold a book and Willow, who loved books, had taken on their early education. Poor Clover had inherited Dad's weak lungs and a severe chill had carried her off. Now the family owed two weeks' rent and ten shillings to neighbours who had lent it to buy special food for the dying child. Mum was right when she said there would be gossip, but that didn't mean the neighbours wouldn't help out. Just as Mum helped out whenever she could.

'Poor folk have to stick together,' she often said. 'No one else cares about them.'

Mum had always paid the burial club sevenpence a week, even if she had to go short of food herself to do it. The idea of a funeral without proper ceremony was pure horror, but death meant there were many bills to pay. The death certificate, a laying-out woman, the gravediggers, the hearse attendants, flowers, a black tie for Dad; in the end it had come to over two pounds and Mum had needed to borrow another pound from the local money-lender to add to the insurance money and would have to pay her back somehow, plus the interest, and all this only to have Clover laid in a communal grave with seven others. Sometimes Willow wondered if that hadn't been the most agonising pain of all.

Driven to distraction by the plight of his family, Dad had gone out looking for work, anything, to earn money. He had ended up standing outside a cabbies' shelter, calling them if a fare turned up, for which service they had given him food. He had brought most of it home and for a few days it had saved them from the worst miseries of hunger. Then a passenger, thanking him for his help, had tipped him twopence and Dad had been promptly arrested for begging. He had spent a week in custody and this morning had been sentenced to three days in jail.

Clara tried to stem her weeping, but still the tears fell on to the sacking apron she wore over her pinafore on washing days.

'Prison,' she said bitterly. 'Prison for a man like your dad. And for what? For bein' given twopence for callin' a cab. It's cruel! Cruel! That's what them above us are like, our Willow, an' don't you forget it. Bastards, all of them! Oh, I shouldn't use such words, but they do seem to relieve my feelin's. He's never done no one an ounce of harm. When he was in custody I told the neighbours he'd gone away for his health. I don't suppose they believed me, but they pretended to. But now he's been jailed for beggin' his name will be in the newspapers an' they can't pretend any more. The disgrace!'

Willow reached out again and this time Clara didn't flinch as her daughter laid her hand awkwardly on her shoulder. 'Don't cry, our Mum, everyone knows that Dad isn't a bad man.'

Clara shook her head and moaned. In the past, Willow had sometimes been kept home from school because her young strength was a boon to her mother who took in washing. Willow had helped with the work, especially the mangling, standing out in the yard in all weathers turning the handle. Now she had to be up very early to give a hand before the factory hooter sounded, and toiled early and late when Mum had a special order. She was frequently very tired, and lately always hungry. The two shillings a week she brought home was swallowed by the family's desperate need and certainly wasn't enough to help assuage Willow's own adolescent appetite, increased by heavy work.

'In the court someone said Dad was lazy,' sobbed Clara. 'They knew he'd lost his job through illness but they kept sayin' he hadn't tried to find another. He did try, but no one will take a sick man when there's plenty of strong ones needin' work. Don't you never think that Dad was lazy, our Willow! He's done all he could for us an' give us all he could, but it seems as if fate's against him. He went on carryin' coalbags a long time after he should have stopped, till in the end he just couldn't lift them no more.'

'I'd never think our Dad was lazy,' said Willow hotly. 'He used to be strong an' he always had work.'

'No, he was never strong,' said Clara. 'Mum didn't want us to wed, but I didn't meet another man I liked as well. He's a lovely man, really he is.'

'You don't need to tell me that. He's a champion. No wonder you wanted to wed him. I remember how he used to lift me up in the air an' toss me about. I used to scream, but I knew he'd never drop me.'

A brief smile shone through Clara's tears. 'That was when we was first married an' we only had you. We got enough to eat in those days. I never fell for another baby for ages, then suddenly all the others came along.' She sighed. 'Fancy you rememberin' that far back.'

'I don't ever forget what Dad used to be like. Now he doesn't seem to mind what goes on round him.'

'What's that supposed to mean?' Clara's temper was swift to kindle, though equally swift to die.

Willow said, 'You got to admit, Mum, that our Dad doesn't bother much with us now, not even the little 'uns.'

4

'He do mind about you! He do! He was dreadfully upset about Clover. He's just too bloody tired an' ill with his bad chest to show it, that's all.'

Willow seemed to be driving Mum to further oaths that she would later regret. 'I know that,' she said soothingly, 'I didn't mean anythin' nasty.'

'Aye, I reckon you do know an' I know you love your dad.'

Clara sighed. They had eaten their meal of mashed potatoes flavoured with a piece of onion and drunk cups of tea without milk and must now return to the wash-house. Clara had taken on more customers and Willow used her midday dinner time to help. The boys fetched and returned the washing in their go-cart, made by themselves from wood they had filched from a woodyard. Clara disapproved of stealing, but the man who owned the timber-yard was fat and rich and wouldn't miss a few small off-cuts which would probably have been burned as rubbish anyway.

She got up, smoothing down her apron with red hands almost as rough as the sacking. There could be no putting off the work.

The Riches, with their six surviving children, occupied one room downstairs and two upstairs in the small terraced house in Barton Hill and shared the back wash-house with the Tuckers, the true tenants, as they did the outside privy and the strip of barren garden. They were lucky that only two families had to share and at least they had a cold water tap and a good boiling copper. Unfortunately, there was no passageway from the front of the house to the garden and the Tuckers had to come through the Riches' living room to get to the amenities at the back which was a source of constant irritation to Clara, especially when Mrs Tucker carried out the night-soil bucket. She knew that in using it her landlady was being both practical and kind by not traipsing through at night when the three boys, Joe, Sam and Alfred, were sleeping on a mattress on the living-room floor, but still she resented it. Mrs Tucker had even had a cooking range fitted into her own front living room when she began to let rooms.

Clara knew of many women who had constant battles when they were obliged to share cooking facilities. Tomorrow was one of Mrs Tucker's days to use the wash-house and Clara's work must be finished and ready for ironing by then when it was due back.

The door opened and a small girl walked in, rubbing sleep from her eyes.

'Jasmine!' Willow picked up her sister and cuddled her. She was just four and the person Willow loved best in the world, perhaps because on Clover's birth and subsequent ill-health, the little girl had been so often bereft of her mother's attention.

Jasmine put her arms round her big sister's neck. 'Why's Mum cryin'?' she asked anxiously.

'I'm not, my love,' said Clara, dabbing at her face with a piece of rag. 'I got a bit of onion in my eyes. It makes them water.' She took a deep breath and her face set into its usual tired but determined, lines. She was thirty-three and looked much older.

Clara got up to spoon food on to Jasmine's plate and Willow disengaged her arms from where they still clutched her neck. They were thin, too thin, but like the rest of them Jasmine was now living chiefly on potatoes and bread. Once Dad had earned twenty-three shillings a week and Mum had just about managed, even with all the children. Now their days were a nightmare struggle. During the little time she had left over Willow ran errands for the neighbours, scrubbed their steps for a penny and minded their children, and eleven-year-old Joe got up at five and delivered milk and hurried home from school to deliver groceries in the evenings. In spite of all their efforts one week the family had been forced to exist on five shillings and fourpence. It was this which had sent Dad out in desperation.

Willow kept Jasmine on her knee while she ate, smoothing her hair with a tender hand, and Clara sat down again lethargically.

'Is there a puddin'?' asked Jasmine.

'You know better than to ask,' snapped Clara.

Jasmine's lip trembled and Willow hugged her and kissed the top of her head. 'Don't cry, my love, I'll be gettin' a rise when I start on bonin' the corsets, then I'll buy you somethin' nice for your puddin'.'

'Ooh, thanks, Willow.'

'Have they told you when they'll be movin' you up?' asked Clara.

'The other girls say it won't be long. There's another run-about startin' next week an' I'm sure to get put on the bonin' table.'

'Cocky, aren't you?'

Willow shrugged. Words were tumbling round her brain, but she couldn't utter them. It would only make her mother's burden heavier if she complained that her boredom with the repetitive, brainless work which she was forced to do was getting beyond her endurance. She'd left school at thirteen, having no difficulty in passing the exam which permitted children to leave early and go to work. She had told no one that her headmistress had called her into her study and informed her that she was one of the brightest children she had ever taught and that if it were at all possible she should go on to secondary school and maybe become a teacher. Willow had felt thrilled, even as disappointment had gnawed painfully at her. An interesting future was an impossible dream. There would be no further education for her. She didn't know anyone who'd been able to go on after fourteen, no matter how bright, not in their circumstances, anyway. The grocer's daughter had, and the ironmonger's son, but they were well-off with new outfits every Whitsuntide and special clothes to go to school and shoes instead of boots for Sundays. Not that she wanted to become a teacher. She knew exactly what she wanted to be. An apprentice to a good dressmaker. Dressmaking! To spend her days sewing fine materials, pressing the seams, finishing off beautiful garments by hand, adding extra touches like those she saw in the fine shop windows in Park Street where posh Bristol people went, and putting into practice a few ideas of her own. In her innocence she had believed that a

7

job in the corset factory would offer her some satisfaction, but soon she hated the sight of the never-ending yards of thick pink cotton. She sought to satisfy her craving for beauty by altering the things Mum bought at jumble sales for a halfpenny or a penny so that they fitted better, and whenever she could, adding something, perhaps a small frill round the neck, or some tucks in the bodice.

She had Gran Riches to thank for her skill with her needle. Gran had been in service as a nursery maid in a big house before her marriage and had been taught to sew well by the ancient Nanny who presided over the nurseries. Gran lived two streets away. Last year, in 1908, the Old Age Pension had been brought in and now she got five shillings a week to add to the four shillings from the savings Grandad had left when he died. Like many another old person, Gran praised Mr Lloyd George to the skies. Her small room cost her one and sixpence a week and she was comparatively well-off and had been able to stop taking in sewing. The extra money had arrived just in time to rescue her from poverty, for her hands were really too stiff and knobbly with rheumatics to go on. Willow reckoned that if it weren't for Gran they might all have collapsed from hunger. Gran ate frugally and gave what she could to her son's family, but even there they had been unlucky. She had been laid low by a bout of influenza and had been so bad that Dad had got frightened and called in the doctor and money had to be found to pay him and for the medicines he prescribed.

Gran had loved her life in a big country house and had been responsible for the flower names of her grand-daughters. Except for Willow. Gran had been away visiting a friend when Clara's firstborn had arrived three weeks early and Clara, town-born and bred, knowing Gran's preference, had chosen Willow, thinking it was some sort of flower.

Jasmine slid off her sister's knee and ran back upstairs to collect her doll. 'Look, Willow, those naughty boys have dented it again. Joe was fightin' our Alfred.'

'Those boys! I'll soak her in a drop of Mum's hot washin' water an' she'll be as good as new,' promised Willow. She removed the scrap of flowered cotton she'd made into a dress for the small celluloid doll, and the tiny knickers to match which were the delight of Jasmine's life. 'Now get out your book an' try to copy your letters, an' when you go to school your teacher will be amazed.'

Jasmine laughed delightedly as she went to one of the cupboards which flanked the black iron range and got out a tattered primer and a stub of pencil. Willow settled her at the scrubbed kitchen table, before following her mother to the wash-house. She found the smell of green soap, the starch, even the steam, pleasantly clean, though she hated to see her mother having to work so hard. One day, she vowed silently, one day I'll get some money and Mum will never have to do washing again for Them. Us and Them. Them and Us. The words were a constant refrain among the people Willow had grown up with. They were rich and lived splendid lives; They were responsible for the miseries of the poor; one day They would be brought down by Us and everyone would have enough to eat and fine clothes and holidays.

Gran Riches said, 'They are different from us because they and their children are born into wealth and don't know any better. Now the Liberals are in parliament things are changing. There's my pension, for one, and the miners are getting an eight-hour day.'

'There's still a lot of unemployed,' Willow had pointed out.

Gran had agreed sadly. 'True, but the hunger marches will make people sit up and take notice. And there's the Suffragettes. They're nearly all well-off women, but they're trying to get us all the vote. People will listen to them. You'll be able to vote one day, Willow.'

Her reply had been non-committal. If she ever had plenty of money she wouldn't waste time marching the streets with banners and fighting policemen. She'd use it in her own business.

She placed the little celluloid doll in hot water and when the dents had filled out, laid it aside to cool, then it was time to race back to the factory.

After work she persuaded her mother to sit with her and have a cup of tea before they had to lift the sodden linen to the heavy wooden rollers of the iron mangle.

'Mrs Riches!' The voice came from the passage.

Clara jumped. 'It's Mrs Tucker,' she hissed, 'an' I know what she wants.'

Mrs Tucker came through. 'Sorry to disturb you, but I can't wait no longer. You've got to give me somethin' from the rent. I got my own rent to pay, an' as you know, it's due every Friday. I've kept it up for two weeks without troublin' you, but I'm short this week an' it's no good me tellin' the landlord I haven't got the right money. He don't care two hoots.'

Clara wiped her forehead. 'I know, Mrs Tucker, I know. You've been patient.'

Mrs Tucker continued as if she hadn't spoken. 'Ten shillin's a week this house costs me an' I only charge you three an' six, though you've got as many rooms as I've got. I've been good to you, you can't deny it, lettin' you have the extra room when you needed it—'

'I pay you a shillin' a week for it an' it's only a tiny place,' said Clara sharply.

Mrs Tucker drew back her chin. 'I never said you didn't pay!' she snapped.

'No,' said Clara, capitulating, 'you're very good, Mrs Tucker, I've always said so—'

'But my hubby says I've got to get the money you owe. A fine thing it'd be if we got turned out an' all because you didn't pay me proper. I've let it go without complaint because you've been good tenants an' you're clean and quiet, not like some round these parts I could mention.'

'I'll give you what I can,' said Clara desperately.

'How much?'

'Would you take five shillin's now an' let me catch the rest up later?'

Mrs Tucker seated herself on a wooden chair. She was plump and rosy and better dressed than many in Barton Hill. Her husband worked in a local factory and she'd only ever borne three children. There were rumours that she 'did somethin' to stop havin' babies'. No one had gone further into the question. It wasn't a fit subject to talk about. She folded her hands over her bosom. 'The report on Mr Riches is in tonight's paper. I'm sorry, I really am. There'll be some who'll say spiteful things, though I'm thankful to say I'm not one of them. Now if you pay your rent proper, you can stay here as long as you like an' folk will see that you're still welcome in a respectable house even when your hubby's let you down so bad.'

Willow saw the colour flame into her mother's pale face and clenched her fists, praying inwardly that she would keep her temper. They could be thrown out on to the street and then it would surely be the workhouse for them. The threat of the workhouse was a constant terror in their lives; sometimes Willow thought it was feared more than prison. At least in prison you knew when you were coming out.

Clara breathed hard. 'I'm really thankful we can stay, Mrs Tucker. My husband isn't a bad man, that you know. He never begged from anyone. He only got a tip, like servants do.'

'What do you know about servants? Oh, of course, old Mrs Riches was one, wasn't she? Did she get tips?'

'Not that I know of, but she used to hear the others talkin'. The upper servants made a deal of money from the nobs.'

'Is that a fact?' Mrs Tucker stood up. 'So you'll be givin' me five shillin's, then. Tonight, mind. I got to have it tonight. I'll make up the rest, though what my hubby will say—'

She left and Clara, who had risen to her feet in her agitation, sat down heavily on the chair the landlady had vacated. 'Sometimes I can't abide that woman,' she muttered. 'She's so satisfied with herself. Well, it's true she turned out the extra room for us. She's not a bad woman, really. I can't grumble.'

Willow had heard it all before. 'Where are we goin' to get five shillin's from, Mum?'

Savagely, her lips set, Clara walked to the wash-house and

11

rubbed a pillow case up and down the scrubbing board so hard Willow feared she might wear a hole in it, then she wrung it out and dropped it into the boiling water in the copper. 'There was pink stuff on it,' she said. 'It's my belief that some so-called ladies paint their faces. Disgustin', that's what it is. No good woman needs paint on her face. An' she must have gone to bed without washin' it off. It makes you wonder what sort of lives they lead.'

As Willow turned the mangle her thoughts drifted. She wondered all the time what sort of lives were led by the rich. Whenever she could she walked to the Downs and watched them as they promenaded with their parasols in summer, their furs in winter, taking in every detail of their outfits. She saw nurse-maids pushing perambulators bearing babies who were beautifully clothed in white linen and silk, all smocked and tucked. She knew from Gran Riches that in every wealthy house there were maids to wash and iron and goffer and care for all the fancy clothes. She saw small boys and girls playing with hoops or balls, and sometimes the girls carried beautiful dolls and made her wish with all her heart that Jasmine could wear a velvet coat with a big lace collar and a hat with flowers and carry a doll with a lovely china face. Even the dolls had clothes that took her breath away with their opulence.

The washing was almost done; sheets and towels were out on the line; the airing was hanging near the ceiling on a frame which went up and down on a pulley; small things were draped on a wooden horse, and the living room smelled cleanly of soap.

Clara said, 'I'll have to go an' see Gran. I hate doin' it. The good soul's worked hard all her life, an' now when she ought to be takin' things easier she's got us to worry about.'

'She doesn't mind,' said Willow. 'Of course, she wishes that our Dad wasn't in trouble, but she won't mind helpin' out.'

'Again!' said Clara grimly.

'You're not angry with Dad, are you?'

'Whatever makes you ask such a stupid thing?'

'I'm sorry, Mum. You sounded so cross. Who are you angry with?'

'No one. I don't know. I've never understood why some have got to work till they drop an' others never do a hand's turn an' have money to burn. But don't you ever think I'd take it out on Dad. The dear man—' Clara's voice broke.

Willow waited a moment, then said, 'Would you like me to go to Gran's, Mum?'

Clara cast her daughter a grateful, half-ashamed glance. 'Would you, love?'

Clara seldom used the word 'love'. She had neither time nor energy for the softer emotions, but when she did Willow felt she'd go anywhere, do anything, to help her.

'Course I will, but I'd best finish the manglin' first.'

'No, run along now. Take our Jasmine with you. Poor kid's not been outside the door today. Tell Gran I'll pay her back just as soon as I can.'

In spite of her resolution Clara hadn't been able to prevent a hopeless note from creeping into her voice. Pay Gran back, thought Willow. What with? She longed to be able to do something to take the defeated look from her mother's face and help Dad to get well again. She ran through the hot, narrow streets to her grandmother's, hating what she had to do.

A figure stepped from a doorway and blocked her path. 'Where you goin' in such a hurry?'

'Get out of my way, Sidney Moor! I've got no time to waste with you!'

Willow tried to sidestep the boy and he moved in front of her. The manoeuvre was repeated twice and Jasmine gave a little sob of fright that spurred her sister to anger. 'If you don't let me pass I'll yell for the cops!'

'Huh! Do you think a cop'll come because you yell? They got better things to do.'

'Like catchin' your brothers stealin' and puttin' them in jail,' jeered Willow. She was sorry the moment the words had passed her lips. However obnoxious Sidney might be he

13

wasn't responsible for his family's crime-ridden behaviour and, as far as she knew, he hadn't been in trouble himself. And now, oh God, Dad was in prison and anyone spiteful enough could point a finger at her. She stared up at the boy. He was only fourteen, but tall for his age. His face had grown red with anger and his pimples stood out like beacons. His hair was shaved to his head after the latest family outbreak of head-lice.

'I've got a good mind to wallop you,' he cried.

Willow breathed deeply to regain a measure of calm. 'Look, Sidney, I'm sorry, really I am. I didn't mean what I said about your family. You made me cross.'

For a moment the boy remained staring down at her, his light brown eyes suffused with rage. Then the rage died. 'I like you, Willow,' he said.

His sudden change of mood disconcerted her. 'Who cares what you like?'

'I care.'

'We've got to get on,' she muttered and he stood to one side and allowed them to pass. As soon as they had got by him Willow began to run faster than before, dragging Jasmine behind her.

Gran Riches opened the door of the downstairs room she rented. It contained little furniture, a table, chairs, a cupboard and a bed, but it was spotless and always smelled of lavender and baking and peppermints. Willow loved it. There was a small fire with a hob and oven and Gran managed to cook everything she needed there. And best of all, the joy of her heart, there was an ancient rocking chair which still moved gently on the rag rug by the fire.

'Come in,' said Gran. 'I've baked a few scones for tea. I've just put some in a paper bag and was coming round later with them, but you can save my legs. They swell up something cruel in the summer. Sit down, Willow, my love, you look all hot and bothered. I'll get you a drink. And how's my little Jasmine? You're out of breath. You didn't ought to make her go so fast, Willow.'

'I don't mind,' Jasmine assured her. 'There was a nasty boy, but Willow told him off good an' proper.'

'Is that so? Willow's a real good girl. Here, drink this.' Gran poured milk into an enamel mug which she handed to Jasmine. 'An' I'll get you a scone.' She turned to Willow. 'She's a deal too thin. Just like poor little Clover,' she added under her breath.

'No, *not* like Clover,' said Willow fearfully. 'Jasmine's strong.'

'I hope so.'

'Dad's in the paper,' blurted out Willow. It wasn't at all what she had meant to say, but she couldn't bear to talk of any possible weakness in Jasmine.

Gran nodded. 'I know. What's been done to him is evil! My son's a good and honourable man. He's always ailed, poor lad, and this won't help him. When he comes home, we'll all rally round him. Now you drink this up. It's milk and water with a spot of sugar. It'll do you good, make you strong. You'll need your strength even more when your dad comes home.'

'That's emptied your jug. Shall I fetch you some more milk?'

'No, I like a cup of tea without milk now and again. Stop wriggling and rest a while.'

'I can't stop. Mum's still got a heap of washin'—'

'And you're doing the mangling like the fine girl you are. Clara won't mind you staying a minute or two. Here's a scone. I didn't have any currants to put in them and I've not got any butter, but a spoonful of jam makes them taste that much nicer.'

'Jam! Home-made jam!'

'One of the women I did a bit of sewin' for owed me some money and asked me if I'd take it in jam. She'd got some free fruit from somewhere. I couldn't say no. She's a feckless body or she'd do her own sewing, and her husband's worse than her, but there it is. Some folk are just naturally daft. Anyhow,' Gran Riches smiled, 'I reckon jam's as good a way to pay as any I know.'

Willow sat looking down at the scone which dribbled dark red sweetness on to Gran's blue and white plate. Her mouth watered, but she wouldn't take the offering before she told Gran why she'd come. Without raising her head she said, 'Mrs Tucker's been on at Mum.'

'Is it the rent?'

'Mum had to promise her five shillin's tonight an' doesn't know where to get it.'

Gran nodded and said, 'It'll be Grandad's billy-can again and he'd say so himself if he was here, God rest his soul.' She reached it down from the mantelpiece where two china dogs stood guard and took out four shilling coins and two sixpences. 'Take this to her, along with the scones. And you can have a pot of jam, too. What do I want with two?'

'Gran, you're so kind! I don't earn much, but one day I will, I'll make money somehow an' I'll pay you back. An' our Mum won't ever have to take in washin' again, an' Dad can have a doctor to him every day an' all the medicine he needs.'

Gran nodded, then looked searchingly at her. 'I met your headmistress at chapel last Sunday. It was raining and we stood a while in the porch and got talking about you. She was full of how clever you are and how you could have been a teacher if you'd stopped on.'

Willow glanced at Jasmine. She was too busy filling her mouth with scone and jam to pay any attention.

'Why were you talkin' about me?'

'She'd heard of little Clover's passing and was tellin' me how sorry she was. She asked after you and mentioned a talk she'd once had with you. You've not told your mum an' dad, have you?'

'How could I? I couldn't go on at school when they needed money so bad!'

'It's a wicked shame! But don't despair, our Willow. Just remember, no matter where you have to go or what you have to do, use your brains and you'll better yourself. And while you're about it, try to improve your speech. You know your grammar. Don't be slip-shod. Girls who are well-spoken can go far.'

That night, as Willow lay awake in the double bed she shared with her sisters and which filled the tiny room, she wondered what her life would have been like if she had stayed on at school. She had seen posh girls on their way to the secondary school in their smart navy and white uniforms and always a stab of painful envy lanced through her. She turned carefully, so as not to disturb Jasmine and Marigold. My children will go to school for as long as they want, she vowed, then smiled ironically into the darkness. She was dreaming again.

Chapter Two

On her Saturday half-day Willow prepared for her favourite pastime, an expedition to the Downs, acres of grass studded with trees and shrubs overlooking Clifton Gorge and the suspension bridge over the River Avon, where there was room to run and good air to breathe.

'Our expedition,' repeated Jasmine gleefully as she trotted about the living room, tucking a packet of bread spread with Gran's jam, and a bottle of water, under the slatted seat of the ancient coach-built pram. The boys had fallen on the jar of jam and used most of it on the hunks of bread they had taken with them to eat after their swim in the Feeder Canal, but Willow had stealthily extracted some generous spoonfuls before they got at it and hidden them in a jar covered with a bit of linen under her bed. Jasmine knew this and the secret had kept her convulsed with mirth all morning. The Downs were too far for such a small girl to walk all the way, Willow said, so Jasmine would ride a while and walk a while, especially up the steep hills on which Bristol was built. Willow tied the ribbons on Jasmine's sun-hat which was pale yellow with a floppy brim; she herself wore a grey flannel tam-o'-shanter.

They said goodbye to Clara who smiled faintly. 'Off again, our Willow. You're daft to go so far just to look at the nobs in their finery.' Her smile became a grimace. 'Especially after they put your dad in jail.'

She said something disparaging about 'the nobs' every time Willow made the long trip to the Downs, but the reference to Dad was going too far. Willow said hotly, 'I hate what they did to him as much as you, Mum, but I'm goin' to learn everythin' I can about them, an' one day—'

'One day!' jeered Clara, but her voice was kinder. She'd finished the washing for the week, she and Willow had scrubbed the floors and front door step and polished the few pieces of furniture with a mixture Gran made from linseed oil, turpentine, vinegar and spirits of salts, and now she was looking forward to an hour with her feet up and yarn in her hands – yarn which had been painstakingly unpicked by Willow from old garments bought in the latest jumble sale. Clara was singularly bad at knitting and Willow usually had to pick up dropped stitches and reknit whole chunks, but her mother seemed to find the clicking of the needles and the repetitive movements soothing and her daughter loved her too much to resent the need to rescue her. Even the knowledge that her beloved husband was in prison couldn't entirely rob Clara of her pleasure in the brief relaxation, the time to do something other than work.

Marigold came into the kitchen and stared at her sisters with an angry glare in her hazel eyes. She was twelve and given to moods of pure rage which occasionally erupted. Her family couldn't understand why and it made them nervously anxious to placate her.

'Would you like to come with us?' asked Willow. She held her breath. Marigold had never accepted the invitation before, but there was always a first time. If she came all the pleasure would vanish from the day. Even little Jasmine was anxious. She kept well away from Marigold whose fingers could deliver a bruising pinch. Marigold looked at the pram disparagingly. 'No!' she said.

'Are you stayin' home?'

'I'm goin' out to play.'

Willow left, thankful also on Clara's behalf. Marigold's presence was disruptive. She pushed the heavy pram out on to the pavement and tried to forget the haunted, shamed expression which hadn't left her mother's eyes since Dad's disgrace. She wondered how they were treating him in prison. Surely they'd see how frail and ill he was?

She walked steadily on, across the railway bridge at Lawrence Hill, to Old Market which was wide enough for the trams to rattle and sway along four abreast, carrying folk who could afford the pence to ride, and still leave room for horses and carts, carriages, and the occasional noisy, smelly motor car. On past the shops in Castle Street and into St Augustine's Parade where they paused to look at the ships in the dock. Then it was up steep Park Street and along Queen's Road where the rich people shopped, and up Blackboy Hill, the steepest of them all. Then before them stretched the Downs. Most people carried their picnics further on where the widest areas of grass enabled them to run their dogs, fly their kites and play cricket without risking the hazards of breaking windows, and small children could enjoy themselves without going near the road. Willow stopped at the fashionable part where the nobs took exercise and from where she could watch the big houses which overlooked the Downs. Everyone was filled with the same idea, to take in air, enjoy the sunshine and watch the others. Willow was thankful to rest. Having had the advantage of plenty of food in her early years she was strong, but it was a long distance from home.

'Can we have our picnic now, Willow?' asked Jasmine, though she knew her big sister would shake her head.

'Not until we've seen them.'

'What if they're not here?'

'They will be. They always walk on the Downs before tea in August.'

'Where do they go when they're not here?'

This had once puzzled Willow. The two Maddison young ladies were never in Bristol for the whole of the year. They arrived quite late in summer and left in the autumn. She had asked Gran about it and Gran had said that they would certainly be in London for the society season and probably had other houses to visit as well as those of friends. Willow had been astonished at the idea of a family needing more than one house, especially when the Maddisons' Clifton dwelling was so big. The house had many tall windows, some of which opened directly on to the finely-shaved lawns. Willow had gone one day to look at it through the big wrought-iron gates, after Gran had returned from a holiday with an old friend, a recently retired servant, with more information about the Maddisons.

'She knows a lot about them,' said Gran. 'They've a house in London, a place in Devonshire, much bigger than the one in Bristol – it's their country seat, that's what they call it – and a lodge in Scotland that they use for shooting, though the ladies of the family don't shoot.'

'What do they want with so many houses? How can they live in them all?'

'They use them at different times of the year,' Gran had explained.

'They should let other people stay in them when they don't want them,' said Willow indignantly. 'We could have holidays there.'

Gran had laughed. 'Oh, there are others living there all year round. Servants stay on to take care of things.'

'Do they get wages for that?'

'Of course. They get board wages. They have a lovely time with plenty to eat and the run of the house and grounds.'

'I don't understand. How can the Maddisons give wages to people for just livin' in their houses?'

'They're rich,' explained Gran, 'and that's the way rich folk live.'

'How much money does Mr Maddison make?'

'Oh, he doesn't work. His family have been well off for generations. His wife's family, too.'

'How much have they got?' Willow's blue eyes had been wide.

Gran laughed again at her indignation. 'I don't know. Many thousands of pounds, I reckon. I shouldn't think they could count it exactly. My friend said the young ladies will have a fortune each when they marry and the two sons will get even more.'

Willow's mind had failed to encompass such wealth, and she wondered why some people lived easy lives, never knowing hunger and want, while others toiled all the time and never even got enough to eat. Dad was right when he used the term 'Them an' Us' with such scathing contempt. Unlike Dad, however, she wasn't going to be mistreated by Them. She would make money and one day she'd stare them out on their own ground. She'd ventured to say so once to her father and he'd just gazed at her with his weak, watery blue eyes, then shaken his head.

Willow spread an old blanket on the grass and she and Jasmine sat down. Carriages pulled by immaculately groomed horses rolled along the road, conveying ladies who held up parasols to protect their complexions from the sun. When they inclined their heads to acquaintances, their faces were almost hidden by huge, highly decorated hats. There were a few gentlemen, some on foot, some on horseback. Many times the ladies' carriages stopped and then loud, cultured voices and tinkling laughter floated across the grass to where Willow watched and waited.

The Misses Maddison usually chose to walk, giving Willow a far better chance of studying them, and she waited breathlessly. She had sounded sure to Jasmine, but she nursed a secret dread that they might not come. It had been raining earlier, but now the sun was high and hot enough to dry the grass and they would surely appear, their beautiful figures in their beautiful gowns drawing young men to them.

'There they are,' she breathed and knelt to get a better view, trying not to gawp, as Gran called it. Both young women were lovely in their different ways. Gran had discovered their names, too. Violet, the elder, was the taller and prouder of the two. Today she wore a lavender-coloured gown and a matching hat which was decorated with a wide purple ribbon and dark red flowers. Frances had on grey silk chiffon and a wide hat covered with big, flowing feathers. They held their dainty parasols in gloved hands and tiny reticules hung from their wrists.

'They're so beautiful,' said Willow reverently.

'They've got pretty faces,' said Jasmine. She had seen

them before and had no interest in them, but she knew that her sister liked a response.

'I don't mean their faces, though they're lovely, I'm talkin' about their clothes.' Willow pulled out a tattered notebook and a stub of pencil from her apron pocket and began to sketch quickly.

Jasmine sighed, but knew it was useless to get impatient. Her sister wouldn't be satisfied until she had noted down every detail of the Maddisons' clothes. They fascinated her because, said Willow, they were the best-dressed women who ever came to the Downs. Later, at Christmas, when she was given the usual paint box by Gran, she would colour in the drawings. Jasmine didn't understand Willow any more than did the rest of her family, but she put up with her odd ways because she was Willow, the dear big sister who loved her and sometimes made her dreams come true.

Today the Maddison girls were escorted by a young man. He bore a resemblance to them and Willow said confidently, 'That'll be Edgar, their young brother. Gran told me all about him. He's left school and is supposed to go to university, but he doesn't want to. My, but he's elegant! And look, Jasmine, that must be their little sister, Winifred, behind them with her nurse.'

'Is she ill?'

Willow laughed. 'No, all rich children have a nurse to look after them.'

'One *each*!' For a brief moment Jasmine forgot the jam sandwiches. 'Winifred's dressed all in white like an angel. An' look at the doll she's carryin'! It's dressed just like her. I bet it's got a lovely china face with pink cheeks and real hair, too. Oh, she's lucky to have a doll like that!'

'She is, but I don't suppose she's much like an angel with that red hair,' grinned Willow.

'Don't angels ever have red hair?' Jasmine yawned, not really interested in the answer as she kept her longing eyes on the doll. She sat up straight. 'Look, Willow, there's a motor car.'

Heads turned to watch the smart turn-out driven by a man

in a leather helmet and goggles which must have made him very hot but were required wear for a sporty motoring man. The car belched smoke and fumes, like a dragon – only at the wrong end, Willow said, making Jasmine giggle. The driver saw the Misses Maddison and waved, turning the steering wheel so that he would come to a halt near them.

Winifred had been walking slower and slower, deliberately dawdling, and was behind the others with her bored-looking nurse. She was a discontented child who liked to be the centre of attention and she had an opportunity when the car slowed down. She darted out into the road, calling, running towards it, waving to the driver.

Everything seemed to Willow to move in a slow, deliberate pattern. She had time to imagine the child, not much older than Jasmine, falling beneath the car wheels, imagine her body, torn and bleeding. Winifred's brother and sisters hadn't seen the child's reckless action and the nurse seemed transfixed with horror. Willow began to run, her legs as heavy as in a nightmare. There was a loud scraping of brakes as she reached Winifred and snatched her up, almost from under the front wheels. The ladies cried out, the nursemaid went white and the driver leapt out, tearing off his hat and goggles.

'My God, that was the bravest thing I ever saw! What a heroine! Are you hurt, young 'un?' he asked Winifred.

She glowered furiously. 'That rough girl made my new frock dirty with her nasty *dirty* hands. And look at Ermyntrude!'

'Who?' The man looked round.

'My doll, silly,' said Winifred.

'Oh, yes, I see, but you are all right, aren't you?'

Violet and Frances, their brother, the nurse and the driver made a circle around Winifred, exclaiming excitedly while they checked that she really was unharmed.

Willow could hear her whining about her doll. The driver took it, dusted it off and handed it back. 'Not a scratch on her face, though Nursie will have to wash her clothes and maybe she'll need a bandage somewhere.'

Violet said, 'You're such a fool, Reggie.' Her words were chiding, but her manner flirtatious.

'What about the girl who saved her?' asked Reggie.

They all turned to face Willow who had eased herself on to the grass where she sat feeling odd. Her only pair of stockings was torn beyond repair, through the haze she wondered how she would get more, and there was a long rent in her one good dress that she had made herself from a jumble sale skirt donated by a large lady.

'Are you hurt, little girl?' asked Frances gently.

'I say,' said the driver, 'you've ruined your gear. Bad luck.'

'My what?' Willow had banged her head hard and it hurt.

'Your clothes, he means,' said Frances.

Violet tapped her well-shod foot impatiently. 'She will soon recover. Nothing appears to be broken. Pay the girl something, Reggie, for heaven's sake, and let us go. There is a crowd positively staring at us.'

'Eh? What? Oh, yes.'

Edgar said disgustedly, 'Violet is right. We are in the middle of a scene!'

Reggie hesitated. 'Perhaps the girl needs medical attention.'

Violet looked down at Willow, her dark eyes appraising her as if she were a lost dog. 'Do you need a doctor? Wriggle your arms and legs.'

Willow moved cautiously. Everything felt all right, if sore, but her head wouldn't behave itself at all. She tried to peer past them at Jasmine, but her eyes were misty.

Reggie, obeying another angry command from Violet, pulled coins from his trouser pocket. 'How much should I give?' he asked.

'How should I know?' snapped Violet.

'What d'you usually give when you knock people down?' asked Edgar.

Reggie began to splutter. 'I do not usually—'

'Will you give her something and let us have done with

it,' interrupted Violet. 'I abominate being stared at in such a vulgar way. I wish to return home *now*.'

'If you don't want to pay her, I will,' exclaimed Edgar, 'though it was your fault.'

'The child ran in front of me. I couldn't possibly stop quickly enough. Nobody could.'

'Don't get huffy,' said Edgar. 'Just reward her and we can go home.'

They were drawing quite a crowd, some of whom were definitely hostile.

'Knocked 'er down with his nasty motor car.'

'They shouldn't be allowed.'

'Horses was good enough for my father, and they're good enough for me.'

'Rich folk always 'ave to buy the latest thing.'

'An' he's 'alf killed 'er with it. Poor little thing!'

Others, the people one knew, were too well bred to stare, but they were passing and re-passing, obviously amused.

'I am going home,' snapped Violet, but she didn't make a move which would have isolated her from the group.

Reggie said, 'Try to stand, little girl. If you do I'll give you a bright new sovereign.'

His words came distantly to Willow. A sovereign! She tried to get up, but the faces above her began to weave in odd circles.

'She's going to faint,' cried Reggie. Willow felt horribly ill and prayed that she wouldn't vomit; and she was terrified for Jasmine, who, she hoped, would still be with the pram. She tried to tell them to keep an eye on her little sister, but her tongue wouldn't move. Then she lost consciousness.

She came to in a strange room, lying on something soft and smooth, her nostrils filled with the scent of flowers. Her head was throbbing. She opened her eyes. She was beneath a high ceiling which was decorated with plaster fruit and leaves. A large picture hung on the wall directly ahead. She tried to move her head to examine the rest of the room and felt sick again.

'Now don't you be ill in here,' said a voice. A young woman in a dark gown, white apron and bib and frilly cap with flowing ribbons bent over her, looking down in a kindly way. 'You're in Mrs Maddison's morning room. You can't be sick in here.'

Willow breathed deeply and the horrible feeling left her. Why was she lying here? She tried to remember and the throbbing in her head grew more insistent.

The door opened. 'How is she?' The voice was anxious. Someone bent over and Willow saw Frances, hat removed, her abundant fair hair secured by tortoiseshell combs.

Memory returned. Jasmine! 'I've got to go,' said Willow. She sat up abruptly, the room swam round her and she sank back with a groan.

'Be still, won't you?' said the maid impatiently.

'Now, Nora, that's no way to talk to her. She is obviously worried about her little sister. She's perfectly all right,' said Frances. 'She is in the kitchen tucking into cake and milk.'

Willow closed her eyes and heard Frances say anxiously, 'We cannot send her out in this state. I think we had better ask the doctor to look at her. She may be quite seriously hurt.'

Willow tried to tell them that doctors cost money, then remembered that money was of no consequence here.

She heard another voice. 'A doctor? Surely there is no need for that! She's probably used to bumps and bruises. Her kind lead quite rough lives.'

'Violet, that's so uncharitable!'

Violet, the haughty one of the sisters. Through Willow's bemused state of consciousness surged a violent dislike of Violet Maddison. She wanted to get up and tell her just what kind of a life was led by her family, how honest her mother was, how generous Gran Riches, how respectable – no, they could never be that again. Not now Dad was in prison. A tear forced its way under her closed eyelid and trickled down her face.

'Violet! You've hurt her feelings!'

'What! Do not be ridiculous, Frances!' There was a swift rustle of petticoats and the slam of a door.

Frances sighed. 'Stay here, Nora. The doctor is with Miss Winifred. I will ask him to come here when he's finished.'

The door opened and closed and Nora said, 'I don't know what Mrs Maddison will say when she hears the doctor's been to see you. A fine thing, to be sure.' Willow opened her eyes. The ceiling no longer spun. 'It'd have been much better to have took you to the kitchen. Cook would soon have put you right with one of her potions, but Miss Frances would have you carried through the front door and now your boots are messing up the sofa. I can tell you, Mr Steadman – that's our butler, though I don't suppose a girl like you would know what that is – well, he was very shocked. "You could have knocked me down with a feather," he said, when he came into the kitchen. "If Miss Frances hasn't had a street urchin took into the morning room and laid out on the Regency satin sofa, and her in her outdoor boots." I don't reckon you're hurt as bad as Miss Frances thinks, but she's too kind by half. Any beggar can get a sixpence out of her.'

'I'm not a beggar,' gasped Willow, 'an' I'd like a drink of water, if you please.'

'Well, you've got manners, I'll say that for you. Lie still as a mouse and I'll get you a drink.'

Before the maid returned Frances came back. 'Where is Nora?' She sounded displeased.

'Please, ma'am, I asked for water,' said Willow.

Frances looked chagrined. 'Water, to be sure. I should have thought of that. How remiss of me.'

'It doesn't matter,' said Willow.

'It does matter. I should have given you more consideration. If one of my friends had suffered as you have, I would have offered water or wine immediately.'

Willow's goodwill towards Frances subsided. She had been placed firmly in her own class. Beneath her gentle manners Frances was no different from the others.

The doctor arrived and examined Willow. 'Quite nasty

bruising about the head, but no concussion. She'll be as right as rain.' He looked down at Willow who stared into his bearded face. 'It's bed for you, my girl, for two or three days. Then call your own doctor and he'll tell you if you're fit to return to school.'

'I don't go to school. I work.' Willow was filled with seething fury. Bed! Call your own doctor! He knew nothing of her circumstances and cared less, but he should have guessed from her appearance that she didn't come from well-off people. She couldn't afford to stay off work and lose money, or maybe even get sacked for malingering, and there was no money for a doctor.

'Should she have medicine?' asked Frances.

'Mmm, maybe so. A little soothing syrup. I'll send some round.'

'I don't live here!' said Willow.

'No, no, of course not.' The doctor's eyes travelled over her clothes, her worn boots, her stockings. 'No, I see.' He appeared to look at her properly for the first time. 'Give me your address. I dare say I can get some medicine to you by tonight.'

'It doesn't matter,' Willow snapped. 'My gran will make me somethin'. People say her medicines are better than any doctor's, an' a lot cheaper.'

He flushed. 'How dare you?' Then he stopped, silenced by Frances who held up her hand. 'Send the medicine here and I will see it is delivered.' She turned to Willow. 'You had better take what the doctor orders, dear, and don't worry about the cost. I will attend to it. It's the very least I can do after you saved my little sister.'

Willow blinked. She had forgotten the reason for her being here. 'Is she all right?'

'She is, thanks to you. My mother is out and Father is in Scotland or they would offer their own thanks.'

Willow didn't answer. She felt much improved after a glass of water to which a little wine had been added. It gave her a hazy feeling which was pleasant after the ghastly sick giddiness. Frances went away to arrange transport for the girls and Nora gave Willow her arm to the kitchen. Her first impression was of its size. The whole of their three rooms would be lost in here. A huge range was set in the length of one wall and copper pans, shining bright as gold, and enormous ladles and spoons, hung on the walls. There seemed to be a great many people in various uniforms.

'There's the little heroine,' said a fat woman in a print dress as deeply pink as her cheeks, a voluminous apron and plain white cap.

'This is Mrs Narracott, our cook,' said Nora. 'And the gentleman in black is Mr Steadman, our butler. The one in livery is the footman.'

There was a rush of feet and Jasmine hurled herself upon her sister. 'Willow, I thought you was dead,' she shrieked. 'Oh, look at your stockin's – all torn. An' your dress is dirty. What'll our Mum say?'

'Careful,' laughed Nora, 'or you'll knock your sister over and she's had enough of that for one day.' She turned to a lofty woman in brown bombazine. 'Could you find her a pair of stockings, Miss Jebb?'

'I dare say I could. Miss Violet won't wear any with a darn, however small.'

'That's Miss Jebb, the young ladies' maid,' whispered Nora, as she pulled out a chair for Willow.

'Pleased to meet you,' said Willow, taking Jasmine on to her lap. Her head was aching badly and she wished she was at home. A sudden thought struck her. 'How will we get the pram into the carriage?'

'The what?' asked Mr Steadman.

'The pram. Our pram. The one we came to the Downs with. Where've you put it?'

Heads were turned inquiringly. 'Did anyone bring it in?' asked Mrs Narracott.

'Not that I know of,' said Mr Steadman. 'Oy, Steven,' he called, 'go and find out about the pram.'

Steven, a boy near Willow's age, with a smudged face, dirty hands and a dirtier coarse apron, came from a side room. He was stocky with straight black hair cut so close that it stuck up like one of his own blacking brushes and as he passed Willow he poked out his tongue at her. Nora gave a good-humoured swipe at him as Willow returned the grimace with interest.

'Did you see the face she made at the bootboy?' gasped Miss Jebb. 'What a little heathen!'

Willow knew from scripture lessons at school what a heathen was and was indignant, but forgot it when Steven returned to announce that the pram must have been left behind on the Downs.

'Oh, no! Someone will have stole it for sure,' she wailed. 'What am I goin' to tell our Mum? We'll never get another. She's had it since I was born an' we need it for lots of things.' It was true that the old pram was in constant use but in the forefront of Willow's mind was the fact that, without it, she couldn't take Jasmine for their weekly visits to the Downs, she wouldn't have the heart to leave her behind, and her chief pleasure in life would vanish.

'What a fuss to make about a pram!' sniffed Miss Jebb. 'It's probably very dilapidated by now.'

Mrs Narracott was kinder. 'She says it's all they've got. Go an' look on the Downs, Steven. No, on second thoughts, you're too dirty. We don't want folk thinking that the Maddison servants don't wash. You go.' She nodded to the footman. 'Ask upstairs exactly where the accident happened.' She turned to Willow. 'Your little sister's been telling us what you did. You're a brave lass. Would you like a cup of tea, or maybe a glass of lemonade?'

Willow accepted the tea gratefully. Jasmine chose lemonade. 'It's lovely,' she said. 'It tastes different from what we get at home. We haven't had any for a long time,' she finished sadly. 'It costs too much.'

'Will you listen to the poor mite?' exclaimed Mrs Narracott. 'Have another glass, my dear. We make it ourselves from pure lemon juice and best sugar.'

'Do you?' said Jasmine. 'I didn't know you could. We get ours from a bottle, though usually we drink water.'

'Quite right too,' said Mrs Narracott. 'Water's best for little girls. Lemonade should be a special treat.'

'You've got a lot of saucepans an' things,' said Jasmine looking around curiously. 'Lots an' lots more than us.'

'I expect we have to cook for lots and lots more people than your mother,' said the cook.

'Hasn't anyone ever told you that children should be seen and not heard?' demanded Miss Jebb sourly.

Jasmine looked chagrined and Willow said, 'Don't talk to my sister like that!'

'It'll soon be time to serve afternoon tea,' said the cook quickly. 'Let's get the trays laid up.'

Jasmine and Willow were fascinated by the many luxurious preparations for so simple a meal as tea. Then the footman returned to say that the pram was safe and he'd left it outside.

'Did you find the jam sandwiches?' asked Willow, 'an' the blanket?'

'I never saw any food or a blanket,' said the footman.

'Oh, dear. Wasn't there anythin' there?'

'Never saw anything but the pram, and that's so old no one would want it.'

Willow felt like weeping. All her lovely drawings, the work of months, had disappeared.

'Have you lost somethin' precious, my dear?' asked the cook.

'Yes, my drawin' book an' pencil. I dropped them when I ran.'

Miss Jebb threw up her hands. 'Did you ever hear the like? A drawing book and pencil. Miss Violet and Miss Frances practically save her life and she's bothered about some old book and pencil. Well, it looks as if you'll have to buy more.' She glared at Willow.

Willow's speech failed her. Surely someone in this crowd understood poverty? Surely someone knew what it was like to have to scrape up the farthings?

The footman said, 'Is this it?' He drew out her book from his apron pocket. Two pages were torn, but it was otherwise intact. 'I didn't see a pencil, I just found this on the grass. I didn't realise it was yours.'

Miss Jebb took the book, holding it gingerly, as if it were contaminated. She turned the pages. 'Well!' she declared indignantly. 'If the little hussy hasn't been drawing Miss Frances and Miss Violet. The cheek of her! Look at this, Mr Steadman.'

The butler extracted a pair of pince-nez from his waistcoat pocket and examined the drawings. The others remained silent and waited. He looked sternly at Willow. 'Who gave you permission to draw your betters?'

'There's no harm in it,' she said.

'No harm? No good either!' pronounced Mr Steadman.

He handed the book back to Miss Jebb who turned more pages, tearing one of them further.

'Be careful!' said Willow.

Miss Jebb stared down her nose. 'Don't you order me about. Only Mr and Mrs Maddison and my young ladies do that in this house. Well, I never! The pages are full of Miss Violet and Miss Frances! Here's one that must have been done last year. Miss Violet got that ermine stole and muff just before we left for the country. You recall them, don't you, Mr Steadman?'

'I most certainly do. Young woman, what do you mean by this?'

Mrs Narracott peeped over Miss Jebb's shoulder. 'They're very good drawin's,' she said unexpectedly. 'You've got to admit that. And she's coloured them in, too.'

Mr Steadman examined them again. 'They do have a certain quality,' he said. 'Who is your drawing master?'

Willow blinked. She knew from Gran that the gentry had teachers for special subjects, but even so stately a butler as Mr Steadman could surely not believe that someone dressed like her, pushing her sister in an old pram, could afford a drawing master!

'I don't suppose she's got one,' said the cook amicably.

'No, I haven't,' said Willow.

They were interrupted by a bell which clanged over the

green baize door leading to the house. 'Miss Frances,' said Mr Steadman. He tugged his waistcoat over his portly figure and Willow wondered how many meals he had eaten to produce so much flesh. Her sick feeling gone, her mouth was watering with the delectable smells coming from the range.

Miss Jebb left to answer the bell.

'Are you hungry?' asked Mrs Narracott of Willow.

'I am,' said Jasmine eagerly, and everyone laughed.

'Quite an engaging child,' said Mr Steadman. 'How old are you?'

When she told him he asked, 'What is your name?'

'Jasmine.'

'Jasmine! That's a bit fancy, isn't it!' declared Nora.

'What's *your* name?' asked a woman who hadn't spoken before. She was tall and thin, dressed in black, with a bunch of keys at her waist.

'Willow.'

'It can't be!' exclaimed Nora.

'Well, it is!'

'That's a tree,' said the lady in black.

'I know that, but my mum didn't.'

'Whatever do you mean?'

Willow said, talking fast because she knew they would find her story amusing and she wanted to get it over with, 'My gran was born in the country an' wanted us all to have flower names, the girls that is, of course, but Mum had me when Gran was away an' she thought Willow was a flower.'

There was a general burst of laughter and she flushed angrily.

'Don't look at us like that, my girl,' said Mr Steadman, controlling his mirth. 'You've got to admit it's a funny name and a very funny story.'

Hot, angry words were ready to spill from her and it was fortunate that Frances, followed by her maid, arrived to inquire after her. 'There is transport waiting for you,' she said. 'Jebb, did you bring the things for the child?'

'I've brought down some stockings, Miss Frances.'

'What about the frock? She'll need one to replace hers.'

'You aren't going to give her one of yours!'

Frances said, 'There is one laid ready on my bed.' Her voice was even, but there was a note in it which sent Miss Jebb hurrying to the door. As she went she directed a resentful glance at Willow and her face went red with anger.

Willow didn't care. She'd never meet the nasty woman again and she was glad of it.

'We're ready to go, miss,' she said respectfully, 'but we lost our sandwiches an' the cook said she would give us some food.'

'But of course. Mrs Narracott, what have we got? Wrap up a nice pork pie. A big one.' She turned to Willow. 'I dare say you have brothers and sisters?'

'Yes, miss, an' they're always hungry, especially my brothers.'

Everyone laughed again, as if she had made a joke, when she had been desperately serious. A pork pie! How big would it be? When she saw the size of it she was astonished. It would feed them all tonight and tomorrow. Mrs Narracott hadn't finished. She found an equally large apple pie, a loaf of new-baked bread and a crock of butter. 'You can keep the crock,' she said, 'it's got a chip in it.'

Frances asked, 'Have we no sweetmeats? All children love them.'

'To be sure,' said the cook. She went back to the pantry and returned with a paper bag. 'Macaroons and raspberry cream bon-bons, all made in this very kitchen,' she said, handing the bag to Jasmine. 'Now, keep your fingers out of there until you see your mum.'

Frances frowned. 'Jebb is taking her time. I think I'll see what she is doing.' She returned soon after with a brown paper parcel. She looked cross with her face all pink and Willow saw how very pretty she was, though not as pretty as Violet who was a real beauty.

'Can you walk easily now, my dear?' Frances asked,

and Willow nodded her head, then wished she hadn't as it hurt.

'Don't nod like a donkey,' said Nora.

Frances laughed. 'Come along, children.' She led them through a side door to the road where Reggie's motor car stood. He was already in the driving seat.

'Up in the back with you, girls,' he said jovially. 'The pram's stowed on the luggage rack.'

Willow's eyes shone, but Jasmine hung back. 'Gran says they're dreadful things,' she protested. 'Why can't we go in a regular carriage, or the tram?'

Frances gave her easy laugh. 'You'll love it, I promise, and you'll be home in no time.' When Jasmine still showed reluctance she said, 'There's your sister all ready and waiting. Don't forget she's not feeling well.'

Jasmine, helped by the footman, climbed into the car and clung to Willow. Frances handed them two filmy scarves. 'Wrap these around your heads to keep off the dust,' she advised. 'You may keep them.' As the girls stammered out their thanks, the door was closed upon them and they were driven away.

'I don't like it,' complained Jasmine. 'It's noisy an' it smells.'

'It's lovely,' said Willow. 'One day I'm goin' to have one of these with a hood that goes up an' down, just like this one, an' I'll drive it myself, an' won't everyone be jealous?'

Jasmine said nothing. She was used to her sister's flights of fancy.

Their return caused a sensation in the street. Mum came running out at the unaccustomed sound of an engine. Reggie swept to a stop in front of the house pointed out by Willow and gave a loud toot-toot on the horn. He had been tooting all the way home and even Jasmine had enjoyed that. He climbed out and handed the girls down as if they were ladies, and Willow had a job not to laugh at the expressions on the neighbours' faces.

'What's happened?' asked Mum.

Reggie held out his gloved hand and Mum put hers out

uncertainly. He grasped it and said heartily, 'Your girl's a heroine. Saved a young friend of mine from serious injury, if not worse. Got a bit of a bump on the head, don't you know, so I brought her home. There will be a bottle of medicine sent over later. Oh, and I'd like to give a small contribution in token of my own thanks. I would never have forgiven myself if I'd run over a child.'

Mum shook her head disbelievingly as the pram was unstrapped and lifted down as carefully as if it had been the young ladies' hat boxes. Willow decided that she definitely liked Reggie. As he drove away, they all watched him until he gave a final wave and turned the corner.

In the house Mum opened her hand and showed them two gold sovereigns. 'Look what he gave me.' She stared down at them, and a couple of tears rolled down her cheeks.

'Mum, don't,' begged Willow. 'Aren't you glad to get the money? You can pay off Mrs Tucker an' the money-lender an' still have a bit left over.'

Clara looked at the girls as if she didn't see them and Jasmine was frightened and began to sob. Clara came to herself and held the gold tight in her hand as the adventure was related to her. Willow was made to lie down until the evening meal was ready. Clara invited Gran and they sat round the table and ate half the pork pie and apple pie and exclaimed over the delicate sweetmeats which Gran said were everyday things in a nob's house. Mum set aside generous portions for Dad who was expected home on Monday. Willow was feeling much better after one of Gran's remedies and a sleep. She leaned back, replete for once, and considered what it must be like to live in a house where you could stretch out a hand to a bell and have food sent up whenever you felt hungry and plates of macaroons and raspberry cream bon-bons when you wanted a treat. Mum had waited until Willow recovered before opening the parcel handed over by Frances. Willow gained an impression of stockings and something in blue serge, before her headache suddenly grew worse and Mum bustled her off to bed for the night. She slept, only waking

37

when Jasmine came up and Mum took the opportunity to spoon syrup into her mouth. 'A man in a fancy uniform brought it,' she said. 'He said to tell you that it'll make you better.' The syrup tasted pleasant and gave Willow a warm glow and beneath its influence she drifted back into sleep.

The next morning she was waited on in bed and given her usual slice of bread with margarine luscious with the remainder of Gran's jam.

'Your gran's one in a million,' said Mum. 'I tried to give her some money. I wanted to pay her back a bit for what she does for us, but she said she hadn't no use for it. Said she's got all she needs.'

Willow washed her meal down with a cup of sweet tea, then climbed gingerly out of bed. Except for her sore head and a few more bruises which had manifested themselves, she felt well. Downstairs, Mum and Gran watched her examine the contents of the parcel.

Willow lifted out the serge. 'It's a dress. I think it'll fit without alteration.'

'Blue serge,' said Mum, 'an' plain as a pikestaff!'

'It'll be one of the young ladies' frocks from when they were in the schoolroom,' said Gran.

'Such plain stuff,' said Mum. 'I'd have expected somethin' better from rich folk like the Maddisons, though I don't know why. They never give a thought to the likes of us.'

'Now, Clara, do you want our Willow to go to the factory in chiffon and lace?'

Mum said nothing. Gran was right, of course, but Mum didn't want to admit that one of Them had done something decent. Even the food hadn't moved her. 'After what our Willow done they should have given her a *big* reward.'

'But the young man gave you something,' Gran reminded her.

'Not as much as she deserved.'

Willow picked up the stockings. 'Look at these,' she said reverently. 'Black silk, an' only needin' a darn in one of the toes.'

'What good will they be to you?' said Clara.

Gran said, 'There's no pleasing you today, Clara Riches. Not that I wonder at it with our poor Arthur where he is.'

'I think Miss Jebb put in the silk ones,' said Willow. 'She said that Violet never wore stockin's if they'd been mended. Frances must have packed some more. Here's a pair of wool and two of lisle, an' they don't need a thing doin' to them.'

'Who's Miss Jebb?' asked Mum, fascinated in spite of herself by Willow's experiences in the rich household. Willow was pleased to describe all that she could recall.

On Monday morning Dad came home. Willow had already left for work. She returned that night to hear her mother anxiously chiding him. 'You've not touched the good victuals an' they'd do you the world of good.'

Willow stood unnoticed in the doorway as her father said angrily, 'I don't want charity from those buggers.' There was a quality in his voice which she had never heard before. 'They've shamed me – they've shamed us all – an' I never did a thing wrong. I've got to live now with the burden of a prison record, an' the way I feel I hope I won't last long.'

Willow gave a cry of protest and Clara turned to her. 'Try to talk some sense into your father. He won't eat any of this good pork pie.' Her voice was rough with impotent anger and fear.

'Come on, our Dad,' begged Willow. She pushed the plate of pie and hot potatoes towards him. 'This isn't charity. I *earned* it. Look!' She pulled back her hair. 'See this bruise, black an' blue it is. An' I've got more bruises in places that no good girl can mention.'

Arthur smiled faintly and she coaxed, 'Come on, Dad. I've paid for every mouthful.'

Looking into her earnest, pleading face, Arthur picked up his knife and cut into the pie.

Clara sighed in relief and beckoned Willow into the

scullery. 'Let's leave him be. I've got a pile of washin' to dampen down ready for ironin'. If you feel up to it you can help me with that. We'll wait a bit for our food. The boys aren't back yet and it'll give our Dad a chance to pull himself together.'

Chapter Three

The doctor's medicine made Willow too sleepy for her to take regularly and go to work. Her bruises ached, especially the one on her head, but nothing must rob her of the promotion which could bring her wages up by as much as a shilling. On the Wednesday following the incident on the Downs she returned home to find her mother holding a letter, a rarity in their household.

Clara handed it to her. 'It's for you.'

The heavy cream envelope was too precious to tear. 'It's like real drawin' paper,' she said.

Clara exclaimed impatiently and Willow slit carefully across the top of the envelope with a knife and drew out a sheet of matching paper. There was an address engraved in black. 'It's from Miss Frances Maddison, Mum.' She scanned the note swiftly.

Jasmine and Marigold jostled her noisily. 'What does it say? Tell us.'

'She says her mother's back now an' is very grateful to me for savin' her little girl from havin' an accident. She wants to reward me—'

'Is she givin' you money?' cried Marigold. 'How much?'

'No, she's not said anythin' about money. She's offerin' me a job.'

'But you've already got one,' said her sister in disgust.

'Yes, but this is different. She says I can go as a maid in their house in Devonshire. Gran says it's very big. There's no tellin' what I might end up as. A lady's maid perhaps. Gran says they get a lot of sewin' to do – I'd like that. Rich ladies wear real good stuff.'

41

'You want to go?' Clara sounded doubtful.

Seeing her mother's anxious face, Willow's enthusiasm was curbed. 'I can't leave you, Mum. Who'd do the manglin'? An' Dad's not at all well.'

'Who says so?'

They turned as Arthur came into the kitchen. 'Don't I get a say about what's goin' on in my own family?' His words were authoritative, but his voice held an alarmingly bitter note. No matter what had happened before he'd always taken it on the chin, but the latest blow had changed him. Since leaving prison he had small wish even to go outside the house.

Gran had said sadly, 'They've broken his spirit. I'm afraid he'll turn his face to the wall.'

Something in her expression prevented Willow from asking the meaning of the phrase, but it sounded bad.

Clara said, 'Come in, Dad, an' sit by the fire. Marigold, pour your dad a cup of tea. The pot's all ready on the hob.'

'No,' said Arthur. 'First I want my question answered.'

'Of course you do, an' you shall,' Clara assured him. 'Wait until Dad's ready, Marigold.'

Willow read the letter to her father. He was silent for a while. 'Do you want the job in Devon, child?'

'Not if it means that Mum has to work twice as hard. She gets that tired!'

Colour flared on the skin stretched over Arthur's cheekbones and Willow wanted to bite her tongue as he said, 'She does too much, that's for sure.'

Clara flashed her a furious glance.

'I wonder what kind of job they're offerin' you?' Arthur said. 'Here, let me see the letter.'

They were silent while he slowly made out the words for himself.

Clara said, 'It's bound to be a good one. I mean to say, if someone pulls your kid out from under the wheels of one of those smelly motor cars you'd treat her right, wouldn't you? An' if they've got more than one house they must be as rich as – as a duke maybe!'

Arthur asked, 'How old are you, Marigold?'

'Twelve, Dad. Did you forget?'

He smiled. 'How strong are you?'

She frowned. 'Why?'

'You could help Mum with the washin'. I don't know why you haven't taken your share before this.'

Willow knew. Her sister looked after her skin, spending any money she could get hold of on lotions and creams. She wouldn't let anything ruin it.

'I don't want to end up like Willow, doin' nothin' but work.'

'You can spare time for your mother. Life isn't all play.'

'She's still young,' said Clara. She thought a lot of Marigold.

'Willow's been turnin' that mangle since she was ten,' said Arthur.

Clara looked at Willow as if seeing her for the first time. 'So you have. You've been helpin' me all these years.'

'An' never a complaint, as far as I know,' said Arthur.

'You'll do it, Marigold, won't you?' begged Willow. 'By the time you go out to work, I might be *somebody* an' I could get you a good job.'

Marigold said deliberately, 'Thank you for nothin'. I don't want to end up as somebody's servant.'

'Less of your cheek,' snapped Arthur. 'Your gran was a servant an' look how well she turned out. You go, Willow, an' make the most of your chance.'

Her heart leapt. 'Gran's told me heaps about the way rich folk live. Their servants get wages *an*' their board an' have a real good time.'

'Gran was in an easy place,' warned Clara. 'You might not be so lucky.'

'She'll make the most of it,' said Arthur.

Clara frowned. 'I'm not too sure about it. She's due for promotion an' a rise at the factory, an' she could end up as forewoman. With her brains, she could do anythin'.'

'Mum learned a lot in service,' said Arthur. 'She'd have been a head nurse for sure if she hadn't got married.'

'I know that, Arthur, but Gran's biddable an' Willow isn't. She's got a quick tongue too. If the place doesn't suit she won't get her job back. There's too many lookin' for work.'

'She must have her chance. It's up to you, Willow. What do you say?' Arthur persisted.

She could no longer hold back her enthusiasm. 'I'll be biddable. I'll obey them.' Her thoughts were spinning in delicious patterns. She'd be in a house where the nobs lived, be able to watch them, learn their ways, see their lovely clothes and draw them. Being a lady's maid was an important position, Gran said. Willow thought of Miss Jebb. Well, she wouldn't be like her, all sour and nasty.

'Does it say when they want you to go?' asked Marigold. Her chin stuck out belligerently. 'Maybe they'll ask you to scrub the floors. You won't be so high-falutin' then.'

'No, they'll have special servants for that,' cried Willow. 'If I accept I've to write to Mrs Maddison an' she'll send me a list. I'll run round an' ask Gran what that means.'

She returned, disheartened. 'I'll need to buy my workin' dresses.'

'What?' Clara was angry. 'The meanness of some folk, an' them so rich an' showy-off. It's a scandal. Well, we'll just have to see what we can do.'

'Mum, you can't!'

'I'll leave off my baccy for a bit an' not go for my pint at the pub.' Arthur's face twisted in a grimace. 'I've not got much inclination for goin' out, anyway.'

Willow looked at them, loving them, pitying them, yet almost angry with them because they wanted to martyr themselves for her.

The list said that two print dresses were needed and a black one for afternoons, black stockings and plain, serviceable shoes with rubber soles and heels. Mrs Maddison required her servants to wear decent underclothing and have a good black costume and hat for attending church. Aprons, collars and cuffs would be provided.

Willow stared at the list. 'That's the end of that, then. We can't buy all this stuff. I can't go.'

'I'll borrow the money,' said Clara. 'You've got your heart set.' Having made up her mind she disliked being thwarted.

'No, Mum. You'll have to pay back the shillin' in the pound extra an' you still owe some money. You can't do it.'

'What does it say about pay?' asked Arthur.

'Ten pounds an' all found.'

'Every week?' Marigold shrieked.

'No, every year, but it's paid monthly.'

'Is that a lot of money?' asked Jasmine. She was dreadfully torn. She wanted Willow to get a fine job but the thought of her going away was heart-breaking.

Willow lifted the small girl on to her lap. 'It's not bad.' She scribbled a few figures. 'I'll get sixteen shillin's a month an' I won't need to spend a penny, so I can send it all home. It's twice as much as I get now, Mum, an' you won't even have to feed me.'

Gran came to tea and read the list. 'When you get there, Willow, you must tell the housekeeper that you need stuff for your dresses and she'll provide it. You can make them yourself. They're sure to have a sewing machine somewhere.'

'Why didn't they say so?' Willow's eyes shone. 'That's much better.'

'They'll still expect you to pay,' said Gran. 'They'll stop the money out of your wages.'

'What!' cried Clara. 'That's really mean. She'll only need to buy special workin' clothes for them. They ought to pay.'

'They don't see it that way,' said Gran. 'If you worked elsewhere you'd buy your clothes, so why not with them?'

Them and Us, thought Willow bitterly. She was sick with fury at what she considered the Maddisons' penny-pinching.

'I can hardly believe it,' said her mother. 'Them with all their money an' they make a poor girl buy her own maid's outfits.'

'It's a regular thing,' said Gran. 'I made my first frocks before I took up a post. Any colour print will do. We'll get some and I'll help with the cutting out and sewing.'

Hope flooded Willow, then she looked doubtfully at her grandmother's knobbly hands.

Most of the remainder of Reggie's money paid for half the cost of the material and Gran, insisting that Clara must keep a little in hand, found the other. She had a friend who supplemented her income by sewing and possessed a sewing machine. 'She'll lend it to us for tuppence an hour,' Gran explained. 'She must charge or she'll be losing money.' Gran allowed for generous seams. 'You're still growing, my love, and you'll need to let them out.' The sewing was finished quickly and Gran produced a rather rusty black costume. 'This is what I used to wear to church. It'll fit you with a bit of alteration, and I got a mourning bonnet from the pawn shop. We'll put a bit of ribbon round it. And I bought a black dress that only wants a few stitches. You'll have to manage with your boots for now and put by a bit each week for shoes.'

'I promised to send Mum all my money.'

'But you must be properly shod.'

Willow touched the ironed dresses with a reverent finger. They smelt clean and new, so different from second-hand stuff. Maid's dresses they might be, but they were the first unused garments she could remember owning. They were a soft shade of pink with small, slightly pinker flowers. She kissed her grandmother. 'You're an angel. I've unpicked this old black shawl an' I'm goin' to knit a small jacket in case it gets cold. Will I need it for work?'

'You might. It depends on what they give you to do. You must be inside or they wouldn't have asked for an afternoon frock.'

'Do some maids work outside?'

'No, my dear. "In the house" means the other side of the green baize doors that separate the servants' quarters from the family. It's always polished wood on their side, with a brass handle, but covered with baize on the servants' side and with an iron handle.'

'Did it take you long to make friends?'

'I was a nursery maid, thought to be a cut above the others, though I could never fathom out why. Our old nurse was a regular tartar; if she thought someone was presuming, it was straight to the housekeeper to complain and she insisted that the nursery maids didn't hobnob with the staff. I got a bit lonely sometimes. Still, if you want to get on you mustn't mind a bit of loneliness.'

When Willow handed in her notice the factory manager was annoyed. 'I had high hopes of you, Miss Riches, and here you are, throwing away everything you've worked for. I just hope you don't live to regret it, that's all.'

'I won't,' she assured him happily.

She met Sidney Moor on her way home. His hair was growing in patchy stubble and his face had even more spots. 'They say you're goin' away,' he said without preamble.

'They say,' mocked Willow. 'Who says?'

'Everybody in the street.'

'Nosey parkers! An' what's it to you?'

'Nothin'.'

Willow was nonplussed. He was the most unprepossessing-looking boy she knew, but she felt sorry for him. In spite of his terrible background he had kept out of trouble and that must take some doing. For the first time she wondered what his life was like at home.

'I'm goin' to Devonshire,' she said.

'What for?'

'I'm goin' to work in a very big house.'

'As a servant?'

'As an *upper* maid, if you must know, though I don't suppose you know what that means.'

'Oh, yes I do!'

'How?'

'I read about it in a book.'

Willow stared. 'You like readin'?'

Sidney's face reddened. 'Is there somethin' wrong in that?'

Willow hastened to pacify him though the idea of his reading at home where the only things the others studied were racing papers and court summonses astonished her. 'Of course there's nothin' wrong,' she assured him. 'Books are lovely. Where do you get yours?'

'From the library in the tobacconist's shop. Have you got books of your own?'

'Some. Dad bought me *Pilgrim's Progress* an' *The Vicar of Wakefield* an' we've got others, all from church sales. An' Gran Riches has kept all my grandad's books.'

'Do you like learnin'?' he asked, encouraged by her softer tones.

'Yes, I do. I'm goin' to be *someone* in this world. I wish I hadn't had to leave school.'

'I wish I could stay on,' said Sidney, 'but I'll never be able to. Dad'll have me at work when I'm thirteen.'

Willow looked sympathetic and he stepped closer. She wrinkled her nose at the unwashed smell of him. 'We'll both amount to somethin', eh, Willow?'

'I have to get home.'

He called after her, 'We'll both get somewhere, you'll see. You can bet a bob on that!'

A week later Willow left the factory and packed her belongings in a small tin trunk supplied by Gran. She found it difficult to sleep the night before she began her journey to Buddleigh Manor. She pictured herself, elegantly dressed in black. In her imagination the made-over pawn-shop dress miraculously became silk and she was carrying a silver tray which held a letter. A letter from a lover, perhaps, to Frances or Violet. A forbidden lover! Willow's reading was catholic and forbidden love was constantly depicted in magazines Clara got hold of from the houses she washed for. She might even be asked to accompany one of the young ladies on an elopement. She smiled into the darkness, the only sound that of her sisters' soft breathing, then she sobered. That kind of activity wouldn't get her to the top. Her imagination soared in a different direction. A royal personage would visit the manor and be so impressed by the tall, well-dressed maid that she would ask Willow to join her household. Either she would become the friend and confidante of her mistress, or marry a nob who came to stay – there must be some nice ones. There was Reggie, for instance. She grinned. He was kind but not bright; he would never do. She would attract someone rich and clever. A prince, even.

She awoke feeling nervous and her optimism withered as she looked out of the bedroom window into a grey, wet day. The whole family gathered downstairs to wish her goodbye and suddenly it seemed impossible to leave them, they were all so dear to her, but Clara gave her a little push. 'Off you go. Write to us.'

She was to make her way to Temple Meads Station. Joe had offered to find a substitute for his job so that he could carry her box, but she had refused. It wasn't heavy and the trams ran just down the road. Gran had said her goodbye the night before, handing Willow a small purse containing three shillings. 'You'll feel better with a bit of money in your pocket, my love. Now don't lose your ticket.' (The Maddisons had sent it.) Willow assured her she wouldn't. It was hardest leaving Jasmine who was pale but dry-eyed. Willow hugged her tight. 'Be a good girl for Mum.'

The train journey was exciting. Willow allowed a man to lift her trunk on to the luggage rack and sat beneath where she could watch it. She clutched a brown paper bag containing her bonnet. On her head was a straw boater Mum had got from a friendly cook. Willow had adorned it with a rose fashioned from a leftover bit of pink material. She carried other scraps in her trunk in case one of her dresses got torn, a fear that quickened her heart. At a small country halt the train stopped and the guard informed her that this was where she got out. She watched the train huff and puff its way out of sight and sound and stood on the short deserted platform, her trunk at her feet. The silence was eerie, quite unlike anything she had experienced before. There were no cart wheels on cobbles, no children at play, no chugging sounds of machinery at work. The rain had given way to sunshine which was hot on her back and gradually she became aware of birdsong, of cows lowing, of sheep bleating; somewhere a horse neighed, the only sound with which she was familiar. Otherwise nothing, not a human being in sight. She sat down on a bench near a small stone building and was startled when a door opened and an elderly man in railway uniform appeared.

'Where are you supposed to be going?' he asked sternly, as if she had no right to be there.

'I'm expected at Buddleigh Manor,' Willow answered, trying to sound as grand as Miss Jebb.

The station-master's face split in a grin. 'You'll be the new maid.'

'Yes, have you heard about me?'

'No, but I'm right, aren't I?'

'How can you tell?'

The man touched the side of his nose. 'I'm a good guesser.'

'How do I get there? I don't even know which way to walk.'

'You can't carry that trunk so far, though it's a quarter the size some of 'em turn up with. Someone's sure to be along to fetch you.'

'When?'

'Do they know what time you arrived?'

'I wrote and said.'

'Then you just sit there and wait.'

Willow sat and waited. She waited for an hour, feeling first disgruntled then anxious. Had they forgotten her? Didn't they want her? Would she have to get a train back and face the mockery of the neighbours? And what about her lost factory job? And where would she get enough money for a ticket? The Maddisons hadn't sent a return.

The clip-clop of hooves floated to her on the balmy air

and the station-master poked his head out. 'That'll surely be someone come for you. The lane outside only comes to the station.'

Willow picked up her trunk and walked to the little wooden gate set in the fence. A high-sided carriage stopped and the driver, a young man in gleaming polished boots, shirtsleeves and striped waistcoat, said, 'You the new maid?'

'Yes.'

'Climb aboard.'

Willow climbed. She felt absurdly disappointed. Of course it had been foolish of her to expect a motor car like Reggie's, or a proper carriage and pair. The coachman had to turn sideways to hold the reins and seemed disinclined to talk as the docile pony trotted between hedges fragrant with blossom, merry with birdsong, busy with bees droning in the heat.

They had travelled about a mile when Willow asked, 'How far is the manor?'

The man said, 'What's it to you? You don't have to walk.'

Willow felt annoyed. He didn't have to treat her like this. 'Is it nice there?' she asked loudly.

The man looked at her, startled. 'It's as nice as any place is when you're in service.'

'Please, are you in service, or—?'

'Or what?'

'I don't know.'

The young man said, 'I'm a groom. Did you think I was one of the Maddisons?'

'I didn't know.'

'You don't know much then, do you?'

'No.' Feeling that a little more was needed, she said, 'It's good of you to fetch me.'

The man gave her a sideways look. 'Better than you know. It's not the usual thing to ask a groom like myself to drive a governess cart. It's built to keep children safe and it's a woman's place to take the reins, but the governess has got one of her headaches.'

'I'm sorry.'

'You needn't be. She's a stupid, ugly creature and lets Miss Winifred walk all over her.'

Willow felt nervous as she remembered Winifred's spoilt behaviour and a wave of sympathy for the governess flowed over her. 'Are they kind to you?'

The groom laughed, suddenly friendly. 'They're all right, I suppose, better than many. You get plenty to eat and there's enough servants to do the work.'

The remark puzzled Willow. 'Why shouldn't there be?'

'It's easy to tell that this is your first place. You should see some of the houses I've worked for. Mean? As mean as dirt! Not enough maids, no butler, one of them only had a parlourmaid to open the front door, and even hired carriages. I ask you! The master and mistress keep a good house. Of course, they're rich. I'm aiming to be head groom before I've finished. Maybe something even better.'

Willow had an impulse to tell him that she would one day be a lady's maid, but decided against it. 'Least said, soonest mended,' as Gran said.

'We'll soon be at the top of this hill and you'll see the manor. It's very old. Set in a valley.'

'What's your name?'

'Andy Hunnicott. What's yours?'

'Willow.'

'Willow! What sort of a name is that?'

'It's mine,' she flashed.

'All right, keep your hair on. What's your last name?'

'Riches.'

'It can't be.' Andy laughed loudly. 'What a name for a servant!'

Willow turned her head huffily and only looked round when the governess cart stopped and Andy said, 'There's Buddleigh Manor,' with as much pride as if it had been his.

Willow looked down into the valley and gasped. A great, grey stone house, bigger than she could have imagined, sat serenely in the sun, a gleaming river coiling halfway round it before it curved back on its journey to the sea. 'Is it a castle?' was all she could think of.

'It's got turrets, though someone stuck them on in Queen Victoria's time. I suppose you could call it a castle, if you've a mind. *They* call it a manor.'

'It's got pillars in front.'

'"Portico" is the right name.'

'I've never heard of that.'

'No? I expect you'll hear a lot of new things in Buddleigh Manor.'

Willow fell silent, wondering how life was lived in such a place. It made the Maddisons' Bristol house look small.

He drove the little cart to the back of the manor and the pony clattered into a cobbled yard, where Andy leapt down and held its head. 'Down you get. Take your trunk through that gateway. The kitchen door's opposite.'

Willow glanced round curiously at the stables and coach houses which were in better condition than most of the human dwellings she had seen. She went through the gate. On the other side were more cobbles. Clothes lines were strung across one corner and a small girl in a hessian apron was pinning out dishcloths. Willow opened the door and found herself in a stone-floored vestibule with stone stairs leading to the basement. She hoisted her tin trunk on to her hip. At the bottom of the stairs was another corridor at the end of which stood a door. She pushed it open nervously to discover a kitchen whose size matched the house. Several pairs of eyes regarded her, then someone said, 'You must be the new maid.'

Willow looked at the speaker, a short, stout girl in a plain white apron and cap. 'Yes.'

'I'm Prue, the cook.'

'But I thought Mrs Narracott – do they have a different cook in every place they go?'

Prue looked round to see if the others were listening. 'Cocky, aren't you?'

'Sorry,' muttered Willow.

'How do you know Mrs Narracott?' demanded Prue.

'I met her in Bristol.'

'Is that so? Mrs Narracott's the head cook; the master and mistress take her whenever they go to stay in another of their residences. She's the best cook in England, the master says.'

'Is she?'

'Can't say. That's what *he* says and who am I to argue?'

There was general laughter and Willow shrank inside. The three humble rooms, where she'd left her family in crowded fellowship, seemed a terribly long distance away. There, she was important, Mum's helper, Dad's nurse sometimes, the children's minder. Here, she was nobody. Well, let them laugh. She'd never reveal how scared and homesick she was at this moment.

Prue said quite kindly, 'The family's away, but they'll be here in a few days, then the guests will start arrivin' an' we'll all be rushed off our feet so you'd better learn all you can as quick as you can. Now, that gentleman over there readin' the newspaper is Mr Norris, the under-butler, over there's Henry Jefford, the footman, and the girls are all maids like yourself. Polly, that's the redhead with her cap on crooked, is first housemaid, Nancy's second housemaid. The other servants will be down with the master and mistress.'

As Prue pointed out each one, the under-butler gave her a haughty stare, the maids waved and Henry winked.

Polly straightened her cap with a grin and Willow said, 'I see.' She didn't see at all. She would never be able to remember all the names and this was only part of the staff. Gran must have been in service in a smaller place.

'What's your name?' asked Nancy.

Willow said warily, 'Willow Riches.'

'Good lord! What sort of a name is Willow?' Mr Norris lowered his newspaper.

'It's *my* name.'

Prue said, 'Stop laughin' at her, do, it's not her fault. Nancy, show her up to her room. Unpack your trunk, Willow, then come back down for tea. I expect you're hungry.'

As Willow followed Nancy up a flight of steep, narrow stairs covered in brown lino, she realised she felt hungry and hoped that Nancy couldn't hear her insides rumbling. She wondered what they had for tea in such a place. The stairs seemed to go on forever. Every so often they passed a door and, just as Gran had described, they were covered with green baize and had iron handles. They reached the attics and Nancy opened a door and said, 'This is where you'll be. You share with Aggie and Ivy. Come down as quick as you can. Tea's almost ready.'

'Who are Aggie and Ivy?' asked Willow, but Nancy seemed not to hear and hurried back to the cosy comfort of the kitchen.

In the room, Willow put down her trunk with a sigh of relief. There was a large brass bed, a chest with three drawers with one leg repaired with unvarnished deal, a wardrobe with a faulty door catch so that it stood open a few inches, a wash-stand with jug and basin, and a slop bucket below. Under the bed she saw a chamber pot and realised that she would have to perform a private function in front of strangers. On the wall hung a small mirror and opposite a sepia print of the coronation of King Edward the Seventh. She pulled open the wardrobe door and hung her clothes on hooks, but decided not to touch the chest until she found out which drawer she was to have. She placed her hats on top of her trunk and brushed her hair, fighting as always to control its dark waves and curls. Should she put on one of the print dresses? She decided against it and began the long descent to the basement. She had reached ground-floor level when the temptation to peep inside the house overcame her and she pushed open one of the green baize doors. She couldn't see much, so she pushed harder and stepped forward and tripped over the deep pile carpet to land at the feet of someone she recognised – the young brother of the Maddison girls.

'Good God! Who are you?' he exclaimed. 'And what the devil do you mean by leaping at me in such a fashion?'

'Sorry,' she gasped, climbing to her feet. 'I fell. I didn't mean to startle you.'

'I should damn' well think you didn't! Don't let it occur again.'

'No.'

'No, *sir*.'

Willow turned to go and was detained by a firm grip on her arm. Her first instinct was to take the action she would at home and land a hefty smack on his face. She stopped herself just in time.

Edgar stared at her, smiling, but not pleasantly. 'You've got fine eyes and you wouldn't be bad-looking if you had a bit more flesh on your bones.' He regarded her carefully. 'I must say, you have execrable taste in clothes.'

Willow hadn't come across the word 'execrable' before, but she knew it meant something nasty. She had decided to save the blue serge for best and had travelled in her black dress. When she remembered the way that Gran's rheumaticky hands had sewn a bit of blue braid round the neck and cuffs, how satisfied they had both been with her efforts, her indignation almost spilled over in angry speech. She pressed her lips together.

'Don't do that with your mouth, girl. Has anyone ever told you you have a pretty mouth? Very pretty. Especially this bit.' He touched her lower lip with his finger.

Willow had always craved a rosebud mouth like heroines in stories had. Her lower lip was full and her brothers said it reminded them of a fish. She had ignored them, but she resented this man's mockery and was disgusted by his familiarity. When he began to trace his finger round her lips her self-control went and she bit it.

'Ouch! You little wildcat! What a devil of a temper! You had best watch your manners if you wish to remain in my family's service.'

'No one told me I'd have to let men paw me about!'

'Paw you about!' He would have said more, but Henry appeared, whose eyes widened at the sight of Willow. 'There you are! Sorry, Mr Edgar, she's the new maid. She must have got lost. She doesn't know her place yet.'

'She makes that perfectly clear. Speak to someone about her manners. Make sure she knows what is expected of her in future.'

Henry grasped Willow's shoulder hard and shook her. 'Go on down to the kitchen the same way you came up.'

'Wait a moment,' said Edgar. 'Haven't I seen you somewhere before?'

'Yes, sir, on the Downs in Bristol.'

'Well, I'm dashed. You're the girl who created a beastly scene.' Willow opened her mouth to protest, but was quelled by a dig in the back from Henry. 'Mind you,' said Edgar, 'she did pull Miss Winifred from under a car so we had better let her off this time.'

'Yes, sir.'

Willow scuttled down the stairs, fearful of the moment when Henry told the others what she'd done when she'd only been here for less than an hour. The servants were in a hall adjoining the kitchen, seated round a table laid with a checked cloth. She looked disbelievingly at the food. Ham, cold beef, hot sausages and potatoes, hard-boiled eggs, tomatoes, cucumber, crocks of butter and several loaves.

Henry entered and she looked at him fearfully. He told them of the scene with Mr Edgar. 'He said he held out his hand and she bit it.'

To Willow's surprise there was a gale of appreciative laughter.

'She never!'

'She did, she did!'

The laughter rang out again and Willow realised that the looks directed at her had become quite friendly. She smiled.

Prue warned, 'I suppose he was tryin' it on. Lots of young gentlemen do. Leave them as fast as possible and say nothin'. If you tell the mistress she'll blame you, never the young gentlemen, and you'll lose your job. You got away with it this time, but you mustn't go into the house again unless you're called. Now sit here and tuck in.'

The kitchen suddenly seemed warm and friendly and Willow couldn't resist the food. If only she could have taken some home. She reached out for a piece of bread spread thickly with butter.

Henry said through a mouthful of cold meat, 'Our new maid's a dark horse. It seems she's already met Mr Edgar on the Downs in Bristol.'

There were meaningful 'ohs' and 'ahs' at various pitches. 'What were you doing on the Downs with Mr Edgar?' asked Polly.

'Seems she saved Miss Winifred from being run over,' said Henry.

'Is that right?' Prue sounded impressed. 'So that's why you got the job. There's a village girl who wanted to come here.'

'I didn't know. I don't like to think of puttin' her out of work,' said Willow.

'She wasn't all that suitable,' Mr Norris said. 'She was too rough. The vicar wants a maid. Perhaps she'll go there.'

'She hoped to be in a grand house,' said Nancy.

'I'm sorry for her, but I like bein' here.' Willow was feeling bolder. 'My gran was in service. A nursemaid, she was, an' she told me a lot.'

'Did she now? Then you won't need any teaching.'

There was another burst of laughter and this time Willow joined in and made a hearty tea. She wanted to ask what her duties were to be, but decided she had drawn enough attention to herself for one day. They might get cross with her if she pestered them and she liked them in this good humour. Her job would be in the house. After all, she had her black dress.

That night, Willow lay awake for a long time. At home she usually slept easily until morning. The day had been long and she was tired, but she had spent much of it just sitting in a railway carriage and hadn't been called on to do any work. She had eaten like a king at tea and again at supper and her stomach, unused to such richness, felt bloated and uncomfortable, but what preyed most on her mind was her position in the house.

Ivy had turned out to be head kitchen maid and Willow was to be second kitchen maid. She felt betrayed. What did you have to do for these people to be given a decent job? Not even first kitchen maid – though, as Ivy had pointed out, she wouldn't have known what to do. Willow was slightly mollified when she discovered that there were lowlier positions. At each meal food was sent to the bootboy who ate in his room. 'Can't have him at table,' said Mr Norris. 'He's never clean.'

And the girl she had seen pegging out dishcloths was Aggie, the scullery maid, under-sized, short-sighted, scrawny, and probably a little slow mentally. She had waited on the servants' table, assisted on and off by Ivy, and had fumbled a dish of potatoes and dropped the lid which had smashed.

'That's more out of your wages,' said Ivy.

Tears had runnelled the grime on Aggie's face and her nose had run and Prue told her to go away and wash her face. Willow couldn't help feeling sorry for the girl and wished she had the courage to speak out, but Gran had advised her that the way to be comfortable as a maid was to get on good terms with the upper servants. She knew that Mr Norris was watching her closely, monitoring her every move after the scandal of her brush with Edgar. After eating her fill she had sat on at the table with a cup of tea with creamy milk and white sugar, listening to the banter and laughter, determined to make herself a valued member of the kitchen staff.

It had been a dreadful come-down to realise that Aggie was to be a bed-fellow. Ivy took the place next the wall, Willow was on the outside and, between them, like a small piece of greasy meat in a sandwich, lay the scullery maid. Willow had not had a bed to herself within her memory, but she found Aggie's unwashed body repugnant, quite unlike the familiar smell of her sisters. She recalled her final night at home, when Jasmine had clung to her, weeping to think of her beloved sister going away for a long time. With tears pouring down her cheeks she had begged her to stay. Willow swallowed hard. Her arms felt empty. Who would tell Jasmine her bedtime story? Even if Mum had time she read so badly that there was no pleasure in it, Dad was getting more down-hearted every day and the boys were scathing over babies' stories.

'Learn to read, Jasmine,' she had advised her, 'then you won't need anyone else.'

'I will, I will, I'll need you!' Jasmine hadn't been comforted. Her face had been twisted with grief and wet with tears.

Eventually nature asserted itself and Willow slept, to be awakened at six by Aggie.

'Wake up, won't you? D'you always sleep this heavy? You never even moved when Ivy an' me climbed over you. I got to go. I've not got time to waste. Hurry, there's a lot to do. Your boots are under the bed.'

Wondering what her boots had to do with Aggie, Willow slipped out of bed and discovered that they had been highly polished. She was embarrassed over the patches Dad had stuck to the soles and the worn, scuffed toes, but the bootboy knew his job. She certainly had never seen them shine like this. She put on her new print dress, smoothing it over her hips, feeling incredibly smart. Downstairs, Ivy greeted her with a frown, all the chumminess of the night before gone. 'You'll have to get up at five when the family gets back. I hope you're not a slugabed.'

'No, sorry, but I couldn't get to sleep.'

Ivy relented. 'Have a cup of tea, the pot's on the range, then we must get on. The others will be down for breakfast at seven an' there's a great deal to do before then. Aggie's blackleaded the ovens. You can sweep the floor – don't forget the butler's pantry through there. Later you can scrub his shelves – he expects everything to be spotless. They'll all be here soon an' tomorrow we'll do the housekeeper's room. If she finds a speck of dust, there'll be ructions. Aggie can help with the scrubbin' while I cook servants' breakfast. When the dishes are done it'll be your job to wash all the dishcloths and hang them outside. Aggie did it yesterday because I was busy.'

Ivy paused for breath and Willow looked at Aggie, her arms engrimed with blacklead, and wondered how she ever managed to wash anything properly.

The others came down hungry for their breakfast. Aprons and caps had been produced for Willow and this time she did the serving, before going out to the huge wash-house to check that the fires were ready for the laundry maids who came from the village.

'Serve from the *left* side, do,' said Prue. 'Your hair keeps fallin' down, your cap's on crooked, don't tip the servin' dish! Heavens above, I suppose the day might come when I get a kitchen maid that's been trained by somebody else.'

Willow obeyed, biting her tongue to keep it still. The housemaids disappeared upstairs with their boxes of polishes, dusters and brushes to carry out their multitude of duties before Mr Edgar's breakfast was served by Henry at half past eight, while Ivy took up a heavy tray to Winifred, her governess, and the nursery maid.

To Willow the day seemed long and chaotic. When she sat down to eat her meals her head was spinning. That night Ivy showed her how to keep her hair secure beneath her cap and lent her some hairpins, and by teatime the next day a work pattern was beginning to emerge and she felt she had a niche in this great house. Even her stomach was coping with the food. In fact, the more she ate the more she wanted. She still couldn't forget those at home on their niggardly diet, but she still ate as if she had been starved for years. She would send money to Mum as soon as possible. Wages were paid at the end of the month and Prue said they were lucky because in some houses the servants had to wait three months, or even a year.

'Tomorrow's the last day of freedom,' sighed Prue over supper.

The others groaned. She said to Willow, 'I bet a bob you

think you've been workin' hard, but just you wait until the family arrives. There'll be Mr Steadman, the butler, and Mrs Westerby, the housekeeper –' Prue pulled a face '– not to mention Jenny, the head housemaid. She's been at her sister's helpin' to look after her sick husband. Then there's Miss Jebb and *Miss Brayton* – she's Mrs Maddison's maid and has enough airs an' graces for a queen. And Mr Maddison's valet, Mr Elwood, an' Mrs Narracott's comin' too, of course, an' things will really hum in the kitchen.'

Willow felt panicky. More names. She recalled Mrs Narracott's kindness and said, 'The cook was nice when I met her in Bristol.'

'Nice is as nice does,' said Henry. 'She's better than some, but everything has to run like clockwork. It's bad enough when it's just the family, but wait till the guests get here and she's got forty more to feed, plus all the ladies' maids and valets coming down here to eat and always demanding this and that for their work. Very hoity-toity some of them are and nothing's ever right. Then we'll have two tables in the servants' hall, and dessert and coffee to be taken to the upper servants in Mrs Westerby's sitting room. Oh, yes, you'll see how nice she can be. Just keep out of the way of her soup ladle, that's my advice.'

The others laughed, half scandalised, half amused, as they recalled memories of dilatory kitchen maids and bootboys being belaboured by the great soup ladle.

Chapter Four

After a few days Willow could scarcely remember any other kind of life. She was kept busy from early morning until late at night and fell into bed too exhausted to do anything but sleep. Aggie was the first to rise. She seemed to have a built-in clock which told her when it was time. Then, all too soon, her grubby hand was shaking Willow who rolled out of bed, pulled on her uniform and descended to the kitchen to begin the everlasting tasks.

Mrs Maddison and her two elder daughters arrived at Buddleigh Manor. Mr Maddison was deer-stalking, and would return soon with friends. Then there would be picnic hampers to make up for river trips and shooting parties.

'Don't they ever stop killin' things?' asked Willow.

Prue looked surprised. 'They've always done it. Some of them will be fishin', too, though I can't see what pleasure they get standin' in cold water for hours when they can easily buy what they want from the fish-monger.'

'That's enough of that talk,' said Mr Steadman. 'It's not for you to criticise your betters.'

Prue made a face; only Willow saw it and she had a job not to giggle. She liked Prue and was starting to realise life was not all work. There were times, short to be sure, when she sat in the servants' hall, comfortable and well-fed, enjoying the gossip of the lower servants about Them upstairs. They enjoyed their freedom when their seniors were in the housekeeper's room drinking Mr Maddison's wine.

'Does he know they drink it?' Willow asked Prue.

Prue shrugged. 'Don't really know, though I think he

must turn a blind eye to it. After all, he pretends not to notice his wife's carryin' on.'

She stopped as Mrs Westerby entered. 'You have had long enough for your meal,' the housekeeper said. 'It's high time you got back to work.' She directed a look at Prue which made her quail. Polly had told Willow that she was a distant relative of the Maddisons' fallen on hard times which Willow found confusing. If she was related to them, why didn't they give her money and not oblige her to work?

Prue was everywhere, supervising, demonstrating the way things should be done, chiding, but she was an even-tempered girl and Willow liked her. Mrs Narracott took most afternoons off and spent them in the housekeeper's room or visiting local friends. Before she returned, the big kitchen table must be scrubbed white, dried and set out with the tools of her trade all ready for cooking dinner.

Willow was sent often to the pantry and couldn't see how the vast array of delicacies would be used up. There was also a game larder where beautifully plumaged birds hung, head down among hares. She had once assumed it to be the place where someone played games, which had given rise to another bout of mirth among her fellow-servants.

'Mr Maddison always sends us grouse,' explained Ivy, 'an' the hares are off the estate. They hang there, sometimes until they're maggoty, then they're cooked and eaten.'

'They eat *bad* meat?'

'They like it. They don't think it's bad.'

Tennis afternoons and river picnics and other outdoor amusements were organised for the expected guests, provided the fine weather held. Mrs Westerby relayed the orders to Mrs Narracott and Mr Steadman, and interesting titbits of news were discussed and gradually filtered through to the bottom of the servant hierarchy. Willow was mystified when certain names were mentioned which made the others giggle and wink. The guests began arriving, most of the younger ones in motor cars, the more conventional in carriages. Willow spent her long days with her hands deep into food. There were mountains of it. Potatoes to peel, carrots to scrape, onions to prepare while her eyes stung and watered. She scaled fish, handing them on to Prue who filleted them with sure strokes of her long, sharp blade. Ivy wasn't allowed near anything which would make her fingers smell because she was engaged in making preserves. Hour after hour she stirred cauldrons of fruit: greengages and cherries; blackcurrants and plums; redcurrants for jelly, which meant that the fruit had to be strained through a jelly bag, drop by drop.

Aggie, coming into the kitchen one day in a rush in answer to a summons by Mrs Narracott, blundered against the bowl and spilled its clear red contents over the floor. Willow was then able to see the cook in one of her rages. She clouted Aggie and shrieked her fury while the scullery maid wept, rubbing her face with hands scraped red-raw by the silver-sand and salt with which she cleaned the copper pans, using her fingers as buffers. Her nose began to run which sent the cook into another paroxysm.

Mrs Narracott had lifted her hand to strike another blow when Willow, unable to bear the maid's distress, cried, 'No!'

Mrs Narracott transferred her baleful glare to Willow. '*What* did you say?'

Everyone stopped to enjoy the novel scene. Willow, inwardly horrified at her own temerity, said, 'I said "no".'

Mrs Narracott's mouth opened and closed a couple of times, then she half ran at Willow, her heaviest ladle ready for action, and Willow raced out of the kitchen. She lingered in the yard, uncertain of what to do, wondering if she'd be dismissed. She saw Andy who waved but she was too dispirited to respond. Eventually, knowing there was no help for it, she returned. Everyone was busy at their duties, Ivy cursing quietly as she prepared another great mound of redcurrants.

Mrs Narracott turned. 'You've decided to come back then? There's a pile of spinach waiting to be cleaned and more to come. You're behind in your work.'

No matter how fast Willow worked on the vegetables, the gardeners brought more. It was like being on a treadmill. Ivy must have felt the same as she coped with peaches, pears and nectarines for preserving whole. At the end of the day Willow helped Prue to carry the jars down to the cool, dry cellars. She looked round in amazement at the number of carefully labelled jars of jams, preserves and vegetables.

'More food! How can they possibly eat it all?'

Prue said, 'Don't you worry, it'll be ate up by the next season. Cook has her work cut out to keep the supplies up for the Friday to Monday guests, weekends to you, and of course there are the ones who stay for ages. Soon we'll be startin' on the mincemeat an' candied peel an' puddin's for Christmas.'

'Fancy gettin' ready for Christmas already,' said Willow, with memories of herself hanging round a butcher's shop until it closed on Christmas Eve to try to get a bit of meat going cheap, and Gran coming round to make a jar of mince for a few tarts.

That night, as she was helping Ivy to clean the kitchen before going to bed, Mrs Narracott called her into the empty servants' hall. Willow stood quaking as the cook frowned at her. She said, 'You should be dismissed for cheek, but I'm letting it go this time. You're a good girl, nicely tempered on the whole, and I'm pleased with your work.'

'Thank you, Mrs Narracott.' Willow couldn't leave it there. 'Aggie—'

'Yes, Aggie! She makes me so cross I don't know what I'm doing sometimes. She hasn't the brains to be anything but a skivvy, she's not really suited to work here at all, but I don't know what would become of her if I got rid of her. She's not all there –' the cook pointed to her temple '– and she's too free with the boys.'

Willow was astonished. 'But she's—' She stopped.

'Plain, were you going to say? She's no picture, though she looks better when she's had a wash and put a clean dress on, and there are some who don't bother looking at a girl's face because they're only interested in her other parts.

Now, finish your tasks and go to bed, and don't ever dare to interfere in my kitchen again.'

At the end of August there was an air of jubilation among the servants. In the comparatively quiet period after servants' dinner and before tea Mr Steadman would hand out the wages. Willow found the work light today as she dwelt on Clara's pleasure at opening an envelope containing a postal order. It would be little more than a week's pay, but it would help. She went to the housekeeper's room when she was called and stood waiting. Mr Steadman had a cash box in front of him. Mrs Westerby sat beside him entering figures in a ledger.

'Ah, Willow,' said the housekeeper, 'Mrs Narracott speaks well of you. Continue in this way and you will prosper.' Willow listened with half an ear. 'You may go,' said the housekeeper.

'But what about my wages?'

'Newcomers are paid at the end of their first full month.'

'I've got to wait for another month before I get any money?'

'Don't raise your voice to me,' said Mrs Westerby coldly. 'Those are the rules. You should be grateful we are holding back less than two weeks of your remuneration.'

Willow wanted to scream with rage and frustration. All that work and nothing to show for it. 'That means the Maddisons have had me for free,' she said, 'an' they're so rich.'

Mr Steadman tried to pacify her. 'Time will soon pass.'

'That's no good to me. My mum—'

'Be silent!' The butler lost his temper. 'Mrs Westerby, I can't imagine what induced the mistress to take on such a girl as this!'

'She wished to show her gratitude for a service rendered, but I agree. I believe a sum of money would have been a better reward.'

Willow glared at them. 'That "service" was saving Miss Winifred's life!' She turned and fled, managing to get as far as the bootboy's room before she released her pent-up emotion in angry tears. She had thought she was alone until someone touched her shoulder. Steven Kerslake, the bootboy, was watching her.

'Isn't there anywhere in this bloody house where I can be on my own?' she cried.

He grinned. 'Language!' He'd been making Japan blacking for boots and his hands were stained black and there was a big smudge on his face. His teeth shone white in the gloom.

'I hope you didn't mess up my clothes when you touched me,' snapped Willow, dashing her tears away.

'You ought to keep on people's good side then you'd feel better.'

'They're mean pigs! Mean an' cruel! They won't pay me my money.'

'You're luckier than some of us. Some have been workin' years an' all that time the Maddisons have held back three or four weeks' wages. They're only keepin' a couple of weeks of yours.'

'Only a couple of weeks! My mum needs my money. A few shillin's would have helped. Now I've got to write an' tell her she's to wait another month.'

'Some folks don't pay their servants till the year's end.' Steven spoke in a matter-of-fact way which restored her balance.

She said nervously, 'I think they'll turn me out after the way I spoke.'

Again Steven grinned. 'Mr Steadman won't. I've seen him lookin' at you. People forget I'm here. I'm like Aggie, I don't know who my folks are. Someone left me on a doorstep in the village. They think people like us don't have feelin's, so they ignore us an' I see a lot more of what's goin' on than they know.' He winked.

Willow stared at him, trying to imagine what life was like when all you knew about your parents was that they didn't want you. She said, 'You're wrong about Mr Steadman. He's old. Married, too, I suppose.'

68

'He's not much above forty an' he's not married. Neither's Mrs Narracott nor Mrs Westerby. They just call them missus. I think that Mrs Westerby, for all they say she's really one of the nobs, wouldn't mind marryin' Mr Steadman. You'd best watch out. If she thinks you've got a chance with him—' He stopped, as Willow's hand connected with the side of his face.

'You cheeky devil!' she yelled. 'You've got a mind like a sewer!'

She hurried to the kitchen where Prue shouted, 'Where the hell have you been? I need the mushrooms chopped, and after that you can prepare the horseradish, and have you forgotten it's your week to keep the kitchen clean and uncluttered? The floor's covered in flour.'

Willow chopped mushroom after mushroom. She wanted to cry, to sob over the burst bubble of her hopes. The horseradish gave her an opportunity to weep, her tears of vexation unnoticed among the ones extracted by the stinging fumes. She thought of the slap she had given Steven and regretted it. She had vented her fury on someone who was in a much worse position than herself. Damn Them and all their ways! They turned servant against servant while upstairs they floated through their lives, cossetted and cared for by the toiling army downstairs, changing their costly outfits four or sometimes five times a day. Willow wondered if Gran knew that some of them spent time in beds they had no business in. Ivy said that Mrs Maddison had been sweet on a certain lord and it was rumoured that Winifred was his daughter.

If Willow hadn't been so busy and so disappointed she might have laughed over her former dream of life in a great house. The butler and housekeeper held complete sway over the servants. Although it was only early September, her feet ached with the cold of the stone floor of the kitchen. Her high-buttoned boots had been much criticised. She had resented this, but now she understood that the rule was sensible. At this rate she'd soon have chilblains. She would need to buy some better footwear as quickly as possible. While her hands were busy she had time to think about her family. Was Dad getting stronger? Did Marigold make a fuss about turning the mangle? Was Jasmine still weeping for her big sister? She had every other Sunday afternoon off and a whole day every three months, with an occasional half day on Saturday. Ivy said it was better than a lot of places, but it didn't give her time to travel to Bristol even if she'd had the money.

There had been one improvement. Ivy had complained to Jenny about having to sleep three in a bed. Jenny had told Mrs Narracott who relayed the information to Mrs Westerby.

The housekeeper sent for the two kitchen maids. 'I have inspected the bed in your room. It is large. Surely there is room for three? Not one of you is plump.'

Ivy plucked up courage and said, 'It would be all right if Aggie didn't smell so. That's true, isn't it, Willow?' She was obliged to agree.

The housekeeper's mouth turned down in distaste. 'Someone should oversee her ablutions. Surely you have shared a bed before?' she said to Willow.

'Yes, ma'am, but only with my sisters.'

'I see. You may go, Ivy. Willow will remain to sign the wages ledger. You failed to do so at the proper time and your rail fare has been entered.'

To the girls' relief a camp bed was set up in their attic which left almost no room to move, but since they spent so little time there it didn't matter.

The greatest advantage in Willow's new life was the food. In this respect Mrs Maddison didn't stint her servants. They couldn't expect the delicacies eaten by 'them upstairs', but there was plenty of good, plain food and Willow ate steadily at every meal. Already her dresses were growing tight and on a half day she let them out. The Maddisons expected their staff to be present for at least one church service on Sundays. Even Aggie was sent off looking reasonably clean for 'her weekly dose of God' as Ivy put it. She was made to sit at the back in a corner where she fell asleep and had to be poked awake when the hymns were announced. The Maddisons occupied their own front pew and this was the only time that Willow saw them. Winifred's nurse was there, a different one from the girl on the Downs who had been dismissed for incompetence. A woman in dark clothes and wearing spectacles must be the governess. Andy Hunnicott had been wrong when he called her ugly, but she certainly wasn't pretty.

Once, when the family were a little late, the servants waited outside until their betters arrived. The Maddisons and their guests strolled unhurriedly through the church-yard, greeted the vicar and passed through the Gothic portals. Willow was able to feast her eyes on the beautiful clothes and startling hats of the ladies. Mrs Maddison was as pretty as her daughters and looked almost as young. Willow thought of Clara. Life wasn't fair.

Willow was ordered upstairs to see the mistress. Henry had brought the news and she was nervous. 'Have I done somethin' wrong?' she asked Prue.

'Search your conscience,' she advised, too busy gutting a salmon neatly enough to be sent whole to the table to be bothered with questions.

Mrs Narracott frowned. 'The mistress wants you after lunch. You'll have to change into your black dress and put on a clean apron, collar and cuffs. You've been chopping onions so mind you wash thoroughly.'

'I will,' Willow assured her. Having decided she had done nothing to deserve a reprimand her heart began to thud with excitement. At last she was to wear her afternoon dress to meet Winifred's mother. This was what she had been waiting for. Mrs Maddison would express her gratitude to her daughter's rescuer and tell her that soon she would be in training as an upstairs maid. She followed Henry through the green baize door into a car-peted corridor, wide enough to hold semi-circular tables

71

on which stood statues and vases of flowers. It was lined with pictures.

'You'd best not gawp like that in madam's boudoir,' said Henry.

Willow found it difficult not to stare when he knocked on the door and announced her presence. The room was a bower, the walls hung with cream paper patterned with tiny pink roses. Deeper pink rugs lay on the polished floor and a small writing desk with chair to match stood near an open window through which wafted sweet, autumnal scents. Mrs Maddison reclined on a sofa in a gown of cream silk-muslin over pale green silk. A lace bolero was secured at her throat by a pearl brooch, lace flounces foamed round her ankles. Standing by her side was Mrs Westerby in dark poplin, her keys, the badge of office, at her waist, her hands folded in front of her.

Willow stood still, drinking in every detail of her employer's clothes.

'Have you done with looking at me?' asked Mrs Maddison laconically, though Willow detected a note of disapproval.

'It's rude to stare,' said Mrs Westerby.

'I'm sorry,' said Willow, blushing. 'Your dress is so lovely.'

Mrs Maddison laughed, a brittle sound, and it occurred to Willow that her remark had been tactless.

Mrs Westerby said, 'Say, "madam" when you address your mistress. She's not yet trained, madam, though cook tells me she is a willing worker.'

'I am delighted to hear it. I am sure that, given the correct guidance, her manners will improve.' Mrs Maddison turned her attention back to Willow. 'I sent for you to express my appreciation for your timely intervention on my daughter's behalf.'

Willow supposed she must be referring to the accident and wondered why she had to dress it up in such long words. 'Thank you, madam,' she said.

'I had inquiries made and discovered your family to be in quite dire circumstances.'

Willow waited, then because her employer seemed to expect something more said, 'Mum has a terrible job makin' ends meet.'

Mrs Maddison's brows rose slightly. 'It is not that to which I refer. I am speaking of –' she lowered her voice '– the fact that your father has served a term of imprisonment.'

'*No*, madam.'

'What! Do you deny it?'

'My dad was locked up for three days an' nights an' he had only taken a tip for findin' someone a cab.'

Mrs Maddison raised white, beringed hands, then let them fall into her lap, looking round at her housekeeper.

'How dare you take that tone with your mistress?' said Mrs Westerby.

Mrs Maddison said, 'I suppose the girl naturally has a lot to learn, coming as she does from such a home.' She turned to Willow. 'It is against my practice to employ someone without a good background. I have made an exception of you, but you must show yourself worthy of trust.'

Willow waited for more. Mrs Maddison couldn't possibly understand exactly what she had done or surely she would offer more substantial thanks? 'How is Winifred?' she blurted. 'I got some nasty bruises myself.'

The two women gave her incredulous looks. Mrs Westerby said, '*Miss* Winifred, if you please, Willow. I can only beg your indulgence for her, madam. I will make sure she is properly instructed.'

Willow's stomach was churning. Words she had heard in the factory, bad words, rose to her lips and it was with difficulty that she held them back. How dare that woman lie there and get more emotional about the incorrect use of her child's name than by an act which had saved that same child's life? Willow didn't want praise; all she hoped for was a chance to better herself. She forced herself to remain calm. She couldn't change Mrs Maddison and she still saw Buddleigh Manor as a chance to improve her prospects.

'I'm sorry, madam,' she said, 'I forgot.'

Mrs Maddison looked faintly amused as she asked, 'Did I hear your name aright? Willow?'

Mrs Westerby frowned. 'I will change it, of course, madam.'

'You should already have done so,' said Mrs Maddison coldly. She turned to Willow. 'I shall overlook your lapse, though it must not happen again. You have a fine opportunity here and, in time, may even become a cook. Now I will give you some advice. I pay generous wages and in this house you can have few expenses. Save your money, place all you can spare into a savings account. Steadman will help you there. Do not send all your money home. Too many servants do so and their families fritter it away.' Her eyes travelled down to Willow's feet and rested on her ankles revealed by her maid's dress. 'You need to spend some if only to buy a pair of decent shoes and a smart frock.'

The words 'fritter it away' almost drowned out the rest of Mrs Maddison's speech and Willow had to hang on to her temper. Her mistress looked briefly into her eyes and Willow had the impression that the woman knew exactly how she felt and was passing part of a boring afternoon tormenting her.

Mrs Maddison yawned and reached for a magazine. 'Send her away, Westerby. We must allocate more rooms. Mr Maddison will soon be arriving with his guests.'

Back in the kitchen the others stopped work to hear what had happened. Willow, still furious, told them. She left out the bit about her father.

'Usual stuff,' said Ivy, 'except for your saying "Winifred".' She laughed, then groaned as one of the gardeners came in. 'Oh, lord, not more apples.'

'It's been a good year for fruit,' grinned the gardener. 'I'll be bringing lots more before the crop is finished.'

'Go up and change back into your pink frock,' said Mrs Narracott to Willow. 'You're falling behind in your work again.'

That night, as they were undressing, Ivy said, 'You don't want to take any notice of them upstairs. They can't help the way they are.'

'They're goin' to change my name.'

Ivy laughed. 'They often do it. I'm glad my mum gave me a plain one. Your mother can't have been in service, that's for sure, or she'd have called you something plainer.'

'My mum –' Willow struggled to get her words past the enormous lump in her throat '– my mum never thought of me goin' into service. I had a good job in a corset factory, but workin' here I can send more money home.' She thought of all the love she had left behind, of Clara's endless struggles and her efforts to keep up Dad's spirits, of how Mrs Maddison had so casually insulted him.

'Homesick?' asked Ivy. 'You'll get used to it. We all do.'

'My dad's not very well.'

'That's not what I heard,' said Aggie. She spoke so seldom they often forgot her presence.

Willow stared at Aggie. 'What do you mean?'

'Is it true he's been to prison?'

'Who told you that?' cried Willow. 'How do you know?'

Aggie shrugged. 'Things get about.'

'Only three days, and he hadn't even done anythin' wrong,' cried Willow. 'He only took money that was given him as a tip.'

Aggie shrugged. 'Pokey's pokey.'

The door flew open and Polly said, 'What the hell do you think you're playing at, yelling like that? Get into bed and shut up. We all need our rest.'

It took Willow a long time to sleep and the following day found her listless, bitterly resentful over the slur on her father, and vulnerable when she thought of the gossip which must be going on behind her back. But she wished she hadn't shouted at Aggie whose life was so hard. She tried to imagine what it must be like to spend long hours standing in the lonely scullery, up to the elbows in water, sore hands stinging. At least she didn't have to clean the shoes. Each night, Steven Kerslake collected every pair in the house which needed attention and sat up late in his small, gloomy room, burnishing leather until it gleamed. He then bedded down in the same room. Willow wondered if he got nervous, being the only one downstairs at night. All the other male indoor servants slept at one end of the attics, the females at the other. Between them was a door to which Mrs Westerby and Mr Steadman held keys.

'So there's no hanky-panky,' giggled Ivy, 'but it doesn't always work. The girl before you was sent away because she was expectin'. It takes more than a locked door to stop that kind of thing.'

Willow sent off the money Gran had given her to her mother, using a postal order which Polly bought from the village, and a letter written on a piece of shelf-lining paper. She kept sixpence for herself. In the letter she made light of her situation. One morning she was handed a letter from Gran. The envelope also contained an ill-spelt effort from her brothers, and a stick drawing of a maid in mob cap and flowered gown from Jasmine, accompanied by dozens of crosses for kisses. From Gran's letter she learned that Mum was grateful for the postal order and they thought that Dad was getting stronger. There were no grumbles. Reading between the lines, Willow understood that Dad hadn't found work. He now had two things against him, his poor health and his lost character. Mum had found two more ladies who needed a washer-woman and went out to do a little cleaning. Willow groaned as she pictured what that meant to Clara. All sent love, even Marigold. Willow tucked the envelope into her pocket as a talisman. At night she slept with it under her pillow.

She used her next Saturday afternoon off to walk to the village, a distance of about one and a half miles, where she bought writing paper, envelopes and a stamp and sat in the sunshine on a bench outside the public house and wrote home.

When she returned to duty Mrs Westerby sent for her. 'What were you doing patronising a public house?'

'I didn't! I wouldn't!'

'You were seen.'

'I'd like to know who by. They're tellin' lies.'

'You are being insolent again. Really, I despair of ever training you.'

'But honest, I didn't—' Willow began, then stopped, remembering. 'I sat outside one to write home.'

'I see. In future please choose somewhere more elevating to rest. It is not good for Buddleigh Manor to have servants generating gossip. There is an excellent bench in the churchyard.'

'Yes, madam.'

'Your response is correct, but your manner – the way you look at me—' Mrs Westerby paused. 'Why did you accept the position as servant here?'

'I wanted to better myself.'

'You are not going the right way about it.'

'No, madam.'

'Is that all you have to say?'

There was a great deal more that Willow wanted to say, but she feared that if she tried to speak tears of indignation would spill over. Pride held her fast and Mrs Westerby waited a moment, then said coldly, 'You may go.'

Willow thought she had been working hard, but when every spare room in the manor held guests the past seemed almost restful. She had previously marvelled at the quantities of food sent upstairs, but what they sent now made that seem niggardly. It appeared that rich folk needed constant nourishment, from the early trays with tea or coffee and bread and butter to the bedtime trays taken to every room, carrying Vichy or Malvern water and an assortment of sandwiches. At breakfast the table and sideboard were covered with dishes containing porridge, fish, omelettes, devilled kidneys and bacon, all kept hot in chafing dishes. There was an assortment of cold meats, scones, honey, marmalade and fresh fruit. The meal for guests began at eight-thirty when gentlemen and some ladies appeared in riding gear to eat standing while grooms waited with their mounts. Breakfast lasted until everyone had been served, some of them in their bedrooms.

'Too lazy to get up,' snarled Ivy, as she prepared yet another tray.

Luncheon followed which could be up to twelve courses and created mountains of washing up, after which the ladies retired to rest after their exertions, then came down in trailing tea gowns, the flowing draperies concealing the fact that just for once they had left off their corsets. The bread must be transparently thin, the scones just warm, the toast crisp, the brioches perfect. There was an assortment of cakes and always ginger biscuits and patisseries. 'In case the King arrives,' explained Mrs Narracott in a rare communicative mood. 'You never know,' she said, 'when His Majesty will take it into his head to pay a visit and it would never do to be unprepared with his favourites. I hear his health isn't all it should be, poor soul.'

Dinner was at eight-thirty, for which the nobs needed another change of clothes, another twelve-course meal, lasting an hour, or two, or three, and just in case anyone felt their strength to be flagging, snacks were served before midnight. Mr Steadman had to make sure that the wines which were served with every meal except breakfast were correct, and he looked after the glasses and silver. Ivy picked out the best of the fruit to send upstairs with every meal. Aggie was on a treadmill of dirty dishes and greasy pots and pans.

After a disappointing summer, it was fine and sunny for harvesting and picnics. All the outdoor staff lived in cottages on the estate and, mercifully, ate at home when they could, but the beaters and loaders had to be fed. On top of that there were the visiting ladies' maids and valets to be catered for in the servants' hall. They sat, of course, at the high table, waited on by the kitchen maids and Henry. All were seated in order of their employer's precedence and Willow was astonished at the fuss they made about who was superior to whom.

At night she could scarcely stay awake to undress and went straight into a heavy sleep which was never long enough, but gradually her body adjusted and she began

78

to feel her old vigour returning. She had to let out her dresses over her bosom. She had no time to look in the mirror except to fix her cap, but one morning she realised that her features were changing. The strained, hungry look had gone; her eyes, her best feature, now shone with blue brilliance while her skin was rosy with health. She had been blessed with good teeth. Others noticed and Henry had twice tried to slide his arm round her waist. The second time he was detected by Mrs Narracott who flew into one of her rages and boxed his ears.

She railed at Willow, now re-christened Lily. ('At least it's a pretty flower,' said Prue.) 'I hope,' cried Mrs Narracott, 'you aren't going to go to ruin like the last girl.'

Willow flushed. 'No, I certainly won't, and there's no call to think I would. I didn't ask Henry to touch me.'

'No, and I didn't see you push him away like a good girl would.'

Willow fumed. Henry had approached her when her hands were thickly covered in scone mix which Prue had asked her to make for servants' tea. If she'd slapped some of the mixture on his face the cook would have been even more annoyed. She didn't dwell on it. Her position meant that everyone except Aggie and Steven could tell her off. She must just hang on to her hope of advancement.

She had discovered the reason for the giggles when the names of certain guests were mentioned. Mrs Westerby and Mr Steadman knew that some men, unaccompanied by their wives, were given rooms near ladies with whom they had dalliance during the night. Name cards were placed in tiny brass frames on each door so that no one could be embarrassed by a mistake.

'Where I live,' said Willow to Ivy, 'they don't call women like that ladies.'

Ivy agreed. 'If we do anything of that nature we get dismissed, like the last girl. Only fourteen she was and hardly knew the time of day.'

'Who gave her a baby?'

Ivy shot her a sideways look. 'I don't know. She wouldn't tell. I keep myself to myself and you must do the same.'

It was the advice meted out by Mum and Gran. It was not necessary. Willow had no intention of getting involved with boys who might impede the realisation of her dream.

Chapter Five

One evening, when dinner had been served upstairs and the kitchen cleaned, Willow relaxed in the servants' hall. She was tired and knew she should go to bed, but she lingered, listening to the chatter. The hall was large and quite sparsely furnished, but one end had been transformed into a cosy corner. It was centred round a fireplace which had been lit against the chill of the September night and before which were comfortable chairs and large cushions. Willow was sitting on a cushion, curled up at the other maids' feet. A fireside rug was pleasingly patterned and soft.

The upper servants, along with the visiting valets and maids, were enjoying the hospitality of the housekeeper in her sitting room – 'Pug's Parlour' everyone called it, though no one knew why – making free with Mr Maddison's wine and drinking their official allowance of beer. Mrs Narracott had gone to visit friends on a nearby farm.

Polly was stitching a tear in a tablecloth, grumbling about the depredations of the laundry maids on the household linen. Nancy was working on a garment which was a froth of white silk, lace and broderie anglaise. She held it up and said crossly, 'Look at this. It's Miss Violet's. It's Miss Jebb's place to mend her clothes but she always tries to get out of sewing. This time she says she's hurt her wrist, but I noticed she didn't have any trouble passing a dish of potatoes.'

Polly said, 'If you ask me, she's passing herself off as something she isn't. Andy Hunnicott is sure he saw her when he was working as a bootboy in London, and she was a housemaid then.'

'That doesn't surprise me,' said Prue.

Willow asked tentatively, 'Is it wrong to try to improve your position?'

'Not at all,' said Jenny, a ladylike girl who didn't chatter readily, 'but it isn't a bit of use to say you can do things when you can't. You get found out in time.'

'Not when there are women like Nancy, daft enough to cover up for her,' said Prue drily.

'Jebb pays me. She gives me nice things that Miss Violet has thrown out.'

'Not often,' said Ivy.

'No, but it makes a difference. When I went home last time I wore the muslin blouse that only needed repairing under the arms. It was highly thought of by my friend.' Her blush indicated that the friend was male.

'What are you mendin'?' asked Willow.

'Miss Violet's new petticoat. *She* says she tore it the other evening dancing. *I* heard different.'

Prue, perched on the edge of her chair, her hands towards the blaze, said, 'If Mrs Narracott hears you talk like that she'll give you what for.'

Nancy was unabashed. 'Miss Violet was very lovey-dovey with Sir George Trembath. Henry said so and he should know, he was there.'

'As if Miss Violet would let a footman catch her out!' Prue was scornful.

'Miss Violet,' said Polly, 'wouldn't notice if Henry was standing right beside her. She usually doesn't see servants at all. He was carrying round a tray of champagne and went out on to the terrace to offer them some.'

Prue snorted with irresistible laughter. 'He knows better than to go on the terrace! If anyone wants a bit of a cuddle, that's where they hide. He must have done it deliberately.'

'Of course he did.' Nancy laughed. 'And he saw Sir George about to give Miss Violet a kiss. She jumped back so quick that Henry swears he heard something tear. Sir George must have been very close if his foot was on her skirts. When Henry offered them wine she pretended to have something in her eye.'

'That's a good 'un,' grinned Prue. 'I've used that myself. I'm surprised that she bothered to pretend anythin' to a footman.'

'It shows she was flustered,' said Polly. 'Perhaps they really were kissin'?'

Nancy sighed and picked up the work again. 'She would have to tear this petticoat. It's new, her favourite, and covered in flounces. It should be mended with the pattern still right, but I can't seem to do it. I've unpicked it twice. If I do it again it'll be full of holes.'

'What of it?' said Ivy. 'Let Miss Jebb get the blame.'

'No. If I do this for her she's promised to give me some gorgeous feathers for my hat. Damn and hell!'

Jenny jumped. 'If you're not careful you'll need to put money in the swear box. I've a good mind to tell Mrs Narracott.'

'You won't,' said Nancy. 'Look at this. It's in a dreadful tangle, worse than when I began.'

Willow leaned over and inspected the sewing. 'Would you like me to try for you?'

The others regarded her with astonishment.

'You're a kitchen maid,' said Nancy scornfully, 'and a second one at that. What do you know about this kind of sewing?'

Willow held back the sharp retort which rose to her lips. The sight of a lovely garment being ruined was too harrowing to let pass. 'I like sewin'. What you're doin' wouldn't be half so difficult if you had a pattern to follow.'

'Well, I haven't, so what's the use of saying that?'

Willow drew her precious pencil from her apron pocket. 'If I had a bit of paper . . .'

Interested, Jenny produced an envelope and extracted the letter. 'Here, use this, though I don't see what good it'll do.' Nancy held out one of the broderie anglaise flounces and Willow examined it, then began to draw, following the intricate pattern until she had a perfect match on paper.

'Well, I never!' said Prue. 'It's like a real paper pattern!

I remember now, Mrs Narracott said somethin' about your drawin'.'

'Can you sew that well?' asked Nancy.

'I think so, though my hands are a bit rough an' I can't get rid of the onion smell.'

Nancy said eagerly, 'I can cure that.' She darted away and returned with sprigs of parsley.

'Cook'll kill you if she finds out you've taken that,' said Ivy.

'She won't know if you don't tell her. I pulled a bit off each bunch. Here, Willow, rub your hands with it and it'll get rid of the smell. Then use this cream. I made it myself for my hands.'

By the time Willow had used the cream which smelt of almonds her hands were definitely less rough. She picked up the petticoat. For a moment she had a strong desire to press it to her, to bury her face in its scented folds and enjoy the sensation of luxury. Then, holding the torn flounce over a darning mushroom, she began to sew. At first she trembled at her temerity. She had never attempted anything like this before, but her nerves stilled as beneath her skilful fingers the frayed tangles began to disappear, until finally there was no sign that there had been any damage at all.

'You're a hundred times better than Jebb!' declared Prue. 'An' cleverer than Nancy.'

Willow glanced at Nancy nervously, expecting her to be resentful, but the good-natured girl was smiling in relief.

Prue said, 'You'd better not let on that Willow did the mendin' or her life won't be worth livin'. Jebb's a jealous woman an' can be really spiteful.'

'Is she spiteful to you, Nancy?' asked Willow.

'Not often, but she'd be sure to pick on you. Whoever heard of a kitchen maid sewin' this good?'

Reminded of the rigid hierarchy of the servants' domain, Willow squirmed. A kitchen maid! One day she'd show them. She would! Miss Jebb had disliked her since they had first met in Bristol, but Willow suddenly felt jubilant. She possessed a skill worthy of a lady's maid and she could acquire others. That night she lay beside Ivy feeling quite optimistic.

Her high hopes proved to be ephemeral. The servants guarded their positions and their rights and she began to wonder how it was possible to climb to the top, especially since the others had advantages denied to her. Jenny's father was butler on a nearby estate and she had been brought up to life in a country mansion. Nancy, a shop-keeper's daughter, educated until she was sixteen, had gone straight into training as a housemaid. Polly's mother had been widowed young and Polly had attended a charity school for servants and left it highly trained. Ladies' maids needed to know a host of things, the very existence of most unknown to Willow. She watched unobtrusively when one of these haughty beings visited the kitchen to make up some special lotion or cream demanded by her mistress, and couldn't understand how they knew so much. She asked Nancy about it.

'They're usually taken on as maid to the girls in the schoolroom and get trained up by the senior maid. If you've got ambitions in that direction, I should forget them. Learn to cook. Good cooks need never be out of a place.'

Willow was mastering some kitchen skills but she made up her mind she would never apply for a job as a cook. To do so would firmly establish her place in life and there she would remain. She even felt a sneaking admiration for Miss Jebb who had worked a miracle.

She passed her fifteenth birthday in October. The day was marked by a letter from home containing a few words laboriously assembled by Mum and Dad, news from Gran, and drawings from the younger children. She learned nothing new about the situation at home and suspected that it was bad, though Gran had cheered her by saying that the money she sent Clara was helping.

Soon after her arrival at the manor she had bought herself a pair of the required type of shoes with money which Mrs Westerby had insisted on lending her, not from any notion of kindness but because her pernickety mind couldn't bear anything out of place. Willow paid her back a shilling a month, and had to admit that once she'd got used to leaving off her boots she liked the feel of the shoes which were sturdy enough to protect her feet from the cold kitchen floor.

One morning she hurried into the kitchen just after five o'clock to find Nancy looking gloomy. 'Miss Jebb's sent another of Miss Violet's things to be repaired. This time it's a lace blouse. I wish I'd never begun this. I've made a rod for my own back.'

'An' mine,' said Willow drily. 'Don't forget I help.'

'And I've paid you!'

'With Miss Violet's unwanted underwear. I can't imagine where you think I could wear a pair of black satin knickers with a hole in the leg.'

Both girls fell into giggles. 'You can keep them until you've got a boyfriend,' said Nancy.

'I bet you'd look nice in them,' said a voice, and Steven poked his head round the door.

Nancy rushed at him and boxed his ears. 'Nasty little sneak!'

'I'm not then,' he whined. 'I didn't mean to listen.' He darted away. 'Knickers!' he yelled.

Willow blushed, but Nancy giggled again. 'He knows far more than he should, scruffy doorstep brat.'

She left with her housemaid's box to clean the drawing room. Then she and Polly would make sure of perfection in the guest bedrooms which would be occupied tonight by the Maddisons' eldest offspring, James, and his guests. He had been in Marienbad with his fiancée, Lady Mary, and her parents, the Earl and Countess of Somervell.

The bustle occasioned by the arrival of the new guests astonished Willow, but by the afternoon they were settled in, the pots and pans required for preparing an extra-special luncheon cleared away, and the maids were drinking tea.

'The Somervells are very wealthy,' said Jenny. 'Wealthy people always take heaps of luggage wherever they go. They carry huge trunks and portmanteaux and hat boxes.

86

Well, they don't *carry* them, of course, the servants do that. Mr James and Lady Mary have been engaged for ages.'

'Two years,' said Prue.

'What are they waitin' for?' asked Willow.

'Lady Mary's not ready to settle down,' said Nancy. 'Can't say I blame her. You can have a lot of fun if you're rich. Once she's married she'll have to behave herself, at least until she's had a few babies.'

Willow remembered some gossip. 'Then will she go with lovers, like Mrs Maddison?'

Jenny said hastily, 'For heaven's sake, Willow, guard your tongue.'

'But I thought everyone knew already.'

Polly exclaimed, 'That doesn't mean they talk about it! If you can't keep a still tongue in your head, we'll all end up dismissed.'

'Sorry,' muttered Willow. 'Where's Marienbad?'

Nancy said, 'It's a health spa, abroad somewhere. The Lamberts go every year after the season.'

'Who are the Lamberts?'

Polly sighed. 'Lambert is the family name of the Somervells.'

Willow didn't see why they needed more than one name, but she filed away the information in her head as something else to learn. 'Fancy eatin' so much you have to go abroad to recover.'

'It's not just the food,' explained Polly. 'It's all the gadding about and staying up late.'

'We have to stay up late,' said Willow, 'an' we never get a rest.'

Later she asked Prue, 'Isn't Lady Mary worried that Mr James will get tired of waitin' for her?'

'Fat chance! With her money she could get anyone, an' he knows it. The Maddisons are rich, but Mr James has got very expensive tastes. He goes everywhere with her. He's very jealous.'

'Is she so beautiful?'

'Not really. She seems gentle. She never goes out with the guns, but he does – every day.'

Mrs Narracott arrived in a temper because she had walked two miles to visit friends and they weren't in. 'I sent them a postcard,' she said.

'Perhaps it didn't get there in time,' said Willow placatingly.

Mrs Narracott glared at her, then round the kitchen. 'The table's not been scrubbed today,' she screeched. 'And what's this bowl of breadcrumbs for?'

'Apple Charlotte,' said Ivy.

'I said vanilla soufflé. Bring out the things I need, and be sharp about it.'

It would have been foolhardy for anyone to tell her that the table had been well scrubbed, or to point out that the menu she had left them distinctly said Apple Charlotte, but as Ivy scurried round the kitchen the cook said, 'Never mind. You've done the breadcrumbs. I might as well use them. I need patty-pans, too. Oh, they're already here. Is the bain-marie ready for the sauces?'

Willow and Ivy whisked about the kitchen on their soft-soled shoes like demented spirits, while Prue worked calmly on the trout which was to be served with a red wine sauce. Willow was told to spread forcemeat on thin slices of veal. 'And woe betide you if you tear any,' said Mrs Narracott. Eventually, her temper cooled and preparations for dinner continued in an atmosphere of reasonable tranquillity. She even managed to pay Willow a compliment. 'You're getting on well, Lily. I'm pleased with your progress.'

Willow's gratification was overshadowed by the reminder of her new name. Ivy gave her a sideways glance as if she didn't care to see the second kitchen maid praised. Gran's life in the nursery must have been easier than this, Willow thought. She never said a word about living on tenterhooks most of the time.

The weather became wet and cool and Mr Norris reported that Mrs Maddison was hard put to keep her guests entertained.

Willow thought they must be exceedingly hard to please. Just being in Buddleigh Manor, waited on hand, foot and finger, should be enough for them. On a day when the sun shone between grey clouds and a soft breeze sent the remaining russet leaves floating down, Willow decided to use her afternoon off to look round the grounds. A shooting party had taken some of the guests to a neighbouring estate in search of partridge and pheasant which were proving elusive this year; the ladies were mostly in their rooms yawning over books and magazines, a few in the morning room talking. Servants were forbidden to go near the gardens when the family was in residence, but nothing had been said about the park. Her leisure time began at three o'clock and she put on her black coat and hat. The bonnet Gran had given her had been ridiculed by the housekeeper.

'But the list said bonnet,' Willow had protested.

'That is only a form of words,' said Mrs Westerby icily. 'It is a list which has been in use for a great many years. Naturally one expects servants to have the intelligence to follow the fashions. I can't think how you could have thought that such a monstrosity could have passed inspection. What was your mother thinking of? It was singularly stupid.'

That was too much. 'Mum's not stupid,' retorted Willow.

Mrs Westerby said nothing for a moment, giving Willow a glare which unnerved her. 'Get yourself a hat,' she said.

Prue had rescued her by giving her a shape which Willow had adorned decorously with black ribbons and a small bunch of feathers.

In a stand of trees she stopped to breathe the cool air. She'd had little time to get to know the countryside, but she identified the dank smell of mushrooms and wet, decaying wood. At first she had missed the sounds of the street, the rumble of carts, the calls of children playing, the screams and yells of quarrelling neighbours, the punctual wailing of the factory hooters, but once she got used to the manor she soon enjoyed the difference. She scuffed her feet through the leaves which released more odours and sent droplets of water into her shoes, making her stockings damp. She walked on, out of the trees, until she came to the lake and sat on a bench watching the water fowl. She was lost in thoughts of home, wondering what they were doing. So she failed to notice that someone was approaching until her arm was grasped and a voice said, 'You again! Don't you know that this seat is reserved for your betters?'

Startled, she looked up sharply into the face of Edgar Maddison whose mouth was fixed in an unfriendly grin.

'I didn't know. Sorry,' she muttered, and made to rise, but he clasped her other arm and held her fast.

'Let me go, please,' she pleaded. Then belatedly added, 'Sir.'

'You hate calling me sir, don't you? I dare say you resent calling my mother madam?'

She thought of Mrs Maddison and her careless attitude and could have poured out a torrent of resentment, but she remained silent. If she just waited he would have to let her go. He couldn't stand there for the rest of the day, holding her down and taunting her. She stared into his eyes which were filled with mirth. His wanton amusement angered her and she tried to free herself.

'It is not a bit of use your struggling. I am much stronger than you.'

'You've got bigger muscles, that's all!' she flashed.

She had annoyed him. 'And what is that supposed to mean?'

'You heard,' she muttered.

'Common little guttersnipe,' he said, so softly it might have been an endearment.

Willow let herself go limp. It was the only way she could control her fury. 'My parents didn't rear me in a gutter, sir,' she said, her voice now as soft as his. 'They gave me as good a home as they could and they taught me decent manners. Unlike yours.'

'Is that so?' Edgar's voice betrayed his resentment, but his grip on her arms lessened. 'That's not how Reggie described things. You remember Reggie? He took you, your sister and a dreadful old pram back to Barton Hill.'

'I remember him. A nice man. I'm sure he wouldn't say anything unkind.'

'Are you? He said—'

'I'm not interested in what he said. I suppose he's just like the rest of you.'

'Oh, and what's that like?'

'Snobby, sneering, greedy people who don't care a damn about the poor.'

'My God, a budding politician! And swearing too. My mother would be fascinated to learn what you think of her, not to mention the bad language.'

'Your mother might be interested in learning how you molested a defenceless woman.'

Edgar shrugged. 'She might, but which one of us do you think would be punished? Sent away?'

Willow saw her job vanishing. She had handed this boorish, spoilt youth an opportunity to undermine her. No one would speak up for her. Second kitchen maids were two a penny. She felt she'd bite out her tongue rather than ask Edgar's pardon, but she'd die of shame if she was sent home, disgraced. The news would spread round the Barton Hill streets like a fire.

She looked away from him towards the lake and said, 'I'm sorry.'

'For what?'

'For sayin' things about you an' your folk.'

'And?'

'For swearin' at you.'

'Say, "I should not have done it".'

'I shouldn't have done it.'

'No, that's wrong. You must repeat my exact words.'

Willow did so.

'Now say "I was wrong",' he commanded.

She was so choked with fury she could barely form the words. 'I was wrong.'

Abruptly he released her and she rubbed her arms. 'Liar,'

91

he said. 'You are not sorry at all. You meant every word of it, damn you! And what's more, you are right. We are all the things you said – and worse.'

Willow was astonished. His voice had lost all trace of mockery. He was angry, but not with her this time.

She felt sorry for him and laid her hand on his arm. He shook it off. 'Don't touch me.' He looked very young. His face was screwed up as if he might cry.

She sat and waited, then he startled her by laughing. 'What a ridiculous scene! Do you know, you are much prettier than when last I saw you. Give me a kiss before you go.'

'No!' Willow got up and tried to escape, but he held her easily.

'Only a kiss. That's not much to ask.'

'Maybe not to you!'

'A kiss, my girl.'

'I won't.'

'I say you will.'

'You can take it by force, but I won't give it. I might come from a poor family, but we believe in keeping ourselves to ourselves before marriage, and behaving ourselves afterwards.'

'Ourselves to ourselves,' he mocked. 'It sounds just the sort of thing a girl like you would say.'

'What sort am I?' asked Willow, playing him at his own game.

He looked non-plussed for a moment, then said, 'I would like to find out. I really would. Come now, girl, explain to me what you mean by "ourselves to ourselves". You shall not go until you tell me.'

'It means I won't kiss you!' she cried.

He pulled her to him and twisted her arms behind her back, holding her close. It was painless unless she tried to move. He bent his head to kiss her. She turned her face at the last moment and the kiss landed on her cheek.

'Such soft, smooth skin,' he murmured, 'and not a pennyworth of powder or rouge. I know ladies who would give their right arm for a complexion like yours.'

'Do you insult them, too?'

'I kiss them sometimes. They like it, especially the older ones.'

'You make me feel sick!'

He was angry again. 'What do I care for the opinion of such as you? A skivvy who spends her life with her hands in greasy water.'

'You've even got that wrong,' she snapped. 'Your sainted mother employs an orphaned half-witted child to do that.'

'Take care. You go too far.'

'*I* go too far! What about you?'

'Now you *shall* kiss me.'

'I won't! Let me go.'

'Not until I've tasted your lips. Come, girl, just a little kiss. Your mouth is the most delicious thing I've seen in an age.' His tone was softly seductive.

After all her brothers' mocking insults about her mouth he couldn't have picked on a more direct way to flatter her. Every instinct told her she shouldn't yield an inch, yet she was driven by an impulse to face him.

'That's much better.' He touched her mouth lightly with his, caressingly, gently, and she found herself responding in a way which surprised and alarmed her.

'May I go? Please?'

He wasn't laughing any more. He stared down into the depths of her eyes as if he was searching for something. 'No,' he said, 'of course not. It couldn't be.'

'What do you mean? What are you talkin' about?'

'Run away back to the kitchen. I shan't find what I'm looking for in you.'

He released her and she ran full tilt through the woods, tripping on hidden roots, stumbling among the bushes and leaves, out across the park and back to the house, scared by his words, wondering what they meant. She entered the safety of the kitchen so fast she collided with Prue who just managed to hold on to a jug of cream.

'For heaven's sake, Lily.'

'My name's Willow,' she yelled. 'My bloody name is

Willow.' She didn't know why she shouted. Something had happened out there which mystified her, which had opened a window in her nature that she hadn't known existed. She wanted to be alone and raced up the back stairs, arriving hot and panting in the bedroom. Aggie was there, standing in her petticoat, washing herself with cold water and a rag. She stared at her red-faced room-mate, then grabbed her grubby dress to put back on.

Willow snapped, 'You can't dress yet. You're wet.'

'Are you cross with me?'

Willow took a deep breath. 'No, I'm not cross with you. Why should I be? I'll go away an' you finish your wash in peace.'

'Thanks,' said Aggie. 'See, I know why Mrs Westerby had the camp bed put up for me an' I don't really want to smell bad cos I know you an' Ivy don't like it. She used to make me sleep right on the edge of the bed before you came. I can't help smellin', honest. The work's so dirty an' I get ever so tired.'

Willow felt deeply ashamed. She resented the treatment meted out to her, yet she had behaved with equal thoughtlessness to the scullery maid. She looked at the bowl of water and back at the girl. Aggie was much thinner than she had realised, with a childish body. 'You should fetch up hot water and use soap,' she said.

'Ivy don't like me touchin' it. She says I could even make soap dirty, an' if I try to fill a can with water someone always gets on to me an' says I should be doin' somethin' else.'

'I'll get some water an' you're welcome to use the soap, Aggie. Tell Ivy I said so, if she asks.'

Prue and Ivy were in the kitchen making sandwiches for tea. Silver cake-stands stood ready filled and bread was cut and muffins waiting to be toasted.

'Fancy comin' in to the kitchen on your day off,' said Prue. 'An' what happened to make you rush in like a scalded cat, an' swear too?'

'Nothin'. I was in a hurry. Now I want hot water.' She

dipped a jug into the huge pot of water which was kept on the hob.

'Have you seen Aggie?' asked Prue. 'The little slut's gone somewhere without askin' a soul. She'll feel the weight of my tongue when I see her, and if Mrs Narracott finds out she'll feel the weight of her hand.'

Willow evaded a direct answer. 'If I see her, I'll tell her she's wanted.'

Aggie had already poured the sooty, greasy water into the slop bucket. She put her hands joyfully into the warm water, sliding the soap between her fingers and sniffing at it. 'Oh, it hardly hurts my sores at all, not like the stuff I use for work. That's awful.'

Willow gave her a washrag. 'Put plenty of soap on it an' give yourself a treat,' she advised kindly. 'I didn't know you disliked gettin' dirty.'

Aggie said matter-of-factly, 'I didn't notice it that much until you came an' I saw how you keep yourself clean, much more than Ivy does, an' you smell nice an' your hair's so shiny. I'd like to be like you.'

The merriment above stairs gained impetus, ceasing for only a few hours at night, and there was a constant bustle of valets and maids below stairs, demanding fuller's earth, stale breadcrumbs and powder-blue for removing stains, using the flat-irons or steaming velvet over boiling water and ammonia so that the kitchen was filled with pungent fumes. They commandeered the table in the servants' hall to clean precious jewellery or revive black lace with tea or beer, and upset the laundry maids by giving them orders to pay particular attention to some garment or other. Willow was fascinated by the upper servants and all that they did, and learned as much as possible.

Miss Jebb was giving Nancy more and more work from both Violet and Frances and much of it was passed directly to Willow. To keep up she had to relinquish much of her spare time. The others advised her to refuse, but Willow carried on because she was learning a great deal about the cut of fashionable clothes. Also, in spite of feeling weary at times, she delighted in handling the lovely things which the young ladies treated so carelessly, especially Violet who took part in various sports fearlessly and often recklessly. A fall at a hedge kept her to her room for several days, but didn't even dent her passion for riding. It meant a lot of extra sewing to repair her flowing velvet habit, a garment previously unknown to Willow, who made drawings of it.

Nancy nodded at the riding habit. 'It's pretty, isn't it? I can't abide Miss Violet, but I've got to admit she looks grand. Miss Frances doesn't like horses. She really prefers a bicycle. Miss Frances can sometimes be quite nice.'

Willow didn't answer. She didn't consider that Frances had been so nice to her, not enough to bother to see again the girl who had saved Winifred.

Nancy said morosely one evening, 'I wouldn't mind if they handed down *all* their cast-offs for us to take our pick, but they don't, although they're always buying new things.'

'What do they do with the ones they turn out?' asked Willow.

'Give them to charity sales.'

'Isn't that a good thing?'

'Maybe, but I think they do it for show. If they were really charitable they'd see the needs of those that work for them.'

'It's not only that,' declared Prue. 'They'd rather be struck dead than risk meeting a maid in something they'd once worn.'

There was to be a ball with over a hundred and fifty extra guests and Mrs Narracott was in a permanent bad temper. 'I'll hand in my notice. I've got a friend in London and her employer gets Fortnum and Mason when they've got a big do, but they expect me to have everything ready on the dot and it's difficult to prepare ahead when the ice box isn't big enough to keep everything fresh.'

Prue said she always grumbled like that when a large party was planned.

'Could the Maddisons afford to get things sent from London?' asked Willow.

'Of course they could,' said Nancy, 'but the master and his friends complain all the time about Mr Lloyd George's Budget. He calls it "a war budget to wage warfare against poverty and squalidness", but *they* don't see it that way.'

'He gave my gran a pension,' said Willow.

'Any woman of good character can get one now,' said Polly. 'It's little enough, but upstairs go on and on about income tax being raised to help lazy folk.'

Willow was amazed to learn that anyone with an income over five thousand pounds a year must pay a super-tax of fivepence on top of the usual one of a shilling and sixpence in the pound. 'Five thousand pounds *every* year?' she asked incredulously. 'How could anyone spend that much?'

Mr Norris laughed. 'Mr and Mrs Maddison get much more than that and he's not the richest, not by a long chalk.'

As Willow worked she often fell to day-dreaming, a habit which Mrs Narracott tried hard to eradicate. In her dream she saw herself earning five thousand pounds a year, driving to the house in Barton Hill in a lovely motor car, filling her family's hands with gold sovereigns while they thanked her with tears of gratitude in their eyes. A clout across the back of the head put an abrupt end to her fantasy.

'What the hell do you think you're doing?' shrieked Mrs Narracott. 'You've let the sauce boil and now it's curdled, and the fish is ready to go up and there's no time to make more. Well, it'll have to be black butter sauce and I'll get the blame for changing the menu. And as for you, you can go back to peeling potatoes until you learn to concentrate.'

Willow rubbed her head as Prue hurriedly tossed butter in a sauté pan, cooked it until it became nut-brown, then added parsley and vinegar and cooked it for a further minute.

'I'm really sorry, Mrs Narracott,' said Willow. 'I know I wasn't payin' attention. I won't let it happen again.'

Mrs Narracott scowled then said, 'Apology accepted.

Have you chopped the mint really fine? Right, add the sugar and vinegar. The mutton's going up next.'

Willow obeyed. The cook wasn't a bad sort, and she was clever and hard-working. In spite of having to cater for so many extra people, she coped. Since arriving at the manor, Willow had heard tales of the treatment of servants in some households which made the hairs on her neck rise. Things here could be a lot worse, though she wasn't any nearer to achieving her dream. All the intricate sewing she did was passed off by Miss Jebb as her own.

Chapter Six

Arrangements were completed for the ball during which Violet Maddison's engagement was to be announced.

When Steadman relayed the latest news to the kitchen staff, Willow said, 'She's goin' to marry Sir George Trembath, then?'

Steadman gave her a look in which indignation and disbelief were mingled. 'In the first place,' he announced, 'you are not to speak to me unless you are spoken to. In the second place, I cannot think why you should say such a stupid thing.'

Willow wished she had kept quiet. Now everyone in the room was looking at her. Even Steven was peering in at the door, grinning. 'I thought she was sweet on him,' stammered Willow.

Mrs Westerby looked down her nose. 'Sweet on him! What a vulgar expression. Though –' she sighed '– no more than I could expect from you. Miss Violet has accepted an offer of marriage from Viscount Radcliffe, Lily. He is Lady Mary's brother. In future, please keep your scurrilous thoughts to yourself.'

Willow hadn't come across the word 'scurrilous', but she knew its meaning must be unpleasant. Steven overheard her asking Ivy about it, but she knew no more than Willow. He said, 'I've got a book that'll tell you.' He went to his room and returned with a dusty, finger-marked dictionary with tattered pages, some of which were loose.

Ivy looked astonished. 'Whatever can you want with that?'

Steven flushed beneath the grime engrained in his skin.

Several of the loose pages floated to the floor. As he picked them up he muttered, 'I won't always be a bootboy.' Ivy laughed, then stamped off as he gave her a murderous look.

'I suppose you think I'm funny too?' he growled, glaring at Willow.

She said mildly, 'No. You've surprised me, but I don't think you're funny. I love books, too.'

Steven relaxed and whispered, 'Do you know, there's a library upstairs. *They* hardly use it at all. I sneak up sometimes after they've gone to bed. I take my candle an' go an' look at them. I dare not touch them, but lookin's better than nothin'. Some are huge and some are tiny, but they're all covered in leather. They make the room smell like the ridin' boots I clean, all leathery an'—' His voice trickled away. 'I don't know enough words yet to explain things properly, but one day I will. I'm only up to "E" so far, but I read as often as I can an' one day I'll know all the words, an' then you'll see! An' what's more, I'm goin' to learn to talk proper. People take more notice of you if you do. I can't abide Mrs Westerby, but she talks nice an' everyone listens.'

Willow knew there was more to the housekeeper's dominance than speech, but she didn't argue. She watched Steven as he riffled through the pages and read out, '"Scurrilous. Grossly or obscenely abusive or defamatory."' By the time they reached 'obscenely', they were united in condemnation of Mrs Westerby's unfair criticism.

The ballroom had been opened up and the wide expanse of floor polished, the long crimson velvet curtains taken down, shaken outside then stored, and rich golden ones put up. Flowers were massed, bronze and gold chrysanthemums, white dahlias and delicate, mauve sweetpeas, all displayed against autumn foliage. Log fires were already alight so that the red-hot ash would keep the lightly clad ladies warm, and the brass fenders had been burnished.

The kitchen was now in a fever of preparation and Mrs

Narracott was everywhere, her sharp tongue and heavy correcting hand busy as she drove her minions along. The ball supper was to be mainly cold, but there were still the meals to be sent upstairs. The task seemed impossible to Willow, but everything was ready in time to be carried to the dining room. Nancy said that estate workers had brought in two huge folding tables and erected them and from somewhere had appeared dozens of small gilt chairs for both the supper room and the ballroom. White linen tablecloths had been produced and washed and starched so heavily in the laundry that they crackled when ironed.

Dinner was served at seven, and while the family and house guests were in their rooms preparing for the ball, Mrs Narracott said that anyone who wished might creep up the back stairs and take a look at the supper tables.

Nancy went with Willow. They gazed from the door of the room as if looking into Aladdin's cave. Huge mirrors reflected the beauty of polished wood. A delicate chandelier holding snow-white candles hung in the centre of the room whose floor was carpeted almost to the wainscot in a pattern of large rust and gold medallions on a linden green background. Willow took this in quickly before her eyes went to the array of delicacies she had helped to prepare. Sole in aspic, chicken creams, game pie, tiny sandwiches beneath glass domes to keep them fresh, cheeses on a platter to be served with water biscuits and grapes, mounds of fruit from the hot-houses, including pineapples, the first she had seen. There would be hot dishes too, clear soup and devilled lobster, and there were eight different sweets waiting in the cold larder. She gazed at the silver candlesticks, the tall silver stem vases of flowers and delicately drooping ferns. There were table napkins folded into fans, and an array of gleaming cutlery.

She wished with all her heart that she was a young lady, dressing herself in a fairy-tale ballgown, ready to descend to enchant her dancing partners and later to enjoy the food. If – no, *when* – she attained the position of lady's maid, she would be able to watch everything, her hands would be as white as Miss Brayton's and Miss Jebb's and she would be permitted to wear fashionable clothes.

'To think,' she sighed to Nancy, 'all this to celebrate an engagement. Where I come from people just get married, an' sometimes they can hardly afford the licence. Miss Violet's so lucky. Don't you wish you might marry a lord one day?'

'What's the use of wishing any such thing? Neither of us will ever live that kind of life. In any case, I wouldn't want to marry Lady Mary's brother. "Lord Randy", he ought to be called. They say no woman's safe with him. She'll never be able to trust him.'

'How awful! The poor thing! Someone should warn her before it's too late.'

Nancy laughed. 'She knows, don't you worry. She's got her eyes on his money; her sort always wants more, especially if a title goes with it. And of course,' she added reflectively, 'he's handsome. Well, maybe not handsome exactly, but you can understand women falling in love with him.'

'Maybe she thinks he'll settle down after marryin'?' suggested Willow.

'Maybe, but I doubt it. I'd love to eat the supper, though. I've never tasted half the stuff. They'll have dozens of bottles of champagne, too, the lucky things. Come on.' Nancy's voice grew suddenly urgent. 'We've been too long. We've got to give the others a turn. At least Mrs Narracott kept back a few nice things for us.'

The musicians arrived and were given beer and sandwiches in the servants' hall. Later, when the gentry were busy with supper, they would get a proper meal. For the first time Willow realised just how much rested on the shoulders of the cook and understood Mrs Narracott's quick flights into temper. As she helped clean the kitchen she wondered who Edgar would dance with and if he would try to kiss any of his partners. The thought drifted unexpectedly into her head; equally unexpected was a slight pang.

The kitchen staff had a little time to slow down and eat and Willow learned the delights of salmon mayonnaise and rhum babas rich with cream and redolent of strong spirit. Later, valets and ladies' maids drifted into the kitchen and the maids described the gowns worn by their mistresses. Willow listened avidly, wishing with all her heart that she could see them. She was sewing a rent in Miss Frances's nightgown, a confection of handsewn nainsook with Valenciennes lace insertions.

'I can't think how she came to tear it so badly,' she said to no one in particular. She wished she had held her tongue when Miss Tomlin, the Countess of Somervell's maid, said, 'In our establishment *I* do all the fine sewing. We don't hand it to a kitchen maid.'

Miss Jebb had discovered that Willow had taken on much of the sewing. She had not liked the idea, but had been forced to accept it. The more indebted she became to the second kitchen maid the more she disliked her. Even hated her, Willow sometimes believed.

The idea made her nervous and she had spoken to Nancy about it. Nancy had said, 'She's got an ungenerous nature. She thinks it's lowering to be beholden to you. And she's afraid you might tell upstairs.'

'I never would!'

'No, but I suppose she judges people by her own nasty ways.'

Miss Jebb, who was sipping tea and nibbling a macaroon, looked up sharply. 'Willow is a trained seamstress,' she lied. 'I permit her to perform the more mundane repairs.'

'What she's got there doesn't look mundane to me,' said Miss Tomlin mischievously.

'No, and it doesn't to me either,' said another maid, joining in the fun.

A valet leaned over and peered closely. 'No, you're right. It looks complicated, but I'm only a man. How would I know?'

'I'm sure you would know,' said Miss Tomlin coquettishly. 'You're so clever.'

Miss Jebb stopped eating and glared at Willow, furious at the attention she had drawn to her occupation, while

Miss Tomlin and the valet indulged in a a few flirtatious moments. When the lady's maid looked away, Willow breathed more easily.

But the servants soon resumed the sport of tormenting Miss Jebb. 'Where did you learn to be a seamstress?' Miss Tomlin asked Willow pointedly. 'You must have attended a sewing school, though you look a bit young for that.'

'I didn't need to,' said Willow. 'My grandmother is very clever an' passed her skills on to me.'

'She must be clever,' said the valet. 'Sewing *and* teaching.'

'Yes, she is,' agreed Willow, glad of the change of emphasis.

'Did she attend a special school?' asked Miss Tomlin, doggedly determined to talk the matter through.

'I don't think so,' said Willow. She kept her voice low and concentrated on her stitching. 'She was a nursery maid and learned a lot from the nanny in charge.'

'Ah, yes,' said the valet portentously, 'nannies are a breed apart. No wonder you can take on Miss Jebb's sewing.'

Willow didn't answer. One glance had informed her that Miss Jebb was boiling with rage. The lady's maid sat for a few moments longer then got up and left, giving Willow a vicious look as she passed. The only good thing was that Miss Brayton wasn't present to hear, thought Willow. There was already rivalry between the two ladies' maids. Miss Brayton descended to the kitchen as seldom as possible. As Mrs Maddison's personal maid of many years she was granted certain privileges, one of which was to take her meals upstairs in her room next to her mistress's.

The servants left the door to the backstairs ajar so that they could hear distantly the music coming from the ballroom. The frantic preparations were over and the lull below stairs continued.

Mr Norris bowed to Nancy. 'May I have the pleasure of a dance?'

She, mischievous eyes cast down in spurious modesty, replied, 'Delighted, I'm sure.'

They waltzed around the kitchen. 'You dance beautifully, Lady Nancy,' said Mr Norris in a plummy voice.

'Thank you, sir.' Nancy fluttered her lashes.

'And you have a simply divine figure. Such a pleasure to hold it in my arms.'

He gave her a quick squeeze and Nancy giggled and although Mrs Narracott tutted it was obvious she was controlling a smile. Mrs Westerby, fortunately, was upstairs, ensuring that nothing could go wrong. She would have come down sharply on talk bordering on the bawdy. Willow laughed delightedly with the others, but she ached to be above stairs to watch. This afternoon during tea she had begged to be allowed to wear her black dress and help the upper servants to carry round trays of champagne.

Mrs Narracott had refused absolutely. 'You're a long way from that, Lily, and the way you carry on, I sometimes wonder if you'll ever get to such a height.' She had poured herself a cup of tea, hot and strong, from the metal teapot kept on the range.

As she was in a good mood, Willow had ventured to ask, 'What is it that I do wrong, please?'

The cook had surveyed her, small eyes made smaller by the plumpness of her face. 'Perhaps I spoke a mite hastily. You're a good enough girl and you do as I ask, but you're too dreamy and a dreamy kitchen maid won't ever rise higher. Look at the way you sometimes let things burn.'

Excited by the mounting festive atmosphere, Willow had said, 'I'll do better, honest, it's just that—'

One of those inexplicable silences had fallen and suddenly everyone was listening. She had been about to say how much she missed school, how bored she often was by her work, but she checked herself. 'It's just that I've never known this kind of work. A corset factory is a very different place.'

'I should blooming well hope it was,' said Henry, and there was general laughter in which Willow joined, before her mind began to wander in just the way Mrs Narracott deplored.

Because the housemaids had been exceptionally busy,

Willow had helped Mrs Westerby with the great baskets of flowers brought in by the gardeners. She had carried another basket for the discarded stems and leaves and followed the housekeeper, silently marvelling. Wherever she went in this great house she was surrounded by a rich elegance which could only have been acquired by many years of discriminating collecting. She had no idea of values, but she had a natural appreciation of beauty and grace. Her eyes roamed curiously. She had noticed a small curtained alcove near the ballroom . . .

The kitchen dance had grown in size. The order of precedence meant that valets of high-ranking members of society partnered the maids of equally high-born ladies. Some of the maids partnered each other and no one had eyes for her. If she left quickly they wouldn't notice and she could creep upstairs and hide in the convenient alcove. Some of the revellers would surely stroll along the passage, giving her a glimpse of their finery. She slipped away and raced up the back stairs to the ground floor where she entered the main house. Only Henry saw her. He was on duty in the hall. His mouth fell open as she scooted across the marble tiles and down the corridor where she hid behind the curtain.

It seemed as if the guests had been waiting for her and several began to stroll along the wide corridor. The downstairs rooms as well as upstairs were lit by gas, the candles being used more as decoration, and in the clear light Willow had a good view as she held the curtain a little to one side and peered through the crack. She drank in the vision of pink silk with white lace insertions worn by a young girl, probably a debutante, her white gloves stretching above her elbows, her headdress of silk daisies and tiny pearls.

She was accompanied by Sir George Trembath and Willow wondered if he would try to kiss the girl and what she would do. He was tall and thin and Willow sensed a wiry strength beneath the faultless cut of his evening clothes. It had something to do with the way he moved. In fact, all the society folk she had glimpsed walked in a certain upright, proud way which she resolved to cultivate.

Her sharp eyes detected subtle changes in fashion. And she was sure that some of the young women were wearing the new, lightly boned ribbon-corsets, so that their clothes flowed softly over the natural curves of their bodies. She had learned about this from Nancy who had a half-on, half-off friendship with Miss Jebb who enjoyed talking in a superior way of fashion details with which Nancy regaled the other maids.

The ladies, with their escorts in attendance, passed to and fro, their skirts swishing and rustling, voices mingling, flower scents wafting, helping Willow to forget time and lose herself among the treasures of silk and satin and taffeta, chiffon and muslin, real and artificial flowers and gems of every kind, sparkling and winking in the glow of the lamps.

When Violet passed on the arm of her fiancé she surpassed everyone. Her gown had been produced, at great cost, by the fashion house of Worth. Willow stared at it, loving the amber satin patterned with pale violet scrolls and the large fan of amber feathers. Violet's gracefully long neck was encircled by a necklace of pale amethysts and diamonds set in gold and on her head was a circlet of gold and purple velvet pansies, each flower's heart holding a tiny jewel.

Willow leaned so far forward she was in danger of toppling out and her heart beat hard at the idea of being discovered. She had lost trace of time until she realised with horror that the band was quiet and guests were sauntering by in small groups towards the supper room. It must be eleven o'clock. *Eleven?* She had been absent for over an hour and Mrs Narracott would be wildly angry. As soon as the corridor was clear she leapt from behind the curtain, then heard voices approaching and darted into the library – empty, thank heaven – and hid behind the open door. Even in the extremity of her anxiety she noticed the smell of books which Steven had described.

Please, God, send everyone away, she begged. If you do, I'll be good for evermore.

She shrank back as several people entered, fortunately leaving the door open. 'Whisky, gentlemen, or Cognac,' said a male voice. 'And do feel free to smoke.'

There were general cries of relief as glasses were clinked and smoke began to drift from cigarettes and cigars.

'Good idea of yours, Maddison,' said one man. 'Champagne is all very well, but it's not my tipple. Fills you with gas without the kick you get from spirits, and the ladies, bless 'em, don't care for smoke.'

'Most don't,' agreed someone, 'though some smoke themselves. I've seen them with cigarettes.'

'An abomination on the lips of ladies,' spluttered Mr Maddison.

'And we all know what we expect from the lips of ladies,' drawled Sir George Trembath, his tone implying more than his words. There was a burst of laughter and he continued, 'Now then, Maddison, give us all a glimpse of the latest addition to your collection.'

'Certainly.' The voice was only a couple of feet from where Willow stood quaking. 'It's ivory. Very beautiful.'

Her nerves were ragged. If only she'd had the sense just to walk along the corridor past the men. They wouldn't have taken a scrap of notice of her.

'By God,' said one of the men, 'that's a superb piece of artistry.'

Sir George said, 'A carved relief ivory plaque. Good lord! Those Chinese are devilish ingenious in more ways than one. They think up an endless number of positions. Look at those two!'

There was more laughter mingled with expressions of appreciation, and there was a timbre to their voices which made her even more uneasy. She heard the opening of a cupboard door and the click of a lock. Mr Maddison said, 'Wouldn't do to let the ladies see it.' Then there was the creaking of leather as someone sank into one of the deep armchairs. More talk followed, much of it concerned with money and the fact that Asquith and Lloyd George seemed bent on ruining the country with their new welfare ideas.

'Damn People's Budget!' said Mr Maddison. 'Thank God the Lords will never pass it. The Liberals will have to go to the country.'

'A general election,' agreed the others, 'and the sooner the better.'

Willow couldn't understand their condemnation of the man who had given Gran her five-shillings-a-week pension. A clock gave out high, melodious chimes and Mr Maddison exclaimed, 'We must go, gentlemen, before the ladies begin to ask what has become of us.'

There were more murmurs and laughter and at last they left. Willow was about to make good her escape when someone else entered and began to wander round the room in a seemingly aimless fashion. She came to a decision. She would walk out as if nothing untoward was happening. After all, why should a guest query the presence of a servant? She sidled out from behind the door, took a step forward, and too late recognised the occupant of the library. Edgar Maddison!

'You! Here! What are doing?' he asked.

'Nothin', sir. I had a message. I have to go back to the kitchen now.'

'This is not in direct line with the kitchen.'

'No, sir, I thought I'd take a quick look at the books.'

Edgar said, 'You're not a very good liar. Somehow I don't think your stay in the manor will prove a long one. Looking at the books, indeed! What are you really up to? You had an assignation, perhaps? Lucky devil to be favoured by a girl as pretty as you.' Before Willow could answer, he said, 'A lady has lost a jewel. A brooch in the shape of a ribbon bow, set with small diamonds. A trembler brooch. I don't suppose you know what that is?'

'No, sir.'

'It has fine gold wires on the ends of which are more tiny diamonds. The whole thing trembles when moved. It is not

109

of great worth, but belonged to her late grandmother and she values it. Have you seen it?'

'No, sir. If I had I would have handed it to someone.'

Edgar said, 'She says she was in the library for a few minutes and she is sure she lost it here.'

'Then it must be here, sir.'

'Maybe. You weren't on an errand, were you? A kitchen maid belongs downstairs.'

'How would you know about the life of a kitchen maid?' she said, suddenly angry.

His eyebrows went up. 'You really must try not to be insolent. An impossible goal for you, I should surmise. But I will indulge your curiosity by explaining that as a child I went anywhere I pleased which included the kitchen. Mrs Narracott gave me nice things to eat. Satisfied?'

Willow flinched at his sardonic tone. 'Thank you, sir.'

'Come, tell the truth and shame the devil. Why are you here?'

'I wanted to see the clothes.'

Edgar automatically glanced down at his perfectly cut evening suit.

'Not the men's! The ladies'!'

'Why?'

'I like lookin' at pretty clothes.'

'I see. At least, I think I do. Oh, now I remember, one of my sisters said you liked to draw costumes. Clever little puss, aren't you?' He took a step closer and looked her up and down. 'You are prettier than ever. There is a bloom about you . . .'

Willow waited for no more. She turned and fled, heedless of whom she might meet.

Mrs Narracott was too busy to do anything except shriek at her to help load the trays with the pudding dishes. 'I'll talk to you later,' she finished.

Willow was truly contrite. She knew that supper had to be well over before twelve-thirty which was the time planned to announce Violet's engagement to the guests.

At one o'clock, Mrs Narracott assembled the staff in the

servants' hall and, as tradition dictated, Miss Violet and her fiancé came to break the joyful news and encourage the servants to raise their charged glasses to a happy future. Willow looked curiously at Lord Radcliffe. His chin was long, his jowls heavy, his lips full, and when he received the servants' toast his eyebrows rose towards his thinning hair. Was he mocking them? wondered Willow. He was supposed to be a lady-killer. He wasn't handsome, but there was something about him, a kind of predatory air that could be attractive. Would he be faithful to his wife? How dreadful it would be to have a husband who went with other women. Dad wouldn't do a thing like that. The thought sped through her mind that Dad had neither energy nor money to do anything much, and the memory of home, even with its deprivations, mingled with her weariness and almost brought her to tears.

Violet spoke. 'My fiancé and I have to thank you, Mrs Westerby, and the staff, for helping to make the party such a splendid success, and also for the delightful flowers.' Her distant tones were not relaxed even in so informal an atmosphere.

'It was a pleasure, madam,' murmured the housekeeper in an equally cool voice.

'A deuced good turn out all round!' said Lord Radcliffe.

'Thank you, too, Cook, for all your hard work. You have performed miracles as usual.'

Mrs Narracott went red with pleasure but Willow wondered if Miss Violet could even remember the cook's name.

The ball went on and on and it was almost daybreak when Willow fell into bed. Mrs Narracott had given the kitchen maids leave to lie in until six. Even Aggie, stupefyingly weary, was granted the concession.

'How bloody kind of her,' muttered Ivy before she dropped off. Willow closed her eyes, longing for the blessed respite of sleep, but it didn't favour her. She kept falling off the edge of wakefulness, then awoke with a jolt as the memory of her evening's adventures kept her alert. Or was it the memory of Edgar that invaded her active brain?

On the following morning Willow went downstairs, unrefreshed and yawning.

'Come on, my girl,' said Prue, 'this won't do. We all have to set to with a will an' make sure everythin' is spick and span before breakfast.'

'Can't we even have a cup of tea?' asked Willow.

'Don't be stupid!' Prue snapped, her good humour eroded by weariness. 'Of course we can eat somethin'. I mean before family breakfast. Where's Henry? The lazy pig hasn't appeared yet an' there are all the breakfast trays to carry up.'

'Are they all eatin' in bed early this mornin'?' asked Willow, stuffing down bread and butter. She didn't feel like eating yet, but knew if she missed this opportunity she would soon be ravenous.

'Try not to be dense,' said Prue. 'Here, leave that an' carry this tray up to the dinin' room. Ivy, fill two toast racks, that should be enough for now. Will you stand there all day?' she screeched at Willow. 'How can they go ridin' before havin' a bite to eat?'

Willow groaned. 'Why do they have to get up so early? An' don't they ever stop eatin'? It seems like it was only minutes ago we were feedin' them.'

'It's not our place to pass comment,' said Ivy.

Willow muttered beneath her breath and Ivy said, 'If you're sayin' somethin' about me, I'd like to hear it.'

Willow had been mocking Ivy's virtuous little speech, but she said, 'I was still goin' on about them upstairs.' As she carried the heavy tray she spilled some milk. Nancy was laying the table. Already the sideboard was covered with cold meats. 'Half the milk's on the tray,' she scolded.

'Sorry, it's so heavy, an' it isn't half the milk!'

'Don't answer me back! It's Henry's fault.' He appeared, buttoning his waistcoat. 'There you are, and about time. If Mrs Westerby or Mr Steadman find out you didn't begin work until well gone six, they'll murder you.'

Henry murmured something which was clearly rude, making Nancy giggle. 'Well, get to work now. Willow, go downstairs. You shouldn't really be here.'

The rest of the guests awoke more slowly and at ten-thirty there were still a few eating a leisurely breakfast.

Mrs Westerby had already handed over the menu for the day so they were surprised to see her in the kitchen so soon. 'Mrs Narracott, call your staff together if you please.'

The cook's face reddened in anger. 'If we all stop work, lunch is bound to be late.'

The housekeeper stared at her grimly. 'I am waiting.'

The staff assembled and Mrs Westerby said, 'Last night, at the height of the celebrations, a lady who is a house guest lost a brooch. Has anyone found it?'

'If they had we'd know by now,' said Mrs Narracott indignantly, 'because they would have handed it in.'

'They had a great deal to do and it might have been forgotten,' said Mrs Westerby. 'Everyone worked well.'

'Well, thank you, I'm sure,' said Mrs Narracott.

This time Mrs Westerby turned her cold eyes on the cook. 'You will be able to return to your tasks far more quickly if I am not subjected to unnecessary interruptions. Now, I ask again, did one of you find a brooch and forget to tell someone? If so, and the brooch is recovered, the matter will be overlooked.'

'What does it look like, ma'am?' asked Prue.

Mrs Westerby described the brooch exactly as Edgar had done. 'So you see,' she finished, 'although the brooch is of comparatively small value, the lady is very upset by its loss.'

Willow's heart was hammering. Many of the assembled staff knew that she had been upstairs for over an hour last night and Edgar was aware that she had been hiding in the very place the brooch was supposed to have been dropped. She wanted to cry out, 'It wasn't me! I didn't touch it!' but realised the foolishness of such a response.

Mrs Westerby's eyes travelled over the servants and came to rest on the housemaids. 'You will clean every room thoroughly, including the corners, and behind and beneath every piece of furniture. Henry, you will assist the maids. If the brooch is not recovered Miss Brayton will accompany me as I look in the maids' bedrooms and Mr Norris will help Mr Steadman in the men's quarters. The kitchen staff will continue to prepare lunch and come out one at a time when called. There must be no interruption of the guests' routine. Meanwhile, not one of you is to go to his or her room.'

'She might have dropped the brooch outside,' said Mrs Narracott, her bombast all gone. This was a serious matter for the servants, who were always the first to be suspected.

'The weather was not warm enough to tempt the lady to walk in the garden,' said the housekeeper, 'and, in any case, she says she was in the house the whole evening.'

'Does she have any idea what time she lost it?' asked the cook.

'At ten o'clock someone admired it. Around eleven she missed it.'

Willow's eyes were fixed on Mrs Westerby in dreadful fascination. How long would it be before she discovered that the second kitchen maid had had the temerity to spend an hour upstairs, the exact hour during which the brooch had vanished?

Mr Norris came into the kitchen as Mrs Narracott said, 'There were a good many guests last night. How can you be sure that one of them—'

Mrs Westerby gave her a look which froze her tongue.

Mr Norris said to the housekeeper, 'Mrs Maddison wishes to see you at once.'

When Mrs Westerby had gone the others besieged Mr Norris with questions and he did his best to answer. 'The lady who lost the brooch has had an attack of hysterics and a doctor has been sent for.'

'She sounds like a very silly woman!' said Mrs Narracott. 'Just the sort who would lose something and give endless trouble!'

Mr Norris shrugged. Later he informed them that the

housemaids' search had not produced a result. 'They've decided a servant's got it.'

'They're going to search all our rooms,' said Jenny.

Mr Norris said, 'I can't think why they should imagine one of the kitchen staff could be guilty of theft.'

Mrs Narracott groaned. 'Well, there can't be any let-up in the work.' She stopped abruptly as her glance fell on Willow. 'I almost forgot—'

'What?' Jenny was sharply suspicious.

'Nothing,' said the cook. She issued swift orders, then beckoned Willow to her side. 'Stand by me and watch how I separate eggs. You put the yolks in one bowl and the whites in another.' She said quietly, 'You were upstairs last night. I never did get to ask you what happened. What were you doing?'

'Just lookin' at the lovely clothes,' said Willow, trying to keep her voice steady.

'You must have been hidden somewhere. Where were you?'

Willow told her and the cook's hand slipped. 'Drat it! I've put some yolk in with the egg whites and they'll never whip. Ivy, fetch a basin over here quick and separate a dozen eggs.'

Mrs Narracott told Willow to follow her and marched down the passage to the pantry. Inside, she said, 'I've not known you long, but I'd have staked anything you were honest.'

She peered closely into Willow's face. 'You didn't pick the brooch up, did you? If you did, tell me now, and I'll think of something to say that won't involve you.'

'I didn't see the brooch.'

'Are you sure? Perhaps you thought it a bauble without value. A kitchen maid could easily make such a mistake.'

Willow coloured, her heart hammering. 'How can I make you believe me? I didn't see it.'

'Did anyone catch you upstairs?'

Willow hesitated. 'Yes, Mr Edgar.' She explained what had happened.

'Do you mean to tell me he asked you about the brooch *last night*?'

'He did an' I told him what I'm tellin' you. I didn't see it.'

'I can't save you now, my girl. Sooner or later suspicion's bound to fall on you.'

'But I've not done anythin' wrong! I only watched the people!'

Mrs Narracott shook her head. 'Come on, back to the kitchen. Bring something with you so it'll look as if you've been helping me. Another basin of eggs. The way things are going this morning, I'll probably need them.'

The men were taken first, one by one, followed by the housemaids, then the kitchen staff. The butler, housekeeper and cook were regarded as above suspicion. 'So far,' said Mr Steadman, 'they've kept the news from the other guests, but it's bound to leak out. Pray we find the damned thing. The stupid female admits the catch was faulty. If she'd had it seen to none of this would be happening.'

Each servant returned from the search indignant.

'Bloody cheek!' muttered Henry, and Mrs Narracott for once didn't reprove him.

'What happens?' asked Willow.

'You'll find out. You were upstairs last night, weren't you?'

'Yes, but I didn't take the brooch! I wouldn't! Henry, what happens when you get called out?'

'They go through everything you've got.'

'They even take off the bedclothes,' said Nancy, 'and look carefully at the mattress to see if there's any sign of recent sewing in case we've hidden something inside. I can't think when we've had time to sew anything since last night.'

'Have you been in a search before?' asked Henry.

'Yes, once. In my first place a necklace was missing and they found a housemaid had pinched it.'

'What happened to her?' asked Willow.

'She was sent off without a reference. You had to feel

sorry for her. She was getting on and would never get a decent job again.'

'Poor thing,' said Willow.

'She was lucky they didn't prosecute her,' said Nancy.

'I hope you don't agree with stealing from your employer!' said Jenny.

'Of course I don't,' cried Willow.

Prue said, 'Jenny, please don't keep Willow talkin'. Ivy needs a hand with the fruit.'

Right at the end Aggie, Ivy and Willow were sent for and had to stand and watch as Miss Brayton, beneath the housekeeper's cold gaze, conducted a thorough search. First through Ivy's neat pile of clothes. Then through Aggie's untidy heap of underwear as Mrs Westerby tutted. Finally they came to Willow's drawer. She heaved a sigh of relief that the whole horrible episode was nearing its end. Again Mrs Westerby tutted, this time at Willow's underwear which was neat and carefully mended, but worn, then Miss Brayton removed her spare pair of stockings and held up something she had found.

'Hand it to me,' said Mrs Westerby. She took the object and lifted it to see it better by the light of the candle she held against the gloom.

Her voice was pure ice. 'What have we here, Lily?'

The brooch was as it had been described. Willow saw how the tiny diamonds trembled delicately on the gold wires and sent thousands of pinpoint lights darting through the attic room.

Chapter Seven

Willow was hustled along the corridor by Mrs Westerby, whose bony fingers dug like steel into her neck and whose ears affected not to hear her protestations of innocence. Jenny held on to her arm while Ivy followed with her things. Mrs Westerby opened a door at the end of the corridor. 'You will remain here until you are told to leave.'

Ivy scuttled in and put Willow's clothes on to a narrow iron-framed bed and left.

'You *can't* treat me like this!' she cried. 'I haven't done anythin'.'

'Perhaps in your view stealing is not wrong,' said the housekeeper. 'In the opinion of the majority it is a crime.' She paused then said, 'I have always been surprised at the way you wormed yourself into Buddleigh Manor with a jailbird for a father.'

Willow gasped at the unexpectedness of the attack. 'He's not!' she yelled. 'He's not! He's a good man!'

'Be so good as not to shout at me,' said Mrs Westerby.

'Hush, now, Lily,' reproved Jenny, in gentler tones. 'You'll only make this worse for yourself.'

The two women left, the door closed behind them and Willow heard the click of the key in the lock. It was difficult to believe that she was actually a prisoner. She tried the door. She knew it wouldn't open, but she rattled the handle in an agony of misery and frustration, then sat on the narrow bed which barely fitted into the tiny box room, her mind seething with anger and outrage. The room was little more than a cupboard. Now, she supposed, the matter of the thieving kitchen maid would be discussed by

– by whom? She had no way of knowing. Was it important enough to reach the exalted ears of the family? Possibly the housekeeper and butler could decide such an unimportant matter for themselves and just hire another girl. No, stealing was a criminal offence. They might send for a policeman. She might end up in prison. She shuddered. And what had she done? Simply hidden to watch ladies in their beautiful gowns. Yet the brooch had been found in her drawer. Someone had put it there, but who? Who disliked her, hated her enough to do such a dreadful thing?

Willow sprang to her feet and paced the room angrily, three steps one way, five another. She had to duck to avoid hitting her head on the sloping roof. There was a tiny window in the ceiling above, through which she could see the sky. It was grey. She felt terribly confined and a wave of panic swept over her. She contained herself. No one would hear her screams and she would only make herself feel worse. Then she had wild thoughts of dragging the bed beneath the skylight and trying to escape on to the roof, but she wouldn't be able to reach the window and where could she go then? She threw herself on to the hard mattress and curled up, her hands over her face, breathing deeply, struggling to control herself. Eventually her panic died, to be replaced by deep anger.

She thought of Dad and began to understand something of his suffering at being unjustly imprisoned. No wonder his spirit was so badly damaged. She began to think again about the brooch. She knew she hadn't touched it, but someone had. Who had had the opportunity? Any number of people, she realised, and it didn't matter now anyway because she had been identified as the thief.

She was surprised when she heard someone in the room. They were standing by the open door, holding a chamber candlestick. The sky above the window was dark. She realised she had been asleep.

Mrs Westerby's cold voice reached her. 'I fail to comprehend how one with a guilty conscience can find it so easy to rest.'

Willow sat up, rubbing her head which ached a little. 'I haven't got a guilty conscience,' she retorted.

'Come with me. You're wanted downstairs.' That was Mr Steadman.

'Does it take two of you to fetch me?' asked Willow, investing her voice with as much sarcasm as her shaky nerves would allow.

'Insolence will only do you further harm,' said Mrs Westerby.

'Further harm? How's that possible? Between you you've blackened my character for ever.'

'Get up,' urged Mr Steadman. 'The sooner you face facts the better.'

Willow finally moved and swung her feet to the floor. 'What time is it? I wonder the family can get on with both of you up here,' she said.

'Sarcasm becomes you no more than insolence,' said Mrs Westerby.

'What's time got to do with anything?' asked the butler.

Willow said steadily, 'I need to – to wash and—'

The housekeeper interrupted her. 'I will take you. Come.'

Willow followed the housekeeper down the backstairs to the female servants' closet. Her bladder felt as if it was bursting, but she was so inhibited by the knowledge that Mr Steadman and Mrs Westerby were waiting for her that for a moment she thought it would be impossible to relieve herself. She felt refreshed after splashing her face with cold water and tidied her hair as best she could without a comb. She went to replace her cap, then stuffed it into her pocket, tossing her head. She was damned if she'd put on her mark of servitude in a house where she was being treated so unjustly. She realised that she was very hungry. 'What time is it?' she asked Mrs Westerby again.

'It is ten o'clock.'

'At *night*! I've been shut away for all those hours, with no one caring what I might need?'

'Be silent. Are you ready now?'

'Yes. Where are you taking me?'

The housekeeper didn't answer. Willow's eyes widened in surprise as she was conducted to the first floor of the main house. Mr Steadman left and she once more found herself standing in Mrs Maddison's boudoir. There was a strong smell of lavender water and Miss Brayton stood by her mistress holding a bottle of smelling salts.

'So there you are,' said Mrs Maddison petulantly. 'Wretched girl! You have been the instrument of ruining for me a very special house party. All the guests are old friends of the family invited especially to celebrate Miss Violet's happy news, and you have spoiled much of the joy I was experiencing over my dear daughter's engagement. I feel quite ill. You have given me a headache. What have you to say for yourself?'

'After you've pronounced sentence, do you mean?'

'Such insolence,' said Mrs Maddison in die-away tones. She lifted a lavender-scented handkerchief to her nose and the lace of her négligée fell back to reveal her white, rounded arm. Willow had a vision of Clara, her arms deep in a washing tub, cleaning up the mess made by just such people as this woman.

'Do not glare at me like that,' said Mrs Maddison. 'You are fortunate that I have asked to see you. Most servants in your position would have been turned out by now, but Miss Frances intervened on your behalf. She believed I should interview you. Besides, I engaged you – I thought – that is, Mr Maddison thought . . .' Again her voice trailed away, then she said, 'Your master is very angry. He has always insisted on obtaining servants on personal recommendation. He has turned out to be quite right. Miss Frances is inexperienced in these matters, though she was trying to help you. She has even suggested that I give you a second chance.'

'But does *she* think I stole the brooch?' demanded Willow.

'I assume you are referring to *Miss Frances*,' said the housekeeper coldly.

'Such bad manners,' muttered Miss Brayton.

'Bad manners! How would you feel if you were falsely

121

accused? I didn't touch the brooch! I never even saw it.'

'The evidence is conclusive,' said Mrs Maddison. 'Lying will not help your cause.' She leaned back against the cushions piled behind her. 'Never again will I take a servant on trust as haphazardly as I took you. This is the kind of thing that happens.'

Willow listened to the cruel tongue which demeaned her and angry words of passionate rejection of what was being done to her flowed into her brain. She tried to speak, but could only gasp.

'You have nothing to say to me? That does not surprise me. I took you, a child of a slum dwelling, and gave you a position in a good home. Now I wish you to tell me, before these witnesses, why you have so abused my generosity as to steal from a guest?'

Willow's voice returned. 'I didn't! I didn't!' she began angrily, but abruptly her anger was undermined by misery at being the victim of such injustice. 'Mrs Maddison,' she said, 'madam, please believe me – I would never steal. Never! Not from anybody. I wouldn't!' Tears filled her eyes and spilled on to her flushed cheeks.

'Control yourself,' said Mrs Westerby. 'If you are innocent, why are you crying?'

'Do guilty people cry?' asked Mrs Maddison curiously.

'Oh, some of these girls are good actors, madam,' said Mrs Westerby. 'This one has been a nuisance ever since she joined us, with her day-dreaming and her mistakes. One of the gamekeepers told me he saw her taking her ease in the park on her afternoon off, before she was sent packing by Mr Edgar. She simply doesn't know her place.'

'Is that true?' asked Mrs Maddison of Willow.

'I walked in the park, yes, but I didn't know it was wrong.'

'You don't sound too sure,' said Miss Brayton.

Willow hesitated. It was true she had doubted the rightness of using the park.

Her hesitation cost her her credibility. 'You see, madam,'

said Mrs Westerby, triumphant. 'She is well aware of her wrong-doing.'

'I didn't even see the brooch,' said Willow doggedly.

Mrs Maddison yawned, hiding her open mouth behind her fingers. 'Thank God we are all having an early night. The ball was so enervating, but *such* a success, in spite of all this.' She waved her hand towards Willow.

Willow waited, dashing away angry tears with the back of her hand. It was as if she only became visible at Mrs Maddison's behest. 'What are you goin' to do to me?' she asked aggressively.

Miss Brayton flung up her hands and Mrs Westerby glared.

'Do you not know?' said Mrs Maddison. 'You must leave my house, of course.'

'Did you bring me here just to tell me that?' Willow felt reckless now. What had she to lose? 'Any of your servants could have passed on your message. You shouldn't tire yourself out like this.'

Mrs Maddison looked confused. The girl's words were the kind she expected from those about her, but not in that tone.

'Shall I take her away, madam?' asked Mrs Westerby.

Mrs Maddison frowned, then yawned again. 'Yes. She must be kept apart from the other servants, of course. We would not want them corrupted. See to it, Westerby.'

Willow made a last desperate attempt. 'Mrs Maddison, please listen to me. I'm not a thief, truly I'm not. If I had found the brooch, I would have handed it to someone. Please, please, believe me—'

Mrs Westerby's hand dug into the soft flesh of her neck again and she was propelled rapidly from the room. She was physically strong and for a moment was filled with wild ideas of fighting, then they were in the corridor and Mr Steadman appeared and grasped her tightly and all thoughts of escape were hopeless. She had been arrested and condemned, but not tried. Even the worst criminal was entitled to a trial.

She was returned to the small, gloomy box room, where

a solitary candle had been lit, a plate of thick bread with a scraping of butter and a glass of water placed on the small cupboard, and a chamber pot left under the bed. The preparations infuriated Willow even more. They had always planned to bring her back here. They were convinced from the start of her guilt. She knew she should be relieved that the police were not involved, but she was too angry to be logical.

When the sounds of footsteps had died away she made up the bed with the blankets which had been thrown on to the mattress and crawled in. She missed Ivy who was reasonably friendly and well-fleshed and warm, she had already slept for hours during the day and it was a very long time before she drifted into uneasy rest. Her last waking thought was that at least she wouldn't have to answer to the name of 'Lily' any more. No, not quite her last waking thought. She wondered if Edgar's kiss in the park had also been seen and reported.

In the morning the door was opened and Prue entered. 'Here's your breakfast. They said you were only to have bread, but I've sneaked up a bit o' bacon.'

The last thing Willow felt she could face was bacon, but she was grateful for the thought. 'What's goin' to happen to me?' she asked.

Prue tossed her head. '*They've* given orders that we're not to speak to you, but I think it's a shame the way they're treatin' you.'

'Do you, Prue, do you? Then you don't believe I took the brooch?'

Prue went red. 'I'd better go or they'll start on me.'

She left Willow in even deeper despair. Even Prue, kind and companionable as she was, thought her guilty. She started on the food and forced it down, fearing that it could be a long time before she got more. Then she washed and dressed and sat on the bed and waited. She had no means of knowing how long it was before the key was turned and the door opened. She expected a vengeful Mrs Westerby, but Miss Brayton stood there. She was frowning, yet there

124

was something in her eyes . . . vindictive pleasure, Willow realised.

'You're to come to madam's boudoir,' was all she said.

Questions were tumbling around Willow's brain, but Miss Brayton walked very fast, obviously not prepared to speak. Once more she stood in front of Mrs Maddison and once more Mrs Westerby and Miss Brayton stood like courtiers by their queen.

'Lily,' said Mrs Maddison, then stopped. 'Lily . . .' she tried again. 'Oh, dear, this *is* so difficult.' She waved her hand in Mrs Westerby's direction.

'It has come to Mrs Maddison's notice,' said the housekeeper, 'that you were not responsible for the theft of the brooch. You are therefore reinstated in your position as kitchen maid.'

Willow stared. The sudden release of tension made her feel nauseous. She gulped and swallowed.

'Have you nothing to say, Lily?' asked Mrs Maddison.

Willow stared at her mistress for so long that a flush stained her cheeks.

'Why does she look at me so?' she asked Mrs Westerby.

The housekeeper dug a bony finger into Willow's back. 'Will you not answer your mistress? She has given you good news. You can at least remember your manners and say thank you.'

They had been ready to throw her out without even a hearing and now she was expected to be grateful. 'Thank you? Thank you for humiliatin' me? Thank you for imprisonin' me? Thank you for lettin' me out? Why have you? What's happened?'

Mrs Maddison gasped. It seemed, thought Willow, as if she was perpetually able to dismay her. She wanted to giggle. Then she wanted to shout and stamp and scream at the injustice of the power of Them over Us. Dad had been so right.

'Please,' she said in as mild a tone as she could manage, 'will you tell me what has made you change your mind about me?'

Again Mrs Maddison allowed Mrs Westerby to answer. 'A witness has come forward who has exonerated you.'

'I see,' said Willow. 'No, I don't see. What—'

Mrs Maddison said abruptly, 'For God's sake, take her away, Westerby! Give her the news somewhere else. I'm quite devastatingly weary. If the girl does not wish to offer her thanks to me—'

Willow was pushed from the scented room into the corridor and down the back stairs to Mrs Westerby's sitting room. It was surprisingly large and comfortably, even luxuriously, furnished. The housekeeper seated herself in an easy chair by the fire, but left Willow standing. 'A witness has spoken on your behalf.'

'A *witness*. Who?'

Mrs Westerby frowned. 'You have not been dismissed on this occasion, but I doubt if you will last long in Buddleigh Manor. You are altogether too impudent.'

'Who?' insisted Willow.

'The bootboy,' said the housekeeper at last.

'The bootboy? Steven?'

'Kerslake,' said Mrs Westerby. She rubbed her long dry hands together with a slight rasping sound and set her thin lips as if she couldn't bear even to discuss a bootboy. 'He saw someone enter your bedroom, heard a drawer opening and closing. Someone who had no need to go to the attics.'

Willow's mind spun. No need to go to the attics! Steven certainly had no need. But it appeared that he was not the thief. Was it someone in the family? A guest? One of the upper servants? She stood very still.

'The person has been confronted by the witness, and broke down and admitted guilt,' said Mrs Westerby. 'No blame attaches to you, though I must point out that if you had not been upstairs spying on the guests you would not have been suspected. I never want to hear of such a gross misdemeanour again. That is all. You may go.'

'Go? Who stole the brooch? Who put me in such a dreadful position? Surely I've a right to know?'

'A right? You have only the rights your employers give you.'

'Then I'll go upstairs and ask one of them,' she yelled. 'Why shouldn't I be told? It was my life they were about to ruin.'

Mrs Westerby stared coldly at her, but a look of trepidation flickered in her eyes. She was responsible for the conduct of the people beneath her and already she had permitted the lives of the servants to impinge uncomfortably on those of her employers. 'Very well, Lily,' she said coldly, 'I will tell you. After the ball, when the guests had retired and you were in the kitchen, it appears that Kerslake waited until Mr Steadman and Mr Norris had made their rounds and put out the house lights. He saw Miss Jebb behaving in what he said was a suspicious way. She was "creeping about", was his term. He followed her and watched her go into the room you share with the other kitchen maids. He heard a drawer open and close, then Miss Jebb came out. He was concealed in the shadows, but he says he saw by the light of Miss Jebb's candle that she looked – as he said – "full of beans and grinning". He says he told no one because he believed that one of you was to be the victim of some harmless practical joke. When he realised what had happened, he went straight to Mr Steadman.'

'Oh, how brave of him! Mr Steadman must have been very angry that he was upstairs.'

'He most certainly was, as were we all.'

'I must thank him,' said Willow.

'Whether or not you thank him is up to you. I have his home address in my book. Naturally, he has been dismissed.'

'But he's not done anythin' wrong!'

'That is hardly a matter for a kitchen maid to decide. The bootboy is not allowed upstairs for any reason whatsoever and it has been discovered that for some time he has been in the habit of creeping up to look at the library. At least, that is what he told us. A very unlikely story. Mr Steadman and I decided that he must go.'

'But he *was* lookin' at the books,' cried Willow. 'He loves books.'

'You knew of his activities?'

'He told me once.'

'I see. You merely reinforce my belief that you will not last long here. As for Kerslake loving books, that is a ridiculous notion! A boy like that can barely read or write.'

'Yes, he can, an' he's teachin' himself more. He wants to make somethin' of himself. He's a really nice boy when you get to know him.'

Mrs Westerby looked incredulous. 'Get to know him! You have had the opportunity of mixing with some highly regarded, well-educated servants, and you chose *him* for companionship? Furthermore, you must have done something extremely unpleasant to Miss Jebb to make her so angry with you.'

'I've never hurt her,' said Willow. 'In fact—' She stopped. It was because of her sewing that Miss Jebb had been humiliated. Servants gossiped endlessly and she had given the visiting maids and valets ammunition for their quick tongues. What had happened to Willow was an act of revenge, a determination to rid herself of the troublesome kitchen maid.

'You have remembered something?' said Mrs Westerby.

Willow hesitated, thinking of the malicious pleasure of Miss Brayton whose rival had put herself in a position from which she would never quite escape. Smarting painfully from the raw wound of suspicion and rejection, she shrank from worsening Miss Jebb's degradation.

'Where is she? Has she left yet? Or do you have her in prison somewhere in the house?'

Mrs Westerby's eyes glittered. 'Miss Jebb's fate has not yet been decided upon. We have shown her a certain amount of leniency because she owned up to her wrong-doing – although, it must be said, only after a lengthy interrogation by Mr Steadman and myself.'

Willow's sympathy subsided. She had been forgiven for something she hadn't done, Steven had been sent away because of his courageous honesty, but Miss Jebb was to receive compassionate treatment. There was no understanding the situation. She felt drained and shaky. 'May I leave, madam?'

'I would be very much obliged if you would.' Mrs Westerby's voice was coldly scornful.

On the following day, Miss Jebb had all her meals sent upstairs, appearing only once in the kitchen to steam a velvet jacket. She spoke to no one, but sent a baleful look in Willow's direction as she left. The subject of the brooch had been forbidden as a topic of conversation in the kitchen, an order which had been disobeyed in whispers, except by Mrs Narracott. Sympathy was definitely with Willow.

'It's a disgrace to treat you so,' said Prue.

Henry had said, 'In a way I feel sorry for Jebb. Poor thing, she's worked her way up to lady's maid, even though she's not a good needlewoman.' He received black looks and subsided, though Willow respected his compassion. Her angry indignation had kept her awake for most of the night, but she was too overwrought to feel tired. Several times she considered leaving, but necessity held her fast. She might not get another position, certainly not one in a great house such as Buddleigh Manor where she was receiving such excellent training in the ways of the gentry. It went against her spirit to succumb to injustice, but the thought of her parents and their need for money held her fast. Once again, she was called upstairs.

She entered Mrs Maddison's boudoir, which was rapidly taking on the overtones of a well-upholstered torture chamber, to be confronted by Mrs Maddison, Mrs Westerby and Miss Jebb. Violet, draped elegantly on a chaise longue, stared out of the window. As Willow entered she turned and put up her white hand to smooth her hair. Her engagement ring flashed.

'Lily,' said Mrs Maddison, 'we are in a dilemma.' Miss Jebb twisted her hands nervously. She was very pale. 'Miss Jebb has something she wishes to say to you.'

The maid tried to speak, gulped, then said, 'Lily, I'm sorry for what I did. I hope you'll overlook it.' Her words tumbled over themselves. She raised her eyes and looked at Willow, who saw with a jolt that Jebb really did hate her.

'Why did you do it?' she asked.

'I was angry with you. Remember how the visiting servants made fun of me because you gave me a little assistance with the sewing? They upset me badly with their nasty tongues and I just lost my reason. I was going to the ballroom to peep at my young ladies and found the brooch. It had been dropped in the corridor before the guest and her gentleman friend ever reached the library.'

'So that's settled,' said Mrs Maddison. 'I am told, Lily, that you sew quite well.'

'Yes, madam.' Quite well!

'And that Miss Jebb allows you to give her a helping hand?'

'Yes, madam.' A helping hand! She did much more than that!

'She has afforded you an opportunity usually denied to a kitchen maid and you must make the most of it. A girl with sewing skills may aspire to a position as housemaid.' She sighed. 'Well, that is that. It has all turned out to be rather trivial.'

That seemed to sum up her approach towards her servants. Rather trivial. If Miss Jebb left she would find it trivial, or if Willow had been banished without a character. As for Steven, he was entirely below her notice.

'The matter is not quite finished, madam,' reminded Miss Brayton gently, her eyes shooting sparks of vengeful pleasure at Miss Jebb.

'No, indeed,' drawled Violet.

'Ah, I had forgotten. Pray explain the position, Westerby.'

The housekeeper said tonelessly, 'Miss Violet does not wish to lose the services of a maid who has always proved hard-working and reliable. She would be obliged if you would forgive her so that matters may continue in harmony as before.'

Harmony! thought Willow. How little they knew about their servants.

'We are waiting,' said Violet. She glanced at her watch. 'For God's sake, hurry, and let us have done with this tiresome charade. I have a fitting for my wedding gown.'

'She's said enough,' muttered Willow, abruptly thrown into fellow-feeling with the wretched lady's maid.

'Miss Violet must be the judge of that,' said Mrs Westerby.

Miss Jebb said, 'Lily, you must – they say you must speak your mind clearly.' She thrust out a hand to Willow who grabbed it quickly, so heartily sick was she of the entire episode. Miss Jebb's hand lay in hers, cold and limp, for a few seconds.

'I forgive you.' Willow sounded almost spritely, suddenly remembering the many religious novels she had borrowed from Gran in which scenes similar to this were constantly enacted. All that was missing were the flowing penitential tears. She gasped as she controlled the laughter which bubbled in her throat.

Mrs Westerby gave her a look of frowning suspicion.

'There, that is definitely settled,' said Mrs Maddison. 'We did not wish to dismiss a maid who has given such good service for a number of years. Perhaps now I can take my rest before I have to change for dinner. And thank God the mystery is solved. Brayton, I wish to be left in peace for an hour.'

Willow stood her ground. 'What about Steven?'

Mrs Maddison gazed at her incredulously. 'Steven? Who is he?'

'Kerslake, the bootboy who had the habit of roaming through the house at night,' said Mrs Westerby. 'I have dismissed him and engaged another lad from the village. The new one comes from a good home. I should never have employed a boy like Kerslake. His parents are unknown.'

'You have your answer,' said Mrs Maddison, giving Willow a faint smile which was more a grimace than an expression of pleasure. 'Mrs Westerby was kind enough to give Kerslake a chance and he spoiled it.'

Willow opened her mouth to protest again, then closed it. What was the use?

'May I go, madam?' asked Miss Jebb.

'You may,' said Mrs Maddison. 'I trust that Miss Violet will be wearing the Poiret rose chiffon frock with the fur trimming. Lord Radcliffe is coming to dinner.'

'It's all ready for her, madam.'

'She must wear the pearl choker with the diamond centrepiece with it, and do not forget the pink silk roses.'

'No, madam, I won't forget.'

'The choker is such a superb engagement gift,' enthused Mrs Maddison to everyone in general.

'Indeed, yes, madam,' came the murmurs, except from Willow who stood seething with indignation at the contrast between the importance given to Miss Violet's outfit and the lack of humanity shown to Steven.

Miss Jebb left, throwing her a glance in which relief was mingled with loathing, and Willow was firmly dismissed. Later she described the scene to Mrs Narracott.

'You might have imagined the look,' said the cook. 'After all, you've been treated very badly and your nerves must be all over the place.' She paused then said reflectively, 'Mind you, some folk resent being forgiven.'

'I don't understand why they're lenient towards Miss Jebb an' cruel to Steven,' said Willow.

'That's an easy one to answer. Miss Violet threw a fit when she heard that Jebb might be dismissed. She said she didn't care tuppence for all the fuss made about the brooch, that it wasn't worth the fuss, and that the silly girl who lost it had only herself to blame. The gentry put up with quite a few goings-on among the upper servants, especially when they've been trained in their ways for years, and ladies particularly hate changing their personal maids.'

All the visiting servants were absent, readying their masters and mistresses for dinner, and Mrs Narracott went on, 'We've managed to keep the affair a secret from outsiders so far. The guest was told that the brooch had been kicked by accident beneath one of the brass fenders in the ballroom and was found by the head housemaid. No one here wants a lot of malicious gossip spread about. It's best all round if you try to put it behind you, like everyone else.'

'Except Steven,' said Willow miserably. 'He's out of work, an' all because he tried to help me. I didn't know he was so brave.'

'No, it surprised me. He could have just let events take their course, poor lad, but he'll get a position somewhere. He's ready to do anything to get out of—' She stopped.

'To get out of what?'

'I suppose I shouldn't say so, but I've always thought he'd have been happier in an orphanage than with the people who brought him up. They said it was their Christian duty to a child that was left on their doorstep, but duty's had a lot more to do with his rearing, I reckon, than Christianity.'

'I'll visit him on my next half-day,' said Willow.

Mrs Narracott stopped crumbling her pastry flour and fat and gave Willow a sideways glance. 'If you see him, it might make him feel better. I'll be interested to hear what happens.'

Willow kept her word and on her next half-day she walked to the village, past farm houses and cottages through whose windows she could see preparations for Christmas. She arrived at Steven's dwelling. The front door was impeccably painted in dark brown, there was a highly polished door knocker and the net curtains at the window were pristine. She hesitated. Everything was altogether too perfect. She glanced again at the front window where the curtains hung in mathematical folds. She wanted to turn back, but she couldn't abandon Steven. She banged the knocker. The door was opened by a thin woman with grey hair brushed smooth and secured in a rigidly unattractive way by a plain wooden comb.

'Yes?'

'Are you Mrs Kerslake?'

'I am.'

'Please might I see Steven?'

'Who are you?'

133

'My name is Lily. I'm a maid at—'

'I know where you're from,' interrupted the woman. 'You're the hussy who got Steven dismissed.'

'That's not fair! I did nothin' wrong.'

'You sneaked upstairs to watch the gentry in their sinful finery and everything that followed was your fault.'

'No, it wasn't, it wasn't! They had no reason to doubt my honesty an' poor Steven was tryin' to protect me because he knew I was innocent.' The wind was keen and Willow shivered.

'Who's out there, Martha?' called a man. 'There's a terrible draught coming in.'

The woman set her thin lips and stood back, motioning Willow to enter. She led her along a small passageway with a wooden floor scrubbed as white as Mrs Narracott's table and into a kitchen. A man watched them enter.

The woman said, 'This is Lily, the maid from the manor that got Steven turned off.'

Willow opened her mouth then thought better of it. No sense in antagonising them further. 'Please, may I see Steven?' she asked again.

'What for?' demanded the man. He too was thin and unwelcoming.

'I'd like to tell him how sorry I am for what happened, but mostly to thank him for the way he sacrificed himself for me.'

The woman's eyes opened wide. 'Sacrificed himself for you! What an expression to use about a mortal. The Lord sacrificed Himself for us all. Are you comparing Steven with Him?'

Willow blinked. She had learned more about religion from the enforced church attendances since she came to the manor, but she was out of her depth. 'I'm not comparin' him,' she began, 'but he did—' She was halted by the uncompromisingly frigid looks she was getting from the Kerslakes. How had Steven, reared in such a place, turned out to be so warm-hearted?

'Did what?' demanded Mr Kerslake.

'He saved me from being dismissed.'

'As I see it, he was sent away for sneaking round the women's bedrooms.'

'No,' protested Willow, 'not sneakin', he was followin'—'

'I know what he said he was doing,' interrupted Mrs Kerslake. 'He shouldn't have been there, not in any circumstances, and he was dismissed because it wasn't the first time. He's had a habit of creeping round the manor.'

'Only to look at the books in the library,' mumbled Willow, thrown completely off balance by these two sanctimonious, unyielding people.

'There's only one book a body needs to read,' said the woman, 'and that's the one Mr Kerslake has on his knee. I'm referring to the Bible, the story of our Lord Jesus and His ancestors. No one needs aught else.'

Willow, not having been invited to sit, still stood in the centre of the room. A pot bubbled gently on the range, giving out a savoury smell. She had been so nervous at the idea of visiting Steven that her appetite had failed her during servants' mid-day dinner and the smell made her mouth water. A kettle steamed and hissed and a coal shifted, giving out sparks. The range was black-leaded to a steely glint that could only be arrived at by relentless applications of polish, the furniture was sparse and scrubbed, the rug on the floor spotless. On the walls there were religious sepia prints. Over the range was an embroidered text: 'The Fear of the Lord is to Hate Evil', it proclaimed. On another wall was a second text: 'The Wicked Shall Fall by his Own Wickedness'. There was no comfort to be had on the third wall which insisted: 'No Man is Compelled to Evil'.

She felt she must make one last effort. 'Please, Mrs Kerslake, may I see Steven? Only for a minute. It's my half-day, you see, an' I won't be able to get here again for a while, perhaps ages, because the manor's goin' to be full of guests at Christmas.'

'Oh, aye, that I don't doubt,' said Mrs Kerslake. 'Full of sinners eating and drinking themselves to an early grave, and committing other sins, terrible sins, expressly forbidden by

Our Lord. Sins of the flesh—' Her voice was rising into a chant.

'Martha, that'll do,' said Mr Kerslake sternly.

Willow was surprised to see colour stain Mrs Kerslake's cheeks as she obeyed her husband.

He said to Willow, 'You can see Steven in our presence. Martha, go and fetch him down.'

Steven was clean. That was the first thing which struck Willow. There was a fourth motto over the door. 'Cleanliness is Next to Godliness', and she had a picture of him arriving home in disgrace and his mother getting out her scrubbing brush and soap and removing the ingrained grime by mercilessly attacking his skin. She held out her hand and Steven took it awkwardly. 'I just wanted to tell you how sorry I am you've lost your job. It was very good an' brave of you to tell what you'd seen. You don't deserve to suffer.'

Mr Kerslake snorted. Mrs Kerslake remained where she was, standing as straight as the bamboo cane hanging beside the range. Willow wondered how often Steven had known its sting.

'I was glad to help you, Willow,' he said.

'Willow!' exclaimed Mrs Kerslake, all the suspicions of her arid mind alerted. 'She said her name was Lily.'

'Lily's what they changed it to,' said Steven.

'By "they" I suppose you mean her employers? Lily is a much more suitable name. Willow! It's outlandish.'

'I never thought they'd get rid of me,' said Steven ingenuously.

'Do you mean you wouldn't have told Mrs Westerby the truth if you'd thought you'd be dismissed?' Mr Kerslake's voice was harsh and a look of trepidation filled Steven's eyes. Willow longed to help him. Whatever answer he returned she knew the Kerslakes would find fault.

'I think I should,' said Steven.

Mrs Kerslake's voice was gritty. 'If you'd been intent on doing your duty in the sphere of life it pleased God to place you, you would still have honourable employment.'

Willow and Steven looked at one another and for an

instant their eyes exchanged messages. Sympathy, understanding, something more and indefinable which caused Willow's heart to beat harder.

'You've said your piece, young woman. Now you can go,' said Mr Kerslake.

'What will you do next?' she asked Steven.

'I said, you can go!' Mr Kerslake was quietly furious.

'You heard what my husband said. Go!'

Steven took a deep breath. 'It's begun to snow, Mother. Can I see Willow – Lily – as far as the manor gates? She's not been this way before and might lose herself. It'd be only Christian charity.'

The end of the speech was a good stroke and finally the Kerslakes agreed that he could be out for fifteen minutes. No longer.

'One Sin Doth Provoke Another', graced a further canvas in the passage, and over the front door, in case you hadn't noticed the others: 'Sin Brings its Own Punishment'.

Outside Steven seized Willow's hand and they raced together through the swirling flakes, until breathlessness from the exercise combined with the crazy laughter which had overtaken them forced them to stop.

'Aren't they a right pair?' gasped Steven. 'Thank God they're not my real parents. Do you know, I did all the sewing on those texts?'

'You embroidered them?'

'Yes, Mother made me. She said I'd remember them longer.'

'And do you?'

'Remember them? Oh, yes.'

'They're all about sin and punishment and evil. There's nothing happy about them.'

'No, happiness isn't important in our house. Sin and evil are everywhere.' There was a disturbingly worried note in Steven's tone, as if, thought Willow, he half believed it and it scared him.

'I've never seen them in church.'

'Oh, no, they think that people who go to church are

ungodly. They're Methodists. There's a small chapel in the next village. The minister preaches for hours. Some services last all morning.'

'Do you like that?'

Steven shrugged. 'Not in the way they hope. I get a chance to stop still for a bit an' listen to proper speech and learn new words.'

Willow held her hands to her heart which was calming down. 'Oh, Steven, don't let them make you like them, not ever. Read all you can. You said you're goin' to be somebody, some day. You will be, I just know it.'

They ran again until they reached the big iron manor gates which were open to allow the entrance of the first of the Christmas house party.

There they stopped and regarded each other once more. Steven bent forward and gave Willow a kiss right on her snow-cold, damp lips, then turned and raced away, his skinny figure soon swallowed by the whirling storm.

Chapter Eight

Christmas for the Buddleigh Manor servants was an almost unending grind of work. Every bedroom was occupied, some of the younger guests needing to share, a situation which was not resented in view of the Maddisons' reputation for hospitality.

'It's all right for them,' gasped a sweating Mrs Narracott on Christmas Day, as she leaned over the range with its coals kept red-hot to maintain the temperature of the ovens, then peered into a great cauldron of brisket stewing to make clear soup for tomorrow's dinner. Again Willow marvelled at the amount of beforehand preparation required of the cook in a large household, as if the day itself wasn't enough to think about. The cook moved with surprising speed, considering her weight, to the immense stove set in the middle of the kitchen. Today, them upstairs were having an easy lunch. 'They call it easy,' grumbled Mrs Narracott. 'They ought to come down here and see how easy it is.'

Willow knew that preparation of the smoked hams had begun weeks ago to bring them to their luscious fulfilment, that even the production of a simple-sounding mushroom sauce needed days of attention, and that the fruit had been immersed in syrup throughout the summer.

'Doesn't Mrs Maddison have any idea of how overworked Mrs Narracott is?' Willow whispered to Prue.

Prue winked. 'She did suggest once sendin' out for food, but the truth is our dear old cook doesn't want anyone to think they can buy stuff as good as what she makes.'

Henry, overhearing, said, 'I think she's right there. I've tasted shop stuff and it doesn't beat Mrs Narracott's.'

It was unfortunate for him that the cook caught him gossiping and whacked him across the buttocks with her heaviest rolling pin. 'You don't know anything about posh London food shops.'

'Ouch!' Henry rubbed his hind-quarters. 'I was sticking up for her, too,' he muttered as he passed Prue and Willow who had their heads bent industriously over their work, desperately trying to stifle their giggles, Willow pounding pheasants' breasts for tonight's soup, Prue making tiny sandwiches with bread so thin it was practically transparent. Ivy was preparing sandwiches for the staff's mid-day meal. No daintiness needed here as she sliced doorsteps of bread, covered them thickly with butter and slapped lumps of beef and ham between them. They would be eaten within minutes and the servants would return to work. Occasionally Mrs Westerby looked in, apparently unexcited by the festivities, her sharp eyes travelling over the length and breadth of the kitchen. Neither she nor Mrs Narracott acknowledged the presence of the other. Not until the housekeeper had gone did Mrs Narracott mutter a few choice phrases about interfering, nosy busybodies that wouldn't know how to use an oven if one jumped up and burnt them. Dinner was served upstairs at eight o'clock and to Willow's eyes was absolute perfection, though Mrs Narracott still grumbled.

'Take no notice,' said Prue. 'She's never satisfied.'

In an odd way Willow felt that she saw the world through the cook's eyes and understood her obsession with perfection. She felt it, too, when she caught sight of a beautifully gowned woman who knew how to wear her clothes and how to complement them with the proper jewellery: it actually made her mouth water, as if the woman had been a set-piece of confectionery.

It was time to lay up the huge trays which were carried up by the male servants, while the housemaids walked behind bearing lighter trays of sauces. When the dirty dishes had been returned and washed up by Aggie, assisted on this special day by the kitchen maids, the table scrubbed and the floor swept, Mr Steadman hurried into the kitchen. 'They're on their way,' he said. 'Get in line.'

Willow felt excitement bubble inside her. 'They' were on their way with presents for the staff. She thought of the many marvellous things they had the money to buy and her eyes shone with anticipation.

Mr and Mrs Maddison walked into the kitchen, smiling broadly. At least, Mrs Maddison was. Mr Maddison had merely stretched his mouth across his teeth in something more resembling a grimace. They were followed by Frances and Edgar. Both men carried big garden baskets containing brown paper parcels.

Mrs Maddison ceremoniously called her servants one by one, reading their names from a list, and Frances handed out the gifts which were accompanied by a crimson silk rose for each woman and a cigar for the men, and wished everyone a happy and prosperous new year. When Willow stepped up nervously to receive hers she glanced up and caught Edgar's eyes. He was smiling at her in a way which made her heart jump. She tried to tell herself it was all imagination, but she knew he liked her, there was no doubt about it.

'Hurry along there, my girl,' ordered Mr Maddison abruptly.

'Darling, really,' drawled Mrs Maddison, 'it's Christmas and she's nervous. Come along, Lily.'

Willow received her parcel with a small curtsey and retired to wait for the ceremony to be finished before examining what she'd got. She wanted to hold on to her delicious anticipation for a while longer and watched the others untying the string and revealing their gifts. Mrs Narracott had received a length of black material which rustled and crackled, and a selection of hat trimmings. Prue's cloth was a beautiful sky blue and Ivy's a dusky old rose. Willow could wait no longer. She tore off the wrapping paper and was filled with such disappointment and resentment that she tasted bile. A length of dismal pink print awaited her needle to make into a working gown.

141

Mrs Narracott said, 'Now, don't you be fretting, Lily. The mistress is being kind. After all, you're growing all the time and you'll need to make another dress soon. And you've got the lovely rose.'

Willow wasn't consoled. Her present dresses could have the seams let out again and, even if they couldn't, she wanted something colourful, something which rustled when she moved, a dress that would make her feel like somebody.

Willow waited on the tiny halt which she had last seen five months ago. To her astonishment the entire house party had packed and moved from Buddleigh Manor to other houses for the New Year festivities and Mrs Westerby had given several of the servants time off, including, to her great surprise, the second kitchen maid.

'Your work is improving, Lily,' she said in her cold way, 'and you bore yourself well beneath punishment suffered for a misdemeanour committed by someone else. That she should be kept on!' She stopped, evidently feeling she was saying too much to a mere kitchen skivvy. She might have spoiled Willow's joy at the thought of seeing her family again by adding, 'I trust, Lily, that you will return ready to work more and daydream less,' but Willow hardly heard the final sentence. She was too busy imagining herself at home for three days. As the train approached, she wished that she was returning dressed in something other than Gran's costume, but the wish was put firmly aside. Mum needed her money, and all the admonitions from senior staff about previous stitch marks which showed when she had let out the costume and the heavily mended state of her underwear couldn't change her mind. She had borrowed a small portmanteau from Prue and stepped from the tram feeling happy and grownup.

As she traversed the streets of Barton Hill she began to be uneasy. She'd forgotten just how narrow they were; she'd forgotten the ever-present smell of earth closets; she'd forgotten the odour which wafted out of some of the houses when the doors were opened.

Marigold opened the door to her knock and each girl stared at the other in surprise. Marigold had grown shapely in the few months Willow had been at the manor. 'Oh, it's you,' she said without enthusiasm.

Willow kissed her, then Jasmine peeped round the living-room door and erupted along the passage, throwing herself on her sister, laughing and crying all at the same time. Willow picked her up and hugged her. Clara came out to see what the noise was about. She looked more tired and haggard than ever, but she welcomed Willow with a kiss.

'You should have let us know you were comin',' she said. 'I'd have got in somethin' special.'

This was said just to be sociable and Willow knew it. Clara, struggling with poverty all year round, was especially poor at Christmas because of her determination to buy everyone a gift, however small, and provide a good dinner of pork roast, sausages and stuffing. Willow walked into the living room. 'Where are the boys?'

'They're fetchin' coal,' said Marigold.

'Will the yards be open this time of night?' asked Willow. 'It must be after six.'

Marigold laughed. 'They've taken the pram to Lawrence Hill station to see if they can pinch a bit.'

'They haven't!' snapped Clara. 'It's only lumps lyin' about on the ground. Poor stuff, most of it, that nobody wants.'

'Except us,' said Marigold cheekily.

'It isn't stealin',' said Clara, giving Marigold an angry look. 'Lots of folk go an' collect it. Nobody seems to mind.'

'Some do,' said Marigold with an air of satisfaction which made Willow's hand itch to smack her. 'One of the Moor brothers got took by a policeman when he was pickin' up coal the other night.'

'Which one?' demanded Clara.

'The eldest. They reckon he'll have to go to Reform School.'

'What if one of our boys got arrested?' Willow asked, anxiety roughening her voice. 'Is it worth the risk?'

Marigold said nastily, 'I dare say our Willow's forgot how we live, while she's been in a rich house eatin' good food an' keepin' warm with plenty of fires.'

'Give over, do,' begged Clara. 'You do look well, Willow.'

'You're gettin' fat!' said Marigold.

'She's not, she's not,' cried Jasmine. 'She's lovely.'

Clara motioned Willow to sit in a chair beside the range, making her feel like a visitor, unintentionally shutting her outside the family.

'Have you brought our Christmas presents?' demanded Marigold.

'Your sister's hardly been in the house a minute an' she's sent her wages to us, as well you know.'

'Still, I dare say there's plenty of pickin's at Buddleigh Manor,' insisted Marigold.

'Pickin's!' exclaimed Clara. 'What a way to talk. You'll come to a bad end, our Marigold, the way you go on.'

Willow said gently, trying to defuse the atmosphere, 'I've made a new dress for Jasmine's doll an' penwipers for the boys an' a lace collar for you, Marigold. I earned the stuff by doin' a bit of sewin' for Miss Frances.' (The collar had taken her hours to repair.) 'I've brought somethin' for everyone. Was Christmas a good time?'

'Huh! Your money's all been used up by the doctor's bills,' grumbled Marigold.

Willow's heart gave a little jump. 'Who's been ill enough to need a doctor?'

'Dad,' answered Marigold shortly.

'Is he worse, then? How is he? Where is he?'

Clara said unhappily, 'Your dad's not gettin' any better. In fact, he's worse. He keeps to his bed a lot of the time, though not as much as the doctor says. He gets fed up with doin' nothin' and seein' nothin' but bare walls, and then he comes downstairs an' we've got to keep a good fire goin'. An' I've been told to feed him well.' She sighed. 'Even the doctor knows that's near impossible in our state.'

'He gets meat more than once a week,' said Jasmine, her

144

tone making it clear that she was proud of the fact, not envious.

Willow put the portmanteau on the kitchen table and opened it. 'I brought hardly any clothes, Mum. Just a change of vest and knickers. The rest is stuff Mrs Narracott sent you.'

The three watchers' faces lit up as Willow produced a smoked ham, some of Cook's best sausages, a jar of sweet pickle and a pot of preserved plums and, wrapped carefully in a linen cloth, a big chocolate cake.

Clara was delighted. 'Dad can have somethin' really good tonight. I've got potatoes an' a few carrots an' I'll fry some of the ham.'

'I don't suppose we'll get any?' Marigold's perpetual anger flared again.

'Of course you will,' said Clara in a conciliatory tone and Willow realised that she was a little afraid of her daughter's temper. 'Apart from anythin' else, it wouldn't keep, not the ham anyway.'

'I don't need any,' said Willow. 'Marigold's right. I'm lucky to have plenty to eat every day.'

Clara took the ham to the wash-house to put it in the close-meshed hanging frame as a precaution against the rats and mice. Willow followed her out and asked, 'How bad is Dad? Does the doctor say he'll get well soon?'

The flickering light of the candle Clara carried threw shadows over her face and she looked quite cadaverously thin, her cheekbones emphasised by the pallid skin stretched over them, her eyes hollow. She shook her head helplessly, at first unable to speak, then said, 'The doctor don't hold out much hope. Well, none, really. Dad's lungs are hardly workin'.'

Sadness spread through Willow like a dense cloud. 'I'll go up an' see him.'

'Wait a minute.' Back in the kitchen Clara opened the oven door and took out a hot brick which she wrapped in a flannel vest. 'Here, take this up an' bring down the other one. It'll be a lovely surprise for him when you walk in. I'll be up in a minute with a cup of tea.'

Willow held the hot brick close to her body as she climbed the stairs. She had forgotten how steep and narrow they were. Even the back stairs at Buddleigh Manor were spacious in comparison. She tapped on the bedroom door and entered when her father answered.

He was lying on his side, his back to her, staring through the window at the darkened sky. Willow slid the brick beneath the bedclothes and took away the cold one.

'Thanks,' muttered Arthur, turning his head. In an instant he sat up, staring at Willow as if she was a ghost.

'How did you get here?'

'They gave me a few days off. All the nobs have moved on to other houses. I had no time to let you know.' Willow spoke rapidly while her mind registered the fact that Dad's breathing was shallow and rasped in his throat and his voice was husky. He reached out and lit a cigarette which made him cough until beads of sweat stood out on his forehead.

'Dad, should you be smokin'?'

Arthur frowned. 'I hope you haven't come home with a fancy notion that you've a right to criticise your elders? If so you'd best go back.'

Willow hid her hurt. 'Sorry, Dad, it's so worryin' to see you like this.'

'Like what? Off you go. Tell Mum not to bring anythin' up. I'll be down directly.' She turned to leave and he said, 'Willow, my love, I'm really glad to see you.'

She smiled at him, then returned to the living room where she helped Clara lay up the table, the centrepiece of which was the chocolate cake. Marigold mixed up a teaspoon of bright yellow mustard and Jasmine put a spoon ready for the pickles, while the vegetables bubbled on the hob. Willow took her portmanteau to the bedroom. On the threshold she stopped, then entered slowly. Surely it couldn't always have been this small? Surely the wallpaper had not been so discoloured or the ceiling plaster so cracked? The room she shared with Ivy and Aggie was almost luxury compared with this. And had the house always smelt this way? For all the vigorous use of Gran's home-made polish, the odours of too many people living in a confined space pervaded it. She had to make a conscious effort to smile before she re-entered the living room, hearing by the cacophony that her brothers were back. When she opened the door the three boys rushed to embrace her and she forgot everything else in her love for her family.

Dad came down and was seated nearest the fire. Clara put a plate of steaming vegetables with two thick slices of ham in front of him.

'Look, Dad,' shrieked Jasmine in an ecstasy of pleasure, 'there's mustard *an*' pickles as well.'

Dad looked and threw up his hands in exaggerated astonishment, making Willow remember the times when he'd been such a live spark, making them laugh. 'I wonder which good fairy we've got to thank for this?' His smile at Willow was warm.

'It wasn't a fairy, Dad!' cried Jasmine, jumping up and down. 'It was our Willow!'

'Shut your noise, for pity's sake,' said Clara, but she was beaming with pleasure as she ladled out portions of food.

'Now then, Alfred, that's enough,' she reproved, but she was still smiling as he dipped the spoon into the pickle once more and ducked, grinning, as her hand swept harmlessly past his ear.

'Where's Gran?' Willow asked. 'Can't she come round? Has anyone told her I'm home?'

'She's visitin' a friend over Kingswood way,' said Clara. 'She'll be back soon an' Joe's been round with a note – he's a proper scholar, is our Joe – an' I've put some food by for her.'

Willow studied the eldest of her three brothers. He'd washed sketchily. There was coal dust beneath his finger-nails and a black tidemark framed his face. His dark hair stood up in a spiky halo, but his blue eyes, so like her own, were bright as sapphires. He hadn't grown much in the past five months and Willow was suddenly afraid for him. He needed feeding up. The memory of the food shovelled out to the pigs on the manor home farm tormented her. Joe might grow up with a weak body like Dad's. Her heart twisted at the idea. His salvation would surely lie in his capacity for brain work. 'Do you like readin' an' writin'?' she asked him.

Joe grinned. 'Readin', yes. Writin's not bad, but I don't like it so well.'

'You must keep on with your education,' said Willow earnestly. 'All of you must. There are good jobs to be had for an educated boy or girl.'

'Hark at her,' Clara jeered softly, but the pride in her voice gave Willow a glow of joy. 'I suppose you think you know it all now?'

Willow shook her head. 'No fear. I've a long way to go.' She smiled, but inside her there was a knot of anger against a society which seemed always to be pushing poor children, however clever, into mindless occupations. Unless there was a miracle, they would all have to leave school as soon as they could earn.

While they munched on the delicious chocolate cake and washed it down with tea, Willow handed out her presents. She had added a few bon-bons she had been permitted to make to the boys' penwipers, and even Marigold couldn't hide her delight at the exquisite lace collar. Willow had made the doll's dress from a piece of left-over cotton print and Jasmine was enchanted, especially when she unwrapped a tiny white apron and cap for which her sister had sacrificed a handkerchief.

'It's all exactly like yours, Willow,' she cried.

When the children had finished exclaiming, Willow brought out a small tissue-covered parcel and handed it to Clara who opened it slowly. She stared down at the crimson silk rose lying on a box of Prue's petit-fours, and some colour stole into her cheeks. She picked up the rose and fingered its softly glowing petals. She said nothing for a moment, then her voice became husky. 'My, won't I be smart? I'll wear it the first time Dad an' me can go out together.'

'I thought you might sew it to your hat,' said Willow. 'If you like, I'll do it for you.'

'No thanks, love, I'll do it myself.' Clara wrapped the rose up tenderly and placed it in the cupboard and Willow knew as surely as if she could see the future that Clara would sell the rose for as much as she could get. She turned to give her father the pack of cigarettes she had bought, along with Henry's cigar which she had acquired for threepence. 'This is for you, Dad,' she said.

'Thought you told me I shouldn't smoke!'

Willow shrugged ruefully. 'You will, anyway. You might as well have somethin' good.'

Gran came hurrying in before they'd finished eating and Willow kissed her, enjoying her special scent of peppermint and the lavender she sprinkled in the drawers. Joe jumped up and gave her his seat near the fire and Clara fetched out a plate of vegetables keeping hot in the range oven and added ham and pickles.

'I suppose Willow brought these home?' Gran said. 'The cook must be a good sort.'

Willow felt pleased that here was someone who understood her life at the manor. It made her feel less of a stranger.

Willow and Jasmine attended to the dishes then they all sat around the fire which had been replenished with the coal brought home by the boys. It burned clear and bright and odourless, unlike the usual coke which gave off fumes which crept acridly up nostrils and into mouths. Willow told them about Buddleigh Manor and its occupants. She selected the stories carefully, giving them a picture of the funny side of service in a great house: how Ivy had slipped on a patch of grease on the kitchen floor and dropped a perfect fruit jelly which had landed in her lap, ruining her clean apron, and how Mrs Narracott had shrieked and slapped her, then charged around trying to discover who had been so careless as to drop the grease in the first place and not clean it up.

'Did she find out?' asked Jasmine, her eyes moist with tears of laughter.

'No,' said Willow. 'We all knew it was Aggie, but we didn't let on.'

'What's Aggie's job?' asked Clara.

'She does the washin' up,' said Willow. 'She's a funny little thing. She goes to sleep in church and someone has to keep nudging her or she snores. I think she must have somethin' wrong with her nose.'

She described the scene when Violet had come down to show off her engagement ring, and the family visit at Christmas, bringing gifts.

'What did you get?' asked Jasmine, still hugging herself in joy at having her beloved sister home, and the centre of an admiring group.

'A beautiful piece of pink cloth,' said Willow enthusiastically.

She made it sound as if her life at the manor was one long round of pleasure. She told them how she had hidden in a curtained alcove to see the lovely gowns and nearly fallen out, and they laughed loudly, Dad loudest of all, until he began to cough and Mum and Gran insisted on his returning to bed. He didn't protest which frightened Willow. She tried to describe the manor to them, but out of all its grandeur they were most impressed by the idea of lavatories built like thrones and painted with flowers, which flushed clean, and bathrooms where hot water flowed.

'I should like to see that,' said Jasmine.

'People like us never get near luxuries like that!' stated Marigold. 'How did you see them, Willow, when they forbade you to go upstairs?'

She laughed. 'When everyone had left the manor and Mrs Westerby was away for a day, Jenny, that's the head housemaid, took me upstairs an' said I could use the guest bathroom as long as I didn't tell the others.'

'Why?' demanded Marigold loudly.

'Hush your noise,' said Clara. 'Go on, our Willow.'

'I was surprised, but I get on well with Jenny. Anyway, she ran the hot water an' left me. I found a jar of bath salts that made the water go blue and smelt wonderful. I didn't dare stay long and had to use one of the servants' rough towels, but it was lovely.' She paused, looking into a distant future. 'One day I'll have a bathroom of my own an' I'll let you all use it.'

'One at a time, I hope,' said Joe, and Clara was so interested it was a minute before she took in the saucy undertone of the remark.

She shook her head. 'You'll use that cheeky tongue of yours once too often.'

Willow walked Gran home before ten o'clock. It was cold and a bitter wind blew. 'I'm worried about Dad,' said Willow.

Gran was silent for a moment or two, then she said sadly, 'My poor boy isn't going to recover. I'm sorry you had to come home to such bad news, but when he – when – it – happens you may only learn of it through a letter and the shock will be less if you know what to expect.'

Willow cried rebelliously, 'You sound so calm, Gran! I can't bear the thought!'

'You'll have to bear what the Lord sends, the same as me. I've buried my husband and half a dozen babies. My Arthur's lungs are well-nigh useless and getting worse, and it's no good blinking the facts. Thank God he's had such a good wife as Clara. He's known nothing but love all his life and he'll leave some of himself in each of the children. In you, my love, too, don't forget that. He was never strong, but he's always been gallant.'

Willow fell silent and Gran said, 'Now then, my girl, let's hear a bit of the other side of your life at the manor.' She hobbled along with a walking stick in one hand, her other clutching Willow's arm. Her rheumatics played her up these cold nights, she explained without a trace of self-pity. They arrived at Gran's lodging and Willow relit the fire. As it crackled and flamed they sat in front of it, sipping cocoa, Gran's rocking chair scarcely moving as she held her hands round the warm cup and Willow told her everything.

'You've had a bad time,' said Gran sympathetically, 'but you've come through it well. So the bootboy stepped forward to clear your name? What a brave little fellow he must be. He'll find it hard to get a job without a reference.'

'Don't the gentry understand at all what our lives are like?' asked Willow angrily.

'No, and the sooner you accept it, the better for you. How can they understand when from the day they can walk they've only to stretch out a hand to call a servant? They can't help the way they are, any more than we can.'

'Some of them live bad lives,' said Willow.

Gran asked sharply, 'What do you mean?'

Willow explained about the cards on the door and the men and women who played night games, and Gran shook her head. 'It wasn't like that in my day. It's the influence of King Edward. I've heard about some of the carrying on in his court. He makes favourites of ladies who don't behave virtuously. Some of them are high up in society, some are actresses, they're all good-looking. The old Queen would have nothing to do with their like. Queen Alexandra is a good woman, too, but she turns away from things she prefers not to know.' Gran changed the subject. 'Have you seen much of the nursery?'

'No,' said Willow. 'If I didn't know that Winifred is brought down to the drawing room for an hour a day at teatime, I should think she didn't exist. I only see the nanny when we go to church. The nursery maid just comes down for trays or clean laundry an' she hardly speaks to us. She thinks she's a cut above us, Prue says.'

'Things are no different from my day, then. You won't have had any trouble with the young men of the house,' said Gran, 'seeing that you never get upstairs.'

Willow hesitated and Gran looked searchingly at her. 'It never does a servant any good to let the young gentlemen – or their fathers, or the gentlemen guests, for that matter – become familiar. I hope you haven't forgotten that?'

'I didn't forget, Gran.' Willow told her about Edgar, trying to make it sound amusing, but Gran didn't laugh. 'You know you must *never* let anyone take liberties with you.'

'I didn't. I slapped him.'

Gran grinned in appreciation. 'I'm glad! Impertinent young man.' She went to the cupboard and brought out a parcel tied with blue ribbon. 'Here's your Christmas present, my love.'

'Oh, Gran, you shouldn't have!' Willow's words ended in a gasp of pleasure as she lifted wool and cotton underwear worked in the finest of stitches and trimmed with narrow lace. She kissed Gran, fighting tears. 'How did you know? Your poor hands—'

'Don't take on,' said Gran. 'Every stitch was a pleasure to me. You haven't grumbled but I dare say your old vests and knickers have been commented upon.'

'If ever they say anything about my underwear again it'll only be in admiration,' said Willow, kissing her soundly.

On her way back Willow thought of Edgar. While talking to Gran she'd realised she was reluctant to speak his name aloud. Some of the faces in Buddleigh Manor were rather hazy in her mind, but she saw his clearly, the boyish features too often spoilt by the petulant turn of his mouth, his eyes dark with mischief as he'd tried to kiss her. As she turned into the road leading home she met Sidney Moor, who fell into step beside her. In the yellow glow of a street lamp she saw that his hair was still scrubby, but he had fewer pimples and he had surely grown an inch. He was tall enough now for her to have to look up at him.

'How have you been gettin' on with your job in Devon?' he asked.

'Quite well, thank you,' she said politely. 'I have to work hard.'

'Don't you mind bein' a servant?'

'No, but I don't intend to be one always.'

'I expect you'll have servants of your own one day.'

Willow glanced at him to see if he was joking. His head was sunk into the collar of his thread-bare suit which was turned up against the cruel icy wind. His nose was red.

'Your Mum's been ever so good to me,' he said. 'She makes a real home for her folks and she lets me share it sometimes. She's more of a mother to me than my own.'

'Mum's got a good heart.'

'Yes.'

'I was sorry to hear about your brother.'

His expression didn't change. 'He asked for it. They all ask for it.'

'That's not very charitable.'

'It's the truth. Now two of my sisters are gettin' up to tricks as well.'

'Stealin'?'

'Worse.' Sidney's voice was sharp.

'Worse?' Willow was horrified at the thought his words conjured up. 'You don't mean—'

'Yes, I do mean. They say all they've got to sell is themselves, an' Mum an' Dad just take the money they bring home.'

'But if they get caught, what will happen to them? Won't they end up in prison, too?'

Sidney looked startled. 'I don't know. I suppose you're down on them?'

'I didn't say I blamed them. I said they're askin' for trouble an' so they are. I can understand why they do it, but I think they're mad. Much better to get on without riskin' prison.'

Sidney let out a long sigh. 'I wish my family was like yours, Willow. Whenever anythin' bad happens in the district the police are round at our house, and whenever one of them sees me I get a dirty look. They'd arrest me as soon as look at me if they could. But I'll never give them the chance. Never!' he added grimly.

He had changed in more than looks. The spirit that held him straight in the face of his family of thieves and prostitutes had hardened. She said, 'I think you'll get on well one day.'

He looked down at her. 'You really do?'

'I really do.'

When they reached his home he wished her goodnight and she hurried home to find that Clara had sat up for her and had the kettle boiling for a night-time drink. She produced a bottle of Camp coffee, a luxury she must have bought for a Christmas treat, and Willow drank a cup of the thick, pre-sweetened liquid made with water and a little milk. It was nothing like the coffee served in the manor. She went to sleep that night feeling like a traitor, as if by that thought she had let everyone down.

Willow returned to a Buddleigh Manor which was almost placid now that all the family but Miss Winifred had gone. Miss Brayton and Miss Jebb had accompanied their mistresses and the atmosphere in the kitchen quarters was close to a holiday one. Although Mrs Narracott made sure that time was well used, work was undertaken without a sense of urgency. No matter how much Mrs Westerby complained about the time it took to scrub the kitchen floors, the corridors, the back stairs and outside steps, to empty the cupboards and wash the shelves, to take down the soiled curtains to give to the washer-women and put up clean ones, and perform all the multifarious duties the manor required, Mrs Narracott permitted the kitchen maids to continue without haste. The unlucky housemaids were constantly grousing about being under the housekeeper's eye at all times as they gave the manor an extra-special clean. However, it was easier to endure when each evening they could look forward to dishes which the kitchen staff now had time to prepare, and which normally the servants never tasted. When Mrs Westerby complained about the expensive ingredients the cook told her that she was experimenting with new dishes while she had the chance and the food couldn't possibly be allowed to go to waste.

'As I have said many times, Mrs Narracott,' grated the irate housekeeper, 'food never goes to waste here. There are always the pigs on the home farm.'

Mrs Narracott screeched with rage. 'The pigs! Give my lovely new dishes to pigs? I'll do no such thing, and well you know it. The staff enjoy them.'

Prue told Willow that the arguments occurred whenever the family went away. 'Mrs Westerby won't tell them anythin' because she knows that no one will scold Mrs Narracott.'

Willow had time to sew for herself. She was growing so fast she was outstripping the seams and hems of her dresses and she began to make a new one from the pink material, reflecting that whoever had chosen the gift for her had been quite right after all. She would unpick the seams of the other two dresses and turn them into one.

The visitors had left generous tips and Mr Steadman had allotted each servant his or her share, according to status. It helped to make up the board wages. Willow carried out her work, glad that with every passing day she was growing more proficient. Her increased health and stamina enabled her to cope with the long hours and still have time for herself. Yet beneath her outward cheerfulness was the knowledge that back in Bristol Dad's illness was claiming more and more of his feeble strength and she wished with all her heart that she could share the last of his life.

Chapter Nine

After weeks away, the family returned to the manor, bringing only a few guests, and life resumed its normal course which meant the customary long hours for the servants. Willow was relieved that Miss Jebb only came into the kitchen when it was unavoidable. The lady's maid quite clearly detested her.

Mrs Narracott said, 'You'd think she'd be grateful to you, Lily, but that's often the way things go. Some people let false pride stand in the way of everything.'

Prue said, 'You shouldn't have forgiven her, Lily, an' then she might have been dismissed.'

'That's uncharitable,' said Mrs Narracott.

'I know what it's like to be poor,' said Willow fervently. 'I wouldn't wish it on my worst enemy.'

Prue laughed. 'What enemies do you have, Lily? Apart from Jebb, that is?'

'None, I hope, though I'm not very sure about Mrs Westerby.'

'No one's sure about Mrs Westerby,' said Prue.

'That's true,' said Mrs Narracott. 'I've been here since I was head kitchen maid, that's before the old Queen died, and I've never known her make a friend.' She got up from the chair where she'd been enjoying a short break. 'Come on, we've got to get tea for upstairs.'

Jenny, Polly and Ivy were all in bed with severe colds and Nancy was clearly sickening and sniffed constantly, so Willow had been ordered to put on her black dress to help serve tea. When she went to change she was terrified that she might have outgrown the afternoon dress, but she managed to squeeze into it and her stiffly starched apron concealed the fact that her breasts were pressed so hard into the material that their contours looked like cushions. She was shaking with nerves as she picked up a tray of sandwiches and followed Mr Norris who struggled with the weight of the silver tea service, Henry who carried the cakes and scones, and Mr Steadman who carried nothing at all.

When she entered the smaller drawing room her eyes went involuntarily to the ladies' tea-gowns and it was with an effort that she crossed the room, eyes cast demurely down, to wait while Mr Norris placed the butler's tray on the frame built for the purpose. Henry and Willow laid their plates on small occasional tables and it was her duty to retire, leaving the men to serve. She turned at the door and curtsied, her eyes greedily noticing more details of the sumptuous gowns. Frances was the only one who took any notice of her and gave her a small smile. Then, just as she was closing the door, Edgar, who had been lounging in a bored fashion by the window, turned and raised his brows humorously at her, just as if he understood the workings of her mind. She ran down the back stairs to the kitchen.

When she burst in Prue almost dropped the dish of oranges in jelly she was carrying to the cold pantry and Mrs Narracott, who was frying small slices of stale bread to make cheese croustades for tonight's savoury, jumped and sent a spurt of hot fat on to the back of her hand.

'Really, Lily!' She sucked her burn. 'You know better than to rush about like that.'

'I'm ever so sorry,' said Willow. 'Can I get you some liniment?'

Mrs Narracott shook her head. It was impossible to dislike her unusual kitchen maid. 'I'm used to it. My hands are as tough as old boots.'

Willow put on an enveloping apron because she was to help carry up the dishes for dinner and must keep clean and applied herself to chopping sorrel, chervil, and the tenderest lettuce leaves ready for the chicken soup. As the kitchen staff worked their way towards the family dinner her mind wandered. Maybe tonight she would have an opportunity to add drawings of the tea-gowns to her growing collection? She went over the details, committing them to memory, and almost cut off the end of her finger. She glanced round quickly and was thankful to see that Mrs Narracott had her back to her. Consequently, she was startled to hear the cook ask, 'What've you done now, Lily?'

'How did you know? I mean, nothin'. I've done nothin'.'

Mrs Narracott turned her large person and surveyed her second kitchen maid. '"Nothing" wouldn't cause you to gasp like a landed fish. Let me see your hands.' Willow spread them out. 'I suppose you nearly cut yourself. Day-dreaming again.'

That night Willow was completely happy as she hurried up and down the stairs with the many dishes her employers and their friends needed to protect them from hunger. For once, she didn't make painful comparisons between the bare existence at the bottom and life at the top. Her mind was too full of the beauty of the dinner table with its mitred table napkins standing sentry until the white hands of the gentry shook them open; of the array of wine glasses, so delicate that they looked as if they might shatter if someone held them too tight; of the flowers and vines and candles which decorated and illuminated the table.

Most of all she looked at the ladies, wondering how they felt in their heavenly gowns. The older women wore the delicate sweet-pea hues in vogue for the past few years, but the younger blazed in startling reds, greens and blues. Willow longed to know why the two groups were so different, how the young women had discovered the new colours, how it was that they all blossomed forth in them at the same time? She could carry styles and colours in her head, and had only to close her eyes to see the gowns in their full glory painted, as it were, in her mind's eye.

Somehow she would find out all she wanted to know. If she behaved herself tonight it might lead to something better and she concentrated on the tasks in hand, so much so that Mr Steadman paid her a compliment. Ivy was feeling better and had come downstairs. She was sitting by the kitchen fire, privileged because of her illness, clutching a large cup of cocoa. She looked resentful on hearing Willow praised. She had her revenge, however, because Willow soon caught her cold and had to lie in bed, irritated and bored by turns.

She took longer than the others to recover. Mrs Narracott visited her each night – the cook never usually climbed the many stairs to the attics before bedtime – and looked concerned.

'Your constitution isn't as strong as it might be, Lily. I expect it's because you've not had enough good victuals at home.'

Willow bristled and the cook said, 'Calm down, my dear, I don't mean to insult your parents. They must be having a dreadful struggle now your dad's so bad. I shall see you get plenty of chicken and bone broth, and a good tonic wouldn't come amiss.'

She didn't forget and Willow began to feel better, though she wrinkled her nose at the tonic which was bitter.

'That's the stuff they put in to strengthen your blood,' explained Mrs Narracott.

Willow asked how much money she owed for the medicine, but was told that Mrs Westerby had authorised it from the housekeeping. 'She's a stickler for "proper procedures" as she calls it,' said Mrs Narracott, 'and makes it her business to see that sick servants are looked after. Leaving them lying in bed disrupts routine.'

When Willow came downstairs she expected to resume work, but Mrs Narracott would have none of it. 'Put your coat and hat on. You need fresh air to put the colour back in your cheeks and walking will strengthen your legs. We've had a lot of rain, but it's cleared up for a while and you'd best make good use of the time. Don't forget, you mustn't go in the garden, and it's best to stay out of the park. Walk towards the village.'

It wasn't raining, but the sky was cloudy and the air damp and cold. Willow walked briskly, to counteract the chill, deep in thoughts of home. She was startled when a big dog rushed up to her and frisked about her. She stopped and looked up, straight into Edgar's eyes.

'Down, boy,' he ordered. 'Heel!' The dog obeyed reluctantly, his tail wagging.

'Did he frighten you? I'm sorry,' said Edgar.

Willow said, 'No. Is he yours?'

'In a way. Mrs Maddison doesn't encourage animals in the house so the head gardener looks after Horatio for me.' The dog, hearing his name, leapt up and Edgar once more brought him to heel. 'He's not very well trained, I'm afraid. He's barely out of puppyhood and I can't give him as much time as I should like.' He scratched the dog's head, sending it into wriggling spasms of joy. 'You've been ill.'

'Yes. How do you know?'

'Miss Frances told me.'

'How did she know?'

'She is interested in your welfare.'

'Is she?' Willow's doubt was evident.

'Oh, I know she doesn't do much about it.' He sighed. 'I'm afraid we are all rather lax. I am glad you are well again. Should you be out on a day like this?'

'Mrs Narracott said I should. I won't have much time for walking after I return to work.'

'When will that be?' He actually sounded interested, though Willow suspected he was amusing himself on a dull afternoon.

'It doesn't matter to you, Mr Edgar,' she said, putting a slight emphasis on his title, and began to walk away.

She found herself held back. 'It does matter.'

The haughty glance she cast on his restraining hand couldn't have been bettered by a duchess. Edgar laughed delightedly and Willow was fascinated to see that his laugh wiped all the petulance from his features. He released her.

'Thank you.'

'Not at all.' He gave her a small bow. 'May I walk a little with you?'

He was behaving as if she were a somebody and although

she remembered Gran's warnings, she wanted him to stay with her. Surely, there could be no harm in a walk?

'What if someone sees us?'

'What if they do?'

'Your parents would be angry to know you were with me.'

'We're going in the same direction, that's all.'

'Excuse me, but you were goin' in the opposite direction.'

'I was just about to turn.'

Willow laughed, her eyes brimming with mirth. 'No, you weren't.'

'You're pretty, even when the tip of your nose is pink.'

She stepped back, immediately suspicious, and it was Edgar's turn to laugh. 'What on earth have people told you about me? I'm harmless, you know.'

'No one's told me anythin' about you. My gran warned me not to get friendly with the upstairs people. She said it isn't done.'

'Isn't done! Good lord.'

'She also said it could be dangerous to a girl.'

'Your gran seems to have had a lot of experience in these matters.'

'Do you mean she's right?'

'Yes, indeed, in some instances, but she's not making allowances for a man who just enjoys your company.'

'Until someone young and pretty and rich turns up.'

Willow stalked off in the direction of the village. By the time she had hurried a few hundred yards she was out of breath and realised that her illness had taken a greater toll of her strength than she had appreciated. To add to her discomfort rain began to fall. Not gently, but in huge, sploshing drops which promised a real downpour. She raised the umbrella Ivy had lent her and discovered it to have several holes and a web of uncovered spokes. She looked round her. To one side was a low wall behind which stood a herd of cows who regarded her inquisitively from their shelter beneath a tree. It was winter-barren, but might have afforded a little respite if she hadn't been petrified at the idea of braving animals which looked very large close to. On her other side was the high boundary wall of the manor. The overhanging branches of trees growing in the park clattered above her in the rising wind. She felt nervous, as if she had strayed into an alien land. In town there was always a handy shop doorway to shelter in. At the sound of footsteps she looked round and saw Edgar with his dog now on a tight leash, and was filled with an emotion which wasn't only relief.

'What a spiffing umbrella, Lily,' he said.

She looked skywards, through the skeletal frame, and rain plopped into her eye. Laughter bubbled up and Edgar grinned. 'We must get you to shelter or you'll be ill again.'

She couldn't argue with this as the rain began to fall in sheets. He grabbed her hand and hurried her to the huge wall, clearing away some small evergreen bushes to reveal an ancient wooden door. 'Through here,' he ordered, opening the door which creaked on rusty hinges. Fifty yards on there was a wooden structure built into the low branches of a large cedar.

'What is it?'

'It's a tree house, or what's left of it. I built it when I was young. I used to fancy myself master of my domain, with my own gate to the world outside.'

He brushed away some twigs and crumpled brown leaves and Willow climbed in. He tethered Horatio to a thick growth of rhododendron where the dog could get some shelter and followed her. The tree house was too low for them to stand so they sat listening to the drumming on the roof. A few spots seeped through and Edgar put the umbrella up again and crouched close to her beneath the covered part. His head was almost touching hers and Willow felt intensely vulnerable.

He turned to look at her. 'You needn't be scared of me.'

'I'm not.'

'Well, you look it.'

'I'm not,' she repeated. She could hardly tell him it was her own weakness which scared her. She was terribly aware of him, of the clean scent of his hair which mingled with the faint smell of expensive cigars, of his athletic body.

'How old are you?' she asked abruptly.

'Nineteen. How old are you?'

'Fifteen.'

'Is that all? I thought you were older.'

'Well, thanks very much.'

Edgar laughed softly. 'I only meant that you seem more mature, not that you look ancient.'

'Poverty makes you grow up early,' Willow almost snapped.

'I suppose it does. Is your family very poor?'

'Yes.'

'How many times has your father been in jail?'

Willow gasped and began to struggle from the tree house though it was raining harder than ever.

Edgar grasped her and held on to her.

'Let – me – go!'

'I shall do no such thing. You could catch your death of cold.' His voice had taken on nannyish overtones and Willow smiled in spite of herself.

'That's better.'

She sighed. 'I suppose you imagine people of my class go to prison quite often.' Briefly, she told him what had happened and was pleased when he expressed his indignation. 'If he had had a lawyer to represent him he would have got off.'

'If he'd been wealthy enough to employ a lawyer,' retorted Willow acerbically, 'he wouldn't have been in court at all.'

'That's true.'

They fell silent, watching the rain making muddy pools on the sodden ground. Again Willow felt the dangerous tug of her feelings towards this man and began to edge away from him. Considering the size of the tree house that was virtually impossible. He grabbed her and slid his arm round her waist. 'Hang on, you're going to topple out.'

She stiffened. 'Don't do that!'

'Do what?'

'You know very well what! Take your arm away.'

'I'm just being friendly. You've decided again not to trust me and here I am, saving you from a wetting and possible pneumonia.'

'You're not! You're makin' advances.'

He shouted with mirth. 'Making advances! What an expression! Lily, darling, just think of the state you would be in if you tumbled into a puddle.'

'Don't call me darling! And my name's Willow. Mrs Westerby changed it.'

'Willow. How pretty. You're such a darling. I am not going to molest you, but I always think of you as a darling.'

'You probably never think of me at all.'

'That's where you're wrong.'

'You weren't very friendly on the Downs when Miss Winifred ran in front of the motor car.'

'No, that's true. You'll have to forgive that. We gentry live in horror of making a public scene, don't you know?'

He had spoken in a silly haw-haw voice and Willow laughed. She couldn't deny that she enjoyed the feel of his arm about her. She had to be stern with herself not to lean against him. She turned her head. His face was inches from hers, the pupils of his eyes were large and what she read in them bothered her. Then his face came closer, slowly, giving her time to stop him. He was going to kiss her. And she wanted his kiss. At first his lips barely brushed hers, then the kiss grew deeper, his tongue touched her lips gently, probing and pushing until, instinctively, she opened her mouth. He pulled her close, so close she could feel his heavy heartbeats and his hands began to wander over her body. She should stop him, she must stop him. He undid the buttons of her coat and cupped a breast, his fingers brushing over her hardened nipples. She dragged herself back to sanity.

'No!'

He released her, his mouth compressed into a thin line, his cheeks flushed. 'I beg your pardon, Willow.'

She said nothing. Her heart was hammering as she tried to control her longing to hold him, to let him do anything he wanted.

'The rain has stopped,' said Edgar. He stepped out, regardless of the puddle beneath the tree house. 'There was always a puddle here after rain.' He put his hands beneath Willow's arms and helped her to jump clear, steadying her on the carpet of wet, dank-smelling, slippery leaves, then untied Horatio. 'I'll see you safely home.'

'No. I prefer to go alone.'

'I swear I won't touch you again.'

'No,' she said shortly, to hide her grief at the knowledge that she must keep away from him when she longed to stay with him.

'Very well.'

She hurried off, not looking back, though she sensed that he watched her out of sight and was confused by her own feelings of mingled disappointment and relief that he had permitted her to go.

Willow was determined not to give Edgar an opportunity to test her resistance again. On her free time she always looked round warily before she set off for her walk. It worried her that she couldn't keep him out of her thoughts; he invaded her dreams. More than ever she wished she could be one of the young ladies upstairs, one who visited the manor, wonderfully gowned, perfumed and bejewelled, with hands as smooth as silk. Hers were getting more rough and red by the day however much she rubbed grease into them. Since the episode of the brooch she had not been asked to do any sewing and regretted the loss of the opportunity to handle beautiful clothes. Jebb made no attempt to hide her loathing whenever they met which was as seldom as possible; she now followed Miss Brayton's example and had her meals sent upstairs.

Willow heard that Edgar was going to Oxford University and told herself she was thankful that temptation was put out of her way. In spite of her vigilance he managed to meet her on one of her forays to the village. She turned, prepared to hurry back the way she had come, then decided she was being ridiculous and faced him.

'I just want to say goodbye,' he said politely.

'Well, you've said it. Goodbye.' She tried to pass him, but he put out a hand. He hadn't touched her, but she stopped as if he had. 'I heard that you didn't want to go to Oxford,' she said flippantly. 'Changed your mind?'

'You changed it for me. It's best I go away.'

Willow gazed up at him, regret clear in her eyes.

'Don't look at me like that or I shall kiss you right here and now. You care about me, don't you?'

'No! Yes, in a way. You know you're puttin' me in an impossible position. I don't intend to become any man's bit of fluff.'

This brought a twisted smile to his lips. 'Did Gran teach you that?'

'No, it's an expression I picked up from the scullery maid.'

He took her hand in his and held it. 'Goodbye, Willow. Say goodbye nicely.' His tone was flippant, but Willow sensed that it masked unhappiness.

'Goodbye, Mr Edgar,' she said, firmly placing the barrier of their stations between them.

She felt miserable when Edgar had gone. Even knowing he was under the same roof with her had given her a pleasant glow. It's just as well he is away, she told herself, or who knows what might have happened?

Buddleigh Manor was in a state of funereal gloom. King Edward, that staunch arbiter of pleasure, had died. The event drew the servants together in rare intimacy.

Mrs Narracott shed tears. 'We've entertained His Majesty more than once in London and down here. Such a gracious gentleman.'

'He was enjoying a holiday in Biarritz only a few weeks ago,' said Mr Steadman. 'And he always insisted on getting up and dressing, even on the day he passed on. He kept on with state business almost to the last minute.'

'He loved this country of ours,' said Mr Norris.

'What did he die of?' asked Prue.

'I'm not sure,' said Mr Steadman. 'The poor man was subject to bronchitis and I've heard it weakened his heart.'

Henry lowered his voice. 'I heard that Mrs Keppel was sent for and by Her Majesty, too. Fancy her letting her husband's mistress attend his death bed.'

'I heard that!' snapped Mrs Narracott. 'And I don't believe a word of it. It wouldn't have been proper, not proper at all. And Queen Alexandra's always been a very proper lady.'

'You are quite right, Mrs Narracott.' Mr Steadman gave Henry an indignant glance. 'Only those with low minds would believe such a thing.'

The Maddisons went to London for the funeral. When Ivy heard of the crowds that had flocked from the East End to line the route of the procession, she muttered to Willow, 'What a fuss. He never did anythin' for the likes of us.'

'I suppose they'll cancel everything for a while,' mused Mr Norris. 'No Ascot. That'll upset folk.'

'That's not all that'll upset some people,' said Jenny. 'The new King and Queen are much more severe in their behaviour. I dare say there'll be a lot who won't get invited to the palace any more.'

She was right, and Norris was wrong. Many ladies who had been acceptable at the court of the late King were struck from the list of desirables by Queen Mary. Royal Ascot was held as usual with one incongruous difference. Everyone was dressed from head to toe in black.

Edgar seldom came home from Oxford, spending most of his vacations with friends. Willow was recognised now by everyone in the servants' hall as a hard worker who never shirked her duty. Prue was engaged to be married to a farmer's boy and Willow was allowed to perform quite a number of the minor cooking tasks, though Ivy protested if the second kitchen maid ever appeared to usurp her place.

'It's awkward,' said Prue to Willow. 'You're better at cookin' than Ivy. In fact, I don't mind tellin' you that Mrs N's got an idea of makin' you second cook after I leave, but she can't think of how to get round Ivy. The cook's the boss, I know, but Ivy could make life nasty.'

Willow was glad that her talents were appreciated, though she couldn't see the cook promoting her over Ivy's head and wasn't sure that she wanted her to. She had always treated the first kitchen maid with respect and they had become quite good friends. Aggie, after futile attempts to keep herself clean, had sunk back to her original grubby self, only washing when Ivy roughly insisted on it. Willow remonstrated with Ivy who said, 'We have to share a room with the brat an' I don't take kindly to stinks.'

The house was in a continual bustle. In March 1912, it was announced that the wedding of Miss Violet Maddison and Lord George Radcliffe would take place on 1 May at the bride's country home. From that moment, both above and below stairs, the house revolved around Violet.

Miss Brayton paid one of her rare visits to the kitchen. 'Miss Violet's will be one of the great weddings of the year. And then she will be presented to Their Majesties again as a married woman.'

After she left, Prue said incredulously, 'Is that true? Will Miss Violet's weddin' be one of the great ones of the year?'

'Why shouldn't it be!' snapped Mrs Narracott, suddenly belligerent. She considered it as a personal attack if anything, however remotely applied, appeared to reduce the status of the family to whom she had devoted so much of her life.

'No reason,' said Prue. 'I just wondered, that's all. I don't know about such things the way you do, Mrs N.'

The cook was soothed. 'Well, I admit I don't have first-hand knowledge of who's going to be there. You tell her, Jenny. You hear things.'

Jenny was happy to oblige. 'The guest list is amazing and nearly everyone has accepted. Dukes, earls, viscounts, some of the richest people in England, plus a few of the foremost artistic folk. Mrs Maddison didn't want them. She said it would make people think they were bohemian.'

'What's that?' asked Ivy.

Jenny said, 'I'm not absolutely sure, but I think it means they live odd lives. It appears that writers and artists are a bit strange. That's what Mrs Maddison says, anyway, but Violet insisted on them being asked. She says she's going to be a great hostess and have all the most interesting people to her house, and that includes bohemians.'

Willow thought, I could have looked up the word in Steven's dictionary. She missed him. He had been sent away from the village and his cold-hearted, bible-thumping guardians would not say where he was. On one of her visits home Willow told Gran about Steven and Gran had bought a pocket dictionary second-hand and sent it to her. Willow followed Steven's example and began to enlarge her vocabulary. She looked up the word 'bohemian' and discovered that it meant unconventional. She was taking great care over her speech and read the magazines bought by Mrs Narracott. The stories were sentimental and often silly, but their grammar and punctuation were correct and added to her store of learning.

Every time Willow visited her family Dad looked more frail. She wondered how so skinny a body, racked with coughing, kept going. Clara was untiring in her resolve to keep him with her and Willow thought sadly that her mother's obsession was all that held him clinging to the narrow thread of his life. Clara was bone thin, her face more lined. In spite of a larger contribution from Willow whose wages had risen to eighteen pounds a year she still worked at the wash tub to pay doctors' bills. Willow's heart ached for her. Jasmine had begun her formal education and her teachers were delighted with her. Joe had left school at thirteen and had got a job in a local boot factory, proud to be contributing to the family income, Sam was about to leave school and Alfred could hardly bear to wait another year to follow his brothers, talking of the job he would get.

Clara confided to Willow, 'Marigold worries me. She stops out far too late at night. I gave her a good hiding more than once, but last time she threatened to hit me back. That wouldn't worry me,' she said grimly, 'but it would worry your dad. He hates to hear any of us quarrellin'. I just hope she knows what she's doin'.' She lowered her voice. 'Her monthlies began early. She's been a woman for three years.'

Willow didn't need to be told the significance of this latest information. 'You don't think she goes with boys, Mum?'

'I don't know. I just don't know about her. An' she's so pretty.'

Willow wondered yet again if the time would ever come when she could help one of the family to get a better education. She loved them all so much and always left them reluctantly. But as soon as the train approached the tiny Devon halt she was filled with curiosity as to what had happened at the manor during her absence. She had learned that a great deal of training was needed to become a lady's maid and had decided that her ambition was all but impossible. A job as a cook was far more attainable and looked more attractive than she had thought. Families depended on their cooks and a really good one need never be out of a job. She would have a reasonably good income and wield influence over the people above stairs, who tried never to antagonise the cook, and enjoy total power in the kitchen.

Soon after the wedding announcement, Willow was summoned upstairs. 'Who wants me?' she asked Henry.

'Miss Frances. She's in her room. She says to go straight up.'

Willow straightened her hair and pinned her cap on firmly, checked to make sure her hands were clean and hurried to the second floor.

Frances called her in. She was seated in a chair, the window open to the scents of damp, disturbed earth where the gardeners were forking and raking everything to perfection.

'Hello, Lily, you look well. One would not recognise you as the girl I met on the Downs.'

'No, miss. Thank you, miss.'

'As you know, my sister will be leaving us soon. She is taking Jebb with her. I must confess I've never really taken to her, but Miss Violet says that she does not want the bother of training up another maid.'

Willow felt that something was expected of her and said, 'I hope Miss Jebb will be happy in her new life.'

'Do you?' Frances smiled. 'You are a forgiving soul, aren't you, after what we put you through. I was so relieved when it was proved that you were innocent of wrong-doing, especially as it was my recommendation which got you taken on in the first place. I really was distressed for you.'

'Were you, miss?' Willow heard the sarcastic tone of her own voice and added hastily, 'That's nice of you.'

Frances gazed at her, raising brows which were as fair as her hair. She looked very pretty in a blue morning gown with white tucks about the high neck, and Willow noted with interest that she had chosen the new higher-waisted line, and that her skirt, when she moved, displayed fine pleated inserts which would give her good leg room to walk.

'Do you still draw fashions, Lily? I see you are studying my gown.'

Willow coloured. 'I'm sorry, miss, I didn't mean to stare. Yes, I draw as often as I can.'

'I suppose you don't have very much time for frivolous occupations?'

Willow wanted to tell her that her drawing wasn't frivolous; that it was, in fact, one of the most important things in her life, but she said only, 'Not much time, miss.'

'My mother says that Westerby gives a good account of your work.'

'I'm glad to hear that, miss.' Surely Miss Frances hadn't got her up here just to chatter? She should be in the kitchen making pastry and baking it blind ready for it to cool in time

172

for the fruit flans. Mrs Narracott said that pastry making was one of the most important and difficult branches of cooking. 'Ivy's hands are too hot and heavy, but yours are perfect,' she had commented, throwing Ivy into a rage.

'You're wondering why I've asked to see you?' said Frances.

'Yes, miss.'

'How would you like to become my maid?'

Willow stared. 'I beg pardon, miss?'

'I shall need a personal maid when Jebb leaves in May. I discovered that you were responsible for the delicate stitching which she was supposed to have mastered so suddenly. I didn't say anything about it to Miss Violet or my mother because I felt sorry for Jebb, but I would be glad of your skills.' She smiled ruefully. 'I do not spend as much of my dress allowance on clothes as my sister. I buy books, and pictures, and pretty pots and vases. You didn't know I was by way of being a collector, did you, Lily?'

'No, miss.'

'Well, what do you say? What is your answer?'

'Do you mean you want me to take over from Miss Jebb?' Willow was stunned by this sudden upturn in her life. 'Why me, miss? I mean, I've never even been an upper servant. I'm the second kitchen maid.'

'Are you? Is that a nice position? I've wondered sometimes what it must be like to work in the kitchen. Quite exciting, I should think, when there's a dinner party or a grand ball.'

Willow couldn't think of an answer to such an uninformed comment.

'I am sure you could do the work I ask,' said Frances. 'I am not exacting, and you have proved yourself honest, reliable and intelligent.' Willow felt flustered. Frances was such a bewildering mixture of ignorance and understanding. 'If you begin at once you will have time to learn my ways from Jebb and I dare say Miss Brayton won't mind lending a hand.'

'I will be taught by Miss Jebb?' A hundred images flashed through Willow's mind, of herself and Jebb spending the next couple of months together, one hating her pupil, the other mistrusting her teacher. Fearful to place herself in such an unbearable situation, she said, 'I don't think I'm ready for such a big promotion.'

'I am sorry to hear that. I believe you would master the job excellently.'

Willow suddenly realised what she was about. She was turning down the very position she longed for! Her wits must have dulled. She thought again of Jebb's vindictiveness. She wondered again if she could deal with it, but as if her ambition had taken on its own life and spoken through her, she said, 'Yes. Yes, please, Miss Frances. I'd like to try.'

'What changed your mind?'

'Er – you did, miss.'

Frances smiled happily. 'Then that's settled. I'll see Westerby and she'll arrange matters. Run along, Lily, and tell them the good news in the kitchen.'

Willow ran along. Tell them the good news in the kitchen! Another incidence of Miss Frances's naivety. Pretty well everyone would be furious or resentful or both but she was so excited that she blurted out the information loudly as soon as she entered the kitchen, before she saw that the housekeeper was there. Everyone stopped moving, as if they had been turned to stone, looking like statues in the game which Willow had once played in the Bristol streets.

Mrs Westerby stared disbelievingly, colour staining her usually pallid face. She opened her mouth and tried to speak. Then she said harshly, 'Why have you all stopped work?'

The servants bent to their respective tasks, taking sly peeps at the melodrama going on in their midst. The housekeeper beckoned Willow to follow her and once more she stood in Mrs Westerby's room. The housekeeper seated herself and looked Willow up and down. 'Pray explain your extraordinary outburst just now.'

'I'm sorry, madam, I know I shouldn't have burst in the way I did, but I was so excited over my news.'

'You must have made a mistake. Miss Frances could not have engaged you as her maid. It is unthinkable.

Unheard of. You are a kitchen maid, and barely trained at that.'

'I'm tellin' the truth. Ask Miss Frances if you don't believe me.'

'Insolence!'

'I don't mean to be insolent, madam.'

'You cannot help it. It has been born and bred in you.'

'No, it hasn't,' cried Willow, incensed at the slur on her family.

'You see, you cannot even conduct a conversation without raising your voice.'

'Insulting my father and mother isn't a conversation.'

Mrs Westerby tapped her fingers on her chair arm. Willow waited.

The housekeeper spoke. 'I should not have implied criticism of your parents.' It was as near an apology as Willow would get and more than she expected. Mrs Westerby got up. 'I shall go and see Mrs Maddison. Meanwhile, return to your kitchen duties. Apply yourself diligently and put all thoughts of such an unthinkable promotion out of your head. It will not happen.'

Chapter Ten

Mrs Westerby's misgivings were disregarded, for Willow was elevated to her new position.

'At present you will continue to occupy the room with the first kitchen maid,' said the housekeeper, 'but later you will be allotted Miss Jebb's room.' Her tone was expressionless; her eyes held animosity.

Willow hadn't thought about having to spend her nights with Ivy and Aggie and couldn't have foreseen the depth of the resentment felt by the head kitchen maid. Ivy scarcely spoke to her at all and then only to say something unpleasant. Sometimes, in the past, when they had been less weary than usual, they had tumbled into bed and there had been whispered, giggling chatter and interesting speculation about their employers. Now that Willow had access to the ear of the gentry all the fun had stopped and more than once she came to bed after an engagement of Frances's had kept her up late to find that the hot water bottle had been left on the floor to get cold. Once she could have curled up comfortably, enjoying the warmth of her sleeping partner, but now even in her sleep Ivy seemed to sense her presence and pulled away.

Life upstairs was no easier. She and Miss Jebb were trapped in their mutual dislike and if Willow had been forced to rely solely on the resentful lady's maid for instruction she would have learned very little. Fortunately for her, Miss Brayton took a hand. Willow was aware of the fact that her enthusiasm for teaching had more to do with a wish to annoy Miss Jebb than to be of service, but she didn't care. She needed all the help she could get.

She had expected Jebb to be annoyed at the sudden elevation of the kitchen maid, but hadn't realised how much she could damage her prospects. Twice she had deliberately given Willow the wrong information and if Frances had not been forbearing Willow feared she would have found herself back in the kitchen. Once she had been instructed to clean her mistress's brushes and combs. She had, on Jebb's advice, placed the drying brushes so near the bedroom fire they warped and had to be replaced; the tortoiseshell combs should not have been washed at all and the teeth had split. Only later did Willow discover that the brushes should have been dried in the sun, or over a mild heat, and that the combs should have been cleaned with a special brush. That had happened during the first week of her new job. She had held her tongue, wondering if somehow she had misunderstood the advice.

On the next occasion she had, again on Jebb's advice, rubbed so much oily pomatum on Frances's newly washed hair that it had had to be washed again, making her late for an engagement. Each time, Miss Jebb had loudly commented on Willow's stupidity. Still she held her tongue. Frances was pleasant to work for, but hated any kind of conflict; much of her gentleness was born of weakness. After that, Willow refused to do a thing unless she had watched another servant do it first, or checked with Miss Brayton.

Willow found an unexpected ally in the form of Mr Maddison's valet. Mr Elwood was a short, thin man who always wore black. When he had taken a meal in the servants' hall he had seated himself in his place near the butler, eaten a modest amount of food, then melted away back to his duties. No one paid much attention to him, but now she discovered his worth. From him she learned the intricacies of keeping Miss Frances's clothes in perfect condition without washing them and thereby detracting from the quality of the cloth; which of the aromatic mixtures would keep moths away; how to clean feathers. Miss Brayton, spurred on by her desire to keep ahead of the valet, stepped up her teaching and Willow

177

committed to memory the names of the substances which every lady's maid should be able to command: essence of almonds, olive oil and rosemary for a hair pomatum; white wax and oil of almonds which, with other ingredients, must be used to combat freckles should any lady so far forget herself as to sit in the sun without a sunshade and incur any; and the invaluable and seemingly limitless uses of vinegar and fresh lemon juice. Miss Jebb watched and listened, expression sour, her manner surly.

One day Willow asked, 'Mr Elwood, didn't Mrs Maddison object to my being offered my new position? After all, I'm not experienced.'

Mr Elwood smiled. 'Miss Frances chose her time well. She gave her mother the information rather casually when the mistress was making one of her many lists for the wedding. I'm not sure if Mrs Maddison absorbed the query properly at the time. But don't worry, Lily, the young ladies are accustomed to getting their own way and your appointment is not likely to be disputed now.'

Willow's promotion rankled with most of her former work-mates. Even Prue talked to her only grudgingly at first and the housemaids, especially Jenny, were resentful.

'You can't expect anything else, I'm afraid,' said Mr Elwood. 'If a lady's personal maid was to be trained up from the staff it should have been an upper servant. To be honest, I've never heard of a promotion like yours, though Miss Frances knew what she was doing. You learn faster than any girl I've met.'

Willow appreciated his approval, but she said anxiously, 'I can understand their being annoyed, but I did think they liked me. Jenny's absolutely furious.'

Mr Elwood looked up briefly from the felt hat he was renovating with a mixture of benzine and water. 'When Jenny learned that Miss Jebb was going with Miss Violet, she had hopes of taking the maid's place. She's well qualified to do so, coming from a good home, educated and well-spoken.'

'Oh, dear, I didn't mean to upset anyone.'

'Of course you didn't. Will you stick it out? Do you feel like going back to the cosiness of the kitchen?'

'The kitchen isn't all that cosy when Mrs Narracott gets going,' said Willow ruefully.

'So I've heard.'

'Besides, this is what I want. When I came here I didn't know what life in a great house was like. I was beginning to think I might never be anything but a kitchen servant. I'm not going to give up now.'

'That's the ticket, my dear.'

Mrs Narracott, too, had been less than friendly but as the wedding day came near she paid little attention to anything that hadn't to do with food. The bride cake had been made weeks ago and was maturing in the pantry waiting for a professional confectioner to arrive from Exeter to cover it with marzipan and fancy icing. There were to be twenty-five different dishes for the wedding breakfast, four of fish, eleven of meat and game, and ten sweet dishes, while the gardeners were nursing along fresh fruit and exotic flowers in the hot houses and Mr Steadman and Mr Maddison held solemn conferences about the wine and liqueurs. Willow stayed out of the kitchen as much as possible, but there were some procedures which couldn't be tackled upstairs. She enjoyed watching the pre-wedding bustle and gradually most of the staff resumed their friendship. Only Ivy remained coolly aloof. Willow had missed the bustle of the kitchen and relished seeing what went on before so grand an affair as a wedding.

The kitchen was completely dominated by the preparation of the mountains of food which would be needed to feed the two hundred and fifty people invited to the reception, as well as close friends who had already arrived to stay. Prue told Willow that Miss Jebb now made quite frequent visits below-stairs. 'She's just showin' off because she'll be maid to a viscountess,' said Prue. Willow could well believe it. A mistress as beautiful and graceful as Violet, who was about to become extremely rich as well as the wife of a member of the nobility, was a walking advertisement for her maid.

Jebb had almost ceased to work for Frances, leaving Willow to manage as best she could. She told the kitchen staff about the wedding gown. 'It's so wonderful it quite took my breath away. Silver brocade, embroidered in white silk with roses and orange-flowers, and a twelve-foot train. Six pages will carry it – they'll be dressed in white satin shirts and black velvet knickerbockers. And there are six bridesmaids in the palest pink you can imagine, and six groomsmen to partner them. She'll wear white satin shoes with a tiny heel and she'll have white stockings. Her bouquet is to be white, too, roses with the thorns removed, and white satin ribbon. And the clothes she's taking away with her! And her underwear!' Miss Jebb's eyes rolled to heaven. 'I haven't the time to tell you the half of it.'

'Won't she have any colour at all?' asked Prue.

'Yes, indeed. You should just see Lord Radcliffe's present to her. Presents, actually. She's got a diamond tiara to hold her veil in place – that's made of old lace and was her great-grandmother's – and he's given her a necklace and bracelet to match the tiara. The jewels flash like fire whenever she moves. He's also bought her an ermine cape. I'm to wear a new gown and be ready in the background with the cape in case the weather turns cool,' she said importantly. 'Our Mr James is going to be best man to Lord Radcliffe. They say that because he's going to marry his lordship's sister he's like one of the family.' She left, saying, 'I'll have to be about my duties. Later this afternoon a photographer is coming to take pictures of the bride.'

Ivy said, 'Fancy havin' her photo took before the day! I'd be afraid. It's just askin' for fate to take a hand an' ruin everythin'.'

'I hope not,' said Willow.

Ivy, suddenly remembering that her former friend was there, flounced off. Willow remained to make strong tea for the renovation of a black lace shawl. She had listened avidly, though she had known some of the details of Violet's ensemble, and decided she'd rather have a husband she could trust than the presents.

180

She said so to Mrs Narracott who looked shrewdly at her. 'I dare say you're right. Never having been married and never wanting to be, I can't rightly say. Some society ladies don't seem to care overmuch that their husbands get up to that sort of thing, and some of the ladies are no better than they should be.'

Willow nodded, then remembered that Edgar would be home for the wedding and she would be far more accessible above-stairs. She didn't want to think of Edgar. She asked, 'Mrs Narracott, when is Mr James going to marry Lady Mary?'

The cook shook her head. 'Heaven knows. They've been engaged long enough. It's my opinion she's none too keen. He's as rackety a fellow as Lord Radcliffe. They make a fine pair.'

'Why is she engaged to him if she doesn't care for him?'

'Family pressure,' said Nancy. 'Both sets of parents think it's a good match.'

'My parents wouldn't make any of us marry someone we didn't like,' said Willow.

Ivy had come in with a bucket of coal. She laughed mirthlessly. 'Girls like us are lucky if we find a respectable chap to wed at all. Not everyone's lucky, though now you've wheedled yourself into a fancy job, I suppose you'll manage it.'

'Don't tell me you'd have refused a promotion,' snapped Willow, tired of the way Ivy goaded her.

Ivy went red. 'I'd never be asked, not in a million years. I should have known a girl with book-learnin' like yours would push her way to the top. An' of course, you've got the looks.'

'I can't help the way I look, Ivy.'

'None of us can,' said Prue. 'An' not every man wants a pretty wife. I mean, look at me!' She grinned. 'My man prefers an ordinary girl who won't be tempted to stray. I never will.'

'Nor would I,' said Willow.

'No, but you might just wander a bit beforehand, from what I've heard,' said Ivy.

'What do you mean?' Willow was incensed.

'I speak as I find,' said Ivy. 'A little bird told me that a certain kitchen maid who's recently got too big for her boots was seen in the grounds kissing a certain young gentleman.'

Willow went cold. So she and Edgar had been spotted. 'I've never encouraged any improper advances,' she protested.

'There's ways of sayin' "no" that can mean just the opposite,' taunted Ivy.

'They're not my ways,' cried Willow.

'Stop this at once,' ordered Mrs Narracott. 'Ivy, take yourself off to the pantry and make more room on the shelves. You'll have to crowd the things a bit.'

Ivy slammed out in a temper.

'She's jealous,' Prue said to Willow unnecessarily.

'I wish she wasn't.'

'You can't blame her,' said the cook. 'You're very lucky to rise to lady's maid so fast. Poor Ivy doesn't want to end her days as a servant. She would love to be married.'

'With her temper, chance will be a fine thing,' said Prue.

Mrs Narracott looked so annoyed at this unnecessary remark that Willow was afraid she might box a few ears, but she just tutted loudly and told Prue to get Ivy back to prepare the vegetables.

Willow had never ceased being troubled by thoughts of Edgar and was grateful that her hours had become so crammed with tasks that she had little time to devote to her day-dreams. At night she usually slept without difficulty. Sometimes, though, especially when she was cold, she lay awake listening to Aggie's adenoidal breathing and Ivy's soft snores, unable to dismiss the memory of Edgar's eyes, the feel of his mouth on hers. She thought of him so much that when she actually met him outside Frances's room she assumed for a few brief seconds that he was only there in her imagination.

He sprang into worrying reality when he said, 'Willow! Dear little Willow! I'm delighted to see you. I have heard of your promotion, and I'm really happy for you. That is, if you are happy?' he ended. He sounded as if he were truly concerned and Willow had to remind herself that people of his sort had had centuries to polish the art of concealing their feelings behind a mask of politeness.

'I enjoy my new job,' she said primly.

'Then I am happy for you,' he returned, mimicking her tone.

The barriers between them were melted by her laughter.

'Have you missed me?' he asked.

'What a silly question to put to your sister's maid! Of course not. Not for a single minute.'

'Oh, how disappointing. I had hoped for a few fleeting moments of your thoughts.'

'You're breaking my heart.'

'Nonsense! You haven't got a heart.'

'Do you enjoy Oxford?'

He shrugged. 'It's all right in parts. I enjoy the company of some of the fellows. They have a good social life going.'

'That should suit you.'

'How vinegary you sound.'

'You should take the chance to study. Some would give their eye teeth to go to university.'

'I would willingly relinquish my place to them.'

Willow thought of Joe and his keen brain; of herself lacking the schooling she wanted. 'You've got so much!' she burst out. 'And you don't care about it.'

He wasn't in the least put out. 'I know. Life isn't fair.' He reached out suddenly and pulled her towards him.

'No! Not here!'

'Not here? Does that indicate that you are willing to kiss me in private?'

'No! Not at all, but especially not here. Miss Frances is in her room,' she whispered urgently, 'and Mrs Maddison is with her.'

'They can't see through the door.' He glanced around

and laughed softly. 'In fact, there's no one to see.' He planted a kiss on her mouth. It could by no means be called passionate, more like the casual ones she received from her brothers. All the same, her face flamed, and her heart raced. Then Miss Jebb came out of Violet's room and saw them. They had moved apart but were still too close and Willow's blush was like a beacon. Jebb stared hard at them, her lip curling, before she made her way towards the back stairs.

'Damn!' Edgar was genuinely regretful. 'I was only giving you a friendly hello. Do you think she noticed?'

'Noticed? She's probably racing downstairs to tell the kitchen staff that she saw that hussy Lily being embraced by Mr Edgar. Oh, yes, she noticed all right.'

'Does it really matter?'

'Of course it does! Everything matters in this house.'

'My sisters won't take heed of servants' gossip.'

Willow said hotly, 'It wouldn't occur to you, would it, that when you speak of the servants you're talking about people I have to mix with every day? They could make my life hell. It's bad enough as it is.'

'What do you mean?' he asked sharply.

'Oh, nothing. Let me pass, please. Sir!'

His face darkened, he opened his mouth to say more, but closed it and allowed her to enter Frances's room. Frances was standing on a wooden stool in the centre while around her fussed a dressmaker and her assistant. Her mother sat on the edge of an easy chair watching, her face distorted by anger. The gown had been delivered from London and found to be too long.

'How dare you make such a mistake!' she had raged on the telephone. 'We travelled to London to purchase a Worth gown and *this* is the result. I shall insist on a reduction on my account.' When it was suggested that she and Frances return for another fitting her fury had increased. 'I shall most certainly not be put to such inconvenience! The dressmakers must come here.'

They had arrived an hour ago and were busily pinning

up the gown. Charles Frederick Worth had died some years before and the firm was ably carried on by his sons and still patronised by the smartest women who flocked to the store in Grosvenor Street. Apparently it was unheard of for the fitters to get a measurement wrong. Willow felt sorry for the quaking dressmakers because she knew that the apparent mistake had been brought about by Frances's leaving off the heavy corseting still required by Worth's gowns. She was so slender that she didn't need to have her figure confined into shape, and the heavy satin, high-waisted gown flowed over its wearer's body and descended to the floor unimpeded by whalebone.

When the alteration hands had finished and left Frances was amused. She considered the whole episode to be extremely funny and would no doubt relate it to her friends. 'Just think, Lily,' she said, 'if Mama finds out about the corset and makes me wear it on Violet's wedding day, my gown will be too short. Imagine the commotion.' Willow could easily imagine and she shuddered and wondered if someone would blame her.

When the bedroom was empty Willow busied herself in tidying it. This was a task she thoroughly enjoyed. She loved the feel of the fine lawn and silk and nainsook underwear with its broderie anglaise and lace trimmings. She held the lace of a petticoat to her face. It was delicately scented with rosemary and hadn't been worn. Miss Frances had a way of changing her mind several times when dressing and Willow always carefully folded the discarded underclothes and hung the abandoned gowns of silk and velvet, feathers and fur, in the wardrobe which took up almost the whole of one wall, checking carefully for buttons missing, rents or soiled patches.

Today no work was needed and she had time to spare – and time was what she struggled to achieve. She picked up the magazines which Frances had perused over her late breakfast in bed. Opening them she saw names which were becoming familiar to her, and reproductions of gowns which fascinated her. Some of the magazines were French: *Les Modes*, *Gazette du Bon Ton* and *Le Figaro*.

Willow couldn't understand a word of the text, but the illustrations she understood very well and worked out how the clothes must have been cut. The English magazines carried articles on artists and designers too, Georges Lepape and Madame Paquin who, while Willow had been struggling to become an efficient kitchen maid, had enjoyed a huge success in an Exhibition in Brussels.

She read of Whistler, George Braque and Pablo Picasso. The first artist was praised, but harsh criticisms were made of the other two and she wondered why. The black and white illustration of an 'abstract' work by Braque puzzled her, yet in an odd way the shapes, horizontal and vertical, drawn it might seem haphazardly, pleased her. The brilliant colours of the new wave painters – 'Fauves' – were described and she realised that the latest gowns favoured by many young women had been inspired by them. The colours of the clothes mirrored the palettes of the painters, and their straighter, more severe lines owed much to the abstract artists. Somewhere there was a world where art in every form flourished and vibrated with new ideas which flowered and ripened and she longed to discover it.

Above all, she thrilled to the accounts of the *Ballet Russe*, and Serge Diaghilev, Leon Bakst and Nijinsky. She was able now to distinguish the designers of clothes from the stage designers, the visual artists from the dancers. One day, she promised herself, one day she would visit the shops and theatres and see everything, but most of all she wanted to go to Paris to see the innovators, the men and women who were creating styles which would change fashion for ever.

April had produced showers and some unseasonably cool weather, but 1 May, Violet's wedding day, was clear and bright. The servants were up at five and Willow suspected that Mrs Narracott hadn't slept at all, so heavy-eyed and crotchety was she.

All the staff who could be spared were permitted to

stand outside the front door and watch as the wedding party left for the church. A procession of carriages and pairs was ranged along the drive and a bevy of sweating nannies shepherded the excited pages and flower girls into their vehicles, muttering dire threats beneath their breath to those who got over-excited. Then the bridesmaids and groomsmen took their places. Frances gave the servants a smile. Edgar smiled, too, and Willow was sure he had allowed his glance to linger on her. He looked so handsome in his morning suit and top hat, and so out of her reach.

Finally, the bride's father helped her into her carriage which was resplendent with white ribbons and drawn by matched greys with jingling, gleaming brasses and white rosettes.

'Miss Violet looks too beautiful to be real,' sighed Willow.

'She does that,' agreed Ivy, her unfriendliness forgotten for the moment in the drama of the occasion. 'I wish I could have a weddin' dress like that.'

The coachman and footman wore livery and top hats and for a moment Willow didn't recognise Andy Hunnicott who had met her at the station when she had arrived. The driver's long whip curled about the horses' ears without actually stinging them, Andy folded his arms and the carriage rolled down the drive to the church where the 'pretty country wedding', as Mrs Maddison had termed it, was to be solemnised.

'Pretty country wedding!' said Mrs Narracott, as they all hurried indoors. 'It'd have been a lot easier if she'd held it in London and engaged a hotel for the reception.'

'You'd have preferred that?' asked Jenny, slyly.

The cook snapped, 'Of course not. It's just that *they* never seem to understand anything that happens down here.'

Frances's room was chaotic, but Willow was glad to get back to it. For the first time she truly appreciated the difference in her life. She knew to the last task what would be happening in the kitchen and she sat for a moment and revelled in serenity and peace. Miss Brayton had been dispatched to the church porch to arrange the gowns perfectly before their wearers walked down the aisle and Jebb was packed ready to leave with Violet, Lady Radcliffe, as she would be, and had lost interest in Willow. Frances had tried on four petticoats and three pairs of knickers before she was satisfied that they wouldn't spoil the cut of her gown. Mrs Maddison permitted the discreet use of face-powder and Frances had tipped a whole box on to the carpet. Willow went to work and by the time she heard the bells ring out from the church tower the room was clear and the powder-covered furniture dusted. She heard excited voices as young women came upstairs and Frances led a bevy of them into her room.

'Lily,' she cried, 'set to work with a will. We have brought you torn hems, a missing button, a lady who needs a restorative . . .'

The room was filled with girls who laughed and chattered like so many pastel-coloured birds. They entered with a swoop, and left as precipitately, and again Willow cleared up the mess. As she worked she became aware of the lost comradeship of her former workmates.

'Count your blessings,' she muttered, recalling one of Gran's phrases. One of the greatest blessings of her new place was the rise in her wages to twenty-one pounds a year – an unprecedented increase. Mrs Westerby had fumed, while Willow was delighted to be able to increase the size of the postal order she sent to Clara. Gran had written to tell her that with the extra, plus the bit of money the boys brought in, Mum had been able to take in less washing.

'It's lucky you got such a wonderful raise,' Gran's letter had read. 'Your dad needs a deal of looking after nowadays.'

Every time Willow remembered the words she felt grief and rebellion rise in her like gall. She was imprisoned here while Dad grew weaker and more sick. She wanted to be near him, to see him every day as the others did, to give a hand in nursing him.

Frances leaned back in an easy chair, watching her maid

mend a tear in her riding habit. 'You're so clever,' she said. 'But are you clever enough to keep secrets?'

Willow looked up sharply. 'Secrets?' She remembered the time when she had imagined herself as a messenger in an illicit love affair. Since working at Buddleigh Manor she knew that such clandestine behaviour would earn instant dismissal.

'Don't look so startled. They're not very wicked. Well, they are not wicked at all.'

'Perhaps you had best not tell me,' said Willow firmly.

'I think I shall, though not today. You could be of help to me.'

Frances travelled with her parents to London for the Private View at the Royal Academy and Willow and Miss Brayton went with them.

'Such a bore,' yawned Frances when she returned to the rented house. 'I cannot bear walking round staring at hundreds of pictures, smiling practically without ceasing.'

Willow almost gave way to angry indignation. She would give a great deal to look at pictures. She said levelly, 'I'm sorry, miss.'

'Are you, Lily? I don't believe you are.'

'Don't you, miss?'

'No. Come now, admit it.'

Willow smiled. 'I would like to go to an art gallery, miss.'

Frances waved her arm in an exaggerated fashion. 'Then you shall go to the ball.'

'What?'

'Think of me as the fairy in the pantomime. Don't tell me you've not visited a pantomime? Nanny took us every year.'

'I went twice, Mum says, but I was too young to remember. Afterwards they couldn't afford it. My father's never been strong and was often out of work.'

'Poor you.' Frances frowned. 'Why don't you go to the National Gallery on your afternoon off? You will find a feast of art there.'

'I've never been out by myself in London!'

'You will be perfectly safe. I am sure it cannot be difficult to find the direction.'

Willow asked Mrs Narracott about travelling around London.

'It's easy,' she said. 'Find a main road and take an omnibus.'

Willow did find it easy and spent all her time off visiting art galleries and stores, especially those which sold materials and gowns. She wore her summer clothes: a muslin blouse, pin-tucked, with long, lacy sleeves and a lace Peter Pan collar which had once belonged to Violet, and a navy serge skirt. Her outfit was completed by white cotton gloves and a straw boater with navy ribbon beneath which she pinned her abundant hair. She examined her appearance in Miss Frances's cheval glass. The severe style suited her well. She returned from these expeditions swamped by new impressions. To think she might have spent her life not knowing that London was so filled with glorious beauty.

There were days when she felt weary. Frances's life was filled with parties, operas and balls, and often as Willow helped her out of her clothes in the early hours of the morning she chattered about the men she had met. The name Ernest Bickford came up often.

Mr Bickford, it appeared, was unparalleled. He was tall, handsome, and much sought after by society mamas as a husband for their daughters, a fact which seemed to spur Frances on. 'I think he likes me best,' she enthused.

'You could be next down the aisle,' said Willow. 'That's if Mr James doesn't marry Lady Mary first.'

'I wonder?' smiled Frances. 'Mr Bickford hasn't made a declaration. It is much too soon.' She had just returned from the customary stroll in Hyde Park in which Mr Bickford had joined her and Mrs Maddison and she looked extremely pretty, the colour of her complexion matching her pale rose gown. 'Oh, Lily, do you think I might be falling in love?'

She grew exacting over her appearance. Mr Bickford liked women to be dressed in a feminine way, but not too frilly.

Mr Bickford enjoyed plays and books of a serious nature. He smoked an occasional cigar and drank in moderation. His mother acted as hostess for him until he should be married, when she would be tidied away into the Dower House. When he first came to dinner Willow managed to catch a glimpse of him by peering through the carved balusters. He was handsome in a way, but his face was narrow and his mouth stern. She wondered why Frances favoured him. Perhaps it was the attraction of opposites. Frances was energetically encouraged by her parents, which didn't surprise Willow when she discovered from Mrs Narracott that Ernest Bickford was richer than Lord Radcliffe, had led an exemplary life, had political ambitions and would be just the man Miss Frances needed to curb her frivolity.

Frances had also made a special friend. Miss Jane Barton was not pretty, but she had animation and a strong will and Frances was inclined to follow her dictates. Except in one instance. When Willow overheard Miss Barton advising Frances not to get too fond of Mr Bickford, Frances rebelled and said coolly that it was none of Miss Barton's business. Willow wondered if Miss Barton was after Mr Bickford herself; she took a decided interest in politics. She was also a champion of women and Willow wondered at Mr and Mrs Maddison's allowing the friendship, but apparently Jane was socially unimpeachable.

'Mr Bickford does not care for Miss Barton,' Frances blurted out one day after she had been riding with him in Rotten Row.

Willow didn't reply. She didn't care for Jane herself. If it came to that, she didn't much like the sound of Mr Bickford either; she wouldn't want a man who tried to control her as strictly as he did Frances. Perhaps that was why she felt such ambivalence over Edgar. He was strong-willed, wanting his own way, trying to push her into situations which suited him, yet he could be understanding and kind and she still felt drawn to him and missed him. She hadn't seen him since the wedding. He had gone to America. Frances had said, 'Perhaps he will meet an heiress there. He's the younger son and it would be best for him to marry a fortune.' She had laughed. 'He would probably do better here. London is full of wealthy American girls just longing to be joined to an old family, preferably a titled one.'

Chapter Eleven

In August Mr and Mrs Maddison left London (she reluctantly) and went to Scotland for the shooting. Frances and Willow were to go to Mynster, the family seat of the Lamberts. Only Winifred and the nursery detachment had gone to the Bristol house before departing for a seaside holiday.

Frances was excited. 'Mr Bickford has been invited to Mynster and my brother James will be there. I wonder if he and Lady Mary will make a date for their wedding? I know that Lord and Lady Somervell are annoyed at the long delay.' Willow had once been puzzled at the profusion of names owned by a single titled family. She had asked Henry about it.

'It seems the aristocracy need a lot of different ones,' he said. 'I think it goes with owning a lot of different things.' Willow knew now that the Somervells were the parents of Violet's husband, Lord Radcliffe, and Lady Mary.

When Frances spoke to her, as she sometimes did, in a familiar way about her family, Willow never answered, having decided that an answer wasn't really required of her and could at best be tactless. And she had soon discovered that Frances had a disconcerting way of allowing her maid one day to give an opinion, and on another pulling her up sharply.

'Lady Mary is so sweet,' enthused Frances. 'I just long for her to become a proper sister.'

She paused and Willow said, 'Will there be many other guests, miss?'

'I don't know. There may be, though we already have

enough for tennis and croquet during the day. There are sure to be dinner parties and a dance.'

She wandered off, leaving Willow to pack her gowns, a skill she had learned from Mr Elwood.

Mynster was in Gloucestershire, a long, two-storey building in dark grey stone. The moment she saw it, Willow loved it.

She asked the coachman, 'Is it very old?'

He was elderly and morose. 'Yes.'

'How old?'

'Hundreds of years. And it's always been lived in by the same family.'

'How wonderful.'

The coachman glanced at her and was moved by her obvious admiration. 'Once upon a time,' he said, 'there was an abbey here, but Henry the Eighth pulled it down. Then Queen Elizabeth gave the land to the Lamberts, a Protestant family, and handed over the titles with it. It seems that some of the Lamberts had a rough time under Queen Mary.' As if feeling he had been loquacious enough for one day, his mouth shut like a trap and nothing Willow could say would make him open it. She sat back, revelling in the sunshine, studying the meadows and hedges which were gloriously alive with colour and bird-song, until they arrived at the great gates of Mynster. The coachman growled, 'They're the original gates, but the walls are new.'

'How new?'

He merely grunted thanks to the aproned woman who ran out of a small stone gate-lodge to open the gates. The walls, which must have been ten feet high, were composed of bricks faded to a deep, glowing pink. Just the right colour for a gown for Frances.

Willow supervised the unloading of the luggage and asked the footman and housemaids to carry it to her mistress's room, following them feeling almost like a young lady herself. The room was empty, but Frances had been in residence for half an hour and it was already muddled. She had been fetched from the station by her brother James in his new Daimler and her motoring mantle was thrown carelessly on to a chair, her hat and veil on the bed and her gloves on the floor. Willow busied herself putting them away, then turned her attention to unpacking Frances's trunks and hat boxes, sighing with relief when she saw that most of the clothes were uncreased. She decided to descend to the kitchen to borrow a flat iron. A footman told her the way and nervously Willow pushed open the green baize door leading to the kitchen. A number of pairs of eyes turned to her and conversation stopped. It was just the same as when she had first gone to Buddleigh Manor.

She smiled and introduced herself and the cook invited her to take tea with them. She went with the others to the servants' hall where the kitchen maids were ready to wait on them. Precedence was as strict as that in the manor. Lord Somervell's valet was paired by Lady Radcliffe's maid, Miss Jebb, Lord Radcliffe's valet led Willow, the butler held out his arm for Lady Mary's maid. The others formed themselves into pairs and joined the housekeeper who was already seated at the head of the table and tea was served, a substantial one which Willow needed. Her appetite had increased since good food had always been available to her. Fortunately, the only weight she had gained was in the right places and she caught several of the male servants eyeing her. One of them, a footman, winked, an action which was seen by the butler who clearly marked his subordinate down for a good ticking off.

When Frances returned to her room, still wearing her travelling gown, she was in high spirits. 'There you are, Lily. I fear that my emerald green taffeta is a little creased. I want to wear it tonight. Mr Bickford is very fond of green.' On being assured that Willow had arranged for the immediate use of an iron, she bubbled on, 'I always forget how sweet Lady Mary is when I'm not with her.' Just like her fiancé from all accounts, thought Willow. 'I wish that stupid brother of mine would marry her. Do you know, Lily, I've a suspicion that the earl is becoming rather tired of Mary's procrastination. I would almost bet that a date will be fixed during this visit.'

Willow held up the gown and Frances stepped into it. In Willow's opinion her mistress's fair, rather fragile beauty was all but eclipsed by the shining green material, but when she had ventured to suggest something paler she had been put sharply in her place. 'Strong colours are all the rage. I felt a positive idiot at Miss Violet's wedding, though of course we all had to wear pastel shades.'

Willow brushed her mistress's hair and dressed it off her face, swirled into a crown embellished with tortoiseshell combs studded with tiny semi-precious green stones. The small, pretty face needed a few curls over the forehead and round the ears, but again Willow's proposal met with opposition by Frances who had the means to follow fashion slavishly, without the taste which would make her look her best. Her evening gloves and shoes were white, as was her feathered fan, and her earrings were of gold. She surveyed herself in the cheval glass with satisfaction. Late that night she came to her room looking downcast and allowed Willow to remove her clothes and place a wrap round her.

'Do you feel unwell, Miss Frances?'

'No.' She sat at her dressing table while Willow unpinned her hair. 'You're rough tonight! You're hurting me!'

'I'm sorry, miss.'

Willow began to brush the soft fair hair with long strokes.

'Ah, that's soothing.' Frances closed her eyes and Willow saw a couple of tears roll down her cheeks. 'Lily, I was so full of happiness when I went down to dinner, but Mr Bickford—' She stopped, biting her lip. Willow helped her mistress into bed and as she turned off the gas, leaving her with a lighted candle by her bed, Frances said, 'Tomorrow you may get rid of the emerald silk gown. I hate it.'

Mynster, Willow discovered, was very different from Buddleigh Manor. To begin with, the place was full of dogs. Each member of the family owned at least two and they were adored and pampered and allowed the run of the downstairs rooms. Lady Mary's favourite, a tiny pomeranian, slept wheezily on her bed. Everything was old and looked it, the family portraits needed cleaning and the dogs had torn the carpets and upholstery, yet the overall impression was one of comfort and serenity. The atmosphere in the servants' hall, despite its occupants' attention to protocol, was relaxed, the housekeeper a welcome visitor. The summer lingered and the tennis court was used daily, which kept Willow busy ensuring that the supply of her mistress's tennis whites never ran out. Frances seemed to have recovered from her disappointment and spoke often of Mr Bickford.

'Did you get rid of my green taffeta?' she asked Willow.

'Er, not exactly, miss.'

'What do you mean?' Frances was annoyed.

'I thought of an alteration which might please you.' She went to the wardrobe and drew out the taffeta gown. 'I've taken the ivory lace over-tunic from the brown frock you say you've never cared for and tried it over the green. It isn't fixed, of course, because I need your approval, but see how well the lace tones down the colour. If you like it, may I suggest that you wear it with a big lacy bow around the knees which will transform it into a proper hobble skirt – all the rage,' Willow finished cunningly.

Frances frowned, then smiled. 'Lily, you're so clever. Do please transform the gown for me. Can you have it ready for tomorrow night?'

Willow spent most of the day sewing. When she went into the corridor on her way to the kitchen to use the flat-iron, she found her way barred by Edgar.

'You!' she said stupidly.

'Why not me?'

'I thought you were in America.'

'Well, I am not. I returned yesterday, and when I discovered that you were not in the manor I hot-footed it over here.'

'Oh.'

'I missed you, Willow.'

'Please, sir, let me pass.'

'In a moment. Tell me you missed me.'

'Did you find an American heiress?'

'What?'

'I was told you were searching for a rich wife.'

'Is that so? When do you finish work? Never, I suppose. My family are tartars with their maids. Do you get an afternoon off sometimes?'

'That's no concern of yours.' Willow tried to side-step him and again he blocked her way. 'Let me pass! Miss Frances wants to wear this gown tonight. She has a special reason for doing so.'

'What reason?'

'I don't know. Ask her.'

'I'm asking you. I shall not allow you to pass until you tell me what you think.'

Willow stared up into his face and softened. You couldn't use the word beautiful about a man, but if you did, it would surely apply to Edgar.

'Are you satisfied?' he asked softly.

She felt colour creeping into her face. 'Mr Edgar, I shall be told off by Miss Frances if I don't get this done. It's almost time to dress for dinner and I have to iron the seams. I've altered the gown to suit her.'

'Clever little Willow.'

'I'm not so little. I'm not all that much shorter than you.'

'That's true,' he agreed blandly. 'You must pay to pass. One kiss.'

'Someone might see. You embarrassed me before.'

'You see, you do want to kiss me. You're only afraid.'

'So would you be if your livelihood and your family's depended on keeping a job. If your mother heard a breath of scandal about me—'

'One kiss,' he begged.

She capitulated. He was selfish and careless, but she wanted desperately to feel his lips on hers. 'One,' she said.

He kissed her, his mouth gentle, his hands not touching her. She broke away and he allowed her to hurry past him.

'Mr Bickford complimented me on my gown,' said Frances that night. 'Do you know, Lily, I don't think he realised it was the same one he so disliked the first time I wore it.'

'Most men don't take much notice of a woman's clothes,' said Willow. She was gratified that her skill had been put to the test and passed.

Inevitably, it seemed to Willow, Edgar happened to come along whenever she was alone. When everyone had gone on a picnic and she thought she was safe from him, he actually entered his sister's bedroom and sprawled in an easy chair, watching her tidying.

'What a messy girl Frances is. Don't you ever get fed up with her?'

'It's not my place to get fed up.'

'No, but I'd bet a tenner you do.'

'You'd lose your money. I've never been so happy.'

'I could make you happier.'

'I wish you wouldn't say those things. You know you don't mean them.'

'If you believed I did, would you be more friendly?'

'No, and anyway you don't.'

'But I do! And to what "things" precisely do you refer?'

Willow stopped work and gazed at him steadfastly and it was his turn to colour. 'Willow, you know I want terribly to kiss you. You are the prettiest girl I have ever met.'

'Nonsense!'

'It's true.' He sprang up and came to her, grabbing her arms. 'It's true and I know you want me as much as I do you.'

His kiss this time was deeper and as she felt his tongue moving on hers Willow pushed herself close to his body, straining to hold his mouth. He released her arms which crept round his neck, her fingers entwined his hair. She heard the soft footfall just in time and jumped away. 'There's someone outside.'

'Good God!' Edgar darted across the room and took cover behind a chaise longue.

There was a cursory knock and Miss Brayton walked in. 'How are you, Lily? You look rather dishevelled. Mrs Maddison has arrived. She doesn't care for shooting and has decided to join the family. To be honest with you, I think she has hopes of arranging a wedding date for Mr James. I know the earl and countess are impatient.'

Willow wasn't surprised at Miss Brayton's sudden friend-liness which was probably being used to infuriate Miss Jebb.

'I'm well, thank you,' she said, answering the first question and, because of Edgar's unseen presence, refusing to be drawn on anything else. She managed to steer the conversation along tedious lines and soon Miss Brayton left, looking disappointed.

Edgar crawled out from behind the chaise longue and dusted his knees. 'Phew! I'd forgotten the maids. What fascinating conversations you have, though I wish you had not stalled Brayton whenever she began to get interesting. Do you know everything about us?'

'I shouldn't think so. Now, will you leave! You could get me dismissed.'

'Then you could come and be my personal servant,' said Edgar cheerfully. He stared into her eyes. 'You'd like to box my ears, wouldn't you?' He stepped back in simulated fear. 'Please don't,' he pleaded, laughing, 'you've got the muscles of a prize fighter. I remember.'

His ability to make her laugh always breached her defences. 'I'm going downstairs,' she said. 'Even you won't dare to follow me to the hallowed precincts of the servants' hall.'

'Correct me if you like, but hasn't your vocabulary increased? Yes, it has. I like the way you walk, too, the way you carry yourself – and your speech is different. I do believe you've bettered yourself.'

The mundane phrase, so beloved by some of the working-class folk to whom she belonged, so despised by others who had no wish to emulate the nobs, irritated Willow, emerging as it did from the lips of this brash young aristocrat. He had suddenly become one of Them and she despised herself for her weakness in liking him so much. Gran had told her tales of servant girls ruined by young gentlemen, then simply turfed out to fend for themselves. She wasn't going to relinquish her ambition for the sake of a few stolen kisses. His instinctive rush to hide made it clear that anything between them must be kept clandestine.

'How kind of you,' she said. 'At least, I think you meant to be kind. Now I'm going.'

'You have not heard the last of me,' growled Edgar, twirling imaginary moustaches. This time she waited until he had left before she laughed. Drat the man! He could get round her so easily, but she wasn't any man's for the taking, certainly not one who could have no respectable intentions towards her.

Frances came bursting in and kicked off her shoes, threw her shady hat on the floor and plumped down on the bed. 'My sister Violet—' she began, and choked over the words. 'Lady Radcliffe has been shopping in Paris. I've just looked into her wardrobe and it's absolutely crammed with the most heavenly gowns you ever saw. Who would have supposed that the Empire line would become so popular? It was the fashion in Napoleon's time. The colours! Brilliant scarlet, heavenly blue, bright yellow – oh, I feel so cross! Why can't I go to Paris?'

'Can't you, miss?' asked Willow.

'No. Mama sees no necessity for it. She is exceedingly irritated with me because my allowance for the month is gone and I've had to borrow from her. I could not afford the fare of a tramcar.' Her face suddenly lit up. 'Lily, I've just remembered! You are so clever with your needle. If I let you see my sister's gowns, do you think you could copy them? You made over my green so beautifully!'

Willow was startled. 'Fixing a lace overdress is very different from copying haute couture.'

Frances was startled. 'Where did you learn that expression?'

'I take the liberty of reading your magazines, Miss Frances. I hope you don't mind?'

'Of course I don't. I'm glad. You must have seen the Ballet Russe-inspired gowns by Poiret?'

'Yes, miss, but those styles are beginning to pass and Monsieur Poiret is not the only designer. There is Madame Paquin. Her clothes are very elegant and she uses colours better suited to you than those of the Fauve painters. And then there's John Redfern of the Maison Redfern; he was one of the first to bring in the Grecian line, and his suits and gowns are seen everywhere.'

Frances's mouth didn't quite drop. 'How much you know! You amaze me, Lily!'

'It's all in your magazines, miss.'

'Is it really? I must read them more carefully in future. Could you do it, do you think?'

'Do what?'

Frances said impatiently, 'Turn one of my gowns into the very latest style. I will not be outdone by Lady Radcliffe, I will not!' She sounded like a petulant child. Willow half expected her to stamp her foot.

'I can try, I suppose,' she said soothingly.

'Good.' Frances raced across the room to her wardrobe. 'Is there anything here? How about this?' She dragged out an almost new Prussian blue gown. It was entirely wrong for her, but when Willow thought of the consequences if she ruined it she felt faint. It had cost a great deal of money.

'What if I can't manage it? What if I spoil it?'

'Oh, don't worry. Whatever happens I will take the blame.'

Remembering the way in which Frances had held herself aloof during the episode of the lost brooch, something she could not have failed to know about, Willow felt doubtful. She picked up the gown and stroked its silken folds. The temptation to work on it was too great to resist. 'I'll try, Miss Frances.'

'Thank you, Lily, you are an absolute gem.' She raced out and returned quickly with an orange tunic embellished with black velvet spots and a red collar. 'I took it right under Brayton's nose,' she laughed. 'I said I wanted to try it on to see if the colour suited me. She was furious, but nothing to what Violet will be if she catches me. Quick, Lily, draw it and it may give you some ideas.'

Nowadays Willow was at liberty to carry her pad and pencil in her pocket and she hurriedly drew them out. Her pencil raced over the paper. 'I can't possibly match that gown,' she said. 'There, I've finished drawing it. You had better return it. I have an idea . . .'

'I knew you would.' Frances hurried out and was back again in moments. 'Now, what are you going to do?'

'Your gown has the higher waist,' said Willow. 'I need some gauze, pale blue or pink.'

'Pink?' Frances looked doubtful. 'I am sick of pink. Mama always insists on my having pink gowns.'

'Where can I get gauze?' asked Willow.

'There's a village nearby which has a good drapery shop. It's a little too far to walk. I'll get someone to take you there.'

'Shall I show you my idea first?'

'No. I trust you. Just do it. I should like to wear it tonight.'

'That's impossible. I can do it by tomorrow night if I can use a sewing machine.'

'There is bound to be one somewhere. Ask the house-keeper. Oh, dear, I must run. I should be downstairs. Mr Bickford is waiting to take a stroll with me before dinner. Quickly, get out my Oxfords. No, don't bother, put your hat on. The shop may close at any moment.'

When Willow reached the stable yard she was dismayed to find Edgar waiting with a pony and trap.

'How did you get dragged into this?'

He bent to give her a hand up. 'Not dragged, Willow.

Frances asked me to engage a coachman and I engaged myself.' He flourished his whip over the pony's head and it pulled the trap over the cobbles and out on to the drive. 'I understand that you are anxious to reach the village before the shops shut?'

'I suppose I am.'

'Why so lugubrious?'

'None of your business.'

'I suppose it is something to do with my sister? Something she prefers to keep secret.'

'Suppose away,' said Willow, clutching the low side of the trap as the trotting pony skimmed it along the road. She arrived at the shop just as it was about to close, but the smiling owner was pleased to serve the maid of one of the young ladies visiting Mynster.

'Such a lovely lady, the countess,' she said, 'and Lady Mary – the sweetest girl you could wish to meet. Gauze, is it? I've got plenty in white, but not much in colour. Pale pink? No, but I do have a good length of pale blue – ordered by a customer, it was, an' never fetched.'

Willow paid for the material and took her seat in the trap. Edgar drove well and she leaned back, her eyes closed, enjoying the breeze. They stopped. 'Are we there already?' She opened her eyes. The trap had pulled up beneath an avenue of trees which gave a greenish hue to the filtered sunlight.

'Stop frowning, Lily-Willow,' he said. 'That slips off the tongue quite nicely, doesn't it? I maintain that you are the prettiest girl I ever met and I don't care tuppence that you began in our kitchen.' He wound the reins around his wrist and slid along the seat towards her.

She moved away until she was in danger of falling out. 'Drive on, please. Miss Frances wants me to refurbish her gown for tonight.'

'Liar,' he said softly. 'She's already told me it's going to be ready by tomorrow.'

'Well, she did want it. And if you don't let me get back, I'll be up all night sewing.'

'You're up practically all night in any event, waiting for Frances to come to bed.'

Willow set her lips. He leaned forward until he could see her face. 'Nothing you can do will make your mouth any less kissable.'

Willow was abruptly angry. 'Leave me alone! I mean it! I've no intention of allowing you to disrupt my life. Not ever! You're taking advantage of my dependence in your house, and now here! I don't even know where I am, or how to get back to Mynster.' She was tired, and disgusted with herself when her voice wobbled.

'Willow, I haven't made you cry, have I?'

He sounded so tender, so genuinely regretful, that she would have liked to turn to him and surrender to the impulse which could only land her with insuperable problems.

'No, I'm not crying. Edgar, please call off your pursuit. You can have your pick of so many well-born, beautiful women who'd be glad to fall in love with you. Why persecute me?'

Edgar was silent. Then he slid back to the driving position and the trap sped on until it arrived once more in the stable yard. She picked up her parcel, a groom ran to the pony's head and Edgar helped her down. He didn't look into her face and she ran into the house, seething with a mixture of regret, longing and unhappiness that threatened to burst forth in frustrated tears.

Willow took out the bright blue gown and hung it on a hanger over the wardrobe door. She measured it before kneeling to cut the gauze, after which she made her way to the small room leading off the kitchen where a sewing machine stood on a table ready for use. She hemmed the raw edges of the gauze and returned and pinned it on the gown in the way she had visualised.

When Frances returned she looked flushed and happy. 'Mr Bickford is a very interesting man, Lily.'

'I'm glad, miss.'

Frances saw the gown. 'It's so pretty! How did you do

it? Blue gauze, too. Delightful! Quite delightful!' She was so bubbling over with determination to be appreciative that Willow wondered what had taken place with Mr Bickford.

'I've only pinned it by the inside seams,' she said. 'I needed your opinion before I actually begin. If it goes wrong you'll never be able to wear it again because it'll be ruined.'

'Oh!' Frances pouted. 'I had hoped to wear it tonight.'

'I told you, Miss Frances, it's impossible to complete it in so short a time.' The enormity of Frances's expectations left Willow breathless.

'Can I have it by tomorrow?'

'I'll do my best.' A best which would be enhanced, she reflected, if Frances didn't always leave the room in such a state of chaos. As soon as she had gone down to dinner and Willow had tidied, she began her work. She took a long piece of gauze and draped it round the shoulders of the blue gown. It fell to the floor in hazy folds and she drew the ends back to the waist, creating slim panniers. She secured the high waist with gauze, forming a built-in sash just beneath the bosom. As she had envisaged, the gauze toned down the Prussian blue to an acceptable shade and the parts of the original gown which were left uncovered were not enough to dominate the whole. She had removed four blue silk ornamental buttons and sewn them to the sash in a square. When she had finished she stood back and surveyed her work and was actually surprised. It looked good. It looked right.

She stretched her aching limbs and glanced at the bedside clock. It was two o'clock in the morning. She had forgotten to go down for servants' supper and was very hungry. She decided to descend to the kitchen and get herself a snack. She found bread and cheese and made herself a cup of cocoa, then returned to continue her vigil. On her way she met Miss Brayton who looked very tired. Willow realised, for the first time, that the maid was growing old. What happened to elderly spinsters when they were forced to give up work? Did a servant ever manage to save enough to live on?

'Another late night,' said Miss Brayton. 'Where have you been?'

When Willow told her, she said, 'I hope you tidied everything away.'

'Of course. I know better than anyone how annoyed the cook gets if things are disturbed.'

Miss Brayton nodded. 'I get weary waiting. I wish I could cat-nap, but that blessing is denied me, unlike Mr Elwood who can sleep in an instant. It keeps him looking young. Can you sleep easily?'

'When I'm in bed. I don't try until I'm there.'

'Youth,' said Miss Brayton. 'I've forgotten mine.'

When Frances came to bed at three o'clock, she was glittering with excitement. 'Mr Bickford is such an entertaining man, Lily. He has hopes of entering Parliament – as a Tory of course.' A shadow passed over her face so swiftly that Willow might have imagined it, then she was chattering again. In bed she sat up. 'Have you done the gown? Where is it? Show it to me!' When she saw it she stared hard. 'Isn't that style called "pegtop"? I think I saw one rather similar in a magazine.'

Willow was delighted that she had created something recognisable. 'Yes, Miss Frances. It's the very latest thing.'

'You're a gem, Lily, a positive gem.' She yawned. 'God, I'm tired.' She snuggled beneath the bedclothes. 'Goodnight.'

'Goodnight, miss.' Willow put the clothes away and turned out the gas, then she went to the small room allocated her on the same landing. Tomorrow she would ask Frances to repay the money she had spent in the village shop. She only hoped she'd get it.

She didn't. Frances was dreadfully sorry. 'Too naughty of me, but I will repay you as soon as I get my next allowance. It is due in September.'

She looked appealingly pretty in her new gown. She wore a simple necklace of sapphires and earrings to match. In a mellow mood she permitted her maid to tease out a few curls to frame her face and wore a dainty headdress of blue satin with a curling blue feather. Willow watched her go down to dinner, feeling both triumphant and apprehensive.

After the meal Willow was surprised when Violet came into the bedroom. She gave a bobbing curtsy. 'Lady Radcliffe.'

'My sister says you made the gown she is wearing. I do not believe it. It is in the pegtop style and where would you learn such skills? You are not capable.'

'I didn't make it,' began Willow.

'As I suspected.' Violet looked into the cheval glass and touched her own gown with reverent fingers. 'I chose this after looking through a book of designs drawn by Georges Lepape for Poiret – he is the greatest designer in Paris and Lepape one of the greatest artists. Which means, of course, in the world.'

'It's beautiful,' said Willow, and meant it, though she wondered why her ladyship was troubling herself to talk to such a lowly member of the household. Her eyes devoured the flowing muslin skirt which stopped at the ankles, the draped over-tunic of silk which reached the wearer's knees, where it was edged with fur and wired to make it stand out from the body. The entire gown was a poem in white and grey with hand-embroidered pale pink and green flowers executed after the style of the modern painters. Bangles rattled on Violet's arms and a rope of pearls adorned her neck. She looked overwhelmingly lovely and Willow stored away impressions to set down later.

'I shall go now and tell my sister how naughty she is,' said her ladyship, clearly revelling in the idea.

Willow was alarmed. 'Miss Violet, I beg your pardon, Lady Radcliffe, please wait a moment.'

Violet turned, her chin up, her haughty gaze meant to demolish an importunate servant.

Willow rushed on, 'I didn't *make* Miss Frances's gown, but I altered it.'

'Altered it?'

Willow explained and saw Violet looked extremely irritable. 'Where did you learn such skills? Am I not correct in believing that you were promoted from the kitchen?' She gave the last word the same inflection she would have given to 'hell'.

'Quite correct, my lady, but you may remember that I've always been interested in fashions? I've drawn them for as long as I can recall. I used to sit on the Downs in Bristol and wait for you to come along and draw you. Your clothes were always so marvellous.' She had hoped to placate Lady Radcliffe with her rather unctuous words. She failed.

'I do recall some idiotic incident on the Downs, though I cannot remember your part in it.' Violet swept out, still obviously furious, though no more so than Willow.

'Idiotic incident! Your part! I can't think why she should be so angry,' Willow said later to Miss Brayton, 'when she's got the whole of the fashion world to pick from.'

'She's got a jealous nature,' said Miss Brayton. 'Probably she can't bear to think she could have taken you as her maid and didn't.'

'Do you think she'll want me now?'

'She may try, she hates to be outdone, but Miss Frances can be stubborn. You'll be of tremendous use to her when she runs too quickly through her allowance, which lately she's done every quarter.'

Frances retired that night in a gleeful mood. 'My sister saw the new gown. She is so cross.'

Willow decided that silence on the matter of Violet was the safest course to take.

After a few weeks the family returned to Buddleigh Manor, mostly satisfied in their various ways. Lady Mary had been persuaded to give a firm date for her wedding which was to be solemnised in London in the spring of next year. The countess and Mrs Maddison set things in hand immediately, before Mary changed her mind. Willow had caught sight of her a couple of times. She had thought Frances had a delicate look, but Mary looked as if a stiff breeze would blow her away. She was small and slender, thin really, her face heart-shaped, eyes blue, features regular. There was nothing about her that was unattractive, yet there was nothing particularly striking. She would pass unnoticed in a crowd. Willow wondered how she would fare married to the ebullient James. She had made friends with one of the Mynster housemaids who told her of the 'goings on' of James and Lord Radcliffe. 'They're a pair of demons. No girl's safe from them.'

'Servant girls, do you mean?' asked Willow.

'I said girls and I mean girls, and that includes maids. A couple of ours left suddenly durin' the past year. One was –' she lowered her voice '– expecting. The other was too good-lookin'.'

'Do you mean she was dismissed for being pretty?'

'Yes, I do. The countess doesn't believe in putting the maids in harm's way. Of course, they can't do much about the other sort.'

Willow breathed, 'What other sort?'

'The ladies, real born ladies who come to stay. Mind you, the men only flirt with them, as far as I know.' She dropped her voice again. 'Unless they're married, then it can be a free-for-all.'

Willow remembered the visitors to Buddleigh Manor. 'I was told that there was a lot of creeping about in the night at house parties.'

'I don't think it happens so much now. King George and Queen Mary don't hold with such goings-on.'

Willow listened, fascinated by the stories of the secret world of lovely women and their rich protectors. 'They're no better than street women,' she said.

'I suppose not,' said the maid, 'but they live much nicer lives than street walkers, from all I've heard, and a far richer one than ours.'

Frances was happy. Mr Bickford had not made a formal declaration, but she was sure he would. Miss Brayton said that Miss Frances might have to be patient for some time to come because Mr Bickford was not one for rushing into things.

'I don't understand why she cares for him,' said Willow. 'He sounds so dull and looks very stern.'

'She doesn't see him as dull. She sees him as a strong man who'll take care of her. She could never stand on her own two feet.'

Jane Barton was now a regular guest. Mr and Mrs Maddison had decided to like her because her presence at Frances's side seemed to subdue their daughter's excitable spirits.

Violet came on a visit to Buddleigh Manor with Lord Radcliffe and appeared to be perfectly happy with her marital bargain, though there had already been whispers about her husband's behaviour with other women. Violet was supposed to be jealous so Willow assumed that she simply hid her feelings, or perhaps had never loved her husband. Perhaps it was enough that she was so extremely rich that a room had to be converted to accommodate the clothes she was for ever buying.

Frances swung between extremes of emotion. Envy of her sister when she was shown yet another gorgeous garment, or beautiful fan, or splendid coat or hat; disapproval when Miss Barton pointed out that Lady Radcliffe led a totally useless life and cared nothing for the sufferings of the lower orders. Willow heard snatches of conversation when she was in Frances's dressing room and Miss Barton was haranguing Frances over the selfishness of the wealthy.

Edgar came back to the manor with the rest of his family, but Willow saw him only from a distance.

He came to her one day when she was walking in the kitchen garden. 'I'm leaving,' he said.

'Are you?' She bent to pick a sprig of mint, rather straggly now in autumn. She chewed on it, enjoying its aromatic tang.

'You don't care at all, do you?'

'That you're going away? It's not up to me to care.'

'Willow, ask me to stay.'

She looked up at that, and stared straight into his dark eyes. They were filled with pleading, but she shook her head. 'I'll never do that.'

He kicked a stone into a bed of brussels sprouts.

'That won't do them any good,' said Willow, 'and if the gardener sees you—'

'Damn the gardener! Damn everything! Damn you! What's wrong with me?'

'Your language, for one thing.'

'You are sparring with me again. I can never get a straight reply from you.'

'I thought I'd just given you one.'

'And you really mean it? You do not wish me to stay near you?'

'Go away. Go and find someone who'll welcome your advances.'

'You love my advances.'

Willow breathed deeply. 'I've no right to them and you've no right to make them to me. Find yourself a suitable girl.'

He turned angrily and strode away, taking much of her heart with him.

Chapter Twelve

On her eighteenth birthday Willow received her usual letter from Gran. As always it was full of family news, the latest exploits of the boys, Jasmine's increasing beauty, but right at the end she wrote, 'Try not to worry, my love, but if you could get leave to visit your dad, it might be as well.'

Not worry! Willow went hurrying to Frances and said she was needed at home.

'Home?' Frances looked surprised. 'Oh, I see, you mean Bristol.'

'I mean my home,' retorted Willow, too annoyed by Frances's lack of understanding to be anything but sharp. With difficulty she modified her tone. 'My father's health is worse. My grandmother thinks I should see him.'

'How bad is he? I mean, can't you put it off for a few days? Remember, Mr Bickford is coming to stay. And Miss Barton.' A shadow passed across Frances's face. 'I wish they weren't going to be here together.'

The obvious question would have been: why did you invite them together? Willow knew the answer. They were two strong-willed people, each of whom would have no difficulty in making Frances believe that an invitation was expected, each determined to dominate her. Willow wouldn't have put up with either of them; the idea of marriage to an autocratic husband repelled her, and she disliked the way Miss Barton constantly harangued Frances. Jane Barton was a suffragette and absolutely committed to the cause of votes for women; Mr Bickford, a prospective Tory member of Parliament, was absolutely against the idea;

and Frances was in perpetual turmoil as she listened to one or the other.

'You see,' she had explained carefully to Willow, after a visit by Miss Barton, 'I do think that women should have a say in what happens to them.' Then, after Mr Bickford had spent a few days in Buddleigh Manor, 'I have serious doubts about our ability to fashion our own lives. I think Mr Bickford is right, Lily. Women are not constitutionally created to take a leading role. Their place is in the home, caring for the children, ensuring that their husbands have a haven to which they can return after a day's toil.'

Willow listened to both views with equal distrust. A large number of women in Britain had no hope of turning their homes into a haven, however much they tried; poverty, endless child-bearing, husbands often made into bullies by overwork, or no work at all. Their lives were a constant nightmare and she wasn't convinced that gaining a vote for women would alter a state of affairs in a land in which money determined the style of life enjoyed. Vaguely, she supposed, one day women might be equal, meanwhile she'd go on striving to reach the place where money was to be had. Her mind flew to Edgar. He would have given her luxury, but at a price she was determined never to pay. She didn't see herself as a kept woman in a silk cage any more than a dominated wife.

'Well, Miss Frances?' Willow prodded. 'May I take a few days off?'

'A few days?'

'Maybe only two. It depends on what I discover at home. Miss Brayton will maid you, or Jenny.'

'They do not have your way with my clothes and hair. Mr Bickford always admires me when you send me downstairs.'

Willow sighed. Her will was stronger than her mistress's and she knew that simply waiting was often the best course to take.

'Very well,' said Frances. 'You may go.' Having made her decision, she became animated. 'Of course you must go. I do hope you find it's a false alarm. Your father has been ill for some years, hasn't he? I expect this is just unfounded anxiety on your grandmother's part. Elderly people do tend rather to fuss, don't they?'

Willow didn't bother to point out that Gran was the most steadfast person she knew and not the sort who created unfounded alarms. She packed a small portmanteau, was driven to the station, and arrived in Bristol on the first available train.

The front door of her home in Barton Hill was always open and she walked straight in. The landlady met her with a solemn expression. 'There you are, Willow. I wondered when you'd come home.' A note of reproach had crept into her voice which Willow ignored. In the past four years she had acquired the veneer of her employers.

Mrs Tucker flushed. 'Of course, I knew you'd come home as soon as you could.'

'Of course.'

'I'm so sorry about your dad.'

'Has something happened?' Willow's voice was sharp with fear and Mrs Tucker hastened to amend her words.

'He's still with us, dear, but very weak.'

Clara greeted her eldest daughter with a look of profound relief. She kissed her. 'I didn't know you were comin', my love. I suppose Gran told you about Dad?'

'Yes. How is he?'

'Not so well. Not so well at all. Go on up, he'll be glad to see you.'

Willow hoped she had concealed her shock when she saw her father. It seemed impossible, but he was thinner than ever.

'Willow,' he said, his voice full of love, as if his severe illness had freed him from all constraint.

'Dad.' She bent to kiss him.

He turned his face away. 'You mustn't. The doctor says I shouldn't breathe over any of you. Your mum don't give a toss,' he said proudly, 'she gets into bed with me every night.'

His pride in Clara's devotion brought Willow close to tears. 'Of course she does.'

'No of course about it.' He spoke harshly, then softened. 'Willow, what brought you home? Is it holiday time?'

'In a way. I've been given a few days off.'

'That's good.'

His eyes closed and she realised that he had fallen asleep as easily as a baby. She crept downstairs where Clara had made a pot of tea and produced a few of Gran's scones. 'I've missed Gran's cooking,' Willow said.

'Go on with you! You've been gettin' better stuff than we can make.'

'Richer perhaps, but not better than Gran's cakes. Mum, how ill is Dad?'

'Pretty bad.' Clara paused. 'Very bad. The doctor says he can't understand what's keepin' him goin' at all.'

'He'll never give up,' said Willow.

'We all have to give up some day. I just hoped your dad could be spared a few more years.'

Willow couldn't think of a reply and if she had she couldn't have uttered it through throat muscles paralysed by tears.

She sipped her tea, then asked, 'How is Gran?'

'Beginnin' to feel her years.'

Later Willow knocked on Gran's door and was shocked at the change in her too. She was bent and walked with difficulty and her eyes were red-rimmed and watery. Willow kissed her and the familiar smell of mints and lavender filled her with fresh regret that so much of her life was spent away from the family she loved.

'I knew you'd come,' said Gran.

They seated themselves in front of the fire which the autumn chill made necessary.

'Should I leave my job to help nurse Dad?' Willow asked.

'Certainly not! No, my love,' Gran added in softer tones. 'We can manage. The children are good.'

'But Mum looks worn out.'

Gran stared into the fire. 'She is worn out. She's a good woman. She deserves better.'

'I must come home!' Willow cried.

'My dear, we can do all that's necessary for my Arthur's comfort. I know how hard it is for you to leave him now, but Clara depends on your regular money. She can't do without it, especially now we have to pay doctor's bills. Besides,' she smiled, 'you've got ambitions and although your father may not say much, he's as proud as a peacock that you've risen so far in such a short time!'

Again Willow felt the weight of misery roll over her and Gran said gently, 'Don't fret, my love, you do your best. How's the sewing going these days?'

'I seem to do more and more. Miss Frances has asked me to make her a gown. She's bought a length of fine silk – difficult to control – it slides all over the place.'

Gran smiled. 'What you should do is sew tissue paper into the seams, that'll hold the material still, and later it's easy to tease the paper out.'

'Thanks, Gran, I should have written and asked.'

'How do you manage for clothes when you take so little money for yourself?'

'I manage fine. I go to all the local church jumble sales and buy as much good stuff as I can. Little do the posh ladies of the district realise that their discarded finery ends up on my back. They don't recognise it after I've finished with it.'

Gran laughed, then said, 'Willow, I know a lady's maid sometimes makes garments for her mistress, but I'm very surprised that she expects you to cope with a formal silk gown. The Maddisons are very wealthy. Surely she can afford to buy her clothes?'

'She's never got any money. I suspect she gives a lot of her allowance to the suffragettes.'

Gran looked startled. 'That's the militant side of the women's movement, the ones who burn and destroy things. You don't want to get mixed up in any of that. It's all very well for middle-class women to pass some of their idle time on such matters; it does a poor woman no good at all.'

217

'Don't you think we should have the vote?'

'Certainly I do, but what I say is, let those who can afford it do the fighting while the rest of us make a living as best we can.'

On her way home Willow heard footsteps behind her and was joined by a tall young man whom she didn't recognise. She marched on indignantly until he said, 'Too proud to talk to old friends, Willow?'

She stopped to take a closer look. 'Sidney Moor! You're so different.'

'True. And so are you.'

He was at least six foot tall and very thin. His wrists stuck out from his jacket sleeves, his trousers barely covered his ankles. He no longer suffered from acne, though the scars remained, giving him a piratical appearance that was oddly attractive. When he raised his cap to her, he revealed hair that was straight and thick. He had an air of determination and authority.

'It must be years since we met!' she exclaimed.

'Two, to be exact. I've been away too.'

'Where?'

'Several places. I tried to work in Bristol, but my family's reputation made it difficult. Impossible, at first.' He stopped speaking and glancing at him sideways Willow saw that he was angry. 'However,' he continued smoothly, 'I tried other towns, Manchester and Birmingham among them, looking for decent work. I found some in the north.'

'Are you back in Bristol now?'

'I am. I've got a job in a corset factory in Kingswood. I've worked my way through the departments quickly and the boss says I'm certain to become an overseer. And I'm saving my money. One day, I'll have a business of my own.'

Willow was astonished. Even if his clothes weren't much good, Sidney had smartened up his speech and his future ambitions were clearly thought out.

'I admire you,' she said sincerely.

'Thanks. And I admire the way you've managed to

improve yourself. With a mum and dad like Mr and Mrs Riches to give you encouragement' – he hesitated – 'don't think I don't care for my family. I do, but I'm much happier with yours. Will you be staying long?'

'Only for a few days. Dad's so unwell. I want to give Mum all the support I can.'

He nodded. 'Quite right, too. She needs you. She's got a lot to put up with, what with your dad and Marigold.'

Willow stopped and faced him squarely. 'Marigold? What about her?'

He subjected her to a steady gaze. 'I thought you'd know. Marigold's been dolling herself up and going out with boys much older than herself.'

'You must be mistaken. Mum would have told me.'

'Perhaps she doesn't know. Marigold's cunning. She behaves at home, but when she gets round the corner she slaps on paint and powder.'

'How do you know?' Willow demanded angrily.

'I've seen her.'

'Oh. I suppose it didn't occur to you to tell Mum?' Willow wished the words back as soon as she'd said them. Barton Hill folk didn't snitch on one another.

But Sidney gave her answer thoughtful consideration. 'You're probably right. Maybe I should speak to Mrs Riches about it, but in our house, the greatest crime you can commit is to tell tales.'

'Yes, I see. Thanks. I'll have a word with Marigold.'

Her sister indignantly denied everything. 'What nasty busybody's been fillin' you with lies?' she demanded.

'Someone I can trust.'

'Oh, I suppose it was Sidney Moor? I saw you with him. He can talk, comin' from a family of jailbirds.'

'He's never been to jail.'

'It was him, wasn't it?'

'He has your welfare at heart.'

'Huh! I don't think!'

'Is what he said the truth?'

'All right,' Marigold capitulated. 'I do put on a bit of

paint. Only a dab of face rouge and powder and a bit of colour on my mouth. There's no harm in it.'

'Good girls don't paint!'

'Good girls don't paint!' jeered Marigold. 'Who says I'm a good girl? Oh, don't start again, our Willow. Of course I'm good. I just like a bit of fun.'

'Bits of fun can have disastrous consequences.'

'I know how to look after myself.' Marigold's eyes were bright with resentment. She had grown tall and extremely pretty with a cloud of dark hair framing an oval face with a perfect complexion. Her figure had matured far more than Willow's at the same age and she would have no trouble in passing herself off as older than her sixteen years.

Willow felt afraid for her. 'What do you do? Where do you go? I understand how frustrating life can be sometimes, but I wouldn't want to see you hurt.'

'The only thing that hurts me is havin' no money, an' I'm sick an' tired of it!'

'What's that got to do with you painting your face?'

'Nothin'! Well, in a way it has. I've got some very nice boy friends who take me places. Music halls and theatres. There's no harm in it, Willow, honest.'

'What do they expect in return?'

'Oh, you've got a foul mind! Just my company, that's all. They like me. I can't expect anyone in this family to understand that!' She flounced off and Willow heard a door slam.

If she hadn't been so preoccupied with her father's illness she might have tried to discover for herself what Marigold was up to. She did attempt to question her again, but her sister's brief moment of conciliation was over. 'I don't have to tell you anythin'.'

'Maybe not, but you shouldn't deceive Mum.'

'Don't you think she's got enough problems without me worryin' her?'

'Of course I do, and I don't want you to bring home any more.'

Marigold tossed her head. 'As if I shall. Anyway, she

probably guesses I have a good time, but she's too worn out to care much.'

'How can you say so? She does care!'

'Well, don't try tellin' her stories about me because she won't want to hear them.' Willow was afraid this was true. Clara could barely cope with her desperately hard life. Marigold made a surprise attempt to placate her sister. 'Stop worryin', do. I can take care of myself. I've got girl friends an' we go out in a crowd.'

Willow felt somewhat comforted. If Marigold was always in a crowd she couldn't come to much harm.

She decided to speak to Gran, her refuge and advisor. Gran sighed, 'Boys and girls these days seem different from when I was a girl. I blame it on the late King. He seemed nice enough, but his morals weren't very good. If Marigold's bent on getting into mischief no one will be able to stop her. But don't worry, she was born one of the knowing ones, not like you, my love.'

'The knowing ones?'

'Haven't you noticed? Some girls seem to understand how to take care of themselves from their cradles, others learn the hard way and some never learn at all.'

Gran looked weary and Willow pressed her no further. She stayed at home for four days, each one filled with love and the evidence of sacrifice. Her youngest brother Alfred, twelve now and dying to leave school, asked if she'd brought home any food. When Willow explained that a lady's maid didn't have the same access to food as a kitchen maid he grinned ruefully. 'I think I'd have stayed in the kitchen, then.'

On the third morning, Willow received a letter from Frances, asking her how much longer she would be away. 'Mr Bickford will arrive soon,' she wrote, 'and I did so want to greet him in my new gown.' Willow could almost hear her querulous voice and had a strong impulse to write back and say she was never returning. But she said her goodbyes feeling happier. Dad had perked up a lot after her arrival and was able, with help, to come downstairs for a few hours a day. All the same, Willow's heart ached when she turned at the corner of the street to wave. Dad was there, struggling to breathe properly as he sat on a kitchen chair in the doorway. Jasmine waved frantically. She was growing fast and maturing; she didn't beg her beloved sister not to go, though her heartache was plain to see.

The silk gown was finished just in time for Mr Bickford to admire it.

Frances said, 'He paid me a very nice compliment.'

Willow wondered how such a dry stick got his tongue round a compliment.

'He said,' continued Frances, 'that my gown gave me the serenity of a matron. I think it was because of the lace fichu at the neck. He does not care to see too much of a lady's skin displayed. I can tell that by the way he looks at Lady Radcliffe.'

Willow was astounded. Was that how Frances, aged twenty-two, wished to see herself? With the serenity of a matron? Mr Bickford had arrived in his usual garb, black frock coat, grey-and-black-striped trousers, white waistcoat and collar, black tie and grey spats. He looked, thought Willow, as if he'd been born in them and went to bed in them. Once she had seen him in tennis whites, looking, she thought, like a starling in dove's plumage. He was the last man she would have thought Miss Frances would choose.

The struggle between Mr Bickford and Miss Barton to dominate her still raged beneath the surface. Frances had seldom mentioned the suffragettes to Willow, so it came as a surprise when one day she said softly, 'What would you say, Lily, if I confessed I had told you a little fib?'

Willow glanced up at her mistress whose hair shone gold in the rays of winter sun which beamed through the window, whose blue eyes were glittering with an inner excitement. 'It's not my place to criticise you, Miss Frances.'

'No. But I did tell you a fib. Actually, it was quite a whopper. It is true I collect little antiques, but that's not where most of my money goes.'

'No, miss?'

'No, indeed. Lily, have you heard of the suffragettes?'

'I've read about their antics. The newspapers are often full of them.'

'You think of the suffragettes' activities as antics?'

Frances sounded cross and Willow said soothingly, 'I'm far too busy to think much about them at all. I know they believe they're doing something for women. I know they mean well.'

'Mean well!' Frances frowned. 'Mean well! They are out there suffering dreadful things so that we women can have the vote.'

'Yes, miss,' said Willow, carefully putting her mistress's morning gown into the wardrobe. 'What will you wear for tea, Miss Frances?'

'Oh, anything! I don't know. I won't be taking tea. I'll wear the striped skirt, my new lingerie blouse and white buckskin shoes. I'll need my motoring coat, too, and a hat and veil. Mr Edgar says he'll take me for a drive.'

Willow was startled. She had thought Edgar was in the north, visiting a friend with a very pretty sister who possessed a fortune in her own right.

'I don't think he made much headway with the lady,' said Frances, as if reading her thought. 'He says he is visiting us before going to America again.' She got up and wandered restlessly about the room. 'Life can sometimes be so drab. I don't believe there's anyone under the age of forty staying here at present.'

'No, miss,' said Willow, getting out the specified clothes, her mind focused on Edgar. Frances's pretty mouth was turned down at the corners and Willow wanted to use one of Gran's sayings when anyone pulled a face: 'If the wind changes, you'll stay like that.' She smiled at the memory.

'You are laughing! You find me amusing?'

'No, miss, not at all.'

'I'm a bore – a pest – is that it?'

Willow turned to look at her mistress. 'Of course not,

Miss Frances.' Willow wondered what she would have said if she'd answered, 'Yes.'

'Oh, how beastly I'm behaving to you, Lily, but you deserve it, really you do.'

'I'm sorry, miss.'

'You should be. Don't you realise that women, carefully brought up women, are going to prison and suffering torture for our sakes?'

Willow decided to keep to herself her opinion that anyone who deliberately put themselves in danger of going to prison must be crazy. What she had learned of the hunger strikes and the forcible feeding of women appalled her, but they didn't come out of prison moneyless, jobless, with a family dependent on them. 'They're very brave, miss.'

Frances's mood changed. 'They are, aren't they? Lily, I'm about to tell you something which you must never divulge to a living soul.'

Willow felt apprehensive and even more after Frances had spoken.

'I have friends in the WFL.'

'What?'

'The Women's Freedom League.'

'I see, miss.'

'No, I don't think you do. Our league grew tired of the ladylike behaviour of the old suffrage movement, though they too are beginning to tire of a passive role. Naturally Miss Barton and I are on the side of those prepared to use any means in their power to gain our rights.' Willow was unsurprised to hear that Miss Barton embraced violence to reach her goal. She wondered if Frances had any notion of what it meant to be committed to a cause.

'You see, Lily, the peaceable women have gained nothing from all their protests, marches and pamphlets. None of their so-called parliamentary friends have uttered a word lately unless they were heckled into it. We are dreadfully tired of broken promises and believe in showing the men what we women are capable of.'

Frances's growing excitement alarmed Willow who stopped

work to look at her mistress. 'Are they the ones who throw bricks through windows, miss?'

'Yes! Isn't it splendid to be so courageous!'

'Have you ever joined in?' asked Willow nervously.

'No, but I intend to.' Willow thought that a note of uncertainty had crept into Frances's voice and decided to play on it. Frances could be infuriating and selfish, but she was vulnerable and easily persuaded.

'Do you think you're being wise?'

'I don't suppose I am, but I can't disappoint the others, can I? Did you read about them in the spring when they marched round the West End of London smashing windows with bricks and hammers? The police arrested a hundred and twenty. Poor dears! Miss Barton says they received abominable treatment. The status of political prisoner was denied and some were imprisoned with hard labour. Dreadful! Simply dreadful! And the printer who produced their weekly newspaper was so terrorised that many of the columns were left blank at the time. They took away our freedom to speak. Miss Barton says I should have been among them.'

'Why?'

Frances twisted her hands nervously, 'She said it was my duty.'

'It's lucky Miss Barton doesn't get caught.'

'Oh, but she has been and she went on hunger strike, and says she will do so again if she has to. It's a good thing that my parents don't know.'

Willow understood why Frances was always so nervous after she'd been with Jane Barton. She couldn't begin to imagine the depth of the Maddisons' rage and humiliation if one of their daughters were to be arrested and jailed.

'Miss Barton tries not to get caught. Some of the women seem to go out of their way to be arrested. I don't share that particular enthusiasm.'

'I'm glad to hear it, miss.' Willow began to tidy the dressing table.

'Stop that,' said Frances, 'and listen to me. Lily, I've been given a specific task to perform by the WLF who wish me to prove my beliefs. Thank goodness it has nothing to do with arson.'

'Arson! That's starting fires, isn't it?'

'Yes, and it's very dangerous. I could never do anything like that. Fire frightens me, especially when the women use bottles of petrol.'

'What have you to do?'

'Nothing very brave. Just accompany Miss Barton to London and throw a stone through a window.'

Willow stared at Frances who looked almost childish in her pale pink wrapper, her baby-fine hair curling on her shoulders, her eyes troubled.

'Oh, miss, don't do it,' she begged.

'Miss Barton says I must to show my good faith.'

A very unladylike epithet for Miss Barton sprang to Willow's lips. She held it back.

'Your parents—' she said.

Frances shrugged.

Willow played her trump card. 'What about Mr Bickford?'

That went home. 'I know. He would be so cross if I was arrested.'

'Cross' was not how Willow would have described Mr Bickford's probable reaction. Frances would be lucky if she ever saw him again. 'Don't do it,' she begged again. 'You might lose Mr Bickford altogether.'

Frances gazed at her almost in relief. 'You're right, Lily, so right. I'll tell Miss Barton. I'll think of an excuse.'

'Just say no.'

'Yes, I will. I'll just say no.'

Jane Barton arrived on 3 November and from the moment Frances was in her company she was enslaved. Willow watched her mistress grow more and more worked up to the point where she regarded the window-smashing as a mission.

'I shall be going to London on November the fifth,' she told Willow.

'A bonfire party, miss?' Willow asked resignedly.

'Yes, in a way.'

'How long shall I pack for?'

'Several nights. I don't know how long I'll be. Put in my dark tweed suit, fur felt hat and my boots.'

Willow did as she had been instructed. On the morning of the fifth, Frances looked at her in surprise. 'You are not ready.'

'Am I to come with you? You didn't say.'

'Of course you must come. I need you.'

Willow hastily threw some things into her small portmanteau and was ready in her black clothes and shoes. She settled her mistress in a first-class carriage and found her seat in third class, enjoying the illusion of freedom on the journey. She wasn't surprised to find Miss Barton waiting at the station to meet them.

'There you are, my dear Frances! I am so glad. I should have known you would be brave.'

Willow's spirits dropped, but Frances's eyes lit up at the praise. Willow knew how scared Frances was, but Miss Barton took her enthusiasm for granted. They were driven to her house in Kensington, where Willow was given a small room. She was feeling more and more uneasy, and by the time Frances rang for her was unsurprised by the information that tonight the suffragettes had targeted many windows to smash. She made one last effort to dissuade Frances from taking part.

'You're risking your future. It's not too late to draw back. Please, let's go home – you know you want to.'

Frances shook her head. Her eyes looked as if she'd been mesmerised, as indeed she had by the unswerving persuasion of Jane Barton and others like her. 'You don't understand, Lily,' she intoned in a sing-song voice. 'Everyone is turning against women. The Liberal Party and even the Irish Nationalists. They fear that if we are given the vote an election might bring down the government and support for the bill for Irish Home Rule will disappear. And there is also the Reform Bill which will give the vote to many more men.'

Willow was even more alarmed. If Miss Barton wasn't careful Frances would be ill. Presumably, if that happened, she would be chalked up as another martyr to the cause.

'Miss Frances—' she began.

'It's no good arguing with me, Lily. In the beginning, when I heard about the bravery of the suffragettes, I was timid, but now I must prove that I care.'

'And that proof means performing a violent act?'

'Yes.' Frances's voice was almost inaudible. 'I gave my solemn oath.'

'Surely that was extracted from you before you knew what it meant? It wouldn't be wrong to break it.'

'I swore on the Bible!'

'Oh, Miss Frances!' Willow felt disgusted with Jane Barton. 'What if you get caught?'

Willow hadn't heard Miss Barton enter and jumped when she snapped, 'That will do. Are you ready, Frances? And you, Lily?'

'Me? If you think I'm coming—!'

'Please, please, do,' begged Frances. She was a picture of terror and Willow wondered if she actually would throw a stone through a plate-glass window. If she managed it her legs would turn to jelly, or she'd be so paralysed by horror she'd be an easy catch for the police. Maybe if Willow went along she could stop the mad act.

'I'll come,' she said shortly.

'Good,' said Miss Barton. 'I can trust you to take care of her. I have business elsewhere.'

'Won't you be with me?' Frances was astonished.

'It doesn't need both of us to destroy one window.' She left.

'She's so brave,' said Frances. 'I do wish I was more like her.'

'She's gone,' said Willow unnecessarily. 'Let's just get a train and return to the manor.'

'You need not accompany me,' snapped Frances. 'No one would blame you. After all, you are only my maid. No one expects *you* to be brave.'

228

Willow doubted that Frances was aware of what she was saying, or of the disdain in her voice, but all the same the words stung. She followed her mistress who ordered a taxicab to take them to Oxford Street.

Frances crept along the pavement like a criminal. The night was clear save for a few drifting clouds which reflected back the red light of Guy Fawkes bonfires. They passed a number of stores.

'Which window are you going to break?' Willow asked, anxious now to get the thing over with and hurry to safety.

'I don't know. Miss Barton says any large store will do.'

Willow was exasperated. Was ever a woman so unfitted for the task? 'Why not break a street lamp?' she suggested. 'Quite a lot of women do and you can choose one away from the shops.'

'What a good idea. But, no, I must obey my instructions. A big window is much more expensive to replace than the glass in a street lamp. I have to break the window, shout "votes for women" and run away fast.' Frances stopped and withdrew a large stone from her muff. Her teeth were chattering with terror as she aimed her missile. Twice she failed and Willow fetched the stone back, feeling like a gun dog, almost laughing, albeit hysterically, at the absurdity of it. By now Frances was shaking so much she dropped the stone twice and each time Willow picked it up. The third time she decided the only way to get Frances safely clear was to act herself.

'Stand back,' she ordered, then drew back her arm and hurled the stone with all the force she could muster, but not at the plate-glass window which was filled with opulent, beautiful clothes. Even in her nervous state she couldn't bear to see them ruined. The stone landed squarely on a street lamp which shattered, showering the pavement with glass. 'Votes for women,' she shrieked.

She turned to Frances, but she had gone, then dark forms materialised and she was seized by two men. They wore ordinary dark suits. She struggled, but her arms were held cruelly tight.

'Let me go!' she yelled.

They laughed and held her tighter and she increased her resistance.

'This one's strong! Now stop fightin' and let's get on with our job. We're policemen though we might not look the part.'

Willow refused to give up and kicked out wildly, until one of the men squeezed her breasts while the other took hold of her coiled hair and pulled it viciously. They went on torturing her until the pain destroyed her power to resist and pinioned by strong arms, she was lifted off her feet by the larger of the men and carried away. The other kept hold of her hair. Her eyes filled with tears of rage rather than pain. 'You disgusting bullies, you're hurting me!' she yelled.

'Stop caterwauling.'

'You don't have to hurt me like this! You're both bigger than I am!'

The policemen still held her tight. 'You've just deliberately damaged property and you'll be charged with same, though perhaps they'll be lenient if you tell us who the other one was.'

'Which other one?'

'The woman who made off before you threw the stone.'

Willow fell silent.

'Come on, miss, tell us. Give us her name. The judge won't be so hard on you if you do.'

'Judge?' Willow was horrified. 'You know I can't tell.'

'She doesn't care about you. She left you.'

'No, I can't tell!'

'Please yourself.' They laughed as they hustled her to a police station. The place was crowded and noisy with women who had been arrested. They were in varying states of dishevelment. A delicate-looking girl in expensive clothes had a large black and purple bruise over one eye, another a split lip. Many had had their clothing ripped. Willow was dropped and leaned against a wall, watching them. She caught sight of Jane Barton struggling among the others. She also saw that suffragettes were not just from the middle and upper classes; here were women in poor garments, their hands work-roughened. One of them, quite young, suddenly produced a hammer from beneath her shawl and smashed it down on the desk, breaking an inkpot and sending a blue-black stream across the desk on to the presiding sergeant's clothes. He gave a bellow of rage and a constable slapped the girl so hard she fell into the arms of her friends.

Willow was sickened by the violence. But Frances would organise help. It wouldn't be difficult. She had never attended a rally before so no one could bring a charge against her. Surely she'd come soon and get Willow freed. She must.

Chapter Thirteen

Willow should have known that Frances would lie low. If the police got hold of her name and address she would rate more than a passing mention in the newspapers, and reporters would certainly attempt to interview her parents. She would give everyone a plausible reason for her maid's absence and wait for her return. Willow had almost succeeded in reassuring herself when she was stung back to reality. A well-dressed girl leaned forward, seized the desk book and flung it through the station window. She was punched, hard, in full view of the others who began shrieking and yelling, 'Bullies! Cowards! Wicked brutes! Votes for women.'

'Get their particulars and throw the lot of them in the cells,' the sergeant bawled. 'They can cool their tempers down there.'

The women refused to move voluntarily and were man-handled roughly while, with immense difficulty, the sergeant in charge took down names and addresses. Willow gave her Bristol address, though it was unlikely that she would be mentioned. She was a nobody and there were plenty of famous women – or notorious, depending on how you viewed it – whose names would be made public.

The sergeant glared sourly at her. 'Do you mean you came all this way to make trouble? You could just as well have chucked a stone in Bristol. Take her down.'

By this time any patience the police might have felt had vanished and they didn't bother to ask her if she'd go quietly. A large policeman simply grabbed the back of her neck and a handful of clothes and hurried her down the stairs so fast that he ripped her coat. He locked her in a small cell with three other women who sat on the plank beds and chattered excitedly about their exploits. One was a rope maker, two were biscuit packers. Even here it seemed that they were segregated by class into cells. Willow was exhausted and lay down, her back against the cold, damp wall. She closed her eyes and tried to forget herself in sleep but it was impossible. The other women in the station cells kept up a constant noise, shouting and singing and calling out their war cries, and in the end Willow went beyond rest and waited apprehensively for the summons which would take her before a judge, wishing she had a little of the dedicated fervour which carried the others along so bravely.

She was tried in Bow Street before an angry-looking magistrate. Asked if she had smashed a street lamp, she replied, 'Yes.'

'No shame,' said the magistrate. 'Not one of you has shown any shame for your unwomanly conduct.'

She had given her age and in view of her youth and the fact that she had no previous convictions the magistrate said her sentence would be light. 'Seven days with the option of a ten-shilling fine.'

'Seven days!' Willow gasped. 'In prison?'

'With the option of a ten-shilling fine,' she was reminded.

It might as well have been ten pounds.

'I must go to prison?'

The magistrate leaned forward. 'I am glad to see the effect your just punishment has on you. Perhaps now you will sever your connection with this immoderate group of females.'

Willow felt like telling him that the behaviour of the authorities was more likely to send her straight into the camp of militant females, but she held her tongue. Things were bad enough. The Black Maria waiting for them looked like a hearse. She climbed in, controlling her shaking legs. More and more women were crammed in although the roof wasn't high enough for anyone to stand upright and when they drove off they were wedged too tight to fall. Even here, their spirits hadn't flagged. Jane Barton managed to put a scarf with the suffragette colours through the grille window and sang, 'The March of Women', her voice ringing as clear as if she was off on a picnic.

In Holloway Prison they were formed into lines where wardresses as grim as the grey prison walls studied their names and particulars of their sentences. They were then locked away, three or four to a cell. The others tried to be friendly towards her, but her thoughts were of her job. How long could Frances keep up the deception? But, of course, she was at Jane Barton's house. She would simply telephone home and say she had decided to prolong her stay a little. Willow felt calmer as things grew slowly quieter, then the door opened and she was ordered to step outside. She asked what was to become of her, but the wardress just nodded her to go on, prodding her in the back when she walked too slowly. She was given a medical inspection, pronounced fit, then ordered to strip and handed a coarse gown and an apron, both marked with arrows, and told to wait in the passage with others.

'I'm not a criminal,' she said. 'Why do I have to wear these terrible clothes?'

The wardress laughed harshly. 'You shouldn't mind them. They were designed by your fellow suffragettes. They make them when they're inside. *They're* proud to wear them.'

'Well, I'm not!'

'Perhaps this'll make you go home and behave like a decent woman.'

The wardress read out the prison rules and Willow finally found herself alone in a tiny cell, the furniture a fixed plank bed on which, precisely folded, were two sheets, blankets and a quilt. There was a chair and a moveable washstand, a slop bucket and two tin plates and a mug. A small electric light was fixed to one wall. On a hook hung a yellow badge made of material which bore the number of the prison block and the number of the prisoner. Willow was ordered to attach the badge to a button on her bodice. From now on she would be known as number ten. Seven days stretched before her like an eternity. Dad must have felt like this and he hadn't done anything wrong at all. At least she had brought this on herself. She recalled the stone she had sent smashing through the street lamp and felt a stirring of bitter humour and a kind of consolation in the fact that she was being punished for a crime she had actually committed.

Her buoyancy didn't last long. In the evening she was ordered to hold out the pint pot for gruel made of oatmeal, water and no seasoning, a lump of bread was dropped on to her plate – later she was to learn that it weighed six ounces, no more and no less – and there was water to drink. Willow wondered what the gently reared women made of food like this. They didn't really have to fight for a cause and risk jail. Belated admiration for them grew in her. She tried to eat, but her insides were churning with nerves and she left most of the food.

When the wardress returned she stared hard at the uneaten food. 'Not another of you! Well, you'll soon learn how we treat hunger strikers.'

Willow thought she'd never sleep in this dreadful place, but she was exhausted and when she awoke she was hungry. After she had emptied her slop bucket she held out her tin dishes. Breakfast was exactly the same as supper, but she drank all the gruel and ate the bread. It was tasteless and disgusting, but it filled her.

The wardress grinned. 'Thought better of it, did you?' She ordered Willow to clean her dishes with three pieces of rag that looked none too clean, making her do it three times before she was satisfied. Next she must fold her sheets and blankets to precise measurements. A bucket of water and a piece of bath brick were produced with which she was commanded to scour the cell floor.

It was a relief to be taken to the workroom to sit among the rows of women and given a man's shirt to sew. Many of the suffragette prisoners had friends with them, and she wondered if Miss Barton was here. She tried to find her. Even seeing her would help, as a familar face in a bizarre situation always did. She was ordered to keep facing the front. Later she learned that prisoners who refused to eat were kept in their cells.

Three days passed in boring monotony. Willow wondered how the ordinary prisoners kept their sanity when they were in for months, even years. Poor creatures. Some of them were so worn down by their fight to survive, prison might seem a refuge.

On the fourth morning, wardresses went along the rows of cells, unlocked the doors and left them ajar, ordering the women to remain where they were. Willow was nervous, wondering what new torment was about to begin. Then the horror started. From the other end of the row of cells she heard a woman screaming and the shouts of women and men! God, what were they doing? She began to shake. Voices called from other cells, exhorting friends to take courage, and Willow realised that Jane Barton was in the next cell to hers and remembered that she had vowed to go on hunger strike if she was arrested.

Terrifyingly, slowly, the sounds came nearer, until Willow could hear the shrieks being stifled by ghastly choking and vomiting. Forcible feeding! She had heard of it, but hadn't understood the dreadful reality. When the crowd of wardresses and doctors entered Jane Barton's cell, Willow heard every agonised sound.

'Open your mouth,' a man ordered. 'It will go easier on you if you do. I am a doctor. I do not wish to hurt you.'

Willow waited for a reply, silently begging Miss Barton to obey.

The doctor's voice again. 'Very well. If you insist.' Jane Barton's cries were muffled by her tightly closed lips.

The doctor said, 'I can't get through her teeth. Hand me the pointed one.' The terrible screams began as the girl's mouth was forced open. 'Give me the gag. Good. Now the tube.'

When the dreadful choking and gurgling began Willow couldn't bear it. She knelt by the hard bed and covered her ears, but she couldn't shut out the sounds entirely. She thought they would echo forever in her head.

At last the horrifying noises stopped and the other prisoners were fed and taken to work. This time Willow sat through the long hours, knitting socks, her mind imprisoned by the terror of the morning. When she was returned to her cell for supper the door was left ajar and once more the screams of agony reached her. Unbelievably, the barbarity continued during the remaining days of her sentence. She wondered how women, so many of them delicately reared, could withstand such torture.

On the morning of her release her possessions were returned to her, she signed a receipt book, and was turned out into the chill air. Several ordinary prisoners were released with her and hurried off into the November fog. One was holding a baby beneath her inadequate shawl. Willow stood for a moment looking about her, dazed. Where was Frances? She had counted on her being here.

'She isn't here,' someone croaked. Jane Barton was behind her, leaning against the prison wall. She was very pale and her lips were cut. She smiled. 'I'm not a pretty sight, am I?' Her smile revealed torn and bleeding gums and Willow instinctively went to her and put her arms round her in support.

'You are a good girl,' Miss Barton said in her rasping voice, pausing between words as if each one was a struggle. 'What happened to Frances?'

'She ran away.'

'Before or after you threw the stone?'

'How do you know I threw it?' Willow dissembled.

'She abandoned you, didn't she? Word gets around, even in prison. You didn't betray her. You're a good girl,' she said again.

'Isn't anyone coming to fetch you?' asked Willow.

'They'll be here. I dare say the fog has delayed them.'

As she spoke a car was driven slowly across the damp, gleaming cobbles. 'Here they come now.'

Women jumped out and half carried Miss Barton to the car, praising and cheering her. They looked inquiringly at Willow who said, 'I'm expecting someone.'

Jane Barton gave her a pitying look. 'Frances won't come. Bring her along,' she said to her friends. 'She's a heroine.'

Miss Barton's house was luxurious by any standard. After prison it seemed like a palace. A maid showed Willow to a bathroom where a steaming bath awaited her and she luxuriated in the scented water which drove away the prison smells. It reminded her of the illicit bath she had taken in Buddleigh Manor. Abruptly her worries returned. She must get back there with a good reason for disappearing for over a week.

Miss Barton had been put to bed and a doctor called. After he had left, Willow went to see her.

'There you are, my dear,' she said.

'Miss Barton—' began Willow.

'Jane to you. You're one of us now.'

'No,' said Willow. 'I'm not. I can't afford to get mixed up in anything like this.'

Jane looked disappointed.

'My father is slowly dying and my mother is struggling to keep the family. My wages are a help to her.'

'Lots of poor women are with us,' Jane said wistfully.

'I know, and after what I learned in prison I respect them, but I can't embrace a cause which can lead me to prison and poverty. My family suffer so much through lack of money and I feel I have it in me to help them. Ever since I was little I've been determined to make something of myself and relieve their problems. I shall pack today and return to Devon.'

Jane closed her eyes, holding out her hand as if to implore silence. Willow stared down at her white face, her bloody lips the only hint of colour, and silently lauded her for her courage. She wandered across the room and looked out of the window. Elegant women in carriages or motor cars were being driven to elegant shops. She returned to the bed when she saw that Jane's eyes were open.

'Has Miss Frances left any messages for me?' she asked.

Jane motioned her to a bedside chair and Willow sat down. Clearly something was amiss.

'Frances had to go home,' said Jane, 'but she left five pounds for you. She said it was all she had. I shall add more.'

'I won't need your money, thank you. Five pounds is more than adequate to get me back to the manor.'

'But, my dear, you do need it.' Jane reached across to her bedside table and handed Willow a newspaper. 'Read this.'

The news of 'The Latest Suffragette Outrages' was on the front page and gave a full account of the 'disgraceful proceedings on the night of November the fifth', listing the names of the 'perpetrators', including Willow's.

'Oh, no! Do you think the Maddisons have seen this?'

'I know they have. Frances telephoned my house this morning and discovered that I was being released at the same time as you. I should have been kept in longer, but they let me out because the forced feeding has weakened my heart which was never healthy. The last thing they want is for someone to die beneath their torture. They will probably arrest me again when I recover. Frances asked me to look after you.'

'I knew she wouldn't just abandon me.'

'No.' Jane sighed. 'But, my dear, you can never return to Buddleigh Manor.'

'Why? That can't be true! I only followed my mistress's instructions. I only went with her to take care of her.'

'I know, but that is not how Frances's parents see it. They believe you led her astray.'

'How can they? If she told the truth—' Her voice trailed away.

'Exactly,' said Jane. Her hand went to her throat and Willow took a glass of water from the bedside table and held it while she sipped. 'You are strong, used to coping with life. I am very fond of Frances, but I know she is weak.'

'Yet you persuaded her into behaving as she did. You are responsible for this whole ghastly mess!'

'I cannot blame you for being angry, but the responsibility is not mine. It belongs to the men who refuse to grant us our rights. Oh, if only you could understand what having the vote would mean to you.'

'I suspect it'd mean very little to women like me. It wouldn't relieve our poverty and illness.'

'It would give you the opportunity to change things with a simple cross on a voting slip.'

Prison with its poor food, the lack of exercise and broken nights had affected Willow to the point where she was utterly weary and the latest blow so dispirited her she couldn't continue arguing.

'What has Frances told her parents?' she asked.

'That you are a member of the Women's Freedom League and that you got her to go to London by telling her that you were attending an orderly meeting. She said she went out of curiosity and that she was astounded when you smashed a lamp.'

Willow jumped to her feet, blazing with fury. 'I saved her. Without me she would have been arrested.'

'Without you,' said Jane gently, 'she would have been unlikely to carry on at all.'

'Yes, she would,' snapped Willow. 'You'd have taken her with you and she'd probably have ended up in jail with you and that would have ruined her marriage prospects with Mr Bickford. She has sacrificed me. I hadn't thought she cared so little for me—' The steam suddenly left her and she said wearily, 'I'm sure she doesn't love him. I can't imagine why she would care tuppence about losing such a bigoted man. I can't see how she'll be happy with him.'

'He certainly would not be my cup of tea.' Jane painfully summoned a smile. 'Frances is dazzled by his future. He is rich, don't you know, very rich, and has a great deal of influence. I am sure he will be elected to parliament, and urged on by her parents she sees herself meeting all the famous in the land. If that does happen, she will be most dreadfully bored, though she does not realise it, poor girl.'

'Poor girl!'

'I can understand your indignation. Lily, I am disappointed in you.'

'Are you really? And by the way, my name is Willow. I'll never answer to Lily again.'

'They changed it? I am not surprised. A very conventional family, the Maddisons.'

A conventional family. Willow had done the Maddisons another favour and this time it meant the end of her job, the end of four years of solid hard work, with nothing to show for it, not even a reference. 'I shall write and ask her for a reference,' she said. 'It's the least she can do.'

'It will be of no use to write. Frances says she has promised her parents that she will report immediately any contact you try to make with her.'

'Her promises mean nothing,' said Willow. 'I'll try.'

Jane touched her shoulder. 'You are a game girl. Throw in your lot with us. We shall see you don't go hungry.'

'No! I sympathise with you, but I can't join you. If you really want to help me, I need a job. I am a hard worker and an excellent seamstress.'

Jane shook her head. 'All my staff are devoted to the cause. I can't employ someone who is not entirely with us.'

'Do your servants actually go out smashing windows?'

'Every one of them is prepared to take risks. Won't you give it more thought?'

'No, I can't.'

'I see. Fetch my purse, please.' She handed five pounds to Willow. 'This is from Frances.' She added another five. 'And this is from me.'

Willow looked down at the money and temper overtook her. 'Keep your damned money! Frances owes me something. You don't!'

'Do not be a fool!' Jane's voice cracked and she held her hand to her throat. 'Take it, please,' she whispered. 'You need it. You have earned it. If ever you change your mind about our cause, you will be welcome.'

Yes, I have earned it, thought Willow. She took the ten pounds and turned to go. Jane called her back. 'Go to my dressing table and bring me the carved box.' Willow obeyed and Jane opened it and produced a brooch. 'Each one of us who has been to Holloway is given this special decoration. It's by way of being a medal. Here is yours.'

The brooch depicted a portcullis emblazoned with a broad arrow in the suffragette colours of purple, green and white, with silver chains hanging on either side.

'Thank you,' said Willow without enthusiasm.

'Promise me one thing. When women get the vote, promise me you will use yours.'

'I promise.'

She left Jane Barton's house, clutching her case, with one shilling and sixpence in her purse and ten pounds wrapped in a handkerchief and tucked inside her corset. Ten pounds! And ten shillings would have saved her from prison and secured her job. Frances could have provided the money easily. She railed at the silken cocoon which money wove around Them, binding them so thoroughly that they never actually understood the needs of the very poor. Miss Barton had been kind in her way and Frances had left her some money, but neither of them could even begin to imagine her dire situation and her *loving* duty to her family.

As she began to walk along the wide pavement, wondering what to do next, a housemaid ran after her. 'Miss Maddison left you a letter. I forgot to tell Miss Barton about it. She told me to catch you.'

The envelope bore a Bristol postmark and Willow sat on a convenient low wall and opened it. It was from Gran and was short. 'Dear Willow, you should come home as soon as possible. Your dad is extremely ill. Gravely ill, the doctor says. I hardly need to tell you what that means. Don't delay.' She ended with love.

Willow turned the envelope, dazed with shock. It was dated November the second and must have been received at the manor before Frances had taken her to London. Had Frances deliberately kept the letter back, fearing that what was in it might dissuade her maid from accompanying her to London? She knew of Dad's serious illness. Or had she simply forgotten it? Willow went straight to the railway station and, arriving in Bristol, took the tramcar for Barton

Hill. As she turned the corner of her street she saw that the neighbours' blinds and curtains were half drawn. She raced to the front door and into the house.

Clara was sitting by the fire. She looked up. Her face was pale and drawn, her eyes lack-lustre. 'Willow.' Weak tears rolled down her cheeks. 'I'm glad you're here, my love. I thought you'd have come before.'

'I couldn't. I didn't get Gran's letter until today. Mum, how is he?'

Willow felt a huge weight pressing on her. Before Clara spoke she knew the answer. 'Dad took a sudden turn for the worse an' passed away two days ago. It's a shame you couldn't have been with him. He'd have liked that.'

'Where is he?' Willow was devoured by grief, bursting with violent emotions of love, sorrow, regret, fury.

Clara's eyes went to the ceiling and Willow slowly made her way upstairs. Dad lay in a plain coffin on the bed he had shared with Clara. His cheeks were sunken, but he looked peaceful. Willow kissed his forehead, then knelt by his side and laid her head against the wood of the coffin. She made no sound but inside she said his name over and over. She told him of her bitter pain that he had died before she came, she prayed for him, clumsily because she wasn't used to prayer.

She wondered if there really was a heaven like they said in church and if she'd meet him again. She couldn't move, she didn't want to move, her anguish was so great, but would be greater still if she left him. She was shaking with cold when a hand on her shoulder made her look up.

Clara said, 'Shall I bring you a cup of tea, my love, or will you come downstairs?'

Willow stared at her mother and tried to speak, but no words came. 'Come on, Willow, come downstairs with me. He's at peace now, poor man, after all his suffering.' Clara helped Willow up and, moving like an automaton, she followed her mother.

Clara poured her a cup of tea and Willow asked, 'Did Dad ask for me?'

Clara hesitated, but her emotions were too raw, too pared to the bone, to dissemble. 'He asked, my love, of course he did. You were our first. We both had happy memories of your birth. But don't worry. Dad knew that you'd have come if you could. He sent his love.'

Willow drank her tea, not tasting it, her mind still upstairs.

Clara said, 'The neighbours have been real good to me. I've not been able to put any money by. The doctor's bills—' Her voice broke, then she went on, 'He was kind. I'm glad we called him in. He gave Dad medicine that eased his pain. The neighbours have had a collection an' given me thirty shillings. I'll need more, of course, but I can borrow enough to give our Dad a decent funeral.'

'Don't worry, Mum, I can help out.'

Clara looked up. 'How? You send me all your wages.'

'Upper servants get good tips.'

'I remember Gran sayin' so,' said Clara.

Willow said, 'He'll have a decent burial, all right, and what's more we'll buy a ham and make sandwiches and you can ask who you like back for a bite. I can give you five pounds.'

Clara's eyes opened wide. 'Five pounds! That much?'

In the face of her mother's startled gratitude, Willow felt hypocritical, but she had to keep something back until she found a job. Telling Clara now that she had been sent from the manor in disgrace would be too much of a blow.

'You're a good daughter. One of the best.' Clara stood up and leaned on the mantelpiece, one hand covering her face, the other held out to prevent any more talk. Willow went to her and put her arms round her. She could feel Clara's shoulder blades, sharp through her thin dress. She needed more food, she needed rest, and she desperately needed the money Willow had earned at the manor. A great hatred of Frances and the Maddisons dug itself into her consciousness and sent down roots.

* * *

244

One by one the family came home and greeted Willow with relief, as if she would be able to make things right again.

Jasmine put her skinny arms round her sister and nuzzled her face, wet with tears of grief and love, into her neck. 'Where were you? Our Dad wanted you.'

Willow shrank from the stab of pain. 'I came as soon as I could, love.'

Even Marigold was subdued, and shock and distress were written on the boys' faces.

Alfred and Sam arrived together. Sam was ashamed and angry because he'd failed the labour test and couldn't work yet. Willow kissed him. He wasn't bright, but he was good-natured and kind and eager to run round to Gran's to tell her that Willow had come. He waited until Gran had put on her hat and coat and accompanied her back, his hand under her elbow, slowing his pace to her faltering steps. Gran's health had deteriorated further. She had been sprightly, in spite of her rheumatics; now she was very bent, very old. She embraced Willow, appreciating her double grief. 'You didn't hear about your dad in time,' she said. 'My poor girl.' Willow blessed her understanding which was like balm on an open wound.

Joe returned late from his overtime job as errand boy to the butcher. He propped his heavy bicycle with its huge wickerwork basket over the front wheel against the wall and raced in. 'Willow! I heard you were here.' He too looked as if a burden had rolled from him. They all relied on her, the eldest, the one who had branched out so successfully. 'I'm ever so glad to see you,' he said. He had to bend to kiss her.

'How you've grown in such a short time. You're taller than me.'

'I'm gettin' on well, an' I can get cheap meat and sausages an' stuff late on a Saturday night. It helps out.'

'It does that,' said Clara, smiling at her eldest son.

'Can't stop,' he said. 'I've still got meat to deliver – that's if no one's pinched it off my bike. I'll get a terrible row if they have. See you later, Willow.'

* * *

The funeral was well attended. In spite of his long spell of inactivity at home, Arthur Riches had kept plenty of friends and they came, wearing the darkest clothes they could muster from their meagre wardrobes. Willow wore all black because that was all she had with her. As the family followed the coffin up the chapel aisle a tall man turned to look at her. Sidney Moor. Again. It seemed he was determined to be a part of the Riches family in any way he could.

Willow watched the coffin being lowered into the ground, her whole body aching with misery. The November fog swirled around them, icy and wet. Jasmine wept quietly all through the ceremony, Clara kept her handkerchief pressed to her shaking lips, the boys fought off unmanly tears. Marigold was very pale and looked angry as if Dad had done her a personal spite by dying. Gran leaned on her stick, staring into the open mouth of the grave, her face set and expressionless.

When the last words had been intoned, they trooped home, followed by the guests. Mr and Mrs Tucker, whose wreath had been the largest, seated themselves with properly lugubrious expressions. Gran was given a place of honour by the fire and anyone in the street, any one of Arthur's friends who could attend, crowded in. Mrs Tucker permitted some of the ladies to sit in her room; the men overflowed into the scullery where they started on the keg of beer.

Clara had invited Sidney. 'He's been such a good lad,' she whispered in response to Willow's question. 'He played draughts with your dad an' cards, an' read to him. Dad enjoyed his visits.'

When the guests were munching sandwiches and drinking strong tea Willow eased her way to Sidney. 'Mum's told me how kind you've been. Thank you. Thank you very much.'

'I did what I could to help your mum. I was fond of your dad.'

'I can only say thank you again. Wouldn't you prefer

to join the men in the scullery? There's plenty of beer for all.'

'I'm not much of a one for beer, thanks. How's your job going?'

Willow said evasively, 'I've got to make my way in the world, now, more than ever.'

'Because your dad has gone?'

'Yes,' she said, the truth of her jobless position wafting over her like a chill wind.

Sidney said, 'It's a long while since he added anything to the purse. In fact he's been a drain on it.'

Willow's eyes opened wide with shock. 'How could you? At his funeral!' Her voice had risen. She lowered it when she saw several heads turned their way. 'How could you say something so ungenerous?'

Sidney stared down at her. 'I'm only stating the truth. I thought you'd prefer it. Because I see things straight doesn't mean I don't sympathise. I know that if he'd had the money to go to a sanatorium up in the mountains somewhere he might have lived for many more years.'

Willow couldn't answer. He was right, of course.

She produced two bottles of sherry, a decent one, having learned something about wine at Buddleigh Manor, an extravagance which would help Clara to look back on Dad's funeral day with pride. She had borrowed tumblers and wine glasses from Dad's local pub free of charge and they toasted the memory of the dear departed. The men stuck to the beer, but the women polished off the sherry, something they usually tasted only at Christmas and only then if they were going through a good spell. The guests left, several of them happily tipsy. They wrung the hands of Clara and Gran and Willow, and kissed the other children. Jasmine, who loathed being kissed, kept smiling through the rather slobbery goodbyes. She's growing up well, thought Willow.

There were further compliments about Arthur and then the house fell quiet as, the ceremonial of the funeral over, the family lapsed into their private grief.

* * *

Willow returned to London after a week. She'd bought a return ticket and she had three pounds and a few coppers left with which to begin again. She had come close several times to telling Clara the truth, but hadn't been able to bring herself to destroy her mother's pride. After the burial Clara had been complimented many times on her fine eldest girl with her posh job in a great mansion. A lady's maid, as everyone agreed, wasn't like being a servant at all and there were so many prospects and she might easily marry above her. With her looks she was bound to be sought after.

As the train clattered over the rails Willow pondered on her situation. She must write to Mrs Westerby asking for her things to be sent on, with the small amount of pay to which she was entitled, but that had to wait until she had an address. She had decided that although Henry wouldn't have the easiest access to the Buddleigh Manor mail he was resourceful and liked her and would agree to forward letters. On her way to Bristol, she had wondered if she'd be able to confide in Gran and draw comfort from her sympathy but had recognised at once that she had borne enough. Arthur was the last of her children and she had taken his death very hard.

She thought of Frances's total lack of concern over the vital letter about Dad. The memory would wreck her peace of mind for years, perhaps for ever. Willow turned her face from the other occupants of the carriage, struggling to control her distress with which anger had become so intermingled she couldn't separate them. And already she missed her family. There had been so much to do, so many to care for and loved ones to mourn with. Now she had no one who could share her sense of loss.

Chapter Fourteen

In London, Willow's first task must be to find a room; her second, a job. She'd had no experience in seeking accommodation, but a friendly porter advised her to look through newspapers or in tobacconists' or small general shop windows. 'Decide on the area you want to be in and have a walk round,' he suggested.

'I don't know enough about London to know where I want to be,' said Willow. She was anxious and nervous as people swirled round her like flocks of birds, all knowing their way home. No, not all. There were the down-at-heel tramps, the drunken men and women who rested a while then were moved on by the police, and the women in clothes that were a little too fine, a little too flamboyant, who whispered into the ears of passing men. Willow hadn't been aware of these people when she had visited London for the first time. She too had been shielded. The security given by her job with the Maddisons had enabled her to turn aside from suffering. Well, she had her eyes open now and pitied the women, but she couldn't allow herself to think about the unfortunates. Perhaps they had once arrived in London seeking work.

The porter had removed his cap and was scratching his head. He looked like a family man with his well-fed paunch and affable manner. 'Haven't you got a friend to advise you?'

Willow shook her head.

'Have you got some money? Enough to carry you on until you find work?'

'A little.'

'You'd best make your way south of the river then to

Blackfriars or Walworth. Living's cheaper there, and if you're careful you can find a nice lodging. Mind you, there's some rough folk.' He frowned. 'You don't look cut out for . . . I wouldn't want any of my girls . . . well, good luck, and be careful. If you want directions, ask at a shop. There's some pretty funny people walking about.'

Willow thanked him. She assumed he was referring obliquely to the so-called white slave traffic of which Prue seemed to know a good deal. She had been full of stories in which young women had mysteriously disappeared, never to be seen again but known to be sold into brothels abroad. Willow was neither foolishly naive nor over-bold, and she was aware that she must take care. She had a map from her previous excursions in London and soon worked out the way to Walworth. She hadn't before ventured on the subterranean railway, but did so now. At first she was nervous to be going so far below ground, then came the rushing winds caused by the speeding trains, and noise and echoes, but once aboard a train she was exhilarated by the incredible speed.

Getting out at Blackfriars she found a tobacconist's shop and, sure enough, pinned to a swinging card inside the door there were advertisements of all kinds. One particularly took her attention. It read: 'Room to let over small family business, modest rent. Help in house required in return for small wage'. She asked for the address and the tobacconist looked at her hard. Apparently satisfied with what he saw he scribbled down the address. Hard Street, Walworth, Willow read.

The shop turned out to be a grocer's. It was busy with women buying the day's supplies. Some were respectably dressed, but most were poor and shabby and some wore tattered gowns and wool shawls so ancient that their original warmth must have gone. Willow waited, watching them, listening to the blandishments as they tried to persuade the woman behind the counter to 'Let me 'ave a loaf o' bread, just till payday, missus. I've got nothin' to give the kids.'

Some were successful and filled a shopping bag with goods

'on the slate', others were turned away. One particularly persistent woman refused to leave until the shopkeeper himself came from the back in his large white apron and hustled her out. 'It's no good. I'm sorry about the kids, but you haven't paid a penny for over three weeks. If I was to run my business like that none of us would have anything.'

Willow ached for the disappointed woman, who stood outside and yelled obscenities until the shopkeeper threatened to call the police.

When the last customer had left the woman asked politely, 'Now, what can I do for you, miss?'

'I saw your advertisement in the tobacconist's window. I wonder if I might have the room – that's if it hasn't already gone.'

The woman's attitude altered subtly. 'I thought you was a customer.'

'I may well be,' Willow smiled, 'but I need somewhere to live first.'

'What, may I ask, is your line of work?'

To say she was a dress designer would have been impossibly pretentious. 'Dressmaking,' she ventured.

'I see. Why here? The district's full of women trying to make a living with their needle.'

Willow was silent and the woman said, 'How old are you? Eighteen? Did you lose your last job?'

'I was no longer required. I was a lady's maid, but my mistress married and decided she preferred a different girl.' Willow mixed fact with fiction, hoping it sounded true.

The woman nodded then said, 'Some of them nobs don't give a toss for their servants. I thought you was in mourning with you wearing black, but I suppose that's your uniform. Haven't you got any more luggage?'

'I'm to send for it when I get settled.'

The man had returned. 'Where, might I be so bold as to ask, was you employed?'

Willow hesitated. 'With a family called Maddison.'

'Have you got any references?' asked the woman.

251

'No.'

'No references. Could you get one?'

'I'm sure I could,' Willow replied, thinking of Mrs Narracott.

'I've taken quite a liking to you. You're honest. I can always tell,' said the woman complacently. 'What say, Charlie, shall we let her have the room?'

He nodded, leaned across the counter and shook Willow's hand. 'I'm Charles Wade and this here's my missus, Betsy.'

Willow greeted them politely, giving her name.

'Whoever christened you that?' marvelled Mrs Wade.

'My mum,' said Willow.

'Still alive, is she?'

'Yes.'

'Where do you come from? You talk quite nice, but I can catch a bit of accent.'

'Bristol.'

'Is that right? We been to Weston, haven't we, Charlie. We took the kids there once. It was ever so muddy when the tide went out. It went out so far you couldn't hardly see it. Still, the sands were nice and safe. Why don't you go back and get a job in Bristol?'

Willow was beginning to think that even the comfort of a decent room was too big a price to pay for such inquisitiveness, then Charlie said, 'Give over, Betsy. She seems awful nosy, miss, but it's only because she likes to be of help.'

His tone was teasing and Mrs Wade smiled, though a little frostily. 'Come on, girl, I'll take you upstairs.' As they climbed the stairs she explained, 'Charlie and me live in the room back of the shop and sleep up here. I'm not getting any younger, all my kids are scattered around Britain and there's no one to give me a hand about the place.' She stopped, panting, on a half-landing, one hand beneath her plenteous bosom. 'You never answered my question about Bristol. Why don't you go back there?'

'I think I'll do better here. London's got so many opportunities.'

'Yes, you're right there. What does your father do for a living?'

Willow's stomach contracted at the suddenness of the question. 'Dad died recently.' She found the words difficult to say.

Mrs Wade said, 'Sorry, girl, my Charlie's right. I am too nosy sometimes.' At the head of the stairs she threw open a door. 'Here's the room. My girls used to sleep in it. We use the boys' room for storage now. Five boys and five girls I had, and all but the one girl alive and well today. She was always ailing, poor kid. The rest of them was perfect. Good food, I put it down to. We always had good food to give them. You heard me refuse that woman just now. I expect I sounded hard to you, but you've got to be a bit severe in business or your own kids would starve.'

The room was square, furnished with a double bed, a small bedside cupboard, a chest of drawers and a wardrobe. A table and chair stood beneath the window. On a washstand was a jug, a basin and a small pot painted with lurid roses. 'The public baths are quite near,' said Mrs Wade. 'Charlie and me go there once a week.' She opened the bedside cupboard to reveal a chamber pot as brilliant with roses as the washstand set. 'The lav's out the back.' Linoleum covered the floor and in front of the small fireplace piled with paper and wood was a rag rug. It was scrupulously clean and very cold.

Mrs Wade shivered. 'It's not had a fire in it since Christmas when the family came. It'll soon warm up. There's a coal shed out the back near the lav. Now, about the work I want done . . .'

Willow settled quickly into the Wades' routine. Up at six to make sure the shop was tidy and clean and the shelves well stocked for the eight o'clock opening by which time there was always a queue outside. Mrs Wade prepared breakfast, a substantial one of porridge, bacon and egg, and Mr Wade swept the outside pavement and washed the shop windows.

Willow then helped with the morning customers in between doing the house chores. Mrs Wade lent her a sewing machine, or rather, she deducted a shilling a week for its hire, and Willow's evenings were free, enabling her to get on with her sewing. She had enough to eat, coal for her room and pleasant people to work with, but she was discontented. To earn enough to send home she had to take on any sewing job she was offered, however boring, however time-consuming. This was not at all what she had in mind. She remembered her dream, her determination that she would make it come true, and felt trapped.

The Wades gave her time off at Christmas and she was able to go home. Clara was glad to see her, her eyes lighting up at the sight of her daughter, but she soon sank back into lethargy.

'She's not getting over Arthur's death,' said Gran. 'I haven't either, but I'm old and more than ready to go.' She silenced Willow's protests with a wave of her hand. 'Death's a friend to the old, my love, but your mum isn't so old. She should be getting more out of life, but poor women have a hard time of it all round.'

'If only I could earn more.'

'You do what you can. You've got to stick where you are and get to the top.'

The top! Where was that? She never seemed to get nearer. Every day there was the struggle and every night the realisation that the goal looked just as far off.

Sidney Moor was made welcome on Christmas Eve. He was now quite at home with the Riches. He brought a bag filled with wrapped gifts and placed them under the tree, as usual a spindly affair.

Clara brought him tea, already milked and sweetened. 'How's the family?' she asked.

Willow cringed inwardly at the idea of asking after the Moor family of jailbirds and street girls, but Sidney wasn't put out and Willow realised that this was simply a continuation of a frequent discussion. 'My brother's out again, tougher than ever. The others are still inside. And Nellie got fined.'

Clara shook her head, tutting. 'Why can't they go straight? You've managed it.'

'We're all made different, Mrs Riches. They can't help their natures.'

'I suppose not. Is business good?'

'I've got two new customers, good ones.' He turned to Willow who had been sitting quietly by the fire, happy to be with her family, content for a while to let her problems wash over her. 'Would you like to see my factory?'

'*Your* factory?'

'The others have had a look round. Soon I must go back to work – a couple of last-minute customers – but there's time.'

Clara said, 'Why not, love? He's proud of what he's done and quite right too. He worked it all out.'

'I had a good think,' said Sidney, 'and decided that women always want corsetry of some kind or other. Even if they wear their shoes into holes, they try to keep their bodies together.'

'He's clever, isn't he?' said Clara. 'I'd never have thought of that.'

'You've convinced me,' said Willow. 'I'll get my coat and hat.'

The factory was a small tin-roofed shed not far from the Feeder canal. As Sidney opened the door he said, 'It's only a start, Willow. I'm going to expand.'

'Like the corsets,' said Willow mischievously, bringing a smile to his lips.

Two girls sat at power machines stitching at the strong pink cotton material commonly used for corsets. Willow knew both of them from schooldays and they grinned at her companionably.

'We've only done the cheaper range up to now,' explained Sidney. 'I can sell those easy enough round here. I can't afford to employ anyone else yet and the girls do every-thing, strapping, lacing and finishing but they're good workers and make sure that the corsets are really well made.'

'Who puts the steels in?' asked Willow.

Sidney laughed. 'I forgot you started in corsets. The girls take some home and I've got a few outworkers. They'll be along later to collect their bundles.'

'Can you make a living for all of you with only two machines?'

'Yes. Not a rich one yet, but one day I will. I'm getting some special orders. The steam power will serve more than two machines and I'm keeping a look-out for bankrupt businesses to buy more. If I can get into the fashion trade I'll be able to really charge.'

'How do you find customers?' Willow was intrigued.

'I go round shops touting and I'm not above turning my hand to sewing when it's necessary.'

'You've got it all planned.'

Perhaps a wistful note had crept into Willow's voice. Sidney gave her a sympathetic look. 'It's a pity your job takes you so far away. You must miss your family. Perhaps one day you could work for me. I'll be able to make you an overseer, even perhaps the factory manager – that would open people's eyes, wouldn't it? A woman as factory manager.'

'It certainly would.'

When Willow arrived home Clara was preparing tea and as soon as Joe arrived they ate. Willow had bought flour, butter and currants and made a large fruit cake. As she drew it carefully from the oven she remembered briefly the dozens of different confections which Prue and Mrs Narracott produced for the Maddisons who ate the food sent above stairs with keen appetite, careless of those toiling below. She'd never be like them. She laughed inwardly, ironically. She might never get the chance. At the moment she was further than ever from turning her dream into reality.

As she cut into the still warm cake, extravagantly luscious with currants, she said, 'Who would have guessed that Sidney Moor would turn out so well?'

'I would,' said Clara, accepting a small piece, more to please her daughter than from any wish to eat. 'Anyone who comes out of the Moor family without ever bein' in reform school or prison must be strong-willed.'

'And good,' said Jasmine. 'I like Sidney a lot. He's always kind.' She was seated as close to Willow as she could get, often reaching out to touch her sister to make sure that she was real. Her unwavering devotion both touched and worried her sister. Each night Jasmine demanded stories of Buddleigh Manor and its inhabitants and Willow obliged, her mind jumping ahead of her words to make sure she didn't repeat a story, embellishing a few.

Arthur's death was too recent, emotions too raw for them to enjoy Christmas, though they tried. On her last night Willow lay awake, listening to the even sounds of her sisters' breathing, wishing she hadn't got to leave them. Even Marigold had behaved quite well. Willow had a suspicion that this was a deliberate move to dissuade her sister from asking too many questions. The following day Willow set off, her heart heavy at the thought of all that she was leaving behind. And she was worried too. In spite of Marigold's efforts she had cornered her sister and asked some pertinent questions. She had received a flow of denials, statements, promises and, she suspected, lies. 'I told you, there's no harm in anything I do,' Marigold declared. 'You shouldn't badger me like this.'

In London, Willow settled back into her routine which she found more repetitive and boring than ever, working as a shop-assistant, more often as a housemaid, making conventional gowns for the wives and daughters of local tradesmen who looked scandalised if she asked for more than a pittance of payment and hinted that there were plenty of other seamstresses who would be glad of the work. Willow knew this to be true. Gradually she became impervious to the ill-tempered protests of clients who wanted a lot for a little and, if they had asked for pretty extras in lace or fur, just waited until the diatribe was over then held out her hand for the money. The fact that they paid and came back was proof enough that she was the best. They were small triumphs, but her first.

She got plenty of exercise in the house and shop, but needed time to walk outside. She'd forgotten how unhealthy the air of a town could be. Bristol was bad enough, but London was worse, with its tens of thousands of smoking chimneys. In Bristol she had seen poverty far worse than her family's, but had accepted it, as children accept most things. Now the truly pitiful state of so many almost destitute people became clear and she began to understand why women like Jane Barton withstood so much suffering to gain power for them. The Riches had had to struggle, but at least they all pulled together and their home, however humble, was a refuge. Here, in street after street, there was little but poverty and despair and men and women took on any work they could find, however degrading, the women scrubbing doorsteps, shelling peas or peeling potatoes in hotel kitchens, the men shovelling coal or horse manure. They all laboured to buy food, but as often as not defeated, degraded, needing something to deaden their misery, disappeared into one of the public houses which proliferated and quickly got drunk on beer at twopence a pint.

The children who were old enough to go to school got a midday meal of soup; they were the lucky ones. Not all families were feckless, of course. She learned that late on a Saturday night the poor bought two pennyworth of block ornaments from the butchers – pieces of meat trimmed off the joints, sometimes weighing several pounds if the butcher had had a good day. The very poorest bought giblets or lights and Willow knew she would have to be literally starving to stomach them. After buying the meat, the most desperate hadn't a penny for the gas or coke for the fire and it was common to see women and children trudging with anything they could find to the pawn shops.

The best-dressed women were, she soon discovered, the prostitutes who swarmed out of their hideaways in the early evening. The less successful sold themselves locally; the younger, prettier, cleverer, took the tube to Victoria where they met 'a better class of customer', as one of them later explained to Willow without a trace of self-consciousness. Several of them shopped in Wade's and expected and received good service, because they always paid promptly in cash.

'You've got to serve all sorts in a grocery shop,' said Mrs Wade, sniffing contemptuously.

Willow was non-committal. It was easy to despise them from a position of respectable strength. Some of the girls were unfriendly, others downright hostile – jealous of you, was Mrs Wade's verdict – but some were eager to chat. Two in particular Willow liked. Edna and Muriel were well spoken and polite, and both had a sense of fun. When the Wades weren't in the shop they shared a joke.

Muriel said one day, 'How much d'you make here?'

When Willow told her she gave a little scream. 'We make that in half a day in Victoria. You'd never believe how eager some of the men coming off the trains are. You'd think their wives hadn't given them a good you-know-what for years.'

'I'm not surprised,' said Edna. 'I've seen photographs of some of their wives.'

Both girls shrieked with mirth. The jollity was cut short when Mrs Wade walked in and glared at them. 'Serve the young ladies, Miss Riches,' she said. 'There's unpacking of supplies to do before you've finished.'

She'd put a slight emphasis on the word 'ladies'. Willow felt humiliated for them, but Edna grinned and Muriel winked.

On their next visit Muriel said, 'You'd do better working with us. Much more pay.'

Edna frowned, 'She's got to make up her own mind.'

Muriel continued undaunted, 'We'd show you the ropes, and we've got good protection. If a man looks like cutting up rough with us, he gets taken care of.'

'That's good. Who takes care of him?'

'Our boyfriend,' Muriel said.

'One between you?'

Willow had spoken lightly, teasingly, but Edna flushed. 'We don't mind sharing, do we, Muriel?'

'Not us,' declared Muriel, though she didn't sound convinced.

'I've other ambitions,' Willow explained carefully, not wanting to hurt their feelings, 'and besides, I don't think I'd be very good at – what you do.'

Muriel laughed. 'It's easy. Money for nothing. Well, nearly nothing.' Her pretty mouth curved in a wide smile which revealed perfect white teeth. She had reddish-brown hair and used make-up discreetly, as did Edna. 'You'd need hardly any make-up,' continued Muriel. 'Perhaps none at all. What do you think, Edna?'

'She'd have to wear a bit. It'd be expected of her, but not put on with a shovel like some. You're wasted serving behind a counter.'

'It isn't all I do,' said Willow. 'I'm a dressmaker, too.'

She was interrupted by another small scream from Muriel. 'A *dressmaker*. That's one of the worst-paid jobs of all.'

Edna, who was quieter, and with her light brown hair and eyes and delicate complexion looked more like a Sunday School teacher than a prostitute, said, 'Do you need work?'

'I have plenty to do, but I can always use more.'

'Would you make a dress for me? I'd like a really pretty one to wear when my boyfriend takes me out. We're going to the theatre tomorrow.'

'I should be delighted, but I'm afraid I can't make it ready for tomorrow night.'

'I want one, too,' said Muriel.

'Of course.'

'That's settled then,' said Edna. 'We'll bring you some patterns.'

When they were there Willow enjoyed their company, but they left her feeling sad. One day they would look old and used and have to join the others on their way down, taking on any man they could get, standing against a wall, for a shilling or less.

One day when they came to the shop, Muriel was heavily veiled.

'Aren't you well?' asked Willow sympathetically.

Muriel just shrugged and murmured something unintelligible, but Edna said, 'The bastard gave her a beating.'

'Who?' Willow was bewildered.

'Our boyfriend, Cyril. Just because she wanted to come to the theatre with us the other night. You're daft, aren't you, Mu, because you know he never takes us out together. One of us has to work. "Keep the money rolling in," is what he says.'

'But he took you last time and we're supposed to go in turns,' said Muriel.

'Can I help it if he likes me better?'

Muriel muttered ferociously and moved towards Edna, and Willow hastily asked them what they had come to buy. The more she heard of Cyril the less she liked him. She knew that their word for him was a euphemism. He was a pimp, something she had learned about very quickly. Pimps were despised by everyone except women who, however badly they were mistreated, actually loved them.

'I was silly,' said Muriel who had quickly regained her composure, 'it was just that I really wanted to see *Hullo Tango*. Ethel Levey's in it. She's so pretty and clever. I wish I had her talent, then I wouldn't have to walk the streets.'

'Give over,' advised Edna. 'You could have gone into a different job, a factory or shop or even as a typewriter girl in an office. You're quite clever. You wanted work that would earn you good money.'

'I didn't know what I was letting myself in for.'

'She's down in the dumps,' said Edna, 'and no wonder. Cyril's got big fists.'

Willow's brain reeled in the face of her matter-of-fact statement. 'How bad is it?' she asked Muriel, as Edna tangoed round the shop singing, 'He had to get under,

Get out and get under—' She invested the words with such naughty overtones that the others laughed. 'It's from the show,' she said.

Then Muriel shrugged and threw back her veil. Willow was shocked. One eye was blackened, there was a bruise under her chin and her lip was split.

'He's a brute! Why do you stay with him?'

'He doesn't hit us often and only when we ask for it,' Muriel answered.

'No woman asks for that,' Willow protested.

Muriel closed the conversation by reading out the shopping list and Willow wrapped up their order. She said, 'You won't be working tonight, Muriel?'

'Of course I shall. I'll use stage make-up. The clients never see me in a good light.'

'Where do you take them?'

'Curious, aren't you?'

Willow flushed. 'Sorry.'

'I'm only teasing. We take them to St James's Park, or sometimes to the garden of an empty house. Some clients want us to go to their own place with them. That can be a bit tricky.'

'It's warmer and more comfortable,' said Edna.

'It can be dangerous too.'

'Not with Cyril watching out for us. More than one fine gentleman's got his nose bloodied when he's tried to get funny, and the best of it is they don't dare complain to the police or their relatives will find out what they've been up to.'

'Yes, he looks after us well,' said Muriel.

Willow tried to picture Cyril. He'd be tough, big and sneaky-looking, probably over-dressed too. He was none of these. When he walked into the Wades' shop one morning, Willow moved forward to serve him.

'Mrs Wade's out.' His words were more of a statement than a question. 'Where's Mr Wade?'

'Up in the storeroom. Do you want to see him?'

'No, it's you I came to see.'

262

Willow waited politely, not taking her eyes off him. He was about five feet ten, well-built, conservatively dressed and nicely spoken, as Gran would say. His light eyes surveyed her equally thoroughly, but without causing offence. 'I believe you know me by reputation,' he said.

'I'm sorry, I don't think—'

'Muriel and Edna have told you of me.'

'You're Cyril?'

'Yes, you look surprised. What did you expect?'

'A bully,' said Willow.

His eyebrows raised a little, the skin round his eyes crinkled in a small smile. 'Because I chastised Muriel? She needed a good hiding. She doesn't mind. She was jealous of Edna and she'd think I didn't care about her unless I hit her.'

Willow was unimpressed. She'd seen wife-beating and knew the excuses the men gave for their brutality.

'I'm working,' she said coldly. 'I've no time to gossip.'

He stayed where he was, his eyes roving round the shop from the well-stocked shelves, to the saucepans and kettles and brooms dangling from ceiling hooks, to the big tins of biscuits stacked in front of the counters. 'Do you enjoy working here?'

'Yes.'

'I don't believe you. My girls tell me you'd prefer to make good clothes.'

Willow stayed silent. She hated Cyril's presence.

'You haven't much to say for yourself.'

'No. Not to you.'

He smiled, broadly this time, tipped his hat and left.

Willow stayed up long hours working on the gowns for Edna and Muriel. They came for their final fitting and looked at themselves in Willow's mirror.

Muriel's was an apple-green silk tunic over a draped bottle-green dress. It had pink lace sleeves and a matching fichu. Edna's was quieter, as befitted her genteel appearance, a crêpe de Chine oyster brocade with cream lace.

'My, aren't we fine?' cried Muriel, twisting to see the back. 'We've never looked better.'

They paid two pounds ten shillings each, plus the cost of the material, and handed it over without the slightest hesitation. After they had gone Willow looked down at the money. Five pounds! For work she had thoroughly enjoyed doing. If this went on she'd even be able to save, to return to Bristol, set up her own business and be near her family.

Edna and Muriel brought friends and Willow was able to send home enough money to ensure Clara's well-being and peace of mind. Henry still acted for her so that her letters carried the right postmark.

Muriel dashed in one evening before she began work. 'Cyril wants you to meet him,' she explained breathlessly. 'Could you go to the Lame Duck pub in the next street at seven tonight? He going to suggest something that'll help you. Mind you go.' She hurried out without waiting for an answer, apparently thinking that a summons from Cyril was tantamount to one from royalty. At first, Willow had no intention of meeting Cyril, but by seven she was free and she was tempted. She'd never been one to shirk a new experience and a drink in a pub with a pimp was certainly a new one. In fact, entering a pub at all was new to her. Besides, she wanted to see just what kind of proposition a man who lived off the bodies of women could possibly try to tempt her with. He was everything she disliked, but he wasn't a fool, so it must be something interesting. The bar was filled with noisy customers and she drew back, but a young man in a long white apron caught sight of her. He had been told to watch out for her and she was directed to a small lounge where Cyril rose politely at her entrance.

'You came. I knew you would.'

Willow was infuriated that she had proved him right. 'I can't stay for more than a few minutes. I've plenty to do.'

'I'm sure you have. You're a very busy girl. What will you have to drink?'

He bought wine for her and whisky for himself. Willow

took a sip of the wine and grimaced at its sour roughness. She put the glass on the table.

Cyril laughed, but even his laughter was muted. 'You're quite right, my dear. It's execrable stuff.'

'You asked to see me,' she said, keeping her tone business-like.

'I did. I've got a proposition.'

'If you think for one minute that I'm going to work for you—' Willow rose, shoving her chair back with such haste it almost toppled.

'Calm down,' he said evenly. 'I'm not expecting you to follow Muriel and Edna.'

'I'm not prepared to do a thing for you! Not one thing!'

'Why did you come to meet me then?'

She frowned. 'Call it curiosity.' She sat down and said the words she'd wanted to say since she'd met him. 'It's a wonder to me that any man can make his living by putting young girls out into the street.'

'My girls don't do badly out of it and I'm watchful to see that they're not exploited.'

She stared at him. 'What do you think *you're* doing?'

'I'm giving them a living. They were both out of work and suffering privation. Now they share a comfortable flat and have plenty to spend. They haven't grumbled, have they?'

The question was rhetorical and Willow didn't answer. Cyril wasn't put out. He simply smiled his bland smile. His face expressed a gentle calm, but his eyes held menace. She looked down at his hands. They were large. She imagined them closed into fists, crashing into Muriel's face and wondered why she was here.

'I must go,' she said.

He put his hand on her arm to detain her and she had a job not to shrink from it.

'I'll not waste your time, or mine,' he said. 'I've seen the gowns you've made. They're beautiful. How would you like to set up in business for yourself with me as a backer?'

For a few seconds Willow felt that the world was full of joyous singing. Her own business. A place to develop her ideas and ambitions. Her euphoria quickly died. 'Why should you want me to do anything of the sort? Don't you earn enough money from your girls?'

Her contemptuous tone failed to move him. 'They're good workers, yes, but I can see you succeeding to the point where rich women patronise you.'

Willow felt she was struggling in thick mire. This ghastly man was opening a door for her which, if she walked through it, could mean the realisation of her dream. All she needed was the money to set up and she was sure she would succeed. She asked, 'Just an ordinary business?'

'Ordinary,' he assured her.

'Why?'

'Suspicious little girl, aren't you? Well, I will admit I have another motive. You see, my dear Willow, there's nothing like a respectable thriving business – and I'm sure it would thrive under your direction – to lull suspicion.'

'Suspicion of what?' But she already knew the answer.

'With your gown shop as a front I could accommodate perhaps a dozen girls in a really big house. You can keep all the money you make and have a share in the profits of the house. All I'd want is for you to let the girls and their clients go through the shop.'

'You're crazy!'

Cryil shook his head ruefully. 'Quite right. I knew you were clever. Of course they mustn't go through the shop. We'd need a place with a back entrance. What do you say?'

Willow sat half stunned by the impact of the horrible picture he was painting. 'You are offering me a share in a *brothel*?'

'Keep your voice down.' For the first time he looked rattled.

'A *brothel*,' she repeated. 'How dare you? How dare you!'

'Calm down, my dear. You took the girls' money and were glad of it. You knew how they earned it.'

'It isn't the same. It isn't!'

'Certainly it is.'

'They need clothes wherever they work.'

'I quite agree, but no ordinary employment would enable them to afford the gowns you've made for them. And the fact is they got the money working for me, and you know it.'

'I charge them a fraction of what those gowns would cost anywhere else.'

'Exactly. And with me you would be able to earn a great deal more money.'

'By getting me to shield your disgusting trade!'

'Your own exclusive business. All you'd have to do is run your gownshop and simply close your eyes to anything else. We should both make lots of money and so would the girls. You've seen for yourself that Muriel and Edna live carefree lives.'

'Except when you beat them! And when they've lost their looks, when they catch some foul disease, what then? I've seen some of the poor women crawling about the streets, picking up a few coppers where they could. You should be ashamed! My trade is an honourable one. Yours is—' She wanted to say more, to repudiate him with such venom that even he would cringe, to spit in his face. She was impotent in the face of her absolute disgust. She walked out.

Chapter Fifteen

From the time Willow walked out on Cyril she got no further commissions from Muriel and Edna and the Wades' shop also lost their custom. She missed their friendly talks. They had staved off the loneliness which the Wades did little to dispel. Other girls came, but she didn't get on close terms with them and her isolation emphasised her deep grief as she thought of her mother and the children struggling on without Dad. He had been helpless before he died, she had scarcely seen him for four years, but he had still been the head of the family, loved and needed.

Then Mrs Wade came back from tea with the vicar's wife and a few church ladies, her face red with fury and embarrassment. 'You're getting the shop a bad name,' she raged at Willow. 'To think that our vicar's wife had to complain. And one of my oldest friends came to you for a fitting for a Sunday gown and met two *street girls* on her way down from your room.'

'I'm sorry.' Willow paused. 'But I thought you knew about them? They make up the best part of my business.'

'Indeed! You ought to be ashamed! And how was I to know who they were?'

'But many of them buy their food here and have done for ages. Without their custom your shop wouldn't be half so successful.'

'Don't you argue with me, my girl. I can't help it if a few floozies pass themselves off as decent women. Most of our customers are respectable. Wade's is the best in the district.'

'That's why the girls come here,' said Willow in an

attempt to calm the furious woman. 'There's no shame in selling them food, is there?'

'Did I say there was?'

'Then why should I mind making their clothes?'

Mrs Wade went a deeper shade of red. 'It's not the same.'

Willow sighed. The lines between morality and sin could get very blurred, especially where money was concerned.

'I never *knew* what they were!' cried Mrs Wade. 'And even if I suspected, it's not the same as letting them into our private quarters. For all I know they might be telling local thieves what I've got and where it's kept.'

'But they only come up the stairs to my room. They never look into your rooms, I make sure of that.'

'No, it won't do! It's got to stop! I'll have no more floozies up my stairs.'

Willow felt desperate as she saw her chief source of income going down the drain. 'But, Mrs Wade, you'll lose more than you realise. Some come to see me then buy their groceries.'

'You think we can't do without you, do you?'

'No, I didn't say that—'

'I should hope not. Whatever you do makes no difference to us. I never had this kind of trouble before, and I'll not have it now.' She had whipped herself into a fury. 'Best thing is for you to pack your bags and get out.'

Willow was horrified. 'But, Mrs Wade, please! You and Mr Wade say I work hard. You've always praised me.'

'We can get another girl. We don't have to have one who's bringing disgrace to our name. And another thing – that *nasty* Cyril never came here before you arrived.'

Willow was angry at the injustice. 'I have nothing to do with that beastly man! I never would!'

'That's what you say. You was seen with him in a pub. Nice thing that is for a girl who's living in my house.'

She had goaded Willow into unwise retaliation. 'You must have a good team of spies to know that.' Mrs Wade opened her mouth for another tirade and Willow said quickly, 'All right, I'm sorry, I admit it was silly of me to meet him, but I soon told him I wasn't interested in what he had to say.'

'And what was that? Did he offer you a place in his string of girls?'

'No, he didn't. And I told him to leave me alone.'

'You could have said that here. You didn't have to go drinking with him. It won't do! You've got to go, now, and I know Mr Wade will agree.'

It was useless to try to reason with her. 'Let me at least find another place first,' Willow begged.

'No! You're to leave at once.'

She cooled off later and agreed that Willow should stay for two more days. 'By that time I expect you'll have settled something,' said Mr Wade hopefully. He smiled warmly, almost too warmly at her, a smile intercepted by his wife who glowered, making Willow wonder if she was being sent away for a reason unsuspected by her and very different from the one which Mrs Wade had given.

Willow found herself once more in a position where she needed accommodation. It must be local, here where she was building her reputation as an excellent dressmaker. She couldn't expect to find an arrangement as beneficial as the Wades', enabling her to send much of her profit to her mother. Henry sent on her letters faithfully and Gran wrote every week now. She was full of praise for a grand-daughter who could earn money so successfully. Willow remembered phrases from her last letter. 'Your mum's beginning to look better. She doesn't have to take in so much washing now. The boys are earning too, but it's the money you send that makes all the difference. Be careful, though, my love, you must take care of your own needs. I know how fussy mistresses can be and it won't do for you to dress in shabby clothes when you've got such a high position. I'm glad to hear that your sewing is coming in useful.'

Coming in useful. If only Gran knew! She had been to the third advertised local room to rent and been turned down by the landlady who, it appeared, was a friend of Mrs Wade. The first two places had been dirty and foul-smelling and she had refused them. On the afternoon of the second day's grace granted by Mrs Wade she was peering at the many cards pinned to a small shop doorway when she heard her name and turned to see Edna and Muriel.

Her questions came immediately and without thought. 'What are you doing out at this time? Shouldn't you be resting?'

Muriel shrieked with mirth. 'We're starting early. You'd make a kind madam if you had the inclination.'

Willow smiled. 'Well, I haven't!'

'We know,' said Edna. 'Cyril's furious with you.'

'Good!'

'What are you looking for?' asked Muriel, gesturing to the cards.

'A place to live. Mrs Wade's decided she doesn't want me there.'

The girls looked discomfited. 'Is it because of us?'

'No. The vicar's wife was scathing about some of my more flamboyant customers who came upstairs for fittings.'

Muriel giggled and Willow laughed. 'It's no laughing matter, really,' she said. 'Mrs Wade's a hypocrite. She doesn't mind serving anyone downstairs.'

'We did help to get you turfed out, didn't we? It amounts to that,' Edna said reflectively.

'And you need somewhere to live,' said Muriel.

'And work,' said Edna. 'And I'm afraid you won't find decent digs round here. Cyril's spread the tale that you're a loose-moralled woman.'

Her tone was so matter-of-fact that it took Willow a moment to make sense of the words. She was appalled. 'That's *slander*. It's illegal. But who'd listen to a worm like him?'

'There are some who don't know what he does, others are afraid of him. He's rich and can make things unpleasant for someone he takes a dislike to.'

'You know what a slimy brute he is!' exclaimed Willow. 'Yet you stay with him.'

'He's got his good side, love.'

'I haven't seen it! Hell! Now I'll have to begin all over again in a different district and it could take ages to get established, and I won't have the Wades' wages, small though they were.'

'Could you go back to Bristol?' asked Edna.

'I could but I won't, not like this. I want to go home a success.'

The girls exchanged glances then Edna said, 'How would you like to live in Bayswater?'

'Why there?'

'Because it's a better neighbourhood and I've got a cousin who lives in a good house there. I'm sure she'd help you. She and her friends could easily afford your frocks and pay more for them than we do.'

'You're both so kind. You've been my only friends since I arrived in London.'

They looked pleased, though Edna said, 'If you see Cyril, for God's sake don't tell him we helped you. I'll write a letter to my cousin. Her landlady's got rooms she hardly ever lets out because they're up too many stairs. I think she'd be quite glad to have someone take one, especially a girl who's as handy with her needle as you. My cousin's name is Mabel really, but she calls herself Claudette because she thinks it's prettier.'

Edna kept her word and Willow caught a tube train to Bayswater and found Tottingham House. It was narrow and not as tall as the houses either side. Somehow the difference gave it a discreet appearance, like a nervous girl who hides in her mother's apron folds. The paintwork, curtains, brass doorknocker and mud scraper were immaculate. The door was opened by a pretty maid in white apron and cap who looked about fourteen.

Willow handed her the introductory letter given to her by Edna. It was addressed to Mrs Bliss and the girl invited her to wait in the hallway. It was wide and contained a highly polished table with a large green plant in a yellow pot and a tray which held letters for posting. There was also a box fixed at head height with pigeon holes, each with its own key and labelled with a name. The general air of cleanliness and serenity was continued in the landlady's living room.

The woman gave her a shrewd look when the maid showed her in. She was stout, seated at a desk where she had been entering figures into a ledger. She said, 'Please sit down. I'll not keep you long.'

Willow sat in a comfortable chair near a coal fire and held out her cold hands to the blaze.

'Bring the young lady a cup of tea,' said the woman. 'Do take off your coat.'

'Thank you.'

The tea was brought and the woman left her desk to pour it into a porcelain cup. She settled her large, severely corseted body into a chair which had taken on her contours and offered Willow a selection of home-made cakes, then she leaned back, lighting a narrow cigar from which she blew clouds of blue smoke while she subjected her visitor to a long scrutiny.

'Do you always wear black?' she asked.

'Not always, but it's serviceable and the frock is well made. I can't afford to waste it.'

'It's certainly well made, but it looks like a servant's dress. Are you a servant?'

'I was a lady's maid,' said Willow steadily.

'Lost your job?'

'Yes.' The woman's attitude was serene and unhurried, as if this interview didn't matter at all, and Willow was provoked into saying, 'It wasn't my fault.'

'Came to London seeking your fortune, eh? And decided to venture into Bayswater where the streets might be paved with a bit more gold than you've seen up to now?'

Willow gave a little smile. 'You make me sound like Dick Whittington.'

'You see the funny side of things,' said the woman. 'An

asset in any type of work so long as your clients don't think you're laughing at them. So you'd like to take rooms here?'

'Yes, please.'

'You're pretty. Take off your hat and let's have a proper look at you.' Willow obeyed. 'My, yes, you're very pretty. Good figure, too, and nice teeth. Edna says you won't mind an attic. It's ten shillings a week.'

Willow gasped. 'How much?'

'That's the price, my dear. I look after my tenants and you'll soon have enough work to manage the rent and have a lot more besides. The girls here know they're in a good place and pay me well. The second-floor apartment is two pounds, the first two pounds ten, and the ground floor three. What's your speciality?'

'Sewing,' said Willow.

The woman looked startled. 'Sewing? That's a new one on me.'

'Is it? What do your other tenants do? They must be very clever to afford such rents.'

'They are.'

'Well, I'm afraid I can't earn that kind of money. My family – I need to send as much as possible home.'

The woman nodded. 'That's what a lot of young ladies do. Now, I've taken to you. I don't often take to people, but I like you and I'm sure you'll do very well. Give the attic a try. I'll only ask for a small percentage of your profits until you get going.'

Ten shillings was more than Mum paid for her three rooms and the woman wanted some of her earnings as well. Willow didn't like the sound of it, but she had to sleep somewhere. 'I'd like to see the room,' she said. 'I don't mind stairs. In service, you get used to them.'

'Your clients won't like them, though, but I suppose you've thought of that. I've never had a girl who wanted to go above the second floor, but if you think you can make money up there—'

'I'm sure I can. I shall be trying to get rich clients and I

274

won't ask them to climb all those stairs. I'm sure to be able to visit them in their homes.'

The woman's eyes opened wide. 'Visit them in their homes? I've never heard the like! Well, you learn something new every day. You'll have to tell me just how you manage it. And you'll need to give me a card setting out what you do for the gentlemen.'

'I don't sew for gentlemen, only ladies.'

The stare Mrs Bliss gave her this time was very long indeed.

Willow was suddenly nervous. 'What did Edna put in the letter?'

'She said you were down on your luck and needed a place to work. She forgot to mention what kind of work. Dressmaking!' Mrs Bliss laughed loudly. 'You really are a dressmaker. That Edna's a silly fool. She should have made it clear. I've got her cousin here. A very superior girl.'

Willow stood up. She felt nervous, disappointed and ashamed all at the same time, and she wanted to get out of here with the least possible embarrassment. 'I'm sorry. There's obviously been a misunderstanding. Edna knows I won't do – her kind of work.'

'Pity. You really are a good-looking girl. I'm surprised that their nasty pimp hasn't tried to seduce you.'

'Cyril? I told him to leave me alone.'

'Did you, though? You're not daft. Edna's stupid to stay with him. There are plenty of houses who'd give her protection.'

'She says she loves him.' Mrs Bliss shrugged and Willow said, 'I'd better be on my way. I must have a bed for tonight.'

'You can stay here.'

'No, I think not.'

'It's all right, my dear. I don't operate a white slave trade. If you want to spend your life sewing in my attic for a little when you could live in luxury and earn a lot that's your affair. My girls will be glad to have a handy dressmaker and they'll advertise your frocks – if they're good enough, that is.'

'They are.'

The woman nodded. 'I like a girl who's sure of her trade. What's your last name? Edna forgot to say. Riches? Willow Riches? Are you sure? I mean, is it really yours or a made-up one?'

'It's really mine.'

'Well, it's certainly different. I'm Anabel Bliss. Bliss by name and Bliss by nature, my gentlemen friends always said. Still do. Some of them come to see me after all these years, though often now it's just for a chat and a drink, anything to get away from their wives.' She rang for the maid. 'This is Maisie. She'll show you up. She's to have the room next to yours, Maisie.'

Maisie was a little shy, but friendly and attractive with her fair hair and light blue eyes. The room was quite small. At least, it was small after Buddleigh Manor and even the room at Mrs Wade's, but it was certainly larger than the cell in Holloway. Would she ever wipe her mind clean of that horror? Everything was spotless, and the bed, wardrobe and chest of drawers matched. Round the edges of the floor lay linoleum so highly polished it looked as if the square of carpet was a raft afloat on it. The washstand held a large china jug and matching bowl. There was a gas fire and Maisie pulled aside a curtain to reveal a small alcove in which was a small scrubbed wooden table holding two gas rings on a metal tray, a saucepan, frying pan and kettle.

'If you want to bake,' said Maisie, 'you can use madam's kitchen, provided you give due notice to Mrs Harris, our cook. If you want her to cook for you she'll ask a small fee. There's a wash-house and a small drying lawn out the back. The washerwoman will help you as well, if you pay her. The facilities for you are on the floor below.'

'Facilities? Oh, the lavatory, do you mean?'

'And bath. Madam believes in giving her girls the best. Facilities, madam calls them. She's very particular about the way we speak.'

'Who usually has this room?'

'It's a spare, really. The last girl has gone to the Edgware

Road, though how she'll get on there I don't know. Mrs Bliss said she should never have let her in, and told her to leave. Mrs Bliss is very good at reading people. That girl wasn't the right kind for this house. This is one of the best. I hope you'll be happy here, miss.'

'Thank you,' said Willow. Maisie evidently understood the nature of the house and its occupants. 'The park is so near, isn't it? I enjoy walking.'

'Do you, miss? I don't. I was born in London and never been anywhere much. I'm just waiting till I'm old enough to improve my position here. Madam's very strict and she won't have anyone working from the house before they're eighteen. She's a good sort, is madam.'

'I see. How old are you?'

'Seventeen, miss. I look younger than my years and madam says that's an asset. I've not long to wait and I'm learning a lot. Here's your key and a key to the front door. Let me know if you've got luggage you want fetched. We've got an odd-job man.'

After stowing away her few possessions Willow wrote to Henry and went out to the post, buying provisions on her way back. She cooked herself a pan of bacon and eggs and ate it with slices of bread and lots of butter. That night there was much activity in the house, the voices of men and women laughing and talking, the constant tread of feet up and down the lower stairs. Eventually she slept and when she awoke early the house was as quiet as a tomb.

Willow settled easily into Tottingham House. Gradually she met the other occupants. There were three, one on each floor. Maisie explained earnestly that Mrs Bliss could easily have accommodated more: 'But she gives each girl a bedroom and sitting room and a kitchen all of her own,' she said as proudly as if she were describing a palace. 'You should see their rooms. And all the decorations are changed for a new girl, once Mrs Bliss decides she's right for us.'

When Willow was invited to a formal tea by each girl in

turn she saw what Maisie meant. Comfort with respectability was the style and each girl's apartment was a setting for her special type of beauty. Angelina had a sweet baby face, with a pouting delicate mouth and auburn hair. Claudette was fair with blue eyes and a voluptuous body. Carmen was black-haired, dark-eyed and sultry. They each in turn expressed surprise that Willow refused to use her beauty to make money, but they made her welcome, and even more so when they discovered her sewing skills. When she had arrived Willow had nothing to display and not enough money to purchase good material, but she soon discovered that Bayswater too held jumble sales, some of which, because of the better financial state of the residents, turned out to be gold mines. She took to haunting church halls on crowded Saturday mornings, fighting her way through the crowds at the sales to gather up gowns of velvet, silk and satin, rubbed and worn only round the hems and under the arms, old lace shawls, finely worked cambric and muslin underwear too voluminous to agree with the present fashions – all tumbled together on the stalls and on sale for coppers. She bought scarves and feathers, hats and fans, fine leather gloves and pieces of fur – anything from which she could create something to tempt a woman's purse. She also bought a wool coat and a serge costume and made them over into decent outdoor outfits for herself. Mrs Bliss had a sewing machine which she hadn't used for years and the odd-job man whose large muscular body was in direct contrast to his brain, carried it upstairs.

Toby might be known as the odd-job man, but Willow had no difficulty in picturing how easily he would throw out any client who became a nuisance.

She took the measurements of the three girls and with her basic materials was able to cut enough good stuff to make three gowns. At the fittings they were ecstatic.

'Scarlet!' cried Carmen. 'I look my best in scarlet. And with black lace inserts.'

'I've never seen you in anything better,' pronounced Mrs Bliss, who had puffed and panted her way to the first floor where Carmen was extending the hospitality of her room to the others. Angelina who worked on the ground floor was expecting a client and must keep her room orderly.

'What about *me*?' asked Claudette. She turned round slowly to display the pale blue satin and silk crêpe brocade gown which fell to her ankles.

'Can you walk in it?' asked Carmen. 'It looks tight, even for a hobble skirt.'

Claudette moved gracefully across the room. 'Willow's cut a short slit in the front,' she explained. Claudette wasn't really beautiful, for her eyes were a little too small and her mouth too wide, but she radiated sexuality.

They all turned to examine Angelina who was in a cream crêpe de Chine gown with pale pink lace inserts in the sleeves, a fichu of lace and silk, and a scattering of tiny pearls on the bodice. She looked like a modest English beauty, until she glanced at them sideways from half-closed eyes. Willow had no difficulty in picturing the way men were attracted to her.

'I wish I could wear my frock today,' said Claudette. 'Hurry and finish them, Willow. Can you make us some more?'

'When you've paid me I can buy more stuff, or if you like you can select your own material and I'll fashion gowns to your preferences.'

'You can do that?' Mrs Bliss was astonished.

'Yes. I've done it for years. I began on doll's clothes for my little sister.'

Mrs Bliss laughed. 'It's not the same. The girls had better bring patterns.'

Willow hardly heard her. Mention of her sister brought a wave of longing for her family, and a resurgence of grief for her father which wouldn't go away. The others caught her sadness and fell silent.

'They can bring patterns, can't they?' asked Mrs Bliss.

'Of course,' agreed Willow. 'But I get great pleasure from using my imagination. I want to be a dress designer. It's what I've always wanted.'

* * *

Willow settled happily into her new life. Now she could spend her time sewing without the many chores Mrs Wade had demanded. The girls had readily paid four pounds for their gowns. She could have asked more and next time she would. She had no compunction about doing so. They got exclusive frocks from her and they knew it. They were a marvellous advertisement. Discreet and well-spoken, they were able to operate in the best hotels. Usually they brought clients back; sometimes they accompanied the men to their hotel rooms, though only those known to them. They each had regular 'gentlemen friends', and with their lovely faces and alluring figures were marvellous advertisements for Willow's clothes. She got so many orders that for the first time she could send money home and still save.

One day Maisie tapped on her door. When she entered she stayed just inside, her eager gaze taking in the gowns in varying stages of completion, the swathes of material, the vivid green satin which Willow was sewing for one of the few local beauties who could carry off such a colour. Willow had rented another attic room to hang her creations in, for an extra three shillings a week. Mrs Bliss was delighted with her unusual lodger.

'Yes?' said Willow impatiently to Maisie.

'Oh, sorry. I was looking at the beautiful frocks. There's a gentleman downstairs.'

'What of it?'

'He's asking for you.'

'What! What's his name?'

'Mr Kerslake, miss.'

'Who? Kerslake? I don't know – my God, not Steven!'

'I don't know, miss. He says you're old friends.'

'Please tell him I'll be down in a few minutes. I can't leave my sewing – I'm doing a neckline.'

When Willow entered Mrs Bliss's parlour where she was happily entertaining the male caller she looked in amazement at the man who rose to greet her. He wasn't especially tall, about five foot nine, Willow reckoned. His dark hair fell over his forehead in a broad wave, and his eyes were dark too. He was familiar, yet unfamiliar. She stared at him. Steven Kerslake? Steven was a grubby little bootboy. Then his mouth curved in a smile.

'It is you,' she exclaimed, going forward to shake his hand. 'Steven! After all these years. Where have you been? What happened to you?'

'Sit down, do,' urged Mrs Bliss, thoroughly enjoying herself. She claimed to be a romantic and this meeting with a long-lost male had all the qualities of a good magazine story. 'Give the poor man a chance, Willow. I've sent Maisie for tea. You'll take tea, Mr Kerslake?'

'Yes, please. And do call me Steven.' His voice was well-modulated. 'As to where I've been, it's a long story. I've worked all over the place at anything I could get, but now I'm where I've always wanted to be – in my own shop.'

'A shop! What do you sell?' asked Mrs Bliss, nodding her thanks to Maisie for the tea tray. 'Milk? Sugar?'

'Yes, please,' said Steven. 'I sell books.'

Willow laughed delightedly. 'Books! I might have known. You were always mad about books.'

Mrs Bliss looked disappointed. She had hoped for something more exotic. She wasn't a reader, except for *Home Notes*, a women's magazine, and a brief glance through a daily newspaper.

Willow explained, 'When I began in service I was only the second kitchen maid, and Steven—' She stopped. 'You don't mind my telling Mrs Bliss about you?'

'Why should I? I'm not ashamed of anything I've done.'

'Good. Steven was the bootboy. I was always wallowing in food and he was always covered in blacking.'

Steven grinned. 'You paint a pretty picture.' He glanced down at his boots which were polished to mirror perfection. 'I've never forgotten what I learned.'

'He used to have a tattered old dictionary and we'd huddle in his dark little room at the manor and look up long words.' Willow laughed at the memory.

'You're prettier than ever,' he exclaimed.

Mrs Bliss beamed. This was more like it. 'She's a real beauty, and clever with it. She's a dressmaker. A very exclusive one. My girls won't go to anyone else now.'

'Your daughters?'

Mrs Bliss swallowed her fifth cake. 'Bless you, no. My girls. They work from the house.' Her exaggerated wink left no space for doubt.

Steven coloured. 'Willow—?'

'No, she doesn't,' said Mrs Bliss. 'She only sews.'

He stared hard and Mrs Bliss said severely, 'Now don't you go doubting her. I happen to know she had an offer from a man prepared to set her up in her own gown shop if she'd let him operate his kind of business behind the scenes and she refused, his business being the same as mine. Mind you,' she continued, 'I'm not sure she did the right thing there. It's hard for a girl to get on in the world when she's poor and got no influence.'

'She did the right thing,' said Steven. His tone reminded Willow of his parents' fanatical religion.

'Yes, you're right,' agreed Mrs Bliss blandly. 'You have to have your heart in it to make a living. Willow's got hers set on sewing.'

'I'm glad,' said Steven. 'Will you come out with me, Willow?'

'Come out with you?'

'Don't act daft, girl,' said Mrs Bliss, her cheeks flushed by the fire, the hot tea, and the seven little sweet cakes she had now consumed. 'The man's giving you an invitation. It's time a gentleman gave you an outing.'

'I see. Yes, I'd love it.' Willow smiled. 'Will you take me to see your book shop?'

'My God!' Mrs Bliss rolled her eyes. 'I despair of you sometimes, Willow.'

Steven called for her the next afternoon. He looked approvingly at her dark blue coat and the hat with a long feather around the wide brim, and down at her neat ankles and black kid shoes with tiny bows. 'Fashions have changed, haven't they?' he said. 'When a woman has such pretty ankles as yours they should be on display.'

Willow eyed his dark city suit and bowler hat. 'You're very natty yourself.'

'I have to be. I'm building a clientele of well-heeled men. I'm getting good stock – I learned more than I realised in the manor library – and they come in to browse and buy. I'm saving money to purchase better books.'

'How did you find me?' she asked.

'I went to visit my parents. After I was dismissed from the manor Mum and Dad sent me to a farm miles away and told the people to work me as hard as possible to drive the devil out. They were old acquaintances of Mum and obeyed her. In fact, they were glad to because it meant they got more work out of me. In the end I walked out.

'I decided recently to visit my parents and when I asked for you at the manor Mrs Narracott said you'd left some time ago and she didn't know why except she believed it had something to do with Miss Frances. She said to give you her best wishes if I found you. Then, on my way out, Henry told me your address. He was sure you wouldn't mind.'

'I'm so glad he did. Henry's been a great help to me.'

'He's a good chap. But why do you let your family think you still work at the manor?'

'Because Mum's had enough to bear without worrying about me. I mean to be successful before I tell them anything.'

They turned into Hyde Park and strolled in the sunshine. The scattered snowdrops beneath the trees with their yellow-green spring foliage, the unfolding buds of golden crocuses and the birdsong lent the park a country air. 'I walk here when I can,' said Willow. 'I miss Devonshire.'

'What did Frances do to get you dismissed?'

Willow walked on slowly. It would be such a relief to tell the whole story and she was sure she could trust him.

She spoke swiftly and finished, 'So now you know.'

Steven stopped her and faced her, holding her arms.

'You're a heroine. I think you're wonderful. How could Frances abandon you like that?'

'She's very weak-willed. Perhaps it was a blessing in disguise, as Gran would say. I might have stayed in the manor until I was too old to do anything much. They were cruel to you, too, dismissing you the way they did. It was my fault.'

'No! They don't care. None of them do. Mrs Narracott told me that Miss Violet – Lady Radcliffe, that is – decided she wanted a French maid and found an excuse to throw Miss Jebb out. No one knows what became of her.'

'Poor thing. She's not very clever.' Willow, her nerves soothed by Steven's sympathy, told him of the way she had learned of her father's death, though it was still an agonising memory and it hurt her to speak of it. 'I hate them,' she finished.

Steven held her hand. His was strong, square and warm, with a little dust beneath the fingernails. 'Be careful. Hatred's a powerful emotion. It won't affect them, but it might damage you.'

His shop was on the ground floor of a narrow building in a street off Trafalgar Square. It was lined with shelves of books. An elderly man looked up from cataloguing and stretched his shoulders. 'I'll be on my way now you're back, Steven.'

'Willow, meet Mr Mason. He takes over when I go to sales. Mr Mason, this is Miss Willow Riches, a friend of mine from years back.'

Mr Mason shook Willow's hand. His was brown-spotted and dry. 'I'm happy to meet you, my dear. Steven works too hard. Try to get him to a theatre or one of those bioscopes – the moving pictures.'

Willow smiled. 'I'll see what I can do, but he's never happier than when he's surrounded by books.'

'Sensible fellow.' He put on a rusty black frock coat and a top hat and shuffled off.

'You must be doing well if you can pay an assistant.'

'I don't pay him what he's worth,' said Steven, 'because

he'll only accept a little. He's got a small pension and his life has been spent among books. He'd come in for nothing if I allowed it.'

Willow looked round her, sniffing the delicious scent of leather and paper and floating dust. There were books piled on the floor and stacked on the oak counter and more in the living room. 'I need more space,' said Steven. 'The upper floors are used for storage by a local ironmonger – he's my landlord – but there are two rooms behind this one. They've been neglected and are damp. I shall set them right gradually and take the back one for my quarters and the front one to extend the shop.'

'Where do you sleep?'

'Here.' Steven laughed. 'This sofa lets down at either end. It's enough for me. Take the chair by the fire and I'll bring you something.'

'Can't I help? Where's the kitchen?'

Steven drew aside a small curtain to reveal a single gas ring on to which he set a kettle of water. 'You may pour the tea.' He produced a box of cakes, delicious and expensive and she filled large blue and white breakfast cups and bit into a chocolate eclair, scooping the abundant cream which squirted from the sides into her mouth with her finger.

Steven laughed and handed her a napkin. 'It's wonderful to see you here,' he said. 'I've never forgotten you, not for a single day. I thought you looked beautiful in your maid's dress.'

'We were only overworked children.'

'I pictured you growing up. I couldn't look for you until I had something to offer you.'

This was getting altogether too serious and Willow asked mischievously, 'How did you know I wouldn't be married with several babies?'

'It was a chance I had to take.' He raised his brows. 'Anyway, you'd have had to start young for all that. You're not nineteen yet.'

'You remembered.'

'I remember everything about you. You were the only one

285

in the manor who showed me any respect. I hung on to that memory when things were very dark.'

'All these years?'

'Don't tease, Willow. I'm serious.'

'Respect isn't a basis for a deeper relationship,' Willow said gently.

'It is for me. I want to marry you.'

'Steven! You're going too fast.'

'Is there someone else?'

'No.'

'That's settled then. You're my girl.'

Willow laughed. 'Bossy, aren't you?'

'I am when I want something.'

'Don't rely on me, Steven. I've other plans.'

Chapter Sixteen

Disappointingly, Steven had no news of any other Buddleigh Manor servants. 'Mrs Westerby was on the rampage,' he said with a grimace, 'so I was only there for a few minutes.' He called regularly and took Willow out, several times to see the new bioscope moving pictures and once to watch a new young actress, Sybil Thorndike, of whom great things were predicted. Their early friendship ripened. After a childhood like his he could have been bitter, but he wasn't. He was kind, but stopped at the point of self-martyrdom, he was neat in his person and hardworking. Although disapproving of the profession of Mrs Bliss's girls, he treated them with courtesy. He was an equable, steady companion.

'He's in love with you, Willow,' said Mrs Bliss.

'He's not got eyes for anyone else,' agreed Carmen.

'If I'd met him before I began to entertain gentlemen I would have grabbed him,' said Claudette.

Willow was rather sorry for Claudette who was losing the sparkle which had made her attractive. Marriage would have suited her much better.

'He'd marry you tomorrow,' sighed Angelina, who was romantic at heart.

Even Maisie expressed an opinion. 'He's just the kind of gentleman I hope I'll have as a regular when I start work.'

'If you had the chance of a husband, would you take it?' asked Willow.

Maisie's eyes opened in an apparently ingenuous stare which would soon be worth guineas to her. 'No! I want to have an apartment like the others and earn lots of money. Then I can buy my own house.'

'You'll set up like Mrs Bliss?'

'Yes, that's my intention. If you didn't spend so much time working up in the attic you'd see what a lovely life you can have if you keep your head screwed on right.'

Willow discussed this with Steven who said, 'It's up to everyone to make the best of themselves.'

'But she's so young to have worked things out that way! And she looks like a schoolgirl.'

Steven said, 'Some men find schoolgirls the most attractive of all.'

'Aren't you shocked? After the way you were brought up. I mean, your parents being so religious.'

He frowned. 'Part of me is shocked. I suppose I'll never get over their hypocritical behaviour, but the world is tough when you're poor. Did you know that Maisie was abandoned as a baby, like me?'

'No.' Willow was pensive. 'She's never said anything about her past to me.'

'When you get to know her she sometimes likes to talk, but you're always so busy. She admires you for that. "To each his own God-given talent," is the way she puts it.'

Willow was surprised. From what she'd heard about God she wouldn't have expected Him to be on Maisie's side. The thought made her laugh and when she told Steven what amused her, after a slight hesitation he laughed too. She was happy in his company. He was calm, one might almost say phlegmatic had he not been saved by a sense of fun. He'd make a good husband one day. Did she love him? She wasn't sure. She didn't know how you were supposed to tell. She confided her plans, her dreams, her ambitions to him, and he listened attentively.

'I've been introducing styles made popular by the Ballet Russe and its Bakst decor,' she said and he nodded. She never had to explain the arts to him, another thing she liked. 'I don't do them for Angelina, of course. The strident colours and bold outlines are quite unsuited to her colouring, but Claudette, and especially Carmen, can carry them.'

'I saw the Diaghilev dancers last year,' he said. 'They're

brilliant, especially Nijinsky in *L'Après Midi d'un Faune*. He created almost as much of a sensation with his skin-tight costume as he did with his dancing.'

Willow clasped her hands. 'How I wish I could see them. French clothes have become very influenced by them.'

'And now you're making them?'

'Yes, a few.'

'Do I detect a doubtful note?'

She smiled ruefully. 'They don't get displayed in the homes of the rich and famous. That's the clientèle a designer needs. That's where real success lies.'

'Sorry, I can't help you there, love.'

She said impulsively, 'You help me a lot, Steven. You understand so much.'

'I'm gratified. Would you like to see the Ballet Russe?'

For a moment Willow was speechless. 'See them? How? When? Where?'

'How? By accepting my invitation. When? Quite soon. Where? In Paris.'

'*Paris!*'

'I'll look after you. It isn't the sinful city it's supposed to be.'

'Isn't it?' she laughed. 'But, Steven, I can't possibly go with you to Paris!'

'Why?'

Reasons chased through Willow's brain. Women didn't go on trips with young men, especially not those which continued overnight. She had a pile of work waiting. She shouldn't squander money. She could have thought of more, but she didn't. She said, 'I'll come. But separate rooms, mind. No hanky panky.'

Steven grinned. 'I'll get everything arranged then.'

Mrs Bliss regarded Willow with approval. 'Ooh, la la!' she said. 'Paris, eh?'

'Steven says it isn't really a sinful city. He says they have an honest view of things.'

Mrs Bliss winked. 'They've got the right attitude to sex so prudes call them sinful.'

Willow, having been influenced by so many contradictions in her relationships, wasn't altogether sure what was the right attitude to sex and thought she wouldn't learn through Mrs Bliss. 'Anyway, he's booking separate rooms,' she said. 'And I've insisted on paying my own bills.'

Mrs Bliss beamed. 'He's such a wise boy for his years! I'm a strong believer in keeping up appearances, and being in separate rooms has never kept a pair of lovers apart yet, though I think you should let him pay.'

'We're not lovers. Maybe I should have refused?'

'Nonsense! Go and enjoy yourself. Have a look at the fashions. They'll give you fresh ideas.'

'They will, won't they?'

Mrs Bliss just smiled.

Being in Paris in May, thought Willow, was like going to heaven. She had enjoyed the journey and had discovered that she was a good sailor, while poor Steven had needed to remain out on deck for fresh air and didn't eat or drink a thing.

As they landed he said, 'Sorry, Willow, I've not been much of a travelling companion so far.'

'No, thank goodness.'

'What do you mean?' He looked hurt.

'You're so blinking efficient in everything you do it makes a change to find something you can't.'

'Is that how you see me? Efficient? That's more like a servant's reference than the description of a friend.'

'Of course you're much more than that.'

When they had boarded the train to Paris, he said, 'Am I more than that to you?'

'What?'

'Am I more to you than efficient?'

She turned away from the window to look at him and there was something about his eyes and in his expression which made her pause before she replied, 'Yes, you are more than that to me. You're just about the best friend I've ever had.'

'Thanks, Willow. Don't forget that I intend to be more than a friend.'

'Maybe.'

'I shall make you care for me.'

'I hope you can,' she said, and meant it. A woman married to Steven would gain a husband who was loving, considerate, charming – surely everything she could possibly want?

He had arranged for them to stay near the Luxembourg Gardens. The paint on the front door of the hotel was peeling in the warm sun and the building had a leaning, rakish look, giving the impression that it needed the support of its terraced neighbours, like a good-humoured drunk. Willow was enchanted. The inside was clean, functional and tranquil, and Madame *la patronne* welcomed them with a smile. She gave them two keys and wished them a pleasant stay.

'I slept here last time I came over,' explained Steven. 'The only meal they serve is breakfast, but the city is full of small restaurants. Also, there are lots of bookshops on the *quais* nearby, some of the best in the world.'

'I see.' She smiled. 'Another good reason for choosing this hotel.'

'Do you mind? Do you want somewhere different?'

'No, it's lovely, thank you. Do you buy foreign books?'

'Of course. Some of my customers ask for them.'

'But how can you know what to buy if you don't speak the language?'

Steven laughed. 'I've been taking lessons in several continental tongues. I'm not fluent, but I already know enough to get by.' It seemed as if he would never stop surprising her.

They had arrived in the evening and Willow had seen people seated at tables outside the restaurants, served by brisk waiters, while the appetising aromas of a hundred dishes wafted everywhere, engendering in her an appetite which she felt desperate to appease.

She was delighted to join the other diners in the Paris twilight.

'Are you hungry yet?' she asked Steven.

'I certainly am. One thing about sea-sickness, it soon goes when you land.'

He called for wine and Willow sipped at it, then drank it as the others did, as liberally as if it had been water. Steven ordered the dishes in French and Willow devoured onion soup with cheese, lamb cutlets with mushrooms and béchamel sauce, and orange fritters.

She leaned back, replete, and Steven filled her glass yet again. 'Do you know something, Steven?' She paused, pondering on the fact that she had lost some control over her diction.

'No, what?' Steven waited smilingly for her to speak again.

'I've just realised that Mrs Narracott knows about French cooking.'

'Naturally. All good cooks do.'

'Do they?'

'Of course. Drink up. We've half a bottle still to get through.'

'I hope you aren't trying to get me drunk, Steven Kerslake.'

'As if I would! I'm introducing you to a bodily glow which matches the brilliance of Paris.'

'Because if you are,' Willow sorted out her thoughts and then her words. 'Because if you are, you needn't think I'll let you take advantage of me.'

'As if I would.'

'Because Mrs Bliss said—' Willow stopped. She might put ideas into his head, though she suspected that he had ideas there already.

'I can easily imagine what Mrs Bliss said.'

'Because I've only come here to see the ballet and to look at the fashions. I've a living to make.'

'Of course you have, sweetheart.'

'I'm not—'

Steven gently removed her wineglass from her hand. 'You've had enough. If you take any more you'll lose the pleasant feeling.'

'Don't you dictate to me!'

'As if I would!' he said again.

'You're laughing at me.'

'I know. It's because you're so deliciously sweet.'

Willow pondered this. 'I'm not sure I like being called sweet. It sounds rather silly.'

'Then I won't say it.'

'You're very obliging, Steven. Very obliging,' she repeated, in case he had missed the point the first time.

He guided her to the hotel, his arm beneath her elbow, led her upstairs, opened her bedroom door – and said goodnight. Willow undressed and lay between linen faintly scented with herbs, and thought of him. Her body was giving out new messages. If he'd asked if he could stay she would probably have said yes.

She awoke the next morning with a dry mouth, but no other sign of her indulgence, except a pensive wonder at her naughty thoughts of the night before. She ate croissants and drank strong coffee, wondering how Parisians went to work on such a meagre breakfast. Fortunately, Steven was of the same mind and they found a restaurant serving omelettes.

When they had finished eating he said, 'We must make the most of the day if you're to see the sights.'

He took her to the Eiffel Tower, the Arc de Triomphe and the spacious Place de la Concorde, and she gazed at everything appreciatively before suggesting tentatively that she would like to see the artists.

'A girl right after my own heart,' said Steven, 'but I knew that already.'

Willow could have lingered for days watching the artists busy at work in the streets, their pictures displayed on railings, and had to remind herself that she must conserve money and not buy several pictures which attracted her. One day, she promised herself. And the shops! They went to the Rue Faubourg St Honoré and the Rue de la Paix and they were an enchantment. She watched rich women paying large sums for exquisite clothes and stared greedily at the ones they wore and was suddenly homesick for her rooms in London where her swathes of cloth and her jumble sale bargains awaited her return. She got out her notepad and pencil and Steven warned her that if she were caught 'stealing' the model creations she would probably be thrown into the street, but he obligingly shielded her with his body while she made notes and quick sketches. She felt drunk on beauty.

'It's my turn now,' said Steven as he led her to the banks of the Seine where stall after stall of books were on sale, tended by men and women who appeared to be prepared to wait there as long as there was a single person interested in their wares.

There were few books in English so Willow wandered on until she came to antique stalls where she bought small pieces of jewellery for Mrs Bliss and the girls and a bead necklace for herself. At one she discovered a box containing loose beads and broken necklaces and damaged brooches, and gathered a treasure trove for her future work.

After they had eaten they returned to the hotel and changed their clothes. Willow wore a short-sleeved blue gown whose severity contrasted delightfully with its wide embroidered lace collar. The filmy lace had once graced a stole worn by a woman of fashion and she had been keeping the ensemble for a special occasion. With it she wore a navy hat with a pale blue feather. Her gloves (also bought at a jumble sale and carefully mended) were navy and reached her elbows. Her shoes and stole matched. Steven smiled his appreciation as she stepped into the horsedrawn cab which was to take them to the newly built Théâtre des Champs-Elysées where the first performance of *Jeux*, a *poème dansé*, was being presented, with music by Debussy and choreography by Nijinsky who was also dancing. It was the theatre's opening night, too, and it was crowded with distinguished people, interested in its modern architecture and excited at the thought of a new work which would assuredly be a vehicle for the great dancer.

Jeux had no plot. Two girls in tennis outfits played ball and were joined by a young man, whereupon they forgot the game and danced with him until another ball was thrown from the wings. It was deeply unconventional, strident, and in the opinion of most of the audience tedious and unacceptable. Their angry murmurs grew in volume until the music was drowned by catcalls and booing. Nothing could obliterate Nijinsky's power and beauty of movement, or his determination to finish what he had begun, and he danced until the end when he was hooted off the stage. Willow was fascinated by the ballet and the anger around her which stimulated rather than frightened her, but her chief interest lay in the Bakst stage décor with its vibrant colours and sweeping lines and she scribbled notes in the semi-darkness.

Afterwards they strolled in the Luxembourg Gardens, among lovers and dog-walkers and families with children who couldn't tear themselves away from the velvet Paris night.

Steven took her to a small café where they drank hot chocolate and ate little cakes and she leaned back in her chair in a state of euphoria, dazed as she was with happy memories, warmed through as though she still sat in the sun, feeling an upsurge of affection for him. She slid her arm through his as they made their way to the hotel. Tomorrow evening they must leave for London, where both had business engagements, but tonight stretched before them.

'Thank you,' she said fervently. 'I'll always remember Paris with you.'

He covered her hand with his own. 'That's a wonderful thing to say, Willow. You really mean it, don't you?'

When they arrived at her room he kissed her and she responded, yielding to the magic of Paris, to his enveloping masculinity. Her hands began to wander over him, touching him without reservation in an instinctive wish to please. He gasped.

'Willow,' he began, 'do you know—?'

'No, don't speak.' She drew him into her room and held him close.

'I'm not made of iron,' he said. 'I wonder if you realise what you're doing to me?'

'Do you object?'

'God, no. I want you. I've always wanted you.'

She entwined her fingers in his hair. 'Even when you were a grubby little bootboy?'

'Definitely.'

'You couldn't have. You were too young.'

'Is that what you think?' He laughed softly. 'You don't know much about boys, do you?'

She didn't answer, but lifted her lips for another kiss, one which went on until she was drowning in pleasure. He tried again to speak, but she held her hand over his mouth. Her body was hot with the sensations which had disturbed her last night, but now they were far stronger and wouldn't be controlled.

When they broke apart she undid the hooks and buttons of her gown which Steven helped her to lift over her head, displaying her modern, lace-trimmed underwear which revealed almost as much as it hid. She sat on the bed and he was quick to remove his clothes, his shining eyes fixed on her. His body was square and strong, the muscles rippling, the skin pale and unblemished. She held out her arms and he pushed her back against the pillows and knelt beside her to take off her cambric and broderie anglaise petticoat and her light corset, undoing the hooks with careful fingers, then removing her frilly knickers. He rolled down her stockings with trembling hands and she lay naked before him, basking in his fascinated, covetous gaze. He climbed on the bed and lay beside her, one arm thrown over her, looking down into her face.

'Willow,' he said, 'you're the most beautiful woman I've ever known.'

'Out of how many?'

'Don't joke, my love. Not now.'

She turned and clasped her arms round his neck and his eyes became opaque as he caressed her, teasing her until she reached a tumultuous pitch of need. Then he entered her. There was a moment of brief discomfort, before he moved slowly and lovingly until he brought her to a climax, waiting until then to enjoy his.

They lay side by side, their breathing slowing.

'Are you happy, my darling?' he murmured.

'Very. Are you?'

'Ecstatic. I'm glad I was the first.'

'It hurt hardly at all. From the things the girls told me—'

'Don't! Don't compare yourself with those girls!'

'Does that worry you so much?'

'You're above them.'

Willow felt a stirring of unease. 'They're my friends. The best I've got. Muriel and Edna and Mrs Bliss and her girls helped me when I was desperate.'

'That doesn't make them your equals.'

'For heaven's sake, Steven!'

He sat up, his broad back turned to her. 'They could have chosen honest work. Good women do. Women like you.'

'Don't set me on a pedestal.'

'Why not? You are above the ordinary run of women.'

Willow's euphoria died, leaving her sad. 'Don't spoil tonight,' she begged.

'I'll never willingly spoil anything for you, Willow.'

He began to dress. Before he left he kissed her, his lips moving on hers in a passionless caress. 'I never want to make you unhappy.' He turned at the door. 'Sleep well, my love, my Willow, I'll see you in the morning.'

She sat up in bed, her arms around her knees. She had enjoyed unreservedly her first experience of love-making, but it didn't make her feel committed to Steven. Was that loose behaviour? She had wanted him to stay, but his manner had deterred her. Had she been contaminated by her association with the girls? No, they had given her an uncomplicated, rational attitude towards sex.

She slept until the *patronne* knocked on her door and later Steven greeted her with a subdued demeanour which didn't fool her. His eyes were brilliant with happiness.

'Good morning, my darling,' he said. 'Are you ready for the day's pleasure?'

'I most certainly am.'

They did touristy things and over lunch Steven asked, 'Are you still enjoying Paris?'

'Can't you tell?'

'Yes, though you seemed cross with me last night. Do you wish we hadn't?'

She smiled. 'Of course not. I enjoyed every minute of it.' He frowned and she said, 'Is it wrong to feel that way?'

'No,' he said slowly. He glanced around the small café. It was almost empty but the few who were there were celebrating a birthday and making enough noise to cover their conversation. 'I'd have expected a touch of – I don't know how to say it – but you took it so much in your stride.'

'I can't help liking love-making.'

'It means more than the act itself, you know.'

'Of course. Last night was a gorgeous episode between friends.'

'Is that how you see it?' He looked troubled. 'I see it as a beginning.'

'A beginning? To what?'

'Marriage, of course.'

'Marriage! I'm not getting married, not for years.'

'I'll wait, but you'll change your mind,' he replied confidently. 'And, Willow, my love, if anything should come of last night, you know we'll get married straight away, don't you?'

'Nothing will come of it,' she said.

'Perhaps you don't understand what I mean,' he said gently.

'Oh, yes, I understand very well, but you've no need to worry. I've learned a lot about certain matters from the girls.'

298

He flushed and the veins stood out on his temples. 'You mean you used something?'

'I most certainly did.'

'But how did you know I'd—'

'I didn't, but I lay awake the night before thinking of you and I rather hoped you would. I made my preparations.'

'What?'

'You're shocked, aren't you?'

'Women shouldn't know about preventives. They should leave that kind of thing to the men.'

'Did you have something with you?'

'No, of course not. I couldn't have known—'

'Then it's a good job I understood what to do, isn't it? The last thing I want cluttering up my life is a baby.'

'Is that how you look on motherhood?'

'No, it's how I see it at present. It's fine for a man to have children, it doesn't prevent his working, but I couldn't care properly for a baby and give the energy I need to work.'

Steven looked relieved. 'So it's only a temporary thing, this unwillingness to become a mother?'

'You put it too glibly, Steven. I've seen Mum suffer over and over again. You don't "become a mother", as if you wake up in bed one morning and find this sweet little bundle waiting to be loved. You carry a child inside and it gets heavier and heavier and you go on slaving away, looking after the rest of the family, and give birth in pain, and when it's all over you get up no matter how you feel and stagger on until the next baby. It's practically destroyed my mother and many others like her. No, I intend to reach the top, to have money, to be safe and make my family safe. And when – if – I marry, I shall make sure that I never have a child I don't want. And if that shocks you, I can't help it.'

He said, 'I've never thought much about that side of women's lives. My foster parents had no children, that's why they adopted me, though why they bothered has puzzled me for years. They seemed to hate the sight of me.'

Willow said slowly, 'That's sad.' She was thoughtful.

'Perhaps you reminded them that they'd failed – people do expect married couples to have babies.'

'They didn't have to take it out on me. It wasn't my fault.'

'No, of course not. Well, you're not like them, thank goodness. You're generous and sweet, with a lot of love to give.'

'Thanks. I dare say you'll change your mind, Willow. Your woman's instinct to hold your own child will overcome your objections.'

She didn't reply. Steven wanted to think of her as a domestic young woman; she wasn't and never would be, but if it made him happy, why argue? No matter what she said it was clear he didn't want to relinquish his image of her.

He stopped walking, holding her back by her arm. 'Do you love me at all, Willow?'

'Don't ask me,' she warned gently.

'Surely you wouldn't have let me – do what I did – unless you loved me?'

'I care for you, but I don't think I'm in love with you. I'm sorry.'

They walked on and Steven said anxiously, 'You may be mistaking your feelings. After all, you let me into your bed, your first lover.' She didn't answer and he said, 'I'll have to be content with that, for a while. Deep down, you do love me, even if you don't realise it yet.'

Again she felt disinclined to argue. She had made herself clear and Steven chose to close his eyes to facts.

He looked at his serviceable watch and sighed. 'We'll have to pack and leave soon to get the boat train.'

'I know.' Willow sighed with him. 'This has been the best two days of my life, Steven.'

'I feel that way too.'

'I don't know how to thank you enough.'

'Last night you gave me all the thanks I want and far more than I expected,' he said. 'Now, we can't leave Paris before you've taken a walk in the Bois.'

They wandered among the fashionable people who strolled

300

and gossiped in the sun, many of the women wearing gowns and hats designed especially for them, displaying small pieces of discreet jewellery, parasols shading them and protecting their complexions. Most were accompanied by a man dressed almost uniformly in frock coat and top hat, spats and a cane and white gloves.

'How smart everyone is,' exclaimed Willow.

'They look a bit starchy to me, but the French are conventional at heart.'

'That's not what I've heard,' said Willow. 'I was told they were naughty.'

Steven said, 'That sounds like Mrs Bliss.'

'Yes. I dare say it's no different here from England. The men live one kind of life on the surface and a different one underneath. Some of the women too.'

'You shouldn't know those things!'

'Well, I do. I discovered that much when I was a maid. I listen and learn.'

'Obviously!'

'Don't bite my head off. Mrs Bliss's life wouldn't suit me and I can see that there's really no future in what her girls do.'

'Thank heaven for that!'

His sanctimonious attitude provoked her and she said, 'Unless, of course, I fail as a designer and have to become a madam with all the prettiest and most skilful girls I can find.'

'Willow! You don't mean it, really, do you? You're not thinking—'

'Of setting up a brothel? No.'

Steven looked relieved. 'At least the French have imported one splendid fashion from us,' he said. 'There are tea rooms in the Bois and we're just coming to one.'

They sat down and drank tea and ate cake and Willow feasted her eyes on sights that she might not get to see again for a long time, though this taste of Paris had made her even more aware that she must keep an eye on the French capital's great designers and their exclusive houses.

'Oh!' she exclaimed. 'I thought I saw Edgar Maddison!'

'Did you? I suppose it's possible,' Steven said with a pronounced lack of enthusiasm. 'He hasn't a living to earn and probably comes to Paris quite often.'

Willow glanced at his set face and knew she had upset him by even mentioning a Maddison and wished she'd not spoken. She had unsettled his equilibrium enough and tried to make it up to him. 'Having lots of money doesn't make a man. I admire one like you who can begin with nothing and make something of himself.'

She was rewarded by a smile. Glancing over his shoulder she realised that she had indeed seen Edgar. He was strolling near them with a woman on each arm, both extremely chic.

'I did see him, Steven,' she said quietly, 'but he'll never notice us. And if he does he won't remember us. And even if he did he won't acknowledge us, not a couple of his mother's former servants.'

'I don't think he ever knew of my existence,' said Steven. 'I was just one of the nameless inferiors who lived below stairs. When it suited them, they chucked me out, just because I looked at their books. Mrs Westerby told me I should go home and learn better manners from my parents. Parents!'

Willow looked at him sympathetically, then back at Edgar. He wore a suit which had clearly come from the hand of a bespoke tailor and contrasted noticeably with Steven's ready-mades.

Steven turned and followed her gaze. 'He's seen you.'

'What?' Her attention had been taken by the women's clothes.

'He's coming over,' said Steven.

Edgar walked his companions to their small table and bowed. 'Miss Riches,' he said formally, 'what a pleasant surprise. Please permit me to present Mrs Thurley and Mrs Stewart? Ladies, Miss Riches.'

The women held out their hands and touched hers briefly.

Willow said, 'May I introduce Mr Kerslake? Steven, this is Mr Edgar Maddison.' Steven caught the mischief in her voice and it helped salve the sting of having to be polite to a Maddison.

'May we join you?' asked Edgar, and not waiting for an answer he lifted his hand and a waiter came at once and placed chairs at the table.

'We can't stay long,' said Steven. Edgar's eyebrows rose slightly at his belligerence.

'I quite understand, my dear fellow,' he said. 'Paris is too fascinating to sit around talking.'

'I always think that part of her charm is that one does just that,' said Mrs Thurley in bored tones. 'Of course, one does it in London also, but it isn't the same.'

'Why is that, I wonder?' asked Mrs Stewart.

Mrs Thurley just managed to smother a yawn. 'As a race we set far too much store on being active. Don't you agree, Miss Riches?'

'I keep active, certainly,' said Willow.

Her voice was as distant as Mrs Thurley's and Edgar said, 'I must say they made a wise decision to open tea rooms. What say you, Mr Kerslake?'

Steven smiled briefly. 'I quite agree.'

Willow said, 'Steven, we ought to go shortly, we have to catch the boat train.'

'How sad.' Mrs Thurley was obviously even more bored by this information, and by the café and her newly met companions, and her gaze wandered.

Mrs Stewart said, 'What a shame that you must leave this enchanting city on so delightful an evening. Are your engagements so pressing that you cannot extend your stay?'

'Unfortunately they are,' said Willow, managing to sound regretful when laughter was bubbling inside her. Her engagements! Appointments in Bayswater with the local ladies of pleasure. She caught Steven's eye, but he gave not a glimmer of a smile.

The waiter brought tea and Mrs Thurley shook her head.

'Not for me, thank you.' She stared past Willow who was studying her hat, a velvet toque with a halo of aigrettes. It was just a little overdone with its twelve-inch plumes, more suitable for evening wear, which gave her a brief flash of rather malicious pleasure.

'I'll pour.' Willow had no idea why she had said it. Or why she hadn't got up and walked away as soon as she caught sight of Edgar. When she recalled his insulting kisses and the way he had condoned her dismissal by his failure to intervene, she felt she hated him most of all the Maddisons. Memories crowded in and she slopped a little tea. 'Sorry,' she mumbled.

Mrs Thurley looked at the spilt tea and at Willow with equal distaste. She poured milk wishing that she could empty the jug over Mrs Thurley's over-done hat.

'What brought you across the Channel?' asked Edgar.

Before Willow could say a word Steven said, 'My fiancée has never left Britain before. I thought it would be a pleasant little holiday for her, especially as so many seem convinced that war is threatening.'

Willow had read of the rumours of unrest but had paid little heed so had nothing to say on the matter, and she was so annoyed at being described by Steven as his 'fiancée' that she couldn't, in any case, find words. She had seen that Mrs Thurley's eyes brightened whenever she looked at Edgar. Did she have designs on him? She was not beautiful like her companion, but judging by her outfit she was certainly rich. Both women were older than Edgar.

The men's air of antagonism dissolved like snowflakes in a fire at the mention of war.

Edgar said rapidly, 'There are so many countries already fighting and others longing for a signal to begin. King Edward knew what he was doing when he encouraged the Entente between the British and the French governments.'

'He did that!' In his excitement, Steven's acquired accent slipped a little and Mrs Thurley caught Mrs Stewart's eye in a slight grimace. 'One good thing,' continued Steven,

'Mr Churchill's been put in charge of the navy and he's building it up.'

'It's fortunate for us that he is. Germany has the most formidable army in Europe and is also developing its fleet,' said Edgar. 'I too have an unpleasant feeling that it will come to war. What is your opinion?'

'I'm afraid it could,' said Steven.

He didn't sound afraid. In fact, both men spoke of war enthusiastically and looked as if they'd welcome a call to arms.

Willow missed the rest of the conversation because Mrs Stewart leaned towards her and said smilingly, 'These men and their talk of war. I sometimes think they want to fight. Let's discuss a far more interesting topic. I have been longing to know who made your costume. The cut! The style! And the colour! Saxe blue and plain but simply divine. A costume like that makes one feel positively overdressed, does it not, Mrs Thurley?'

Her eyes ranged coldly over the costume. 'Very smart,' she conceded.

'Do tell,' begged Mrs Stewart. 'Where did you get it?'

Willow had a mischievous impulse to say, 'Actually I grabbed it from a jumble sale stall in Bayswater, and as it had been made for a lady with impressive girth I was able to cut out enough cloth for myself.'

'I went to my usual source,' she said instead, smiling.

Mrs Stewart laughed. 'And you are not going to divulge it, are you? I cannot say I blame you.'

They turned their attention again to the men. Edgar was saying, 'Lord Fisher has predicted that war will break out in October 1914.'

'And we'll be dragged in,' said Steven.

Mrs Thurley stifled another yawn, but in a way which would catch Edgar's notice. He rose. 'Forgive me, ladies. We are boring you.'

The two women got to their feet and said their goodbyes, Edgar bowed and so did Steven, and the three strolled away,

Willow following their course with a keen eye to the cut of the women's skirts from the rear.

'That Edgar's not so bad when you get to know him,' said Steven. 'He talks a lot of sense. Did you see much of him when you worked as lady's maid?'

'He was usually away visiting and travelling. Steven, why did you introduce me as your fiancée when you know I'm nothing of the sort?'

He coloured. 'It was an impulse, but I'm glad I did. You'll be engaged to me one day and I decided to warn that fellow off. He's got a reputation for being fast and he was giving you the eye. He always has a woman with him and often not of the best class.'

'That sounds snobby,' said Willow sharply.

'Maybe, but it's what his family would say.'

'Well, you can't make such an accusation against him today.'

Steven looked sideways at her. 'I'm not so sure. Those women aren't what they set up to be.'

'What are they?'

'I reckon they're from what is known as the demi-monde who sell themselves exactly as Mrs Bliss's girls, only for a higher price to selected clients.'

'No, I can't believe it! They seemed so respectable, so well-bred.'

'It pays them to appear respectable, and in fact some are from good families whose fortunes have dwindled.'

'What makes you think that they are like that?'

Steven shrugged. 'They look at men in a certain way. Even me, when they thought I was beneath them.'

Willow was fascinated. 'Do they go into society?'

'Since King Edward died, most are now on the fringes.'

'I should have told them I made my suit!' exclaimed Willow. 'I might have got some custom.'

'Is that all you've got to say?'

'We all have to make our living.'

'That seems to cover every sin with you.'

They drove to the station in an irritated silence.

On the train as they steamed away from Paris Steven produced a flat parcel. 'Let's not fall out, my love. I bought these for you. Just something for your work and to help you remember our first time in Paris.'

'I'll never forget,' said Willow, glad that their brief coolness was over. She opened the parcel. Inside were two luxury magazines, *La Gazette du Bon Ton* and *Le Journal des Dames et des Modes*. 'Oh, how wonderful!' she breathed. 'They've got the coloured illustrations by Georges Lepape and George Barbier and Charles Martin. They're superb, but so expensive.'

'They're in French, of course, but I can help you there.'

'The pictures are so gorgeous I hardly need the words. Steven, you shouldn't have, but I'm delighted that you did.' She kissed him impulsively on his cheek, which embarrassed him in front of the other passengers.

I wonder if Edgar would have been embarrassed? wondered Willow. Damn! Why should he intrude into her thoughts? He was a Maddison, uncaring of those he considered beneath him. She had, as it happened, fallen on her feet, but his family didn't know that. Yet, today in the Bois, Edgar had recognised her and made the first move and unfortunately she hadn't forgotten him. On the contrary, she had known as soon as she set eyes on him that she had missed him and wished she could see him again. And, worst of all, she suspected that had it been he to whom she had made love last night she would have been swamped by far more turbulent sensations. Poor Steven. She had given him her body but none of her heart.

Chapter Seventeen

Back in London life took on its usual pattern, though Willow was troubled by contradictory feelings. One moment she hated Edgar because he was a Maddison; the next she wished with all her heart that he was available to her. Her ambivalence made her snappy with Steven.

'What's up with you?' he asked one evening after they had been to a bioscope.

'Nothing . . . I don't know. I think it's stupid to spend money to watch jerky little figures on a screen where it looks as if it's always raining and have to listen to someone bashing out tunes on a tinny piano.'

'Then we'll go to the theatre.'

His easy compliance irritated her. 'Do you always want the same as I do? Haven't you any preferences?'

'I prefer the theatre. I thought you preferred the moving pictures. And, as a matter of fact, I'd be happy spending my free time just reading.'

'You should do it then! I've always got plenty of sewing to get on with.'

Steven said patiently, 'I want you to take time off. You need it. I don't want to see my future bride with huge bags under her eyes.'

'And that's another thing—'

'All right, so you're not my future bride yet! But I'll make you care for me.'

'I don't see why you bother.' Willow was exasperated. 'There are many young women who'd welcome a nice fellow like you with open arms.'

'I want you.'

London was busy catering for the season, when the rich and privileged took up residence. Each new debutante hoped to attract a man of whom her parents could be proud, while the girls who hadn't managed it the first time round were anxiously preparing for another onslaught. The debutantes dreamt of love; their mothers told their daughters that they must not permit foolish sentiment to interfere with their chance of a rich union which would bring love in its wake. The young male scions of the wealthy and aristocratic families had slightly different aims. They were seeking a good time. Their parents had identified which of the new season's girls they would welcome as family members and it was up to them to make good use of the knowledge. Breeding the next generation from the right stock was vital, said their fathers; fun was what you indulged in discreetly with a separate class of woman.

Mrs Bliss's girls were excited, too, each of them looking forward to renewing contact with old clients, and meeting new ones. They dreamt of money and maybe a faithful protector.

Willow and the girls were taking tea with Mrs Bliss, as they sometimes did in a quiet moment. She had greeted Willow's return from France with a searching look which had melted into one of mischievous pleasure. 'You've done it, haven't you?' Her bluntness brought colour rushing to Willow's face. She didn't bother to ask what the madam meant. In this house lost virginity was merely a matter of expediency. It could only be sold once, though when Mrs Bliss had had a little too much to drink she told them tales of the past and how the madams used alum and fish bladders to make a gentleman believe he was a young girl's first lover. 'Ah,' she said now, 'there's something about a girl who's experienced the joys of love for the first time.'

'Good lord, I hope not everyone is so perceptive.'

'No, most folk go round with their eyes half shut. It's different with me. Is Steven going to marry you?'

'He says he is.'

'You sound gloomy.'

'I'm not ready to settle with anyone. He shouldn't have introduced me as his fiancée.'

'Who to?'

'Some people we met in the Bois de Boulogne. I knew one of them before.'

'A handsome young man, was it?'

'What makes you ask?'

'Just the look on your face.'

'How do I look?'

'Dreamy. Is he someone you fancy?'

'Good lord, no. He was my employer's son and didn't care tuppence about the servants. I didn't have much to do with him.' Mrs Bliss kept her eyes fixed on Willow who coloured. 'All right, when I worked for his family he tried to kiss me. That's all there was to it. I soon told him what I thought of him and I'm not likely to meet him again.'

'That's all right, then,' said Mrs Bliss, wriggling herself into her armchair like a spider settling into the centre of her web.

The girls were enchanted with Willow's description of Paris and the clothes.

'I wonder how I'd get on over there?' said Angelina.

Mrs Bliss's face took on a wary look. 'You'd have to learn the lingo first.'

'What we do doesn't need words,' said Carmen, her dark eyes glowing with mirth.

'That'll do,' said Mrs Bliss. 'I won't have such vulgar talk.'

Willow's bank account was growing steadily, but not by much, although she had so much work she was forced to engage an assistant. This meant that she had to add another two and sixpence a week and extra food and rent to her expenses. Bridget was short, plump and plain and was getting stouter on three good meals a day, a luxury she had never before enjoyed. She was only fourteen, and Willow was sure that she wouldn't interest Mrs Bliss. She was excellent at sewing, especially by hand, her needle darting expertly in and out of the cloth. She came, she said, from a very large family in the East End and was delighted to be offered a refuge where the work was enjoyable, food was abundant and good, and the company not stuck up. Willow had taken her measurements and had acquired material enough for her to make herself a couple of pretty frocks.

Anastasia, a friend of Carmen's, wanted a special gown and Willow was anxious to satisfy her. She was the regular lover of an aristocrat who paid her well at present to keep herself only for him.

'She doesn't, of course,' said Carmen.

'Isn't that cheating?' asked Willow.

'Who cares? Her lover will drop her like a hot cake as soon as he finds someone he likes better. She's got to keep up her contacts and practise her special skills. Seems old Lord Whatsit only wants straight sex.' It was a measure of how matter-of-fact Willow had become about the house and its occupants that she saw this as fairly logical.

Bridget had no illusions about what the girls did and admired them immensely. 'You wouldn't want to be like them, would you, Bridget?' Willow asked one day, after her assistant had talked at length about their beauty and their earning power.

'Me?' Bridget laughed hilariously. 'My face and figure will never be my fortune. I'll be lucky if I ever get a fellow of my own. I'm goin' to learn everythin' about sewin' an' then I'll be able to keep myself.'

'Have you never had a boy friend?'

'One or two took me out but they were only after one thing an' when I wouldn't give in to them they dropped me – an' they weren't very polite about it either. I didn't mind much. I didn't like them in the first place, but all my friends had boys so I thought I'd give it a go.'

Willow had seen the perfect material for the new gown in Harrod's. Anastasia had a flawless oval face with grey-blue eyes and long, sleek dark hair which she plaited and wore like a crown. Willow envied her when she tried to discipline her own unruly curls. Anastasia had, said Carmen, enough money to retire when she wished, plus a great deal of expensive jewellery.

'Why does she keep on working?' Willow asked.

'She's not ready to retire yet!' said Carmen, quite shocked.

'Do you have that kind of money?' asked Willow, and when Carmen shook her head asked, 'How has Anastasia managed it?'

Carmen looked pensive. 'She demands more than we dare. She's managed to fool people into thinking she's secretly a Russian princess who's run away from home and is in hiding from a disgusting old suitor. She tells them she was never brought up to earn her living and has nothing to sell except her body. She says this flatters the men because then they think they're more attractive than a Russian nobleman.' Carmen gave a shriek of mirth. 'Actually, she was born in the next street to mine in Clapham. She wanted to be an actress only she wasn't good enough but once had a small part in a play with a Russian princess in it and she copied the actress. Now she's done it so long and so well I sometimes think she believes it herself.'

Anastasia had demanded silvery grey satin, with a black and silver bodice and a red and gold cloak, as she had seen in an illustration by George Barbier in one of Willow's magazines. She was willing to pay well. The mix of colours might seem extreme but Anastasia would carry them off with her usual flair. It was a marvellous order. Willow went out shopping in a pale blue silk costume, a straw hat decorated with silk cornflowers, and carried a parasol in her gloved hands. She set off in the sunshine. She had set Bridget some plain sewing to do and for once allowed herself the luxury of time just to wander. She spent two delightful hours window-shopping, then drifted round Harrod's, intoxicated by a store with an incredible eighty or more departments, gazing with interest at the ready-mades, the millinery and shoes, and covetous of the giant swathes of material. There were a number of rich girls out with their mothers, their supply of gloves and stockings and evening shoes needing replenishment. Willow watched them unobtrusively, marvelling at the way they ordered everything to be sent to their London address, even so small an item as two pairs of white kid gloves. She noted the almost cringing attitude of the shop assistants who could be dismissed arbitrarily if they upset the wealthy clientèle. When I have my salon, Willow vowed, I'll not have my workers terrified out of their lives. She gave a small smile at her dream which was still so far from fulfilment and a young man raised his hat and returned her smile. She blushed and hurried away. She had already noted that the material she required was still there and went to buy it, as if the man's smile had triggered off a reaction against dawdling. Passing an elegant display of tailored wear she turned her head to get a better look, when she heard a voice say, 'Willow!'

She knew the voice and turned slowly to see Edgar, his hat in his hand as he greeted her. 'Don't scowl at me, Willow. Aren't you pleased to see me?'

She longed to stay with him. 'I'm afraid I'm busy,' she said, 'so if you'll excuse me I must be on my way.'

'Won't you have tea with me? I know a place where they serve the most delicious pastries.'

'No, thank you.'

'You used to be more friendly to me,' he said reproachfully.

'Maybe. That was a long time ago. Besides, I'm not hungry.'

'Good God, do you have to be hungry to eat a pastry? I look upon it as one of life's bonuses.'

'That's because you've never had to make it yourself.'

Edgar looked contemplatively at the ceiling. 'Would it make you happier if I promised to learn how? Would you teach me?'

Willow smiled unwillingly. 'Don't be silly.'

'Why not?'

'Because it's silly to—'

'It's silly being silly?'

313

Willow laughed outright and Edgar smiled. 'That's better. Now, can I take you to tea?'

'What would your parents say if you were seen eating with me?'

'What could they say?' He stepped back and examined her from head to toe. 'You are so chic no one would ever guess that—' He paused.

'That I was your kitchen skivvy?'

'Now you're cross with me again. Please, don't be. I always thought you a most superior skivvy, and in any event you rose to be my sister's maid.'

'Yes.' Willow paused. 'How is your sister?'

'Frances? She's married.'

'Oh. Is she happy with Mr Bickford?'

'I hardly think so. He never takes her anywhere which might offer her the smallest opportunity to get into a scrape. After what happened to her in London he's very strict.'

'What does she say about the incident in London?'

'You were there. All I was told was that you had led Frances astray.'

'That *I* led *her* astray?'

'Yes. Didn't you?'

'No!'

Edgar lost his amused, bantering air. 'I should so like to talk to you, Willow.'

'I have shopping to do.'

'Get them to send the stuff.'

'I need it quickly.'

'Let me carry it back for you.'

Willow contemplated him. He was more handsome than ever. How old was he now? Twenty-two?

'You won't dare be seen carrying a large parcel. What would the young ladies and their mamas say?'

'I don't care what they say.'

'You've changed. The first time I met you all you could talk about was the scene we were making.'

'I'm not the callow lad I was. Besides, I've got a motor car outside. Think of the ease with which you'll get home.'

Home! To a brothel! 'No, thanks. I don't need your help. But I will have tea with you.'

He beamed and Willow wondered what had made her behave so stupidly. The idea of getting mixed up with a Maddison was anathema to her and it was disconcerting to discover just how much she longed to remain a little longer with Edgar.

She completed her purchases and he insisted on carrying the brown paper parcel to a nearby tea room where they did indeed sell delicious pastries.

'Now,' said Edgar, 'I want to know *exactly* what happened to you and Frances.'

'What did they tell you?'

'They said that she was fortunate to escape arrest as a suffragette and that it was your fault.'

'And you believed them!'

'I suppose I did. Are you a suffragette?'

'What if I was?'

'I wouldn't mind.'

'How very sweet of you!'

'Now you are being sarcastic.'

'I have nothing to do with the movement. My aim is to become a successful dress designer.'

'Good heavens! How long have you wanted that?'

'I was born with the dream.'

He gazed at her admiringly, then asked, 'Why did you take a job as kitchen maid? You couldn't have got much practice there.'

'More than you'd think, especially after I became Frances's maid. As for being a kitchen maid, I expected something better when I was offered employment in the manor because, if you recall, I saved Winifred from being run over by a motor car.'

'Of course I recall it. I was pretty beastly to you that day.'

'You behaved much as I expected from a member of your class of society.'

'That hurt! Do you still have a low opinion of us?'

'Pretty low.'

'Of all of us?'

He sounded anxious, but he and his kind were experts at dissembling. In fact, she was even beginning to imitate them. In her quest along her chosen path she plucked at behaviour patterns as a magpie selects bright objects. Dissembling skilfully was an excellent way of getting out of embarrassing situations.

'Yes, all of you.'

'Even me?' He worried at the subject like a dog with a bone. She half expected him to lick her hand and the idea made her laugh.

'Do I amuse you?' There was a tinge of annoyance in his tone now.

'No.' She revealed her thoughts and he laughed too. She was relieved, then dismayed at the way he was chipping away at her resolve never to trust a Maddison.

'Why did you stay when you discovered the position you had been given?'

'Once I'd arrived I had no choice. My family needed the money and I'd given up my job in Bristol.'

She had kept her eyes on Edgar's face as she talked and watched the expressions that moved across it. 'You really do dislike my people, don't you?' he said.

'That's too mild for what I feel. I haven't told you everything yet.' She related in flat tones the story of her arrest and trial and prison sentence. 'Ten shillings was all that was needed to pay my fine. Frances spends that sum without a thought. I honestly expected her to appear in court and rescue me. Now, I've got a prison record and I've ended up in – lodgings, sewing for a living.'

'Good God! How ghastly of Frances! To think of you – it's terrible. If only I'd known.' He reached for Willow's hand and she let it lie in his. She liked the feel of his strong fingers, the skin smooth, nails well kept.

'Did you suffer terribly in prison, Willow?'

He was genuinely sympathetic. She said: 'I suffered

316

because of the injustice, the indignity, but compared to what those brave women go through . . .'

'I've read about them.'

'About the hunger strikes? And the forced feeding?'

'Yes. Is it really as horrible as they say?'

The tea room was warm but Willow shivered. 'Far, far worse. I heard them. Oh, God, those poor creatures! And they're still suffering, over and over again. And now everything's got even more dreadful.'

'The cat and mouse policy, d'you mean?'

'Yes. Such wickedness! To let them go until they've recovered their health, then re-arrest them and begin the whole horrible process again. I know of one woman at least whose heart has been weakened by it.'

Willow hadn't thought of Jane Barton for months. A faraway look came into her eyes. 'She looked after me when I left prison, though she could barely stand. She even offered me a home.'

'That was kind of her.'

'Yes, but I had to refuse.'

'Why?'

'I would have had to join the suffragettes.'

'Don't you want the vote?'

'Yes. I hadn't thought of it before prison, but now I would like to see women able to control their own lives.'

'But not enough to be active in their campaign?'

She felt his words to be critical and snapped, 'No, I *must* earn money.' She calmed down. How could he be expected to understand? 'My family need it. *I* need it. I intend to make something of myself. Emmeline Pankhurst has been sentenced to three years in jail. I can't afford that or to end up broken in health. One day we'll be allowed to vote and I'll never forget the women who made it possible. Frances might have learned something if she'd gone through with her task.'

'Well, if it's any consolation to you,' he said, 'she's miserable. Bickford is stingy and domineering. When he's occupied with his business – a determination to get into politics if only in an influential capacity – she has to sneak off even to see her female friends. He expects her to give lavish dinners to politicians and accept their invitations, and they all bore her to screaming point. If she invites her own friends to the house he manages to give off such a disapproving air that they become stilted and stop talking. I know. I went once. Never again.'

Willow withdrew her hand. 'I thought Mr Bickford a cold fish right from the start, but it isn't very brotherly of you to abandon her if she needs your help.'

'Aren't you glad she's miserable?'

'We were talking about you. You're treating her like she did me. Just walking off and leaving her with her worries.'

She expected him to be annoyed, but he wasn't. 'You are right in a way, though I don't think the cases are the same. She chose to marry Bickford. What happened to you was not your fault. You deserve to be helped. I should like to help you.'

'No, thanks. I shall manage my own life. I don't intend to make the idiotic mistake of marrying the wrong man – that's if I get married at all. I've seen little yet to attract me to so-called wedded bliss.'

Edgar said angrily, 'Don't men attract you at all?'

'Not particularly.'

'You prefer *women*?'

'I'm not attracted to women in the way you obviously mean.'

Edgar's face coloured. 'Sorry. Have I shocked you?'

'No.'

'I see.'

'You don't, but it isn't important. Now I must get back. I need to get a gown cut out and tacked ready for tomorrow.'

'All that work in so short a time?'

'I employ an assistant,' she said grandly.

'Congratulations. You must be doing well.'

Willow thought of tubby little Bridget and suppressed a laugh.

Edgar caught the flash of humour and said quickly, 'May I see you again?'

She was taken aback by the fervour in his voice and her reaction to it. Maddison or not, she wanted very much to see him again, but he could prove dangerous to her plans. She shook her head. 'No, I think not.' She rose and he sprang to his feet. 'There's no need to accompany me,' she said, 'I'll get a cab.'

She swept out, leaving him to deal with the bill, and was lucky enough to find a disengaged cab at once. She looked back and saw Edgar standing on the edge of the pavement, watching. She raised her hand. He gave her a brief salute, then was lost to view.

Anastasia was unreservedly pleased with her new gown and paid the sum Willow asked without a murmur. As Mrs Bliss said, 'She won't worry, it isn't her money. She's got that tucked away in a bank and it's not coming out. Her rich gentleman will foot the bill.'

The gown brought a flood of orders which Willow and Bridget laboured to fill, though many came from girls with only modest sums to spend. Mrs Bliss was fascinated by the new interest which had entered her life and ordered Maisie to show the shoppers into her room where they were asked to sit and, if she liked them, entertained them with tea or coffee and a plate of the endless supply of little cakes so beloved by her. She often allowed Willow to take measurements and fittings there.

When each girl had departed she released a flood of information, much of it scurrilous but seldom malicious. 'She's a clever one,' she'd say, 'she'll never want for anything.' Or, 'That one will never get anywhere. Her pimp takes everything she earns.' Or, 'That girl's a fool. Her man beats her regularly. She used to be a real good-looker and I offered her a place here. She wouldn't take it and she's had her beauty knocked out of her. She'll soon be among the dregs and he'll drop her and get hold of someone else.'

Willow tried to be impartial, determined not to be swept into the desperately sad lives of some of the women she served. Mrs Bliss's background knowledge enabled her to modify her designs and adjust her prices to suit their purses and that was as far as she could allow her interest to go.

Gran wrote regularly and Henry forwarded the letters with as little delay as possible. Gran's handwriting was growing more and more spidery and the letters shorter and it was clear that her physical powers were failing. Willow decided that a visit home was imperative.

Bridget was given a pile of sewing to occupy her, but not enough to keep her a prisoner in the attic rooms. When Willow handed her a five-shilling bonus and told her to take some time off she beamed through happy tears. 'You're so good to me, Willow. Better than anyone I've ever known. I never want to leave you.' Willow was moved by her gratitude. The girl was another she must continue to succour.

She caught the train for Bristol on 5 June. The day before at the Derby a frantic suffragette, Emily Davison, had thrown herself in front of the King's horse. Horse and jockey survived, but Emily lay in a coma. Willow barely saw the passing scenery as she thought of the girl with the courage to hurl herself in front of a fast-moving instrument of bone and muscle and galloping hooves. Other people in the third-class carriage talked of it.

'A scandal!' said a woman in a flower-bedecked hat. Willow looked at her appreciatively until she went on, 'She could have killed the horse, an' the jockey for that matter, an' it was His Majesty's horse too.'

No one spoke up for the dying Emily. Willow couldn't let this pass. 'Don't any of you think that Miss Davison was brave?'

The woman in the flowered hat stared angrily at her. 'No, I don't. Them women ought to be strung up, rushin' round smashin' things and settin' fire to them. Someone could be killed.'

'They confine their activities to property,' argued Willow.

'A thundering disgrace,' said a man in a plaid suit. 'They're not proper women. If my wife ever tried to join them I'd give her what for!' I bet you would, thought Willow, her eyes on his beefy hands. 'And anyway, that Davison woman isn't expected to live.'

Willow burned with indignation. Every other passenger was furious with her and she half wished she had never started this, but the memory of Jane Barton choking and gagging in the cell next to hers would never allow her to be lukewarm again about the suffragettes.

'I suppose you're one of 'em?' said a small man who hadn't previously spoken.

'No, I'm not. I've my living to earn.'

'Well, there you are then,' said beefy hands triumphantly. 'You got no room to talk.'

'I sympathise with them,' said Willow, 'and so should all women. And I dare say your wives and daughters feel the way I do. They may hide it, but they want the vote.'

Before the beefy one, whose colour had risen cholerically, could reply, the small man said in his precise tones, '"Outragettes", they call them now.'

'What's that supposed to mean?' asked the flowery hat.

'It's a mixture of words – suffragettes and outrageous, see?'

Everyone in the carriage except Willow laughed. 'That's a good 'un,' said the choleric passenger, slapping his large thigh. 'That's a real good 'un.'

Conversation between the others became general and Willow turned her face to the window.

Joe met her at the station and she greeted him with a kiss which made him squirm. 'Not in front of people,' he protested.

She laughed. 'Sorry, but it's good to see you again. You've grown. And you're so smart.'

Joe almost preened himself. 'I know I'm not very tall, but I work in the shop a lot now an' earn enough to help

321

Mum, an' I've a bit left to go out to the picture house an' have a bit of fun with my mates.'

He carried her case. He was fifteen, strong and bright-eyed. He was worthy of something better in life than a job as a counter assistant. One day she might be able to help him. One day.

'How are you gettin' on at the manor?' he asked.

For a brief moment Willow was taken aback. 'The manor? Oh, yes. Very well, thank you.'

He gave her a sideways look. The tram was rattling along the lines to Lawrence Hill and she took an unexpected delight in seeing the smoky scenes of her childhood. 'You don't sound very sure, our Willow. Is that Miss Frances botherin' you?'

She turned to him. His eyes were anxious, their expression more searching, more understanding than she would have expected from one his age. Then she remembered that he had had to take the place, as far as possible, of their father.

'You've been looking after the family well, haven't you, Joe?'

He was surprised. 'Course I have. It's my duty.'

'You're a good boy. As a matter of fact, I left the manor a while back.'

'What? But Gran's been writin' to you there an' you've answered.'

'I know. Henry the footman's been helping me keep my secret.'

'What secret?' He looked startled. 'Our Marigold's got secrets too. If you're not at the manor, where are you? An' why did you leave, an' why didn't you tell us?'

She laughed. 'I'll tell you all when we're together. And, don't worry, I've done nothing to be ashamed of.'

He squeezed her hand. '*I* know that.'

She was welcomed by the whole family. Clara hugged her tight. 'We've missed you, love.'

The others clamoured for attention. Even Marigold had stayed in until she arrived. Barely sixteen, she was taller than Willow and slender in her green cotton summer frock and straw hat. The truce was over as soon as she took in the elegant simplicity of her sister's Paris-inspired grey silk costume, white blouse and grey hat with saucy feathers pointing in different directions. She plucked angrily at her skirt. 'Where did you get those clothes? How much were they? They look like clothes the rich women wear.'

'They do, don't they, but I made them. I'll make something for you, if you like. You've such a good figure.'

The compliment fell flat. 'I can get my own things,' muttered Marigold. 'I don't know what time I'll be back, Mum.'

Clara protested, 'Not later than ten, love.' There was no reply and Clara said, 'She's completely out of hand. She's often late for work. God knows what she gets up to with her fast friends.'

The others crowded round, Jasmine attaching herself like a barnacle to a boat, following her beloved sister everywhere except the privy.

'Have you got lots of stories about the manor?' she shrieked happily.

'I've got a job,' said Sam. 'When Joe went into the shop I took over as messenger boy. I bet I'll be serving one day.'

'Not if you keep forgettin' where you're supposed to be takin' the orders,' said Joe.

Sam put up his fists in a mock display of boxing and Joe accommodated him. The two milled round until Clara begged for mercy.

'An' I'm workin',' said Alfred. 'I'm workin' in a shop, too.' He looked at Clara somewhat defiantly. He resembled his father in looks but not in constitution and this tended to rile her.

'In a woman's dress shop,' she said distantly. 'It's no job for a boy.'

'Most of the great fashion designers are men,' said Willow, smiling at her crestfallen brother.

He brightened. 'Yes, I've been readin' about them.'

'Is that what you're goin' to be?' jeered Sam. 'A women's dressmaker?'

Willow put a stop to the budding fracas by saying loudly, 'I've got presents for everyone.'

They took her offerings happily. For Clara there was a white crêpe de Chine blouse inset with broderie anglaise and frothy lace.

She held it up. 'I've never had such a thing. Never. It's beautiful. It must have cost you a lot.'

'I made it, Mum. I hope it fits.'

'It will. I can see it will. You made it, you say? You're so clever. I wonder you had time to do it, workin' for Miss Frances. She's married now, isn't she? I saw it in a newspaper. She lives somewhere different, doesn't she?' Clara frowned. 'You never told us that, nor why you're still at the manor when she's somewhere else.'

Willow caught Joe's eye. 'All will be revealed in due course,' she promised.

'What's for us?' The others clamoured for attention until Willow had distributed boxes of chocolate which the boys fell upon, and a straw hat with yellow ribbons for Jasmine.

She had brought Marigold one of the new-style jumpers, a sleeveless tunic resembling a man's waistcoat, and put it aside for later. Joe and Alfred ran round to fetch Gran who needed their support to walk. Willow was shocked by the change in her and kissed her, holding her arms round her, scarcely daring to embrace her for fear her brittle bones might break.

'It's lovely to see you, child,' she said. 'I'm glad they gave you time off.'

Clara made a fresh pot of tea and produced a tin of home-made biscuits.

'I made them,' cried Jasmine. 'An' I can cook other things.'

'She's gettin' good at it,' said Clara. 'She's a great help to me, though I don't take in much washin' nowadays, what with the money my family gives me.' She looked round at them. 'I've been blessed.'

The boys wriggled uneasily at their mother's sudden descent into sentiment. Jasmine handed Willow her tea in a matching cup and saucer. 'We're gettin' ever so posh,' she said proudly. 'Our tea set matches. Here, have a biscuit. See, the plates have got the same pattern on as the cups an' saucers.'

Willow ate her biscuit and complimented her sister. 'Now,' she said, 'I've something to confess. As you've already realised, I'm not with Frances any more. As a matter of fact, I left the manor a while back.'

Clara exclaimed and Willow ran quickly through the events of the past months, allowing them to think that she had been dismissed for wrongly influencing Frances. She omitted her jail sentence. The general opinion was, of course, heavily in favour of Willow and condemnation of the Maddisons.

'And you've got a dressmaker's business?' Gran asked. 'There never used to be much money in that. Times must have changed.'

'Not much, Gran. Women still sweat over work that pays them a few coppers, but I've got clients who appreciate my designs. I brought some drawings home for you to look at. I keep a record of all the dresses I make, with a swatch of the material I used. I've coloured some of the drawings, but haven't had time yet to do them all.'

The exercise books were passed round to be looked at with small interest by Joe and Sam, with cries of admiration from the women, and with silent, appraising respect by Alfred. Willow watched his face as he turned the leaves and knew that he felt as she did about the beauty of clothes. Poor thing, he probably had a hell of a lot of teasing to put up with. One day, she'd offer him a position. One day.

'Why didn't you come to Bristol an' open a shop?' asked Clara.

'I wanted to, Mum, but I didn't like to worry you at first, then I got some very good customers and couldn't really get away.'

The boys went out for a last-minute kick around the

streets with a football and Jasmine departed reluctantly to bed.

Mrs Tucker came to say hello and left, and Clara, Gran and Willow seated themselves near the open window of their living room, enjoying the soft air of summer, even laden as it was with soot and grime.

'Does Marigold go out often?' asked Willow.

'Every night,' said Clara. 'I think she's playin' around with boys.'

'Playing around? Has she got a regular boy friend?'

'She's got too many,' said Clara grimly. 'If she's not careful she'll end up with nobody. Men marry women they respect.'

Gran said, 'She'll get what she's after, whatever that is. I've always said she was born knowing. She's old for her years in *that* way.'

'She's often got more money than you'd expect from her job in the boot factory,' muttered Clara. 'I only hope she doesn't come to a bad end.' Translated, this meant an illegitimate baby or a life on the streets.

'She pays her way here, doesn't she, Mum?'

'She gives me what I ask. I'll never touch money that isn't honestly earned.'

Gran said, 'Oh, come on, our Clara, you're not telling me that Marigold's actually getting *money* from men!'

Willow was thankful she hadn't enlarged on the subject of Mrs Bliss's house. Not that she had meant to, knowing the strict moral views held by her mother.

'So you don't see anyone from the manor, Willow?' said Gran, tactfully changing the subject.

'I saw Edgar Maddison in London recently.'

'What happened?' asked Clara. 'Remember what Dad always said. "It's Us and Them." A boy of his class isn't going to act properly by you, any more than his sister did.'

'Mum,' protested Willow, 'I only had a cup of tea with him in a respectable café.'

'That's all right then.'

'He said that Frances was unhappily married.'

'Serves her right!' snapped Clara. 'She deserves to be after the way she treated you.'

'Couldn't you possibly run your business in Bristol?' asked Gran. 'We miss you.'

'No, not at present. I can't afford to lose my customers. They're mostly well off.'

'What happens when they leave London at the end of the season?' Gran was altogether too knowledgeable.

'There's always someone who wants something done.'

'You don't speak the way you did,' Clara said suddenly. 'You sound posh.'

'It goes down better in my trade, Mum.'

'London! Posh talk! Bristol was always good enough for Dad an' me.'

'I'll come back one day and when I do we'll buy a big house and you shall have servants, both of you, and never do a hand's turn again.'

'That'll be the day,' said Clara.

Chapter Eighteen

Willow couldn't get the memory of Gran's frailty off her mind. She missed her family, and felt it keenly that she was denied the pleasures of watching Jasmine grow up and the boys' steps towards adulthood. And Marigold was causing a great deal of worry. She wondered how she could increase her income and save enough money to set up in Bristol, or at least to visit more often.

Edgar found the beginnings of the answer. He arrived one day at the Bayswater house, sending Mrs Bliss into raptures. She told Maisie to fetch Willow and actually climbed the first flight of stairs herself and waited on the landing, clutching her heaving bosom and panting. Willow was cutting a silk gown and was cross at being disturbed.

'Stop frowning,' ordered Mrs Bliss. She looked at Willow's working outfit of a loose cotton dress and sighed. 'There's a really lovely gentleman waiting for you.'

'Who is it? Maisie says she doesn't know.'

'Ah, but I do.' Mrs Bliss wagged her finger roguishly. 'You didn't tell us you knew such a gentleman, a real toff.'

Willow suddenly understood. 'Edgar Maddison!'

'That's right. And hurry up because he looks impatient.'

'Tell him I'm out,' she snapped.

Maisie gasped and Mrs Bliss caught at Willow's arm. 'Don't be a fool. I'll bet he moves in the best circles. He could be useful to you.'

Willow stopped arguing. 'You're right. But don't leave me on my own with him.'

This suited Mrs Bliss perfectly and she preceded Willow into her living room. 'Here she is.'

Edgar, looking wickedly handsome in a grey light-weight suit, was perfectly at home.

He rose as the women entered. 'Willow, my dear,' he exclaimed, 'how charming you look.'

She scowled, earning herself a frown from Mrs Bliss. 'I've been working,' she said, 'and I've still a lot to get through. What do you want?'

Edgar was impervious to her terse greeting. 'I want to talk to you.'

'I've just told you, I'm busy.'

'Now sit down do, Willow love,' urged Mrs Bliss. 'You can spare time for that. You need a little rest anyway.' She turned to Edgar. 'You'd never credit how this girl works, Mr Maddison. She's bending over her cutting table or a sewing machine day and night. It's not good for her.'

'I take exercise when I can!'

'Not enough, by the sound of it.' Edgar had addressed his remark more to Mrs Bliss than to Willow, and she felt even more annoyed by the fact that she cared that she was not wearing something pretty.

'You look as if you could do with a walk right now,' said Edgar. 'How about it?'

Willow opened her mouth to give him a decided no. She hesitated. He was smiling, but she thought she caught an anxious undertone in his manner. Did he really want to see her, or was he piqued by her reluctance?

'I'd have to change my frock,' she said, 'and I really don't have the time. I'm in the middle of something quite difficult. And besides,' she turned to Mrs Bliss, 'Anastasia is coming round in an hour for a fitting of her velvet jacket.'

Faced with the kind of business which Anastasia brought to her lodger, Mrs Bliss was serious. Money, after all, was money.

'That's true,' she said.

'So you won't come?'

'I can't, Edgar. Be reasonable.'

'When can I take you out?'

Never, was what she should say. He could complicate

every area of her life. 'How did you get my address?' she demanded.

'Steven gave it to me.'

'Steven!'

'Yes. When we met in Paris he told me of his bookshop and I went to call on him and asked where you might be found and he told me.'

She wanted to fire questions at him. Was Steven suspicious? Was he resentful? Did he give the address willingly?

'He spoke of your engagement,' said Edgar gently, sensing her annoyance.

Mrs Bliss's eyes opened wide and Willow was so angry with Steven she said impulsively, 'I'll come out with you tomorrow. Call for me at twelve and we'll have lunch together.'

Mrs Bliss hardly waited until Edgar had gone through the front door before she said, 'Willow Riches, you haven't gone and got yourself engaged to Steven, have you? I mean to say, he's a nice enough chap, but with your looks you could do better, much better. The gentleman who's just left likes you a lot.'

'Not enough to marry me, even if I wanted him.'

'Many a girl has done well for herself through a man like him. Is he rich?'

'I think so. His family is.'

'Then why not treat him kindly? If you do he might take you to posh parties and things. Lord knows, you could do with help to reach good customers. You've said so often enough.'

Willow abominated the idea of relying on a Maddison for anything.

'You're right, of course. And I'm not engaged. Steven told Edgar and his friends that I was his fiancée the day we met in Paris and I couldn't argue and let him down, could I? I don't think he really believes it himself.'

'Maybe not, but perhaps he thinks if he says it often enough you'll drift into marriage with him. It's been known.'

'Well, I'm not going to marry him,' said Willow decisively. 'I don't intend to marry anyone, and now I'll get back to my work.' She stamped upstairs, irritated with both men.

Lunch with Edgar was a luxurious pleasure. He had booked a table at Simpson's in the Strand where they ate fillet steak and lemon syllabub and drank vintage wines and Edgar paid a bill which exceeded a month's income for many a family. Willow couldn't help revelling in the atmosphere of tranquil security, but felt a pang at the contrast between the lives of the needy and the lives of the rich.

'Have you enjoyed your meal, madam?' the waiter asked with all the reverent anxiety one might use in enquiring after a sick friend.

'Yes, thank you.'

The waiter glided away and Willow said, 'It's very different from Lyons. Lunch or dinner there is a shilling and sixpence.'

Edgar looked round him in mock horror. 'For God's sake don't say that here! The idea! Lyons!'

'Snob!' she hissed.

'Guilty,' he acknowledged, so languidly that he made her laugh.

She looked surreptitiously at the other women and was pleased to see that not one of them surpassed her in elegance, even if their jewels were real.

'You're a pleasure to take out,' said Edgar over coffee.

'I am?'

'Indeed, you are. Everything fascinates you.'

'I've never been to a place like this before.'

'Not even in Paris?'

'Certainly not. I couldn't afford it.'

'Didn't Steven pay for you?'

She frowned at him. 'No! I only went on the condition that I met my own bill.'

'I see. You visited Paris with an attractive man and behaved like a nun. What a waste!'

She had happy memories of the pleasant hours spent in

331

bed with Steven and felt like telling Edgar, just to watch his reaction. 'You *would* say so! Steven thought that Mrs Stewart and Mrs Thurley were members of the demi-monde.' As soon as she had spoken she wished the words unsaid. Wine had loosened her tongue. 'I'm sorry,' she said lamely.

'He's right. Clever of him to spot it.'

'You mean they're high-class tarts?'

'I doubt if they'd be flattered to hear that.'

'I don't imagine they would. Are they?'

'Some call them that.'

'Why were you with them in Paris?'

'Mrs Stewart and I went there together. We happened to meet Mrs Thurley. She's not a pleasant woman.'

'I suppose Mrs Stewart is your mistress.'

'Suppose away,' said Edgar calmly.

'Don't you mind people thinking it?'

'Not at all. And don't forget, you live in a disorderly house yourself.'

She stared at him, a flush rising to her cheeks. 'Thank you. Thank you very much. Now, if you'll excuse me I'll get a cab home – to the disorderly house.'

'Simmer down, please. I apologise. You are not the only one who speaks without thinking.'

That was unarguable. He ordered more coffee and liqueurs and she sipped at smooth, sweet Chartreuse while Edgar swirled brandy round his glass and drank it slowly.

'Why do you live there, Willow? No, don't get cross with me again. I ask only out of interest.'

She explained briefly.

'So, you are still suffering from Frances's ill treatment of you?'

'I suppose you could say that. However,' she sat back and looked thoughtfully into the glass of golden liquid, 'maybe she will prove to have helped me. If I hadn't been abandoned that night, I might never have begun my career as a designer.'

'You make a good living sewing for ladies of joy?'

'If that isn't typical of a man! Ladies of joy! They're happy

332

enough right now, it's true, but when their beauty is gone their lives are anything but joyful.'

'You don't have to be a woman to realise that.' She was silent and he said, 'Willow, let us not argue. Don't spoil our pleasure.' Don't spoil *his* pleasure, he meant. That's all he asked of life, it seemed, that it should afford him pleasure. 'If I could get Mrs Stewart to patronise you would you accept her custom?'

'What? Make gowns for her?'

'She goes into society a good deal. Not quite into the highest echelons, but among well-to-do people who have plenty to spend on luxuries.'

'You seem to have a lot of influence over her.'

'As I said, we are very good friends. Now, enough questions, Willow. There are some matters ladies do not pursue.'

'I'm not a lady, or have you forgotten?'

'You would pass for one.'

'Ladies are born, not made.'

Edgar laughed. 'Don't you believe it! Half the male aristocracy spend time in America trying to marry heiresses to fortunes made in trade.'

'You've been there yourself, haven't you?'

'Yes.'

'Did you find an heiress?' She couldn't look at him as she asked.

'I found several, but decided to forgo the delights of wealth in favour of—'

'Of what?'

'Never you mind. Now, about Mrs Stewart. Think of the customers you would get.'

'How can you be so sure?'

'I know clothes, I understand them and yours are superb. I have no doubt that you will be even more skilful when you attract customers with the cash to spend on expensive materials. Will you let me help you? No obligation on either side, I promise you.'

She couldn't hold out against such temptation. 'I'd be delighted to sew for her. How about Mrs Thurley?'

'I dare say she and many others would patronise you if you became the rage.'

'Can I charge Mrs Stewart a lot?'

'If you did not she'd think you weren't worth employing.'

'How shall I set about it?' Now that she had capitulated Willow felt excited. 'When can I meet her?'

'I'll arrange for you to call. She has a delightful house in St John's Wood.'

Mrs Stewart's house was, as Edgar had said, delightful. An elegant, Georgian grey stone dwelling, with the original windows and front door and a neat maid to open it. Willow was nervous. This was one commission she couldn't afford to bungle. She was shown into a pretty drawing room which gave an overall impression of blue and silver grey. Sun streamed through the windows and the maid pulled a curtain across to keep it, she explained, from fading the Oriental carpets. She left then reappeared. 'Madam says will you wait on her in her room?'

Willow followed the girl up carpeted stairs into another sunlit room with a decor of palest mauve and pink. The softly sweet colours of the house were exactly right for a 'lady of joy'.

Mrs Stewart called for tea and poured it into pretty Japanese cups. There were tiny macaroons which Willow refused but which Mrs Stewart ate rapidly. One day she might run to fat, but now she was lovely in the generous way which was going out of fashion. Willow measured her. The maid entered with her arms full of material which wasn't quite purple and wasn't quite puce. Lilac? Heather? Heather, she decided.

'Here's the pattern.' The maid handed it to Willow and retired, taking the tray with her.

Willow studied it. 'I can, of course, follow this, but would you not prefer to have something original?'

Mrs Stewart wrapped herself in a lacy dressing gown. She looked amused. 'What do you picture for me?'

Willow pulled a sketch pad and pencil from her bag and

334

swiftly drew a gown which was plainly cut except for three horizontal pleats which caused a draped effect over the hips. The gown narrowed just below the bust in the new style and the sleeves were full with a fall of lace at the elbow and a matching fichu at the neck.

Mrs Stewart studied it and cried, 'Horizontal pleats! For me? My dear girl, I am not so vain and foolish that I cannot see myself as I am, and I want nothing which makes my rear end look larger.'

'It won't, I swear. The soft draping would conceal the curve of your hips, and the pleating across the front is quite short so that it gives the illusion of a narrower waistline.'

'Are you sure? Can you really give me a slimmer-looking figure?'

'I can,' said Willow, her heart beating fast. She smoothed the sensuous material. 'It's beautiful.'

'It is, isn't it? Very well, I'll allow you the opportunity which Edgar says you need. He's such a dear boy, isn't he?' Willow wondered if Edgar would be paying for the dress.

'When can you call for the first fitting?'

'A week from today, if that's all right. I have other orders to fill, then I can give my time to you.'

'A week? Yes, I'll wait that long. And if you bring it off I shall pay you well and recommend you to others. If you don't, I'm afraid, my dear Willow, you will be sadly out of pocket. The material is costly.'

Later Willow was amazed at her confident daring, but now she was borne up by a combination of hope, need, and strongest of all the ambition to seize this marvellous chance. She dispatched her current orders with the help of Bridget who joined her in working long hours. Steven complained that she was always too busy to go out with him.

Edgar was equally vociferous. 'It isn't healthy to stay indoors too much,' he grumbled. 'And, what's more, you're overworking Bridget.'

Willow glared at him. They were in Mrs Bliss's parlour and for once that lady was absent. Claudette was having a problem with a client who was demanding more in the way of sexual gymnastics than she was prepared to allow.

'You're a fine one to talk about overworking,' she snapped. 'If you want to see it at its worst take yourself into your parents' kitchen and have a look at the servants, especially the scullery maid. A child who's lucky if she gets six hours' sleep out of twenty-four. But what do you care? And you can stop worrying about Bridget. I am paying her extra and shall allow her time off to make up. Unlike your servants, who work all the hours God sends without compensation.'

She had angered him. 'I wish I'd never introduced you to Mrs Stewart.' His voice carried the petulance she remembered.

'Well, you did, and now you can take yourself off and stop bothering me.'

'I've a damned good mind to advise her to cancel the order!'

For a moment she was breathless with fury. 'You would, too, wouldn't you? It's just what I'd expect from a spoiled brat like you, with your toffee-nosed family and your damned Eton education.'

They stared at one another while the air around them crackled with antagonism, then the vision of Edgar, a little under six feet tall, as a spoiled brat in an Eton collar came to them and they fell on one another's shoulders, laughing hysterically.

'I'm sorry,' he gasped.

'So am I.'

'I'll try to be patient.'

'And I'll try to work faster.'

'Would you care to go to a music hall?'

'What?'

'Music hall. You know, comics, singers, naughty jokes?'

'I'd adore to.'

Mrs Bliss came in and looked bewildered at the air of hilarity. 'Well, you two seem to be having fun. I've just had to have a client escorted off the premises. How dare he treat one of my girls as if she was dirt!'

'Quite right,' agreed Edgar.

Mrs Bliss was soothed by his agreement. 'Are you stopping for tea?'

Edgar glanced at Willow. 'I think not. There is work to be done.'

Maisie showed him out and Mrs Bliss said, 'What a lovely young man. Is there any chance you and he might—?'

'None whatsoever! I despise his whole family.'

Her answer was illogical and untrue, Willow reflected, as she climbed the stairs to the attic. There was no reason why he should be punished for his sister's callousness, and she didn't despise him. On the other hand, she couldn't quite respect him. He was too light, too insubstantial.

The gown for Mrs Stewart was a triumphant success. Willow fitted the completed garment on her and stood back. 'You look utterly beautiful,' she said. It was true and when she asked for nine guineas Mrs Stewart paid so willingly Willow decided she should have asked more.

Edgar congratulated her on her success. 'But you could have got more money, you know. The new gown will be going to a ball where people are bound to notice it. You're sure to get commissions.'

Edgar was right. She did receive commissions from women who could pay. Mrs Stewart asked for a pair of the new harem trousers and a tunic to match. Even she would not dare to wear these in public and as Willow stitched at the transparent green voile she wondered if Edgar was friendly enough with her to see her in them.

She said so to Steven who had insisted on her taking a walk in the park. She lifted her face to a cooling breeze as they stepped out of the brilliant sunshine into blue-green shadows beneath the trees.

'I wish you wouldn't speak of such things,' he said.

'Why not? I like to speculate on where my creations end up. I'm going to call the harem outfit *Scheherazade*, after Bakst's stage costume.'

'You're calling your clothes *names*?'

'Yes, why not?'

'It's utterly pretentious!'

'I see you've been studying your dictionary again.'

She had been trying to tease him out of his prudish annoyance, but the problem with Steven was that she never knew where to draw the line and this time she had angered him.

'I wish you wouldn't be frivolous about my studies.'

'Sorry. I know your vocabulary is extensive, but you should understand my work, too.'

'I don't call sewing for rich women proper work. I shall want you to join me in the bookshop one day. My trade is growing fast.'

'Join you in the bookshop? Are you crazy? Why on earth should I?'

'Because I'll expect my wife to be a helpmate.'

'Do you seriously believe that if you keep telling people that I'm your fiancée, I shall eventually marry you?'

'Won't you? After all, since Paris we're married in the eyes of God.'

'I don't consider us any such thing! And you can stop believing that you can bully me into marriage.'

Steven stopped. 'Bully you? As if I ever would! Only brutes are bullies.'

Willow looked down at the daisy-studded grass and swept a semi-circle with the toe of her shoe. 'There are other ways of bullying,' she said gently, 'and they include talking. I shall marry whom, and when, I choose.'

He didn't answer and she looked up to see his eyes filled with pain. 'Steven, I wish you wouldn't.'

'Wouldn't love you, do you mean? Well, I do, and I intend to have you. You're mine already!'

'Perhaps I might have agreed with you once, but my views have changed since I left the manor.'

'Is that attributable to Mrs Bliss's so-called girls?'

'It may be. And to Mrs Stewart who seems perfectly respectable yet makes a living selling herself to men. Certainly I see sexual matters in a different way now I know more about them.'

338

Steven looked hastily around. 'You shouldn't use words like that in public.'

'Like what? Sexual?'

'*Yes*! You wouldn't ever sell your body?'

'No, I shouldn't think so. No, I'm sure I wouldn't. On the other hand, if I fail as a dressmaker—'

'Stop it! Stop it at once! How can you even imagine yourself sinking so low?'

She walked on and he was forced to follow. 'Steven, I see poor souls in the streets who have sunk to the depths of degradation, but I wouldn't be like them.' She wondered why she was torturing him like this when she had no intention of ever setting up as a prostitute. Perhaps she wanted revenge for the way he had glibly assumed control over her future. 'Sorry,' she said quickly. 'I'd rather starve than sell my body.'

Steven laughed in his relief, though it had a harsh sound. 'The less you see of Edgar Maddison the better. I'd bet a week's takings that sooner or later he'll try to seduce you. You won't succumb, will you?'

'Of course not. Meanwhile, he's useful.'

Mrs Stewart's gown had been so much admired she asked Willow if she could see the sketches she had made. Willow obliged. 'I've got them all on a single piece of paper.'

'But they are so beautiful! The preliminary sketches run around the page and my heavenly gown is in the middle. And you've called it *Heather*. It's a good likeness of me, too. I had no idea you were so very talented. Have you christened the harem outfit, too? *Scheherazade*! Perfect! My dear, would you sell the pictures to me?'

'What?'

'Sell them to me, please. I'll pay well.'

'What will you do with them?'

'Hang them on my wall, of course, where they will be seen by my guests.'

'You want the whole thing, including the rough sketches?'

'You've no intention of making other garments the same, have you?'

'No, that's exactly what I don't intend to do, but I need the sketches to remind me of what I've done.'

'Couldn't you copy them for yourself?'

Willow was persuaded and added an astonishing fifteen guineas for each picture to her bank account. She was excited and talked eagerly about it to Edgar.

'I saw *Heather*,' he said. 'She's had it beautifully framed. Next time you visit her you must have a look.'

'Where is the other one? In her bedroom, I suppose.'

He laughed. 'You know, you would be insufferable if you weren't so interesting. I have no idea where it is.'

Willow blurted out, 'She isn't under your protection, is she? You're not paying her bills and just getting her to commission work from me?'

'No, I am not!' He paused. 'I will explain about her and then perhaps you will let the subject drop. I hadn't even left school when she initiated me into the mysteries of love. We enjoyed one another enormously. Lately she engaged the attention of an extremely wealthy and respectable man who is now her only lover. I have an idea he would marry her if only his wife – who is a devil's handmaiden, if ever there was one – would die. Our trip to Paris was a farewell, a last fling.'

'Waiting for a dead woman's shoes?' jeered Willow.

'I thought you liked her.'

'Yes, I do,' she admitted.

'Well, I can tell you with certainty that you wouldn't like his wife.'

The death of the suffragette Emily Davison had shocked many more people than her sisters in the struggle for the vote and the streets had been lined with crowds watching her funeral cortège pass. The coffin arrived from Epsom at Victoria Station and four suffragettes dressed entirely in white, with their distinctive sashes of black and purple, stood guard at the four corners, their arms filled with flowers. Then Charlotte Marsh, the standard bearer, carrying a wooden cross, led the slow procession to King's

Cross Station from where the coffin would be taken to Morpeth, Emily's Northumberland home, for burial. Long lines of women dressed in white, holding madonna lilies, were followed by others in purple and black, bearing irises and peonies. After them came the suffragettes awaiting trial for conspiracy. In their everyday clothes they stood out. The bands played music by Chopin, Handel and Beethoven and many women and some men in the crowd wept and those who had come to jeer were silenced. Willow was there with Steven and couldn't fight back her tears. One woman was being helped along by two friends and with a shock she recognised Jane Barton. She looked prematurely old and it was obvious that she stayed upright with difficulty. As the cortège passed, Jane's exhausted friends handed her over to two others and Willow felt a flash of regret that she wasn't in there among them.

'I know that lady,' she said to Steven. 'She helped me when I came out of jail.'

She had kept her voice low and whispered in his ear. He caught her hand and squeezed it. The gesture was slight but comforting, and it moved her.

On an impulse she called on Jane. The maid kept her waiting in the hall while she consulted her mistress. Willow was invited upstairs. She found Jane lying in bed, her emaciated form barely making a mound in the bedclothes, her eyes dark-ringed.

'I'm sorry to find you so ill, Jane.'

'I am sorry to be so ill.' Jane smiled, revealing more broken teeth.

'They've been torturing you again! Your illness is all their fault.'

'It will be worth it when we get the vote.' Jane's voice was a mere thread of sound.

Willow sank into a chair by the bed and took Jane's hands in hers. They looked deathly white, the veins showing purple. The tips of her fingers were blue and there was a blue line around her mouth. 'You make me ashamed that I've done nothing.'

'Oh, but you have, my dear. We all know about the sacrifice you made for that spineless creature Frances Maddison. You remained silent and took her punishment for her. Why did you?'

'I don't know . . . she's such a weak girl, and I'd had habits of obedience drilled into me. And then there was the oath she'd sworn on the Bible. She tried to fulfil her mission even though she was so frightened. Mind you, I don't know if I would have helped her if I'd known I wouldn't get my job back. That was a terrible blow.'

Again Jane smiled. 'I like your honesty. And you look as if you are managing well.'

'I am. In a way, I suppose I've Frances to thank for that. I might still have been slaving away for her.'

Jane gave a little laugh, then coughed alarmingly and her maid came hurrying in. She must have been listening outside. She took a bottle of linctus from the bedside cabinet and tipped a spoonful into her mistress's mouth.

'Thank you,' said Jane. Her voice had grown fainter.

'You'd best go, miss.'

'Not yet,' said Jane.

'But the doctor said—'

'I know what he said. That's why I want a little longer with Willow.'

The maid averted her face as she hurried away.

Willow asked, 'How ill are you?'

'Pretty bad. I have never recovered from my experiences in prison. Now, my dear, tell me, to whom did Frances swear a Bible oath and what was it exactly?'

'You don't know?'

Jane shook her head weakly.

'She said you had made her swear on the Bible that she would come to London and take part in a violent demonstration.'

'Do you think I would do a thing like that?'

Willow looked into Jane's eyes and said, 'No. Not now. Though I did at the time. She said it simply to make me go

342

with her. I can't understand why she went at all. She was terrified.'

'She's a woman who likes everyone to think well of her. Spineless people often find it easier to agree to others' requests. Poor soul, she's paying a heavy price now.'

Willow wanted to ask her what she meant, but Jane began to cough again and this time the maid would not be put off.

Jane held Willow's hand in a parting gesture and gasped, 'Promise me, promise me faithfully, that on the glorious day when women get the vote you will use yours. Always, and wisely.'

'I swear I will. I've seen such wretchedness since I left home, and so much more among the women with their endless child-bearing.'

'You understand.' Jane withdrew her hand. 'Goodbye, Willow. Take good care of yourself.'

Edgar called and asked Willow to accompany him to a party where there would be dancing. 'Modern, of course. The cake-walk and that kind of thing.'

Fresh from seeing Jane, she was irritated by the frivolity of his life. 'I've no idea how to dance the cake-walk or that sort of thing,' she snapped, 'and anyway I'm too busy.'

Edgar, who by this time had penetrated the fastness of her remote attic, took her sewing from her. She had to let it go for to hold on might have risked tearing the material.

'What is the matter?'

'A friend is very ill. I'm afraid she may die.'

Edgar looked down at her sympathetically then said, 'Would she expect you to stay at home and be miserable?'

'No, that's the last thing she'd expect.'

He smoothed the material. 'This is pretty stuff.'

'It's for Mrs Thurley.'

'What?'

'Mrs Thurley,' repeated Willow. 'Mrs Stewart recommended me. Do you think the colour will suit her?'

'I shouldn't wonder. Now about this party . . .'

In the end it was easier to go than to refuse. The party was in a house in Belgrave Square and was quite different from her expectations. 'I thought it would be in a hotel. I hadn't expected to be taken to a private house. And this must be one of your grander occasions. I suppose I should have known when I saw you in white tie and tails.'

'Are there any other sorts of occasions?' Edgar grinned. 'Now then, Willow, you can't hit me here. What would people say?'

'Aren't you afraid of what your friends will think of me?'

'Of you?' He eyed her carefully. She wore a green satin gown which was draped from her hips to her knees, falling in heavy folds to her ankles. It was trimmed with fur. The fichu was of palest lilac, and tiny green earrings graced her ears. She had tied a lilac satin bandeau round her dark curls and fastened it in a floppy bow. A small gold bird lent by Carmen was perched on the lilac satin. Her diaphanous wrap was of the same lilac material as the fichu. Her gloves were full-length white kid and her silk shoes dyed green. 'You look absolutely splendid,' he said. 'No one will wear anything to touch that frock.'

He was wrong, of course. She couldn't outshine clothes designed by Monsieur Poiret or Madame Paquin, though she was pleased to discover that she recognised their work as clearly as if she could read the labels and was delighted when more than one lady asked the name of her couturier.

She dissembled at first then Edgar said, 'You had better think of a name for yourself. Something fancy, preferably French.'

'Not French! I've not even a smattering of the language. And what's wrong with the name I've got?'

Edgar had given her some lessons in the new dances and Claudette, who liked to dance herself, had practised with her, so she was able to hurl herself into the frenzy of the cake-walk, the bunny hug and the turkey trot. As she and Edgar left the floor, breathless after one vigorous session, she realised that she was being stared at.

344

'My God, both your sisters are here,' she muttered to him. 'One would be bad enough, but both!'

He laughed and led her straight to them. 'Haven't we met somewhere?' asked Violet.

'I believe we have, Lady Radcliffe.'

'Where could it have been? I say, I do admire your frock. Who is your couturier?'

'Riches, Lady Radcliffe.'

'Riches? Is that a man or a woman? A woman? Really? One has never heard of her. You must give me her address.'

'No need. Riches is a woman who calls on her clients at home.'

'Even more delightful.'

'I knew I recognised you,' hissed Frances, who had clearly been drinking heavily. Her fair English beauty was blurred, her blue eyes a little bloodshot. 'I remember you.'

'As I do you,' said Willow, looking at her calmly.

Did Frances read an implied threat there? Edgar said she had never disclosed the truth about the night in London. 'Here's my husband,' she said fretfully. 'I dare say he'll want to leave now he's seen the man he was looking for.'

Mr Bickford joined them and said smoothly, 'Come, my dear, you need rest.'

'Can't we stay a little longer?' Frances spoke in a whining tone which sent shivers up Willow's spine. 'I've never even tried the new dances. The cake-walk looks so jolly.'

'Are you aware,' said Mr Bickford, including them all in his frigid glance, 'that a specialist doctor has castigated the cake-walk as an obsession of the brain, and that a young girl who became physically deformed by it needed six months' rest in the country to recover?' He was deadly serious.

'I dare say he has a special clinic to assist such stricken females,' observed Edgar.

Mr Bickford remained unaware of his sarcasm. 'Of course,' he agreed. 'It is fortunate that someone is trying to help these young people back to mental health.'

'I think he is very silly,' said Frances, 'and I want to dance.'

'I think not, my dear.' Her husband was implacable. 'Come, I will escort you home.'

'I don't want to go home. I want to dance. If I can't do the cake-walk, let me dance the turkey trot. It looks such *fun*.'

Mr Bickford gave her a look of disgust, took her arm firmly and led her away.

'What a fool she is to knuckle under to him,' said Violet to Edgar. She spoke languidly, as if it didn't matter to her one way or the other, and Willow was shocked. Violet looked around the room. 'Have you seen Radcliffe anywhere?'

'No, sorry. How's the Radcliffe heir?'

'He's well. He looks like his daddy,' she added jeeringly.

Edgar led Willow on to the floor for a waltz. 'Such a sweet old-fashioned dance,' he said.

'Are neither of your sisters happy?' she asked.

Edgar sighed heavily. 'I should like just to talk about us.'

'They don't seem happy. Frances was drunk, wasn't she? And Violet sounded sour.'

'Can we talk about them later? Could you manage to enjoy being in my arms?'

'What a sweet romantic you are, to be sure.' But she laughed and gave herself up to the lilt of the music and the charm of her partner.

He called on her the following day in a very happy frame of mind. 'You were a success. People are talking about you and your clothes. You must have cards printed with your name and profession which you can hand out to enquirers.'

She found a small printer who produced cards quickly. He printed a sample which read: 'Riches. Couture Designer. Clients may Purchase Water Colour Sketches of their Unique Gowns.'

'That's perfect,' said Willow. 'I'll need to give you my new address.'

She had agreed with Edgar that she should move. He said, 'You must rent a flat or house in a good part of London.'

'Impossible! I haven't that kind of money.'

'But I have.'

'No!'

She was so emphatic that he flushed. 'The money would be a loan. I would not take advantage of you in any way. It would be merely a business arrangement. You can cut me in on the profits, if you wish.'

'No, I'm sorry, but it simply wouldn't do. Someone would discover you had given me money. I'm serious about my designing. I want no complications to get in the way.'

'Am I a complication?' he asked angrily.

Willow said, 'Of course you are. All emotional entanglements are complications.' This made him laugh, and when she followed it up with a request for advice about finding suitable premises his good humour was restored.

She had lived for so long with Frances that, in spite of everything, she couldn't just ignore her plight. When she asked Edgar about her, he admitted, 'She drinks.'

'I could see that.'

'I don't mean the way one usually does. She drinks far too much and she drinks alone. Bickford has to lock the stuff away.'

'Why does she do it?'

'Bickford leads her a hell of a life. Everything is regimented with him. The house runs like clockwork and is about as soulless. The servants have been with his family for years, and are all old and grim and spy on her.'

'Poor thing. And what about Violet?'

'What about her?'

'There's something wrong there too, isn't there?'

'You haven't taken a course after Dr Freud, have you? All right, Violet has made a terrible mistake.'

'Married the wrong man?'

'Fallen in love with the wrong man. Her husband.'

'And that's bad?'

'It is when the husband is a philanderer who doesn't even take the trouble to hide his conquests.'

'The servants at the manor used to talk about him. If they knew what he was like, surely Violet—'

'I keep forgetting you worked in our kitchens!'

'You can forget if you wish. I can't.'

'Radcliffe can't resist a pretty face and it cuts Violet up no end. He had his eye on you last night.'

'Wouldn't it be odd if the dirty little girl whom she and Frances picked up on the Bristol Downs enticed Violet's husband?'

'You wouldn't!'

'No, you're right, I wouldn't. And she has a son. Hasn't that brought Lord Radcliffe to heel?'

'It's made him worse. He says he's done his duty by his wife and family.'

'Poor Violet.'

'You've a generous heart,' said Edgar.

'But not a large enough purse to move from here.'

He laughed. 'You are a stubborn wench! Did I ever tell you you were beautiful? You are, you know, and your figure is superb. You would be the best mannequin of all to advertise your clothes.'

'And I suppose you can arrange that too?'

'Perhaps. If you will let me. There are still plenty of parties before everyone decamps to Brighton or the more exotic resorts abroad.'

'Or Bristol?'

'The house isn't often used nowadays.'

Willow went full tilt after attracting clients and Edgar, often amused by her, accompanied her willingly to soirées, balls, and parties. Before each one she and Bridget sat for hours sewing so that Willow could always appear in a different outfit, but the work bore fruit. She gained half a dozen wealthy customers and was delighted, though the labour grew heavier. To capitalise on this excellent beginning she absolutely must find a larger place and engage more staff, though she would miss the camaraderie of Mrs Bliss and her girls. And at the back of her mind was always the niggling thought that she should move back to Bristol.

She said this to Edgar who advised, 'Stay in London. You are on your way to success. When you are sure of it you can take on the provinces.'

'Are you advising me disinterestedly?'

He avoided a straight reply. 'I wish you to do anything which advances your career. It's a fascinating one.'

Steven gave the same advice, only his was definitely loaded with self-interest which he didn't trouble to hide. 'I want you near me, Willow. Thank heaven the so-called season is almost over. Edgar Maddison will leave town and probably go jaunting abroad and I'll have you to myself.'

He was serious, but managed to smile as if he was making a joke. His jealousy didn't blind him to the realisation that if he put too much pressure on Willow he would lose what small influence he had over her. And he did have some. He was a friend from the desperate days and the only one who could talk them over with her when she needed a sympathetic ear. He knew her struggles. To Edgar, who had never known anything but wealth, everything was a game.

Chapter Nineteen

Mrs Bliss found a new place for Willow. She was sad at her leaving, but accepted it. 'Mr Maddison's quite right, my dear, we can't have your posh clients visiting you here. I think I know the perfect place and the landlady would like to meet you. She's an old friend and only lets to business ladies – real ones, I mean,' she said with a wink. 'She likes the sound of you, and you'll still be in Bayswater and near enough to pop in now and again.'

Mrs Grigson was tall, pale and thin, and seldom smiled. When she did her face assumed an almost merry expression and her eyes shone. 'She's like a lamp post being lit by a street lighter,' said Edgar when he met her. She unbent at once to him, as most women did.

She took to Willow, too. 'You're a real hard worker, says Mrs Bliss. I like that in a young woman. And you don't gallivant all over the place. Annie Bliss and me went right through school together. I don't think much of what she does, and she thinks I'm daft not to make more money. Well, what suits one don't suit another and we manage not to fall out.'

Willow found her brisk restlessness daunting, but the rooms she offered overcame any slight misgivings. They comprised the whole of the ground floor. One large one at the front would make excellent living accommodation, a long room with side windows had ample space for several machinists to work, and there were four other small ones. All the decoration had been done by an admirer of William Morris, and flowers and birds and ornamental leaves rioted everywhere without a straight line in sight. Fortunately the colours were subdued, they looked as if they might have faded gently over time, and the overall effect was one of controlled jubilation. The furniture was of good quality and appeared comfortable.

'Beautiful, isn't it?' said Mrs Grigson. 'The wallpaper, I mean. I noticed you examining it.'

'Yes, indeed. You must have had very good tenants here for everything to look so cared for.'

'I lived in these rooms until three months ago. That's when my husband passed on. One room is enough for me now I've got to manage the place on my own and I've moved to the first floor. I took as much as I needed of my furniture and some of this is new. He had a bathroom installed off the first half-landing which you can use, and there's a lavatory there and one down here. My husband always paid a lot of attention to the needs of our business ladies, God rest his soul. You'll have to share the kitchen with me. That's if you decide to move in.'

'I'd like to very much, Mrs Grigson. What rent are you asking?'

'Twelve and six a week. It's not cheap, I know, but don't forget there are six rooms. It's threepence extra for a bath and your fires all have penny meters.'

Willow doubted that she'd find a better place. 'I'll take it,' she said.

'Good. My husband always insisted on a proper legal tenancy, yearly or six-monthly, with proper notice to leave given on each side.'

'Your husband was evidently a clever man.'

Mrs Grigson smiled her beautiful smile. 'He was an angel, Miss Riches. An angel. I miss him.'

Toby, Mrs Bliss's odd-job man, hired a barrow and spent a couple of hours transporting Willow's goods to her new address. The girls were sorry to see her leave and begged her to continue sewing for them. 'Of course I will,' she said. 'How could I forget your kindness to me?'

She signed the lease and purchased a third machine and

engaged Bridget's sister, equally plain and dumpy, to use it. Having worked out her finances she was satisfied that with care she would do well. She had a respectable lodging, employees, sewing machines, and a little cash in the bank. She had moneyed clients and would get more.

A week after her move she heard that Jane Barton was dead. It saddened her and she stood unnoticed on the side-lines of her funeral which was conducted with the ceremony of a soldier's, one who had died honourably in battle. Afterwards she learned that Jane had left her a legacy of two hundred and fifty pounds in a codicil added to her will three days after Willow had visited her.

She sat in the lawyer's office, feeling stunned. 'It's a fortune!'

He smiled. 'Not quite a fortune, my dear, but a very tidy sum.'

'It's a fortune to me!'

The lawyer veered between the avuncular and the astonished. This woman was gowned in the highest fashion, in an outfit which must have set her back a good many guineas, yet was proclaiming two hundred and fifty pounds to be a fortune. 'What will you do with it, my dear? Take a nice little holiday? Buy a fur coat? A small motor car suitable for a lady?'

His smile faded in the face of the look Willow gave him. It said very clearly, Don't patronise me. 'I shall use it to build my business, which I'm sure was Miss Barton's intention.' She reached into her handbag and offered him a card on which she had written her new address. 'I have recently moved to these premises and would be happy to call on your wife at any time.'

'My wife buys her clothes in the big stores,' he said, a little indignantly.

'Well, if she changes her mind and would like a unique couture outfit, I shall be pleased to wait on her.' She turned at the door. 'By the way, I designed and made the clothes I'm wearing.'

She had already written to her family telling them about

her move. If she had had the money just one week earlier she might have gone back to Bristol, but it was impossible now; impossible also not to acknowledge the sneaking feeling of relief that she hadn't to uproot herself and begin all over again.

London in 1914 was unusually hot and people enjoyed it to the full. The summer holidays were in full swing. Those who liked raucous fun went to Blackpool or Southend. If they sought bracing air they travelled to Weston Super Mare or Brighton. Families with a little more money to spare and a higher opinion of their place in society favoured Bournemouth or Boscombe. The wealthy clients whom Willow had attracted who had not gone abroad visited her on the few occasions they came up to town, but the rest of the time she relied heavily on Mrs Bliss's girls and their friends. Three of the small rooms had been fitted up as bedrooms, the fourth as a storeroom for work in progress, and she couldn't afford to let up now, with rent and wages to pay and food to buy for three.

She gave her small staff time off to go home for a few days and when they returned they said they were glad to be back. 'Honest, Willow,' said Bridget's sister Dora, 'me an' Bridgie have never had a room to sleep in on our own. I mean, one each, not even havin' to share with each other. It's like a palace here. An' hot water comin' out of that geyser thing! It scared me at first. Now I love it. Mum thinks we're ever so lucky.'

Willow's recreation was taken in the London parks where the grassy areas were lively with other stay-at-homes. The Serpentine was crowded with men and children and she watched them cooling themselves, wishing she could join them. Women didn't disrobe and leap into the water, not in the heart of London, though by all accounts they did at the seaside, some wearing quite scanty bathing suits. Sometimes there was a band and little girls danced, lifting their ragged skirts above their skinny knees.

Steven had gone to see his foster parents, though Willow wondered why he bothered since he always returned depressed by their narrow, sanctimonious attitude.

'Aren't they at all pleased at the way you've become a respectable businessman?' she once asked him.

'I don't think so. They asked what kind of books I sold, and when I said "all kinds" they went on and on, saying I should only sell religious books, especially Bibles. I told them I stocked some of those, but they weren't impressed.'

'Why do you keep trying to please them? It's hopeless and only makes you miserable.'

Steven was thoughtful. 'It must seem masochistic. I suppose it's because they're the only parents I've known and they took me in and kept me from being put into an orphanage. And just think, Willow my love, if they hadn't, I should never have met you.' They had been chatting in his room at the shop after a high tea he had cooked himself. Her hazy sense of well-being, the scent of leather which permeated the whole place, the general atmosphere of content, was euphoric and when Steven began to make love to her she responded. Since Paris their relationship had settled into one of steady pleasure where each gave the other uncritical understanding and sexual fulfilment. Sometimes, Steven was stirred into guilt over their unhallowed arrangement and felt miserable. Once he pointed out that if they had got married when he wanted they could have had a child already and another on the way. He was perfectly serious; in his dream he saw Willow living with him behind the shop, tending a child, expecting another, selling books, cooking meals, serene and content. It was a million miles from her own dream.

Edgar had gone down to Devon after the season ended, had paid a visit to Monte Carlo, but returned to London saying he'd missed her. He tried to coerce her into love-making but she was adamant in her refusal. She wanted to believe that loyalty to Steven held her in check, but in truth she couldn't analyse her reluctance and surmised that to slide into a second relationship would make her feel cheap. Edgar received her constant refusals first with temper, then with fortitude. Today he had joined her in the park. He lay full-length on his stomach on the over-dry grass, gazing up at her as she fanned herself lazily.

'You grow more beautiful with the passing years,' he said.

'So do you,' grinned Willow.

'Be serious, woman. I am.'

'So am I.'

For a moment his mouth took on the petulant look she hated, then he smiled and rolled over, looking up into the leaves of the tree which shaded them from the broiling sun. He picked a daisy and plucked the petals one by one. 'There will be a war; there won't be a war; there will; there won't. It comes out won't. That's a relief. In a way.'

'In a way? Surely you can't want one?'

'It might be exciting. Yes, I'm sure it would be.'

'I think it would be horrible. I don't know how you can joke about it. Why should we fight?'

'You can't have been reading the newspapers!'

'I read them when I've got time. I know that the Turks are at war with Greece and Bulgaria.'

'And with Serbia and the Balkans where most think the flash point will come.'

'What makes you so clever when Lloyd George said only in January that the prospects for world peace have never been so bright?'

'He's closing his eyes to reality. The Kaiser doesn't trust us. He's building up his fleet.'

'He would never go to war with Britain. He's related to our royal family. His grandmother was Queen Victoria.'

'That won't stop him, and it certainly cuts no ice with the little nations or with Austria.'

Willow shivered though the sun had lost none of its power. 'You're just trying to upset me,' she declared, springing to her feet. 'You don't actually know anything, only what the newspapers say. I want to walk.'

'Come back! Must you be so vigorous?'

He got up and ran after her, slipping his arm through hers. 'I won't talk about war again. Let's think of frivolous things. Let's go to the theatre.'

They did and saw George Bernard Shaw's play *Pygmalion* and heard the word 'bloody' used on an English stage, an event which amused some and shocked others. They went to a music hall and sang choruses and laughed at the antics of Little Titch as he cavorted on the tips of his enormously long boots. But the laughter rang too loud and the songs were sung with superfluous vigour, aggression even, as people sought to convince themselves that there could not possibly be a war, not in Britain anyway.

On 28 June, in Sarajevo, an assassin fired a shot into the face of the Archduke Franz Ferdinand, heir to the Austrian throne. Making a desperate but already forlorn attempt to save her husband, the Archduchess threw herself across his body and received the bullet which ended her life. At first Britain took little notice. What was the death of a small foreign princeling to them? But Austria wanted revenge and sent impossible demands to Serbia which, to Austria's private fury, were all met. Such submission did not cool the Austrians who hungered for a war which would teach Serbia, and any other small country, that no one trifled with them. Some nations were desperate to avoid war; others keen to use it to press their territorial claims. Then Germany, in defiance of Britain's ultimatum, invaded Belgium, and with crushing, horrifying inevitability, on 4 August Britain found herself at war. Her young men flocked to the recruiting stations, encouraged by a striking poster of Lord Kitchener pointing an accusing finger and saying, 'Your Country Needs You'. On one September day alone thirty-five thousand men signed up.

Steven's reaction was to propose immediate marriage to

Willow before he joined up. He was in a state of high excitement. 'Lots of fellows are marrying quickly,' he said. 'They feel the same way as me. I know I'll fight better thinking of you waiting for me at home. You can't refuse me now, I need you to run the shop, and it was only a matter of time before we got wed.'

Willow said as gently as she could, considering he had just consigned her own career to limbo, 'It was not, Steven. I've never said I would marry you.'

He looked astonished. 'You've never said you wouldn't. Not properly.'

'I should have.'

'You mean, you really won't?'

'I'm not ready for marriage. I am happy as I am. Besides,' she said, clutching at the nearest straw, 'what if we had a child? Are you ready to bring a child into a world gone mad?'

He seemed dazed. 'You won't marry me?'

'No.'

He leapt to his feet and began to pace his small living room. 'Is it because you're afraid to have a baby?'

'What?'

'Are you afraid of childbed?'

'For heaven's sake, what are you talking about?'

'You said you don't want to bring a child into the world.'

'Steven, stop pacing and sit down.' He obeyed her though he moved restlessly in his chair. 'I am not afraid of having a baby. I hope one day to have a family of my own, most women do, but I just don't want to be tied down at present. I have a career to follow.'

He was single-minded. 'Tied down? Is that how you see marriage with me?'

'It's how I see it with anyone.'

He glared at her. 'Anyone! Do you mean there are other men? Edgar Maddison perhaps. Maybe you've been to bed with him.'

'No, I haven't.' Her patience was growing thin. 'You are the only man I've allowed such intimacy.'

'Because you love me! That's why, isn't it, Willow? Because you love me? I know you do! No woman could let a man do what I did without love.'

As Steven was as familiar as she with the profession of Mrs Bliss's girls Willow thought this a peculiarly silly statement.

He caught her thought. 'You aren't comparing yourself to those women again, are you?'

'Those women are my friends. The only female ones I have.'

'I know, and it's a disgrace.'

'I happen to like them. And what time have I had to meet other women? And where should I find them?'

'There are plenty of decent ones in chapels.'

'Chapels?' She was really angry now. 'Where I could meet women like your mother, I suppose? Sanctimonious, mean-spirited, unkind—'

'Don't talk like that!'

'Don't yell at me!' Willow felt suddenly deflated and very sad. 'Steven, let's stop this. I can't bear to think of you going away after a quarrel.'

He glared at her, his eyes so red she wondered if he was near to tears, then he sighed and took her outstretched hand. 'I never want to quarrel with you, Willow. Please, please marry me. I love you so.'

His response shocked her. He had never told her he loved her in quite that tone of voice. For a moment she considered accepting his offer or perhaps becoming engaged to him, but she couldn't do it. He walked her home, but he wouldn't come in and she watched him stride away, his back straight, his head erect. Already he saw himself as a soldier.

She decided she must visit her family. Who knew what war would bring? There were dreadful rumours of air balloons which could carry bombs to drop on innocent civilians. As the train rattled along the track to Bristol she wondered why civilians were always termed 'innocent'. Were soldiers then guilty? And of what? Of patriotism?

Clara greeted her with a kiss. 'My, you're smart. Jasmine's

358

gone to the shops. She won't be long. The boys are at work.'

'You're looking better, Mum, though you've not put on an ounce of flesh.'

'Do you expect me to when I'm so busy? I seem to spend as much time cookin' as I used to washin'. How did I get everythin' done before you began sendin' me so much money?'

'I don't know. You're a marvel. I've brought you some clothes, a dress and a smart coat, and while I'm here we're going to find a hat to match.' She brushed aside her mother's protests which were only token. Clara was delighted, and proud of her clever daughter, and Willow prayed she'd never find out exactly where she earned much of her money. 'How's Gran?'

'Not so well. This war has hit her hard, poor old soul. She still won't come an' live with us, but I see her every day an' Jasmine an' me clean for her, Jasmine mostly. She's growin' into a really nice girl.'

Gran welcomed Willow tremulously. 'I knew you'd come home, my love. Can you stay with us in Bristol? Families should stick together in times of war.'

'I wish I could.' Willow was saddened by Gran's disappointment. 'I've got my employees to think of as well as myself. I can't let them down.'

Gran smiled. 'You're quite right. I'm being selfish. But, Willow, I'm so afraid of this war.'

'You shouldn't worry. Bristol's bound to be safe.'

'It's not that. The South African war seems like only yesterday. Men go away and don't come back.' She sighed. 'No, they don't come back. Or else they come as wrecks, their poor bodies broken, their minds affected.'

'I've never heard you talk like that before.'

'No! Who wants to speak of old fights? Who wants to think about men who can't work? It's our class that has to face the swords and guns. Have you got a boy-friend, Willow, my love? Will you be losing a lover?'

'I'm not serious about anyone yet.'

Gran nodded. 'Quite right. You're doing what all women should do. Make a pile of money first and then think of marrying. Marigold's going to be rich some day, but—' She stopped.

'What about her?'

'Nothing, my love.'

'What's happening to her? Mum wouldn't talk about her either.'

'She's making money. She tells us it comes from all sorts of jobs, but we think – *I'm* pretty sure – she's selling herself to men.'

'What?' Willow's first, shaming reaction was not caused by her sister's way of life but by the belief that she should be protected in a house like Annie Bliss's.

'I don't say she's actually a street-walker,' said Gran. 'She's got what she calls boy-friends. Generous boy-friends. Only there are a lot of them and they're a sight too generous to her if she's an innocent. I told you, Willow, our Marigold was born one of the knowing ones.'

Jasmine came racing round to Gran's and threw herself into Willow's arms, almost knocking her over. 'Steady on! You're not a baby any more,' Willow laughed, hugging her tight. 'I've missed you, too.' Jasmine at ten was almost as tall as she and as slender as a boy. Her dark curls so like Willow's own were tied back with ribbon. She was pretty, but her attraction lay chiefly in her liveliness, the constant play of expressions across her face. Willow felt her heart contract with love. What if Marigold should inveigle her into emulating her own dubious activities? It seemed unlikely in the light of Jasmine's open nature, but who could tell? Annie Bliss's girls must all have been young and innocent once. For the first time Willow understood Steven's nervousness about her friends. Perhaps part of his eagerness to marry her was born of the fear that she might slide into their profession.

She and Jasmine walked Gran to Mum's and they sat round the big scrubbed table over a meal which Jasmine had helped to cook. There was no shortage of food here now. Slices of luscious pink ham were cut from the steaming joint and served with tiny sugary peas and potatoes roasted in the oven. Jasmine was proud of her achievements and glowed when Clara praised her. Marigold came home late, unrepentant and uncommunicative.

The boys were full of the war. Joe said, 'Willow, do you know that Bristol's got permission to form its own regiment? It's to be called the 12th Service Battalion of the Gloucestershire Regiment, but everyone already calls it "Bristol's Own". Sam an' me wish we could join straight away. Everyone's sayin' it'll be all over by Christmas. I hope it won't. Poor old Alfred's goin' to have to wait ages until he's old enough.'

'Thank goodness,' muttered Alfred.

'Sissy boy,' shouted Joe.

'Pansy,' yelled Sam. 'He thinks he's better than us, with his poncey talk an' his shop.'

Alfred flushed but didn't answer, and Clara didn't reprove them. Willow watched her youngest brother covertly. His hair and skin were fair and it was easy to make his colour rise. He was flushed now and unhappy. Though he said nothing, it was plain that this baiting was a regular occurrence.

Later he said to Willow, 'I'll be thankful if they do join the army and leave me in peace. They make my life a misery.'

'You can't want to see them fighting? They might get hurt.'

'No, of course I don't want that. But the war won't last long and the new battalion is billeted in the Bristol International Exhibition Centre at Bower Ashton – the war's ruined trade – an' they'll probably never even reach France. By the time they've got through a medical and been given their uniforms and done a bit of training – at the moment the recruits are digging holes in Brandon Hill – the war will be over and it'll be time to come home. And I'll have enjoyed a bit of peace and quiet.'

'How's your job going?'

His eyes lit up. 'Fine. I like it. I'm allowed to serve now in the boys' department. They're pleased with me and say I'll make a good salesman. One day I'll be a floor-walker in a frock coat and striped trousers.'

Sidney arrived and was warmly welcomed by Clara. He drove his own car now and managed to persuade Clara to take a drive.

'I've no wish to go anywhere,' said Clara, 'and certainly not in a smelly motor car.'

'Go on, Mum, you'll enjoy it,' persuaded Willow.

'All right. I'll go if you do.'

They stopped in Pucklechurch at an old inn and drank beer.

'You'll no doubt come home now, Willow?' Sidney said.

'There isn't any compelling reason why I should.'

'There is. Families should be together at a time like this. Who knows what'll happen? War is a terrible thing.'

'I can't argue with that, though all the signs are that it won't last long.'

'I don't agree. Already the Empire has been drawn in with men coming from overseas to enlist. If Germany wasn't set on war they wouldn't have invaded Belgium. It's all about territory, Willow.'

'Greed, in other words. And for that people have to die?'

'Yes, I suppose greed's killed more people than anything else.'

'War seems to make people philosophical,' said Willow. But not Edgar. She preferred not to think about him.

'Well, there's nothin' we can do to stop it,' said Clara quickly. 'Let's not talk of fightin'. And there's no need for Willow to come back to Bristol, not when she's doin' so well. The war's bound to end soon. Everyone says so.' Her underlying fear for her sons permeated her voice.

362

Sidney dropped them at their front door. 'I'll see you tomorrow, Mrs Riches,' he said before driving off.

'He spends a lot of time here,' said Willow.

'Yes, he likes to talk to me. After all, the poor lad hasn't got a decent family of his own. All they understand is wickedness.'

Willow enjoyed her few days with her family and said goodbye reluctantly. War still seemed remote to her, even though the railway stations were crowded with young men who shouted and laughed as if they were on their way to a football match. Perhaps they saw it in that light. The cry 'It'll be all over by Christmas' was on everyone's lips and young men, desperate to exchange their dull working lives for the excitement of soldiering, flocked to the recruiting sergeants. She thought of her brothers, the men she knew, among them Steven and especially Edgar.

'Where in hell have you been?' Edgar burst into Willow's living room, after being admitted through the front door by Bridget.

She raised her brows. 'How *very* nice to see you, Edgar. It's *so* refreshing to return from my uncouth, plebeian family to high society.'

'Sorry.' He grinned. 'I missed you. I didn't know where you were.'

'Didn't Bridget and Dora tell you I was in Bristol?'

He said rather sheepishly, 'They did. I thought you'd be back sooner. I was frightened I might have to go without saying goodbye to you.'

She sighed. 'I take it you've enlisted?'

'Of course. I'm to join the Devons, my father's regiment.'

'As a private?'

'Certainly not. As an officer, of course.'

'Of course,' she mocked him.

'Don't you mind that I'm going away?'

She gave his question some thought. 'I shall miss you. As, I don't doubt, will many other girls.'

'I don't care for any other girls the way I do for you.'

'Really? Do you mean I'm the only one you invite to your bed?'

His face darkened with anger. 'What a disgusting thing to say!'

'You haven't answered, though, have you?'

'A man can't get along without a woman now and then. That's easily dealt with. I respect you.'

'But not enough to prevent your asking me for sexual favours.'

'For God's sake, Willow, sometimes your language! I suppose it comes from living in a brothel.'

'I don't live there now.'

'But you still see the girls.'

'I work for them.'

'You talk to them, too, as if they were your equals.'

Willow looked steadily at him. 'If I agreed to sleep with you, whose equal would that make me?'

She had really angered him now. 'It would be different! You know it would!'

'I know no such thing.'

'Are you going to marry Steven?'

'Mind your own business! I shall marry whomever I please. It has nothing to do with you.'

'Yes, it has.'

'Why?'

'Because it has! Because I've known you a long time—'

'So has Steven. Longer than you. When I was kitchen maid he was the bootboy, remember?'

'You know I hate to hear you talk about your past!'

'Of course you do. You're a Maddison and it hurts your pride.'

For an instant Willow caught a glimpse of the vision of herself that she had been crushing for years, of a world where a Maddison could marry a servant.

'I may be killed.'

The words were like a blow to her heart. 'That's unfair and you know it. I wonder how many girls will yield to men

364

after hearing those words? I wonder how many of them will pay for it for the rest of their lives?'

'In what way?'

'Wars bring babies, so I've read.'

'Darling Willow!' He almost laughed in relief. 'Is that what is holding you back? A fear of becoming pregnant? I can promise you you won't!'

She wanted to scream. Men, whether of high degree or low, seemed to have minds that ran on a single, boring track. Edgar's face was alive with eagerness.

'You care only for yourself!' she said. 'You can't imagine, can you, that I might have reasons other than that to refuse you!'

'Then why won't you let me love you? I do care for you, you know.'

'Care for me!' She was quivering with rage. 'You use the word love to persuade me to your will. That's not my view of love. Thank you for nothing, because that's all you're offering me. Nothing!'

He grabbed his hat. 'I'm going! There's no reasoning with you in this state.'

She didn't want him to leave. She wanted him, she always had, wanted to hold him close and give in to any demand he might make. Resentment, sorrow, regret and fury mingled, and fury won. 'If I wished to sleep with you, I would. And you needn't worry, I can take excellent care of my own health.'

Her meaning was unmistakable. He stopped dead, turned and fixed his eyes on her, his face pale now. 'I see. You are experienced in such matters. You've had men already, have you, just like your friends, the tarts? Perhaps if I offered you money?'

'Get out! Get out!' she screamed. 'I hope I never see you again!'

She was left with two damaged relationships. Maybe it was best that way but she regretted many times her final words to Edgar, especially as news gradually seeped through about the conditions the fighting men were meeting. The Germans were by no means the easy conquest which had been promised. On the contrary, they were better equipped and in far greater numbers than the British Expeditionary Force. Right at the beginning, in August 1914, Britain had been stunned by the news that the British and French forces were in retreat. Men had been forced to walk miles, without rest or food. Letters from soldiers had been printed in the newspapers, assuring those at home that morale was high – and that in spite of the fact that in reality troops were falling to the ground, unable to move because of extreme exhaustion and hunger, and were later listed as 'missing'.

For a while, Britain became an odd mix of pockets where war intruded, such as the areas surrounding munitions factories, the large houses turned hurriedly into hospitals and convalescent homes for the wounded, parks dotted with tents and loud with the voices of sergeants drilling recruits, and places where it was impossible to tell there was a war on, apart from the lessening supply of young, marriageable men.

Willow took on any work she could get. Patriotism dictated that clothes should be made to last longer. Orders dwindled, then picked up as Mrs Bliss's girls and their like were sought after by men on leave, anxious to forget the horrors of the battle front in the fleshly charms of pretty women who demanded nothing in return but money. She wondered what Edgar was doing. He hadn't contacted her since she had ordered him out. Memories of him were always quickly banished. Association with him could never bring her happiness. Steven had been declared unfit to fight, but had been accepted into the medical services. Sidney became a corporal quite soon. Willow wasn't surprised. A man who could lift himself clear of a family such as his must possess rare qualities. The notion took her by surprise as she sat stitching the hem of a spectacular gown for Carmen who was expecting her favourite lieutenant to pay her a call. Willow was depressed and was ashamed of her depression because it was caused by the abrupt downswing in her career. She told herself that she was unpatriotic, heartless, self-seeking, but her disappointment wouldn't go away. Perhaps she should have married and produced children. At least she would be contributing something to the world. Fancy clothes were unimportant when men were suffering so terribly. She even considered marriage to Steven. It might be acceptable. He was enterprising and clever. She did not love him, but that could be an advantage, enabling her to hold on to her own career, untrammelled by sentiment.

In the autumn of 1915 Willow was in Bristol when a meeting was held in the vast Colston Hall and Arthur Balfour harangued the audience of five thousand on the need for every able-bodied young man to enlist. The wave of early enthusiasm which had carried so many men off to war had receded and only a handful were moved to come forward. Two of them were Joe and Sam. Willow smiled at their enthusiasm, but her indulgence faded when she learned that the boys had lied about their ages and were accepted, fulfilling their dream of joining the Old Pals' Brigade, Bristol's Own.

Clara wept, but her pride showed through her tears and she refused to intervene. Alfred, who prayed daily that the war would end before he got enmeshed in it, was constantly derided, though, as Willow pointed out, he was only fifteen. The army made a derisory allowance to Clara on behalf of her sons and Willow increased the sums she sent home. In spite of it all, she, along with many other civilians, still felt that the war would be only a brief interlude, though one which was taking a horrific toll in dead and injured. Men were being shipped home with unspeakable wounds, their bodies torn and mutilated by shell and shrapnel. At first they were professional soldiers, but then the volunteers began to arrive on the hospital trains, hundreds upon hundreds sent to Bristol which was considered safe from bombing and shelling and had a large number of medical centres.

The Allies were embedded in trenches running from the Alps to the English Channel and it was promised that they would annihilate the enemy from there.

War had come nearer to home when an aeroplane dropped a bomb on Dover, and people were scared and needed the assurance that this was a solitary exercise. Then German cruisers had shelled Scarborough, killing forty people, including women and children, and injuring some four hundred more. Winston Churchill's declaration that the Germans had risked many ships merely for the pleasure of killing as many English as possible was of no comfort to those who watched and waited fearfully, beginning to understand something of what their menfolk suffered daily. Stories had begun to circulate, of soldiers sent to fight without proper training, of under-age lads as young as thirteen accepted without a check, and when in January 1915 German airship raiders had killed four people in Yarmouth and King's Lynn, it was finally accepted that the war was being carried to civilians. In London, the lake in St James's Park was drained to alter the landscape, and Londoners assured one another, more in hope than faith, that airships would never reach them. People went about their business, getting used to women taking on jobs for which men were once thought indispensable. Women with money formed committees for the care of the Belgian refugees and for the entertainment of wounded soldiers. Dr Elsie Inglis offered her services as surgeon and general organiser and was told to 'go home'. The French were not so foolish and women doctors were encouraged to establish hospitals in France. After that, they could no longer be ignored by the British authorities and a military hospital in Endell Street, London, was staffed entirely by women.

The Suffrage Movement formed a corps of Police Volunteers to protect girls against themselves in the neighbourhood of barracks, camps and convalescent hospitals.

Annie Bliss's girls found the idea hilarious. As Angelina

said, 'Fancy denying the poor devils a bit of 'ow's yer father when they've been fighting for King and Country.' Mrs Bliss frowned at this piece of vulgarity, but had to admit that she agreed.

Chapter Twenty

Through it all Willow kept going, while trying to reassure Bridget and Dora when they were afraid. London was suddenly swarming with soldiers and sailors of many nationalities, as well as members of the Royal Flying Corps, and Mrs Bliss's girls were much in demand. Even on Sunday, which she normally insisted must be a rest day, they entertained young men, some off to war fresh out of school, others, battle-weary veterans. Willow visited the girls late one Sunday night. They were all in Mrs Bliss's sitting room, drinking gin in an atmosphere which had not yet reached the maudlin stage.

Angelina said, her deceptively innocent eyes open wide, 'He said I was his first and I took a real liking to him. He was so young, his body still quite bony, like a little boy's.' She took a long swig of her gin. 'He's going to marry a girl he's known all his life, but the parents won't hear of it yet. She's only seventeen and they must wait till after the war. Mean, I call them. Well, of course, he got excited and a bit scared, though he was bursting with love.'

'I hope you were gentle with him,' said Mrs Bliss.

Angelina was indignant. 'Of course I was. I made him happy, don't you fret, *and* more than once in the hour he stayed with me. Bless his heart.' She could have been a mother praising her child and Willow half smiled.

'What you laughing at?' demanded Angelina.

'Not at you,' said Willow. 'You're a good girl.'

A good girl! If Mum could hear her now! Or see her! The girls were lounging around the living room in various states of undress. Mrs Bliss had loosened her corsets and was bulging comfortably beneath her dressing gown. Maisie tripped back and forth pouring out the gin to which an occasional dash of lemon or tonic was added. In her pert maid's uniform, her body rounded with youth, she looked alluring and exuded an air of quiet self-confidence which added to her attractions. A man would feel deceptively safe with her.

In February, 1915, the Kaiser had authorised Zeppelin raids on London and for the first time the people of the metropolis were flung into a war being fought on foreign soil. The euphoric optimism which had been encouraged by their leaders in the first months finally vanished when people realised that the dead and wounded could be counted in tens of thousands and the old, professional British Army had to submit to the unpalatable fact that the despised volunteers – the citizen soldiers – had passed their baptism of fire with honour and that war could not be waged without them.

Willow took Carmen's new gown to her and had tea with Mrs Bliss who was loud in her indignation. 'More bombs! Fancy dropping bombs on London! Did you ever think such a thing was possible? I didn't, not in a million years. Them Germans must be right cruel buggers to order the killing of women and children.' When she was indignant her assumed air of gentility was apt to deteriorate.

'War is horrible,' said Willow. 'I can't bear to think about it. My brothers are all right so far and so are Steven, another friend – and Edgar.'

Mrs Bliss waited as if expecting more then said, 'The fellows that come here seem to get younger and younger. They ought to be at school, not sent to their deaths. What life have they had?'

Willow couldn't bear to talk of death when so many of the people she cared about were in constant danger. She said, 'Carmen, walk across the room. That's right. Twirl around. Good, it hangs perfectly.'

'Is there a cup of tea for me?' asked Carmen.

'Not till you've taken that dress off. Willow don't spend her time making clothes for you to spill tea on.'

Carmen stalked out.

'What's wrong with her?' asked Willow.

Mrs Bliss sighed. 'She's been daft enough to fall for a lieutenant, as if it will do her any good. He's nineteen and his father's Sir somebody or other. Imagine him taking Carmen home to Mum and Dad!' She laughed raucously, without humour. 'I thought the stupid girl had more sense.'

'There isn't much sense around in wartime,' said Willow. 'And what will it all prove? When it's over things won't have changed much, if at all, except that a few families will be mourning a man. More than a few, by the sound of things.'

Mrs Bliss said, 'That's a fine way to talk with Britain and the Empire fighting off the enemy. What makes you think up things like that?'

Willow had been repeating Alfred's disgusted estimation which was echoed to a certain extent by Steven. She said so and Mrs Bliss shrugged, but although she behaved nonchalantly, she looked tired and discouraged and Willow bent to kiss her when she left. Mrs Bliss caught her hand. 'Take care, my dear. Keep your dream fresh. One day I know it'll come true.'

Marigold arrived on Willow's doorstep late one night carrying a small cardboard case containing the few possessions she valued. 'Let me in, I'm starving,' was her greeting.

Willow fed her, hoping without much conviction that the visit would be short. Marigold was undoubtedly lovely, her dark curls held back by a wide satin ribbon, her hazel eyes large and luminous, her complexion flawless. She was tall, her figure curvaceous, her carriage straight, and she moved with an air of confidence. Her beauty was marred only by an expression which sometimes gave a hard look to her face.

'How's the family?' asked Willow.

'Well, I suppose. Except Gran.'

'Is she ill?'

Marigold had filled her mouth too full of bread and beef to speak. Willow waited impatiently.

'She's just old.'

'But you said she wasn't well.'

'She isn't exactly ill. She's all bent up with her rheumatics and she can't see very well.' Marigold changed the subject. 'Can I stay here for a bit?' She looked round the living room. 'I must say you've got yourself a decent place. It seems like a palace after our house.'

Willow could scarcely refuse her own sister. 'You can stay. How long will you be here?'

'I'll leave as soon as I get my own rooms. You can give me advice on the best parts to live.'

'Best for what?' asked Willow. She knew what Marigold meant and waited with a mixture of resignation and trepidation for her reply.

'A place where I can entertain my friends. My gentlemen friends,' said Marigold, taking another huge mouthful. She swallowed it and said, 'You're good-looking, Willow. You could live a soft life with plenty of money instead of sewing. God, what a prospect! Sitting sewing for years.' She laughed, revealing perfect white teeth. 'I'm going to make money fast and have fun, lots of it, war or no war.'

When the air raids had begun Bridget and Dora had elected to share a bedroom for companionship and Marigold moved into the vacant place. She went out daily and was secretive about her movements. She had plenty of money and shopped ecstatically in the London stores, becoming addicted to Harrod's, Peter Robinson's and Debenham and Freebody.

'Why don't you get Willow to make your clothes?' asked Bridget. 'She's a wonderful dressmaker.'

Marigold tossed her head. 'I want proper stuff. I don't intend to be dressed by an amateur.'

She changed her mind when she found Willow at work on a ball gown for Anastasia who, having discovered that real Russian princesses were nursing the wounded in Highgate, decided to marry a wealthy lover, a widower of sixty-four, who had proposed in an access of excitement brought on by the war. Marigold stared at the heavy scarlet satin on which Bridget was sewing tiny pink pearls, while Dora embroidered a pale pink modesty vest to be sewn into the deep V-neck. 'Who's that for?' she asked ungraciously.

'A Russian princess,' replied Dora.

'There's no need to be insolent,' snapped Marigold who had picked up some autocratic habits from somewhere.

'She's not,' Bridget assured her. 'Princess Anastasia is gettin' married and wants a whole new outfit. Willow's designed it for her.'

'I'd like to try it on,' said Marigold. 'It looks about my size. Give it to me.'

Willow said, 'Do no such thing, Dora, Anastasia will be round herself later. If you want to see it worn you must wait, Marigold.'

She flounced out, muttering.

Dora said, 'Your sister's got a lovely figure, Willow. She'd be a good mannequin. Some shops have them.'

'I haven't got a shop,' pointed out Willow.

But the exchange made her think. War or no war, women still wanted to look smart. Edgar had been useful in introducing her to the well-heeled and respectable, but although some were faithful to her, many had left London, closing their houses for the duration of the war. Bridget and Dora weren't always fully occupied and she had needed to dip into Jane Barton's legacy.

In spite of the war there were those who defied the bombs and the new season began. Willow saw names she recognised in the society pages of the newspapers, among them Mrs Frances Bickford and Lady Violet Radcliffe. She decided to mingle with people of fashion and at the same time look at the many war pictures hung this year, and so attended the Private View at the Royal Academy to which two tickets were obtained for her by Anastasia. She wore a light dress of white muslin, flounced and embroidered, and a small straw hat adorned with black velvet ribbon and moss roses.

'Why can't I come with you?' demanded Marigold.

'You can if you promise not to ogle the men.'

'Ogle the men! What an expression! As if I would! Have you got something nice I can wear?'

Willow lent her one of her new dresses and Marigold emerged, elegant in a broderie anglaise frock with a high-backed collar which framed her face and a straw hat with a wide brim.

They wandered about the hot and crowded galleries looking at the pictures, though Willow was more interested in the women and Marigold was only interested in the men.

'They're either very young, very old, or wounded,' she muttered to her sister.

'You promised!' warned Willow. 'If you jeopardise anything for me I'll throw you out on your ear.'

She sat down, fanning herself, and was joined on the bench by a woman she recognised as Frances. Willow took a closer look and saw that her skin had coarsened, she was puffy around the eyes and she smelt of drink. She looked unspeakably bored and stared at Willow without a single sign of recognition.

'Mrs Bickford?' said Willow.

Frances lifted her chin. 'Have we met?'

'You know me. I'm Willow Riches.'

'Who?' Frances was tetchy. 'I have some faint memory of you.'

'We met quite recently.'

'Did we?'

Willow said coldly, 'Once you called me Lily.'

'Heavens, did I? How very odd.'

Willow's temper was rising. She wondered if this woman, who had created such havoc in her life, was being deliberately forgetful.

'Yes, you remember,' she said, raising her voice. 'We went to London together and stayed with Miss Jane Barton.'

Frances glared at her with bloodshot eyes. 'What are you doing here? How did you get in?' She looked Willow's gown over. 'You seem to have done well for yourself.'

'How are you?' asked Willow.

'Well enough, I suppose.' Frances had removed her gloves and she picked at them, pulling threads from the soft silk. 'Have you married someone?'

Willow knew she meant, have you married someone worth marrying and if not, where did you get the money to dress like that?

'I'm a couturière,' said Willow. She said it calmly, though her heart beat hard at this first public declaration of independence.

'Oh, yes, I remember you used to sew quite well.'

'I sewed very well.'

Frances yawned, not troubling to conceal her boredom, and her sister appeared out of the crowd and stood in front of her, shielding her. 'Frances,' she muttered, 'pretend to be interested, if only for Ernest's sake.' Her eyes flickered over Willow, taking in the details of her fashionable gown. She smiled without warmth. 'We've met, haven't we?'

'We have indeed, Lady Radcliffe. I was just telling Mrs Bickford that I am now a couturière.'

'Is that so?' Violet looked Willow up and down. 'Did you make that frock?'

'Yes, and my sister is over there in another of my original creations.'

Violet turned, then glared at Marigold who was flirting with a man as if she had known him for ever. 'What a lively girl,' she said sharply. 'Have you a business card on you?'

Willow, her hands not quite steady, drew out a card from her small bag and Violet dropped it into hers without looking at it. 'Come along, Frances, I think it is time we left.'

Frances got rather clumsily to her feet and Ernest Bickford arrived in time to steady her. 'Are we leaving?' she asked. Her husband did not bother to answer as he took her elbow in a hard grip and hurried her away.

Marigold finished her conversation and joined Willow who asked, 'Do you know that man you were with?'

'I think you might say I do, though we've only just met. I shall get to know him a lot better. He's going to take me dancing. He admired my gown. You must sew lots for me. I'll pay you the proper price.'

'You can't afford my clothes.'

'I know plenty of people who can.'

'Plenty of men, you mean, don't you?'

'Try not to be naive, sister dear. You know damn well what I mean.' Marigold gave her late companion a small bow, and he saluted her.

'Why isn't he in uniform?' asked Willow.

'He's going back to the front in a week. He had a riding accident while he was on leave. He said he prefers civilian clothes.'

Claudette announced unexpectedly that she was getting married.

After Mrs Bliss had recovered from the shock she said, 'I hope it's not to a fighting man. You could be widowed and left alone with a couple of kids.'

'No, as a matter of fact, I'm marrying a farmer.'

'A farmer! Where on earth did you meet him?'

'I was shopping in Selfridges. I dropped my purse and he picked it up. He's really nice, good-looking too.'

'Does he know what you do for a living?'

Claudette flushed. 'No, though I've told him I'm no angel.'

'That's a good one,' laughed Carmen, subsiding beneath the weight of Mrs Bliss's frown.

'How old is he?' asked Angelina.

'A bit older than me.'

'How much older?'

'He's forty. Well, forty-three to be exact. His father died when he was a boy and his mother was an invalid for years. She died recently.'

'Was he a mother's boy?' asked Carmen.

'No.' Claudette was flushed. 'He said his mother was very demanding and he wouldn't bring a wife home to be tormented by her. It seems she was very jealous. He employed women to look after her.'

'I hope they were good-looking and kind to him,' said Carmen.

'Go on,' said Mrs Bliss, giving Carmen another cold glance.

'He's frank about it. He slept with those that would have him. And why not?'

'Why not, indeed,' said Mrs Bliss enthusiastically. 'Sounds like you've got yourself a good man. I'll be sorry to see you go, my dear, but I'm sure we all wish you the best of luck.'

The Bayswater house had a vacancy which was filled within a few days by Marigold who went straight to work.

'Your sister's a really bright girl,' said Mrs Bliss. 'She's a lot better than Claudette. That one never had her heart in the business, but Marigold –' she threw up her hands '– she's a natural.'

Willow said, 'Good,' and was half amused, half scandalised by her reaction. She hoped that Clara would never find out.

That was the last time Willow was to see Mrs Bliss who decided to visit a friend in the East End. When the air raid began she stayed on and the house received a direct hit, killing all its occupants. She had made a will, leaving most of her money to a sister no one had ever heard of. Recently she had added a codicil and Maisie found herself possessed of a sum sufficient to run the house smoothly for six months. Marigold and Maisie had found they had much in common, especially a burning wish to make money without emotional involvement and both approved of Mrs Bliss's stipulation that Marigold should get a share of all profits for the next year. Maisie genuinely mourned her late mistress's death, but always practical, took over her quarters and had them redecorated in little girl shades of pink and blue.

Angelina and Carmen had invested money on the advice of Mrs Bliss's financial adviser and were not interested in the running of the house. They accepted the situation and business was carried on as efficiently, and possibly more so, than before.

Early in 1916 Willow received a letter from Jasmine telling her that Gran was very ill, and caught the train to Bristol. Everything had risen in price, including fares which were doubly penalised by the addition of the War Supplement. She had decided to travel first class where she might see and be seen by her clients and was entertained for part of the journey by two choleric retired colonels who resented women working as waitresses in the dining car, although they understood that this permitted male waiters to exchange their bum-freezer jackets and stiff collars for His Majesty's uniform. In the end they fell silent, perhaps reflecting on the fact that among the men who had left the Great Western Railway to enlist there were already over two hundred dead and at least five hundred and fifty wounded or taken prisoner or posted as missing, that most difficult of all states which still held out hope.

Marigold had refused to come to Bristol. 'Gran's been on her last legs for years,' she protested, 'and I've a very important client arriving. He'll want to spend at least one night with me.'

Gran had been waiting for Willow. She was propped up in bed. 'I knew you'd come, my love. Jasmine told me she had written.'

'Of course I came. Jasmine said you were ill, but you don't look so bad.'

Gran smiled. 'I'm glad you think so. I wouldn't want to knock on the Almighty's golden gates looking a sight, now would I?'

She died soon after, as quietly as she had lived, and Willow lost her friend, confidante and adviser, one of the dearest people in her life.

'She's been goin' downhill since the war began,' said Clara miserably. 'The dear old soul. I shall miss her. She had a way of smoothin' things over for me.'

Marigold arrived for the funeral looking elegant in black

and left immediately afterwards. Clara was pleased to see the sign of mourning and Willow didn't tell her that Marigold often wore black because it suited her. She and Clara sat drinking tea. Alfred had returned to work, and Jasmine had been persuaded to go out with friends.

'It'll do her good,' said Clara. 'Poor kid. She thought a lot of her gran. She's gone to the moving picture house. She's mad on those bioscope things. Gran wouldn't have wanted her to stay at home and grieve, though I don't know how she can sit watchin' those flickerin' screens. I can't abide it. The only time I went it gave me a headache. She's a good girl, Willow. She's my mainstay these days.' She sipped her strong tea. 'I'll miss Gran,' she said for the hundredth time, staring out of the window. 'She was a link with Arthur.'

Willow's throat contracted. 'Don't, Mum.'

'No, there's too much weepin' and wailin' these days. So many young chaps dead or wounded. You remember Frankie Rathbone? He's home for good with his legs useless below his knees. He rides round on a little cart he pushes along the ground with his hands, and walks on his knees from door to door sellin' cigarettes.'

'He used to win all the races at school,' said Willow. 'He wanted to be an engineer.'

'He's no chance now. It's awful to see him. An' he's not the only one, not by a long chalk.' Clara's eyes went to the mantelpiece where two photographs stood side by side, Joe grinned out of one and Sam regarded the world solemnly from the other. Both were in khaki.

'Do you hear from them often, Mum?'

'They write when they can. They ought to write to you. You do enough to keep the family goin'. I'm able to set aside a bit of money these days so that when they come home on leave I can give them somethin' special. They don't get much leave,' she finished bleakly.

'The money's for you, Mum. You should buy yourself some treats.'

'You don't mind me keepin' it for the boys, do you?'

Clara sounded sharp and Willow said gently, 'It's yours to

do as you like with. If I send a little more will you promise me to have a treat now and then?'

Clara got up and picked up the tea things, rattling them unnecessarily. 'The only treat I want is to see you all come through this awful war safe an' sound. What with them at the front an' you an' Marigold in London, I can hardly sleep at nights.'

'I'm sorry, Mum.'

'We've all got our own way to make. Marigold—' she paused. 'What exactly does she do? She laughed at me when I asked her an' said she's doin' essential war work, but I couldn't get a sensible word out of her. She's always been headstrong. Sometimes I'm afraid for her.'

'She's tough, Mum. She can take care of herself. To tell you the truth we're both so busy we hardly see one another.'

'But what does she *do*?'

'She takes care of our fighting men when they're on leave,' said Willow desperately. 'Makes sure they have a pleasant time to remember.'

'Is it a canteen? I've read about those.'

'Sort of,' said Willow.

The whole civilised world had been horrified to learn that Germany was using poisonous gas and now doctors were faced with horrific injuries they had to deal with as best they could.

Willow scarcely dared think of her brothers, although so far they had come through with only minor wounds. Jasmine read their letters to Clara and answered them at her dictation, then she posted them on to Willow who wrote to the boys and sent parcels with tins of cigarettes and mints, wool socks and canned food. She received postcards in return.

The constant cry from the government was for more men, more munitions, especially now that the big push on the Somme had begun.

Willow, sitting for long hours over her sewing machine,

had time to think about the war and wished often that she and Edgar had not parted with harsh words. She hadn't heard of him since and had no way of knowing if he was alive or dead. Tired though she was, she frequently lay awake thinking about him, picturing him wounded or gassed and she not having the right to be told.

The war showed no signs of ending and Londoners were taking the air raids in their stride, often not bothering to seek shelter. Nowadays, Jasmine wrote, lots of wealthy people, including the Maddisons, had decided that London was too dangerous and made Bristol their base during the season. She always ended her letters with an impassioned plea to Willow to be careful. Then she sent a paragraph cut from the *Western Daily Press*. In a list of officer casualties she had ringed the words, 'Captain Edgar Maddison, missing, believed dead'.

Willow stared at the words, not at first comprehending their significance. She had scanned the lists so often for news of Sam, Joe, Steven and Sidney, and felt overwhelming relief when their names weren't there and she had scanned the lists of officers, searching for the name she most feared to find. Sir George Trembath and the good-natured Reggie were reported killed which had brought the terror nearer. Now here it was, written down in black and white, Edgar was feared dead, and she had to face the overwhelming truth that he held a place in a secret corner of her heart which she had never dared examine. She was swamped by grief, an agony of loss which gripped her whole body and mind and held them in thrall. Some nights she didn't even try to sleep, but paced her small bedroom, trying to contain thoughts of Edgar lying dead on the battlefield, his torn flesh perhaps unburied. She knew that she loved him and had done so for a long time, maybe from the time when she had been a servant. During the days she behaved normally, working and doing a volunteer stint in one of the canteens set up for war-weary heroes returning from the front. On each spell of duty she asked the men if they had heard anything of Captain Maddison. No one had. His image wove its way into her dreams which turned to nightmares of barbed wire, blood and mud, and broken bodies.

Mr Bickford wrote to her: 'Lady Radcliffe and my wife are staying in the Bristol house and wish you to take their measurements for new gowns. They will be at home next Wednesday morning.'

Willow could have fumed in the face of such autocratic behaviour but she travelled gladly, staying overnight with Mum, praying that she might get more hopeful news of Edgar. When she arrived at the house overlooking the Downs she knocked on the front door which was opened by Henry. He greeted her with pleasure. 'You look grand.'

'So do you. Are you buttling now?'

'Under-butler,' he said proudly. 'They said I was too short-sighted to fight. Poor Mr Norris was killed at Loos.'

Willow's heart contracted. There was no escape from the anguish of this war. 'I'm sorry. Really sorry.'

'Yes, it was sad. Do you remember Andy Hunnicott, the groom?'

'He fetched me from the station when I first went to the manor.'

'He died along with Mr Norris.'

'Oh, the poor boy. He had ambitions to becoming head groom.'

'Lots of men won't come home and there'll be a lot more, Mr Bickford says. Lord Radcliffe was wounded, but went straight back as soon as he recovered. And Mr James Maddison – I don't think you saw much of him. He finally married Lord Radcliffe's sister, Lady Mary, and she's just had twin boys – he's in the Royal Flying Corps.' He recalled his duties. 'I'd better tell the ladies you're here.'

'Wait! Is there any news of Edgar?'

'Mr Edgar? Not that I know of. The family reckon he's dead.'

Frances was reclining on a sofa, the one Willow had lain on after the motor car accident. Violet was in an easy chair, reading.

They looked up. 'Oh, it's you,' Violet said laconically. 'Hang on while I finish this chapter.'

Willow waited. She was not asked to sit so she remained standing, but perhaps her indignation reached Violet for she looked up and said, 'Oh, hell, it's a long chapter. I dare say you want to get on.'

Willow took their measurements upstairs in Frances's bedroom. Violet stood as still as a statue, but Frances swayed and Willow asked her to step down from the stool for fear she'd fall. Even then it was difficult.

She said, 'I hear that Lord Radcliffe was wounded. I'm sorry. I hope he recovered well.'

Violet, who had been primping her hair at the dressing table, looked sharply at her. 'Would he have been permitted to return to the front if he had not recovered?'

'I suppose not, but many of our fighting men are so courageous that they refuse to convalesce long enough.'

Violet's voice softened and her eyes grew moist. Willow wouldn't have believed it possible if she hadn't actually seen it. 'My husband is certainly courageous. I fear for his safety.' Then, feeling she had said too much to a mere seamstress, she asked, 'How much longer will you be? We are expecting guests.'

'Not long, Lady Radcliffe, but I must get everything right.'

'I suppose so.' Violet picked up her book, then stood up so suddenly that Frances jumped and Willow dropped her tape measure. 'Do get *on*, Miss Riches. I'm going to my room to change.'

She shut the door with unnecessary force and Frances said, 'She's hell to be with since her precious husband was wounded. I think she believed he was immortal up to then.'

'It's difficult to have someone you love in danger.'

Frances walked to her bedside cupboard, leaving Willow on her knees, and took out a bottle of brandy. 'I think a small aperitif before luncheon would be in order. Would you care for a glass, Miss Riches?'

Willow refused and Frances poured a large measure and drank most of it in one gulp. 'I wish my husband would go and fight. He's supposed to be too useful at home. I would like to see the back of him. Life's so damned unfair!'

Clearly she had forgotten she was talking to her dressmaker and Willow took the opportunity to ask, 'Have you heard anything of your brother?'

'James is off fighting with the others.'

'I meant Mr Edgar.'

'Oh. No, the poor lamb is dead.'

Willow felt sick. 'Have you been told so?'

Frances returned to Willow. 'He's been missing for quite a time. They think he's dead.'

'But you've had no definite word?'

Frances jerked from Willow's hands impatiently. 'Why are you asking all these questions? What has my brother to do with you?'

'I worked in your house once, have you forgotten? Naturally I'm interested.'

'I don't see why. Haven't you done with me yet?'

'Yes. I can manage now.'

'Good.' Frances dragged a dressing gown round her and pulled the bellrope and a maid Willow had not met before appeared. 'Show Miss Riches out.'

In the hall Henry dismissed the maid. 'Did you come all the way from London just to take their measurements? They're born selfish, those two. And lazy. They ring for someone to do the least little thing. They don't take account of the number of servants who've left because of the war. Got time for a cup of tea?'

He conducted Willow to the kitchen where she met a new cook. 'Mrs Narracott's stayed in Devon with the master and mistress,' Henry explained. 'Sit down.' He called to the kitchen maid, 'Bring us some tea.'

She too was unknown to Willow who watched her scuttle about laying up a tray, remembering the times she had done it.

'Prue's married now with kids,' said Henry. 'Ivy's head

kitchen maid in the manor, Polly and Nancy are both
working on the land. Jenny's brother won't last much longer,
but she won't come back. Her sister's got six children and
can't cope.'

'Poor soul. Where's Nora? She was kind to me.'

'She got married. Last I heard her husband had been
killed in France, leaving her with a baby.'

Willow sighed. 'It's all bad news. What happened to
Aggie?'

'She's still scullery maid. She's got no brains at all,
that one.'

Clara was full of questions. 'How's business? It must be
good if you can send home so much money. What sort
of customers do you get? How's our Marigold gettin'
on?'

Willow answered as best she could and was relieved
when Mrs Tucker knocked and joined them for dinner.
'I still call it dinner,' Clara sniffed, 'though Willow says
luncheon.'

'I dare say she's right,' said Mrs Tucker, seating herself
and looking admiringly at Willow's navy costume. 'Did you
make that? My, you're clever. Is Marigold good at sewin'?
I never thought she'd make a dressmaker.'

Willow left the question unanswered and asked some of
her own about the people she had grown up with. So
many were dead, wounded, or ill with diseases contracted
at the front.

Mrs Tucker went through the list, and finished, 'God
knows what'll happen if this war goes on much longer. I
don't know where girls will look for a husband. Are you
interested in anyone, Willow?'

'Not yet.'

'Well, you're a smart girl. You won't need a man to keep
you. I always think if a girl's got a way of earnin' her
money she's much the best off. I've always kept a bit of
your mother's rent money for myself. After all, I run this
house while my husband's out at his job.'

Willow nodded.

'You an' Marigold are doin' the right thing, an' that Jasmine's as bright as a golden guinea. She'll do well.'

'I'm sure she will.'

'Mr Tucker an' me are thinkin' of sellin' up and movin' to the country.'

'You never told me,' said Clara, shocked. 'What'll happen to the house? Are you goin' to sell it?'

'Nothing's settled yet.'

Mrs Tucker left Clara worried. 'I bet she'll give us notice when she decides to sell up. Where would I go?'

'There are other places, Mum. Don't worry.'

'I do worry. I don't want to leave here. All my memories of my Arthur are here, an' there's the boys. I want to keep things the same for them. The few times they've had leave they've come straight home to me. I don't want things to change.'

Jasmine accompanied Willow to the station. 'Will you ever come back an' live in Bristol?' she asked.

'Maybe, one day.'

'Could I come an' live in London with you? I don't mean now, of course, because Mum needs me. Our Alfred isn't much company for her. He works ever such long hours, then he goes to help the wounded at the Temple Meads station, just lightin' a cigarette or holdin' a cup of tea for a man with no hands. That's what he did last week. He gets really upset about it.'

In the train Willow thought about her various encounters. Sidney Moor hadn't called, although he was back home, discharged honourably. 'Poor man, he was shockingly disappointed,' Clara had said. 'He doesn't go out much these days, except to work.'

'Was he injured?'

'No, it seems he developed bronchial pneumonia and never really got over it, so he was declared unfit to fight. He's doin' his best to help and turned most of his factory over to makin' uniforms. He's very busy an' he's taken on several more workers. He's the sort who'll prosper. An' he's a nice lad, too.'

Willow's mind returned over and over again to Edgar. No matter what she was doing, thinking or saying, he was always there in the background. She returned to work with a heavy heart made heavier because she couldn't talk about her anguish to anyone.

Chapter Twenty-one

Willow wondered how it was possible to live as if nothing had happened, when all the time she suffered beneath a leaden weight of grief. Whenever she was working routinely her mind went to Edgar. She wished she'd allowed him to make love to her. How ungenerous she had been! Sometimes she had to get out and walk, fast, in an attempt to outstrip her thoughts, but she could never walk fast enough. During her work in the canteen she looked at everyone who entered, wondering against any trace of hope if some day Edgar might walk in.

She was in Hyde Park and her feet took her automatically to the place where she and Edgar had sat together under a tree and talked of the possibility of war. She couldn't sit down today. Summer this year was damp and cold – and she wore a coat and a tam o'shanter. It had been dry when she left, but a brief, sudden storm had soaked her. She leaned against the craggy bole of the tree, wet, chilly and miserable. The war was so cruel, so bitterly destructive. It made thinking about her work seem trivial, but she still worried. Her business might have collapsed if it had not been for Marigold, Maisie and their friends. Some ladies still braved London and treated themselves to a nice new outfit by 'that clever little couturière who is so inexpensive, my dear'. She closed her eyes, seeing Edgar's face against her lids, hearing his laughter in her mind.

'Penny for them.' The voice was strong and amused. Edgar's voice, so real that she was startled. She opened her eyes and he was there, standing in front of her, pale, a scar running from beneath his hair to his chin. She stared at him, the colour leaving her cheeks.

'Hang on, you are not going to faint, are you?'

'Are you real?' She put out her hand and touched him, ran her fingers over the scar. 'You are real.' Tears poured down her face.

'You've missed me, you really have. Darling Willow!'

'Missed you! They said you were dead!'

'I know. It's been such a lark.'

'A lark?' She stared at him. His eyes were brilliant, his manner almost feverish. 'A lark?' she repeated.

'Yes. I was blown up by a damned shell. Lost all my clothes and my identification. The stretcher bearers – God, they're brave lads, I wouldn't want their job – found me and I was taken to a field hospital. I was too sick to move to Blighty and apparently I lay there for quite a time. No one thought I'd live, but I did, and they sent me to England, then, would you believe it, when I finally came to, I couldn't remember who I was. It was the bash on the head, don't you know. When I did remember I was given leave. And here I am.' He finished on a slightly anxious note, unable to make sense of Willow's reaction.

They looked at one another for a long moment, then they were in each other's arms, hugging, murmuring words of endearment, tasting rain and tears. Once she had put her arms round him Willow felt she could never let him go. They walked across the park, not even noticing another shower and a wicked little breeze that cooled their wet faces. They found a hotel where the proprietor asked no questions of couples who rented a room for a few hours. The brave lads from the front deserved all the comfort they could get.

In the bedroom they were silent as they undressed rapidly and held one another tight once more, their bodies taking delight in the meeting of skin upon skin, before half falling on to the bed. Their coupling was swift and gave relief as much as pleasure.

Edgar lay back with a sigh. 'My wonderful girl. I've thought of you every day.'

'Except when you'd lost your memory.'

He laughed. 'The war hasn't deprived you of your sense of fun. No, I can't remember what it was like not to remember.'

'Did you remember me first?'

'No.' He laughed again. 'The first thing I thought of was a bedpan. The sudden shock.'

'Oh, Edgar. It's been terrible. I – am so fond of you.'

'And I of you. I'm not the first with you, am I?'

'No, there's been one other.'

'Steven?'

'None of your business.'

'Very true.'

Later, after they had lain together, smoking contentedly, their passion was reborn, but this time Edgar explored her body, his hands and lips finding her most secret parts, while she caressed and stroked and kissed him until he writhed and gasped. This time their love-making was slow as they savoured every moment until her body was yearning for a cessation of the sweet torment and he entered her with excruciating control, until he could hold out no longer and they were carried helplessly on a wave of ecstasy.

Edgar pulled the bedclothes over them and slid his arm round her neck, lighting two cigarettes dexterously. 'You used not to smoke,' he said.

It was such a trite statement, but Willow found everything he did and said of all-consuming interest. 'I began a while back, but I didn't smoke much until – I heard about you.'

'Poor darling. And all the time I was being waited on by pretty young nurses.'

Foolish jealousy swept over her. It was a dangerous emotion to feel over a man who had never once said he loved her. Maybe he saw her only as an outlet for his need, just as men saw the girls in Annie Bliss's house. The idea didn't shame her. She loved him so much that at this moment she would be anything he wanted.

They made love for a third time, tenderly, each learning more about the other's needs, before Edgar said sadly, 'I have to go, my sweet. I haven't been to see my people yet.'

Joy spread through her, warming her. 'You visited me first?'

'I needed you.'

'Needed me? Needed my body, don't you mean?' She spoke lightly, to show him she was just joking.

'No, I do not. I could buy a body if I wanted one. I needed you, my darling. My people know I'm all right and I shall visit Buddleigh Manor next. Violet and Frances are going there to wait for me. I've only a short leave.'

Willow refused to think of his going back. She waited, longing for a word of love, but none came. They dressed and she saw him off on the train.

The Battle of the Somme began and by the end of July the 12th Gloucesters were at the front line. They received their first experience of trench warfare in all its bloody horror on September the third when they were ordered to attack the strongly held German positions near a village called Guillemont. By the end of the battle, out of a total of nine hundred and thirteen, Bristol's Own counted three hundred and twenty-four killed or injured. Even figures like these were a drop in the flood of death and agony. More than a million men, British, French and German, were accounted dead or wounded. One of the wounded was Willow's brother, Sam. Joe had been killed.

Willow went home as soon as Jasmine's letter reached her. Clara was sitting listlessly at the kitchen table when she arrived. She looked up, her face pale, eyes dark-rimmed but tearless.

'There you are then,' she said.

Willow put her arms round her mother. 'I came as soon as I heard.'

'Yes, I knew you would. Our Joe's gone.'

Willow's arms tightened. 'I know.' She wanted to weep, but could not in the face of Clara's dry-eyed misery.

'And our Sam's hurt bad. I don't know if we'll ever see him again, either.'

Jasmine had crept quietly into the room and burst into tears. 'Mum, don't. Please don't. Our Sam will come back, I just know he will.'

'You got no cause to say so,' said Clara. 'Every family in this street has lost a man, some more than one, an' lots of men die of their wounds. They say they don't have enough facilities for lookin' after them in the front line. They have to carry them back to field hospitals. Mrs Tucker told me all about it. She reads a lot about the war. Why should this family be different from the rest?'

Silently, Willow cursed Mrs Tucker. What she said was true, but she might have kept it to herself. She had no sons fighting.

'What's this bloody war about, Willow?' asked Clara.

She couldn't answer. She couldn't tell her mother what she believed, that it was about the nations demanding more land. That's what Steven had said last time he was home. Steven talked a lot when he was on leave. Edgar had spoken hardly at all. Mrs Tucker came to offer her condolences to Willow, ending with the information that she and her husband had decided to move to Cornwall where he had been born and were putting the house up for sale. She gave Clara a month's notice.

'How could she!' exclaimed Willow. 'How callous of her!'

'She's never been one for sentiment,' Clara said. 'Oh, Willow, our Sam will get better. I've got to think he will, an' he'll want his home to be waitin'. Tell me what to do. I don't know any more.'

Willow knew, without thinking about it, the course she must take. She saw Mrs Tucker who asked one hundred and twenty-five pounds for the house. It was exorbitant for what was offered, but all building had stopped for the duration of the war and accommodation was increasingly hard to find. Willow's lease expired next month and she wouldn't renew it. She returned to London and gave Bridget and Dora the news. They were sad, but resigned.

'You'll set up again after the war, won't you, Willow?' said Bridget.

'I certainly will.' She spoke with more conviction than she felt. No one knew what would happen when this dreadful war ended. Women might no longer demand couture clothes.

'Can we come back to you if you do open up again?' asked Dora.

Willow assured them she couldn't exist without their expert stitching and they left to work in munitions.

'You're a fool,' said Marigold to her sister.

She was between clients, lounging in a yellow satin dressing gown which became her, as did everything she wore. She bought only the best. 'How can you go on making our dresses if you're so far away.'

'I can't.'

'That's nice, isn't it? A proper let-down. And why can't you? You've got all our measurements.'

'That's not good enough. My clothes must be perfect and that needs fittings.'

'If you'd only lower your impossible standards, you could make money.'

'Maybe I could do something for you when you visit home.'

Marigold pulled on her cigarette which was in a long amber and gold holder. She blew smoke out in a blue stream. 'I shan't have much time for visiting. We're always so busy.'

'I see. Don't you want to see Mum?'

Marigold laughed. 'What on earth for? What have we got in common?'

'You are mother and daughter!' exclaimed Willow. 'Joe's been killed and Sam's badly hurt!'

Marigold still held the power to shock her. She was much tougher and more ruthless than the other girls, even Maisie.

'I can't afford to stop work,' she said. 'I'm saving a lot of my money. I want to go half shares here with Maisie, but if she's not willing I mean to set up on my own. I think she'll agree though. I'm too valuable to lose.'

Willow knew that the apparently vain statement was only the truth. Marigold attracted men like bees round a flower, one with a particularly heavy impregnation of pollen. Carmen said she never gave them anything but what they paid for, no genuine warmth, no real sympathy, even if the client was a young, wounded boy, destined to return to the hell that was now the front line, but men wanted her, basked in her sensuality.

'Do you ever hear from Edgar Maddison these days?' asked Marigold.

'Why should I?'

'Don't snap my head off. I had the idea you were sweet on him. You're daft enough. If you'd any sense at all you'd forget Bristol. I know dozens of girls who'd be willing to pay you well even for cheap frocks as long as they were cut nicely and looked pretty.'

'If you're so well off perhaps you'd help with the cost of Mum's house?'

'You must be out of your mind! Fancy buying that horrible little house. Have you forgotten it's got no bathroom or lavatory, only gaslight or candles and smelly coke fires when Mum can't afford coal. You'll hate it.'

'I intend to see that she can afford coal and a few of the other things that some people take for granted, like decent food and clothes.'

Within four weeks Willow had settled in Bristol in the little house in Barton Hill, now owned by Clara. Willow had used most of her money and lost her business. She had also lost much of the will that had carried her forward and, for the first time, had no clear sense of direction. She knew that Edgar was the cause of her lassitude. Since he had returned to the war zone she had received a single postcard from him, the stereotyped kind which offered a series of messages to be crossed off, or used, and had learned that he was 'Quite well' and 'Going on well'. She knew she had no right to expect more. Willingly and joyously she had given him pleasure; he had made no promises.

She and Jasmine had to work hard to get their mother to take an interest in day to day living. She talked constantly of Sam, wondering over and over when he'd be sent home from France. 'If he's that bad,' she moaned, 'they can't hold out a lot of hope for him. And there's my Joe—' Her voice broke. 'My Joe. I haven't seen him dead. How can I believe it when they've not let me see him? Do you think he had a decent burial somewhere in France, Willow?'

'Of course he did, Mum. This is a Christian country and so is France.'

'That's what they say about Germany,' said Clara bitterly. 'I wonder which side God is on?'

Willow applied for a job to Sidney Moor who gladly took her on to oversee the making of army uniforms and paid her a good wage. She loathed the factory. She hated everything about khaki, its smell, the hideously unbecoming shape of the finished uniforms, its sameness, but most of all its necessity, and was tormented relentlessly by thoughts of the men who would wear it and die in it.

There was a bright spot in her life when the magazine *Vogue* was introduced into Britain. She resolved to buy it even if she had to go without food. She pored over its pages and discovered that Paris showed clothes for wartime work and printed articles on 'Dressing on a War Income', then ran them side by side with delightful, expensive garments with exhortations to wear them and send your man back to his duty carrying with him a dream of loveliness.

Jasmine adored *Vogue*. 'Look at this.' she cried. 'A picture of a Doucet evening wrap of rose panne velvet with tassels. And here it says that women should slim "in order to use less fabric".'

Clara glowered at her. 'That must be for rich women. The poor don't get enough to make them fat.'

Obtaining food had become a constant problem for most and there were queues everywhere for even the most basic necessities. Jasmine had reached puberty and was always hungry. 'She'd eat the plate if it wasn't china,' said Clara dourly. She sighed. 'Our Marigold always had a good appetite. I wonder how she's gettin' on. She doesn't have the time to come to us so I've got it in mind to go an' see her. Jasmine could travel with me if you're too busy.' She somehow made Marigold's busyness sound more important than Willow's.

Willow was hard put not to give her an irritable reply. 'Best not, Mum,' she advised as lightly as she could. 'There's always the danger of bombs in London.' She thought it unlikely that her mother would actually carry out her scheme.

Clara said, 'She don't seem to worry. She's a good girl to throw herself into her war work the way she does.'

'Oh, she is, Mum, she is. I'll write and suggest that she comes here. I dare say she doesn't realise how time's passing.'

She wrote, telling her sister what Mum was thinking of doing and Marigold sent a letter by return of post promising an early visit.

The army had returned a letter written to Joe by Jasmine, dictated by Clara. It had been unopened and was stamped 'Deceased'. Clara had grasped it fiercely, torn it to shreds and thrown it into the fire. The next thing to arrive was a parcel containing his personal belongings stained black with dried blood. When Clara opened it she all but fainted.

Willow and Jasmine got her to bed with a liberal dose of brandy fetched hastily from the pub.

Jasmine was as white as her mother. 'How could they?' she kept crying. 'How could they be so cruel?'

'I don't know,' said Willow. 'I don't understand anything about this war. We're told it's for King and Empire, but I still can't see why we have to fight. Try not to dwell on it,

Jasmine. It can't do Joe any good and he'd have hated to upset us.'

'I know, but I can't help it.'

'Mum needs us to stay calm. Why don't you go out with your friends, my love, and I'll look through Joe's things?'

Jasmine's stomach heaved and she retched. Controlling the sick spasm she cried, 'You *can't!*'

'There may be something there for us. Perhaps a half-finished letter to Mum.'

'I never thought of that. I'll stay.'

Jasmine couldn't bring herself to touch the things so Willow, holding herself in firm check, did so. There was half a packet of cigarettes, a stub of pencil, a handkerchief and a pocket book, tucked inside of which was the beginning of a letter, the pages stiff and congealed with blood, the words unreadable. Jasmine grabbed the book and letter and consigned them to the flames. 'We must never tell Mum,' she said. 'Never!'

Willow found the factory so numbingly boring she decided that she must do something to add interest to her existence or she'd go crazy. She knew that the Maddisons were in Bristol and called on them. They treated her distantly but gave her orders for frocks and she spent much of her free time sewing the bright coloured silks, satins and brocades that she loved. Not that she got a lot of work. They said that patriotism prevented them from having too many new clothes 'when our brave boys are suffering in the war'.

She met Lady Mary, the wife of James Maddison. She was a waif-like creature, with soft eyes and a sweetly-shaped mouth, clearly no match for her husband who rollicked away most of his leaves in Paris. It was no wonder to Willow that she had kept him waiting so long for marriage. Family duty and the war had weakened her and now she took most of her joy from her lusty twin sons. She stood perfectly still while Willow took her measurements for a cream gown, then left to return to the nursery.

'She takes those boys everywhere with her,' said Violet, as she stood impatiently enduring the tug and pull of Willow's hands on her latest frock. 'Imagine how boring and annoying hostesses must find it. Who ever heard of such nonsense?'

Frances, watching with a glass of wine in her hand, was lethargic. 'I suppose she hopes they'll love her. God knows, she doesn't get much out of James.'

Violet threw her an angry warning glance, but Frances just laughed. 'For heaven's sake, Vi, Willow must know about our dear brother. Everyone does. Especially Mary.'

'Do not call me Vi,' snapped Violet.

Winifred Maddison was now thirteen and Mrs Maddison asked Willow to make her a party frock. She had fulfilled the promise of her spoilt childhood and was more autocratic even than Violet. She treated Willow with as much contempt as she treated her governess, a pale, anxious woman who sat in on the fittings. Winifred loved her new clothes, though the information only came to Willow via Henry, who got it from the nursery maid, and she looked undeniably pretty in them. Other parents ordered garments and Willow began to build a different clientèle, visiting little girls who stood in their Chilprufe liberty bodices and frilly knickers while they were measured and fitted, mostly for party frocks of an originality which could not be bought in any store. Children soon outgrew clothes and must have new and there was nothing unpatriotic in that.

When the authorities realised how many medical centres Bristol possessed they were quick to route an enormous number of war casualties that way. The new buildings at Southmead had been built for sick paupers, but were turned over, unused, to the armed services. A Red Cross flag flew over the Bristol Infirmary, where a new ward of two hundred and sixty beds had been taken by the military. The Beaufort War Hospital in Fishponds could cope with one and a half thousand men, and more in emergency beds on the floor, and large houses and schools also took in wounded. Avonmouth was an embarkation point and Bristol was suddenly a garrison city with strict orders to maintain blackout. There were fighting men everywhere in their hospital blues, many on crutches or in wheelchairs, the blind led by sympathetic mates. Every entertainment was free to them and the nights were busy and lively, though the church bells and striking clocks were silenced because it was believed the Zeppelins could steer by their sound.

At first the ambulance trains arrived during the day, but very soon men were being ferried into the city at night too and Temple Meads was busy throughout the twenty-four hours.

Alfred went there every night to help and his absence from home was a relief to everyone. Clara was growing increasingly resentful of his presence and nagged and snapped at him. Willow's remonstrances brought no let-up. Clara cried, 'Why should he be alive an' whole while one brother lies dead and the other probably dyin'?'

Alfred tried to be philosophical. 'She's half crazy with worry over Sam.'

They had received two letters from him, both short, written by a nurse who explained that he was too weak to hold a pencil, 'though coming along nicely', and giving no return address.

Willow offered her services to Temple Meads as an untrained volunteer. The routine was always the same. A period of intense activity, followed by a few quiet moments waiting for the next ambulance train. Enormous urns were ready with coffee and tea, tables were laid with food, there were chairs for the walking wounded and stretchers for the helpless. And always cigarettes. Willow waited with the others, most of whom prayed that someone they loved would not arrive terribly wounded, expected to die, or that a man listed as missing might thankfully turn up.

Then the train would arrive with its grisly cargo. Sometimes the only thing one could do was to light a cigarette or hold a cup for a man who had lost his arms, then write a postcard telling his family he was alive. Willow smiled at the men until her mouth felt stretched in a grimace, when what she wanted to do was weep. The long hours told on her and she grew thin and pale, but she couldn't give up. Then about two o'clock one morning, Alfred hurried to her as she knelt by the side of a boy of about eighteen who was clearly going to die.

'Willow,' he said in an urgent whisper in her ear, 'our Sam's here.'

Willow's heart leapt. She did all she could to comfort the dying youth until a priest arrived, then followed Alfred. Sam lay on the lower part of the double-decker stretcher and she knelt on the cold stone paving and put her arms round him.

He opened his eyes. 'Sis! It's really you! And Alfred! How did you get here?'

'We're helpers,' said Willow. 'Oh, Sam, I'm so thankful to see you.'

'I'm thankful to be here. Got a blighty wound that'll keep me home.'

'I'm glad.' Willow stopped. 'What sort of wound?'

'It's only my leg. Lots of chaps—' He choked, then managed, 'Our Joe – Mum must be—' He stopped again as a spasm of pain crossed his face.

'How bad are you, Sam?'

'Don't worry about me, Sis.' He lowered his voice. 'The chap above me is dyin'. Help him.'

Willow kissed Sam and carried on with her work until at three in the morning the last man had been tended and others came on duty to meet the next transport. She and Alfred had brought bicycles and together rode back to Barton Hill, happy for once, but too weary to talk. The misery of Joe's loss would live on, but at least Sam was home. And safe.

Willow crept into her mother's room which she shared with Jasmine, carrying a lighted candle. Clara was lying curled up on her side. She looked unrested and anxious even in her sleep. Willow touched her shoulder and she woke instantly. 'Arthur?'

Willow felt weak with love and compassion. 'Mum, it's me, Willow.'

Clara sat up. 'What's happened? Not our Sam!'

'Mum, I've seen him. He's wounded, but he's as lively as a cricket.'

Clara began to get up and Willow pushed her back gently. 'Rest a bit longer. It's not yet four, but I couldn't wait to give you the good news.'

'Thank you, love, thank you.' The tears which had been denied Clara before now poured down her face. 'Do you know how bad he is?'

'He told me it was a blighty wound.'

Clara leaned back against the metal bed frame. 'Doesn't that mean it's bad?'

'He looked all right. A bit pale, but that was to be expected.'

'I want to see him.'

'Of course you do. We'll go together. Would you like a hot drink, Mum?'

'I would, though I'll get it. You must be tired out.'

'Not too tired to bring you something. I don't know if I'll sleep anyway, I'm so glad about Sam.' Willow sat on the edge of Clara's bed and they drank malted milk, then she kissed her mother before going to her room.

She fell into bed. I'll have to change places with Alfred, she thought. There won't be room for my sewing machine in the box room. Then everything drifted away as she fell into an exhausted sleep. She awoke in the morning to find Clara offering her a cup of tea and Jasmine carrying a plate of hot toast.

'Fancy, our Sam's all right,' shrieked Jasmine. 'You rotten, mean things not to wake me.'

'Can we help it if you sleep like a dormouse?' smiled Willow.

Clara put a hand to her head. 'Jasmine, stop yellin'.' But she too was smiling.

Sam had been taken to the Infirmary and there his family learned of the severity of his wound.

'We had to amputate his leg below the knee,' said a young doctor.

Clara cried out and he said, 'It's awful, I know, but it was his leg or his life. He understands and he's cheerful. A good patient. And at least he can't be sent back again.' Willow heard the wretchedness in his voice. He might be young, only just qualified, but he had coped with more horrors than most doctors saw in a lifetime.

A raised blanket hid Sam's legs. He seized his mother in a hug and kissed her soundly.

'Sam,' she murmured, 'my boy. Thank God. Thank God.'

Sam winked at Jasmine who stood at the opposite side and she landed a hearty kiss on his mouth. A nurse, all white starch, stopped at the end of the bed. 'Not too much excitement, if you please. Private Riches has been told to remain calm. His wound has not yet healed, not by a long way and he's due to go to the theatre again soon.'

'The theatre?' Clara was bewildered.

The nurse marched on, twitching a sheet into order here, tidying a locker there.

'She means the operatin' theatre, Mum,' said Sam.

'What for? I thought you were gettin' better.'

'I am, but they can't finish off operations properly in the field hospitals, though they do their best. I just need my stump tidied up a bit.'

Jasmine grimaced. 'Poor you!'

Clara's hands clutched the bedclothes convulsively. 'I can't bear to think about it. What you must have been through!'

'I'm lucky to be back. Lots of my friends – so many of Bristol's Own, our own Old Pals – will never come back.'

Clara said, her voice half strangled, 'Joe?'

Sam took her hands in his and said gently, 'We were together to the last, Mum. He was killed outright by the shell that nearly got me.'

'They sent his stuff back. It was all covered in blood.'

Sam said something under his breath. 'Believe me, Mum, he didn't suffer. He couldn't have known anythin' about it.'

Clara closed her eyes and her lips moved.

Willow left the Infirmary and went straight to the factory. Sidney said, 'Where have you been? Good lord, you look like death warmed up. Are you fit to be here?'

'Sam's back. I went to see him in the Infirmary.'

'Badly hurt?'

'He's lost part of a leg, but he seems fine, as jolly as always. He'll never go back to the war and that's a blessing.'

'Poor chap. He'll find it difficult to get a job.'

The private sewing grew more than Willow could handle and Jasmine helped by doing the hems. Even Clara took on some of the plain work, but Willow needed someone who could manage the more intricate stitching.

'Let me try,' begged Alfred.

He caught his mother's glance and flushed. 'I know sewing is women's work, Mum, but our Willow will collapse if she doesn't ease up a bit.'

'A man sewin'!'

'Plenty of men sew, Mum,' said Willow. 'Take a look in my *Vogue*. Lots of the clothes are made by men.'

Alfred learned fast and quite soon was able to use the one sewing machine Willow had brought with her, and they put in a few hours when they could and worked all day Sundays. Willow felt that she had been tired for ever and would never catch up on sleep, but the stories which were coming back from the front stiffened her resolve to keep going. If soldiers could endure and fight from trenches which were knee-deep in mud and water, often without food because the transports couldn't get through, without sleep because of the noise of bursting shells and the rattle of gunfire, then she could soldier on too.

She had kept up her letters to Steven and he knew where to

find her. He was waiting for her at home when she returned from the factory one day. Clara and Jasmine were plying him with tea and cake. He stayed as long as courtesy dictated, then asked Willow to walk with him. As soon as they were out of sight he held her at arm's length. 'Willow, you're so thin, so white. What have you been doing to yourself?'

'No more than the war demands. You don't look so healthy yourself.'

'I've been lucky so far. Many of the medical corps have been killed.'

'Edgar said he wouldn't have your job for anything. He thinks you're by far the bravest.'

As usual Steven seized on the point which interested him. 'You still see Edgar Maddison?'

'He came to tell me he was all right after he was reported missing. I suppose he takes his leaves with his family.'

'Or he follows his brother James's example and goes roistering in Paris.'

'Why shouldn't he? Fighting men need recreation!'

'Don't snap my head off. Can I take you somewhere nice?'

'I don't know. I'm terribly busy. Tired too.'

'Couldn't you spare an hour or two? I've only a short leave. You deserve recreation, too, and I wouldn't mind a bit myself.'

She softened. 'Sorry. I'm edgy. It's—'

'It's the war, my love.'

He had driven down and they went for a run. The car rattled and blew out copious exhaust fumes. 'Sorry,' said Steven, 'it's all I can afford. One day I'm going to get a better one.'

'What's happening to your shop?'

'Old Mason still keeps going and he's found a couple of great-nephews who help him out of school hours. What about your business?'

She explained and he frowned. 'Fancy working for Winifred, that stuck-up little madam.'

'That stuck-up little madam helps to pay our expenses at home and I've got other commissions from her friends.'

'I wish you'd work for ordinary folk.'

'Ordinary folk don't have money.'

'But you've lost your business. The nobs didn't take long to desert you.'

'It's not their fault. It's—'

'The war. I know, I know.'

'And they haven't deserted me. I still make gowns for Violet and Frances and Lady Mary, too.'

'Poor soul.'

'Who's a poor soul?'

'Lady Mary.'

'Well, she is a little droopy, I agree.'

'I didn't mean that. Her husband James was killed. It was in *The Times*.'

Willow thought of the delicate girl who had put off her wedding for so long.

'Poor man,' she said. 'But she might be relieved.'

'Willow! What a dreadful thing to say.'

'I know. I didn't mean it, exactly. But she didn't want to marry him and I think he made her miserable.'

Steven was tired of discussing others. He had stopped the car by the gate to a field. Autumn was close and, following the pattern of this bad-weather summer, it began raining.

'Winter's on its way,' said Willow, 'and we've scarcely seen any summer.'

Steven took her hands. 'You're cold.' He tried to pull her to him, but she resisted.

He swore. 'What's wrong with you? I thought you'd be willing to give me a bit of comfort after what I've been through. I'm not asking for much.' He had attempted to sound jocular, but it fell flat.

She flushed. 'I'm sorry—'

'No, that was rotten of me. I vowed I'd never try to play on your sympathy.'

His self-abnegation weakened her and she leaned over and kissed his cheek.

'You don't love me, do you, Willow?' he said sadly.

'No. I wish to God I did.'

'Who do you love?'

'No one. No man,' she lied.

'I don't believe you. I think it's Edgar Maddison.'

She said nothing and allowed him to take her in his arms. 'I'll not take advantage of you,' he said, 'though I want terribly to make love.' She was silent and he said, 'Willow, be careful.'

'Of what?'

'I don't know what hopes you've got of Edgar – no, don't speak, hear me out. Now that James is dead, the Maddisons will expect Edgar more than ever to marry a girl of his own standing. They'll be looking for someone they can welcome into their home.'

'I know.'

'You say you know, but I think you're still praying for a miracle and that he'll ask you to marry him. He won't. He's become engaged to the daughter of an earl. That was in *The Times*, too.'

Willow jerked herself away from him, unable to hide her anguish, and folded her arms about herself as if she must hold her body together. Steven glanced at her face then turned away, jealous and angry at what he read there. 'I'll drive you home.'

'Not yet! Please! Not yet!' He leaned back and stared ahead. 'Steven, I'm sorry. I always seem to be apologising to you.'

'Yes.'

'I'll get over him. I must. One day.'

'I'm not so sure. But whether you get over him or not, I still love you, I still want you for my wife.'

'I don't deserve a friend like you.'

'Yes, I am your friend. Dearest Willow, I've always been your friend, but I want more than that. I've never looked at another girl. It's always been you.'

Willow hadn't understood just how strong her dreams of Edgar had been until they were snatched from her. She didn't blame him. She could imagine the pressures put on him to marry suitably. Blame him? He had never promised her a thing.

A new horror entered the lives of the family in the small house in Barton Hill. Sam came home from hospital to a welcoming tea party to which many of the neighbours had contributed.

'They're wonderful folk,' said Clara. 'They're all mournin' someone yet they're glad for me.'

Sam, still haggard, smiled and joked and laughed until the revellers left. Then he sat staring morosely into the fire.

'Cheer up, love,' said Clara. 'You're safe now you're home.'

'Our Joe isn't so safe!'

Clara gasped. 'Don't,' she begged.

'Mum's suffered enough over Joe,' said Willow, controlling a surge of anger. 'Why must you make things worse for her?'

'He's got a right to speak his mind,' snapped Clara.

'I know, Mum, but our Joe is gone. Nothing can bring him back. We ought to stick together and help one another.'

'She's right,' said Jasmine. 'Please, Sam, don't go on about Joe.'

He offered to sleep downstairs and leave the larger bedroom for Willow and her work, but she refused indignantly. She changed places with Alfred and had to sit on the bed to use the sewing machine.

Sam became alternately feverishly jolly or broodingly quiet. 'Sam, my love,' said Clara admiringly one day, talking as much to lift his mood of depression as anything else, 'I can't get over the way you manage the stairs with your crutches.'

'Good lord, that's nothin'.' He began to laugh. 'I'm lucky compared to a lot of the men. Of course, some were more lucky than others. Honest, you should have been in our trench one day. There'd been a heavy bombardment from both sides and somethin' landed right by us. We all threw ourselves away, thinkin' the Boche had got us with a shell, but you'll never guess what it was.'

Jasmine, taking her cue from his jolly aspect, smiled in anticipation and asked, 'How can we? Tell us, Sam.'

'It was only the top half of a German officer. Imagine that, an' he was still wearin' his cap.'

Jasmine gasped and ran from the room. Sam laughed heartily and from then on talked constantly of the war, of the horror of seeing friends crucified on barbed wire, their limbs jerking as bullets ploughed into them, of being splattered by the blood and minced flesh of comrades, of the debris of severed limbs and unburied bodies which were often used to reinforce the barricades. He poured out his memories and those who loved him bore it as best they could, waiting for it to stop.

Clara began to dread going to bed because of nightmares conjured by his memories and Willow and Alfred often found her still up when they returned late from Temple Meads. Alfred always went quickly upstairs, but Willow stayed to listen to Clara's desperate fear repeated again and again.

'Willow, Sam said that our Joe didn't suffer, but it sounds as if thousands didn't get killed outright. I can't help thinkin' that Joe might have been one of the unlucky ones. Did Sam see him hangin' on the barbed wire? Was he one of them that died tryin' to hold their guts in? That's what he told us tonight. Will he ever stop?'

Sam did stop, but no one in the Barton Hill house slept easily for a long time to come.

Chapter Twenty-two

In 1917 the German Zeppelins were replaced by wide-spanned biplanes which had a much greater capacity for dropping bombs and in one night in London a hundred people were killed, a quarter of them children. The planes, Gothas, grew heavier and carried larger bombs, and two squadrons of British fighters were pulled back to defend Britain, a move which infuriated the French so much that Haig returned them to the continent and the civilians had to take whatever Germany sent. This led to night-time migrations from London.

On one of Marigold's infrequent visits to Bristol Clara said, 'Come home, my love, there's plenty of war work here. Sidney Moor's always takin' on new girls. His business is gettin' huge. He'd give you a job.'

Marigold refrained from expressing the first reply which rose to her lips. 'Sorry, Mum. I'd love to, but I'm needed where I am.'

Since Willow's letter warning her that Clara might come to London she had travelled down every two or three months, sleeping with her mother in her double bed. She must have purchased specially the cotton nightdress she wore and the plain underwear, for certainly they wouldn't figure in her London wardrobe.

'You're crazy,' she told Willow. 'I'm making a mint of money and you could too.'

'Not your way!'

'What way, then? Don't tell me you're making a fortune from those stuck-up Maddisons and their pals.'

'I'm managing to save a bit towards the future.'

'I hear Edgar Maddison is engaged. To the daughter of an earl. If you had any hopes there—'

'I didn't.'

'Not for marriage perhaps. You know, Willow, I'd bet anything he'd gladly visit you after his wedding if you gave him the ghost of a chance.' Without giving the indignant girl the chance to reply, she continued, 'By the way, guess who turned up on my doorstep one day? Well, you won't, so I'll tell you – Sidney Moor's sister Nellie, the one I used to go around with. She wanted a job in our house. Can you imagine! That common little slut working for Maisie and me?'

'I thought you were friends.'

'No fear! I went out with her because I wanted to know how she worked, and I learned a few things, but I've gone far beyond her expectations.'

'What happened to her when you turned her away?'

'How should I know? Probably gone to a beat in the East End. It's all she's fit for.'

'How can you be so callous about her?'

Marigold sighed. 'Don't go sentimental on me, please.'

As she was getting ready to return to London, Clara asked, 'Aren't you at all afraid of the bombs, my love?'

'It's a bit scaring at times, but I can't desert my post.'

'You're brave.'

'It's a laugh really. At first they had policemen pedalling bicycles as hard as they could round the streets with a notice that said, "Take Cover". Then it dawned on them that only people out in the streets would see it so they got buglers standing in the back of a car, some of them boy scouts. Now they've got maroons that burst in the sky like fireworks and scare people before the raid's even begun.'

'I don't know how you can joke about it, honest I don't.' Clara kissed her warmly. 'Take care of yourself, my love. This family's suffered enough without anythin' happenin' to you.'

Marigold didn't reply, but the look of barely concealed disgust she shot at Sam who was sitting morosely in front of the fire said everything. Fortunately Clara didn't see it, but Willow did. Waiting for the taxi – Marigold never travelled now by tram or bus – Willow said, 'Don't you care for Sam any more?'

'No more than I always did. It isn't a bit of use being annoyed with me. I feel as if I was born into the wrong family. Their kind of life doesn't suit me at all.'

'I can see that!'

'Be honest, Willow, it doesn't suit you. How can it? You had a lovely place in London, a developing business, beautiful clothes. Look at you now. A mud-coloured dress, and your hands!' Marigold drew off one of her gloves and spread her fingers, soft and white, the nails pink. 'Yours could look like this if only you'd give up working in a factory. You can't possibly be happy.'

When Marigold had been borne away Willow went back inside, irritated because her sister was right. She stared down at her hands. She was an overseer, true, but that didn't mean she hadn't ever to handle the heavy khaki and she was always the one called upon to deal with any snags which, because of the shortage of men, sometimes led to her becoming oily and sustaining small cuts and abrasions.

Clara stared at her. 'What's so interestin' about your fingers?' She was snappy, as always when Marigold had left her.

'Nothing, Mum. I shall be glad to finish making uniforms. My hands are so rough sometimes I'm nervous when I'm handling anything flimsy.'

'Our Marigold keeps her hands lovely an' soft.'

Sam looked up. 'I wonder how?' It was a sneer.

The Germans had warned the world that they intended to begin submarine warfare without restriction and in April, 1917, angered by the sinking of the *Lusitania* with the loss of many of their nationals' lives, America declared war on Germany.

Sam was elated. He bought newspapers and read them

avidly. 'We're bound to win now, Mum! And it won't be long.'

He was disappointed to discover that the USA had no intention of taking to the field in France until they were good and ready.

He threw down a newspaper disgustedly. 'Eighty-five thousand men, that's all, an' we have to supply them with heavy arms an' aircraft. An' they send our boys out before they've got time to catch breath.'

'It isn't the fault of the American soldiers,' said Willow.

'Whose side are you on?' he demanded.

'Britain's, of course.'

Sam got to his feet and winced as his artificial leg, which was heavy and cumbersome, dug into another crop of blisters on his stump.

'Britain's got a lot to answer for,' he said argumentatively. 'They sent us into hell, an' for what? For men to die, that's what, because someone wants more power an' land.' He moved awkwardly and his artificial leg slid from under him. He crashed to the floor. Willow and Clara ran to help him up, but he waved them away. 'I can manage! I've got to for the rest of my life!' He hauled himself up and they heard him leave the house, no doubt on his way to the pub.

'The wickedness of doctors,' Clara raged. 'They could have given Sam a better leg. It's horrible! It's so heavy!'

Willow learned of a company in London which supplied light artificial limbs with joints that moved so fluently they enabled the wearer to return to a favourite sport. Enquiries revealed that to have one fitted meant a trip to the supplier and a bill for at least forty-five guineas, as well as travel and accommodation expenses. She decided that somehow she would raise the money; it might prevent Sam from complete degeneration into a bitter, miserable wreck. She wondered how Joe, the clever brother, would have behaved under similar circumstances, and clamped down on the thought. But it was impossible for her to work any harder and prices were rising rapidly. They had done so since the war began and were now a hundred and thirty-three per cent higher than in 1914. In an attempt to beat profiteers and wealthy hoarders who ignored the pleas for voluntary rationing, official food rationing had been introduced, tentatively, in February, 1918, but although the ration cards promised fair shares for all, the goods simply were not in the shops and there was still the endless queuing. Clara and Jasmine took this particular task on themselves and rejoiced when they found something extra to eat. Sam was given the largest portions until he began to put on weight which made his stump more sore than before.

Willow remonstrated with her mother who shrugged. 'I know you're right, Willow love, but I can't seem to do enough for him. I can't stop rememberin' how he's been spared to me.'

Alfred had grown tall, though he was still thin. When he had become eligible for conscription he had gone along, regretfully but bravely, to be assessed. He was turned down on the grounds of his poor physique.

Clara took it as a personal affront for which she blamed Alfred, ranting at him with her sharp tongue. He refused to quarrel with her and she abused him the more.

Willow carried on, shoving the hard facts of her present existence behind her so that she could concentrate on the present, and when the Maddisons introduced more customers to her she found that, after all, she could dig even deeper into her reserves of strength. Some of these wealthy women had husbands who appeared to know what was going on behind the scenes. They said that the war could not possibly continue much longer and Willow took fresh heart and looked towards the day when the horror would stop and everyone could try to repair the frayed fabric of their lives.

Edgar began to write to Willow. He made no mention of his engagement (which had been confirmed by Violet) and neither did she. Their letters were just friendly. Sometimes he unburdened himself of a little of the frightfulness of trench warfare; at other times he joked. The sight of a letter from France on the front doormat kept her happy for days. She knew she was asking for more hurt, but her love for him had grown even without nourishment. It was a humiliation which surely must one day cease. When he finally returned home and married, their friendship would automatically end. She might even make clothes for his bride. The idea tortured her, but she kept it to the forefront of her mind, arming herself against the darts of pain, knowing they would get worse.

At night she lay in bed and read and re-read his letters. 'Dearest Willow', or 'Darling Willow', or 'Best Beloved Willow', they began. He didn't mean it, but just the same she was grateful for the endearments. Perhaps he didn't love his fiancée? Perhaps he really loved her, Willow? She knew it was foolish and useless to think this way. Just as Lady Mary had succumbed to James Maddison, so Edgar would succumb. 'I miss you,' one letter said. 'I shall never forget the loving comfort you gave me when I so desperately needed it. I think of you constantly.' Surely not! If he thought of a woman it must be of his fiancée. It was like him to exaggerate. She loved it, though, just as she loved everything about him. 'Life here goes on much as usual. We shell them and they shell us.' Them and Us. Dad's words, though in a very different context, but of course Dad had been right all along. Them and Us. A man could make love to a woman below his station in life, could even fall in love with her, but not marry her. She looked down at the letter again. 'Tonight I am at –' here the Censor had struck out a name '– tomorrow I go on leave which I intend to spend in Paris. It is an amazing city. One would sometimes think there was no war.'

Willow blew out her candle and lay down. Edgar would be seeking women on his leaves. Women like Marigold. The idea startled her. Would wives and sweethearts be shocked to know that a man went to someone like Marigold for comfort, a clean business-like prostitute? She was helping soldiers, sailors, and the new breed of air fighters to forget the war for a little while. Marigold really was performing war work, of a kind.

There were rumours of a final push by the Allies and Willow was ordered up to the Maddison house on the Downs to measure for gowns and advise on styles and colours, anticipating parties which would celebrate the ending of hostilities. She took colour swatches, an innovation begun since Lady Mary, who had left off mourning, had insisted on a gown of pale beige.

Willow had protested, 'It will make your skin look sallow and negate your eyes which are one of your best points.' Mary had refused to listen, trying to assert her independence; the gown was a disaster.

Then Willow had taken her a length of coral silk and draped it against her and Mary saw at once that it transformed the natural pallor of her complexion to translucent ivory.

Violet and Mary, along with Mrs Maddison and Winifred, were waiting for Willow in Mrs Maddison's boudoir. Miss Brayton, the lady's maid, was also present and she looked coldly at Willow. Her skin had grown appreciably thicker since her days as a servant so she was not the least put out. She took satisfactory orders from all the ladies, Frances, who had refused to leave her bedroom, being the last to see her. Willow found her reclining on a daybed, her husband standing over her, glowering. He had clearly been remonstrating with her and when Willow came in said to his wife with frigid politeness, 'I shall expect you downstairs and ready to accompany me in about an hour, my dear. Be sure to see Brayton first.'

He left and Frances laughed and produced a bottle from beneath her skirts. 'Good thing he did not ask me to get up or this would have slid out and revealed all.' She poured liquor into an empty cold cream pot and tipped it down her throat. Then she looked at Willow in a bemused fashion. Her skin was blotched and her cheeks puffy, her eyes slightly bloodshot and red-rimmed. 'What are you here for?'

'I'm to measure you for your new frock, Mrs Bickford. It's for the victory celebrations.'

'Good lord, has the war ended then?'

'Not yet, but the end is supposed to be in sight.'

'Is that so? Pity someone does not tell the Boche. The casualty lists are getting no shorter. If anything more men are being killed.'

'Please stand up, Mrs Bickford. I'm really very busy. I only have the weekend to complete my own sewing.'

'Goodness!' Frances got to her feet, swaying, steadying herself by clinging to the mantelpiece, her arm stretched over the nursery guard which protected her from the bright fire. 'What do you do with your time? I'm bored as hell. Especially when my husband wishes me to go to a political meeting with him. That is why he is waiting downstairs. You had better be quick because he expects Brayton to dab a little powder and rouge on my face. He seems to think I need it.'

'Could you stand still, *please*, Mrs Bickford?' Willow begged.

'Do you still paint people?' asked Frances abruptly.

Willow looked up, smiling. 'Fancy remembering that.'

'Well, do you?'

'I've no time at present. I shall begin again when the war is over.'

'That's good. That's very, very good. Have you got a sweetheart, Willow?'

'In a way.'

'Goodness. Is it possible to have a sweetheart in a way?'

'I don't want to get married. I've too much to do.'

'What have you got to do?'

She looked down at Willow who knelt at her feet pinning sky blue satin. 'What have you got to do?' Frances repeated.

'Plenty. I work in a factory making uniforms and I am also a dress designer, though this has been curtailed because of the war, but—'

'I dare say you have a little bit of loving from someone, don't you? I am sure you have comforted *someone* before he left for the war. Will you be long? My husband will be very, very cross with me if I am late.'

417

'Not long.'

Frances began to sing in a reedy, quavering voice. '"Another little drink wouldn't do us any harm." How true. How very true. I heard that sung in a music hall. I went with my sister and Lord Radcliffe. He has turned out to be a nice man. A very nice man. He is different since he went to war. He got burnt in his aeroplane and it made him look different and act differently too. Don't you find that surprising, Miss Riches? He is good to Violet now. He is a nice man. I wish I had a nice man. Have you got a nice man, Lily?'

At the sound of the old name Willow jumped and jabbed her finger. She tied a piece of linen tightly round the pinprick which seemed to spew forth an astonishing amount of blood and tried to deflect Frances from her personal questions. 'I'm glad that Lady Radcliffe is happy,' she said.

'Oh, yes, she is.' Frances laughed too long and loud. 'Just think, she might not be able to wear her new gown when the war ends. She's started another baby. I never expected to see my sister so dependent on a man and wanting more children. Soon she will be out here.' Frances held her arms a couple of feet from her stomach and bulged her cheeks. 'She will be so fat. I have never had a baby, have you?'

'I'm not married, Mrs Bickford.'

Frances shrieked with raucous mirth. 'What has that to do with it? I have several friends who have trotted up the aisle in white when they should have worn red. Scarlet for sin, don't you know. I wish I had a nice man.'

Willow wondered why her husband insisted on her accompanying him.

'Are you well enough to keep an engagement?' she ventured.

'Am I too tipsy is what you mean, isn't it?'

Willow wished she'd said nothing. A still tongue in a wise head, as Gran used to say.

'I am sure you have a nice man,' said Frances. 'Mr Bickford is not a nice man. He expects me to go to dreadfully dull affairs. He gets cross with me. Very, very cross. I do my best. He is trying to impress people with his – s-s-s-suitability, heavens, I could hardly say that word – to be a Member of Parliament. It seems that Members of Parliament must have respectable wives.'

Willow decided that continued silence was best and when Mrs Maddison swept into the room a moment later she was glad she had.

'Not finished yet, Miss Riches? Do please make haste. Mrs Bickford has an important engagement.'

Willow finished and stood up. She carefully folded the shimmering material into a piece of white linen. 'I'll return in a week for a fitting, Mrs Maddison, if that's convenient?'

'Perfectly.' She turned away and Willow left, already planning the hectic days ahead.

She was busy with her sewing machine when Jasmine opened the bedroom door. Willow looked up. 'Not now, my love, unless it's something very important.'

Jasmine's eyes were like saucers, and there was a teasing quality about her smile. 'There's one of those Maddisons outside in a green car, a two-seater, what Sam calls a real corker of a car.'

Willow wondered which one wanted to alter her order for a frock, sighed, and went downstairs and through the front door.

She stared at the car, hardly able to believe that it was Edgar who stood by it. He came to her and took her hands. 'Close your mouth, Willow,' he grinned. 'I am real. Don't look like that. I say, you are not going to faint on me, are you?'

She shook her head. 'I thought you were in France. How did you get here?'

'A spot of leave. I decided to spend it in blighty. I could hardly come to Bristol and not visit my best friend, could I? Get your coat and hat and we'll go for a spin.'

Clara and Jasmine were peering at him from the open front door and Sam was staring over their shoulders. 'Wait a moment,' she said breathlessly. 'I must tell Alfred – he's upstairs – he helps me.' Her brother received with a smile the news of her unexpected chance to go out on a pleasure trip. 'Time you had some fun.'

She dropped a kiss on the top of his head and hurried into her bedroom, changing into a smart brown costume and cape to match, and putting on the jaunty hat which went with them. The car was open to the chilly February breezes so she found the gauze scarf given her by Frances so long ago, when Reggie had driven them home from the Downs, and tied it over her hat. Gloves, a small handbag containing the face powder she had begun to use, a clean handkerchief and she was ready.

Edgar had been talking to Clara and Jasmine who watched as he opened the door of the passenger seat and handed Willow in, covered her knees with a luxurious fur rug, then cranked the car and drove off. They were watched also, to Jasmine's grinning delight, by most of the neighbours. Fancy a handsome man in khaki – an officer – coming to fetch her sister in a posh little car! And helping her in like that, and a *fur* blanket. She was ecstatic.

Now that they were alone an awkwardness had set in and Edgar drove in silence for a mile or so before he spoke. 'Thank you for your letters.'

'Thank you for yours,' she said. 'Where are we going?'

'Does it matter?' he said. 'We're together, aren't we?'

Was it enough for her? It had to be. She thought of mentioning his engagement, but didn't. She would snatch this brief time together without sounding a discordant note.

'Will you let me take you somewhere, Willow?'

'I thought that's what you were doing.'

'Don't joke, please. I'm serious.'

She sighed. 'You can take me anywhere you like.'

Again they were silent until he pulled up at a small cottage in Frenchay.

'This belongs to a friend. He has lent me the key. He's still in France.'

Willow waited while he unlocked the front door and gestured to her to go in. The place was warm and a fire burned in the black-leaded grate. 'A local woman keeps it all clean and aired,' said Edgar. 'It's a tiny place. It's used as a retreat.'

He had brought a basket with him and unpacked it, placing the contents carefully on the kitchen table. Two bottles of wine, bread, butter, cheese, and a sponge cake.

'You don't seem short of rations,' she said, though she was uninterested in the food. She knew why they were here and nothing could prevent her being glad.

'I took the stuff from our kitchen. Cook pretended not to see me,' he said.

He removed her cape and dropped it on to a chair and together they went up the narrow stairway into a bedroom which was furnished with a luxurious double bed, leaving little room for a tallboy, a narrow wardrobe and a washstand. A fire burned here, too, making the room pleasantly warm.

Edgar looked her up and down. 'How smart you are. You made it, didn't you?'

'How do you know?' She tried to sound jocular and failed.

'Your clothes have a stamp of their own, a style.'

'Do they?' She was thrilled. Originality was the vital quality needed by a designer.

She stood passively as he undid the buttons of her coat and skirt, then removed his uniform. His muscles were well-developed and hard, all boyishness gone from his body for ever, just as it had from his face. He was a man now who had looked on sights which would leave an impression for the remainder of his life. He watched her as she removed the rest of her clothes.

He dragged the bedclothes down with impatient hands and turned to her. 'Beautiful,' he breathed. 'You are so incredibly beautiful.'

She was trembling a little. Her tongue seemed riveted to the roof of her mouth as she waited for his touch. He held her close, then lifted her easily and laid her on the bed, continuing to stare down at her until her body gained life such as it had not known since last she had made love to him. She wanted him so much, she wanted him with a passion which drove all reason from her mind. She held up her arms and he climbed on the bed beside her and kissed her with a deep, demanding kiss until they were breathless. He explored her as if he had never seen her before and each touch of his hands and lips were a fiery trail of love. She looked at the physical evidence of his own need and touched him and caressed him, making him gasp. He was skilful, far more than he had been; he had learned lessons from someone. The thought drifted through her mind without rancour as she gave herself up entirely to sensation.

Afterwards they lay side by side, so close that their skin continued the caresses; they were warm, hazy with fulfilment, content to be together.

'I'm hungry,' Edgar yelled suddenly, leaping out of bed. 'I shall bring you food. Cover yourself, you shameless woman.'

'If you think I shall let you out of my sight, you've got another think coming.'

He laughed, leaned into the wardrobe and pulled out two dressing gowns, one a heavy tartan wool, the other a flame-coloured cashmere in a smaller size. Evidently Edgar's friend had ideas about what his women should wear.

'I suppose he has something naughty and revealing as well?' she said.

He opened a drawer of the tallboy and pulled out a wine-coloured garment of silk and lace which clearly would reveal more than it hid.

'Exotic, too.' She laughed. 'Race you downstairs.' And she leapt for the door.

'Not fair!' cried Edgar. 'I can't pass you. It's too narrow.'

'What a terrible shame.'

They cut thick chunks of bread, buttered them liberally

and took alternate bites of bread and cheese, washing it down with draughts of wine. Willow felt alive with sensation. One appetite sated they went back upstairs and made love until all passion was spent.

Five hours later Willow waved goodbye to Edgar. As he turned the corner he lifted his arm in the air in a salute, then he was gone and she felt that the world had become a flat, dull plane on which she would merely exist.

Jasmine said, 'He's a lovely man, isn't he, Willow? Is he your boyfriend?'

'He's just my friend.' She took a deep breath and said, her eyes on her mother, 'He's engaged to be married. To an earl's daughter.'

'Oh!' Jasmine was disappointed. 'I wish you could have him. He's handsome and his car is beautiful. No, I didn't mean that quite. I meant—'

Willow kissed her floundering sister. 'Darling, I know what you meant. How about finishing off those hems for me?'

Jasmine went upstairs, regretful, but with her sunny temperament intact.

'Engaged, is he?' said Clara. 'You were gone for five hours and you come back lit up like a Christmas tree. You look to me like a woman in love. You do love him, don't you?'

Willow nodded, unable to speak through a throat tightened by tears.

'He's a Maddison,' said Clara. 'He won't marry you.'

Willow drew a shuddering breath. 'I know, Mum. I've accepted it.'

'You're a fool. With your looks an' brains you could easily get a good husband. What can Edgar Maddison give you? His class always marry their own kind and he's already engaged! I thought you had more sense. The Maddisons! What have they ever given you?'

'They showed me a different way of life.'

'Are you envious?' Clara's voice was sharp. 'Dad an' me did our best.'

'Oh, I know you did. No one could have better parents than mine. The Maddisons have so much yet there seems little love in the family.'

'Money might sometimes be a bigger comfort than love,' sighed Clara. 'I bet the nobs' sons don't have to drag about with artificial legs that weigh a ton!'

The long-awaited German offensive had begun in March of 1918 and any male who could walk and carry a gun was drafted to the trenches, including Alfred.

After all her taunts, Willow expected Clara to be pleased, but contrarily she was not. 'Takin' another of my boys,' she cried. 'I suppose he'll come back like his poor brother, or worse off, or perhaps not come back at all.' She had thrown her apron over her head and wailed.

Sam was angry. He had been the hero and now Alfred would be in first place in the heroism stakes. It was hard for him to take. 'It's bound to be easier for you,' he stormed. 'The Americans are sendin' thousands of men, all fresh. You'll be there to see the war ended.'

Alfred, pale with apprehension which he was too proud to voice, said his goodbyes.

Jasmine was deeply troubled by the departure of another brother to the front and disturbed by the discord caused by Sam. Willow and Clara encouraged her to go out as much as possible with her friends. For over a year the moving pictures had been showing scenes from the battles and Jasmine returned from her first in a state of high excitement caused partly by distress. 'I saw pictures from the trenches! They were so real! Everythin' our Sam's told us about was there!'

When Sam heard, he insisted on going to see these wonders and from then on he went three or four times a week, morbidly fascinated.

'You shouldn't have let him know, our Jasmine,' Clara reproached.

She was downcast. 'Sorry, Mum, I didn't think.'

'That's your trouble. You don't think enough, except about boys.'

'Mum, I don't!'

Willow said, 'If she does it's quite natural at her age. She'll be lucky if she gets a man of her own with so many dead. And Sam could hardly fail to know about the pictures when he can find a full-page spread in the newspaper advertising them.'

He heard part of the conversation and laughed. 'You think about boys, do you, little sister?' He stuck out his artificial leg. 'Would you wed a man like me, Jasmine? Would you like to watch him take off his harness every night an' drop his leg on the floor?'

She ran upstairs and Willow followed to comfort her.

For once Clara was angry with her son. 'You've got no call to say such things to your sister.'

'You say things to her!'

'I'm her mother.'

'An' I'm her brother. Hey, Willow, do you know that Sidney Moor is sweet on our Jasmine?'

'What?'

'He's waitin' for her to grow up.'

'How do you know?'

'He bought me a few drinks t'other night when I met him in the pub. In fact we both got squiffy and he told me he wanted you once, but you'd never have him, so he's goin' to try for Jasmine.'

'She might have something to say about that,' said Willow drily.

'Time will tell,' said Clara. She was pleased. Sidney was an even bigger catch now and Jasmine would have a nice, steady man to care for her. Even his family had redeemed itself. His brothers had gone to war; two of them were dead and three had received wounds and gone straight back to the front. His sisters, except Nellie who, said Clara, had disappeared, were working in munitions.

* * *

The German offensive was resisted by the Allies, and slowly, but surely, the enemy was driven back. *The Times* announced the end of the war, almost laconically, as they had signalled the beginning. The terms of the Armistice were harsh and the *Daily Herald* printed a cartoon depicting the statesmen leaving the council chamber, the Hall of Mirrors at Versailles, and a baby weeping, forgotten, in a corner. It was captioned 'Class of 1940'. The cynical warning that the merciless terms would start another war in a few years' time scandalised some and amused others. Those who feared the future and pressed for leniency were ignored.

Britain had received the unofficial news with relief rather than jubilation. Bristol was quiet on that November morning, though crowds waited outside the newspaper offices. When the end of the war was confirmed the town erupted into celebrations. Paint was scraped from dimmed street lamps, all the bells were rung repeatedly, bonfires threw flames and smoke into the air and Willow, Jasmine and Clara went to the Tramway Centre with Sam. He forgot his grudges for today. He had put on the blue hospital suit of a wounded soldier which he must have kept hidden and his back was patted so hard and so often as he limped along that Clara muttered he'd need a new spine as well as a leg if they didn't give over. He could have got riotously drunk on the amount of beer he was offered had his mother and sisters not kept a stern eye on him. As it was he was only merry. People who had never met before and never would again, kissed, hugged, even copulated, leaving women pregnant by unknown partners, and fifty barefoot urchins in rags marched up Park Street, banging biscuit tins and carrying bunting.

And on the day of frantic joy a thousand people died of influenza. There had been relatively minor epidemics for a couple of years and Clara, Willow and Jasmine had caught it. Many people had been stricken and some had died. Well, that was to be expected. Flu was with them every year and in the aged a lung infection turned to pneumonia and eased

426

them into death. It would pass, people said each time and, of course, it had.

Then there came a second wave, more severe, far more deadly than the previous because, to everyone's horror, it chose the young and healthy for death. Poor nourishment during the war was blamed. Some called it the German Plague, others Spanish Flu. Willow continued to work, fulfilling the orders given her by the Maddisons and their friends, thankful that she could once again concentrate on her dream. She carried the last gown to the house on the tram and fitted Frances, who stood unusually still then fainted.

Brayton came hurrying in at Willow's call. 'I knew it,' she stormed. 'I knew she'd caught it.'

'Influenza?' asked Willow.

'I told the mistress, but she wouldn't listen. No one else has it here. Poor Miss Frances, she's just not fit to resist, she's not herself these days.'

An understatement if ever there was one, thought Willow, helping Brayton with Frances, a role she slipped into without even thinking about it. Looking down at her former mistress, raddled by drink, extremely ill, she consigned her grievances to the past and pitied her. She left soon after and within days had developed a sore throat, followed by a slight cough, then fever.

'You've got it again,' said Clara accusingly. 'That Maddison woman must have given it to you.'

Clara was being less than fair, but Willow knew that the end of the war had brought back torturing memories of Joe and she was edgy. She had surged along with the celebrating crowds, enjoying a drink, glad like everyone else that the long, grim, murderous struggle had ended, knowing that most of those who laughed and cheered around her had lost someone. They hid their shared grief as they gave full rein to their rejoicing, but at the end of the day each reveller had to go home and face reality and as the survivors returned from abroad Clara found the death of her son harder to bear.

Willow had developed resistance to flu during her earlier illness, and recovered well and quickly, but not before Sam succumbed. For some victims, the disease needed only twenty-four hours to complete its destruction. One day Sam had the flu, the next he was dead.

Clara was stunned with disbelief. 'Both of them gone,' she whispered over and over. 'My two sons gone. To think that Sam went through all that an' came home to die.' She turned on Willow suddenly. 'It's your bloody fault! You and those bloody Maddisons. You've killed my boy between you.'

Willow made allowances for her mother's anguished grief, but the words hurt her to the point where she wanted to drown in weeping. She didn't weep, nor did Clara, not where they could be observed. The gentle, tender-hearted Jasmine wept for them both.

Alfred was given leave to attend his brother's funeral. He arrived at the last minute in his uniform and stood to attention by Sam's grave. He looked tired and dispirited. Back at home there were no funeral meats. So many were struggling to come to terms with this new horror, so many were mourning the newly dead, and if they were still healthy they feared to rub shoulders with anyone who might be carrying the dreadful disease. Marigold arrived, looking beautiful in black, though even she was showing signs of strain.

'You aren't ill, are you?' asked Willow.

'No. I had the flu last year. The doctors reckon it's the same strain this time only worse, so those who had it mildly are protected.' She left as soon as she could. 'Sorry, Mum, I've got to get back. A couple of my friends are ill.'

'Have you taken up nursin'?' asked Clara. 'Aren't we as important as your friends?'

'Of course, Mum, but you don't need me. They do.'

Willow stood at the front door with Marigold who said urgently, 'Willow, Alfred was in London. He called without warning and soon realised what I was doing. Do you think he'll tell Mum?'

'I don't know. I thought you didn't care about what people thought,' said Willow.

'I don't. I'm making such a damn good living and I've no intention of giving it up, but I'd rather Mum didn't know because she's bound to make a ghastly fuss. She might even turn up and embarrass someone and I can't put up with that for my clients.'

'Are they all you care about?' demanded Willow.

Marigold peered up the road to see if there was a sign of the taxi. 'I hope it arrives soon. I can't afford to miss my train.'

'An important client expected?'

Marigold ignored the irony in her sister's voice. 'Yes.'

'I see.'

'Damn it, Willow, I do care about Mum. I wouldn't want to hurt her, really.'

'That's a mercy. Who's ill? Or was that just an excuse?'

'Carmen and Maisie are both down with flu.'

'You really are worried about them!'

'You needn't sound so snooty! I don't want them to peg it.'

'No, of course not. Sorry.'

'Not as sorry as I am. Two of the best girls in the business! I need them.'

Alfred was drinking tea and trying to sit still beneath Clara's gaze. Neither he nor Willow could tell what was going through their mother's mind. Alfred looked anxious. When she finally spoke, he flinched. 'You're the only boy I've got now.'

'I know, Mum.'

'Is that all you've got to say?'

'I'm terribly tired.'

'Well, at least you can go to sleep and wake up again, not like our Joe and Sam. They're gone for good. They'll never wake up.'

429

'I know, Mum.'

'Don't keep sayin' that!'

Alfred gave way to a flash of rage. 'Don't keep telling me things I already know! My brothers are dead and I'm alive. That's what's making you so angry, isn't it?'

Jasmine hurried from one to the other as if she could block the bitter words with her body.

'All right, Mum!' Alfred was yelling now. 'I'm sorry I haven't been killed. I'm sorry I haven't even been wounded. I'm sorry I'm still alive. Would you like me to die? Would that help? I'll jump off the suspension bridge, shall I?'

'Oh, don't, don't!' implored Jasmine.

Alfred looked at his younger sister and his wrath subsided. He stared down into the fire as if he might find consolation there.

Clara said, 'I'm sorry. Really I am. I don't know why I say such things.'

Alfred looked up. 'Oh, Mum, I'm sorry, too. I shall miss my brothers. I loved them, you know.' He got up and went to Clara's side, kneeling by her, his arms around her waist. 'I'm grieving too, Mum.'

Clara looked down at him, the least loved of her sons, and her hand went out to stroke his hair. She bent to kiss him as healing tears began to trickle down her face and mingled with Alfred's.

Jasmine stood still, hands clasped, watching them, her lips moving. Willow wondered if she was praying.

Alfred returned to duty without mentioning Marigold. Willow put aside her endless sewing and joined Jasmine and Clara and all those who could walk to help their sick and dying neighbours. She bought as much chicken as she could get, at black market prices, and made huge pans of broth for the convalescents. In some houses whole families lay in bed. Some lived, others died of the pneumonia which followed this particular strain of flu; survival seemed a haphazard throw of the dice.

By the end of the epidemic it was said that half the world had had flu and twenty-one million had perished from it.

Among the dead was Edgar's fiancée.

Chapter Twenty-three

By the early part of 1919 Willow had saved enough to rent the two upper floors of an office in Wine Street, with a separate side door. Alfred occupied a small flat in the attic where he was happier than he had ever been. At night the place was his alone and he used it to work, practising his skills in designing and sewing.

'Fancy a man in a woman's dressmakin' business,' Clara said. She seemed to have forgotten that her youngest son had been to the front, had sustained a wound which meant that he couldn't stretch his left arm fully, and behaved as dutifully and lovingly as any son could while he worked at helping his sister to build a loyal clientèle in Bristol.

Bridget and Dora had joyously returned to work for Willow and shared a bedroom in the Barton Hill house where Clara spoiled them. 'No nonsense about those two,' she declared. 'Nice down-to-earth girls. No fancy notions.'

'I hope I can work for you always,' Alfred said to Willow when he moved in. 'Even when you're rich and famous.'

Willow smiled. '*When*? You mean if, don't you?'

'I know what I mean.'

She laughed. 'I'm relying on you to stay. Do you like Riches for our trading name? It includes you, of course.'

Alfred was overwhelmed with pleasure. 'I'll work until I drop.'

'No need for that, little brother.'

He took exception to the term and ruffled her hair which she had had cut in the shorter style.

It was hot for spring and she worked by an open window. The crowded street below was noisy with horse-drawn and

432

motor traffic which frequently got jammed in the narrow way, sending the drivers into paroxysms of fury. People hurried to and fro in the dusty air which was sometimes malodorous. She enjoyed it all, feeling part of the great commercial life which flowed through Bristol.

A ring on the door was answered by Dora who returned pop-eyed. 'Here's a ladyship come to see you, Willow. I mean, it's Lady Somervell.' For a moment Willow had thought poor nervous Dora had been about to curtsey. Her eyes met Lady Somervell's which were bright with amusement.

'Shall we go?' asked Bridget, rising.

'Not unless Miss Riches wishes you to,' said Lady Somervell. 'I am here on a business visit.'

'I'll make coffee,' said Bridget. Dora followed her, feeling unequal to coping with this ultra-grand visitor without her sister's support.

'Please sit down,' Willow invited. 'How may I help you?'

Lady Somervell took Dora's seat near the window. For a moment she gazed down at the hurrying people below. 'It must be fascinating to have a view like this. Mynster is so quiet.'

'I don't think you'd change, though,' Willow said drily.

Lady Somervell laughed. 'No.' Her daughter Mary resembled her but in the mother's case the white skin was touched with rose, the eyes more lively, brows and hair darker brown, tinged now with silver, and the whole demeanour far more animated. 'Now to the purpose of my call. I do not think that the season will hold its usual pleasure this year – it is too soon after the war.' She paused. 'However, there will be some gaiety and I am hoping that my daughter and my son's wife will take part in it, though at the moment they seem indifferent to the idea. My daughter has always preferred country life and now she has her twin sons she hardly goes anywhere. Her husband was killed.' She paused again. 'My son, thank God, was spared, but he has suffered – is suffering. The girls need a little fun to take them out of themselves.' Her voice grew brisker. 'We all do. I know you have worked for my daughter and Mrs Bickford and Lady Radcliffe, though you may be unaware of their present circumstances?'

'I had heard,' said Willow quietly.

'Such tragedies! But I should not complain. So many have suffered to a much greater degree.'

'Yes.'

Lady Somervell looked at her keenly. 'You lost someone, my dear?'

'My two brothers. One survived without a leg, then died of the Spanish influenza.'

'Oh, how dreadful!'

'Yes. Mum keeps going, but she's different.'

'We all are. The damnable war! But we had to fight it, you know. We had to fight for what was right.'

Willow said nothing.

'Would you come to Mynster for a few days?'

'To Mynster?'

'Yes, please. In my opinion there is nothing like new gowns to cheer women. I am susceptible myself. Do come, Miss Riches. Your work has acquired an excellent reputation, and you are an artist as well as a designer. Could you perhaps bring colour swatches and a few drawings. Will you visit us?' Would I walk there over hot cinders? thought Willow. 'We would make you very welcome. I have made do with my old stuff as long as it was patriotic, but now I can let myself go. I shall be looking for a whole new wardrobe. How about the week after next? I shall send you an invitation, and if you decide favourably, you must let me know the time of your arrival and you will be fetched from the station.'

'Thank you, Lady Somervell. I am happy to accept your invitation, but I can drive myself.'

'You drive? How clever you are! It is an odd sensation, is it not, to move along without horses? I shall never learn to handle a motor car.'

Willow stood up as Lady Somervell rose to leave. 'I'm sorry the coffee didn't materialise.'

'It is quite all right. I am on my way to the Maddison house on the Downs. I shall lunch there.'

Willow took a deep breath and said, 'I must tell you that I was once employed by Mrs Maddison.'

'I have been told, my dear. Mrs Bickford talks about you.'

'She does?' Willow was startled.

'You were her personal maid, were you not? And have recently made frocks for her and Violet.'

'Yes.'

'So you probably know of her indisposition?'

'Yes.' So that was how they described an alcoholic family member.

Willow toyed with the idea of telling the countess exactly how she had begun in the Maddison household, then decided that there could be too much honesty.

'Then I will expect you at Mynster,' said Lady Somervell.

Willow received a formal invitation and smiled at Clara's astringent reaction. 'A house party? Does that mean you sleep there? I hope your nighties are grand enough. What do they want you for?'

'Work, Mum.'

'Dressmakin', d'you mean?'

'Yes, Mum.' She had never managed to persuade Clara to use the word designer.

Lady Somervell had added a note to the invitation: 'Do bring tennis things with you. It looks as if this spell of fine weather will hold.'

Tennis things! She had never held a racquet in her life and wasn't about to make it obvious to anyone. She wondered which of her acquaintances would be present, how much work they would give her, what sort of an atmosphere she would find. The war had ended only a few months ago and sometimes it seemed that the entire land was blanketed in sorrow – or maybe it appeared that way to her because of her mother's enduring grief.

Willow paid a visit to London at Marigold's request. Her

435

sister, who had been asleep, strolled into her living room, yawning. Even in her state of weary deshabille she looked vital. 'Good lord, Willow, what on earth do you want?' was her laconic greeting.

'I thought you invited me.'

'Yes, but not at dawn.'

'It's twelve o'clock.'

'Is that all! My God, I was up until five this morning.'

'Plenty of customers?' Willow asked acerbically.

'Clients,' Marigold automatically corrected. 'And it isn't a bit of use your trying to make me feel guilty. Well, since you're here, I suppose I had better gather the girls together. They want new gowns.'

'Don't be too eager! After all, I've only left my work to travel up to see you.'

'Just to see me?'

'Well, no, I need materials I can't get in Bristol at present. And orders. Good ones. The Wine Street shop is picking up nicely, but I'm after as many customers as I can get.'

'Will you be coming back to London?'

'I hope so, some time. Mum is really devastated by everything that's happened. Losing Sam was the final blow. Sometimes she sits for hours doing nothing, just staring.'

Marigold's eyes had opened wide. 'Good God. Is she going out of her mind? I hope she keeps away from me. I can't abide crazy people.'

'She's not people, she's your mother!'

'You know what I mean,' said Marigold impatiently. 'Look here, sis, if you have to put her away I'll chip in and help with finances, so that she won't have to go to – you know – some ghastly loony bin.'

'Well, that's really sweet of you!'

'You should know by now your sarcasm is wasted on me.'

'Do you make a lot of money?'

Marigold smiled. 'A lot!'

'What do you do with it?'

'I save and invest it. I don't intend to end up in a back-street slum.'

'Maybe you'll get married.'

Marigold laughed. 'Maybe I will, though there's no possibility of that at present. After all, why should I? I have a very comfortable home, maids, a cook, money, and can enjoy love-making when I want to. It isn't always just business.'

'I see,' said Willow, though she didn't see at all. Marigold was an enigma to her. 'Mum isn't *that* bad, and if I have anything to do with it she never will be.'

'What do you intend to do? Bring her to London?' Marigold looked alarmed.

'No, she loves her house. It holds all her memories.'

'Might you stay in Bristol for good?'

'I'll be there while I'm needed.'

'It's you who's the crazy one. Women are crying out for couture clothes and they come to London to look for them. You could make a fortune.'

Maisie came in with a tray of coffee and toast. She looked as neat and pretty as the day Willow had first seen her. She had also kept her appearance of innocence. Willow watched her with interest. 'You look well, Maisie.'

'I am,' she said, 'very well, thank you.' Then she left.

Marigold grinned. 'She's a marvel. I'm thankful we were able to become full partners. You should see how many clients she has.' She rolled her eyes and Willow found herself laughing, and was exasperated with herself for doing so.

After measuring the girls she called on Mrs Grigson. 'Come in, Miss Riches. It's nice to see you, though I hope you aren't after rooms. Yours are let on a long lease. A nice officer's wife and children. He's dead, but she keeps going wonderfully well.'

Willow explained how matters stood at home and Mrs Grigson tutted. 'Your poor mother. She's not the only one who's had her nerves ruined, not by a long chalk. The war's got a lot to answer for, and now it's ended I can't seem to figure out what it was about.'

Willow's final call was on Steven. They had seldom

managed to meet since Willow moved, though they had written. Maybe he had found someone else by now.

He hadn't. The shop looked different. Some of the paint was fresh, the books were classified and stood neatly on new shelving and there was a safe ladder for customers to reach the top shelves and a couple of seats for long-stay browsers. Piles of books on a centre table were offered at reduced prices, an old locked case contained antiquarian volumes. The film of dust proved that Steven maintained the atmosphere beloved of dedicated book buyers.

A young man was seated behind a desk, reading. At her entry he carefully placed a bookmark between the leaves. 'Can I help you, or do you just want to wander?'

'I wondered if Mr Kerslake was in.'

Steven came from the back room with a rush. 'It is you! Come in, come in, do. Eustace, this is Miss Riches.' They shook hands and the young man said, politely, 'How d'you do?'

In Steven's living-room Willow said, 'He seems a rather superior fellow.'

'He's one of Mr Mason's great-nephews. He's seventeen, mad about books. I'm keeping him on full-time.'

'Is the shop doing that well?'

'It's pretty good. I've bought a van and take stuff from people who aren't so well off since the war. There are quite a few house clearances too. I'm getting to know the big dealers and they buy from me.'

'It all sounds exciting.'

'It's fascinating.'

'Will you ever give up the shop and just be a dealer?'

Steven laughed. 'No, thank you. I want to live surrounded by books and I enjoy meeting my customers, however little they have to spend. Some have become friends. Eustace feels the same way. But that's enough about me. What are you up to these days?'

Willow told him and he frowned. 'Does that mean you still won't be working in London?'

'I thought that was obvious.'

'Yes,' he agreed gloomily, 'it is. I wish someone else would take some responsibility from your shoulders.'

'They can't at present.'

While they talked, Steven bustled about, making tea; he produced a chocolate sponge cake and Willow took a bite. 'This is good. Don't tell me you made it!'

'No, I'm a very plain cook. There's a young widow in the next street who's been left with two small children. She bakes for a living.'

'The war again?'

'The war again. Is there anyone whose life hasn't been worsened by it?'

'A few profiteers? Munitions makers? Some are probably sorry it's over.'

'Parasites,' growled Steven.

After tea they lit up cigarettes and smoked for a while in silence which was punctuated now and then by the shop bell and the murmurs of customers.

'Don't you want to go and see what's happening?' Willow asked.

'No, I would much rather stay and look at you. You're a sight for sore eyes.'

'Thanks.'

He laughed, then threw his cigarette into the grate. 'Have you changed your mind yet, Willow?'

'What about?' she asked, though she knew very well.

'About marrying me.'

'I'm sorry, I still feel the same.'

He said, 'So do I. You like books, don't you? I would make you happy, darling. I would, truly.'

He was getting intense and she said gently, 'Steven, I'm not going to marry you.'

'Don't say that! It's too final.'

'It is final.'

'There *is* someone else. There must be.' He pulled her to her feet and held her in a restricting embrace. 'Tell me the truth, please, don't let me go on hoping uselessly.'

'I have told you the truth, Steven, but you don't want to hear it. You don't want to believe it.'

'No, I don't.' He kissed her forehead lightly, then the tip of her nose. The soft touch of his lips was pleasant and the memory of their love-making warmed her body. Then he claimed her mouth voraciously, holding it with his, pressing her lips painfully on to her teeth.

She pushed hard against his chest without effect, and when he eventually released her she stepped back from him. 'You had no right to do that.'

'No right!' His voice rose. 'No right, after what we've been to each other? Have you forgotten? Have you forgotten Paris? Don't you remember the good times we had?'

She dropped back into the chair. 'Of course I do. How could I forget? We had some wonderful days.'

'What about the wonderful nights?'

'Yes, I enjoyed those too.'

He knelt in front of her. 'Darling, I'm sorry I was rough. I never want to hurt you.' He held her hands in his. 'I love you more than ever, but please tell me if there is someone else. You owe me the truth.'

Willow looked down into his troubled eyes. She said, 'All right, Steven. Yes, I am in love—'

'I knew it! I've lost you after all.'

'Yes.'

'Are you engaged to him?'

'He doesn't love me.'

'You're ready to spoil what could be a good life with me for a man who doesn't love you? Is he married?'

'No, I can't explain.'

'Don't tell me he prefers men!'

'What? Oh, no!' She laughed.

'What's so bloody funny?'

'Nothing, I suppose. No, he likes women.'

'But he doesn't like you?'

'Yes, he does. Please stop this. I don't want to say any more.'

'Why not?'

'I find the subject too painful.'

Steven sank back on his heels. 'Too painful! Willow,' he took her hands in his, 'let me heal your pain. I've so much to offer you.'

'I intend to devote myself to my work.'

'Don't mock me!'

'I'm not, oh, I'm not. Steven, my dear, I really do have this urge, this compulsion, to make my dream of becoming a couturière come true.'

'But you'd give it all up for this man?'

She thought for a moment. 'Do you know, I don't believe I would.'

'He might have other ideas.'

'It doesn't matter, does it, since he's inaccessible to me.'

'Does he know you love him?'

'I've never told him so.'

'I'd let you do whatever you wanted. Darling Willow, we could live in a house of your choosing. You needn't come near the shop if you don't want to. You can follow your own career. I'd stay out of your way.'

She was angry. 'I hate it when you debase yourself!'

'Debased, am I?' He was angry too. He rose and dusted the knees of his trousers, slapping them with a heavy hand. 'Debased! Because I want to make you happy.'

'No,' she said. 'I used the wrong word. It takes a real man to act in a humble way sometimes.'

He was not pacified. 'How many men have you met since our Buddleigh Manor days? You couldn't have been in love with anyone when we went to Paris. If you had been you wouldn't have allowed me to make love to you. What's happened since then? I got the impression once that you were stuck on Edgar Maddison.' He must have read some unguarded message in her eyes. 'Don't tell me I've lost you to *him*, after all that family did to you? And to me! Of course, I see now. You love him and he'll never lower himself to you. I never took you for a fool, Willow.'

'I'm sorry,' she said miserably. 'I hate to hurt you.'

'You're the one who's likely to be hurt the most. I feel sorry for you.'

She left soon after, stung by the truth of Steven's outburst, feeling mean and cruel and mortified.

Willow stopped her car at the crest of a hill to look down at Mynster. It was intrinsically beautiful and the brick wall, long since mellowed to a dull pink, acquired an added lustre in the warm sunshine. As yet she had no idea in what capacity she would be received. Well, no matter. Business was business, as Marigold would have said. She put the car into gear and drove on, wondering if Edgar would be one of the guests.

In the past five months she had seen him once, in December of last year when he called unexpectedly. He had driven her to the country where they had stopped beneath trees. The weather had turned mild. It was raining and drops splattered on to the car roof. On the short journey they had enquired about one another's health in a polite and formal way, but when the car stopped Willow had waited, her heart hammering, for what he would say.

'Do you know that my fiancée died of flu?'

'Yes. I'm sorry.' She was, but she couldn't dispel the thought that he was free again.

'I was sorry too. She was a sweet little thing. She had such a short life.'

'One of my brothers survived the war with a dreadful wound, then in twenty-four hours—' She stopped, unable to go on.

He put his hand over hers. 'How ghastly for you. It was such a cruel epidemic.' They fell silent then he said, 'I dare say you know that my sister's husband survived the fighting in a shocking state?'

'Yes, I heard.'

'Hearing is not seeing. The war! The bloody war! How is your mother? And your little sister – Jasmine, isn't it?'

'They're well – more or less. Mum can't get over the horrors.'

'Who can?'

Still she had waited, though she felt a leaden weight in her stomach as the conventional conversation drifted on. Didn't he want to talk about the past? She felt she would go anywhere with him, do anything. Her love, which she had been forced by necessity to dampen down, flared into rampant life.

'How is Marigold?' he asked.

'Well.'

'Still successful?'

'Very.'

'Does your mother know yet what she does?'

'I don't think so, though I sometimes wonder if she guesses and prefers not to talk about it. She never says much about her these days. Marigold visits. She's discreet, I'll say that for her. In Bristol she dresses plainly and leaves Mum money, not enough to make her suspicious, but actually, she gives me extra. When things were really difficult just after the war she was generous.'

'She's a nice kid.'

'Yes.' Willow didn't care for his tone.

'A nice kid,' he had repeated, turning to her and brushing her cheek with gentle fingers. Again she had waited, aching for his hand to move, to caress her as it did in her dreams. 'You're nice too, Willow.'

Then he had started the car and delivered her home, leaving her feeling sick with unrequited desire.

The party at Mynster consisted mainly of family. Lady Somervell was in the hall and welcomed Willow personally, half a dozen of the dogs frisking round her feet; a couple of others, older and more sedate, watched with tails thumping on the oak floor. 'I've given you the blue room overlooking the park, though some of it has been ploughed up to help the war effort. It nearly broke my husband's heart to see a centuries-old sward being desecrated. "Sward" was his word.' She smiled. 'Your room is large enough for you to entertain clients if you wish. Everyone is so looking forward to seeing your new designs.'

In spite of her lovely bedroom, Willow still wondered if she was to be relegated to the position of servant, an ambiguous one perhaps, resembling a governess's, expected to eat upstairs. But Lady Somervell was not another Mrs Maddison. A maid came to tell her she was expected downstairs at seven-thirty for drinks. She had brought with her a frock she had finished quickly for the occasion. Lately, she had needed to restrain her imagination, designing clothes for the wives of respectable shopkeepers and doctors that would be admired, but not cause comment. Here, she could let her ideas run riot. In spite of the war so recently fought on their lands the French fashion trade had recovered fast – in fact, it had never been allowed to lapse entirely – and names Willow remembered, along with new ones, were exciting the world of haute couture. Ankles were now definitely the thing, an innovation which made the slender-legged ecstatic, while annoying the unfortunate females with heavy legs. Madeleine Vionnet's first opening had been ill-timed and war had destroyed her business, but she had reopened, financed by the husband of a leading beauty. Willow wished that Englishmen took such an interest in clothes. *Vogue* kept her up to date and it was useless now for the conventional to insist that lip colour was used only by harlots. Helena Rubinstein was becoming well-known for the delicacy of her face-powder; Poiret was famous for his banishment of the viciously restricting corset; Erté was another whom she admired, especially for his brilliant black and white fashion designs. One day she would issue booklets of her own drawings, just as some of the leading couturiers did.

Her bedroom was furnished in many shades of blue, faded by the action of sun and time and blurred by years of soot from the fire. Willow got out her drawing book and water colours and reproduced some of the heavenly colours. When the maid arrived to help her dress for dinner she washed her paint brushes quickly. 'Sorry to keep you waiting,' she informed the astonished girl who was unused to apologies from guests.

'It's quite all right, madam, only if people are late his lordship gets cross.'

This caused Willow to leap quickly in and out of the bath, before she put on her gown. The maid gasped as the ivory silk slid over Willow's body. 'It's so beautiful, madam. I've not seen another like it anywhere and my master and mistress entertain lots of people. You'll be the envy of all the ladies.'

Willow brushed her hair until it shone and the maid put her headdress in place. She surveyed herself before going downstairs. Her dress had classic simplicity and was skilfully cut so that it flowed over her body like water. On her head was a circlet of the same ivory silk holding two dark rose feathers. Over her shoulders she threw a shawl of the latest Eastern style, of varying shades of pink, ranging from pale to deep rose and holding the merest hint of lavender. Her stockings were beige silk and her shoes were rose with a discreet sprinkling of lavender diamanté. Her make-up was applied with immense discretion. She had no idea how progressive Lady Somervell was, but downstairs she was greeted by her hostess with a truly welcoming smile which encompassed her whole outfit.

The others were in the library. Lady Somervell said, 'I believe you know most of us, Miss Riches? My daughter, Mrs James Maddison, Lady Radcliffe, and Mrs Bickford and her husband. And this is Winifred, the youngest of our guests.'

Winifred had fulfilled her early promise of beauty, but it was marred by a sullen expression as she stared at Willow. 'I remember her. She is my dressmaker,' she said in a tone which brought colour to Lady Somervell's face.

'Miss Riches is a well-known couturière,' she said.

Winifred scowled, but remained silent, while Willow glowed at the compliment.

'And Winifred's parents,' continued Lady Somervell,

'Mr and Mrs Maddison.' Mr Maddison looked at her appreciatively. He had seen his former servant only at very rare intervals and couldn't remember her. Mrs Maddison was under no illusion. Etiquette demanded that she greet Willow courteously, but her voice held no warmth and her annoyance showed in her eyes. 'I was not aware that Miss Riches was to be a guest,' she said.

'Oh, did I not tell you? She is here to show us her latest designs.'

'We have already purchased frocks from Miss Riches,' said Mrs Maddison.

'Yes, but the season, don't you know. Mary hates London, but I should like her to have a pretty wardrobe suitable for the country and I thought that the rest of us might treat ourselves. The Riches designs are so clever.'

Frances looked up, already halfway drunk. 'Ultra-smart, my dears, *ravishing*. Surely you want your daughters to look ravishing in London, Mumsie?'

Mrs Maddison set her lips and Mr Bickford's greeting was icy.

Lady Somervell introduced others, but Willow stopped taking in her words because Edgar entered, walking fast, apologising for being a little late. He stopped as he saw Willow.

'You two know each other?' said Lady Somervell.

'We have met,' acknowledged Edgar.

Willow held out her hand. On one slender wrist she wore an ivory bracelet. This, with small rose-coloured earrings, was her only adornment. Edgar took her hand in his. For a moment she thought he was going to kiss it, then he shook it lightly. 'How pleasant to see you again, Miss Riches.'

Willow felt herself shrivel at his cool greeting.

Conversation was resumed, though Mrs Maddison gave Willow an angry stare from the striped satin couch she occupied.

'I didn't know you would be here,' said Edgar.

'You made that perfectly clear. I'm sorry if I intrude.'

'You do nothing of the damned sort!'

'You're right, I don't! Why should I?'

'True. Are you a guest?'

'What do you think?'

He looked her up and down. 'You're lovelier than ever. I didn't think that was possible. Did you design your frock? Don't answer that, I know you did. You're still in Bristol, aren't you? Will you open up again in London?'

'Which question would you like answered first?' she asked, then the butler announced that dinner was served.

They filed into the hall where they were joined by a man who must be the Somervells' son. Violet went to him swiftly and slid her arm through his. 'Just in time, darling.'

He smiled down at her. At least, Willow assumed from his grimace that he was smiling. His face had been so horribly burned that it was difficult to read any expression. He had lost one of his eyes and the hollow was covered by a mass of white scar tissue. His hands were damaged, too, all the fingers of one hand missing, and only two remaining on the other. Violet was seated next to him in order, Willow saw later, that she might help him with his food.

Willow was seated between Mr Bickford and a young lieutenant, a professional soldier, who had just missed the war because of his youth.

'I say, Miss Riches,' he enthused, 'if you will allow me to say so, I think your frock is absolutely splendid.'

'Thank you. I designed it myself.' No harm in advertising, she decided. He was bound to get married soon and she could gain another client.

The young man begged her to call him Spindle – 'shortened from spindle-shanks, the name I acquired at school on account of my thin legs, don't you know?' He then blushed crimson at his reference to legs. 'Do beg your pardon, most humbly,' he continued, making matters worse.

Willow was amused, but hid it, and he changed the subject. 'I feel an absolute fraud sitting here,' he murmured, 'with George's face so badly burnt and Mary's husband killed in France.'

'You should be glad you missed the awfulness of the trenches,' said Willow.

'Do you think so? I cannot agree. I was looking forward to seeing part of the show.'

'It wasn't a show!' said Willow. She sounded angry because she had just seen Edgar bend his head the better to listen to a girl of about eighteen, brown-haired and pretty, who was seated next to him.

'That's Edgar Maddison,' said Spindle. 'This side of his face looks perfect, though he has a scar on the other. He was lost, believed killed, then he came back.' He sounded wistful.

'A lot didn't,' said Willow. 'Maybe you would have been one of them.'

'A chap would think it honourable to die for King, country and empire.'

Willow sighed. He mistakenly thought she was bored and said quickly, 'Apologise for bringing up the war, Miss Riches. Do you hunt?'

'Hunt? Oh, no, I'm afraid not.'

'Not all ladies have the stomach for it. Do you play tennis? There's a very decent court here.'

'I'm sorry, but I don't,' said Willow, wondering which subject he would dredge up next.

'Do you care for outdoor sports at all?' he asked desperately.

Willow gave the matter serious thought. 'When I was a child I played whip-top and hopscotch.'

'Oh, now you are making fun of me.' Spindle laughed heartily, boyishly, infectiously, and made her laugh, too. She caught Edgar's eye and saw an expression which made her happy. Jealousy! Did he care for her a little? The idea lent her an attractive sparkle.

Frances, who was seated opposite her, peered across a bowl of flowers. 'I love your gown, Willow.'

'Thank you.'

Winifred leaned forward and looked at her sister. 'I hear that Miss Riches calls her gowns names.' She spoke deliberately loudly.

Willow said calmly, 'I merely follow the example of famous designers.'

'Oh? Who?' demanded Winifred.

'Shut up,' snapped Frances. 'I don't know why you are having dinner with us. I'm sure when I was your age I stayed at home and ate with the governess.'

'Perhaps you were too naughty to be allowed out,' said Winifred.

'Frances is right,' said Violet. 'If you make a nuisance of yourself you won't be invited again.'

'I will, won't I, Lady Somervell?' Without waiting for an answer she said, 'What is the name of your frock, Miss Riches?'

Willow thought swiftly. '*Ice floe*,' she said.

'Flowing where?' asked Winifred.

'Floe, ninny,' said Edgar. 'Moving ice.'

Winifred was furious. 'I don't believe that others call their gowns names.'

Willow, already suffering from strain, lost her temper but kept her voice low as she launched into a dissertation on fabrics, painting and design, which included the names of Poiret, Vionnet, Lepape, Diaghilev, Barbier and several others. Winifred fell into a furious silence. Willow finished speaking and realised that everyone was watching and listening and wished she could get up and run, that she had never come, that she could wring Winifred's neck.

Lady Somervell said, 'How interesting, Miss Riches, I had no notion that fashion design needed so much knowledge. I shall be most interested at some time to hear more.'

Conversation buzzed again, but it took a tremendous effort on Willow's part to talk to the young man, while Mr Bickford, who had totally ignored her, seemed to emanate a sharper frostiness.

On the following morning Willow dressed with care in a

cream skirt and blouse with a navy blazer. Her shoes were white low-heeled kid leather. Almost all the men had gone to look at the refurbishment of the stables, neglected during the war when all available horses were needed for the army.

'I kept the brood mares, of course,' Lord Somervell had informed everyone last night, 'and have invested in a superb stallion. I am also seeding the lawn which was dug up for vegetables – damnably stupid to have destroyed it, but it appeared to be patriotic at the time – and soon the place will be as it always was.' His eyes had flickered briefly over the guests, over Mary, over Violet and his son, and over Frances. 'As it always was,' he had repeated doggedly.

They took the older dogs out with them, leaving the half-grown and the new puppies to frolic round the ladies. Lady Somervell laughed, 'They'll all be going to the gamekeeper soon to learn some manners. I enjoy letting them misbehave a little.'

Mrs Maddison opened her mouth to speak, then closed it. She drew her skirts aside when the dogs came anywhere near her. She made her loathing so obvious that Willow wondered if Lady Somervell wasn't being just a little bit provocative in allowing the dogs so much licence. They were banished when the ladies gathered in the conservatory where plants climbed the walls and clung to the glassed-in roof, creating a green bower.

'Listen, everybody,' said Lady Somervell, 'for those of you who do not know, Miss Riches is a couturière. She has brought colour swatches and her latest designs, and now the men are out of the way we can examine them and decide what we would like. We all deserve to indulge ourselves after the past four years.' She glanced up as someone wandered in. 'Edgar, you are not welcome. This is for women only. Why not join the men?'

'All right, if you say so.' The dark-haired girl, his partner of the previous evening, whose name was Kitty Martin, blushed when he smiled at her. Willow had brought a large folio and the designs and swatches were handed round and greeted with varying reactions.

'This is heavenly,' declared Miss Martin. 'Just the thing for me.'

'Let me see.' Violet peered over her shoulder. 'It is a very pretty style. What colour would you choose?'

Kitty turned to Willow who said, 'Periwinkle blue. No belt, the unbroken line will give you height.'

Frances said in a desultory manner, 'How about me, Willow? What should I wear?'

She regarded her former mistress. Her delicate, blonde loveliness was fading. Her complexion was muddy, her eyes bloodshot and bleary, and her mouth had a permanent downward slant at the corners. Her hair was thin and greasy. In that moment Willow, who was not very good at hating, anyway, came irrevocably to terms with what Frances had done to her in the past. If Steven's parents were correct in saying that sin brought its own punishment, then Frances was being punished.

'Dark colours always suited you,' she said. 'Perhaps a midnight blue?'

'I'll have this design,' said Frances.

'No, I think not.' Willow spoke softly. 'That's suitable only for diaphanous material.'

'I like stuff that's light and airy!'

'It is, of course, your choice, but mine would be this.' Willow found a sketch. 'The dress has a tailored appearance, yet it's deceptively full. It would give you elegance and comfort combined.'

'Comfort?' Frances frowned and Willow waited apprehensively. 'What do you think, Mother?'

Willow took the book to Mrs Maddison who was seated upright in a wicker-work chair. She stared at the drawings for so long that Willow expected a cutting remark. Instead she said, her voice holding grudging respect, 'Miss Riches is quite right. I should have it made up in navy.'

'With a few touches of light blue?' suggested Willow.

Mrs Maddison nodded. Later she chose a tailored suit for herself, to be worn with a white piqué waistcoat.

Violet pored over the colours and designs. She had gained

in beauty, her features refined by grief, a gentler look in her dark eyes, her pride and feeling of superiority submerged in her need to care for her grievously wounded, dependent husband. She chose several outfits. Kitty ordered more and other guests, impressed by the fact that Willow had made her own costume and last night's lovely gown, excited by the general air of opulence and acquisition which had been patriotically stilled during the war, were eager to join in. By the time the men returned, Willow's order book was so full she had begun to wonder how she could complete the garments in time.

Lady Somervell asked, 'What is your London address, my dear? We shall all be in town soon.'

'My London address? I will let you know – all of you,' Willow smiled. 'I've been residing in Bristol with my mother while she needed me.'

'Has she been ill?' asked a guest.

'We lost two of my brothers.' There were murmurs of understanding. 'However, I shall shortly be returning to London.'

Willow wondered what was she going to do now? Mum was only happier because she had Dora and Bridget whom she treated like daughters. How could Willow take them away from her? Would they want to stay in the provinces? Yet she must make a success of this magnificent new beginning. There must be a way out of this. She would make one.

Chapter Twenty-four

Willow was awakened by the early morning sunlight slanting across her bed. She lay for a moment, savouring the thought of the gratifying number of orders, then she remembered Edgar and his attention to the pretty Kitty Martin who clearly enjoyed having him beside her. Willow had hoped that he would find a way to come to her side and at least talk to her, but he had kept well away. Card tables had been set up in the library and some of the party had settled down to bridge. Most of the remaining men, including Edgar, had gone to the billiard room, leaving the other guests talking in desultory fashion. Willow had gone to bed at midnight. She was disgusted with herself as she remembered her futile wait. It gave her the impetus to leap out of bed in the morning. It was chilly, the fire in the grate having collapsed into a heap of grey ash, and she stood in a pool of sunlight to dress in a tweed country suit with leather buttons, a black silk sailor hat and serviceable shoes. Going downstairs, she passed a housemaid on her knees brushing the carpet; across the hall another maid was polishing the floor. Her intimate knowledge of the running of a house from below stairs told her that she had committed a small social solecism by rising before the maids had crept into the bedrooms to light fires and she was not surprised by the look of gaping amazement which came from the footman who stood by the sideboard in the breakfast room.

She said brightly, 'It's such a lovely morning I thought I'd get up early and walk for a while,' then was annoyed with herself for giving explanations.

'Yes, madam,' said the footman. He was arranging hot-plates which would presently be filled with boiling water or coals, to keep food warm. A housemaid scuttled in from the hall with her box of polishes and dusters, another carried in cutlery for the table, laid as yet with only a cloth.

Willow would have enjoyed a cup of tea. If she asked for one it would be supplied without comment, but she decided against it and almost laughed to think what a story these servants would carry with them below stairs. She walked to the front door, preceded hastily by the footman who opened it for her.

The day was heavenly, the trees arranged about the park mantled in the brilliant greens of early summer. The air was cool and pure. About a hundred yards from the house there was a stand of trees from which birdsong echoed across the grass. She walked down the flight of steps bordered by ancient stone vases holding pansies, their velvet faces turned to the sun, across the grass which was as soft and deep as a carpet. No wonder Lord Somervell had hated to destroy anything so luxuriant. In the wood it was cooler than she had expected and she hurried through, sniffing at the scents of earth disturbed by the spears of burgeoning plants, and out through the other side. Just ahead of her there was a stream over which a bridge had been built. She strolled to it and stood in the centre, looking down at the clear water. For some reason the memory of her father came to her. 'Them an' Us, Willow. Don't you forget it. You'll always be one of Us.'

Edgar knew this and she was learning the bitter truth of it. She leaned against the parapet and closed her eyes, seeing again the way in which he had fussed over the Martin girl. Willow knew that he was fond of her, but he would never offer her anything other than an irregular relationship and she wasn't such a fool as to accept such a situation. But she wondered how she would bear the years ahead, how she would receive the news of his inevitable marriage, of the birth of his children, without being attacked by the tearing pain of loss.

She walked on towards the ruins of what had been a monastery, destroyed long ago by order of that wilful monarch, King Henry the Eighth. Inside the crumbling walls the sun was quite hot. Wild flowers were being noisily investigated by bees. She sat on a low wall, allowing herself to become enveloped by the quietude which had survived the rape of a lustful king.

She heard footsteps and turned to see Edgar approaching. 'Hullo,' he said, smiling as if they had accidentally met in a busy street.

'What are you doing here?' she asked.

'I saw you from my window.'

'That doesn't answer my question.'

'I like it here.'

She was exasperated. 'Why are you following me?'

He threw himself down on a patch of grass at her feet. 'Don't be so disagreeable. I followed you because I wanted to be with you. I thought we might talk privately.'

'I see. What have you to say?'

'You are still being disagreeable! You used to enjoy my company.'

Rage flooded her. 'Used to is right! That was in the past and that's where it'll stay.'

He looked up at her, shielding his face against the sun, and she realised that his flippancy was a cloak. His eyes held the expression she had seen in Sam's, in Steven's, in other men's eyes, an expression which held the ineluctable stamp of the horrors of a fearsome war. Sorrow, compassion, tenacious love, made her put out her hand to him and he grasped it.

'Willow. Dearest Willow.' He got up and pulled her to him, holding her against him. She savoured the aroma of shaving soap and tobacco, of his own particular maleness, before his lips came down on hers, hard, demanding, dissipating her resolve which melted into clamouring desire. She was helpless against the tide of need and returned his kiss, tasting his mouth, loving it, while her fingers twined in his hair, prolonging the contact. They had to part to draw breath but stayed locked together for a long minute while Willow tried to read on his face the message she craved. Did he want only her body, with perhaps a little token love thrown in? She shivered and he held her tighter. 'Are you cold, my love?'

'No, not really. Not cold.'

He released her and they sat side by side on the ancient warm stones, he with his arm round her shoulders. 'I can answer your question now,' he said. 'I came because I had to. I have stayed away from you because when I see you I can't resist you, and it won't do. I can never forget the sweetness of our lovemaking. If I had known you were to be a guest I would not have come. No, don't pull away from me. Let me talk, I beg of you.'

'If you must.' Her words were ungracious, but she couldn't keep her longing out of her voice.

'You know we lost my brother James?'

'Yes, I'm deeply sorry.'

'Everyone has lost someone. England will never be as it was. So many men, so many of my friends—' He paused, swallowing hard. 'James is dead, and last night Mary told me that she has met an Australian whom she intends to marry.'

'I don't see—'

'Let me finish. She means to go with him to live somewhere in the back of beyond on a damn great sheep-station. She hasn't yet plucked up enough courage to tell my parents, and I can't blame her. They cling to the idea that they can comfort themselves with James's sons.'

'But they surely can't have expected Mary to live the rest of her life without remarrying!'

'No, but they saw her settling down with an English squire, a man whose family they know, and they, the doting grandparents, would take care of the boys while their mother enjoyed holidays with her new husband. My father has already set up a trust fund to cover their education. They hope that she will leave the twins in their care quite often.'

'But Mary adores her sons! How can they believe any such thing?'

'They are desperately sad. Now Mary is in love. She never really cared for James.'

'I got that impression. She kept him waiting so long. I gather that James wasn't all that keen, either.'

'No. It was a marriage cooked up by the parents.'

Willow said, 'It sounds crazy to me. Why should James and Mary have been so compliant? Why didn't they refuse to co-operate?'

Edgar shrugged. 'That's the way our families are, the way a lot of families are in our society. I don't think James much cared whom he married. He just wanted a good time and Mary was suitable to bear his children. He did grow quite fond of her and she did her best to make his home a pleasant one, though she knew he had other women. Poor devil, I'm glad he enjoyed his few years.'

'That kind of thing wouldn't do for ordinary people,' said Willow, then wished she hadn't sounded so horribly smug.

Edgar said, 'Ordinary people? Surely they have an eye to the future when they settle down.'

'Most of them don't earn enough to plan far ahead. I think that love figures largest in their courtships. How does this relate to me?' She asked the question, knowing and fearing the answer.

'Now I am the only son, and they are looking to me to marry well and, darling Willow, they will never consider you suitable.'

He said it almost matter-of-factly and, in spite of her hurt, she appreciated his straightforward honesty. 'Does that mean you once thought of proposing marriage to me?' She had tried to keep her voice light, unwilling to reveal her need to him, but it quavered.

'Yes, it crossed my mind,' he said. Now he was being really flippant, as if he were afraid of revealing too much of his feelings, and it annoyed her.

'God forbid I should upset your parents' plans!'

'Don't say that!' he begged. 'I did think at one time – oh, Willow, I did feel I might have managed to win them over to the idea of a daughter-in-law not out of the top drawer, don't you know,' he ended, trying to lighten the insult his words contained. 'I was still wondering about it when Mary spoke to me.'

'What did you say to her?'

'I congratulated her. She looked happy.'

'Lucky Mary.'

'Yes, lucky Mary. But when the parents learn of Mary's intentions they will be looking to me to supply a wife and produce a child, and as soon as possible.'

'Have they picked out someone for you? The girl you sat with at dinner, maybe?'

'Yes. Kitty.'

'She looks like a schoolgirl! How old is she?'

'Just eighteen.'

'Is she in love with you?'

'She has been told to cultivate my attentions and that is what she does. She doesn't have an idea about love.'

'How do you know?'

He looked at her blankly. 'I don't, I suppose.'

'My God, is all of your society like that? Has it always been?'

He sighed. 'It used to be a great deal stricter. The war liberated some but has imprisoned others. There are so many adjustments to be made. You can't blame my parents for clinging to tradition.'

'And so many girls are looking for husbands,' said Willow. 'I suppose your mother and father have known her since birth?'

'Kitty's mother and mine came out in the same season.'

'Are all rich houses filled with young girls, all looking more or less the same, to be trotted out like heifers at a market?'

'That's a foul thing to say!'

The pressure of his encircling arm relaxed, but before he could take it from her she turned and put her arms around

458

him. 'I'm sorry. Edgar, don't be pushed into this marriage. Please! You are bound to regret it.'

'That has nothing to do with it. I can't let everyone down. The war's given them a rotten time.'

She twisted away from him and sat with her hands clenched in her lap. 'Is Buddleigh Manor entailed?'

'No. Father can leave it to whom he likes. The money, too.'

'Is that your problem? Money?'

'No!' He was annoyed now. 'You brought up the subject of entail.'

'So I did.'

'Father can leave his possessions where he chooses and he won't choose me if I don't conform. Don't interrupt, Willow, please. I have a very small income inherited from my godmother, certainly not enough to keep a wife on. The rest is allowed me by my father. I'm not trained for anything. Without a profession I should be a burden on any woman not approved of by my family.'

Willow turned to him, her eyes shining with relief. 'Is that all? You would never be a burden to me! And you could learn to make money. My brother Alfred is excellent at it. He designs clothes which are snapped up by women who don't aspire to the highest fashion. In fact, I'm thinking of leaving him in charge of my Bristol business so that I can open up again in London. I could travel between London and Bristol, and so could he.' In a rush of euphoria the solution seemed to arrive fully formed and she felt a surge of energy. 'You could work with me, Edgar.'

His reply was like a dash of icy water in her face. 'No, it will not do. The money is only part of it, a small part. My parents need me. If I leave them they would have only the girls. Violet is totally devoted to Radcliffe, quite rightly in the circumstances. Frances is – well, I am sure you know about Frances. She is slowly destroying herself with alcohol. They need me.'

'If they are so desperate to hold you, surely they will fall in with any plan you make about marriage?'

'No.'

She spoke in low, angry tones. 'Do you mean that they would disown you if you chose to marry someone not of their kind?'

'Yes.'

'Yet they profess to love you!'

'Love is not a word which they use lightly.'

'It is not a word I use lightly, either.'

A silence fell between them. Now the birdsong and humming of bees sounded like mockery. If Edgar hadn't been aware of how deeply she felt about him before he certainly must know now. She should feel humiliated. Perhaps that would come later. Right now she realised that, in spite of every warning signal, she had been holding tight to a dream of love with Edgar, and he had just smashed that dream to pieces.

She wanted to walk away, but instead found herself asking, 'Tell me, Edgar, do you love me?'

'Yes.'

His answer was so abrupt, so subdued, that she wondered if she had heard him aright. 'Did you say you loved me?'

'Yes.'

'And I love you very much,' she said, his words unblocking a dam of impassioned feeling.

'I know.'

She made a final plea. 'Then don't throw it away, please, my darling. We've got something which others would give years of their lives for. Tell your parents. Show some courage.'

'It isn't a question of courage. You must see that.'

'So I'm to be sacrificed for some ideal of your family's!'

'Not just you! *I* am part of the sacrifice. And it will be worse for me because you will forge on with your career, forget me in time, and meet someone else, while I shall be married to a girl I respect, admire, but can never love. She's a sweet little thing, but sweetness needs to be leavened by spice.'

Willow sat silently by him. Nothing she could say would

move him. He was rock-solid in the pursuit of his duty. She had fallen in love with him, believing him to be weak. Now she knew he could be strong and he was using that strength against her.

They got up together. She wanted him to embrace her one last time. She wanted to make love to him, right here in the warm May sunshine in the place which had once been holy ground, but she walked away and he followed. Together they moved across the grass which was still a little damp with dew, their feet leaving darker green imprints. Neither had anything further to say. As they neared the house Willow looked up at the beautiful mullioned windows. A curtain moved and she saw that the watcher was Mrs Maddison.

The remainder of the weekend had to be got through somehow and Willow kept smiling. After all, what woman would want to purchase gowns from a depressed, solemn-faced purveyor?

At lunch, Lady Somervell announced that the tennis court was in tiptop condition. 'Thank heavens we decided not to plough it up during the food shortages. Some did so and now regret it.'

'We turned ours over to potatoes. We had to be fed,' argued a lady who had chosen two evening and one dinner gown from Willow's designs. Mrs Judd was a little stout and had taken enthusiastically to the latest fashion news which told her that the old kind of corset was far too restricting, agreeing at last with doctors who had seen disasters caused by displaced organs and lungs pierced by whalebone. Unfortunately, her plump curves were only contained by the new elastic corsets, and not controlled.

'So supple, my dear,' she had exclaimed to Willow enthusiastically. 'One feels a sense of great freedom. However did we manage to wear all those stiff monstrosities with their cruel whalebone?'

Willow could justifiably have pointed out that, though uncomfortable and dangerous, the monstrosities had concealed a great many faults and that her customer's *avoirdupois* could not be kept secret if it was permitted to bulge. She wondered if elastic corsets could be woven to measure, with some non-yielding areas in the places which mattered most? A couturière corset? She must try to find out, and who better to ask than Sidney? She made a mental note to do so. In the meantime she was able to persuade Mrs Judd to accept the latest loose tunic line in heavy silks, and colours which wouldn't clash with her rubicund complexion. 'It falls straight over the underdress to your knees, Mrs Judd, and will give you a slender appearance. And I thought the beautiful jersey cloth – so clever of Chanel to introduce it to fashion – in this lovely autumn brown which will hang as softly as the silk and permit your underdress to show.'

'I like the idea of the tunic,' said Mrs Judd, 'but brown? For the evening? Surely not.'

'It is one of the very latest colours,' said Willow.

'I see.'

Mrs Judd had still looked a little doubtful and Willow said, 'You have lovely shoulders and I thought we might emphasise them with tiny capes. On the grandest of your new gowns we could use a silver or gold lamé. And you must make sure that your jewellery is of the right sort.'

'Yes. How clever! What do you suggest?'

'Amber or gold for the dinner gown. Topaz perhaps, and of course pearls look well on everything. Long necklaces are all the thing just now and will add to the impression of slender length, while distinctive earrings draw their own attention.'

'How clever you are, Willow.' Mrs Judd's words were kind, but she sat staring into the mirror, looking despondent, and Willow felt a little sick. Was she about to lose such a marvellous order? 'What is it?' she asked gently.

'It's my face!'

'You have handsome features,' said Willow truthfully.

'But so red. I blame the time I've spent out of doors. I've always hunted and shot. Brick red!' she finished gloomily.

'Not brick red,' protested Willow. 'And a high colour can be remedied.'

'It can? How?'

'By using make-up.'

'Make-up? But ladies don't! Do they?'

'Not obtrusively, no, but a little green cream patted into your complexion—'

'Green?'

'A primary colour which works against red. Follow the cream with a light dusting of powder and your problem will be solved.'

'I can scarcely believe it.'

Willow wondered if she could come to an arrangement with a cosmetic company and sell the right stuff along with her gowns.

Before Mrs Judd had left she laughed, held out her foot and said coyly, 'My husband takes a most gratifying interest in my clothes, but he is chiefly interested in my feet. He loves them and I give a great deal of my attention to pleasing him in that department.' She had glanced sideways at Willow as she spoke, clearly waiting for a puzzled, or perhaps shocked, reaction, but Willow had learned too much at Mrs Bliss's to react. Her casual attitude was a mistake.

Mrs Judd, clearly a woman of fast-changing moods, was chagrined. 'If I have three gowns in identical styles how will people notice any difference in them? And I might tire of them quickly.'

Willow handled her carefully. She smiled. 'But they will be far from identical. Only the basic shape will be similar. Please, Mrs Judd, leave it to me. I promise that each gown will have a unique finish and will compliment your appearance.'

Mrs Judd smiled, still a little uncertain. 'I shall be in London in two weeks from now, of course, for the season, and I look forward to my first fitting. I shall need one of your cards to telephone your premises to arrange it.'

Willow managed to keep her face composed. Premises? Telephone? She made more mental notes. 'I am in the process of moving to new premises and haven't quite decided where would be most convenient. May I call you?'

'Of course, my dear, though I long for the day when I can visit you and see all the lovely clothes and styles.'

Foursomes were arranged for tennis for which Edgar was to partner Kitty Martin. During the rest of the weekend Willow often found Mrs Maddison watching her speculatively, but Edgar scarcely looked at her and certainly never came near enough to speak and when she left Mynster on Sunday afternoon he was nowhere to be seen. Just as well, she told herself, as she climbed into her small second-hand Lagonda which looked like a baby spawned by one of the huge Rovers, Daimlers or Rolls-Royces. I shall have a motor car like that one day, she told herself. For a few miles the heady sensation which driving gave her, and the exhilaration of having gained a number of valuable clients, were dominant, then her euphoria dwindled as she faced the fact that she had been cherishing a second impossible dream: that of becoming Edgar's wife. It must be discarded; it would be useless and stupid to allow it to weaken her. From now on nothing would be allowed to hinder her ambition.

After her return from Mynster, Willow discussed her ideas with Alfred and he declared himself fully able to cope with the Bristol business, provided she continued to give him guidance. Bridget and Dora agreed to stay with Clara which was a relief, though it left Willow with the need for reliable staff.

In London, she went first to Marigold whose suggestions for workroom sites were outrageously expensive. 'To make money you have to invest money,' she said. Her good looks continued to blossom in her affluent life style.

'That's all right if you've got money to invest in the first place.'

'You could have had. All right, all right, don't bite my head off. My life wouldn't suit you. We've always been opposites. Our rent here is high, but it keeps the landlord sweet.' She smiled. 'He might have asked more but I do him a personal favour now and then.'

'A favour? Do you mean—?'

'You know what I mean, sister dear. The landlord visits me occasionally, and fortunately I like him.'

Willow kept her mind fixed firmly on the matter in hand. 'What do you pay here?' she asked.

'Three hundred a year.'

'*How* much?'

'You heard me,' said Marigold. 'We can well afford it. You wouldn't need that much for a small shop.'

'I've more than a small shop in mind,' said Willow, angered by her sister's careless air.

'It's no good getting annoyed with me.' Marigold stretched her arms above her head and the sleeves of her diaphanous lilac négligée slid down, revealing rounded white arms. 'Why don't you ask Mrs Grigson? She might be able to help, and she's *extremely* respectable.'

Mrs Grigson sent Willow to see the relative of a tenant. Since leaving the army, Rupert Anstey had opened an art gallery between Regent Street and New Bond Street and was looking for a tenant for the upstairs rooms. The building, whose paintwork badly needed attention, was fronted by a window containing three modern paintings and a piece of sculpture of doubtful identity. Inside, there was no one to be seen and Willow wandered round looking at paintings and drawings which were displayed on whitewashed walls. She was fascinated by their bold shapes and high colours.

'May I help you?' She turned to see a man with a shock of red curls who had arrived silently from the back.

'Mrs Grigson sent me.'

'Ah, yes, Mrs Grigson. A jolly decent old stick. She rents rooms to the wife of a friend – ex-friend, I suppose I should say. Poor chap was killed at Verdun. I say,' he looked anxious, 'you aren't going to ask me to display your work, are you? She sent someone last week. All he was interested in was landscape and I couldn't help him.' He waved a hand. 'You see what I sell, or mostly don't sell, at present.' He grinned ruefully.

Willow smiled as she glanced round. 'My work wouldn't fit in here at all.'

'So you are an artist.'

'Not in the way you mean. I take it you are Rupert Anstey?'

'Yes. Sorry. So sorry. How impolite of me.' He stuck out his hand. 'And you are?'

'Willow Riches.'

'I say, what an awfully jolly name.'

'Thank you. I'm here to try to rent the upstairs rooms.'

'Are you really? I say, that's good news. You have no idea how difficult it has been to set up a gallery of contemporary art. Many people don't understand it and they won't even try. Do you like the pictures? You see those on that far wall? Inspired by Otto Dix, but having their artist's original touch. What do you think of them? The one in the middle, for instance?'

Willow stared at the canvas which was brilliantly coloured and depicted a human being – impossible to tell if it was male or female because only part of the head appeared among a plethora of bold squares and lines.

'It's good, isn't it?' said Rupert.

'It's different.' Willow looked again and thought she detected a hand and a necklace. A woman, then? It was altogether an odd piece, but she liked it. 'Yes, it's very good.'

Rupert was delighted. He took her on a short tour, displaying his wares. There were two artists on show; the second was a portrait painter and, incongruously, as a second string, poster designer.

'If Toulouse-Lautrec did it, why can't my chum?' said Rupert. Only when he had finished enthusing over the exhibits did he ask, 'Why do you want the rooms?'

Willow explained and he said, 'Just the thing! A couture dress designer. What could be better? Your customers can walk through my gallery on their way upstairs and, who knows, they may purchase a painting. I'm open from ten in the morning until seven. There is a back entrance, but you need to find your way to it through a simply dreadful patch of garden filled with rubble and usually alive with cats and rats. I tell you what, I'll give you a key and then you will be quite independent.'

'But we don't know yet if we shall suit one another.'

'I'm sure we shall. I can tell.'

'Maybe the premises won't be what I need.'

Rupert clapped a hand to his forehead. 'What an idiot I am. I'll take you upstairs at once.'

'Don't you have an assistant?'

He laughed. 'I can't afford one. The only reason I don't live here myself is because my parents have a house in Kensington and I get free board and lodging. The dear old pater thinks I'm mad, but he's giving me my head, as he puts it, until I overcome the artistic bug, as if I were suffering from measles or something. If anyone arrives they can have a good browse.'

There were two rooms on the first floor and two attic rooms above. Water and gas were laid on and Willow could already see herself working here. The atmosphere was congenial, Rupert being the sort of man one just couldn't help liking. It was when they came to the rent, for which he wanted a month in advance, that her pleasure was severely damped.

'Fifty-six pounds a quarter!' She made a quick calculation. 'That's about four pounds a week!'

Rupert looked at her sadly. 'I know. To stay here at all I must charge you half the rent for which, don't forget, you'll have most of the premises. And it's a good address, near to where your clients shop.'

'I know,' sighed Willow. 'But—'

'You see,' he said confidingly, 'I've no money of my own. In the ordinary course of things my father would never have subsidised me in an art gallery, he cannot stand artistic fellows, but he agreed in a rush of relief that I came home safely from the war. The dear old Dad is subject sometimes to fits of sentimentality which undermine his business sense. Things need doing up here and I can't afford to buy the materials. I dare say you noticed the peeling paint outside?

It must be attended to or the wood will rot. My lease makes me liable for all repairs. The landlord strikes me as being a bit of a profiteer, but since the war fellows like him can get away with overcharging because they still haven't caught up with the four-year lapse in building. And there's been precious little decorating, either. All the workmen one relied on went to fight and so many have not returned.'

'The war,' said Willow. 'Always the war!'

'You lost someone?'

'Two of my brothers. And many of my friends from schooldays.'

'I lost a brother,' said Rupert sadly, 'and two cousins and their father. My uncle was in the regular army. It's up to us who are left to make the most of our lives. Miss Riches, are you positive you can't take the rooms? I do so wish you could. I am sure we would get along like a house on fire.'

'I'm really sorry, but I have neither money nor a father to help,' she finished, then wished the words back; they made her sound as if she was whining.

Rupert was sympathetic 'Poor girl. What kind of clothes do you make?'

Willow took out her sketch pad and pencil and drew swiftly.

Rupert watched. 'I say, you really are clever. Are those gowns you have already sold?'

'No, these are for future clients.'

'Do you have many clients?'

'Quite a few, fortunately, rich ones, but they'll go elsewhere if I can't get the work done soon. I stayed recently at Mynster—'

'Oh, you know the Somervells? They are awfully sweet, aren't they? What atrocious things the war did to them! Look, I'm set on having you here. Could you pay weekly for a time? I simply can't drop the figure.'

They shook hands on the deal and Willow gave her mind to equipment and machinists. The best place to start, she decided, might be in a servants' employment agency. Many people had had to dispense with staff and there would probably be a number of former housemaids and ladies' maids thrown on to a crowded market, or looking for work that didn't entail being at someone's beck and call for twenty-four hours a day. The Bristol shop was doing well, but needed all its profits. She would have to borrow money from somewhere. She thought of Steven, but that would never do. She had no wish to involve him in anything which could lead to encouraging his interest in her. Sidney? He was expanding his own business.

Who was left? Marigold! She might ask her. Where could be the harm in that? This time she had to wait for an hour before her sister appeared.

Maisie greeted her. 'You can wait in the kitchen,' she said. 'We've made it very cosy. I'll tell Carmen you're here. She's free for a while.'

The kitchen had been extensively altered and beside the range there was an electric oven.

The housemaid was new, but Mrs Bliss's cook was still there. 'Newfangled thing,' she grumbled, waving her hand at the oven, 'give me my range any day.'

'We do give you your range,' Maisie pointed out in her calm way.

'And a job I had to keep it! Do you know, Willow, they wanted to take it away, but I said if that goes, I go with it.'

The kitchen had been enlarged by a glass-roofed extension in which plants were growing. There was an electric fire and Willow wondered if clients ever waited here, or if strict punctuality was insisted upon. Maisie excused herself. 'I've a darling old gentleman calling in ten minutes. I must go and change.'

The cook brought Willow a cup of tea and a plate of the little cakes which had been so beloved of Annie Bliss and Willow felt a lump in her throat.

'Go on, eat 'em,' urged the cook. 'She'd be glad to know you kept in touch. I must say, your sister's got a real knack. I always thought no one could be better than Mrs Bliss, but Marigold's up to all the dodges!'

Carmen hurried into the kitchen and grabbed a cup of tea. 'I've got fifteen minutes between clients. How are you, Willow? Where are you working? Can you make me a new gown?'

Willow laughed. 'I certainly hope so. I'll let you know. How are the others?'

'Claudette's settled well. She's got two little girls. Angelina's still with us, though she's thinking of getting married. One of her gentlemen friends has proposed.'

'What about you?'

'Me? No fear. I agree with Marigold. Make your money, then choose what you want to do.'

Marigold looked as satisfied as a well-fed cat when she strolled in, wearing a midnight blue cashmere dressing gown. 'What do you want?' she asked.

'Is that a nice way to greet your sister when she's troubled to call?' the cook said indignantly.

'Can I see you for a minute?' Willow asked.

'I'm here, aren't I?'

'It's a matter of business.'

Marigold's eyes narrowed. 'Business? Money, you mean?'

She led the way into her sitting room, glancing at the carriage clock on the mantel-shelf. There was a pale blue vase containing flowers on the table and a tray with two used cups and saucers. Marigold stretched out a languid hand and rang the bell and the housemaid hurried in, tripped over her feet, and left with the tray.

'She'll have to go,' said Marigold dispassionately. 'Quite pretty, but hopelessly clumsy. Now, about this business talk?'

Willow explained. Marigold was indignant. 'I work hard for my money and only invest it in established companies.'

'I've plenty of orders.'

'From suburban housewives, I suppose?'

'From ladies who want their gowns for the London season.'

'Is that so?' Marigold looked interested. 'Who, for instance?'

470

Again Willow explained and Marigold looked thoughtful. 'I do believe you might succeed. You say the Bristol place is going well, too. What exactly do you need the money for?'

'Sewing machines and furniture. A decent carpet for the clients, a minimum of stuff for one of the attic rooms where I shall sleep. Cash to buy materials and to eat and pay my rent.'

'Your Rupert Anstey sounds nice.'

Willow frowned and Marigold laughed. 'I'll not disgrace you,' she said. She lit a cigarette and smoked for a while. Willow watched her, wondering at the change in her, startled by the realisation that she must have been very unhappy at home. 'I will lend you the money,' said Marigold abruptly, 'but it must be done legally. Have you a lawyer? No, well leave it to me. I'll have a proper agreement drawn up. I shall, of course, expect to be paid interest.'

Willow felt weak with relief. 'Could you possibly let me have some cash now? I really need to get this first batch of orders underway.'

Marigold nodded. 'Very well. Are any of the Maddisons customers?'

Willow said carefully, 'Yes, Violet and Frances, Winifred and Mrs Maddison.'

'Frances drinks, doesn't she? And Violet's got her husband on a string now he's lost his looks.'

'How do you know?'

'I get to hear most things. What about Edgar? Do you see him?'

'Sometimes.'

'You like him, don't you?'

'What do you mean?'

'Your voice changes when you speak of him. It has for a long time. And stop glaring at me or I might change my mind about the money.'

Willow left as soon as she could with an incredible one hundred pounds tucked into her bag. She had already located a reputable second-hand shop and ordered three treadle sewing machines to be delivered the following morning. She spent a luxurious three hours in Harrod's, Liberty's, Dickens and Jones and Selfridges, ordering materials and haberdashery notions to be sent to the art gallery. Afterwards, she strolled in Hyde Park, enjoying the sunshine until, with cruel abruptness, the memory of herself and Edgar walking here came to torment her. She must get back and begin work. Work was therapeutic. Work was the only thing which would shield her from her aching longing for Edgar.

Chapter Twenty-five

Rupert promised to supervise the arrival of the sewing machines and Willow set off for a Servants' Employment Registry. It was situated over a shop. The stairs had a pathway of lino up the middle, flanked by dark varnished boards. Inside she was greeted by a black-suited young woman with very short hair and a severe countenance who reminded Willow of the housekeeper at Buddleigh Manor. Two ladies were waiting, whiling away the time by talking about the dreadful lack of servants since the war.

'They are spoiled for ever,' said one.

'You are so right!' said the other. 'We employed eight and now have only two, a cook and a housemaid. It is quite ridiculous. If things do not improve I shall be forced to take a hand myself.'

The first woman sighed. 'I have only a cook and a general. I suppose they do their best, but the house is large. I need a parlourmaid, but meanwhile have to answer the door myself.'

'My dear!'

Willow wondered how they were faring in the manor. She couldn't see Mrs Maddison wielding a duster or answering the door.

The receptionist motioned Willow to a chair by her desk. 'You are looking for seamstresses?'

'Yes.'

'I wonder at your coming here. We place servants.'

'Personal maids and housemaids can be very skilful with their needles. I also have machines in an excellent condition.' Willow crossed her fingers. The machines were thick with greasy dust and Rupert had offered to clean them while she was away.

'I hope you are not wanting them urgently,' said the girl, without a trace of emotion. 'They are increasingly difficult to find – at least, good ones are. May I ask the nature of your business?'

'I am a couture dress designer,' said Willow, nervousness rendering her voice a little too loud. It penetrated the self-pitying diatribes of the other women and they stared at her.

'I see.' The receptionist wrote something in her large ledger. 'I will send in your name and requirements and Mrs Deacon will see you as soon as possible.'

Willow waited while the other women disappeared, one by one, into an inner room where presumably they were interviewed by the proprietress. They came out looking disgruntled. Three more clients had arrived and their conversation echoed that of the first two.

At last Willow was called and shown to a pleasant room, light and airy and simply furnished. There were cushioned seats and a couple of hard chairs. Rugs covered the floor.

Mrs Deacon was plump and looked motherly, she smiled and nodded a lot. 'You are fortunate, Miss Riches, that I have two women in the servants' waiting room, both of whom claim they can sew and who wish to exercise their talents. Would you care to see them?' When Willow agreed she rang a bell and the door opened. A woman of about thirty entered. She was tall and thin and uncertain. 'This is Maria Booth. Maria, this is Miss Riches who is looking for a seamstress. Miss Riches, if you will begin the interview?'

Willow hadn't reckoned on being monitored; neither had she reckoned on being seated in a cushioned seat, while the prospective employee had to perch on a low wooden chair. It made her feel uncomfortable. 'Have you ever made your living by sewing?' she asked tentatively.

Maria shook her head. 'No, madam. I've been maid to a lady who died. Fifteen years I was with her. Poor soul, she was ill most of the time.'

'Did you sew for her?'

'Oh, yes, madam. I made her clothes, all of them, except lately she didn't want coats and that because she never went out.'

'I see.' Willow swallowed, uncomfortably aware that Mrs Deacon was regarding her amateurish efforts with an air of disapproval. 'Have you brought a sample of your work?'

'Yes, madam.' Maria opened a bag and produced a blouse, tucked and goffered in the Edwardian way, and a nightgown embroidered with flowers in tiny stitches.

'You made these?' Willow was delighted. 'They are excellent.'

She sensed, rather than heard, Mrs Deacon's tutting. It was not the done thing to show such open appreciation of a mere servant which could only lead to a demand for higher wages.

Willow ignored her, feeling on safer ground now. 'I am opening a couture house in London –' how pretentious that sounded! '– and have found suitable premises. Now I need staff urgently to fulfil several immediate orders.'

'Yes, madam.'

'Have you a home in London?'

'Yes, madam, I've taken a bed-sitting room.'

'Are you happy there?' Again Willow felt rather than saw the wave of disapproval from the other side of the desk. What had happiness to do with anything? 'Would you like to work for me?'

'I think so, madam. Please, what's a couture house?'

Willow smiled. 'It's a rather high-flown expression for an establishment which makes clothes.'

'Kind of a dressmaker, then?'

'Kind of.'

'You'll need to see her references,' said Mrs Deacon sternly.

For a brief instant, Willow was whisked back in time and almost reached for her own bag to produce the references which were so essential to a servant's life, then Maria held out two envelopes. One contained an excellent recommendation in a crabbed, elderly hand; the other, equally enthusiastic, proclaimed her worthiness in bold flowing strokes of the pen.

'The first was written by my late mistress,' explained Maria. 'She knew she couldn't last much longer and wanted me to find another place. The second is from her nephew.'

'They are satisfactory,' said Willow. 'Can you begin work tomorrow morning?'

When Maria said she could Willow displeased Mrs Deacon still further by openly displaying her relief. She gave Maria the address of the workrooms, asked her to be there at eight-thirty and the maid executed a neat curtsey as she left.

The next woman came in and a shock of recognition passed between them. Miss Jebb! Looking older than her years, starkly skinny, her hair strained back into a bun, her shoulders a little bent. She walked nervously to one of the hard chairs where she sat gingerly and stared in front of her, lifting her chin defiantly high.

'Good morning, Miss Jebb,' said Willow. 'It's a long time since we met.'

'You know one another?' Mrs Deacon sounded indignant, as if her clients had deliberately banded together to make a fool of her.

'We once knew each other very well,' said Willow.

'Have you worked for Miss Riches before?' asked Mrs Deacon.

A faint flush spread over Miss Jebb's face. 'No,' she said firmly.

'I see.' Mrs Deacon did not see and she waited in vain for an explanation. Finally she spoke to the space between the two women. 'If you are acquainted with one another I must suppose that you both will know whether or not Miss Jebb can fulfil the requirements of the position.'

The thought of taking on Miss Jebb, with all her faults, daunted Willow. She had turned away, but now she looked directly at her and was shaken to see her look of desperation. 'Where have you worked lately?' she asked.

476

'I have been a shop assistant,' said Miss Jebb, then, catching an annoyed look from Mrs Deacon, added, 'madam'.

'You have references?' asked Willow, more to fill the jagged silence than because she wished to know. She wouldn't put it past Miss Jebb to forge her references and, she realised, unprofessionally, she wouldn't blame her if she had. She took the three letters offered her and perused them quickly. One had been written by Violet in an impatient scrawl, on paper headed by a crest, another from a haberdasher on lined paper which was none too clean, the third informed the world at large that 'Miss Jebb was employed by me as a parlour-maid and proved satisfactory'. None of them was particularly reassuring, but it was obvious that she hadn't produced them herself. Willow felt irritated. Why had she to come here today, of all days? Why had not one of the other ladies decided to take on Miss Jebb? One had said distinctly that she needed a parlour-maid. Miss Jebb would have fitted the description. She looked again at the woman who had done so much to damage her life, stared at her thin features and rusty black coat, and a rush of compassion triumphed over practicality.

'When can you begin work, Miss Jebb?'

Miss Jebb looked sharply at her, her face bright with relief she couldn't hide.

'Today! Tomorrow! Whenever you say.'

Her humility embarrassed Willow. 'Tomorrow will be soon enough,' she said. 'At eight-thirty. Sharp!' she added as a sop to Mrs Deacon, then wished she hadn't. To Miss Jebb it must seem like a knife turning in the wound of her cruelly abused self-esteem.

She paid Mrs Deacon the commission asked and went back to find Rupert smeary with grease through which he was beaming broadly. The three machines had been well and truly cleaned and stood in all their bright glory ready for use. 'They are so beautiful,' she breathed, running her finger over the shiny black, gold-decorated machines.

'That is what I thought,' said Rupert.

'You must have worked very hard and fast to accomplish so much already.'

'No, the muck soon came off. I enjoyed doing it, too. I like to work with my hands. I think these are worthy of display in my window.' He laughed to show he was joking. 'Now you must discover if they function properly.'

Willow soon proved that they did and Rupert was delighted. 'By the way, loads of parcels have arrived for you. I've put them all in the other room. It isn't quite so dusty there.'

He insisted on giving a hand with the thorough cleaning on which Willow embarked. He apparently enjoyed rubbing soap on to a scrubbing brush and scraping through accumulated layers of dirt.

'I say, Willow,' he said at one point, 'it looks as if you have been doing stuff like this all your life.'

'Not quite all,' she said, 'but I've done my share.'

'Now you are teasing me. Have you bought any furniture?'

'Not much. Some chairs, two tables and a bed so far.'

Rupert laughed. He laughed a lot in an uninhibited, joyous way. 'I am so glad you decided to come here. You're most awfully jolly.'

Spindle, Willow's partner at the Mynster dinner table, proved to be a friend of Rupert's. He arrived, delighted at meeting her again and was immediately drawn into the work. 'The paintwork badly needs doing,' he said. 'Can I help? I love painting things.'

'He does,' agreed Rupert. 'He's good at it, too, as long as it's not too complicated. He can't take in too much at one time.'

Spindle picked up a damp cloth and threw it at Rupert. It wound itself round his head. He emerged, grinning. 'Ass!'

The following morning Miss Jebb and Maria came to work on time. Willow had spent a good part of the night bending over a large table finishing the cutting out of *toiles* for Mrs Judd's garments. She completed this first, important step before staggering into bed at three o'clock. Rupert arrived at the gallery early for once, still as keen as a schoolboy at a cricket match to follow his unusual tenant's procedures.

'What should I do first, Miss Riches?' Miss Jebb asked as soon as she arrived. Maria was despatched to familiarise herself with the tea- and coffee-making arrangements and Willow invited Miss Jebb to sit.

She sat, hands on her lap, waiting.

'First, you may call me Willow.'

'I don't think—'

'You may call me by my name,' repeated Willow.

'Won't that sound a little odd in front of customers?' The woman was as unyielding as ever.

'I can't keep calling you Miss Jebb.'

'Why not?'

'Because I don't choose to. I like to keep a friendly atmosphere.' It occurred to Willow that she had no idea of the woman's forename.

Miss Jebb looked angry and again Willow was filled with misgivings. 'My name is Jennifer,' said Miss Jebb.

'Good.'

'If you say so, though I would very much prefer that you didn't use it.'

Willow was about to ask why when it dawned on her that the use of Miss Jebb's forename added another dimension to her comedown in the world. 'What would you like to be called?'

'In one of the places I worked the children called me Jebby. I wouldn't mind that.'

'Jebby! Are you sure? Well, if you wish it—'

'Where will you see your customers?' asked Miss Jebb aggressively, to make up, Willow supposed, for the slight lowering of her defences.

'Here. Yes, I know it looks dreadful at the moment, but I'm about to order carpets and all the other paraphernalia which ladies expect.'

'Ladies?'

'My customers. I took a good many orders when I was a guest recently at Mynster.'

Miss Jebb almost gaped and Willow found it difficult not to laugh. Her new employee was making it very clear that she had arrived with a low opinion of the former kitchen maid. She actually sounded quite respectful when she said, 'I remember Mynster very well. It's a happy house. The people there are kind.' Her words strongly implied that no one else had shown any kindness to her and Willow resolved to try to break down the hostile barrier with which Jennifer Jebb protected herself.

The three women worked well together, even if Miss Jebb's attitude was often sullen, largely because she was given only the straight seams while Maria managed more difficult pieces. She knew she wasn't capable of the finer work, but it still rankled. Willow bent over her cutting table until her back ached.

They moved from room to room as each one was papered and painted. Spindle did indeed wield a good paint brush and refused to take pay. Rupert explained that he had oodles of the stuff and nothing to occupy himself with so she was doing him a favour by employing him. Carpets were brought and laid, easy chairs installed for clients, a cabinet containing various wines was brought to a high polish and a telephone installed. Within two weeks the rooms were transformed and Marigold's one hundred pounds had gone.

Mrs Judd was due for her first fitting and Willow picked up the telephone with unsteady hands to tell her so. What if she had changed her mind? What if all the effort and money had been for nothing? The phone was answered by a butler who said he would ascertain if madam wished to speak. While Willow waited she looked round the room. The walls were papered with a beige background with small pale designs which would not clash with clothes being displayed. The carpets were of the same soft beige. There were three large cheval mirrors in the smaller of the rooms for clients to view each aspect of themselves. The easy chairs were covered in the same soft colours, but sported a pattern of animals. Rupert had peered at it. 'I say, Willow, you've got zebras and elephants here. I don't believe I have ever encountered a cream and pink zebra and fortunately never a pink elephant. It's awfully jolly.'

Willow, not relying entirely on Rupert's ready approval of everything, waited anxiously for other reactions. Maria said the rooms were pretty. Miss Jebb said, 'You are very clever, Willow, but of course you always were.' The praise was given without enthusiasm.

Mrs Judd arrived late, giving Willow an attack of palpitations. Rupert had produced a length of brown stair carpet and hung some small, modern pictures both on the stairs and in the workrooms and Mrs Judd looked round appreciatively.

'What a sweet place, Willow! Are my gowns ready?'

Willow managed to look shocked. 'No, of course not, Mrs Judd. I have the *toiles* for you to try.'

'*Toiles?* I don't quite understand.' She smiled as she spoke, uncertain of herself, and Willow pressed her advantage.

'The preliminary shapes cut in muslin. If you will accompany me into the fitting room? Miss Jebb, I shall need you.'

Mrs Judd tried on the *toiles* assisted by Miss Jebb who was quick and deft, proving that she retained what she had learned as a lady's maid and Mrs Judd was impressed, though still confused. 'If it has taken you two weeks to prepare these odd things, how long will my gowns be? As I explained, I want them quickly.'

The serenity of Willow's smile didn't desert her, though nervousness quickened her breathing. 'Now that I have your precise needs, the finished gowns will not take above a week.'

Miss Jebb looked at her in an astonishment that was justified. To complete three original couture gowns in seven days would need a vast amount of work and a great deal of time.

'Couldn't you have made the gowns instead of these *toiles?*'

'If I had,' pointed out Willow gently, 'the slight alterations would have meant unpicking stitches, perhaps marking the cloth, and that would never do.'

Mrs Judd sighed. 'It's my fault. I have eaten a great deal of chocolate lately and some delicious cream cakes. One feels that one can never eat enough after the austerity of the war years. *So* dreadful for my figure, but *so* delicious. I don't think I shall ever attain this new boyish appearance which is suddenly the thing. What do you make of it, Willow?'

'It's attractive on the immature young woman, Mrs Judd.'

'Some older women wear it. I've seen them.'

'Each woman must wear the garments which appeal to her most. Do you see yourself in them?'

'No, though the men seem to like it.'

'Perhaps they only say they do. After all, the poor dears can't fight fashion fads and they go on choosing wives and sweethearts whatever women wear.'

Mrs Judd brightened. 'So they do, my dear, and to tell you the truth, my husband says he likes my comfortable shape.'

'That's the important thing,' said Willow.

'It is, isn't it? Have you seen any of the Maddisons lately?' She asked the question so suddenly that she almost got her fleshy bottom pierced by a pin.

'No, I haven't,' Willow said, 'I've been too busy.'

'Of course you have,' agreed Mrs Judd. 'What *do* you think? Frances made a dreadful scene the other night. At the theatre of all places. We were at the Alhambra to see the Russian Corps de Ballet and I have to admit that their choice was not my favourite: *Scheherazade*, *Les Papillons* and *The Fire Bird*, but one must see them or be left out of conversation. I cannot say I like ballet much at all, but if I must go I prefer *Swan Lake* or something of the sort.'

Willow realised that Miss Jebb was waiting with as much curiosity as she to discover what Frances had done which was so reprehensible.

'And you are sure the colours are right for me, Willow?' asked Mrs Judd.

'Absolutely!'

'What do you think, what's your name – Miss Jebb, is it?'

'Perfectly correct, madam,' Miss Jebb said in exactly the right tone and with the right deferential manner and Mrs Judd relaxed. 'I purchased some green face-cream as you suggested, Willow. My maid had to go to a theatrical shop to find it but it certainly helps my complexion.' She looked around her. 'Where do you keep your other work in progress?'

Willow smiled in a coy way which she privately thought laughable. 'Now, Mrs Judd, if I allowed you to see other couture originals in the making, you would never trust me again.'

Mrs Judd laughed. 'Very true. What was I saying before? Oh, now I remember. Frances Maddison, or rather Bickford as she is now – one cannot like him but one can feel sorry for him. He might have been a Member of Parliament if it were not for her. During the first interval it became obvious that she had been drinking.' Mrs Judd gave a small scornful laugh. 'When isn't it obvious? However, she had taken more even than usual and simply screeched about how much she hated Russian ballet. Well, we were all flabbergasted. She may not like the Russian ballet, but really! Her husband was with her and Lady Radcliffe – not Lord Radcliffe. He doesn't go into public life since his face was burned, poor lamb, and his wife is so devoted to his care . . . Well, Frances went on shrieking and when her husband tried to restrain her threw a glass of wine over him, right in front of everyone. Then she was sick. My dear, it was awful!' Mrs Judd's voice was full of relish and her lips curved in a smile as she recalled the drama which had appealed to her so much more than the ballet. 'In the end Lady Radcliffe and Bickford managed to get her away and take her home. *Such* a burden for the Maddisons.'

Willow murmured something deliberately incoherent

483

which satisfied Mrs Judd who only wanted to talk. On her way out she saw Maria working industriously on a length of emerald satin and said, 'What a delightful colour! I feel quite jealous.'

'It is pretty, isn't it?' Willow said smoothly. 'But far too gaudy for you.'

The word 'gaudy' was sufficient. The gown was being run up hastily for Carmen and it was extremely unlikely that the two would ever meet.

Willow absorbed valuable lessons on that first day. Clients talked without reservation to their dressmaker and everything must go in one ear and stay put if she wanted to remain in business. They wanted to be flattered and reassured about their shape. And never, ever, let one client see material being made up for another. She felt annoyed with herself for committing the latter obvious error. In future there must be a division between clients and sewing machines. Rupert supplied it in the form of a big screen on wheels. It was covered in abstract designs in beige and pale pinks and blues which would not clash with anything.

Willow worked without cease for the next two weeks. Besides Mrs Judd's gowns she had fittings for the other women whose custom she had acquired at Mynster. As yet, no one had paid her a thing and she discovered the sad fact that it was considered amusing to keep one's tailor or dressmaker waiting. She was forced to apply again to Marigold who was in a happy mood, having gained another regular gentleman friend.

'He has simply pots of money,' she cried when she told Willow about him.

'You're beginning to sound like Them,' said Willow, astonishing herself as the old familiar word of her father's tumbled out.

'Them and Us!' said Marigold scornfully. 'Dad was a fool.'

Willow weighed up her next words. If she disagreed she

might put Marigold in a bad mood; if she agreed she felt it would be disloyal to Dad.

She ignored the remark and plunged in. Dad would have understood. 'I'm glad about the pots because I need some more. You'll get it all back, of course.'

'I intend to, my dear sister. How much this time?'

'Another fifty?'

'My God, what do you do with it? Eat it?'

'In a way. I need to keep body and soul together.'

Marigold's eyes flickered over her assessingly. 'I don't know about your soul, but your body's damned thin.'

'It's all the rushing about and the worry.'

'To each his own,' said Marigold languidly.

Willow returned to Riches with money for wages, more cloth, and the freedom to engage the third seamstress she needed.

She wondered if Dora and Bridget had more talented sisters. She seemed to recall them saying something and decided to visit the family. When she arrived at the small terraced house in the East End she was greeted enthusiastically by Mrs O'Hara. 'Come on in, Miss Riches. Sit yourself down an' I'll get a cup of tea.'

The living room, which opened straight on to the street, was spotless, as was the cloth laid over the deal table. 'I get letters from my girls, Miss Riches, an' they're both so happy at work an' at your mother's house. Mrs Riches sounds a real good 'un.' She produced a home-baked sponge. 'My girl Erin made it. She's a good little cook. She sews as well.'

'Does she? As well as her sisters?'

'Better. Erin's good at everything she does.'

'Is she out at work yet?'

'Bless you, yes. She's sixteen. She works down the local grocer's.'

Willow picked up her cup, sipped the strong brew, and tasted the cake, a large slice of which was handed to her on a white plate. 'This is delicious, Mrs O'Hara.'

'Didn't I tell you?'

'You don't sound Irish.'

'That's because I'm a Londoner, born an' bred. My husband's Irish. He's a navvy with a building firm. Doesn't make much money but he's as good as gold with it. Hands all of it to me except a bit for his beer an' baccy. Did you come about somethin' special, Miss Riches?'

'I did. I am so pleased with Dora and Bridget, such good workers and honest with it.'

'Honest! I should hope so!' said Mrs O'Hara. 'I've got a big family an' still more to come an' I've brought everyone up proper!'

Willow was annoyed with herself. She felt she had patronised Mrs O'Hara, just as she had once been patronised, and Mrs O'Hara hated it just as much as she had. It was frighteningly easy to slide into the ways of Them.

She felt dejected and Mrs O'Hara smiled encouragingly, 'Now, tell me what you want. My girls are behavin' right to your mother, aren't they? Givin' her enough to keep themselves.'

'They're wonderful. My mother just loves them, and my brother Alfred who runs the Bristol end of the business couldn't manage without them.' Willow waited for an expression of amazement at a man doing a woman's job. None came and she said, 'I just wondered if you had another daughter I could employ? Erin perhaps.'

Mrs O'Hara laughed. 'I'd not be sorry to see her out of the grocer's. She's meant for better things, is my Erin. We may not be rich in worldly ways, but my Eamonn's very fond of readin' an' he's taught our children a good few things about history an' geography an' he's always given them good books to read. An' I'm good at sewin' an' made sure that my children learned, boys as well as girls.' So that was why she had accepted Alfred's profession without comment. She glanced at the mantelpiece clock. 'If you wait a few minutes Erin will be home. It's her half-day. I've got more girls comin' on, too. The eldest after Erin is Sheila – she's nearly thirteen an' I'm sure she'd like to work for you. I want my children to do somethin' interestin'. I'm glad I've got a lot. They make life worth livin', an' I shan't run short.' She placed her hands around her rotund figure, laughing. 'There's another one in here. So shall I tell Sheila you'll be employin' her when she leaves school?'

'I'm sure I shall need her by then,' said Willow, a little dazed by all this bounty. 'That will be in a year's time, won't it?'

'If you want her she can leave at thirteen. She gets more learnin' at home than she does at school.'

The back door opened and there was a light step in the kitchen. Mrs O'Hara called, 'Erin? Is that you? Here's a visitor for you.'

Erin was as unlike Bridget and Dora as it was possible to be and Mrs O'Hara gave a sly smile at Willow's poorly concealed surprise. She was tall, slim and very pretty, with satin-smooth auburn hair cropped short and a fine-boned face with skin as pale and soft as cream, blue eyes and a mouth with a perfect Cupid's bow. 'Hello, Erin,' Willow managed.

'Here's Miss Riches who employs our Bridget and Dora and wonders if you'd suit her.'

Erin smiled, revealing even white teeth. 'It depends what you want, Miss Riches.'

'Someone who can sew as well as your sisters.'

'I can do that all right. When should I start?'

'As soon as you've worked out your notice at the grocer's, please. Can you use a treadle sewing machine?'

'I've never tried, but I'm sure I could.'

'In one week's time then.'

On her way home Willow sent up a silent prayer of thanks to the generous God who assisted the industrious Mr O'Hara to fill Mrs O'Hara's womb with an apparently unending supply of good, trustworthy seamstresses.

Back in the workrooms she found Violet Radcliffe waiting. Maria had supplied her with tea and biscuits and she and Rupert were entertaining one another with reminiscences. A swift glance told Willow that the screen was firmly in place. Both Miss Jebb and Violet were unpredictable.

'I beg your pardon, Lady Radcliffe,' said Willow. 'I hope I haven't kept you waiting long?'

Rupert had put Violet into a pleasant frame of mind. 'I am early, I believe.' She consulted a small jewelled fob watch. 'Yes, it has only just reached the time of my appointment. I trust you are ready with the final fitting for my new dinner gown?'

'I am indeed,' said Willow. She jerked her head at a grinning Rupert who took the hint and slid away.

In the fitting room Willow and Maria hovered while Violet twisted and turned and examined herself from all angles. The tobacco-brown satin with cream lace suited her. She had always been slender, but now her collar bones were jutting and she was nervy. Rupert had reported that Lord Radcliffe sometimes swung into strange, almost violent, moods.

'The lace hides my collar bones,' she said suddenly. 'I like the whole deisgn. It is quite flattering.'

Maria said, 'Madam is handsome enough to carry off any gown.'

Willow winced. Maria was talking to Violet as she spoke to Mrs Judd and she wasn't surprised when Violet gave Maria a stare which brought colour to the seamstress's face.

'Would you care for a drink?' asked Willow.

'What have you got?' Violet was still studying her reflection.

'Wine, spirits—'

'What sort of wine? Nothing German, I hope.'

'No,' said Willow. 'I have Bristol Cream.'

'Good old Bristol Cream.'

It was impossible to tell if Violet was being mocking or appreciative. 'Don't you have cocktails?'

Willow silently thanked Rupert for his lessons in mixing drinks. 'Of course,' she said serenely.

'Then I will have an Alaskan.'

Willow mixed dry gin with yellow chartreuse, shook it and strained it into one of the good glasses which had been Rupert's opening gift. Violet sipped it, murmured appreciatively, and drained the glass.

'Excellent,' she said, her mood suddenly swinging into affability. 'I am very pleased with the gown, Willow. I am sure my husband will like it.'

Willow was congratulating herself as she carefully folded the satin confection ready to place in one of the large bags printed with the name Riches when Violet said carelessly, 'When will you give your first show? Do you have your own mannequins or does one hire them by the hour or something?'

Willow said smoothly, though her pulses were jumping, 'I shall send invitations out as soon as I am ready, Lady Radcliffe.'

'Splendid. Make sure I get one.'

'I will, indeed.'

Willow was agitated after Violet had left. A mannequin show! She knew that stores showed clothes already made up. Why hadn't she had the sense to give Violet a different answer? She spoke to Rupert about it. 'I could have said my clothes were too specialised to put on parade,' she mourned. 'I promised to send Violet Radcliffe an invitation. What an idiot I am!'

'No,' he soothed. 'You're not. She is a pretty daunting woman. She frightens me to death.'

Willow laughed but went on worrying and into her mind there floated the picture of Erin, the perfect model, and straight after her, the face and figure of Jasmine.

Willow had opened her business knowing that she had much to learn but under the impression that she would soon cope. She quickly discovered that she was practically a beginner. There were times when she lay awake at nights telling herself she must have been crazy to set herself up as a designer. Her study of the gowns worn by the ladies in Buddleigh Manor was no qualification for taking on such a task. Haunting images wove themselves through her dreams: of delicate lace faggoted unevenly to a silk underbodice; ugly, angular applications of braid; corded straps with bobbles falling from them to the floor. She would see Mrs Judd, her face bright red, in a ballooning puce gown; or Violet staring down haughtily from an immense height as Willow tried to cover her bony body with a skin-tight emerald green tunic which reached only to her thighs. She would awaken abruptly, sweating, her heart pounding. Often sleep deserted her completely and she got up and made a cup of tea, deciding that tomorrow she would close down, return to Bristol perhaps. But the new day always brought fresh hope, and even if she considered herself an optimistic fool she went on doggedly with her drawing and designing.

Erin had proved herself clever at tackling tricky bits of hand sewing and enough money was coming in to pay wages and rent and general expenses. But she was often pushed to buy the expensive cloth she needed. If only she could ask for something in advance, but clients had to believe she was backed by solid money.

One morning there was a tap on the door and Mrs Stewart walked in. Willow was happy to see her, though thinking of her connection with Edgar, a stab of jealousy threatened to turn her welcoming smile to a grimace.

Mrs Stewart gazed around her. 'My dear! It is all as it was described to me. Simple, restful, just the place for a woman to purchase clothes.'

'Won't you sit down?' asked Willow. 'Coffee? Tea? Wine?'

Mrs Stewart laughed. 'Coffee, please.'

Willow called, 'Miss Jebb,' and she came from behind the screen making a valiant attempt at a smile. She loathed making drinks for clients, to her it smacked of servitude, but she was easier spared than Maria or Erin.

'How may I help you?' Willow asked Mrs Stewart.

'In plenty of ways, I hope. I have seen some of your gowns – Lady Radcliffe was wearing a delicious one the other night – and Mrs Judd! My dear, how cleverly you managed to hide her bulges. I do congratulate you.' She took the coffee with a pleasant smile which Miss Jebb didn't return.

Mrs Stewart raised her brows. 'What's the matter with her?' she whispered.

Willow frowned. 'Nothing that I won't sort out. I'm so glad you like my clothes.'

'I do. And I like the name of your company. Riches. It flows well from the tongue. Are there more of you?'

'My brother runs the Bristol end.'

'Two businesses? You are even more to be congratulated. Now, I want several garments for the season.'

Willow happily took an order for three evening gowns, two dinner gowns and a costume.

Mrs Stewart pulled on her gloves. 'Do you see much of Edgar?' she enquired, a little too casually.

'Not much.'

'I hear he's practically engaged to another little girl from an unimpeachable family. Didn't he tell you?'

'Of course not! Why should he?' Damn! She should not have spoken so abruptly.

Mrs Stewart appeared not to notice. 'You surprise me. I understood that he thought a great deal of you.'

Willow glanced at the screens, hoping that the whirring of the machines covered a conversation which she couldn't bring herself to end. 'I think you are mistaken,' she said.

'No, my dear, I am not. Of course, you know about our little affair – most enjoyable, and he gave me a superb necklace when we parted. We remained close friends until quite recently and your name cropped up often. Did you send him away?'

Willow made a great play of putting her folio in order and Mrs Stewart said, 'You are right, I am being unforgivably curious, but I thought you were so suited to him. I rather hoped he would choose you.'

Willow looked startled. 'Choose me?'

'For a wife.'

Willow managed a faint laugh. 'How could he? His

brother was killed. He's now the only son. He must marry well.'

'I see.' Mrs Stewart got up. 'I'll return in a week for a fitting, then.'

Chapter Twenty-six

Mrs Stewart was delighted with her new gown. She was still well-corseted and said she intended to remain that way. She told Willow, 'If you had attended Ascot you would have seen some truly awful sights. Women who should know better and who have been known as shapely beauties were bulging and bursting from their gowns.' She shuddered. 'Frightful! I am too aware of my shape to follow that particular fashion.'

She returned unexpectedly as the art gallery was closing and everyone had left Riches.

'Do come in,' said Willow. 'Did I forget something?'

'No, the gown is perfect. My maid simply raved over it and she is French and has a way with clothes. May I sit down?'

'Please do.'

'I want to talk over a matter of business with you. I have a little money I wish to invest and I am attracted to your efforts.'

'You want to invest in Riches?'

'Yes, or rather in you. I have great faith in you and your determination to succeed. Why do you look surprised? You are clearly doing well.'

'Yes, I am, as far as orders go, but I still seem to be teetering on a financial knife edge.'

Mrs Stewart crossed her silk-hosed legs and laughed. 'How very honest of you, but that often happens in the early days of a new company.'

'Does it? Yes, I suppose so. I already owe my sister a large sum.'

'Has the repayment been arranged legally?'

Willow was suddenly suspicious. She was by no means the only woman struggling to make a living after the war; some of them, the unscrupulous ones, would jump at the chance of getting a spy into the enemy camp to uncover a weakness which might be exploited.

Mrs Stewart said, 'I am absolutely genuine, I do assure you. I have enough money to last me for life and I amuse myself by playing the market now and then. I would particularly enjoy being a small part of your fascinating venture.'

Willow considered. That morning she had received a letter from Alfred reminding her that she hadn't visited Bristol for some time and that, although the tailoress engaged to make the patterns and *toiles* was working hard, orders were falling off.

Mrs Stewart said, 'Please, indulge me. I can introduce you to my solicitor who could handle all your business for you.'

'That would mean another bill.'

'Yes, but it might save you problems later. He's an expert in company business and income tax.'

'Income tax!'

'Had you forgotten it?'

Willow had never even given it a thought. In a panic she agreed to go with Mrs Stewart to her solicitor on the following day. The premises of Booker and Castle, Solicitors, were quite near the workrooms and Willow spoke to Mr Booker, a man with a rare capacity for listening. When she stopped speaking she waited, half expecting him to tell her that she was being hopelessly reckless. Instead, he congratulated her, approved of Mrs Stewart's move, and suggested that Willow should go to the bank with the figures which he would prepare, and ask for a loan. In a remarkably short time Willow found herself with an investor and a sizeable overdraft and wasn't sure if she was to be congratulated, sympathised with, or castigated for a fool.

She left Miss Jebb in charge of the workrooms, a move which pleased the embittered woman but led Willow to have doubts as the train carried her further from London on the way to Bristol. She had suggested the idea while reeling under the heady feeling that she was now a real business woman, hoping to soften Miss Jebb into congeniality.

In Bristol she went straight to see Alfred at the workrooms. The sun was strong and Wine Street seemed to be attracting the heat. Even the stones of the road were baking and inside the buildings it had become an effort to draw in enough air. It was far too hot to worry about money. Nevertheless, problems had to be tackled.

Alfred greeted her with relief. 'Thank goodness! Just in time, too. I've a client arriving any minute and she's furious because she says we've cut her new dress all wrong. She wouldn't wait for a final fitting and she's returned the dress and wants her money back. Cora insists she cut it exactly to the woman's shape and it isn't her fault.'

Willow said, 'You're looking very smart, Alfred, and the place is lovely.'

He grinned and kissed her. 'I am pleased to see you, honest, Willow. I'm just so worried.'

'I'm sorry I couldn't get down before.'

His eyes roamed over her dark blue silk suit and hat. 'Gorgeous! Your clothes are plain but beautiful, if you know what I mean. I suppose you made them?'

'No, I cut them out and my girls made them.'

'I wish I had your talent. I can think of new designs, but I couldn't get to grips with the cutting. I thought Cora would help.'

'Let's see what the problem is. First, I must meet her.'

Cora looked mutinous. Her full lips turned down in a pout which made her look like an oversized baby. 'If you don't think I'm good enough, I can go somewhere else,' she said when Alfred walked into the workroom.

'This is my sister, Miss Riches,' he said.

Cora's eyes widened and Willow asked, 'Did you think I was a client?'

'Yes, I did.'

'And you spoke that way in front of someone you believed was here to buy?'

Cora flushed. 'Well, you're here to sack me, anyway, aren't you?'

'Not necessarily. Show me the new dress.'

Cora protested, 'I know I followed the right measurements. I was really careful, but it hangs loose on her.'

'I had better see her in it.'

'Yes, please,' said Alfred. 'She's threatened us with legal action if we don't come up with the money. The material's an expensive one, as you see, but the real harm would lie in the bad publicity.'

The disputed dress hung limply on a faceless figure which did nothing to enhance its fashionable straight lines, the waist lightly defined and sliding down towards the hips. Willow walked round it and viewed it from all angles. 'The low back and neckline are all the rage and I assume she chose the crepe georgette. Yellow. Not an easy colour to wear. Does it suit her?'

'I think it does,' said Cora, 'and Alfred agrees with me. She's got dark hair, though I suspect it's artificially coloured, and brown eyes and rather olive skin.'

Willow said, 'You really have taken note of her requirements.'

'Yes, I have, and anyone who says I haven't is a liar.'

'I do hope you didn't say so to the customer. What's her name, by the way?'

'Mrs Andrew Billington and she makes me bilious,' snapped Cora.

'Customers are sometimes apt to do that,' said Willow calmly, 'but we have to put up with it if we wish to make a living.'

Cora calmed down beneath Willow's equable attitude. 'I'm sorry, Miss Riches.'

'Willow, please.'

Cora flushed. 'Willow, then. Well, I am really sorry, honestly. I didn't mean to upset Alfred and bring you to Bristol when you must be so busy.'

'It's all part of my work.'

Bridget came tearing into the room. 'She's back again. Willow! I didn't know you were here.'

'I'll have a chat with you and Dora presently. Meanwhile, we have a problem.'

Mrs Billington was as Cora had described her. She marched in accompanied by a friend who cast a scornful eye over the shop.

'May I help you, Mrs Billington?' asked Willow.

The woman's eyes opened wide. 'How do you know me? Who are you? The only way I can be helped is by returning my seven guineas to me.'

'I'm Willow Riches, the proprietress. I have come down from London to see you.'

This, Willow noted happily, took some of the wind from the woman's sails. 'I see.'

'I understand that there is a problem over your new gown? I would be grateful if you would take the time to try it on for me.'

Mrs Billington threw a look of triumph at Cora and marched into the fitting area, followed by her friend whom she introduced as Mrs Mappen. The gown slid smoothly over her head and although the fashion was now for loosely draped clothes it was obviously far too loose.

'You see what I mean!' the indignant client said, staring into the mirror and picking nervously at the material. 'I know the waist is supposed to be low, but mine hangs at hip length, and the low neckline practically shows my bosom. I couldn't possibly go out in it.'

Willow nodded. 'May I compliment you on your slender figure?'

Mrs Billington preened herself. 'I've been dieting like mad. We both have, haven't we, Mrs Mappen?'

'Too true,' said her friend.

'It's all the rage now, isn't it, to be thin?' said Willow. 'But it isn't easy to regulate one's food intake. Congratulations on your success. Have you any idea of the amount of weight you have lost?'

'Oh, fourteen pounds easily.'

'And did this happen after your original fittings?'

Mrs Billington realised that she had been led gently into a trap which had closed upon her. She bridled angrily and turned from the mirror to stare at Willow who greeted her fury with a bland smile. Her eyes travelled over Willow's beautiful suit, down to her silk stockings and narrow, silk shoes, and her anger dissolved into a reluctant smile. 'It's my fault, isn't it? I've got thinner.'

Willow said nothing and Mrs Billington said, 'It is *all* my fault. There was a lapse of a month between the fittings and the completed gown because I decided to go to Biarritz. Oh, dear. I really should not have treated Cora so crossly.'

'How generous of you to say so,' said Willow.

'What can you do about it?' Mrs Billington appeared to have developed complete faith in Willow.

'We could attempt to alter it, but that might spoil it. If you wish, I shall keep it as a display garment, and meanwhile perhaps you would care to have us make you another gown? I will go over some ideas with you and take the first measurements myself and Cora and Alfred will do the rest.'

'Can't you stay?'

'I must get back to the London end of the business. The season, you know.'

'London? I had no idea you were a large fashion house, had you, Mrs Mappen?'

Willow thought of the modest rooms above Rupert's art gallery. 'Is the plan satisfactory to you, Mrs Billington?'

It was agreed and Willow called out the new measurements to Cora. As Mrs Mappen decided to buy new clothes, too, a near-disaster was turned into good business.

'All the same, Cora,' pointed out Willow, 'your attitude towards Mrs Billington was not what I expect. The customer is always right.'

'Even when she's wrong?'

'Even when she's wrong.' No further fittings were scheduled for a while and Bridget joined them, followed by Dora with a tray of tea. Regular work and Clara's cossetting had given the sisters an air of confidence which was pleasing. Willow sat and talked for a while, telling them, to their delight, that Erin was proving a great asset, then they returned to work.

Willow discovered that Cora had excellent ideas which she was nervous of using in case she made a mistake. 'The ladies who come here don't really want to be all that different,' she explained, 'and it's hard to know where to draw the line.'

'In future,' said Willow, 'go ahead and try to sell your original ideas. If women don't like them, offer something conventional. I'll send you some patterns from London. Could you adapt them where necessary?'

'Certainly I could. I can't thank you enough. I was scared I'd lose my job, and so many girls have had to give up their wartime work to the returning servicemen and find it hard to get jobs. I was good at art at school and always wanted to do something fancy.'

'That sounds promising. Could you sketch your vision of the finished garments to show the clients?'

'I certainly could. What a good idea.' Willow left with the comfortable feeling that Cora and Alfred would soon regain lost ground.

Clara was very pleased to see her. 'You look grand, my love,' she said, and kissed her. 'An' you smell lovely, too.'

'I've brought you some scent, Mum, and a matching skirt and coat and a couple of blouses.' She looked her mother up and down. 'You haven't changed at all. You are eating properly, aren't you?'

'Of course I am. The pantry's always full of food these days. Those two girls take a lot of feedin'.'

'You don't find them too much for you?'

'Bless you, no. An' our Jasmine's growin' like a beanpole an' eats like a bloomin' horse and never puts on an ounce.

She's got prettier than ever. Last time Marigold came to see us she suggested Jasmine went back to London with her. She said she'd find her a job.'

Willow hid her rage from Clara. 'Did she? What was Jasmine's answer?'

'She just said she wouldn't go. I think she's a bit scared of Marigold.'

'Actually, I may be able to use Jasmine myself.'

'If you asked her, she'd go anywhere. She still thinks the world of you.'

'Would you mind her leaving Bristol?'

'Not if she was with you. I know you'd take care of her, though Sidney might be annoyed.' Clara sat down and fanned herself. 'I can't abide the weather bein' as hot as this. I went in town to see your Wine Street dressmakin' shop yesterday an' it was like an oven. Don't know how Alfred puts up with it. He doesn't seem to mind.' She paused. 'You know, Willow, I thought he was a real poncy-boy to work with women's clothes, but he's not at all. An' d'you know, he gives me money, though he doesn't live here, an' with what you send an' Jasmine's wages an' the O'Haras I do very well.'

Willow looked round the living room. It had been newly decorated in green and pink, Clara's favourite colours. 'Everybody helped,' said her mother. 'Upstairs is the same. In fact, the whole house is like it. Cora's brother's started up in the buildin' an' decoratin' trade an' he gave us a discount. Nice, isn't it?'

'Lovely, Mum. And new furniture too!'

'Yes, I've bought a few things. I got them on the never-never an' I'm always in for the tally-man. Remember how we used to keep quiet an' hide when he knocked at the door? Mrs Tucker never gave me away once. She wasn't such a bad soul, but I'm glad I've got my own house. I've you to thank for that, my love.'

Willow basked in Clara's happiness, though a shiver ran through her at the possibility of failure. It was never far from her mind. She owed so much money and so many depended now on her. And her mother was gentler, older somehow, more frail and needy.

'What time will Jasmine be home, Mum?'

'Tea-time. As you know, she's workin' in Sidney Moor's factory as a run-about. Just like you did. That seems a long time ago. Our Dad was alive, an' the boys. My poor boys.' Her voice cracked and she drew a deep breath. 'I must count my blessin's. That's what they say in chapel.'

'You go to chapel?'

'Most Sundays. Sidney gets us to dress up an' off we go. He drives us in his car an' I feel that posh!'

'I didn't know.'

'Sidney's a good bloke, so different from the rest of the family, I sometimes wonder if his mother strayed a bit.' Clara's hand went to her mouth to cover a smile. 'I shouldn't say that, but honest, it does make you wonder. Mind you, the family's better than it was. Their father fell down one night in the street. Everyone thought he was just drunk again, but when he was still there next day they realised he was dead.'

'That's terrible!'

'He didn't suffer. They say he died of a heart attack before he hit the ground. Since then Mrs Moor's been quieter. Some of the boys stayed in the army, only the eldest's in prison, an' the girls are married, except for the one our Marigold used to go round with. What was her name?'

'Nellie.'

'Fancy you rememberin' that. I heard she was in London –' Clara lowered her voice '– livin' a life of sin, but you can't believe gossip, can you?'

Willow let the subject drop. 'I want to see Sidney while I'm here.'

Clara said, 'I've got an idea he's waitin' for Jasmine to grow up.' She nodded significantly. 'You know what I mean.'

'Don't worry. I haven't got designs on him. In fact, I hope he'll have designs on me, in a manner of speaking. I want to find out if he can supply made-to-measure body supports. Heavy corsets are out of fashion now.'

'Are they really? Well, I always wear mine. I'd feel undressed without it.'

Willow smiled, picturing Clara's rigidly boned, hooked-at-the-front corset. Unlike Mrs Stewart, she didn't need the support. 'Why don't you just try something different? You might be more comfortable.'

'I'm comfy as I am, thank you very much. I've always balanced the washin' basket on it when I had a full load, an' I've got too used to it to change now.'

Sidney was in his office on the top floor of the factory which he had expanded. Willow wondered how he had managed to get a builder when they were all overworked since post-war reconstruction had begun and so many craftsmen had been lost. Cora's brother again, perhaps?

She tapped and entered the office which was comfortably furnished. Sidney looked up and his face brightened. 'Willow! I heard you might be coming to Bristol.'

'Did you? How?'

'I saw Alfred. He was worried about something and said he'd written to you.'

'He would have reached me quicker if he had used the telephone. It's installed in both my establishments now.'

'How grand you sound. I've got one, too. Handy, aren't they?'

'You've become quite grand yourself, and blasé too.' She laughed. 'Can this really be the spotty lad of my youth?'

'And can this be the run-about factory girl? Willow, you look beautiful, and that outfit is wonderful.'

'Thanks.'

'Sit down. Tea?'

'No thanks. I've come with a business proposition.' She explained her idea about made-to-measure corsets and he was immediately interested. 'We already have a few customers who pay more for special corsets. The only problem

502

about London would be the fitting,' he said. 'We can hardly expect clients to travel so far.'

'I've thought of that. I wondered—' She paused and he looked suspicious, though he smiled. 'You wondered what?'

'If you had someone you could spare.'

'To work for you?'

'Yes. She'd have to be a good needlewoman too. I can't afford to employ someone just for corsetry.'

'I do have someone, but I can't let her go. If she's willing, why don't we arrange for her to travel to London regularly?'

'That sounds excellent.'

'Right. I'll put it to her. I won't be long.'

He left and a moment later Jasmine came running in. 'Willow!' She rushed to her sister and hugged her, dislodging her hat. 'Oh, sorry. How smart you look! How long can you stay? I miss you terribly.'

'I have to return soon, I'm afraid. I miss you too, my love.'

'Marigold asked if I'd like to go to London with her. I was tempted because I thought I'd be able to see more of you, but I didn't really want to be with her, an' anyway Mum said no. She was really stern about it. I told Alfred what Marigold said and he was ever so annoyed. He said I was to tell him if she asked again. Marigold looks as if she's well-off. Lettin' rooms must make you rich.'

'Are you happy here in the factory?'

'Oh, yes. I love the work an' all the girls are so nice.'

Jasmine had fulfilled the early promise of beauty. Her hair, as dark as Willow's own, was glossy and more silky and wouldn't get easily tangled, her eyes were of a deeper blue, her mouth more curved. Her height and beauty gave her a mature lustre. The thought of Marigold's offer of work infuriated Willow afresh.

Sidney returned. 'Off you go, young Jasmine, there are several bundles of corsets waiting for you.'

She laughed, kissed Willow again, and dashed away.

'Shouldn't she be on the machines by now?' asked Willow. 'She'd earn more.'

'Strictly speaking, yes, but I can't bear to think of her crouched all day over a sewing machine. She's so full of life I think she'd burst.'

A woman knocked and came in. She was of medium height, stockily built, her greying hair strained back into plaits which were wound round her head in a crown. 'This is Miss Brenda Salter, in charge of our specials,' said Sidney.

'How do you do, Miss Salter?'

'Well, thank you. And you may call me Brenda.'

Willow wondered who was interviewing whom. 'Has Mr Moor told you what I need?'

'Sidney tells me you want me to travel to London to fit your customers with corsets.' Having established procedure, Brenda listened to Willow, nodding now and again. 'That all sounds satisfactory to me, providing of course you can give me a bed for the night if I need it.'

'Of course. Er, my clients are wealthy women,' said Willow uncertainly, wondering how they would take to Brenda.

'If you mean they're toffee-nosed, you needn't worry. I can manage. I tell them what they want to hear and listen respectfully, then get a corset made that's two or three sizes bigger than they say. It always works.'

When she had left, Willow said, 'She's a bit lugubrious, isn't she? And bossy with it.'

Sidney laughed. 'The women love her. They all long to be convinced that she can make them look slim and graceful.'

'It sounds as if she tells whoppers.'

'If you were in the corset trade, you'd know that it's the only way.'

On Saturday afternoon Willow and Jasmine walked on the Downs. 'Just for old times' sake,' Jasmine had begged.

'Old times' sake,' mocked Willow fondly. 'It was only – my God – it was about eleven years ago when Winifred Maddison nearly went under a car.'

'An' you saved her, an' then went away.'

Jasmine's voice broke and Willow slid an arm about her waist. 'I hated leaving you. That was the worst thing.'

'And for me, but I know the money you sent home was needed.'

'Have you kept up with your education? I hoped you'd be able to go on to university.'

'Me? At a university?' Jasmine laughed. 'I can't imagine it. I do read, Willow. Mum tells me I'll wear my eyes out. I won't, will I?'

Willow turned and gave Jasmine an appraising look. Her eyes were large and luminous, exercise had given her a healthy glow, her complexion was perfect. 'No, you won't do that, but make sure you don't hunch over your books for too many hours. What are you reading at the moment?'

'A lovely one. *Three Weeks* by a lady called Elinor Glynn. It's about love and it's so beautiful. I used to read bits of it to Mum, but she didn't like it. I'm glad she didn't because it's a bit naughty – lots of kissin'. It makes me embarrassed.' Jasmine laughed, then put her hand on Willow's arm. 'Look, isn't that Edgar Maddison?'

Willow's pulses raced at the mention of his name. 'No, it can't be, not at this time of year.'

She turned. It was Edgar and he was walking swiftly towards them. He glanced at Jasmine before holding out his hand to Willow. 'Fancy meeting you here.'

'A real coincidence,' said Willow. 'Do you remember my sister Jasmine?'

Edgar gave a slight bow. 'I am sure we cannot have met. I would remember.'

Jasmine giggled and Edgar smiled. 'Where are you going?'

'Nowhere special,' said Jasmine, before Willow could answer.

'Then you can come and have tea with me.'

Jasmine looked at Willow who stood undecided. She wanted to be with him, she longed for it, but her instincts were screaming a warning. He was not for her, never would be, and to be with him could merely increase her longing for him.

'That would be lovely,' she said.

He drove them in a long, low, bright red car with no rear seat so that they squeezed together in the front, Jasmine separating them. 'Isn't she a beauty?' said Edgar. 'Six cylinders. Goes like a dream.'

The sisters understood him to be talking about his car which, Willow noted, was new. Mr Maddison must be feeling pleased with his son. 'I dare say that means it goes fast,' said Willow.

'She certainly does,' said Edgar, restoring the car's gender.

Willow sighed exaggeratedly. 'Men seem to have love affairs with their cars. As far as I'm concerned they are only a useful tool which carry one from place to place.'

Jasmine giggled as Edgar cried, 'Sacrilege!'

He took the road leading away from Clifton. 'You've passed two tearooms already,' Willow pointed out.

'It will be so much nicer to find a place in the country,' he said. 'You agree with me, don't you, Jasmine?'

She sighed an ecstatic yes. 'I wish the girls in the factory could see me now.'

They passed Duchess Park in Stapleton and on to Frenchay Common where Edgar made a slight detour. By doing so he passed the cottage where he and Willow had once spent such a happy time. Willow thought he paused momentarily, but maybe she imagined it, maybe her never-stilled ache for him was playing tricks. They arrived at a tea-garden by the side of the River Frome and Jasmine squealed with delight. She seated herself in one of the garden chairs expectantly and Willow joined her. They were shaded by overhanging trees and the proximity of the water gave a sense of coolness. She fanned her face and gratefully drank the lemonade Edgar brought. The ride had been a dusty one. 'This is just to wet our whistles,' he said. 'Tea follows.'

Willow had to agree with Jasmine when she exclaimed, 'It's like a dream-land.'

The place was green and beautiful and their presence here with Edgar as insubstantial as a dream. Would she have accepted his invitation if Jasmine had not been with her? The answer came swiftly to mind before she could clamp down on it. Yes.

There were children swimming in the river and Jasmine went to watch them. 'I wish I had brought my bathing costume,' she called back.

'I wish she had, too,' said Edgar quietly, his hand reaching out to cover Willow's.

She snatched it away as if he had stung her.

'What's the matter?'

'You know. You have made it clear that there can never be anything between us.'

'We can remain friends!'

'That doesn't mean you can hold my hand.'

'Good God, that's innocuous enough.'

'No,' she said. 'It is not!'

He leaned back in his chair. 'You are right. Nothing I do is innocuous where you're concerned. Oh, Willow darling, I do so love you.'

Her defences fell and she wanted him desperately, now, at once. 'I shall never go anywhere with you again, Edgar,' she said in a low voice. 'It would be best if we never even met.'

'I couldn't bear that.'

'You can't love me as much as you say or you wouldn't condemn me to this.'

'I condemn both of us, don't forget.'

'Yes, but you have your precious duty to your family to sustain you!'

Jasmine returned, her hands filled with wild flowers and ferns. 'These will look lovely on the mantel-shelf. Mum will enjoy them. Alfred bought her a vase.'

Edgar drove them home almost in silence. Even Jasmine was quiet, savouring the wonderful afternoon she had enjoyed with her beloved Willow. She thanked Edgar and leapt from the car and Willow moved to follow her. Edgar grasped her arm. 'Willow, I must see you. Once more. Just once more. I have the key to the cottage.'

'Let me go!'

'Promise me.'

'The neighbours are watching.'

'You surely don't care about a few nosy neighbours.'

'No, I don't, but my mother does and she has to live among them.'

Edgar released her and jumped out to hand her down as Clara appeared at the front door.

'Willow, bring Edgar in for tea.'

'We've had tea, thank you, Mum.'

'There's always room for another one,' cried Edgar.

Willow stared at him angrily as he drank strong tea and talked to her mother. He seemed genuinely interested in all that she told him about the activities of her family and her pleasure in lodging Bridget and Dora. 'Our Willow's really clever,' she said. 'It's a marvel to me how she's got where she is today, with so many people workin' for her. Dressmakin' businesses in two towns, drivin' her own car, an' dressin' just like a lady.'

'It's a marvel to me too,' said Edgar. Willow searched his face for mockery, but there was none. But she still wasn't good enough to marry.

He looked at her once, then carefully avoided her eyes until, reluctantly glancing at his watch, he got up. 'I'm really sorry to leave you, Mrs Riches. It's cosy here, so homely.'

Willow felt sudden pity for him. He had everything money could buy but was denied the comfortable pleasure which Clara inspired. On impulse she walked with him to his car. 'I was glad to see you again,' she said unwisely.

It was the opening he needed. 'Meet me at the cottage, darling, please. I beg of you.'

'I can't. Don't keep asking.'

'But I need you so. Look, I'll be there tonight. If you can get away I'll be waiting.'

She stood watching him drive round the corner, his car

508

causing swirls of dust in the hot road, then walked slowly back into the house.

Willow was preoccupied during the evening. Clara frowned anxiously. 'You're workin' too hard, my girl. You've not an ounce of life in you.'

'I'm sorry I'm not very good company, Mum. I am tired, but I'm strong and young enough to manage.'

'D'you get plenty of decent food inside you or d'you just forget?'

'I eat enough. Anyway, it's the fashion to be thin.'

'A daft one, if you ask me.' Willow glanced at Clara's spare figure, her gaunt face which good living had not yet softened. 'All right, Miss Clever, I'm thin too.'

Willow said, 'I wonder if Sidney would lend me his car? There's a client I want to visit while I'm here.' The decision to go to Edgar was so sudden, the lie slipped out so calmly, that Willow surprised herself.

'Fancy havin' to call on someone at nine o'clock at night!'

'Sometimes the evenings are the only times I can see people.' That, at least, was true. Marigold and her girls demanded her services whenever they happened to have a free evening.

'I'll go and ask Sidney, then.'

Jasmine looked up from her book. 'He's ever so kind. I'm sure he'll lend it to you. He'll probably offer to drive you. I wouldn't mind coming myself.'

Hell! This looked like turning into a mass expedition. Willow half laughed, imagining herself turning up at the cottage with an entourage. Then she sighed. It was no laughing matter. Ever since the afternoon she had been indulging in images of herself meeting her eager lover until she had hypnotised herself into going.

Clara saw Willow's face. 'I think your sister wants to go out on her own. It's probably best. It's nearly your bedtime, anyway.'

'Oh, Mum, I'm sixteen! No one else goes to bed as early as I do.'

'You're lucky you've got the chance. In the old days everyone in the family worked all hours.'

Jasmine fell silent. Whenever Mum spoke of 'the old days' there was sorrow in her voice.

Bridget and Dora came home from a visit to The Globe, the local moving-picture house, and raised Clara's spirits. 'I've kept some soup warm for you,' she said, leaning over the range to stir the pot. Willow had offered to buy Clara a gas stove, but she said they terrified her. 'I've seen one. It makes a terrible poppin' noise when it's turned on an' again when it goes off. It isn't as if we haven't got the front room to sit in if we want to.' The front room was Clara's pride, furnished by courtesy of the tally-man with a square of carpet, lino which was regularly polished to a high shine, and easy chairs. It was rarely used.

Willow slid out and called on Sidney. He was in and didn't need the car. 'It's a bit heavy for you,' he said, immediately. 'I'll drive you where you want to go.'

'It's all right. I can manage. Besides, I don't know how long I'll be.'

'I don't mind waiting.'

'I'd as soon go by myself.'

Sidney opened his mouth to argue again, then capitulated. 'I've a notion I'm being a bit tactless. Sorry. There's plenty of petrol in the tank. Watch out for the second gear. She's a bit fierce.'

Willow climbed in and drove off before anyone else offered to accompany her. The car was indeed heavy and her arms were aching when she reached Frenchay. She stopped on the common, letting the engine run, watching in a desultory way several small boys playing cricket in the gathering darkness. Quickly she put the car into gear. When changing to second she grated the metal so loudly that the boys looked up and cheered. 'Where's yer driver, missus?' one called. Another shouted, 'Women can't drive!'

'Cheeky little blighters,' she muttered as she took the road leading to the cottage.

Edgar was waiting for her and had the front door open

almost before she stopped. He smiled and came to the car with eager steps, opened the door and held her arm as she climbed down.

'I won't break,' she said.

'Darling Willow, I know that. Nothing will ever break you.'

Nothing? She hoped he was right.

They walked into the cottage with their arms around each other and as soon as they were inside Edgar turned and held her close, staring down at her. 'I thought you'd come.'

She wasn't sure she liked that. She pulled herself free. 'You're as sure of me as that?'

'No, of course not. I'm not at all sure of you, but I know you care for me. I've been living on a knife edge for the past couple of hours.'

'You've been here for two hours?'

'Yes, and it feels like a lifetime.' He put his hands on her shoulders and his eyes travelled over her. 'You're lovelier than ever. So elegant too. I suppose you made your outfit? How clever you are. You are all the things I am not.'

She had left off the jacket of her dark blue suit and wore instead a pale turquoise blouse. He smoothed its silky softness with gentle fingers and Willow's body, which had begun its ready response to his presence, began to clamour for him.

'I love you,' he said.

'I love you, too, so much. So much.'

'Sit down, darling. Would you like a drink? I have wine or coffee.'

She wanted neither, she wanted only to be with him, but she asked for coffee, suddenly shy, wary of demonstrating how complete was her enslavement.

He joined her on the low living-room sofa. The grate held a large vase containing a mass of dried flowers and ferns. 'I've missed you,' he said.

'Have you honestly?'

He put his cup and saucer down on a small table. 'You don't believe me?'

'Yes. I wish I didn't.'

'You can't mean that.'

'I do.'

'But why?'

'I have so many responsibilities, so many people depend on me. I can't afford to lose myself in sentimentality.'

'Is that how you look upon our love? As something sentimental, to be avoided?'

'No,' she sighed, 'it isn't.' The atmosphere was becoming too heavy to endure. 'Mrs Stewart buys clothes from me now,' she said. 'She's quite an arbiter of fashion.' She blundered on, 'She's a prompt payer too.'

'To hell with all that!' Edgar removed her coffee cup and slid his arms around her waist. 'God, but you feel good.'

'Not romantic,' she said, 'but to the point.' She rose and he ushered her up the narrow stairway. She remembered their last time here, the frantic passion which had seized them, the memory of which often stirred her, undermining her tranquillity.

He removed her blouse and skirt and she trembled as if this was the first time. Her raw emotion fuelled his need and he ran his fingers over her smooth skin, then pulled down the straps of her petticoat and held her breasts in his hands. 'They're so beautiful, so soft.' He bent his head and took her nipples in turn and nuzzled them, drawing them into his mouth where the movement of his tongue sent her crazy with love and she cried out his name.

'Darling, darling,' he breathed. He pushed her back until she lay across the bed and he unrolled her stockings as deftly as any lady's maid. 'Willow,' he murmured, as he began to explore her with his mouth. She writhed and gasped, 'This isn't fair. You're still dressed.'

He laughed and within moments was standing naked beside her. 'See how much I need you?'

She laughed, too. 'A man's body certainly sends out a clear signal.'

He knelt beside her on the bed, his lips resuming their caresses, while her hands moved over him, smoothing, rubbing, enjoying him. She wanted him so badly it became an ache.

'My darling,' he murmured, 'you're the most glorious, responsive, delicious woman I've ever known.'

And he had known a few. An image of Kitty Martin flashed like forked lightning through her mind and she sat up, her eyes which had been dark with desire narrowing, her passion cooled. What in hell was she doing here, waiting for him to assuage his lust? He chose to call it love, but it was really lust. She hated herself, despised herself for her submission to a man who saw her as a means of gratifying his sexual desires. She dragged at the quilt, pulling it over her nakedness.

'What's the matter?' he asked urgently.

'Get away from me!'

'What?'

'Get away from me! I must be crazy! You don't love me. If you did you would—' She stumbled to a halt. She was damned if she would beg for marriage.

'Willow, please, I adore you, worship you! Don't drive me mad! Is this a tease?' he continued uncertainly. 'It is a tease, isn't it? You've learned new tricks to enslave me.'

'Tricks? You make me sound like a pet animal – or a whore.'

'Don't use that word about yourself!'

'I suppose you think I give myself to any man?'

'No, no, of course not.' He went on sympathetically, 'But I know your sexual feelings are strong and you must have admirers, men who want you. I wouldn't blame you for giving way.'

'Wouldn't you! Wouldn't you, really!' She ran her hands over her face which was damp with perspiration. The cottage bedroom had taken the full glare of the afternoon sun. The window was closed, the air stifling. The room which had seemed to hold everything dear to her was small, cramped, unlovely. 'I'm going home.'

'You can't. You can't do this to me!' He was selfish, she raged, he put himself first. 'Willow, you're behaving like a prude. Why? You were once honest about your needs.'

'What do you know about me? The only needs you recognise are your own. God damn you, Edgar, I hope I never see you again.' She hurried into her clothes, frantic to get away before she burst into uncontrollable weeping.

He grabbed his trousers and pulled them on and followed her down the stairs. 'Willow darling, I'm sorry. Sorry.'

'For what?'

'For insulting you. For suggesting that other men—'

'Yes, I'm sorry too, for believing you loved me. You don't! You couldn't, or you'd understand.'

'I do understand.' His voice was almost a wail, reminding her of the peevish boy he had been. 'You want marriage and I can't give it to you.'

She turned on him, her eyes sparking with fury. 'Why can't you? Am I too common? Not of the right class?'

'Nothing like that makes the least bit of difference to me. You must believe me!'

'Then why treat me the way you do?'

They stood silent for a moment and his grasp on her arm slackened, as he said, 'James was my parents' darling. While he was alive they didn't much mind what I did. If he had not been killed my life would be a good deal easier.'

'So we have to be sacrificed to please your parents!'

'Put like that it sounds melodramatic. It is really quite simple. They've had so much unhappiness. I feel compelled to follow their wishes and marry a girl of whom they approve.'

'And she'll produce blue-blooded babies from her blue-blooded womb and everyone will be happy!'

'Yes.' He was angry. 'Crude, but true.'

'Crude? Why not? I come from a crude society many of whom would despise me for even being friendly with you.'

'You refuse to understand!'

'Oh, I understand all right. It's the war again, always the bloody war. You're using it, too.'

She pulled herself away from him, her final words echoing

in her head as she drove from the cottage, tears coursing down her face, her pride in tatters, and profoundly ashamed because her most powerful emotion was one of desolate longing to go back to him.

Chapter Twenty-seven

Rupert raised his glass and proposed a toast. 'To Willow – and Riches! In more than one sense!'

The guests repeated the words, downing their wine so that Rupert was obliged to refill their glasses, a task he performed with willing relish. He had realised that his essay into the art world was not going to be the success he had hoped. He was too soft-hearted to refuse to hang the works of struggling artists even when he thought they wouldn't sell, and had finally succumbed to his parents' pleas to give it up. In their relief, they paid all outstanding debts. Several of his artist friends were here, tonight, each garbed in his or her own flamboyant fashion, making their bid for originality.

Willow now rented the whole of the shop, the ground floor of which had been decorated in the same unobtrusive colours as upstairs. The window, with a pale blue back-cloth, held a white satin evening gown edged in tangerine, a black velvet cape with a tangerine satin lining, and framed sketches of both garments. In front of the ensemble was a card with the word *Harmony*. It was one of the special display outfits which she had prepared in what little spare time she had and it was eye-catching. Business had increased to a point where she now employed four full-time seamstresses and an apprentice. Her employees were at the party, including Miss Jebb, who maintained her customary sullen demeanour. She was seething with jealousy because she had been kept on plain sewing. After listening to her grumbling and assurances that she had learned much in the intervening years, Willow had given her the chance to work on a more complicated piece and the result had been so bad that it had to be done again, wasting material and keeping Willow up until the early hours putting it right. This seemed to make Miss Jebb even more resentful.

The materials draped around the large ground-floor front room complemented the pictures, which included some of Willow's. Alfred was happy, relishing the atmosphere of money and the slight air of decadence emanating from the artists. Earlier he had pin-pointed styles which would go well in the Bristol shop. 'Neat, not gaudy,' he explained. Women who could afford to pay a little more, the wives and daughters of professional men, wanted something different, but not outrageously so and they found it in Riches of Wine Street. The others, people like the Maddisons, who spent their lives travelling from one pleasure to another, came to Riches of London for their exclusive clothes.

As the room filled and the chatter and laughter grew louder Willow looked around. Not bad, she thought, not bad at all. Clara was here, accompanied by Jasmine who was pink with excitement and drawing many eyes. She was beautiful in a simple, low-waisted, fine wool dress of sapphire blue trimmed with silver. Clara wore a grey suit and a blue hat with a grey feather. She had kept on her gloves, refusing to display hands that were red and rough. 'I can't let you down,' she had said. Willow had hugged her. 'You couldn't do that, Mum.'

When Clara had first arrived she had stood looking incredulously at the window display. 'Willow, my love, I don't want to tell you your job, but you ought to have a lot more stuff showin'. How will people know what to buy? Mr Armitage – you remember him who keeps the haberdashery? – he has his window filled an' he hangs stuff outside an' he does a good trade. His family never go short of anythin' at all.'

Willow had laughed. 'It's the way you have to work in this kind of place. The less there is in the window, the more impressed shoppers are.'

Clara had shaken her head. 'Well, I never. It all sounds peculiar to me, I must say. It stands to reason that the more stuff people see, the more you'll sell. I like the drawin's. You've always been good at them.'

Alfred had brought Mum to town the day before and she was staying with Willow. She had offered Clara a hotel bed, but her mother had been adamant. 'I'm not stayin' in a strange bed in a hotel. You never know who's been there before you. If I can't stay with our Willow I'm not comin', an' that's flat.'

While Clara was upstairs getting settled, Alfred said, 'I hope you appreciate the immense task I've had. Getting Nancy Astor into Parliament was nothing compared to the struggle to get Mum to leave Bristol. She's never been further than Weston in her life and that was only a couple of times when Dad was alive.'

'I do appreciate your efforts, brother dear,' said Willow. 'I wanted Mum to enjoy herself which is why I tried to put her up in a hotel. I thought she'd love all the attention and no work, but it's useless to expect her to be idle. She refused to come down tonight until she'd washed the supper things and put them away.'

Alfred laughed. 'If it makes her happy! You certainly look happy, sis. You are, aren't you?'

'You've just said I am.'

He raised an eyebrow. 'Sometimes you've got a faraway look.'

'Good lord, I must watch it. I don't want my clients to think I'm not actually with them.'

She eased her way through the crush talking to this one and that, then the door opened and Edgar walked in. She hadn't seen him since she had fled from him in Frenchay and she had been deceiving herself if she thought she had conquered her love, as if it was a sickness from which she could recover. As soon as she saw him the old urges became paramount; her flesh tingled, her hands longed to touch him, he turned her into a creature of physical wants. No, not just physical. She loved him with her mind as well as her body and feared she always would. With the percipience that came with love, she knew without watching that he was making his way slowly but inexorably towards her. The crowd and the noise became distant as their eyes met and she cursed herself for a fool.

More guests entered and as people shifted he was momentarily pushed against her. 'How did you get in?' she asked.

'I have an invitation. Do you want to see it?'

'I didn't send one. Who gave it to you?'

'No one. It came through the post.'

'I see. Your mother's name is on my list of clients. I suppose you've taken her place?'

'Mother is at Buddleigh Manor.'

'Heavens! Not doing the season?'

'She's not been well.'

'Oh, I'm sorry. I hope it's nothing serious.'

'I don't think so. She is heart-sick, like so many others these days. Mary has told her of her plans and the thought of the twins going so far away has devastated her.'

'I can understand that.'

'Can you, darling?'

'Don't call me that, you fool! Where's Miss Martin tonight?'

'At the theatre with her parents.' He leaned forward. 'You are still my darling.'

She couldn't control the shiver of pleasure his words gave her; it was all she could do to prevent herself from grabbing him and kissing him. 'How is Miss Martin?' she asked, in an effort to bring herself back to normality.

'She is all right, though I see little of her these days.'

'Fancy! I thought you'd have been engaged by now.'

Edgar shrugged. 'She found someone she preferred.'

She managed to conceal her blaze of pleasure. 'Were your parents furious?'

'They were not pleased. They blamed me for not paying her enough attention. They were right. She's a sweet girl, but I simply could not get excited about the thought of marrying her. I've done her a favour by letting her go. Willow, darling, won't you meet me later?'

She held herself still. 'What for? A few hours of fun and then goodbye?'

'Why not? You're not a prude and you say you love me. You know how matters stand with me. My parents . . .'

'Yes, your parents. You had better be a good boy for them.' She pushed past him, prickly with fury, assuming a smile which became genuine when she saw Mrs Stewart. 'I'm so glad you were able to come. How pretty you look.'

'Dressed, as you will see, in one of your *delicious* gowns.' Mrs Stewart raised her voice just enough to be heard by those nearest. Heads turned and eyes assessed her ensemble, a black ribbed silk dress trimmed with ermine and a black hat with a huge trailing white feather. She gave Willow a tiny wink. 'How are you, Willow? That gown is another masterpiece. You look beautiful in blue.'

They were interrupted by a voluble Mrs Judd, resplendent in a Riches bottle-green gown. 'Willow, my dear child, how lovely to see you prospering. I feel quite maternal towards you. I was one of Riches' first clients,' she said triumphantly to Mrs Stewart, who smiled and nodded her head.

'You were indeed, Mrs Judd,' said Willow, 'and I'm grateful to you for your continued support.'

Mrs Judd beamed, gratified to see that those adjacent to her were listening, then moved away to greet a friend. Marigold arrived, as lovely as ever, in a coral skirt and coat to which was pinned a gold and diamond brooch which matched her earrings. On her head was a daring little hat with a small veil. A man followed her and as they made their way towards her, Willow realised that it was Cyril. Bile rose in her throat. She felt suffocatingly hot. How dare that evil man come to her opening party? He saw her looking at him and gave a cheerful wave and a mocking smile.

'How well you look, Miss Riches,' he said. 'You have come a long way since first we met.' His lizard eyes swivelled round. 'My, my, you have some of the cream of society here.' He looked Mrs Stewart up and down and she, expert in summing up men like Cyril, looked down her nose at him. He was unabashed. 'Won't you introduce us, Miss Riches?'

'Mrs Stewart,' Willow said. 'Cyril. I'm afraid I've never known his surname.' She made it obvious that this was no loss and he frowned slightly.

'You can call me Cyril,' he said. 'You too, Mrs Stewart. All my friends do.'

Willow began to edge away. 'I must see if my mother needs anything.'

Cyril said, 'Your mother's visiting you, is she? I dare say she's very interested in what her girls are doing.'

Willow ignored him and he said quickly, 'Aren't you going to ask after Muriel and Edna? They often talk about you, in a kindly way of course.'

'I hope they are both well.'

'Blooming, my dear. Do tell me the name of that enchanting girl in the blue and silver dress?'

Willow glared at him without replying and vowed that if he ever tried to dig his claws into Jasmine she'd personally do him a mischief.

She couldn't fail to be pleased by the success of her party, but the presence of Cyril spoiled much of her happiness. When everyone else but family had left he followed them upstairs to the attic rooms. He looked around. 'Small, but charmingly done up. What taste your daughter has, Mrs Riches.'

'I know that,' said Clara bluntly. She might be unworldly, but she instinctively distrusted him. Willow went into the small kitchen to make coffee and called Marigold to come and help. Inside, she shut the door. There was barely space for them both and Willow was forced to speak into Marigold's face. 'What in hell made you bring that obscenity with you? I'm amazed that you even speak to him, let alone allow him to escort you.'

Marigold fitted a cigarette into a long tortoiseshell holder and began to fill the kitchen with smoke. 'It's all your damned fault,' she said. 'Apparently he got my address from a girl called Muriel.'

'But why is he bothering you?'

'Because he's that sort of swine.'

521

'What does he want?'

'What do you think? Money, of course.'

'Why should he expect you to pay him?'

'He says he'll make life unpleasant for me if I don't hand over a percentage of the house takings. He's threatened to make an anonymous call to the police and get me closed down.'

'He can talk! He's a blasted pimp, and a vicious one at that. He beats his girls.'

'I dare say.' Smoke drifted down Marigold's nostrils. 'He looks the type. However, he won't beat me or my girls. Toby hated him on sight and would smash him just for the pleasure.'

'So you won't give in to him?'

'I may give him a sweetener. Remember how Kate Meyrick was prosecuted only a a couple of months ago? They called her night club "a sink of iniquity" and took away her licence.'

'You don't have a licence.'

'No, I don't need one because I don't pretend to be running a club, but imagine what they'd call me! I'm not prepared to lose all I've fought for. I've got a gold mine going.'

'But he's not legal either.'

Marigold laughed without humour. 'No, but he runs his business from street corners and can melt away from the police. Actually, I don't believe it's me he's after, it's you. What did you do to him to make him so fiendish?'

'I just made it clear what I thought of him.'

'A mistake. Men like that need to be placated. They are bullies and vain with it. He could make trouble for us both. He's with me now because I feed his vanity. He knows I'm just trying to keep him sweet, but it doesn't matter.'

'How could he make trouble for me? I run a legal business.'

Marigold looked at her sardonically. 'Search your past. There's plenty which could be used against you.'

Willow went cold as her mind roved back, then impatient

voices called for the coffee and Jasmine opened the door. 'Come on, you two, you can chat later.'

During the weeks following the opening Willow worked hard to complete the orders which had come in. Anastasia called, looking serenely happy as she sprawled in an easy chair in the attic, showing plenty of her long silk-clad legs beneath her calf-length skirt.

'What a heavenly gown,' said Willow.

'Lanvin, my dear. The chemise shape. It's becoming all the go in Paris. My husband took me there for a holiday after my ordeal.' Her eyes were filled with mischief.

'What ordeal?'

'My dear, I have a son. He's only a few weeks old. I can't tell you how happy I am. I married Philip for his money. I think he knew it at the time, but he's such a perfect sweetie I've fallen for him.'

'That's good news.'

'Yes, and now there's the baby. Phil's relatives are absolutely furious, except for his sister. She's a sweetie, too. They all expected him to die childless and leave them his fortune. I intend to have more babies, if only to cheat them. Charlotte – that's my sister-in-law – didn't take to me at all at first and it was uncomfortable living in the same house, but then she saw I was determined to make Phil happy and she hates all her other relatives. When I produced a son she was ecstatic. She's positively revelling in her new role of auntie.'

Willow laughed. 'You're wonderful.'

'Not as wonderful as you. I keep seeing the most fantastic clothes and learning that they are Riches models. I hope you can dream up something for me.'

'You bet your boots I can!'

'That's the ticket.'

Anastasia was a marvellous advertisement. Her after-baby plumpness soon went and she was outstanding in any company with her tall, dark beauty. One day, when she

523

was patiently enduring the final fitting for an opera gown, she said, 'Willow, I never see you at any of the grand society affairs.'

'No one invites me,' she said drily. 'Mrs Stewart is often my hostess, but she doesn't have entrée to a number of houses.'

'Would you come out with me sometimes? I should love to have you. My wonderful Philip can open any door. I didn't realise when I married him just what a toff he was. He's only a plain mister, but he's related to half the aristocracy.'

'Wouldn't wonderful Philip be annoyed if you took your dressmaker out?'

'My dear, he'd let me go out with Dr Crippen if I chose to. Well, no, cancel that, I think he'd draw the line there. But he'll love you. I shall ask him if you can make my court dress. I'm to be presented in June. I can hardly believe it.'

Anastasia lost no time in introducing Willow into the circles where the so-called flappers had lost all inhibitions and were taking society over, breaching barriers of convention which had stood for centuries. Willow, attractive, beautifully gowned and lively, was welcomed and her order book permanently full. It was no longer déclassé to work for a living; that was another change that the war had brought about. As Philip said, 'Anyone can run a business these days and remain a lady. Look at "Lucile", the couturière. She is Lady Duff Gordon in private life. And we have Vesta Tilley, a star of the music hall, married to Sir Walter de Freece, and he a Member of Parliament. It's all different since the war.'

Later Anastasia apologised laughingly for her husband's unwitting condescension. 'He doesn't mean anything, Willow. It's just his way of speaking. He's just a darling old stick-in-the-mud. I'm his one rebellion against society.'

'And what a rebellion!' laughed Willow.

Anastasia wasn't exaggerating when she described Philip's devotion to her. He was wholly enslaved and it was fortunate for him that he had picked a girl who, in spite of her beginnings, acted honourably towards him.

Willow travelled to Bristol to visit Clara and to discuss business with Alfred.

Clara said, not altogether approvingly, 'Alfred keeps bringin' me newspapers with your name in, an' sometimes your photo. You're gettin' up to all sorts of society jinks, mixin' with folk your father would have hated. I just hope you're behavin' respectably.'

'Of course I am, Mum.'

'Not like our Marigold, then.'

Willow stared and Clara said, 'Oh, yes, I know. I had my suspicions from the start. So did Gran. She was born bad, that girl, though I don't understand why. Your father was a good man an' I've been respectable all my life.'

'How do you know about Marigold?'

'I paid a little visit to her place in Bayswater the day after your openin' party while you were out an' Alfred took Jasmine to see Harrod's – an' if what she says is the truth, it's bigger than Jones's or Baker Baker's of Bristol, though I can't believe that. I just hope you get enough orders, though why should people come to you when they can go to Harrod's? Jasmine says it's like a town with lots of shops inside it.'

Willow said, 'It's a department store, Mum. My business is run on different lines. I only make clothes to order. Rich women are always searching for something new.'

'Huh! You can only wear one dress at a time. I hope havin' your own place won't go to your head. An' remember, London's not your natural home.'

Willow laughed. 'I won't forget dear old Bristol, Mum, not ever, I promise. You were telling me about Marigold?'

Clara said, 'I went to her house and a maid showed me into her sitting room. Marigold was there loungin' in a pair of yellow satin pyjamas in the *daytime*. There were other girls there, all dressed like the tarts they are. Marigold introduced me, as cool as you like. She seemed to think it was funny.'

Willow could imagine Marigold submitting to fate, finding amusement in the situation. 'The whole place reeks of vice,' said Clara. 'I've never been in one, but it was written all over it. It's – one of *those* places. While I was there a maid came in and told a girl called Carmen that one of her regular gentlemen had arrived early. She excused herself just as if she was goin' out to tea or somethin' and went to meet him. When they'd all gone I tackled our Marigold and she admitted that she an' her friends live off men.' Clara nodded significantly. 'You know what I mean. Shameless, she is, an' to think I've been takin' tainted money from her. I always hoped I was wrong, but I told her she could keep her filthy money in future. I don't want any part of it.' Clara paused. 'Willow, you lived there for a while, didn't you?'

'Yes.'

'You didn't—'

'No, Mum, I didn't. I lived and worked in the attics, though I did make clothes for the girls and was glad to have the chance. I still do. They pay well and on time.'

Clara eyes opened wide in shock. 'So you've been sendin' me money got immorally as well?'

Willow said patiently, 'I make most of it from ordinary clients and that's what I send you.'

'Well, that's a blessin'. But our Marigold, livin' a life of sin! How can she?'

'You said yourself she was born different. I couldn't do it, but she's fair in her dealings with her clients. They know they can trust her.'

Clara winced. 'Clients!'

'Many men aren't happy at home. She gives them a bit of pleasure.'

Clara shook her head angrily. 'It doesn't bear thinkin' about. An' I'm surprised at you stickin' up for her. Mind you don't get led into temptation.'

'I'm far too busy.'

'Too busy is right, my girl. I'm proud of you, an' your dad would have been, but it's time you settled down with a nice respectable man an' started raisin' a family. Is there a boy-friend wantin' to marry you?'

'Not at the moment, Mum.'

'I don't understand it, a pretty girl like you. I'm sure you could get married if you were really tryin'. You used to talk of one called Steven Kerslake. What's happened to him?'

'We're still friends.'

Clara snorted. *'Friends!'*

Sidney had been invited to the opening. He had refused, pleading pressure of work, but had sent flowers. She called into the factory to see him. 'The bouquet was stupendous,' she said.

'I heard about everything from Clara. It's all going great guns. You're a success.'

'I've got the orders,' admitted Willow, 'but it's taking me all my time to draft ideas and make the sketches. I need at least one other machinist and, on top of everything, more and more women want watercolours of their outfits.'

'You'll manage, Willow. You always have.'

He sounded so complacent she felt suddenly annoyed. 'I was thinking of asking Jasmine to work for me,' she said.

His face darkened. 'Leave her be. She's safe here with me.'

'And you think she wouldn't be with me?'

'I know you'd do your best, but you've got too much to do, you said so yourself – and there's Marigold.'

Willow didn't pretend to misunderstand him. 'My God, does everyone know about her?'

'No, your mother let on to me. She was in a state about it and she trusts me. It didn't surprise me after the things she got up to in Bristol. For a while, she had a regular beat on the Downs, she and my sister.' His lips twisted on the bitter words. 'Nellie's in London now. She came home once and told me that she'd asked Marigold for help and was sent away. I don't know where she is now.'

Willow was silent for a while. 'I wouldn't let Jasmine get into any trouble. I love her too much for that and she'd be a help to me. I mean to hold a show and I want her to act as a mannequin. I already have a girl called Erin, sister of Bridget and Dora. Very pretty. The two of them would be a sensation. I shall create a few exclusive gowns to try to attract more women.'

'You can't put your sister on show like that, I won't let you.'

'There's nothing degrading about being a mannequin.'

'Jasmine's not old enough, and I'll have your mother on my side. I shall ask Jasmine to marry me.'

Willow said, 'If she wants to marry you that's fine. I know you'll be good to her. But she must be allowed to decide for herself if she wants to work for me. And if Mum approves . . .'

Sidney said, 'Be very careful, Willow. I'm sure she cares for me and she's not tough like us.'

The conversation turned to business. 'Brenda is excellent,' said Willow. 'She seems to be able to calm the most indignant matron with a mixture of chiding and praise!'

Riches of Bristol was doing well. The work was less complicated, less nerve-racking than the London end. Cora's designs needed only small alterations to make them original.

Before Willow left she spoke to Clara about the possibility of employing Jasmine. 'I'm not sure I like the idea,' said Clara, 'though I know you'll keep a strict eye on her.'

There was no doubt about Jasmine's easily fired ambition to join Willow. It was what she had wanted since the day her big sister had left for Buddleigh Manor, and she didn't care what she had to do. Sidney scowled, but she teased him until he smiled. 'He's asked me to marry him,' Jasmine confided to Willow, 'but I said no, not yet.'

Back in London Willow got down to more work. She was strong and healthy, but the strain was beginning to tell and when one day Edgar called, he was candid.

'You'll kill yourself if you go on like this.'

'What I do is no business of yours,' she retorted, though she couldn't help being pleased at his concern.

'I'm making it my business.'

Willow said nothing. She was on the second floor where

she had set up a dais and chair and was sketching a gown which Erin was wearing, with a good deal more grace and beauty than its new owner would display. 'Take a break, Erin,' she said.

The girl disappeared behind a screen, reappearing a few moments later in a serviceable cotton frock.

As soon as she had gone Willow said, 'In future, if you must criticise me, I would prefer you not to do it in front of my staff.'

'My apologies. To tell you the truth, I didn't really notice her.'

'What? Erin is one of the prettiest girls I've ever seen and you didn't notice her! Come now, Edgar.'

'When I'm near you, I see only you.'

She picked up her pencil again. 'Don't be ridiculous.'

'I am not ridiculous.' His hand came down and grasped her wrist, sending her pencil sliding.

'Damn it, Edgar, look what you've done.'

'I'm sure you have an eraser.'

Willow laid down her pencil and leaned back in her chair. Her back and head were aching.

'Don't you feel well?'

'I'm perfectly well, thank you.'

'You could do with some fresh air.' She said nothing and he looked around at some of the completed watercolour drawings which were waiting for the framer. 'How do you know what frames your clients want?'

'It's simple. They tell me.'

He continued to study the drawings. 'They're very good, but not the best you can do.'

She was spurred into anger. 'More criticism! What do you know of such things?'

'I once saw a sketch book of yours, a long time ago, in the manor. I was impressed then by the lively sense of movement the characters displayed, the way you had caught their individuality.'

Willow's annoyance faded. 'Was I really that good? What am I doing wrong? Sit down. Would you like coffee?'

He shook his head impatiently. 'You are trying so hard to get a good likeness that you are losing your genius for capturing the essence of your sitters.'

'Many of them don't sit for me and the ones that do can only spare half an hour or so. They do their real sitting for oil paintings to hang in the ancestral home. I'm just an amusing diversion they can talk about at parties.'

'Why don't you go back to the kind of sketches you made before?'

'But I used only to suggest faces and figure. Is that what you mean?'

'Yes.' He sat on the dais. 'Draw me, now, quickly.'

Her pencil moved fast as she took in the lines of his body, of his immaculate summer-weight suit, his highly polished shoes and the hat he held on his knees. At first her hand trembled, then he was relegated to the anonymous part of sitter and she completed the picture with a few deft touches, outlining his nose, suggesting his mouth and eyes. She sat silently looking at what she had done.

'Finished? Can I look?'

He stared down at the drawing. 'That's exactly it. You can tell who it is, the clothes predominate, yet somehow you've given me vivid life. I look as if I'm about to leap into action.'

'I see that. But I wonder how my clients would respond.'

'Try them and see. Can I take you walking?'

'You know you can't. We might be seen and you're intended for better things.'

Her voice was as acerbic as his goodbye.

Her first opportunity to try the new style of drawing came the same day when Violet Radcliffe arrived. 'Have you done the sketches I asked for?' she said languidly.

'Not yet, Lady Radcliffe. I wonder if you would oblige me by sitting again for me, just for a very short while? I'm trying something new.'

'New? I'm not sure – well, all right, perhaps for a moment.'

Violet put on her new gown and seated herself, staying still for fifteen minutes while Willow's pencil flew over the paper. Without a word she then got up and sauntered across the room.

'My God, what have you done?'

'Don't you like it?'

'I think so. It's certainly different. I take it you will be adding colour? It is altogether different. How intriguing! When shall I return? Tomorrow?' She returned the following day. 'The new gown was a splendid success last night. My husband and I went to the theatre to see *The Mystery of the Yellow Room*. Such nonsense, but it diverts Lord Radcliffe. You have met him, haven't you, Willow, so you know in what a dreadful state the war left him. He is very self-conscious and this was the first outing I have managed to persuade him to take. I took a box and he sat in shadow.'

'Did he enjoy the play?'

'Oh, yes. There was a time when he would have despised it, but last night he was like a man let out of jail. He has a new interest now. He writes to the newspapers, mostly on political matters. Did you see his letter in *The Times* last week in support of keeping on the new policewomen? He has become a champion of many causes. He is so different from the man I married.' She had no idea that her voice was impregnated with profound relief.

Later, Willow coloured the drawing and stood back to look at it. Edgar had been right. She did have a talent for capturing a likeness without detail. She was both excited and relieved because she could cut hours from her painting.

She had an assistant in the shop, a very superior woman who, however, was not quite as superior as she believed herself to be. Miss Ethel Fowler was forty, a fact which she disdained to hide; her face was plain, her expression severe, though it softened when she was with clients so that they felt flattered right from the start, thus getting transactions off to a good beginning. She could also take on sewing when necessary. Willow had thought she would be ideal for the job and she was proved right. A pretty young woman could have intimidated a plump dowager, an elderly woman might not give confidence to younger clients. As it was, Miss Fowler was able to suggest in a remarkably discreet way that some ladies should attend Riches when the exclusive corsetière would render their figures appropriate to the newest fashions.

She actually talked like that and Willow had reprimanded Erin for giving a lifelike impression of her, though secretly she was amused.

On a hot summer's day Anastasia called. As a privileged friend, she was directed to the room behind the shop where Willow worked crimson-faced over an ironing board. All the windows and doors were open to try to catch what breeze there was and the whirring of sewing machines permeated the building.

'My dear girl,' cried Anastasia, 'do you have to iron in this heat? You look like a pickled beetroot!'

'Thanks.'

Anastasia laughed. 'I've come with an invitation for you. I'm to attend a dance tonight in Russell Square – my dear, it is practically off the map! Do I sound like a flapper?'

Willow laughed. 'Abso-bally-lutely, old girl. I can't go anywhere tonight. I've far too much to do.'

'Aren't you curious to see how your gowns look at a grand dance?' She had touched a nerve and followed through. 'Please come, if only out of friendship for me. I used to long to be part of high society, but a lot of it is very boring. It could be amusing if I had someone to laugh with.'

'What's happened to Philip?'

'Oh, he'll be there, but even with him I can only go so far and there are times when I want to be downright bawdy! At present the most fun I get is watching the faces of Philip's relatives when they see I'm sporting another expensive piece of jewellery.'

'You're shocking!'

'I know, and I love it, and so do Philip and Charlotte – most of the time, anyway. She had retired from society, but now she won't miss an occasion if I'm to be there. She wears clothes she bought ages ago; there's a lot of black, most of it rusty, but she doesn't care tuppence. She's such fun.'

Willow was infected by Anastasia's eager persuasion and allowed herself to think about an evening away from work. 'Yes, I will come.'

'Oh, joyous tidings. Now, is it a day for Brenda? I need some corsets.'

'Nonsense! You're as slim as a wand.'

'Not for much longer. I am once more with child and intend to hide it for as long as possible, then I can spring it on the relatives suddenly. How I look forward to the day.'

'I'm almost sorry for them,' said Willow drily.

'Nonsense! If you had seen the way they treated me at first!' Anastasia lifted her eyes to heaven.

'I can imagine.'

'Mind you wear something original.'

Willow raised her brows. 'Would I do otherwise?'

'I shall have on the adorable pale gold chemise frock which will be a perfect foil for the emerald necklace and earrings Philip has just given me. They'll knock the eyes out of his un-loved ones. I have to go to a boring dinner first, but shall send a car for you at ten o'clock.'

I must be crazy, decided Willow, as she put away her work, but she couldn't control the shiver of excitement at the thought of dancing. Edgar might be there. She dampened the thought quickly, but not before she knew that if he wasn't her disappointment would be keen.

Her dress was a poem of simplicity, a straight green satin sheath around which floated panels of the palest blue. She couldn't hope to compete with the jewellery which was always on display at social events and was content with a modest gold chain and earrings and a tiny satin skull-cap set with marcasites. The car arrived punctually and she found herself waiting in line behind the other cars depositing people at the entrance of the large mansion where the dance was to be held.

A maid took her wrap and she walked towards the music and heard herself announced by the butler. Anastasia was seated by the door, waiting for her. 'Darling Willow, you came. Charlotte, here is my good friend Miss Riches, but you may call her Willow. Everyone does.'

Charlotte, who was indeed in rusty black, raised her patrician brows. 'Everyone?'

'Willow is my marvellous dress-maker. Or rather, couturière.'

Charlotte gave Willow an affable smile. 'You make Anastasia's gowns? Congratulations. You are very clever.'

Philip shook her hand. He was shorter than his wife and a little burly. He beamed and asked her to dance.

'But Anastasia—'

'She will not remain alone for long,' said Charlotte. 'It is most diverting to watch the ranks of eager young men who try to seduce her.'

Willow was whirled into the dance and had no breath to speak as the frenzy of the Shimmy and the over-loud orchestra inspired the dancers. Philip proved to be an expert, throwing himself around in a quite alarming way for one of his years, until his face above his immaculate white tie turned bright red. When the music stopped he mopped his face. 'As you see, Willow, I am not built for such terpsichorean achievements. May I fetch you a drink? The champagne appears to be flowing.'

As he left Willow's side Edgar took his place. 'I am so happy you could come, Willow.'

'Did Anastasia tell you I'd be here?'

'Dance?' He was laughing at her. She hesitated, then he held out his arms and she slid into them and they moved around the crowded floor in a foxtrot which gave them an opportunity to talk. Willow suddenly did not want to. It was enough to be held by him and allow the rhythm of the music and his gently guiding hands to take over her whole being.

Edgar's arms tightened. 'Willow, when you look at me like that—'

He brought her back to earth and she assumed a brilliant smile. 'You dance well,' she said.

'Damn the dancing! Willow dearest—'

'Be quiet. Someone will hear.'

'I don't care. I want you so much.' She glanced up. The pupils of his eyes were distended to blackness. Surely his emotion could be read by others?

'For God's sake!'

'All right, I'll be good. Only say you'll talk to me tonight.'

'We are talking.'

'Privately, I mean. Somewhere here.'

'Are you crazy? If any of my clients get a whiff of scandal they'll go elsewhere.'

'I doubt it. People are used to scandal. There's always a lot of it about.'

'That's nothing new,' snapped Willow.

'That is what I said.'

She gave a reluctant smile. 'If you want real gossip you should go to the servants' hall. If what I used to hear is anything to go by at least half of the upper crust behaves immorally.' She was deliberately reminding him of her humble beginnings, as if she wanted to put him to some kind of test.

He seemed not to notice or care. 'I won't compromise you, I swear.'

The dance ended and reluctantly he returned her to Philip who was waiting with the wine. 'Crowded, isn't it?' he said.

'Like every other event in any season.' Edgar's voice was almost a snarl. 'Hostesses invite at least three times as many guests as it is possible to accommodate.'

Anastasia was brought back by an adoring boy of about nineteen of whom she took a gentle farewell, favouring him with a last lingering look.

'My love, you really should not tease the boys,' said Philip, laughing, then took his wife in his arms for a waltz.

The stairs leading to the ballroom were already half filled by sitters-out of both sexes. They sprawled ungracefully, smoking, drinking, making acidic, frequently scurrilous remarks about the dancers below them.

'The garden room will be reasonably private,' said Edgar.

Willow looked angrily at him before she appreciated the real misery in his eyes. 'Very well, I'll talk to you, but you must slip away first. I want no gossip.'

'Damn the gossips,' he said violently.

'Damn them all you please,' Willow retorted. 'What have you got to lose? I have everything.'

Edgar walked away and Willow decided she was a fool, but having made a promise she would keep it.

Chapter Twenty-eight

The garden room was reached through a small drawing room. It was spacious and hot and exotic plants grew in terracotta pots of many sizes. The scents were varied and unfamiliar, though Willow could detect lemon. Light from the drawing room threw shadows which lent the plants an even more mysterious, foreign appearance. There was a wicker-work table and several cushioned chairs, and an irregularly shaped pool over which hung tendrils of green. Willow waited nervously, doubts filling her. Then Edgar stepped out of the shadows. 'For heaven's sake!' she gasped. 'You scared the wits out of me.'

'I'm sorry. I wanted just to look at you for a moment.' He came close and slid his hands about her waist. 'Beautiful,' he murmured. 'My beautiful Willow.'

'No, Edgar, I'm not yours.' Though I would give years of my life to be, the thought spun crazily out of control.

He bent his head and found her mouth and she couldn't resist him. She didn't even try very hard. Automatically she parted her lips. She wasn't prepared for the violence of the need which surged through her. She put her arms round his neck, pressing him closer.

He lifted his head and looked down into her face which was visible in the muted light. His was in shadow. 'Willow, I love you.'

She put her fingers on his lips. 'Don't spoil our few moments together.'

He kissed her fingers, removed them and put his mouth to hers again.

'I must leave,' she said against his lips. 'I should never have agreed—'

'Will you marry me?'

'What?'

'I said, "Will you marry me?" That's clear enough, isn't it?'

'Is this another tease?'

'It is no tease.'

'I see. Are you planning on a kind of morganatic marriage where I can be kept in the background while the prince does his duty towards his family line?'

'Don't mock me! I am deadly serious.'

'Deadly is right if your mother got to hear of this. She could ruin me, socially and financially.'

'I don't think Mother is that kind of woman.'

'Don't you? Perhaps you've never come up against her ruthless streak. I have.'

'When?'

'A lifetime ago. When I was dismissed from the manor.'

'Oh, that!'

'Yes, that! Have you any idea what it's like to be thrown out of a job without a reference?'

He said impatiently, 'Of course I haven't. Willow, that's all past history.'

'Not for me.'

'But it led you to success. Without it perhaps you would still have been a servant.'

'I might. There again, I might not. Sent from the manor, I might have ended up on the streets along with other desperate women. Your family didn't care either way.'

'Nonsense! You would never have gone on the streets. You would have gone to live with your sister, and I have no doubt that you would have been successful.'

Willow detected amusement in his voice and she laughed shakily. 'What cheek! You don't pull your punches, do you?'

'I wouldn't have mentioned the subject if you were not being so stubborn. And frankly I don't believe you could ever have controlled your rebellious nature and submitted easily to a life of what must surely be degradation.'

'Marigold never seems degraded.'

'Marigold is a born courtesan. I have no doubt whatsoever that she'll end up rich and secure. And as for Maisie – she's incredible. It's like meeting a schoolgirl who is prepared to lift her skirts and pull down her knickers at the touch of a wad of banknotes.'

Willow laughed again, then sank down into one of the chairs and looked up at him. 'Let me get things absolutely straight. You are proposing to marry me. You know all about Marigold and you're willing to take a chance?'

'Yes.'

'My God, you really do mean it. You're asking me to marry you.'

He pulled her roughly to her feet and held her so close she could feel the beating of his heart. 'Yes. Yes. Yes.' He punctuated his words with kisses. 'Will you? Say you will? I'm going crazy with wanting you.'

'Are you? Are you sure it isn't lust that's driving you?'

'No, it damned well isn't! You're in my blood and bones. I shall never find another woman I can be happy with. Think of it, darling. You are my only chance of happiness. You can't turn me down.'

'What happened to your duty? What will your parents say?'

'I shall be sorry to hurt them, but our love matters more than anything.'

'You say that now, but have you really thought about it?'

'I've thought of little else for far too long. Now I can't keep my mind on anything. You fill it. You are in all my dreams. I postpone going to bed, hoping I'll be too tired to dream of you because when I do I go crazy with frustration, yet if I don't I'm disappointed because I haven't held you. I wake to unbearable emptiness.'

'You've never spoken like that before.'

'No. Willow, you love me, don't you?'

She nodded, not trusting her voice.

'Then accept me. Say you'll marry me.'

Overwhelmed by love, she tried to hang on to sanity. 'I won't promise that much, Edgar, but I will become engaged.'

'With a ring? Properly engaged? Publicly?'

'No, not yet. I must have time to get used to it – no, don't interrupt – and you need time as well. If either of us decides that we can't cope, then it's off.'

'After an engagement comes a marriage. How long do we have to wait? Is our wedding to be a secret, too?'

'Don't be silly. And don't scowl. You may be grateful to me when you've had a chance to see the problems we shall meet.' She heard herself mouthing the words like a fool, when what she should do was grab him and hold him.

Edgar scarcely heard her. He held her tight, kissed her eyelids, her nose, her chin, dropped kisses on to her hair, dislodging the pins which held her skull cap in place.

'Willow, you are mine now and I shall never let you go. We'll buy a ring.'

'Which I shall wear on a ribbon round my neck, as in all the best stories.'

'So damned cautious! I find it difficult to reconcile this Willow with the one I've held in my arms and made love to.' Excitement tinged with fear was building up in her. With all her heart she prayed that his first enthusiasm would never falter. Edgar was elated. 'All right, my darling, I'll try to be patient for a time, then everything will be done according to tradition. I *will* make my parents accept you. They must. Why should they not? You are a respectable woman pursuing a respectable profession.'

'Or trade.'

'It's only a word. Lots of people have had to turn to trade since the war.'

Willow's lips curved in a wry smile as she wondered if Edgar had any idea of the slight distaste which had crept into his voice. He couldn't help it and she loved him so desperately it was worth a gamble. For a moment, thinking of her dependants, she wavered, but he seized her hand and hurried her back to the ballroom. They were playing a waltz and he led her on to the floor. Her fingers tingled with life where he grasped them, his touch was sweet on her back. She gave herself up to pure pleasure until she caught sight of Mrs Maddison, sitting with the sulky Winifred, now doing her first season, on the small gilt chairs put out for the girls and their chaperones.

'We've been spotted,' said Willow. 'Are you supposed to be paying attention to some other girl?'

'Yes, but I don't care for her at all.'

'Poor her!'

'Not at all. She doesn't care for me.'

'How could she not? And you so handsome and debonair?'

Edgar laughed and whirled her round with such a burst of speed they nearly crashed into another couple.

When they resumed a more sedate pace, Willow said, 'This is supposed to be a dance, not a chance to embrace. If you don't leave some space between us your mother will probably refuse to buy clothes from me. Besides, I can hardly breathe.'

'Would it matter if Mother got her clothes elsewhere?'

'It most certainly would! She's good-looking, she's kept her shape, she knows everyone and goes everywhere. She boosts my business and praises me as an enterprising young woman. Her attitude could change in a flash.'

The band stopped and the couples left the floor. Edgar led Willow to his mother and sister.

'Not dancing, Winifred?' he asked.

'No,' she pouted. 'I am so unlucky to be a debutante after the war. So many young men are dead.'

Her golden hair with its reddish gleams and her white skin from which all signs of freckles had vanished were set off to perfection by a rose-pink dress and she exuded a delicate perfume. Chanel, thought Willow. Winifred was extremely pretty, but her habitual air of having been hard done by was unappealing.

'Mother,' said Edgar, 'you know Willow, of course?'

Mrs Maddison inclined her head. Willow remembered the scented, spoilt beauty she had first met in the boudoir at Buddleigh Manor. There were subtle changes, something taken away, something added. She was restless, the languid charm of the past gone, obliterated by the war and the death of her beloved son. Willow knew a moment of shame at the idea of Edgar destroying whatever peace of mind she was clinging to.

Willow said, 'Good evening, Winifred. How very pretty you look.'

'I am not wearing one of your gowns!'

'I can see that.'

'Now, now, my dear,' reproved Mrs Maddison with an indulgent smile at her daughter, 'you must not be unkind to Willow. She is a very good dressmaker, which should cause no surprise. When she was maid to Frances she learned a great deal and managed to create all sorts of miracles.'

Willow's lips tightened. 'How is Frances?' she asked impulsively, then wished she hadn't as Mrs Maddison's face clouded over and for a moment her eyes revealed inner panic. 'I believe she is well at present. She is in a nursing home enjoying a rest. Her duties as a hostess can be onerous.'

So they were keeping up the pretence. She could hardly blame them for that. The music began again and an elderly man asked Mrs Maddison to dance. She laughingly refused until Edgar said he would chaperon his sister. Winifred looked furious until a young man appeared and led her away.

'Edgar, you can see how impossible it is. They'll never accept me. Winifred—'

'Winifred is a rude little devil! Always was. Pay no attention to her.'

'It isn't too late to change your mind. Oh, Edgar, we're crazy. Forget my promise and I'll concentrate on work.'

'That's a poor substitute for marriage.'

'So my mother says. You two have something in common.'

When the music stopped and Mrs Maddison returned,

542

Edgar stood to give her his chair. 'Where is Winifred?' he asked.

'She was invited to partake of ice cream by her partner. *Such* a nice young man. The only son of the Cornish branch of the Sellicks.'

The music started up again, but Edgar remained where he was. Mrs Maddison's voice was cool. 'Edgar, Olive is sitting out.'

Edgar cast a cursory glance over his shoulder. He looked back at his mother whose eyes met his with steely determination, then excused himself and took the floor with an eager young girl.

Mrs Maddison patted the seat beside her. 'Won't you join me, Willow? I find these evening engagements rather a bore. Winifred, thank God, is the last of my daughters. Tell me, how goes it at the shop?'

'Well, I'm glad to say.'

'And when can we expect a mannequin display? I believe it was your intention to hold one.'

'Yes, it still is, though most of my work is too individual to show.'

'I see.' Mrs Maddison had lost interest and was watching Winifred.

Edgar returned his approved partner to her chaperon. The room was stiflingly hot, though that was nothing unusual; his face was red, more with frustrated anger than with heat because he had been gently, but inexorably, forced to dance with a flapper who, Willow had noted, had talked all the way through, probably explaining how wonderful it was to be at last a debutante and extolling the parties she had attended. He reached his mother as she was saying, 'I see several of your gowns here, Willow. One can tell them immediately. You have a unique touch.'

'Thank you, Mrs Maddison.'

'Oh, do not thank me, my dear, rather thank your talent.' She was scrupulously polite.

Edgar looked from one to the other, frowned then said, 'Mother, I have something important to tell you.'

His mother's eyes moved in the direction of the suitable young girl, then back to Edgar.

Willow's heart leapt in dismay. She put out her hand, but instead of taking the gesture as a warning, Edgar held it. 'I have asked Willow to marry me,' he said, 'and she has consented.'

Willow was as shocked and angry as Mrs Maddison whose eyes opened wide.

'Willow? *Miss Riches*? To marry you?'

'That's it in a nutshell,' said Edgar, discomfiture at his mother's incredulity spurring him to levity.

Mrs Maddison would never make a vulgar scene. She stared at Willow for a moment. 'We will discuss this at some other time.'

'Of course,' said Edgar. 'Where is Father?'

Mrs Maddison's head was held high, her voice icy. 'He is in the card room playing bridge. You had better inform him of your plan in the morning. Unless, of course, you and Miss Riches have regained your senses before then.'

'You fool!' Willow raged at Edgar as he escorted her home in a taxicab. 'We made a pact. We said no one was to know. You've probably ruined everything.'

'I suddenly couldn't endure the way Mother was treating you. And have you thought what it's like for me? Night after night, I am introduced to young women whom I find tedious. They are bland, without character. Custard against a curry.'

'Don't joke about it! Edgar, I could murder you, and your mother feels the same about me. She hates me!'

'She was overtaken by surprise, that's all.'

'How could you put us in such a dreadful position? If you were set on breaking your promise to me you should at least have told me first.'

'And you would have rejected me.'

'Yes, I dare say I would. I only hope that you haven't wrecked my business.'

He was angry now. 'Is that all you care about? Your business? I *love* you.'

'I know, and I love you, but I must work. I could never live an idle society life.'

'No. I don't suppose you could.'

'Are you prepared for a working wife?'

'I could learn to tolerate her.'

'Oh, thanks! Then there's the question of money. Didn't you tell me you were dependent on your father?'

'Damn! I'd forgotten that.'

His response created an immediate gulf between them. 'Forgot? No working-class man or woman can ever forget the subject of money. Many couples wait for years to marry until they can afford to rent a couple of rooms and raise a family. Edgar, I'm not at all sure about this. We come from such different backgrounds.'

'You could give me a job!'

'I doubt if you'd stick it. Lots of things I do are repetitive and tedious.'

'You suggested it once. I could help with the book-keeping. I am good with figures.'

'Well, that would be useful. Oh, Edgar, why did you have to tell her?'

'My people would never have accepted you. It was useless to wait.' Edgar rubbed his head, making his carefully groomed and slicked hair stand up in spikes. 'I wanted to take the taste of Winifred's rudeness out of your mouth.'

'I had no taste in my mouth. Your young sister has never behaved in any other way to me and I don't suppose she ever will. She's no worse than some of my other clients.'

'She's a brat! After I've faced the dear old pater, I'll give you a telephone call.' The taxi stopped. 'Can I come up to your flat for a while now?'

'No!'

'But we are engaged.'

'If you think that our present, extremely unsatisfactory condition will allow you to make love to me whenever you have the fancy, you had best think again.'

'You allowed it when we were only friends.'

Willow thought of the torment of love she'd endured so long for Edgar. 'I dare say. But if you remember, the last time—'

'You were cruel to me that evening.'

'I should never have come to the cottage. And now, if you don't mind, I have to be up early for work.'

He sighed. 'Willow, you have a streak of steel in you.'

'Please go!'

'If you insist.'

Edgar arrived at Riches at noon the following day. Willow was downstairs in the showroom giving a short lesson in colour coordination to a debutante who wanted a gown of purple and emerald. 'I've seen pictures of gowns like that,' argued the girl. 'My eldest sister has some of them framed. They all follow the colours of the Ballet Russe.'

Willow nodded sagely. 'May I ask how old your sister is?'

'She's twenty-eight. Why?'

'Fashions have changed, they always do. Poiret, Renée, Bakst, Vionnet, Molyneux, de Givenchy have moved them on.'

'I have heard of some of those. They are fashion designers, aren't they?'

'Yes, they work in Paris.'

As Willow had known, the mention of Paris made the girl hesitate and she pressed her advantage. 'Bright colours look well on the right person. Black and white are extremely fashionable at present, though I don't advocate them for you. You are too young.'

'Too young?' The girl was indignant. 'I am out, you know. I am not a schoolgirl.'

'The colours you have chosen would quite swamp your beauty.'

'Would they?' The girl frowned. 'I had not thought of it like that.' She preened herself, watching her reflection in the mirror, then she capitulated, as many women now did before Willow's determination. 'Tell me, what should I wear?'

She glanced at Edgar. She had hoped that by ignoring him she would send him away, but she could see he meant to stay – all day, if necessary. 'Go on upstairs,' she said brusquely and he meekly obeyed.

The girl said, 'That's Edgar Maddison, isn't it? He's *so* handsome. I even like his scar. It was honourably earned in the war, my father says.'

Willow brought her back to the point. 'May I show you a deep blue? It would act as a foil for you and we can dress it up with light shades.'

'I wonder . . . I had better consult my mother before I order. She will be here soon.'

Willow called for coffee and left the girl in the care of Miss Fowler who would never accept nonsense from a chit of a girl and would handle the mother with supreme tact.

Edgar had poured two cups of coffee. He looked up as she entered the tiny flat. There were dark shadows beneath his eyes and he looked strained.

'You told your father?'

'Yes.'

'And?'

'He was furious. He went on at length about duty, a child, my dead brother sacrificing his life for us, and compared him with me.'

'That wasn't fair. You fought, too.'

'No, it wasn't fair. I knew you would understand.'

Though it tore Willow apart to say the words she forced them out. 'It would be better all round if we never saw one another again.'

He took her coffee away and put both cups on the table, making no attempt to touch her. 'Willow, I am all the more determined. No, hear me out. I haven't talked about the war, not many of the chaps do, but it was sheer, unadulterated hell. I vowed that if I got out alive and in a reasonable state of health, I would always seek out true values. I am sorry if this sounds pretentious, but that's how I feel. I hate to hurt my parents, I tried to obey them, but I find it impossible.'

Willow sat down heavily. Here was a man she didn't know, one she had only dimly sensed beneath his frivolous exterior, the essence of the man which surely had been responsible for her love for him.

'If you will have me, Willow, my darling, I'll work at any task you give me. I will go anywhere, do anything, but I must spend my life with you.'

He remained still, his eyes searching her face. She looked at him, looked into his eyes, and knew he was speaking the absolute truth and would never go back on his promise. She got up and said shakily, 'Dearest Edgar.'

He put his arms round her and kissed her gently. It was as if they had come through a scalding ordeal and were at peace.

Edgar's income was considerably reduced and the engagement ring had to be inexpensive, but Willow wore the modest diamond openly with pride. Word soon got about.

Anastasia came hurrying round. 'Congratulations. You've captured one of London's most eligible bachelors.'

'Is that what people are saying?'

'Among other things. You've properly set the cat among the pigeons. I've been to parties where it seemed half of those present were for you and half against you.'

Willow was astonished. 'You can't mean that! They must have better things to talk about than me!'

'No doubt they'll think of something soon, but meanwhile you should take advantage. Phil and I are having an evening function. You must come. And Edgar, of course. You'll wear one of your own gowns and people will stare and admire and you'll get more clients.'

Edgar escorted Willow to Anastasia's party. It was the first time they had been out together since their engagement and it was clear that they were the source of much interest and some malicious amusement. After that, Edgar accompanied her whenever possible. It was inevitable that they would meet members of his family from time to time, but they did not display even a hint of censure. Had Willow been inexperienced she might have believed that they were weakening; she knew instead that they would die rather than allow the world to see their disapproval.

Alfred wrote to say that he had organised a small fashion show and could Willow please come and join in. 'I won't expect you to work,' he wrote, 'just be there to impress the customers.'

She travelled early in the morning. Riches of Wine Street was immaculately clean, every inch of paintwork washed and where necessary refurbished. In the showroom, little chairs were set in rows and a raised walkway with a strip of dark carpet awaited the mannequins. Attendance was by invitation only. As the seats filled Willow was delighted to see how much goodwill her brother had at his command. At exactly two o'clock, she stepped forward and welcomed everyone. She was dressed in a startlingly simple dress of black silk with a wide, draped white collar, a shiny black straw hat and black and white striped gloves. She began her short speech of welcome, looking round at the expectant audience: plumpish matrons and their madly dieting daughters.

'Welcome, ladies. Welcome to Riches. I am Willow Riches. Today Mr Alfred will be displaying examples of our new designs. I hope you will enjoy the experience. If, among the exclusive models, there is anything you would like reproduced in your size, Mr Alfred will come among you during tea and take orders. As always, he will consult you before adding the individual touches which will make your chosen style into an original. Now, let the show commence.'

As the clothes were paraded Willow silently applauded Alfred's choice of models. There were four girls: two pleasant-faced, curvaceous types with whom the older women could identify, and two slender. When tea was handed round in bone china cups, there were plenty of orders.

After the women had left and the chairs were being piled up ready to go back to a local hotel Willow asked, 'Didn't you invite Mum?'

'Of course. She got nervous at the last minute.'

Willow laughed and made her way by tramcar to Barton Hill. Clara stared at her. 'Are you in mourning?'

'No, Mum, it's fashionable to wear black.'

'Well, I don't think I hold with that. I like somethin' a bit cheerful myself. Alfred had this made for me.'

'This' was a sheath of flowered cotton with a small collar. 'It suits you,' said Willow. 'You never get any bigger, do you? I know women who'd give half their lives to be as thin as you.'

'More fools them. I wish I could put a bit on, but it never happens.'

Willow laughed. 'We're never satisfied with ourselves, are we?'

She had to catch a train back that night to be ready for a special fitting tomorrow and the only time she could spend with Jasmine was on the journey to the station. Her sister said, 'Have you got a place for me yet?'

'Not yet, my love, but I soon may have something for you to do.'

When she arrived back at the showroom it was well after hours, though there was a light upstairs in her flat. She opened the door and called and Edgar came racing down to meet her. He hugged her. 'You've been gone an age. I found some braised beef in a pan. Let me warm it for you.'

'No, thanks, there's no need for you to stay. I can manage, though it was good of you to welcome me back.'

'Incorruptible,' sighed Edgar.

'I assume you meant to try to corrupt me?'

The lines on his face deepened in a smile, the last traces of boyishness gone. He was a man and he loved her. 'You must be tired so I'll let you off this time,' he said, 'but you won't always get your own way.'

Rupert was thrilled when Willow asked him to call. 'An

exhibition of your pictures and a few gowns? Yes, it's just the ticket. Give me all the drawings not yet framed and I'll see they get done. And, if I were you, I would write to the people who have your work hanging and ask them to lend it to you.'

'Do you think they would?'

'Of course. Painters do that regularly. Shall I contact them for you?'

'Would you, please?'

Rupert worked in his father's office, but his duties didn't seem onerous or time-consuming and his semi-permanent presence in the showroom was an asset, since he knew all the debutantes and their guardians. He gathered a sizeable collection of Willow's paintings and he, Willow, Edgar, and anyone else who was free, spent a delightful day covering the walls of the showroom.

'I may have a surprise for you,' said Rupert.

Willow looked suspiciously at him. 'Oh? I'm not sure I like surprises when it concerns my work.'

'You will like this one.'

Jasmine was escorted to London by Clara whose previous essay into the capital seemed to have engendered a minor pioneering spirit in her. She explained why she had come when she wouldn't turn up for Alfred. 'No one knows me in London, but they do in Bristol. Besides, I couldn't let Jasmine travel up on her own.' She stood in the showroom gazing round at the pictures. 'What a lot of work you've done.'

'And that's as well as designing and fitting clothes,' said Rupert.

Clara shook her head in amazement.

Jasmine almost danced with excitement and found it difficult to remain still while Willow and the girls stitched and fitted the garments she was to wear. Erin wasn't much better. The two stood only a few feet apart on separate dais and it was impossible to decide which was the lovelier. Remembering Alfred's well-rounded mannequins, Willow had thought of the ladies who flatly refused to diet and wondered where she could find a woman with a good but full shape, who was also tall and graceful and prepared to be stared at.

Steven found the answer. He had accepted the fact of her engagement to Edgar, but remained her friend. Now he brought along Lizzie, the widowed young mother in whom he had become interested. More than interested, noted Willow, when she saw the way he looked at her and it was clear that Lizzie cared for him. She had a soft and dimpled body, a sweet smile and endless patience and was flatteringly dependent on him.

'Don't you ever get fed up with just standin'?' cried Jasmine one day when a dress had been worked on for hours.

Lizzie laughed. 'It's a rest for me, in a way. It's not easy bringing up children on your own.' Her pleasant face clouded over. 'Too many women are in my position. The war—' She glanced at the two eager young girls. 'Enough has been said about that.'

Willow, on her knees at her sister's feet, said, 'If you wriggle again, Jasmine, I shall stick a pin in you.'

Three gowns for Lizzie and four each for Jasmine and Erin were completed, and accessories decided upon, and Willow sent out invitations to clients. The showroom was to be open to guests between two-thirty and four in the afternoon and the show was scheduled for three-fifteen. Rupert was there, almost hugging himself in glee, and Willow soon discovered why.

He had coerced many of the women to come dressed in the gowns which were depicted in the delicate water-colour drawings which they had lent. Rupert said gleefully, 'Wasn't I clever? It gives cohesion to the affair.' He brandished a camera; some women laughingly shook their heads, but others were only too happy to stand beside their depicted image and be photographed. Rupert had thought up another surprise and when the party was at its liveliest and the dress show about to begin, a man arrived, garbed exquisitely in a morning coat, grey-striped trousers and grey spats with a white rose in his buttonhole and a monocle on a black ribbon firmly held in his eye. He sauntered into the showroom. Even Willow, stuck in the workroom much of the time, knew the figure of the man who wrote the most widely read gossip column under the name of Valentine. He could make a reputation with his honeyed pen or break one with vitriolic satire, and his behaviour was so idiosyncratic he could take offence at something which had been too trivial for his unfortunate host or hostess to notice.

He was followed by Spindle. 'I suggested to Valentine that he might come,' Rupert whispered. 'Spindle drove him here.' He watched the columnist as he wandered around looking at the pictures, occasionally peering at a lady whose gown was portrayed. One of the many things he disliked was to be accosted. He spoke only when he was ready and conversation became muted and behaviour modified as everyone covertly watched what the man of influence would do. After what seemed like hours Valentine informed Spindle that he would like to meet Willow. She took the gloved hand he offered in her firm grip, looking steadily into his pale eyes. A spasm crossed his face – was it of mirth? Criticism? No one would know until they opened their newspaper on the following morning.

'I admire your work,' he said.

'Thank you. Most kind,' she responded. 'May I offer you coffee? We are about to display the gowns.'

He swung round slowly and surveyed the table where Maria was waiting with cups and saucers and plates of tiny sugary biscuits which had barely been touched.

'Coffee, please,' he said.

Willow was certain that his whole attitude was sardonic and felt like slapping Rupert for adding this extra weight to her already over-burdened back. The door opened and Mrs Maddison and Winifred walked in. The columnist watched them like a sparrow-hawk its prey. He undoubtedly knew of the engagement of Edgar Maddison and his hostess, as he knew everything of social consequence, and was certainly aware of the underlying currents. It was commonly said that he had a spy planted among the servants in every house in London and even some of the country seats.

Mrs Maddison gave him a faint smile and a wave which he returned with a languid salute. Winifred stared aggressively at him until her mother tugged at her arm.

Music played softly. In the back room Miss Fowler, the dresser, made sure that the apprentice kept the gramophone wound up, played the right records and changed the needle. The sound of soft piano music floated among the guests, a little tinny but pleasing, then the notes of *I'm Forever Blowing Bubbles*. Clara had often sung it to her babies and she began to sing now in her slightly raucous voice: 'Pretty bubbles in the air, They fly so high—' Miss Fowler shushed her urgently.

A pale blue velvet curtain covered the door leading to the back room and Willow stationed herself near it as it was swished aside and Erin appeared, her auburn hair brushed, then burnished with a silk scarf, her deep blue eyes surveying the room proudly, looking startlingly lovely in a turquoise voile restaurant frock. Willow watched Valentine surreptitiously and saw his eyes open a little. Was he bowled over by Erin's sheer beauty? Impressed by the clothes? Erin stalked among the clients, never looking at them, her expression growing haughtier as Rupert announced, 'Erin is wearing *Hyacinth*, one of the exclusive Riches designs. May I draw your particular attention to the tiny handkerchief points round the hem?

'And now we have Jasmine, who is showing a delightful dinner frock. The deep lace insert permits one to see the wearer's skin, yet retains a sense of modesty, while the slightly belled skirt, drawn in at the hem, calls for a small, feminine stride. Please note the partial sash and the bow on the hip. This lovely creation bears the name *Discretion*.'

Willow watched the girls closely. Erin was the more beautiful, but Jasmine possessed an air of vulnerability which enhanced her loveliness. She was suddenly afraid for her. Clara and Sidney were right. Jasmine hadn't got her sister's tough streak. She should stay in Bristol, get married, lead a contented, quiet life.

The two girls were followed by Lizzie in an evening dress of pink georgette which showed to advantage her rounded arms and suited her fair looks. The display ended with evening gowns in which the two younger girls revealed a rather large expanse of flesh. Willow hadn't thought it excessive in the privacy of the fitting room, but here they looked extremely daring. However, they were applauded, especially by the debutantes, and even Valentine patted his thigh, making a silent gesture of approval. Lizzie had refused utterly to show so much skin and was sent out in midnight blue velvet. All three wore the now obligatory long string of beads.

Valentine took his leave as soon as the show was over. He moved through the guests, entirely at ease, acknowledging smiles with nods of his head, accepting without surprise the pathway made for him as if he had been the Prince of Wales himself.

Spindle whispered, 'I think he likes you. It will be so jolly if he does.'

'I hope to heaven you're right.' Willow's head snapped up at the sound of an altercation.

Winifred had bumped into Valentine and knocked his rolled umbrella from where it had been hooked over his arm. She gave a shrill laugh. '*So* sorry,' she said loudly. 'I *do* hope that it isn't dusty.'

Valentine stared at her. 'Miss Winifred Maddison, I believe?'

'Doctor Livingstone, I presume,' retorted Winifred.

Valentine took his umbrella from Spindle who had leapt to pick it up and Valentine replaced it over his arm, and left.

For a moment there was silence, then conversation hummed, the clients undoubtedly discussing the scene.

Willow felt quite ill. 'What do you think he'll say now?' she demanded of Edgar.

'It wasn't your fault. I could kill my sister. But Valentine will surely say something good about you.'

'Of course he will,' agreed Spindle.

'And if he doesn't?'

Spindle flushed and said, 'He must. He likes you. I could tell.'

'Everyone likes you,' said Rupert.

Not everyone, thought Willow, as she caught a glare from Winifred and the cold scrutiny of Mrs Maddison.

The show was pronounced a success and Valentine proved to be kind. He saved his ire for Winifred. 'The Riches gowns were a delight, but it is a pity when one has to encounter a debutante who should be returned to her governess for the counsel she requires.'

Willow felt weak with relief.

Rupert almost danced for joy. '*Everyone* will buy from you now. Valentine is particularly vicious about women who wear unsuitable clothes and I know of a couturier who had to close down after Valentine made mincemeat of him in his column.'

'And you decided to expose me to him?' said Willow. 'I think it's crazy that so much power is invested in a gossip columnist.'

Edgar smacked his hand to his forehead in an exaggerated gesture. 'Don't even think that! He might get to know.'

Chapter Twenty-nine

Edgar helped Willow in every way he could and she grew accustomed to his presence; he became a friend as well as a lover. After the show, when Clara and Jasmine had been seen off on the train to Bristol, at Clara's urgent request – 'I can't leave those girls any longer with no one to look after them' – and everyone had left, he accompanied Willow to her flat. They were tired after the intense excitement of the day, and languorous, and Willow was no match for the demands of her body when he began to caress her. They made love sweetly, their understanding of one another's needs always increasing, and she revelled in every aspect of their mutual passion which could be ignited so readily. After he had left, reluctantly, to keep an engagement with his mother and Winifred, Willow had an early night and lay awake in the darkness, trying to see into the future, wondering how great the power of Edgar's family would prove, how she would react if he broke their engagement.

On the following day she went out to purchase materials. She had access to wholesale warehouses which now willingly opened their doors to her. Afterwards she returned, smiled and chatted to a couple of clients, and went upstairs. A discreet cubicle had been constructed in a corner of the workroom and the noises emanating from it stopped her abruptly.

'Brenda, it will kill me. I cannot get into it. You must have measured me wrongly.' The voice sounded familiar.

'I've made it to your exact size, Mrs Thurley.'

Willow almost groaned. Mrs Thurley had recently become a client, one who never paid on time and owed quite a lot of money. But she must be humoured. She let out a wail. 'What am I to do? I need it tonight for a particular party. How could you have been so careless? I shall go to Harrod's next time!'

Brenda said, 'It's impossible to hide all that fat. When you pull it in one way it bulges out another. You've been eating chocolates again.'

Brenda's direct, uncompromising way was generally accepted, but not by Mrs Thurley. 'That's no business of yours!'

'I beg to contradict you, madam, but a client's figure is always the business of a fashion house and especially of the corsetière.'

Willow tapped and entered the cubicle. Brenda was grasping a handful of flesh which she was trying to stuff into the top of an all-in-one hooked corset. Mrs Thurley had indeed put on weight. She had altered in other ways, too. Her complexion was becoming coarse and an habitually dissatisfied nature had given her mouth a permanent downward curve.

'This doesn't fit me, Willow!' she snapped. 'Mrs Stewart promised me I should get good service here, and now this! The first time I ask you for a corset, you ruin it. How can I wear this tonight? I made it quite clear to Brenda that I want something which holds me together fashionably yet does not restrict my movements.'

'I'm sorry you're unhappy about it,' said Willow. She walked round Mrs Thurley who had been persuaded with difficulty by Brenda, backed by Willow, that she should not attempt to wear the new elastic belt which, on her, would have been a disaster. Willow examined her from all sides as if she had been a statue, while wondering how to get out of this impasse. The woman didn't like her and only came to Riches because others did, and she had a sharp tongue which could damage a reputation. 'Let us begin at the beginning,' said Willow, 'and see what we can do.'

Brenda threw up her eyes, but unhooked Mrs Thurley who stood waiting in her vest and drawers. Brenda tried again, but it was hopeless. Rolls of fat hung over the top of the corset and Willow said, 'Please wait a moment, Mrs Thurley, I think I have solved the problem.' She hurried away and returned with another all-in-one garment.

Brenda frowned ferociously behind the client's back, but wrapped the corset round her and hooked and laced her until her bosom was squashed and she had gained the fashionable tubular appearance, albeit a somewhat large tube.

Mrs Thurley stared into the mirror. 'That is better. This was obviously made for me. You must have picked up the wrong garment, Brenda. So careless of you.' She left the shop carrying a long box bearing the name Riches which contained her precious deceiver.

Mrs Thurley's criticism had rolled easily from Brenda's back but she said accusingly to Willow, 'What are we going to do now? You've gone and given her Mrs Judd's corset and she's coming on Thursday for her fitting.'

'I know. Sorry, but I hate the idea of endangering our good name. If you measured her only a couple of weeks ago she must have been eating like a horse to gain so much weight.'

'Oh, no, damn it! I remember now. I had two other ladies to fit and she arrived unexpectedly and wouldn't agree to wait. I asked Miss Jebb to take her measurements.'

'Miss Jebb?'

'She must have made mistakes, I can't think how.'

Mistakes made on purpose, perhaps, thought Willow. Miss Jebb – Willow could never think of her as Jebby – still displayed a lot of animosity towards her. 'Never mind,' she said to Brenda. 'At least we know it wasn't you who made the mistake and so far, so good. You've got Mrs Judd's measurements and you must get another corset made quickly. Sidney will understand, I know.'

Willow stared down at the letter. It was short and to the point and requested her company at the Maddisons' London house, rented for the season, in order to discuss a certain matter. She felt relieved, as if a blow which she had long been dreading had finally landed. The season was almost over. Some had already left town to travel north for the shooting, or to a spa to seek deliverance from the result of their excesses. Others were off to the casinos in Monte Carlo or Le Touquet, where a few would gamble disastrously.

Winifred's beauty had ensnared the young hope of the Cornish branch of the Sellicks and the Maddisons must be sighing with relief and looking forward to a respectable, approved wedding. Willow decided to try to handle this without telling Edgar and at four o'clock she knocked at the Maddisons' front door which was opened by the butler, Steadman. She felt a slight sense of shock. She had forgotten that she would know some of the servants. She was about to put out her hand but was deterred by his unwavering dignity. He showed her into the drawing room which was quite small by Buddleigh Manor standards.

Mrs Maddison was alone, reclining on a chaise longue in a tea gown, her hair looped back in a loose bun. It was as if the clock had been turned back, and Willow half expected to see Mrs Westerby and Miss Brayton slide through the door and stand behind their mistress. Perhaps the thought was caught by Mrs Maddison. 'I am alone, as you see. My daughters now have their own lives to live. I dare say you have heard of Winifred's engagement? We are all delighted. Won't you sit down? I thought it time we had a chat. Steadman will bring tea soon.'

Close to her former mistress Willow could detect a small network of lines radiating from her eyes and mouth. The tragedies of the past few years had marked her. A small, velvet-upholstered chair had been positioned near the chaise longue and Mrs Maddison waved her hand towards it. It was low enough to bring Willow to her former employer's eye level.

Mrs Maddison waited and so did Willow who had learned a few tricks herself. Unnerve a person by silence and ten to one it would make them break and say something apologetic or idiotic. In the end, Mrs Maddison sighed softly. 'Willow,

I must tell you that your engagement to Edgar does not meet with the approval of his family.'

'I'm sorry to hear that.'

'Are you? Yes, perhaps you are. Do you know that Edgar could marry into any family in Britain?'

'I'm sure he could.'

'He is only infatuated by you because you're different. I suppose the air of success, perhaps a little glamour, which surrounds a couturière, especially a successful one, has made him forget his duty. And, of course,' she added, 'you are pretty.'

'Thank you.'

Mrs Maddison waved her hand, disregarding Willow's acerbic tone. 'I want no thanks. All I want is that you should tell my son he has made a mistake.'

'He's old enough to decide that for himself.'

Mrs Maddison's mouth closed on whatever retort she had been about to make, then she said with determined patience, 'You are a woman of the world. You have seen how society behaves. Everything runs smoothly until someone breaks the unwritten rules, then out come the claws and teeth and another reputation is torn to shreds.'

'But surely Edgar has done nothing to deserve that?'

'No, but have you? Ah, I see that you are remembering something. Perhaps the fact that your father was a jailbird?'

'He was not!' cried Willow. 'He was arrested for taking a tip, as you very well know.'

Her burst of anger disturbed Mrs Maddison and she said unguardedly, 'I believe that such men always have a ready excuse for their bad behaviour.'

Before she could continue her attack the door opened and Steadman, followed by a parlour maid, brought in tea and bread and butter. 'Would you like something sweet?' asked Mrs Maddison. 'Jam? Honey? Cakes?'

'No, thank you.'

The servants withdrew and Mrs Maddison poured tea.

Willow said quietly, though her voice quivered, 'You must not say such things about my father.'

'*Must* not? It is not for you to tell me what I must or must not do.' The voice was quite definitely the one she reserved for recalcitrant servants. She realised it herself and a slight flush touched her cheeks.

'Dad was very ill, Mrs Maddison. He had weak lungs. He had been in bed for ages and shouldn't have gone out into the cold, but we had so little money, he couldn't bear it. He was too frail to regain his job after his illness—'

'What was his job?'

'He worked for a coal merchant delivering coal,' said Willow.

The fine brows went up. 'A coal heaver? Good heavens! Can't you see that you cannot marry my son?' Willow waited, then Mrs Maddison asked, 'Do you love Edgar?'

'Very much.'

'Do *you* truly think you will be happy together?'

'As far as anyone can see into the future, I do.'

'No, you are mistaken. You are deceiving yourself. You brush aside your social differences easily today, and so does Edgar, but sooner or later something will happen which will bring you into conflict with the world, and probably with each other.'

There seemed no answer to this and Willow sipped her tea.

'Have you nothing to say?'

'I can't think of anything. Neither of us will change our mind. This is a fruitless interview.'

'Will no arguments, no recognition of the facts, move you?'

'I will give up Edgar only if he asks me himself.'

'I see. That seems definite enough.' Mrs Maddison stretched out and tugged at the bell pull. Willow thought she had sent for someone to show her out. Instead Mr Maddison, who must have been awaiting a signal, walked in.

'It isn't any use,' said Mrs Maddison, 'she refuses to climb down.'

Mr Maddison stood, legs apart, in front of the tapestry firescreen. He frowned at Willow and his eyes narrowed.

'How much will it take to make you relinquish this ridiculous idea?'

'What ridiculous idea?' she snapped angrily.

'You know I am speaking of your engagement to my son.'

'You are offering me a bribe to disengage myself from Edgar?'

'Call it a gift from a grateful father.'

'You may call it anything you like,' said Willow. 'I have no intention of accepting it.'

'Come now,' Mr Maddison became jocular, 'you cannot tell me that you would not welcome a couple of thousand in your coffers. Think what you could do with it. My wife tells me that you own two dressmaking businesses.'

'I own two couture establishments,' said Willow.

Mr Maddison threw up a hand. 'What's in a name? Whatever you own, you must be able to use such a large sum.'

'Of course I could.'

Mr Maddison smiled at his wife. 'I said she would be sensible.'

'But,' continued Willow, 'I won't take money to betray Edgar. He cares for me as much as I do for him. Why should I hurt him? And why should his parents conspire behind his back?'

Mr Maddison's complexion, which was red and rough from the amount of time he spent outdoors, reddened more. 'Do you know that my son has almost no money but what he gets from me?'

'He told me so.'

'I still allow him three hundred a year. It's enough to stave off starvation.'

'It's enough,' answered Willow, 'to keep an average family in comfort.'

'Yes, you would know a thing like that!' Mr Maddison said. He took a deep breath and again his voice became honeyed. 'Come now, Willow, you are a very pretty girl. Someone will come along whom you can marry without opposition. What man would not want a lovely young woman who can earn herself a good living?'

'Apparently you,' said Willow.

Mr Maddison glared, his none too certain temper roused. 'Unless you agree here and now to break your engagement, I intend to instruct my solicitors to cut off Edgar's allowance completely.'

'That must be your decision.'

'How long do you think he'll love you when he has no money?'

'I don't know, but I shall find out. Meanwhile, he can work for me.'

Mr Maddison banged a fist into the palm of his hand. 'Work for you! Work for a damned dressmaker, a girl who was once a skivvy in my own kitchen! He will be the talk of London! People will find it very amusing. They'll find my whole family amusing. As if there hasn't been enough gossip about us already!'

'If his family supports him the talk will die down quickly,' said Willow.

Mr Maddison strode to the window and back with angry strides. 'I wish to save my son from a degrading alliance. You may believe you have won, but one day he will regret all that he has lost. He will regain his senses and return and you will be left where you belong.'

Willow got up. 'I shall leave. You have insulted me, and Mrs Maddison has insulted my father. Edgar and I will marry when we feel ready. Good day.' She stalked out. Steadman was waiting in the hall and showed her out as impassively as he had shown her in.

Willow decided against a taxi, though she had appointments. She needed to walk off her anger and chagrin. She had lost her temper with Edgar's parents and while it had been satisfactory at the time, it had done nothing to advance her cause. However, the physical exercise helped and when she arrived at the showroom she was able to present a reasonably tranquil face to the world.

* * *

Edgar learned of her encounter with his parents. He came charging into the flat breathless from his headlong run up the stairs. He struggled to get his breath back and speak at the same time. 'Willow, you should not have gone to my parents without me. Why did you?'

'Because I was asked.'

'But you should have told me.'

'I believed I was to talk only to your mother and I wondered – I had a faint hope – that woman to woman we might have settled something in our favour.'

Edgar sat down and accepted a cup of tea. 'Sorry I sounded off at you.'

'How did you find out?'

'Through Steadman. He's an old pal of mine, covered up for me when I was a boy and had done something wrong.'

'He didn't recognise me, or else pretended not to.'

'He remembered you clearly. The situation was unique and put him in a quandary. My father has acted quickly. I have received a letter from the family solicitor informing me that he has cut off my allowance.'

Willow didn't look at him as she waited for what he would say next. He had been pampered all his life; it would not be surprising if he felt so isolated from a familiar and pleasant life that he would decide to return to it.

'Darling Willow, you will have to employ me properly now, or at the very least feed me.'

She turned to him then. He was intent, frowning a little. 'You really mean that?' The enormity of his sacrifice struck her and she said, 'If you can't put up with all this, I'll let you go without fuss.' With only heart-break for me, she thought. She wouldn't say a thing to influence him. If they were to spend their lives together she must be sure he had made his choice without persuasion.

He leapt from his chair, upsetting his tea, and seized her by the arms, pulling her up to face him. 'You will let me go?' he asked fiercely.

'Only if you want it.'

'I shall never want it! I love you. I want to spend the rest of my life with you.'

'You'll miss your family.'

A shadow crossed his face. 'Yes, but I should miss you a great deal more.'

'Darling.' She put up her hand and touched his lips. 'I love you so much.' He nuzzled her fingers. 'Surely your parents will change their minds?'

He shook his head. 'They are both stubborn and I am breaking a cardinal rule: never marry a partner from a class remote from yours.' He kissed her. 'The way I see it, darling, is that you are streets above me.' Again he kissed her tenderly, without passion, soothing her jangling nerves.

Edgar went out, saying he had a little business to conduct. When he returned he was pale and agitated. Willow said nothing to him until the shop closed down for the night and they were alone.

'What's happened?' she asked.

'I went round to see Mother and Father. They were hostile at what they termed "a smear on the family name". I pointed out that you would behave a great deal better than Frances who disgraces her family wherever she goes.'

'That was cruel!'

'They are cruel to us. I was determined to use every argument I could find. I reminded them that Violet was now practically a hermit and that my brother was dead and I was the only son. They just got more furious.'

'I'm not surprised.'

'No.'

'Has your visit achieved anything?'

'It's made them more determined to disown me if I don't come to heel.'

'I see.'

They were sitting side by side on the rather lumpy sofa and he put his arm round her waist. 'Without you my life would have no meaning.'

* * *

Edgar worked at any odd job which could be found for him. He delivered goods in Willow's car, cleaned the sewing machines and kept them properly oiled, even tried his hand at cooking. And he chatted to customers, some of whom visited simply to gratify their curiosity about the rumours of a rift between the Maddisons and their son – 'He is actually working in the shop, my dear'. Miss Fowler cared nothing for the reasons the customers were there. She doggedly sold them designs, or one of the ready-made exclusives. The business was doing so well now that Willow was able to instal powered sewing machines, raise the wages of her staff and send extra money to Clara. She had had two of the attic rooms made into one and furnished it more comfortably and had repaid Marigold. She had become so much 'the thing' that many of her clients visited London out of season for fittings.

Jasmine wrote to thank her sister for the wonderful time she had had in London. She finished, 'If you want me to model for you I will, but I prefer to stay in Bristol. London is so big and noisy. Mum needs one of us near her. And, besides, I've promised Sidney I'll marry him when I'm a bit older.' Willow stared down at the letter. So her little sister had made her decision and there would be rejoicing at home. She had chosen the right way for her. She was vulnerable and easily hurt and Sidney would protect her.

Meanwhile, Edgar found himself a bed-sitting room from where he could walk to work and continued to face up to his new life with determination and humour.

Anastasia called one day wearing a Poiret divided skirt. She seated herself in the showroom, absolutely blooming with well-being. 'Darling,' she said to Willow, 'I've heard gossip.'

Willow, who was on her knees arranging the window display, glanced over her shoulder. 'Heavens! What an amazing thing!' She twitched the skirt of a chiffon gown, frowned, decided it was right and backed out. 'Come the revolution, when everyone has to work for a living, they won't have time for so much talk.'

'Do you think so?' Anastasia was laughing. 'People will always gossip.'

'Are you just resting or is there something you wish to say?'

'Where's Edgar?'

'Out on a delivery.'

'I can't imagine a Maddison working.' She glanced at Miss Fowler and said quietly, 'Willow, could we go to the flat? There is something I must tell you.'

Anastasia puffed her way up the stairs and sank gratefully into a chair. She said, 'You were once acquainted with a very unsavoury man called Cyril, weren't you?'

Willow felt as if a block of ice had landed in her stomach. 'He's the nastiest man I've ever met! What about him?'

'I called on Marigold and the girls the other day and he was there, in her private sitting-room, drinking whisky as calmly as you like.'

'Are you sure it's the Cyril I know? A street-corner pimp who beats his girls if they dare to argue with him?'

'That's the one.'

'I can't understand Marigold. She's usually fastidious.'

'I don't think he was there by invitation. She looked flustered and that's a state I've never seen her in before. I can't tell you anything else because I left quickly. I don't want his impression stamped on my expected little bundle.'

Willow was uneasy after Anastasia's news. Edgar had insisted on putting an announcement of their engagement in the leading newspapers and it had made her feel exposed. The shop was less busy now that many of her clients were on holiday, though not everyone left London. Some could no longer afford to travel. The war and its aftermath had made heavy inroads into fortunes. Men who had always provided well for their families suddenly found that cash was no longer readily available and had gone to work. Some had failed; others had prospered. Resentful wives left their husbands in London to go on extended visits to their luckier friends, but some remained and shopped with Willow whose clothes gave them a taste of life in the old days, and during the summer months the showroom became a friendly meeting place. She had time to work on the autumn designs and Edgar had become really interested. He was considerate when she was tired, and he was clever, and she was able to talk about business with him when he claimed he was enjoying himself 'no end'.

Autumn gave way to winter. Willow had taken on an assistant designer. Anne Withycombe possessed a natural skill which her constant contact with haute couture nourished and refined and Willow was able to enjoy some leisure. Edgar would drive them in her car, a far better model than the first, and they visted Kew Gardens, Windsor, Hampton Court, none of which she had previously had time for. His entire life seemed devoted to her well-being and when she was with him she moved in a permanent glow of love. Following an afternoon spent walking on Richmond Hill in the winter sunshine Edgar opened the door for her and then climbed into the driver's seat. He sat there for several minutes.

'Shouldn't we go back?' she said.

'Look at the deer, Willow. They are magnificent.' He was silent again then he turned to her. 'Darling, I can't go on like this. I want you so much. Not in short interludes. Say you'll marry me soon.'

Willow was taken by surprise. 'I thought we'd agreed to be patient and hope that you can bring your family round.'

'It's impossible! I went home the other day. Father treated me as if I were a naughty schoolboy. Mother was positively arch as if I were a disobedient debutante. It sickened me.'

'They love you,' said Willow. 'Give them a little more time.'

'How can you be so forbearing?'

Willow shrugged. 'They can't help the way they are. If my father was alive he would be as horrified as your parents to know I was contemplating marrying one of Them.'

Edgar sighed, then laughed. 'It's crazy! All right, I'll give them a little more time, but if they haven't come round before Christmas, I am going to marry you if I have to tie you up and drag you to the altar.'

'Caveman!'

'Don't joke.'

'Am I to take your threat seriously?'

For answer he pulled her to him and kissed her, and as always she responded. 'Can I stay with you for a few hours tonight?' he begged.

'Please,' she said.

January was mild and damp, the kind of weather which made people crotchety and disinclined to work, and there were several orders from people who wanted costumes in a hurry for one of the many fancy dress dances which were the rage. Riches now stocked fur tippets, handbags, stockings and scarves so that people could match their accessories, and the run-up to Christmas had been busy with both men and women buying presents. No word had been heard from the Maddisons and when Willow went to Bristol for a few days Edgar agreed, at her insistence, to visit them.

Alfred was making a huge success of the Wine Street shop and planning to move to larger premises in the new year and Clara was happier than she had been for years. She accepted Alfred's role and had stopped taunting him, while Sidney was like another son. Everything was running so smoothly that superstitiously Willow was nervous.

Back in London, on a day when the temperature dropped suddenly and rain turned to sleet which stung the face and rendered the pavements and roads dangerous, Mrs Maddison called at Riches and asked to speak privately to Willow. She climbed the stairs to the flat and seated herself near the large gas fire, holding out her hands to its comforting warmth. 'Winter again,' she said, her voice as bleak as the weather. 'I hate it!'

Willow felt a pang of pity for her. In the old days she had enjoyed the short, cold days when friends flocked to

Buddleigh Manor and she made trips to Bristol or London to attend theatres and concerts.

'Winifred will marry soon,' said Mrs Maddison, keeping her eyes fixed on the hissing flames. 'Her future husband has accepted a position on the west coast of America. She will be a long way away.' She paused. 'And Violet has said that after Christmas, she and Lord Radcliffe are taking the children on a visit to Mary. He has never recovered mentally from his dreadful injuries and on the sheep station he will be isolated. I gained the impression that they might stay there. I will not see my grandchildren grow up.'

'I'm sorry,' said Willow. 'But you can visit them.'

'It is not the same.' Mrs Maddison lifted her chin and stared hard at Willow. 'I have come to tell you that although we think an alliance between you and Edgar will prove a failure, we have decided to humour him. You and Edgar may get married.'

Willow was so shaken she half got up as if to embrace Mrs Maddison, then, meeting her unfriendly eyes, sank back into her chair.

She said, 'Thank you.'

Mrs Maddison's face was flushed. 'It will put an end to the speculation and gossip. Do you read the gossip column written by a character named Valentine? He has dared to ask why we are losing our children one by one, insinuating that there is something the matter with us. When he mentions Frances, he hints that her condition is our fault.' Mrs Maddison swallowed hard, then continued, 'It is unendurable to be the subject of such a scurrilous, cheap column. I must go,' she ended abruptly.

Willow wanted to say something kind, to thank her, but her demeanour was cold and her face set and so the words died. Permission to marry had been granted grudgingly and without pleasure to still the gossips and salvage the Maddison pride.

Edgar arrived at the workroom, having visited his father. 'They've given in!' he said jubilantly. 'I knew they would.'

'Did he tell you that Violet and Winifred are leaving Britain?'

'Yes, lucky for us. We could not have planned it better.' His exultant expression faded. 'You're not happy?'

'Of course I am, to be marrying you, my darling, of course. But your mother is accepting me under sufferance. It isn't a very comfortable feeling.'

Edgar hugged her. 'You'll win them over in time. How could they fail to love you?'

A notice announcing the imminent marriage of Mr Edgar Maddison and Miss Willow Riches duly appeared in the newspapers and curiosity was rife. Brenda was voluble when she arrived for her visit. 'Everyone's asking me about your wedding, Willow. You'd think no one had ever got married before. I suppose it's because they're posh and you're not?'

Clients in London also gossiped, mostly to Miss Fowler, though they might as well have saved their breath. She listened, but told them nothing.

The tradition of announcing a Maddison betrothal during a ball held at Buddleigh Manor was to be followed and Edgar was gleeful when he brought the news.

'They are going to do everything properly for us,' he exulted.

The dance was planned for March and Edgar made many journeys to Buddleigh Manor. Sometimes he stayed the night, telling Willow that his mother had seemed so lonely he hadn't the heart to leave her and Willow wondered how far this emotional blackmail would extend. Had they chosen the only route they could see out of the impasse? A short marriage then an arranged divorce when Edgar was tired of his workaday wife? Divorce was much more common these days. Some no longer regarded it as a disgrace.

One evening, towards the end of the day when the shop was busy with last-minute customers, Cyril walked in. He was well-dressed, as always, sleek and confident. He asked if he could have a private interview with Miss Riches and Miss Fowler called Maria from the workroom and gave her the message to take upstairs. Edgar was out and Willow rejected the request angrily. Maria relayed her reply and then returned. 'Willow, perhaps you'd best see him. He won't go away. He scares me.'

'I'm not surprised. I can't stand the man.' She hesitated. 'But if it's the only way to get rid of him, I had better see him. Ask him to come up, and mind you keep Erin well out of sight.'

'I see.' Maria nodded. 'Can't let a girl pass him by. Don't worry, I'll look out for Erin.'

Cyril took his time climbing the stairs and strolled in casually. He looked round. 'How cosy you are.' He seated himself without being invited, placed his hat and stick on the floor beside him, and lit a cigarette.

'What do you want?'

'Mr Maddison not here today?' His voice bore an inflection which unnerved her.

'He'll be back quite soon.'

'Good. A devoted lover.'

'What do you want?' repeated Willow. 'I'm busy.'

'I came to congratulate you on your approaching marriage. Who would have thought that a girl with your background could have caught a Maddison and actually been accepted by his family? You're a clever girl, Willow. I've said it before and I'll say it again. How is Edgar, by the way?'

His sleek voice got on her nerves. 'How are Muriel and Edna? Any bruises these days?'

Cyril still smiled but his eyes betrayed his anger. 'Not many. I've expanded my business, too. I have four girls now. Nellie Moor who says she knows you – unfortunately she doesn't reach my standards and will have to go – and a delicious armful of sixteen, very saucy. The customers adore her.'

Willow's calm deserted her. 'How can you be so loathsome?' she cried.

Cyril smiled. 'Do you find your sister loathsome?'

573

She glanced at the clock on the mantelshelf. 'I have a great deal of work to do.'

He was impervious to the hint, sitting there taking his ease. He shook his head. 'You work too hard and surely you can spare a few moments for an old – acquaintance.'

She decided that silence would be the best course. He could hardly remain staring at her for long if she wouldn't answer him.

He said, 'So the Maddisons have come round and you will soon be dancing the night away in Devon, among hand-picked members of society? Edgar works for you, doesn't he? What a come-down! Not that I am implying that it's low-class to work. Anything but! I do it myself, of course, successfully. Will he get an allowance from his father? Will he go on working after marriage? Will you? Or will you settle down in the country like a good little Maddison wife? The permutations are of immense interest. They haven't had much luck lately where their offspring are concerned, have they? All about to flee the nest, except Frances, hidden out of sight. Poor Mr Bickford.' He waited, but Willow remained silent. 'Do the Maddisons know that you and your father were in prison?'

Willow couldn't stop her retort. 'Not for any crimes!'

'Some people wouldn't see it like that.'

'Edgar and his family know and that's what matters.'

Cyril smiled, his thin lips barely moving. 'For a while I thought the cat had got your tongue. So they know all about the prison records? And, naturally, you'll have explained the other skeleton in your cupboard.'

'What do you mean?'

'I'm referring to Marigold and her house of pleasure.'

Willow's mouth went dry. 'What my sister does can be of no consequence to them.'

'You don't really think that, do you? Of course they have their own skeletons. They've dealt with Frances very well and without a lot of publicity. But I don't suppose they'd like their posh friends to read in their newspapers that Edgar's prospective bride had once worked in her sister's brothel.'

'As a dressmaker! As well you know!'

'Do I? Does anyone? Of course they don't. Who will believe such a tall story? No, my dear, they may pretend to, but underneath they will be speculating on exactly how you spent your time. Imagine the scenarios. Society functions where every curious eye will be upon you and your in-laws.'

Willow felt ill. He was right. 'Why are you doing this? What do you want?'

Cyril picked up his hat and cane and got up. 'You'll find out. I shall follow your career with interest, my dear Willow. Expect to hear from me again.'

She hurried on shaking legs to the door and stood with her back to it. Her mouth was still so dry she found it hard to get her words out. 'You *shall* tell me what you want! Why are you here? Is it money?'

Cyril frowned angrily and lifted his stick. Willow was frightened, but didn't flinch and he lowered it. 'You've got guts, I'll say that for you. I'll tell you what I want and it isn't money. I've plenty of that. No, what I shall expect from you will be invitations to society functions where I can meet people. The season brings sweet young virgins to town and not all of them are wealthy. The war ate up a lot of fortunes and some of the girls, so I've heard, are quite naughty. I should like to expand into high-class trade.'

'Are you mad?' she said in a hoarse whisper. 'Their menfolk would never let you through their doors.'

'Oh, I dare say they will. I can act very gentleman-like when I try.'

Willow moved from the door. 'Get out!'

Cyril touched the brim of his hat, smiled, and left.

Chapter Thirty

Willow made herself a flame chiffon gown for the Maddisons' ball. The colour suited her and blazoned defiance. She had not been consulted about any of the plans, but Edgar went to Devon often and reported back.

'They're doing it in style,' he enthused. 'Bless them! Who would have thought it?'

'How many guests will there be?'

'Oh, a couple of hundred.' He held her and looked searchingly into her face. 'You are still worried, aren't you? You have no need to be.'

No need! The weeks ahead appeared to be littered with problems. She hadn't told Edgar of Cyril's visit and was shaken when he mentioned it.

'Why did I have to wait for Miss Fowler to tell me?'

'Why should I bother? Who wants to know about a worm like him?'

'Don't pretend to be naive, it doesn't suit you. Why did he come here?'

'He asked me if your parents knew about my father's spell in prison and I told him they do.'

'That spiked his guns,' said Edgar with satisfaction.

'He gives me the creeps. Edgar, what about the other things in my life which would shock your parents? Marigold, for instance.'

'I considered the possible problems before I asked you to marry me.'

'Are you sure? Your proposal seemed more like a spontaneous gesture than a firm decision.'

He wrapped his arms around her. 'Can't you get it into

your head that I love you and want to marry you? Isn't that enough?'

'Of course it is,' she said fervently.

She meant it, but when she had time to think her doubts returned. She wondered if Edgar's parents would continue to use money, or rather the lack of it, as a lever to prise him from her. He could be quite amusing on the subject of shortage of money, but it was a novel experience for him. He enjoyed helping her, but had not yet had time to discover that you couldn't just stop work when you felt like it, and how boring it could get. Riches was doing well, but would need a great deal more time before it would supply the luxuries he had always taken for granted. And he had been accepted gladly by hostesses as an unmarried man with a secure financial future. How would he react if they chose to forget him? Would he miss his gold-lined life? And always, giving her no peace, was the thought of Cyril, mean and vindictive, frightening with his veiled threats.

When her worry became too much to endure alone she told Edgar. He sighed, 'Darling, you must stop thinking about him. The Maddisons can deal with his kind.'

'I'm not yet a Maddison.'

He ran his finger down her face. 'Such perfect skin. Now, we shall have to set an early date.' She smiled, but it was half-hearted, and he said, 'Remember, we have family problems, too.'

'Who doesn't?'

'I suppose it helps to know there are always people worse off than oneself, but it doesn't stop gossip. Tongues certainly wag about Frances.'

'How is she?

'Very sick. No matter what we do she finds drink.'

'She shouldn't have married Bickford. Why did she?'

'She has never faced reality, you should know that. She imagined herself a great political hostess when he would be asked to form a government. Of course, given her weakness and Bickford's intransigence, their hopes were undermined from the start.'

Willow packed for her journey to Buddleigh Manor. 'Don't forget,' she admonished Miss Fowler, 'I shall be back in a couple of days. I'm sure you can deal with anything which comes up in my absence.'

'Then why are you racing round issuing instructions?' Willow smiled. 'Sorry.'

Edgar had gone ahead and she sat in the train remembering herself as a nervous fourteen-year-old on her way to an unknown future. Here she was returning. The impossible dream which had obsessed her was fulfilled.

At the Buddleigh Manor halt the station-master opened the carriage door for her and helped her down, carrying her case to the gate. Willow half expected to see Henry with the governess cart, but this time a liveried chauffeur assisted her tenderly into a large, gleaming car. He coughed gently and said, 'Mr Edgar said to tell you that he was about to drive here himself when Mrs Maddison needed a little advice.'

Willow smiled. 'Thank you.' Her nerves were jumping. Was this to be the pattern for her future? A mother-in-law who put obstacles in the way, a husband obedient to his mother's whims?

She was greeted in the hall by Steadman who handed her luggage to a waiting footman to carry to her bedroom.

For a moment she and the butler were alone in the hall and she said impulsively, 'Steadman, it isn't a bit of good your pretending we don't know one another.' His face remained impassive until she said, 'Mr Edgar told me that you were an old, trusted friend of his.'

At last his expression softened. 'He was a good lad, a bit spoilt, but it's nice to see how well he's turned out.'

Then Edgar hurried into the hall and kissed her on both cheeks, and when Steadman melted away, kissed her lips. 'Everything is marvellous,' he enthused. 'Mother asked me for the colour of your gown and has chosen flowers which won't clash. The head housemaid has been assigned to look after you.'

Willow entered the small drawing room. She had not

expected to feel so stirred. Every part of the manor carried such conflicting memories.

Mrs Maddison got up to greet her, offering her a cool cheek. Mr Maddison left his library and joined them. 'Are you looking forward to the ball?' he asked.

'Of course I am, thank you.'

'I dare say you are nervous,' said Mrs Maddison. 'It will not be easy for you to meet so many people you do not know, but they are our friends and must be asked. By the way, my dear, you did not remember to send me a list of people you would have liked to invite and I quite forgot to remind you. So remiss of me.'

Willow tried to imagine Clara accepting an invitation to the wilds of Devon to dance in a nob's house and found she wanted to smile. 'It isn't important,' she said, 'and I'm sure I shall know a number of the guests through Riches.'

'Ah, Riches,' said Mr Maddison.

Willow said, 'May I go to my room? I should like to change.'

'Of course,' said Mrs Maddison brightly. 'One gets so grubby on trains. All that smoke and grime. We wondered if you might drive yourself down.'

Willow had meant to but her nerves were so jumpy she had changed her mind. 'I decided I would enjoy the rest on the train,' she said.

'I do not wonder,' said Mrs Maddison politely. 'You work so hard.'

A maid was summoned to show Willow to her bedroom. She recognised Nancy who had been third housemaid when Willow worked in the kitchen. Nancy betrayed not a spark of recognition as she showed her into a large room with a four-poster bed and a leaping fire.

'If you want anything, madam, please ring.'

Willow said, 'Right, Nancy, I will.'

The girl turned. 'Lily! I mean, Willow. You haven't got stuck up then.'

'I hope I never will. How many of the servants I knew are still here?'

'Mrs Narracott, Polly's the head housemaid – she'll be maiding you. Jenny had to give up to help nurse her brother. Ivy's still head kitchen maid, though I think she means to apply for a job as a plain cook somewhere. Miss Brayton is maiding the mistress and getting more crotchety every day and Mr Elwood is still the master's valet. I don't think Mrs Westerby will leave until she's carried out in a box and she's as miserable as she always was. When she heard you were coming she went to bed. She said she had a severe headache. None of us believed that!' Nancy paused for much-needed breath.

Willow was disconcerted. Somehow, in the turmoil of coping, she had overlooked the housekeeper. She could never imagine treating her with the distant courtesy used by Mrs Maddison.

'What about Aggie?' she asked.

'Who? Oh, the scullery maid. She was turned off when the mistress found out she was expecting. It was only a matter of time. She was fair game for the lads in the village.'

'Poor Aggie.'

Nancy shrugged, then a tap on the door heralded the entrance of Polly. Nancy said eagerly, 'She's not a bit above herself.'

Polly looked disapproving. 'You shouldn't be gossiping. Miss Riches is a guest.'

'Don't be stuffy,' snapped Nancy.

'You are needed downstairs,' said Polly coldly and Nancy left, making a face behind Polly's back.

Willow had come equipped entirely with creations from her own workroom. For travelling she had worn a grey wool suit and cape. Her dinner gown on the first night was a simple deep blue velvet with a scattering of pale blue diamanté on the bodice; her ornaments a modest necklace and earrings of blue beads.

On the way downstairs she met Mr Elwood who greeted her in his usual quiet manner and complimented her on her gown, her success and her engagement. She joined the others feeling uplifted by his gentle kindness.

'How pretty you look!' exclaimed Mrs Maddison. 'When you become Edgar's wife you will, of course, be entitled to some of our good jewellery.'

Willow smiled, but inwardly seethed. The beads claimed no pretension to importance.

The dance was to be held on the following night, beginning with a dinner to which close friends had been invited. After breakfast Mrs Maddison said, 'I'll ring for Westerby to escort you round to see if you dislike any of my arrangements. She has been in bed with a severe migraine, but is up today.'

Willow's heart beat faster as she waited in the breakfast room. Mrs Westerby entered with her gliding tread and walked towards her mistress without even glancing in Willow's direction.

'Ah, Westerby,' said Mrs Maddison, 'this is Miss Riches, Edgar's fiancée.'

'How do you do?' said the housekeeper.

'How do you do?' Willow responded, in proscribed fashion. 'I'm afraid I can't pretend not to know you, Mrs Westerby.'

The housekeeper's eyes met Mrs Maddison's briefly. 'I hope you will be very happy,' she said, not displaying a single glint of pleasure. She showed Willow all the rooms, as if it were her first visit. 'Now for the ballroom, madam. It is situated near the library.'

Willow had said very little. Everywhere she went she was overwhelmed by memories. They walked past the curtained alcove from which she had once spied on the guests, into the ballroom which was a mass of blooms. Anything which could be brought on in the forcing houses was there in a positive riot of colour. It was a vulgar display and Mrs Maddison must have known it. But at least there was no red to clash with her gown. She was a clever campaigner. Edgar joined them as she was strolling round, trying to keep calm under Mrs Westerby's appraising eyes. She was so thankful to see him she could have fallen on him.

'Where have you been?' she asked.

'Sorry, darling, I overslept. I was up late last night talking to Mother and Father.' He looked round. 'Good God, what a display. Mother seems to have done you proud, though I don't think I would have used quite so many colours. There can't be much left in the succession houses.'

Willow's heart sang. He understood perfectly. 'Brilliant, isn't it, Westerby?' he said, deliberately teasing her.

'It is indeed, sir.' The housekeeper's voice was glacial. Edgar would not be forgiven for choosing a wife who was not out of the top drawer. Willow remembered the strict below-stairs hierarchy. To hell with it!

Dinner was served in the morning room because the dining room was being prepared for the ball supper. Willow knew no one except Mary's parents, Lord and Lady Somervell. She conversed with them and with her neighbours at the table, giving no hint of her annoyance at seeing Edgar placed between two young women who were to spend the night in the manor, both pretty and, Willow supposed, considered suitable. Tonight, she and Edgar should be seated together. Well, no matter how much Mrs Maddison sought to discomfit her she had not been able to prevent her eyes widening in appreciation when her future daughter-in-law came downstairs in her ballgown. The flame-coloured chiffon was cut in a simple sheath of the very latest fashion, and bore all the hallmarks of exclusive cutting and design. A wide belt of crystal embroidery encircled the waist. For tonight Willow had treated herself to a set of perfectly matched garnets.

Mr Maddison's voice cut across the conversation. 'Ladies and gentlemen, I give you a toast. To Edgar and Willow. May their lives together be long and happy.'

The toast was drunk and Edgar's eyes met Willow's. The love in them was unmistakable. It gave her courage. Let his parents have their fun. She would win in the end.

* * *

The ball was a success. Edgar and Willow led the dancing with a slow waltz in which their steps were well matched. They were applauded before the other guests piled on to the dance floor. The band was a good one imported from London, and slow pieces for the more conventional guests were interspersed with jazz. Willow danced every one with Edgar and others and he played his part and took the floor with a succession of young women, some known to him, others just out and carefully introduced to him by his mother.

During the supper interval Violet arrived, having promised to make an appearance. Her haughty beauty had faded and she looked much older. She greeted Willow with indifference.

'How is your husband?' she was asked many times. To which she always replied, 'Well, thank you.'

Back in the ballroom the drummer beat a tattoo and Edgar and Willow went to stand on the raised platform with his parents.

Mr Maddison said, 'My friends, as some of you are already aware, this ball is being held to celebrate the engagement of Miss Willow Riches to my son, Edgar.'

There was a burst of applause. Edgar gave a short speech of thanks. The announcement could not have been kept shorter, but it had been made. The band struck up for a charleston and Willow watched the demented leaping required by the dance which typified the incredible changes which were taking place in society. In her servant days the women had been crushed into the famous Grecian bend by steel and bone and could only sway in stately dances. Now even some of the more mature women had embraced the new fashions and laughed and twisted in the charleston; others had made few concessions to modernity and remained seated on their little gilt chairs, frowning with disapproval.

Willow and Edgar walked behind his parents as they descended to the basement to conform with tradition. Willow stood in the servants' hall feeling unreal as Mr Maddison made the engagement announcement. The servants duly expressed their delight and toasted the young couple, after which they returned above stairs.

'That went well,' said Mr Maddison.

His wife said nothing.

Willow danced until the last guests departed.

'Darling, you were wonderful,' said Edgar.

Now that everything had stopped she was exhausted, emotionally more than physically, and said crossly, 'I'm going back to the kitchen.'

Edgar was astonished. 'The kitchen? Why? There won't be anyone there at this hour.'

'Sometimes I wonder if we aren't making a terrible mistake. We're so far apart in some things.'

He grabbed her and held her close. 'But not in the things that matter. God, Willow, I love you, and I'm proud of you. We've made no mistake, believe me. In what particular way have I annoyed you?'

'The staff will still be clearing up. No matter how tired they are the manor must be ready for the family and its guests in the morning. And in the scullery there will be a child, aching with weariness, her feet freezing from the stone floor, washing endless dishes.'

Edgar was disconcerted. 'It does seem unfair.' He brightened. 'I'll come with you.'

She relaxed in his arms, allowing herself the luxury of an embrace, then gently pushed him away. 'No, it will be better if I go alone.'

He looked doubtful. 'Do you know the way?' He clapped a hand to his head. 'Damn! Of course you do. I'll wait for you.'

Willow hurried along the wide landing to the servants' door and opened it on to the green baize world she would never forget.

Mrs Narracott was busy with the uneaten food. Untouched dishes would be kept for the servants, the others shovelled into a bin for the home farm pigs. When she saw

Willow she was confused. 'It's you, Lily. No, Willow. Sorry, Miss Riches.'

'Thank you for the wonderful supper,' said Willow. 'I know how much work went into it.'

Mrs Narracott beamed. 'It was a real pleasure. I hope you and Mr Edgar will be happy. He's got a good woman in you.'

'Why, thank you.'

Those who had known Willow in the past crowded round, while the others watched, wide-eyed. 'You heard about poor Mr Norris and Andy Hunnicott, both killed in the war?' said Nancy. 'And some of the gardeners never came back and some found jobs with more pay. It's not easy to get people into service nowadays.'

'Did you ever hear what happened to Miss Jebb?' asked Polly.

'I employ her.'

'What? After all she did to you? What's she working as?'

'A seamstress.'

Nancy gave a scream of laughter. 'But she's no good at sewing! And to think she's ended up working for you. You can't help laughing.'

'Why did you take her on?' asked Mrs Narracott. 'After the way she treated you, too?'

'She was down on her luck.'

'Isn't that just like you?' said Ivy, who was more self-assured and friendly. 'Of course, you understand what that's like.'

Before Willow left the kitchen she opened the scullery door. Inside, a small girl leaned over the huge sink, her arms up to the elbows in water to which handfuls of washing soda had been added. The open packet had fallen over and lay on the bench, the crystals spilling out.

The girl looked terrified. 'I've not done nothin' wrong, miss.'

'No, of course not. I came to give you a small present.' Willow opened her tiny evening bag and extracted a golden guinea which she handed to the bemused girl. 'Buy something nice for yourself.'

Edgar was waiting for her and saw her to her room. He put his foot in the door. 'I hate to say goodnight. You're so beautiful. You outshone every other woman.'

'An exaggeration.'

'Not to me. May I come in?'

Willow shook her head. 'I need rest. Besides which, if I let you stay the news will be all over the manor by morning. It won't do.'

'You are beginning to sound like Mother.'

She laughed. 'Go away, my darling. Soon I shall be back at work.'

'So will I.'

'Aren't they going to restore your allowance?'

'Nobody's spoken of it to me and I won't ask.'

On the train back to London Willow began to feel that the whole weekend had been as ephemeral as a dream. As she sank into her seat she realised just how great the strain had been. And it had been horribly increased by the underlying memory of Cyril and his threats. She closed her eyes. At the request of his mother Edgar had stayed on. 'I can't disappoint her, darling, when she's been so good,' he had explained. 'Besides, if I'm well-behaved I may get my pocket money back.'

'Of course your mother wants your company sometimes,' she had said.

So she travelled alone and had time to think. Being with Edgar had been a joy, especially when they had walked through the grounds, rested on the bench by the lake and peered into the tree house, even more dilapidated.

'One day we'll restore it for our children,' said Edgar.

She had other precious memories of the weekend, including the most significant of all. Their engagement had been publicly announced and apparently approved. So why couldn't she shake off the strong premonition of trouble? She was tired and dozed a little, only to jerk awake when

Cyril's face floated into her consciousness. An elderly lady sitting opposite asked her sympathetically, 'Did you have a bad dream, dear? You were moaning.'

'Was I? I'm so sorry.'

Back at work Willow's nerves refused to settle. Marigold visited her one day. Her sister was kinder these days and more composed now that she had ensured her financial security. She removed her white fur coat, revealing the grey suit which was considered obligatory by Paris fashion houses. Hers was embellished by a brooch of diamonds set in gold. She touched it when she saw Willow looking at it. 'Like it?'

'Very much,' said Willow.

'A gift from a grateful admirer. So was this.' She held up her hand to show her sister an emerald ring. 'However, I didn't come here to talk about work, I came to warn you that the gruesome Cyril is peering and prying. Have the Maddisons heard about me?'

Willow shook her head.

'What do they know of the past?'

'They know of Dad's spell in prison a long time ago when I was their maid and, of course, when I worked for them I was arrested with the suffragettes.'

'That's no longer a disgrace. Edgar knows everything?'

'Yes.'

'He's a good chap. I like him. Where is he?'

'Still at the manor.'

Willow poured tea for them both. When she thought of Edgar at Buddleigh Manor, subject to his mother's cunning, she couldn't help being afraid. In spite of outward appearances she had absolutely no doubt that Mrs Maddison would do anything she could to split them apart.

Edgar hadn't felt any such doubt. 'You'll see, darling,' he had said. 'We shall be able to work during the week and come down to the manor at weekends. I'll get a good big car so that we can travel fast.'

Her response had been cautious. 'It's a long way and I

already have to go to Bristol fairly regularly to see the Wine Street shop, as well as my mother and Jasmine, and some of my clients like to engage me at weekends. Part of my success lies in being available.'

They had not resolved that because the conversation had died when he kissed her. They were in her room and that time had made love more from a need for reassurance than passion. Edgar anticipated her sexual needs and fulfilled them. In this, as in every other way, he put her first. If something should go wrong! If she should lose him! The idea terrified her.

'Don't look like that,' said Marigold, blowing out a long stream of smoke. 'What's scaring you?'

'The idea of losing Edgar.'

Marigold laughed. 'Do you always have to expect the worst?'

'In my life I've several times received the worst,' said Willow ruefully. 'I'm afraid I might have got into a bad habit. Marigold, I'm so afraid of what Cyril could do to me, to my marriage.'

Marigold said thoughtfully, 'I wish I could tell you to stop fretting, but he's undoubtedly vile and wouldn't stop at anything to get his own way.'

Cyril arrived in the shop as they were closing. Willow saw the girls out then turned to him. He was taking off a smart wool overcoat, revealing a dark three-piece suit and a white shirt.

'Like the outfit, do you?'

'The suit is nice. The method of paying for it doesn't appeal to me.'

He reddened in anger. 'Miss Smart! I'll make you smart on the other side of your face.' He waited. 'Aren't you going to ask me up to your flat? We could be nice and private there. I know that Edgar's visiting his parents again. Does he miss his mummy and daddy? You'd better be careful, my girl, or you may lose him after all.'

'How did you know—' she stopped.

'That Edgar is in Devon? I have my ways. Well, if you won't listen to me in comfort you'd better do it standing. It's given me a real thrill to see how the Maddisons have been won over. The dance was reported in all the society columns. Even Valentine praised you.'

'I know. He was kind.'

'He wouldn't be so kind if I told him all I know about you.'

Willow knew he spoke the truth.

'You must be generous to me, my dear. Mr and Mrs Maddison don't really want you for a daughter-in-law, do they? They've given in so far, but I think we would agree that they'd find it impossible to accept a girl who once worked in a brothel. My goodness, how uncomfortable Valentine and his like could make the Maddisons. They've had to work hard to kill publicity over drunken Frances and Valentine has already got his knife into Winifred. How much would you offer to keep me quiet?'

For an instant Willow knew what it felt like to want to kill someone.

Cyril laughed softly. 'I'm a lot stronger than you.'

'I couldn't pay you even if I was willing. I've no money.'

'But Edgar's family has lots and once you are married I'm sure he'll have access to it. Now, shall I come upstairs with you and we can work out a deal which will help us both?'

She held on to a display cabinet to steady her shaking legs. 'I won't invite you into my home, not now, or ever. You are despicable, lower even than I thought.'

'Be careful,' he warned.

'You'll never get anything out of me. Never!'

'Does that mean you'll give up Edgar?'

She felt an agony of misery at the thought of losing him. 'He already knows everything. Nothing will keep us apart so you can take your filthy blackmail away.'

'I may have to travel down to Devon to visit the Maddisons then.'

'Do as you damn' well please!' she cried harshly.

He began to stroll to the door, then stopped and turned.

'There's one way you can keep me quiet that won't even involve money. Encourage your lovely little assistant Erin to be nice to me. I've seen her in the street, but she ignores me. I don't like being ignored. She'd draw in some wonderful business.'

'You'd better go,' said Willow in a tone which stopped him smiling. He pulled back the catch on the door and left.

She sank into a chair. She felt trapped. If she was stupid enough to give in to Cyril he wouldn't stop at one payment. She'd be his victim for ever. She spent a wretched night and when Edgar returned the next day told him flatly what had happened.

'The filthy swine. A bloody pimp. And he thinks he can wreck us. The man's a fool! Nothing can do that.'

A tide of relief washed over her. 'Darling, I knew you would say that. But shouldn't we warn your parents?' She laughed shakily. 'They don't really want me to marry you, do they? They'd grasp at an excuse to call off the wedding.'

Edgar put his arms round her. 'You or I are the only ones who can do that. Poor darling. You've suffered so much already for others' mistakes. I did get one thing cleared up. I told Mother and Father exactly how you came to be arrested.'

'Edgar! You didn't!'

'Yes, why not? It won't stop them caring for Frances and it may help us.'

'What did they say?'

'Father couldn't remember much about it. Mother just looked annoyed.'

'What will happen if Cyril goes to Valentine?'

'He may hesitate at printing a story from such a source.'

'He's not the only gossip columnist. Others would report it.'

'If that happens, we'll face it when it comes.'

Willow couldn't go on protesting. It was easier and more comforting to bask in Edgar's confidence. All the same, her worries seethed beneath the surface.

* * *

Willow and Edgar paid a visit to Bristol, Edgar driving them in her car.

Willow had written to Clara with the news of her engagement. 'I saw your photograph in the newspapers,' Clara said, the usual note of disapproval in her voice. 'I must say you looked lovely, and the reporters said some nice things about you.'

Relatives and friends squashed into the little house in Barton Hill to drink, eat, and be presented to Willow's fiancé. Sidney was there, smart in a city suit, looking very much at home and Clara wore a new dress for the occasion, a green wool sheath trimmed with fringes. A toast was drunk to the happy couple and Willow said goodnight to Edgar who was staying in a hotel at Clara's insistence. 'I can't give him the kind of thing he's used to and if he stays here that cat next door might talk. She's got a nasty mind.'

'Mum! She surely couldn't—'

'Yes, she could! She can make dirty talk out of anything.'

Jasmine couldn't sleep. 'Isn't life exciting? Both of us going to get married.'

'Are you sure you love Sidney? You've hardly met any other men.'

'I know. I don't want to try anyone else. Edgar's nice, isn't he? I'm glad we'll both have good husbands.'

She chattered on until her voice dwindled and they slept.

Back at work in London Willow began to dread the peal of a telephone bell, or a summons to go downstairs to the showroom.

Edgar was annoyed with her. 'You'll make yourself ill if you go on this way.'

'I can't help it. Cyril won't give up. I keep waiting for the blow to fall.'

Edgar kissed and caressed her gently. 'It's my belief he will wait until after the wedding when we shall all be more vulnerable.'

'He'll ruin everything.'

'No, he can't. I love you darling, and you love me. That's all that matters.'

Willow wasn't consoled. 'Every day I expect something dreadful to happen,' she said. 'Every time I pick up a newspaper I look at the gossip page first.'

Marigold called. She lay back at her ease, smoking a Turkish cigarette, filling the room with aromatic smoke which mingled with her scent. 'Want one?' she asked laconically, holding out an enamelled case.

'No, thanks. I tried them once. Is this a social visit?'

'My God, you don't waste time on niceties, do you? I suppose you've got work to do.'

'Of course.'

'You work too damned hard.'

'It's paying off.'

Marigold nodded. 'I have to hand it to you. When we were young I thought you were a fool for not exploiting your good looks, but my kind of life would never suit you. You never compromise.'

'Sorry I snapped. My nerves are on edge.'

'I'm not surprised. When I heard what Cyril was threatening—'

'You know! How?'

'He told me.'

'Is he trying to blackmail you, too?'

Marigold laughed. 'He tried, but my business has expanded. I have a number of influential clients who would be very displeased by publicity and are in a position to make life unendurable for him. He prefers not to annoy them, but I'm afraid he'll make trouble for you.'

She told Edgar about Marigold's visit. 'I'm sure Cyril is going to visit your parents. I don't know when, but whenever it is they'll go crazy. Who wouldn't?'

'All he can tell them is lies.'

'How can I prove that?'

Edgar held her close. 'Our wedding date is set and we are going to keep it.'

'Perhaps with an army of reporters seething round enjoying the juicy scandal? Or with the threat of blackmail over us?'

'Yes.'

They were in her flat and she sank down on to the sofa. 'I can't do that to your family.'

'They showed no such mercy towards you.'

He sat beside her and held her close. 'My darling, I repeat, we are going to be married. If we have to step over reporters to get to the church, if I have to punch Cyril out of the way, the marriage planned between Miss Willow Riches and Mr Edgar Maddison will take place. Nothing and no one will stop it.'

She looked into his face. He was neither angry nor scared. He really did accept all that she was and all that might be.

'Do you believe me, darling?' he asked gently.

'I believe you. You must care a lot for me.'

'My love goes beyond anything the Cyrils of this world can do. Don't ever forget that. I'm marrying you with my eyes open and together we'll face whatever comes along.'

Willow felt an immense peace.

They were to be married from the Maddisons' Bristol residence, a concession to Willow's family who usually held celebrations in their cramped house.

'The reception won't be large – the Bristol house doesn't have much room,' said Edgar.

'Which,' said Willow drily, 'is one of the reasons your mother chose it.'

Edgar grinned. 'You're probably right, my darling, but do we care?'

The sun on the stained-glass windows of the church bathed the congregation in rainbows. The organ music was soft and beguiling, the scent of flowers filled the air.

Willow arrived with Alfred who was proud to give her away, and Jasmine, her only bridesmaid, was suitably solemn in pale rose, though the sparkle in her eyes betrayed her inner excitement.

Willow walked up the aisle on Alfred's arm looking hauntingly lovely, clothed in white satin. A white bandeau with tiny rosebuds supported her veil. Rupert Anstey was best man. She saw Marigold who smiled. Her sister was decorous in a cream fringed dress and dark fur and gave her the tiniest of winks.

She had almost arrived at the altar when Edgar turned and she caught her breath at the love in his eyes. He took her hand. To please Mrs Maddison she had accepted an heirloom as a second engagement ring and a gleam of colour from the star ruby vied with the rainbows. Edgar's diamond ring hung on a gold chain between her breasts. She felt her heart would burst from containing so much joy.

The reception was small by Maddison standards, but beautifully managed. Clara tried not to seem too curious but her eyes swivelled from side to side as she took in the dimensions of the drawing room. Willow hugged her. 'Sit down, Mum. Today you'll be waited on.' Clara sampled the food. Afterwards she said, 'Little bits of this an' that! Mind you, it all tasted nice, but I like a good sit-down ham tea myself. I expect the Maddisons did their best.'

Winifred was there, scowling most of the time. She said something quietly to her mother and Willow thought she caught the word 'servant'.

Willow went up to change. When there was a tap on the door she expected to see a maid but Marigold walked in and sat by the window. 'You looked gorgeous,' she said. 'I hope you'll be very happy.'

'Thanks. I shall do my best.'

'I've news of Cyril.'

Willow stared at her sister who was wearing her secretive, cat-like look. 'For heaven's sake! I've been trying not to think about him.'

'I don't blame you.'

'So why talk about him now?'

'I couldn't get to you before the wedding.'

'I mean why talk of him at all? Today, of all days?'

Marigold fitted a cigarette into a holder and lit it. 'I don't think you'll have further trouble from him. The man's a fool.' She took a leisurely drag on her cigarette.

'For goodness' sake! If you've something to say then get on with it!'

'A few days ago he waylaid Erin on her way home. He held on to her arm and insisted that she talk to him. He made all kinds of promises if she would work for him. And then he forced a kiss on her.'

'What? He's disgusting! Erin didn't believe him, did she? She couldn't know what kind of work he meant!'

Marigold shrugged. 'She may not, though a girl with a careful mother like hers has probably had plenty of warnings. But Erin's father and brothers certainly know. They tracked him down and took turns in beating him. He's quite a mess. In fact, he'll never look the same again and he'll need false front teeth. He's in hospital telling the doctors he was hit by a car which didn't stop.' Marigold laughed. 'It's funny when you think of it. He can't tell the truth because the police would get him for procuring.'

'Well, he's been asking for it,' said Willow. 'Thank God Erin is safe.' She paused. 'How does this affect me?'

'Erin's menfolk told him that if he ever came near her again, or did anything to hurt her or her family or her friends, he'd get more of the same.'

'How do you know so much?'

'I got it straight from the horse's mouth. In other words, Cyril.'

'You've been to see him?'

'Yes. I said he was my brother.' Marigold grimaced. 'It went against the grain to claim I was related to him. One thing's sure, he's very sorry for himself and indignant, too. Isn't that a laugh? He was longing to tell someone about the beating and I was his first visitor. He's a coward at heart and it's obvious he's terrified at the idea of more punishment.

Honestly, Willow, he looked so ghastly I almost felt sorry for him. But he deserved what he got. Then two of his girls arrived so I left. I reckon you're safe from him now.' Marigold got up. 'And Edgar will help protect you. You've got a good man.'

She left and Willow sat unmoving for a while. Cyril might still prove a problem, but the likelihood had diminished.

They were to go to Italy for their honeymoon, but had arranged to spend tonight in a small hotel outside Bristol. The guests gathered to wave them goodbye. In her happiness Willow caught Mrs Maddison's hand. 'Thank you,' she said. 'It's all been so lovely.'

Mrs Maddison said coolly, 'I am so glad you appreciate it.' Her kiss brushed Willow's cheek. She was pale and her lips moved in what might be taken for a smile.

Mr Maddison was more forthcoming. 'You look very pretty,' he said, 'and so do your sisters. Especially what's-her-name? Marigold? Damned fine-looking girl.'

When Willow told Edgar he said, 'He's taken a real fancy to her. I shouldn't wonder if he finds his way to her house.'

'Edgar!'

'Have I shocked you?' He was laughing at her. 'Dad has had mistresses from a long way back. Mother has enjoyed the odd fling, too.'

'Well, that's not my idea of a marriage. I'll never stray and I hope you won't.'

'Of course not. I could never find anyone better than you.' He grinned. 'Just think though, darling, if Father did visit Marigold, and Cyril met him and tried to talk. I wonder how the pater would deal with that scum? A horsewhip sounds the likeliest.'

Dusk was falling as they left the house, amid applause and cheers. Edgar was driving a new car, a wedding gift from his parents. Away from the house he stopped to remove the old shoes that were bouncing behind it. When he got back in Willow told him what Marigold had said.

'Good! It's high time someone thrashed that swine. Let's forget him. Are you happy?'

'Very happy.'

'Not at all worried about the future?'

'Aren't you?'

'No, I'm not. Whatever happens now we're together.'

'Just imagine, I used to think you were weak.'

'Just imagine, I used to think you were a forward kitchen maid. Now you're a forward couturière. Willow Maddison, the owner of two grand fashion houses.'

'Are you marrying me for my money?' she asked sternly.

He wrung his hands in spurious nervousness. 'I'd hoped you wouldn't find out so soon.'

'Idiot!'

He laid his hand over hers. 'I am very satisfied with my bargain. Are you?'

'Absolutely, my darling.'

He started the engine and cut back towards the Downs.

'Why are we going back?' she asked.

Edgar said, 'There's something I want to do.'

Willow smiled. 'So I should hope. After all, you've made an honest woman of me.'

'Don't be cheeky. I just want to make the circle complete.'

'What circle?'

He stopped at the Downs. 'Come with me.' Holding her arm he guided her to a spot near the road. 'This is where it all began,' he said. 'This is where you rescued my ghastly sister from death.'

Willow looked round, remembering, seeing in her mind herself, Jasmine, the battered pram. 'Frances was kind to us,' she said. 'Poor Frances. And you were there with Violet and grumbled about the scene we were making.'

'I was insufferable.'

'Yes,' she said, 'you were, but now you're quite nice. Who would have thought it?'

'I warned you about cheek!' He kissed her and she held him tight in a sudden uprush of passion, her tongue flickering against his.

'Come on, woman,' he growled, then yawned exaggeratedly, 'I'm tired. It must be all the excitement. Let's hurry off to bed.'

'Can't you get your mind off sex?'

'No, can you?'

'No.'

They laughed together. A feeling of trepidation floated briefly across Willow's mind at the problems which must lie ahead. As well as coping with Edgar's family, there was her work which she would have to balance against a new kind of social life. She didn't fool herself that it would be easy. She shivered.

Edgar said, 'Are you cold, darling?'

'A little.'

'That won't do.' He put his arms round her and hugged her and she felt safe.

They smiled at one another and, arm in arm, walked to their car.